# TO SET THE STONE TREMBLING

a disquieting book about books
and people who persist in reading them

This is a work of fiction. Names, characters, businesses, places, events and incidents are either the products of the author's imagination or used in a fictitious manner. Any resemblance to actual persons, living or dead, or actual events is purely coincidental.

# JOHN MOSS

## TO SET THE STONE TREMBLING

a disquieting book about books
and people who persist in reading them

**Vanguard Press**

VANGUARD PAPERBACK

© Copyright 2022
**John Moss**

The right of John Moss to be identified as author of
this work has been asserted by him in accordance with the
Copyright, Designs and Patents Act 1988.

**All Rights Reserved**

No reproduction, copy or transmission of this publication
may be made without written permission.
No paragraph of this publication may be reproduced,
copied or transmitted save with the written permission of the publisher, or in accordance
with the provisions
of the Copyright Act 1956 (as amended).

Any person who commits any unauthorised act in relation to
this publication may be liable to criminal
prosecution and civil claims for damages.

A CIP catalogue record for this title is
available from the British Library.

ISBN 978 1 80016 322 5

*Vanguard Press is an imprint of
Pegasus Elliot MacKenzie Publishers Ltd.*
www.pegasuspublishers.com

First Published in 2022

**Vanguard Press
Sheraton House Castle Park
Cambridge England**

Printed & Bound in Great Britain

# Dedication

In addition to my wife, Beverley Haun, my daughters, my grandchildren, in-laws, siblings, and cousins, as named in my bio, I'd like to dedicate all that lies between these covers to the following, listed in historical order of impact on my life as mentors, rivals, critics, friends:

Russell Hannusch, Dick Livingston
Miss Moore, E. Sue King, Mr Ripley
Nick Boyes, Grace Terry, Henry Martin
Martha Plaxton, Cathie Williams, Ed Rowe
A.L. Cochrane, Gib and Carol, Ernie Smith
Primrose Wake, Ian Underhill, Bill Cockburn
Jack Morgan, Janet Newman, Susan Hoblyn, Harvey Pedlar
R.K. Johnson, Max Adrian, Peter O'Toole
David Slocombe, Deb and Leo LaVallee
Walter Martin, Fred Cogswell, Dave Arnason
Judith Steen, John Lennox, Clara Thomas
Margaret Laurence, Sinclair Ross, Chinua Achebe
Chris Armitage, Arthur Ravenscroft, Dave Godfrey
Stan Dragland, Michael Ondaatje, Matt Cohen
Malcolm Ross, Jack McCelland, Margaret Atwood
Bob Kroetsch, George Walley, George Bowering
Michael Hurley, Graeme Dargo, Karen James
Arctic Joe Womersley, Sherrill Grace, Hugh Hood, Jack Haun
Bruce and Carol Hodgins, Dale and Bernice Standen
Jim and Marianne Mays, Tig and Laura
Pepé and Sherry Lazcano, Randy Timms, Elrick White, Andy Phillips
Michael Carroll, Susan Twist at Happenstance Books and Yarns
Alfred Wainwright, Sherry at The Nutty Bean Cafe, Cathy Erb
Lee Radford, Matt and Kelsey, Tim and Yesly
and for making the Boston run an annual event
for over a decade, Dilly and Tim

There may be more; some will be relieved and others annoyed by their careless or willful omission

# Contents

**BOOK ONE: THE LIBRARY OF ENDURING DREAMS** .............. 9
    Chapter One ............................................................................. 11
    The Woman in the Mirror ....................................................... 11
    Chapter Two ............................................................................ 25
    House of Mirrors ..................................................................... 25
    Chapter Three ......................................................................... 43
    Lost in the Funhouse .............................................................. 43
    Chapter Four ........................................................................... 60
    Lost Horizons .......................................................................... 60
    Chapter Five ............................................................................ 77
    Horizon Obscured ................................................................... 77
    Chapter Six .............................................................................. 92
    Camera Obscura ..................................................................... 92
    Chapter Seven ....................................................................... 109
    *Ego Sum Camera* ................................................................ 109
    Chapter Eight ........................................................................ 121
    *Te Provoco Ego* ................................................................... 121
    Chapter Nine ......................................................................... 139
    Provoking the Devil ............................................................... 139
    Chapter Ten ........................................................................... 155
    The Devil in Detail ................................................................ 155
    Chapter Eleven ...................................................................... 172
    Details of a Life ..................................................................... 172
    Chapter Twelve ..................................................................... 189
    The Life of a Woman ............................................................ 189
    Chapter Thirteen ................................................................... 210
    The Library of Enduring Dreams .......................................... 210
**BOOK TWO: THE INVISIBLE LABYRINTH** ......................... 235
    Chapter One ........................................................................... 237
    In the Time of Borges ........................................................... 237
    Chapter Two .......................................................................... 251
    The Labyrinth ....................................................................... 251

| | |
|---|---|
| Chapter Three | 267 |
| The City of the End of Things | 267 |
| Chapter Four | 284 |
| The Cloisters | 284 |
| Chapter Five | 300 |
| We are the Dead | 300 |
| Chapter Six | 314 |
| Plato's Brother | 314 |
| Chapter Seven | 327 |
| Odysseus Ever Returning | 327 |
| Chapter Eight | 342 |
| June 17th | 342 |
| Chapter Nine | 355 |
| The Ghost Sonata | 355 |
| Chapter Ten | 367 |
| MOAB | 367 |
| Chapter Eleven | 380 |
| The Secret Chapel | 380 |
| Chapter Twelve | 396 |
| The Sleeping Room | 396 |
| Chapter Thirteen | 409 |
| Notes in Time | 409 |
| Chapter Fourteen | 424 |
| The Primrose Garden | 424 |
| Chapter Fifteen | 440 |
| Tlön Revisited | 440 |
| **Author's Note** | 455 |

# BOOK ONE: THE LIBRARY OF ENDURING DREAMS

# Chapter One
## The Woman in the Mirror

Anna Winston was struggling to negotiate the sidewalk slush near Yonge Street and College when she glanced up and recognized her own face on a woman approaching the moment before they collided. Careening among strangers, she lost all sense of herself and collapsed in the slurry by the gutter. A throbbing cacophony resolved into voices and screaming and the feint ululation of sirens. Someone helped her to her feet and disappeared into the gathering crowd. She looked around for the woman who looked like herself, saw blood extruding from beneath the wheels of a vintage streetcar, still rocking in its tracks; saw blood splattered on her skirt, blood and viscera near where she'd fallen. Shaken, confused, she slipped away and walked towards her home in The Annex, stopping once, only briefly, to lean against her obscured reflection in the window of a confectionery shop while she scraped scarlet grime from her boots.

Later, being soothed in a warm bath, Anna tried to erase the persistent perceptions of exploding flesh, but she couldn't get rid of the eyes that connected with hers in a moment of recognition. Stirring the water by shifting in slow undulations, she made the waves roll over the length of her body and then she submerged her head, sliding down so her newly blonde hair fanned away from her skull. Another moment surged into her mind and she remembered being jostled; then another, and she saw the woman's dark hair flare in a breeze of hurried movement. Three images in random sequence. The jostling, hair swirling, the eyes reaching out to her own. Anna forgot where she was and inhaled a noseful of soapy water. She surfaced violently, gasping for breath.

After her bath, she gathered her bloodstained skirt, her tights, and the other clothes she'd been wearing, that were piled on the floor, and jammed them into a laundry hamper. She removed a jar of clay-based deep cleansing cream from the back of the medicine cabinet over the sink, pushing a canister of men's shaving foam to the side. She applied a thick mask to her face with the vague notion that it might reduce her sense of revulsion, being symbolically disguised from herself — she believed that symbols could be more efficacious than creams as restoratives. She had once studied literature and philosophy, she still thought a lot about language and thinking. Knowledge filtered through the minds of great thinkers, great writers, connected her to the world and separated her from it — her blessing, her curse, Robert would say, to live so much in her mind.

Anna ate vegetarian that night. She couldn't stomach the thought of cooking raw meat. She drank half a bottle of Beaujolais, holding the very old tulip glass with her thumb pressing the stem against the fore and middle fingers of her right hand, although she was left-handed. The glass was crystal, not glass. She savoured the word *crystal* and thought about words to distract her from thinking. It is not crystalline. Lead makes it musical. Modern crystal has no lead. Glass is a container and a material to make it. She thought about games that words play and smiled at her need to use words to think about how they do it. We dwell in a labyrinth of language, she thought, and was not surprised when Heidegger sprang into her mind, that old fantastical Duke of dark corners who espoused Nazi doctrine and revised our ways of exploring the nature of Being. Heidegger was accompanied in her mind by the original semiotician, Ferdinand de Saussure, who ironically wrote nothing but left an inexhaustible legacy cribbed by his admirers from lecture notes. She also thought about the minotaur, terrible with a bull's head and the body of a man, who lived in the labyrinth on ancient Crete designed for King Minos by the architect Daedalus, and simultaneously she thought of Stephen Daedalus and his slavish amanuensis, James Joyce, who nurtured the illusion that he had created Stephen and not the other way around. The minotaur's name was Asterion; names are important. Asterion was killed by Theseus of Athens. The fantastical Duke was Vincentio in *Measure for Measure* and he was C.G. Jung in the cosmology of Robertson Davies.

Anna thought all of this in the instant between moments of time, while savouring the sprightly fruitiness of the wine, admiring the transparency of the crystal that cast planes of light into unnatural perfect contours, and feeling the damp coolness of her pale hair against the nape of her neck.

Grounded in semiotics, where they converge with linguistics in critical theory, Anna had fled academe to work as a research librarian. She soon discovered her function was approaching atrophy, reduced to irrelevance by universally accessible computers. Still, she felt she must have occasional clients of sufficient influence to affirm her symbolic importance and apparently in sufficient numbers to justify her continued employment. They sought her out on the eighth floor of the Toronto Public Library because the algorithms and silicon chips at their disposal could not rival the allusiveness of an unfettered mind.

She could correlate the magic of light pouring through crystal with wine from Brouilly on the western slopes of the Saône and dry dark stout pouring down Leopold Bloom's gullet by the Liffey while his wife masturbated at home and Icarus soared too close to the sun, leaving

Nietzsche and Kafka cavorting in the darkest shadows of inspired confusion, all in an instant that would have left Google flummoxed, had Google the sense to be aware of itself.

She could think, computers could not. Between moments of time, she could abjure logic for metaphor, facts for abstraction, equivalence for irony, data for emotions and empathy. There was no algorithm for empathy, nor for the horror she endured as she tried to evade the woman scraped into quivering slush under the streetcar.

Anna slumped down in the depths of the blue sofa and stared at the blank television on the opposite wall, affronted by the absence of reflection. Television screens used to mirror the world opposing them. They appeared as alive with potential as toasters. Now they cast only a pall until activated, then dominated with images so impossibly light-infused colour-charged hyper-real that reality could not compete.

She switched off the table lamp but the dull rectangular darkness of the screen remained the focal centre of the room. If she weren't there, if she could observe without being a presence, she suspected it would still shape the room, ordering its small universe in relation to emptiness. She glanced at her open laptop tilted precariously on the sofa beside her. Its Liquid Crystal Display was inert, but the shiny screen projected a reassuring light, and by moving slightly she could catch her own image unresolved in its depths. Yet computers made her uncomfortable. It was not a matter of intimidation, outmoded nostalgia, phobic repulsion. She was not a Luddite. She was a McLuhanite who believed that the brain itself was subject to evolving technology. As writing goes, so goes the mind.

She wandered on a coherent trajectory, tracing a familiar concern. Cursive script had been removed from the school curriculum a generation ago. The links between words formed in the mind and fine motor skills were relegated to and derived from keyboard exercises. In 1439 the blacksmith Johannes Gutenberg made letters into things. They were now reduced to aspects of circuitry linking cerebral impulses to bytes herded by software into accessible clusters. There was no visceral connection. The human mind was superfluous, passive, a neural receptor. Words became incomplete signs, signifiers with no obligation to signify. Before Gutenberg's moveable type, arrangements of letters were synonymous with history and language was autonomous, tangible, copyable, portable. In Mesopotamia five thousand years ago, and separately in Mesoamerica, twenty-five hundred years ago, signs were devised to extend mental function through space and time. Gutenberg gave signs currency among the masses. But then the computer keyboard reduced the minds that deployed them to ciphers in an algorithmic process. Only a few people remained who could think, could do with the mind what computers could not comprehend, could defy logic and make sense.

Anna had such a mind — even if now in the extremity of residual horror its efficacy seemed tenuous. She gave way to the emotionally-charged thoughts her thinking concealed.

The other woman had given no indication she had recognized herself in Anna, in the moment before death, before jostling as they passed — if they jostled. Nothing was certain.

Anna's hair gleamed in the laptop, picking up highlights from the overhead light in the kitchen. The woman's hair had been dark, the way Anna's was before having it bleached and coloured and styled during her extended lunch break a few hours earlier. The woman wore no makeup. She looked unkempt and a little unclean. In the dank evening air, neither wore head coverings.

Anna had often observed herself in the mirror looking exactly like the woman had looked, especially after a weekend grieving and gardening in the tiny lot behind her house. But the other woman would never have seen a blonde looking out from her mirror, a woman with perfect grooming, wearing subtle lipstick and discreet eye shadow and a hint of colour on her cheeks.

Anna reached over and closed the laptop and switched on the table lamp beside the sofa. She had been wearing a winter jacket, good quality. The woman had been wearing a similar jacket, worn and untidy. Even before recognizing their similarity, Anna had noticed neither of them was wearing glasses. They didn't have computer lenses shielding their eyes and interpreting perception, augmenting reality — something which from a spectator's point of view might have seemed alarming, certainly unusual. Anna never wore glasses. There was no legal requirement. She preferred to see what she saw.

She had been carrying a leather handbag. She had dropped it when they jostled against each other. Anna had been carrying the handbag. She had leaned down to pick it up. The streetcar had sideswiped the woman's face, twisting her tumbling against the panel protecting the wheels, twisting her into a mass of blood-drenched clothing and shattered bones as it drew her in like one of those machines that turns branches to woodchips.

Anna rose and walked into the hall in search of her handbag. She went up to the bathroom and bedroom and checked there, then back down into the kitchen, and finally out to the front porch in case she had set it down while retrieving her keys. The keys had been in the pocket of her jacket. No, they had been in her hand. They had been under the doormat.

She returned to the bathroom and checked the laundry hamper to see if she had dropped her handbag in with the soiled clothes. She didn't rummage through. They were blood-spattered and seemed like they belonged to somebody else. Retrieving a green garbage bag from under the sink, she dumped the clothes, even those from the day before, into the bag, tied it closed, and slid it into the hallway.

Standing by the sink, she began to scrub off her cleansing mask. She was comforted by the grotesque unfamiliar image in the mirror. As the clay diluted and washed away, her skin appeared naked, with a pallor that made her feel hopelessly exposed. She applied moisturizer, then carried the garbage bag out to the bin by her back porch, and returned to the living room where she slouched back onto the sofa and used the remote to switch on the television. It was set to the local news channel she had been watching the previous night. With the sound off — she always turned the sound off and on separately — she watched a horrific report of the streetcar incident with close-ups lasciviously avoiding the body parts on the pavement while making sure the viewer was aware they were there, before returning to an antiseptic studio shot of two attractive figures, a pale man and a brown woman, who were severed at the waist by a mirrored glass desk.

What Anna saw, what she thought she saw, what she remembered, was from the perspective of a different accident. In that accident, she was not an onlooker. She turned her head in her memory and observed with no emotion as a body-bag was zipped beside her, catching a shock of Robert's black hair in its teeth. It was hoisted into a vehicle, not the ambulance they were putting her into but another, a dark-sided coroner's van. A siren pierced the air and she had trouble locating its source because she was in the middle of the noise. Then she was in a hospital somewhere. Everything was silent and she slipped into darkness. Time collapsed the way it does in that instant between moments where terror at the sight of an oncoming car becomes horror at the realization of what has already occurred. With drugged apprehension she grasped that Robert was dead, her seventh-month pregnancy was obliterated, and she had miraculously horrifically tragically survived.

Robert's insurance paid off the house. She returned to work.

She had lectured at the university for a couple of years as an adjunct, her meagre stipend supplemented by his postdoctoral fellowship in molecular biology. He had eventually found his research unbearable and accepted a job in the registrar's office. She abandoned her own academic career. She took the library position because books were her passion. She loved to explore among words, opening their deepest recesses, exploring the caverns and mazes of illusion, allusion, shadows, and secrets.

After the crash, when the hit-and-run driver had changed her life utterly, she found in her work at the library a measure of forgiveness for having survived.

During the next four years, consciousness seemed like a curse. She did not identify as a young widow. No one who suffered the loss of a child could ever again be young, and to label herself as the wife of someone who no longer existed seemed spuriously cruel. She existed in the world and there was nothing she could do to change that. She would still be on her own, without her beloved husband, still childless after they had cocooned through the middle of her pregnancy, talking to the baby squirming inside her, whispering to her, singing to her, holding each other, dreaming with excitement and fear and hope as they opened their lives to welcome her in, and then she had been destroyed, he had been destroyed, Anna had been destroyed. Grief was not something to get over but something to endure.

A month ago, her life changed. A man Anna's age had asked her to help in his inquiry on toads. He had been accessing books on the eighth floor since the late fall. From the quality of his clothing, which was somewhat exhausted, usually mismatched, invariably clean, she assumed he was a member of the privileged class who had fallen on difficult times, probably had emotional problems, and was taking refuge from the cold.

"Toads," he said.

It was the first time she had heard him speak.

"Amphibians in the froggish order, *anura*," she observed, without looking up.

"So, you know they're a frog." He seemed surprised. "Most people confuse toads and frogs. They think they're different altogether and actually they're not. Toads *are* frogs."

"I know that," she said. She made eye contact. He wasn't wearing glasses. She realized that since she had first noticed him several months ago, she had never seen him wear glasses, carry a laptop, or defer to a library computer. He read books. "Is that what you need to confirm? That toads are frogs? Or are you looking for toads of Toad Hall, or Margaret Atwood's signature toads, or Shakespeare's ugly and venomous toads, or Philip Larkin's *Toads Revisited*? Cars towed away, poisonous toads, exploding toads, toads in the hole, *Toads on Toast*, three-toed tree toads, toad tasters, horn toads, toad lickers, sin eaters, toadstools, mushrooms, obsequious toadies or sycophants?"

"You're being redundant, and slightly hysterical," he said. "Obsequious and toadie and sycophant mean the same thing; they only imply difference. And toadstools *are* mushrooms."

They stared at each other over the desk between them. She, an attractive woman with dark hair and sad hazel eyes. He, handsome but not boyish in the current vogue, with brown hair, brown eyes crinkled at the edges that made him seem wary, possibly concealing a suppressed sense of humour. He, a little gaunt rather than lean; she, slender, lithe. When she moved, she moved purposefully. He moved with diffidence, as if he were startled by his own capacity for movement. Like a young Jimmy Stewart. She was more like Julia Roberts. Different eras, of course, both ageless in celluloid and silicon bytes.

They introduced themselves and, after that initial encounter, Anna and Sebastian talked nearly every workday, always in the library, always with her desk between them, until one day, two days ago, he asked her for coffee.

They settled in at the nearby Coffee Café on Yorkville. He was well-turned-out and, for a reclusive man, he was surprisingly loquacious. His hair was brushed, his nails were clean, his worn black shoes were polished to a lustrous intensity. He spoke with the air of a man who knew things. He wanted to talk about books and computers as if their discussion were part of a secret agenda.

"You can't say one is better than the other," he declared.

"I can."

"That's like arguing theories of evolution and creationism. It can't be done." He took reading glasses out of his pocket and put them in place. He looked at the menu and ordered a piece of cherry pie. She ordered a soy latte. He asked to make it two. He put his spectacles away. "They're theories to explain different worlds entirely."

"Evolution isn't a theory," she declared. "It's a *word* used to indicate facts, many of which are known and understood, some of which aren't. *Creationism* is a word used to describe a system of *beliefs*. It is not a theory either. It is speculation by the wishfully bewildered."

"Did you know you use oral italics?"

"Only for *emphasis*," she said.

"Well, check your computer, Annie. You'll find both are offered as theories."

No one had called her Annie since Robert was killed.

"The computer is *wrong*," she said.

"Computers aren't right or wrong."

"Sometimes they're wrong. They spew information donated by humans as fact. They're no match for the mind, for art or for poetry."

"They don't intend to be," he said.

"Well, they're not. Here's a test. How would a computer deal with Samuel Beckett's 'I can't go on, I'll go on'? How could a machine grasp the existential complexity of a character who speaks himself into existence?"

"Don't we all? At least Beckett didn't reverse it and say, 'I'll go on, I can't go on'."

"Exactly. That would be simple defeat. He offers despair."

"And that's a good thing?" he asked, as a rhetorical assertion.

"Continuance, the potential to endure until you don't."

"Which would be defeat, I believe."

"Okay, then," she said. "What would a computer do with that wonderful line from Yeats, 'How can we know the dancer from the dance?'?"

"What would you want a computer to do with it?"

"Understand it, explain it, replicate it. Not likely, Sebastian. It's a flawless summary of artistic perfection — among other things."

She had not used his name before. It seemed comfortable. He was a Sebastian. He was charmingly eccentric, perhaps more so because he didn't seem to notice how eccentric he was.

"What about 'To be or not to be'?" she challenged.

"What about it?"

Robert might have asked the same thing as a form of indulgence. Sebastian seemed genuinely intrigued.

"The ultimate existential question," she said. "Nietzsche in a nutshell. A computer could never be so succinct, so precise, so allusive, because a computer cannot capture the myriad implications, the magical possibilities, of the copula verb in all its illimitable contexts. It can only list them."

"But *your* mind can?"

"Can what?"

"Capture the *magical* copula."

"With all I am able to conjure, yes. To be, to be: ranging from what Heidegger called *dasien*, being in the world, to Churchill anticipating Richard Burton's Hamlet soliloquy, declaiming *sotto voce* from the front row of the Aldwych."

"The Old Vic, I believe. And your linking the two, is arbitrary."

"No, it's inevitable. Two geniuses, one a Nazi intellectual, the other the Nazi nemesis — a script, spoken aloud to confound the doubt it conveys; an ontological *proscript*, giving perspective on the nature of Being. And so on and so on. Binaries, complementarities. The connections in my mind were instantaneous. And if you don't follow, well then, you don't. Drink your coffee, I've got to get back to work."

She was exhilarated. She would like to have lingered and the desire made her restless.

"*Perfection*?" he said. He was relentless. "*Magical*? Can something be both?"

"Of course." She couldn't refuse his invitation to preen. "Ezra Pound's poem, *In a Station of the Metro*, do you know it? Of course you know it. But do you? No computer could master its perfect balance of objective correlatives, each side of the poem standing exactly for the other, implying heaven and hell in the spaces between. Only the mind of a great poet could create such a perfectly magical equation." She repeated the title line, 'In a Station of the Metro', and followed with the poem in its entirety.

> The apparition of these faces in the crowd:
> Petals on a wet, black bough.

She drew silence out at the end of her recitation like a round of applause, then dropped the professorial air and spoke conversationally:

"Competitions between computers and people are stupidly misguided, you know. Of course computers can outplay humans at chess; it's a game of logistical tactics. They can do better at *Jeopardy*, a game calling for singular bits of raw information. But a poem! They can only imitate poetry, not create it, not even by random accident." She smiled. "Well now then," she said, allowing the smile to fall away. "I really have to go."

"Wait a minute." He reached over the table and restrained her with one hand placed gently across her forearm. "I wonder, could you answer me something?" He seemed embarrassed. There was a tremor of urgency in his voice. He leaned forward and asked: "Did your husband wear glasses?"

Anna was startled. She had to think for a moment. Her companion was an unusual man. His random curiosity unnerved her.

One afternoon he had casually explained that he had been in an asylum for a while but left undiagnosed. They released him under his own recognizance, he told her. They were sure he would return when his symptoms were more clearly defined. His disclosure didn't frighten her. His candour made him seem endearing and invited her confidence. She had told him about Robert and the accident and losing her baby.

"Sometimes," she answered. "Yes, reading glasses occasionally. Computer lenses at work, of course, but never at home. I think it was my influence. Why do you ask?"

"You don't wear them at all."

"I have a pair but I don't use them. And I don't need reading glasses. What about you?"

"I use spectacles in a place like this, where the ambient light has a fluorescent effect. They're polarized to cut down the glare. Does it strike you as odd or unusual that no one else is like you?"

"Except maybe you," she said. She felt unaccountably exposed.

"We are rare," he said. "You and I. We want reality to be unimpeded. *Un-impeded.* It is refreshing to know you."

"Thank you," she said, then as propriety demanded, she added: "You, too."

"Thank you."

"Why glasses?" she asked.

"Glasses are glasses are glasses. Gertrude Stein comes to mind, yes, and your husband is always a presence. So I asked. Sometimes things are that simple."

"Or that complex," she responded. Colour rose in her cheeks; he was making her uncomfortable, she rose to her feet. She jarred the table and set the flower in a tall plastic vase atremble. Loveliness extreme, the red rose in the vase was real.

She smiled at the gentleness with which worlds collided.

"Glasses are glasses are glasses," she said. "We're back to playing with the transformative powers of the copula, but I have a job to do, I really must go."

He nodded and remained sitting, leaving her to walk back to the library on her own. As she ascended to the eighth floor and settled into her work station, which was essentially an uncluttered desk, one of two within sight of carrels set parenthetically among stacks of reference books gathering dust, she realized how foolish she'd been to be wary or even a little bit fractious. Sebastian was out of synch with the world but no more than she, and with greater detachment. She suspected he was haunted by his own share of demons, but how could there be anything sinister in his awkward attempts to be charming?

The bookish intimacy she discovered with Sebastian had released a craving for intellectual stimulation that, with a pang of guilt, she realized extended back to a time before Robert. In graduate school she had thrived on the informal debates in seminars and colloquia, in pubs and occasionally in beds, where without embarrassment she and her friends could flex their cerebral dexterity, sharing in intellectual triumphs like kids in a utopian sandbox.

When she met Robert, it was different. They explained things to each other. They spoke from the perspectives of their separate disciplines. Discussion tended to set them apart rather than bring them together.

She was unnerved by how liberating guilt made her feel.

She rearranged papers on her desk, then she wandered through the deserted stacks, breathing the familiar reassuring air and struggling to sort feelings from thoughts. A gentle zephyr curled about her as she moved, carrying the melancholy scent of books as they slowly disintegrated, the sweet scent of words shaken loose from their texts, the warm dry scent of an outmoded technology.

She soon lost herself contemplating Sebastian's explanation for the curiosity he had shown about Robert's glasses, when he had pared the word *glasses* down to its literal meaning with repetitive force in a parody of Gertrude Stein. Anna's sprawling response, which she had not articulated at the time, expressed a playfulness evoked by his uncomplicated posturing. She reached past a homonymic cluster that included looking glasses, e-glasses, eye-glasses, drinking glasses, spy glasses, window panes, to consider glasses as symbols and signs, representations of visionary experience, spiritual illumination, or, darkly, humility, signifiers of intelligence, imagination, or insight. She resisted pursuing permutations of the word rose, despite his whimsical allusion, or the radically divergent meanings, as Stein variously indicated, of '*Rose* is a rose' and '*a rose* is a rose', a word is a name or a flower, but always a *word*, and she refused to delve into the numberless memoirs of the Lost Generation in Paris, for whom Stein was the nearly forgotten doyenne. Preoccupied with words, she forgot about her anxiety over why Sebastian had asked about glasses in the first place or why he should be curious about Robert at all.

Although he did not come to the library the next day or the next, she booked an appointment to bleach her hair and colour it blonde, and she decided to ask him to dinner. She had not cooked except for herself since Robert and the baby had died.

She sat forward and touched her fingertips to her face. The skin felt unnaturally taut. She settled back into the sofa's commodious embrace to watch television. She wanted to be distracted from ruminations about Sebastian that would accentuate her loneliness, or about Robert and her unbearable sorrow, or about her duplicate self, whose entire life had collapsed into a single unredeemable instant, or about the squirming of her daughter, impatient to be born. The visceral horror of the last image subsumed all the rest. She trembled and focussed on the screen in front of her.

And as she sat in the semi-darkness, she was afraid. She was not afraid of death, nor of the dead. Part of her longed for both, to be there, to be with them. She was afraid of her own thoughts. In a world predisposed to order over chaos at whatever the cost, retribution for survival seemed inevitable. Her breathing constricted as if she were responsible because she and the woman had looked so alike, a woman who might have been her.

The streetcar *incident*! Without consciously discriminating, she deployed key words to differentiate between what had happened earlier in the day and the *accident* four years ago. An incident was arbitrary, a freak misadventure, while an accident was a disturbance in the natural order of things, a rent, large or small, in the fabric of time. Yet both happened for reasons beyond understanding. The universe was indifferent; even mad people had dreams.

Anna dreamed of her daughter who would now have been four, but the dreams were of someone she could talk to, who would listen, refute, confirm, deny, be nurtured and nurture, laugh, cry, touch, and share with her mother the sorrow of bereavement. Anna seldom dreamed of Robert. She thought perhaps it was a matter of self-preservation. Such dreams were memories not fantasy, and too much to bear.

She smiled at the television. At the device itself, not the content. How improbable that human evolution should have become diverted so far from its natural course by an instrument of our own devising. She thought of the dour prescience of Thomas Hobbes, about the brutish nature of life in a self-conscious world. She thought of Shakespeare, his contemporary, who flourished amid the clash between progress and conviction. Her mind fluttered with excitement. There were times, despite her distressing memories, when the tumbling bits in her mind fell into apt postulations and she found herself happy. She associated Sebastian with those times, when at a loss for words a telling snippet of poetry sprang forward, a philosopher's name that signified an appropriate structure of thought asserted itself, or when an ephemeral emotion, an inarticulable notion, became suddenly palpably clear. This struck her as pleasantly peculiar, since she had known him only briefly but had lived in her mind most if not all of her life.

Time passed. The lamplight that penetrated from the city outside magnified the darkness. She turned on the television and the reality of a *Downton Abbey* rerun displaced her own. She forgot where she was, who she was, until an insistent banging intruded. An acerbic rejoinder by the dowager countess fell flat. Anna rallied, turned off the TV and made her way heavily to the door.

Peering through the security peephole, she saw distended images of two police officers, a man and a woman, shuffling nervously, not talking. She opened the door and stood back, oblivious to the fact that she was in a bathrobe with her hair unattended and her face gleaming unnaturally from residual moisturizer that left traces of luminescence.

"Yes?" she said tentatively, ceding the initiative to them.

"Is this the home of Dr Anna Winston?" The woman had a stricken look on her face.

"It is, but…"

"We have some very bad news, I'm afraid. May we come in?"

"Yes, of course," said Anna, moving back through the foyer into the main hall that opened onto the living room.

"This is far enough," said the man. "We don't want to track snow."

His e-glasses had fogged up and he removed them, gave them a quick wipe, replaced them, and peered at her through a stream of images. The woman removed her own glasses in a gesture of empathy and held them in her gloved hands.

"There's been an accident," the woman said. She hesitated. "Dr Winston has been killed."

"Killed?"

Mistaking Anna's confusion for doubt, the woman put on her glasses again and repeated herself. "Dr Winston is dead, I'm afraid." The policewoman paused, then added, "A streetcar. Very unusual. We're sorry."

"Yes, but…"

"We think she was pushed."

"My God!"

"We think she was murdered."

"Really?"

"There was apparently a struggle."

"A struggle?"

"Jostling, ma'am. Two or three people. Several witnesses — less reliable than one, as they say. We'll have to analyze their video recall."

"Did you find her purse?" Anna asked.

"We did. How did you know?"

How did she know?

"You're here," she said.

"Yes, of course. We'll require you to come to the station in the morning. Here's my card. We'll need information. We'll want to ask you some questions."

There was no reason to think she was Anna. There was no reason to think the mangled cadaver wasn't her.

"Do you want me to identify the body. Where is it?" It! Not her, not me.

"No, ma'am. I'm afraid there's not enough left. Who are you, ma'am?"

"A friend passing through."

"Your name, please."

"Uh, Annesley, Annesley Hall." That was the name of her residence in first year university.

"Are you going to be all right, Ms Hall?"

"I think so. I'd like to be alone, please."

"Of course, ma'am. Is there anyone else here? Do you have someone you can call?"

"It's okay," said Anna.

As the police officers descended the verandah steps, the woman paused and turned back to address Anna, who was standing in the cold at the open door.

"Your monitor wasn't turned on, ma'am. We tried to reach you. We couldn't connect. That's why we came in person."

"Thanks," said Anna. "Good night."

The woman joined her partner. Anna closed the door.

The police had left behind puddles of melting snow that pooled in a depression on the hardwood floor beside Anna's boots, one with a dried bloody sheen where she hadn't quite scraped the leather clean.

As soon as she locked the door, Anna sank to the floor. She lay curled in on herself with her head tilted to the side, her cheek partly on wood, partly on the edge of the small tribal rug she had bought in a splurge before meeting Robert. She tried to sort through the onslaught of words, the barrage of images, that exploded slowly, instantly, inside her head.

Whatever the police might surmise, she was alive. *Cogito ergo sum* — the capacity to doubt her existence proves the doubter exists. She took heart, she could think, she was there in the world. This was not a dream. The blood smear on her boot had a history. It was actual, with colour, texture, transparency. She lay sprawled with her head close enough she could smell the damp leather. This was not fiction. A fictional character could only think what her author thought for her, but Anna could think for herself. It was not hallucination or madness. She could feel authentic grief for the dead from her past and she could feel the genuine dread of a future without them. She could position herself in a present as real as the smell of boots and blood. Yet she knew nothing, nothing was certain.

# Chapter Two
# House of Mirrors

During most of a sleepless night Anna yearned for the antiseptic clarity of René Descartes or Jeffrey Dahmer, the thinker or the killer. As dawn turned to day, narrative coherence took hold. During the last four years she had struggled with the possibility that Robert had been murdered. Such suspicions were a common way people rationalized the arbitrariness of accidental death — she'd been told this before she stopped telling anyone what she suspected. The car that had smashed into them had been stolen, the driver had vanished. It had been a big car, a lethal weapon, and may have accelerated before slamming into the side of their Mazda. No motive was discernable, no reason revealed, but it seemed to her an intentional crime. No one believed her suspicions were justified. Her injuries, the baby's death, had been assessed as collateral damage. Robert was recorded as the primary victim in a tragic accident. Anna's horror was assimilated over time into an aspect of personality. It defined who she was, a woman alone; her's was a story seldom told, even to herself.

She packed a small bag with a few clothes and dressed inconspicuously, wearing a nubuck jacket to complement her patent leather boots and matching purse. The coat from last evening looked shabby in the foyer light. She should have thrown it out. She walked through residential backstreets in the Annex for a couple of hours, then down to a bank and withdrew five hundred dollars at the instant teller from the travel account which was still in Robert's name. His last name wasn't Winston, but she retained access and made random deposits. She liked the continuity, although she had no travel intentions. She had explored extensively before she was married, preferring the cultural wellsprings of Europe to the drugs and sex of Thailand, where her compatriots took frenetic respite before settling into unexceptional lives.

Once the police realized she was alive they would want an explanation for why she hadn't confessed to being herself. She wasn't sure. If there had been a murder, was she the suspected killer? Or had she been the intended victim? She wanted to avoid the police. She wondered if there was anyone anywhere who has never yearned to be a stranger in a world too painfully familiar, who has not wished to hide, even from herself, when thoughts and emotions collide. She wanted to avoid the earnest authorities who had explained away the deaths of her infant and husband as, in effect, an unfortunate wrinkle in 'the universe unfolding as it should'. That was from *Desiderata*. She had an intellectual's contempt for the facile poem quoted by *Star Trek* actors and depthless politicians. It occurred to her she might be paranoid — but people were dead. Her fears and confusion were based on empirical truth, not the maniacal manoeuvres of a wounded mind.

Anna rushed, her head swirled. She took long strides over the sidewalk runnelled with slush, but she did not pay much attention to where she was going until she drew up short in front of the Public Library on Yonge Street. She paused, removed computer glasses from her purse and put them on. No one she worked with had ever seen her wearing them. Most people preferred their world to be shaped by a central source; being isolated that way made them feel less alone. She glanced suspiciously in all directions and went in, tilting her head down and to the side, hiding behind the unfamiliar glasses and a veil of blonde hair. She got to the elevator without being noticed.

The combination of vertical movement in the elevator and the horizontal movement of information projected into the liminal middle distance through her e-glasses induced vertigo and she was forced to shut her eyes until the elevator came to a stop. She knew most people quickly learned to look through the data stream without focussing, allowing it to register in the visual cortex with a minimum of retinal interference. Apart from the occasional contraction of the iris as users aimed with a stare and blinked a command, they appeared fully engaged with the world they occupied and only subliminally possessed by the world that occupied them. This double vision was something Anna had intentionally resisted. She conceded the willfulness but denied that she was disabled — she was told it was like she was colour blind when everyone else perceived colours, like she was tone deaf while surrounded by music. Yet she loved the immediacy of music, the directness of colour. She believed with the strength of conviction that *hers* was not the reduced sensibility.

When the door opened on her floor, she changed her strategy and walked through like she belonged, in spite of the nausea. No one noticed. She didn't stop at her work station but progressed into the shadows of an empty carrel cloistered among the dusty rows of reference books. She settled in to wait. The book left behind by a previous reader was called *Invisible Among the Ruins*. She put away her glasses and read passages at random (the book had seemingly been designed to be read that way), until Sebastian appeared. She saw him conferring with Peter Dearing, her coequal (neither accepted the other as boss), and then watched his body fall slack, as if his suddenly voluminous clothing was all that held up his muscles and skin. He walked slowly in her direction, obviously hoping to console himself in the shadows.

As he moved past her carrel she whispered, with her head still down, her face hidden by hair which he had never seen blonde: "Do you believe in ghosts?"

"Only dead ones."

It was one of those moments when time spins ahead and then backwards, rocking like a car on frozen snow to get out of a rut. Anna was desperate to leap to her feet and embrace him, while Sebastian seemed seized, in the midst of crushing grief, with the possibility that death was an illusion, something as a nihilist he should have suspected.

He stopped, grasping the back of her carrel, trembling, not touching her. His voice quavered. He seemed desperate to follow his spontaneous joke with another, but uttered only a babble of allusive confusion.

"I, you, we, you're blonde, a streetcar, the police, you're dead."

"Be quiet," she said. "Be quiet, Sebastian, sit down, no, not here, in the carrel behind me. Listen. Lean forward, listen. I need you."

"I'm here."

"Someone tried to kill me. I'm probably wanted for murder."

"Which?"

"Both. I think I'm wanted for murder. Someone tried to kill me."

There was an uneasy pause and then he said, "I'm still here."

She felt a disconcerting surge of affection.

They left separately and met at The Coffee Café, where the air was infused with the layered aromas of roasted caffeine and steam-espressed grounds holding winter at bay.

Sebastian commandeered a small table by immediately sitting down. Anna set her travelling bag on the floor beside him and picked up a couple of soy lattes at the counter. She carried them over to the table where he was perusing the menu. When she approached, he quickly folded his spectacles and tucked them into a breast pocket. It hadn't concerned her before, but she couldn't help wondering, if he needed glasses to read, what had he been doing in the fluorescent glare of the library for the past few months? Had he only simulated reading as he pored over various books, including *Tristes Tropique* by Claude Lévis-Strauss, in which toads were likened to human armpits? She had noticed he read it in French. If, if he had read it at all.

Perhaps it was only the light in the Café, but it seemed no more glaring than in the library carrels. He wasn't quite what he seemed to be.

"Saw your death on the news last night," he said cheerfully. He seemed to have recovered from the shock of her inexplicable resurrection. Then he turned appropriately sombre. "They withheld the name. Sounded grisly, tied up traffic for almost an hour."

She offered a wan smile, then proceeded to talk, and the more she told him the more frantic she became to be understood. She needed to feel grounded, to know that she was not floating away on an ebb tide of dread. She told him every detail she could recall about the streetcar incident. She repeated her account of the accident when she lost Robert and her baby. She explained her fears and suspicions. She used the word 'conspiracy', but she couldn't explain its relevance. The more she tried to clarify, the more confusing her account became.

"Occam's razor," he said at last. She was relieved he had interrupted. What he proceeded to tell her was familiar, but she appreciated hearing his voice. "The deep fat friar argued the simplest answer is usually correct. I suppose that's why it's a razor, it cuts through the superfluous stubble. Sebastian of Occam was a Franciscan with a vested interest in simplicity, a theoretical logician — I suppose all logicians are theoretical — he argued that the hypothesis based on the fewest assumptions will generally be best. Ludwig Wittgenstein honed the razor — you might say he stropped it keen — by saying a sign that is not necessary is meaningless. If that seems obscure, try it the other way around: if a sign seems to have meaning, it does."

She gazed at him with a mixture of awe and bewilderment. He spoke of his namesake, a fourteenth century monk, as if they were friends who habitually debated logical parsimony over draughts of beer at their local pub. Had he also made a joke about a deep-thinking corpulent mendicant and saucepans? 'Deep fat fryer.' Was it a joke if he wasn't aware he was making it?

"*Numquam ponenda est pluralitas sine necessitate.*" Sebastian quoted the master, assuming she understood Latin, although his was imperfect. "*Frustra fit per plura, quod potest fieri per pauciora.*" The first statement had enough familiar echoes, she caught the gist, while the second evaded her; she assumed it meant much the same thing, in praise of simplicity.

He leaned back from the table to see her against their surroundings, an industrialized version of intimacy that had become ubiquitous in coffee shops around North America and was spreading to the bistros and cafés of Europe — décor as an expression of entitlement to justify unconscionable prices.

"You know about Occam, of course," he said. "You taught philosophy."

"Mostly literature."

"Ah, they are much the same thing. You have a PhD, you are a doctor of philosophy."

"Aesthetics, the philosophy of literature."

"Critical theory?"

"Cognitive linguistics, semiotics, poetics, deconstructionist discourse."

"The more you talk, the less certain you seem. Evidence of an unsettled mind, of a mind deconstructing, perhaps?"

"So I've been told."

"By your husband?"

"I'm not always the most thoughtful of thinkers, Sebastian. I'm better at making connections than working out consequences."

"So, I imagine you got my little witticism about the chubby friar. And what about your husband?"

"He was a molecular biologist."

"You told me that already. It is a large field."

"He was trying to encrypt DNA to perform set functions."

"Human DNA?"

"At the chemical level, plant and animal nucleotides converge. He was trying to synthesize nanoparticles of nucleic acid, independent of specific life-forms, to function as infinitesimal computing machines." Her response was drawn from half-buried memory, spoken by rote.

"Infusing them with algorithms."

"In effect."

"A terrifying field to work in. As daunting as astrophysics but not so safely ineffable. You will not alter the cosmos with space-time theories of relativity, but you can change the world with quantum-field theory by constructing computers out of self-replicating strands of deoxyribonucleic acid. Yes? Quite frightening, really."

"You seem at home talking about such things, Sebastian."

"A little, yes. It's just talk. I'm especially interested in the *theory of everything*."

"Seriously?"

"Of course. It's a concept in theoretical physics, also called the *final theory*."

"I know what it is. Robert was intrigued."

"So was Einstein."

"I pointed out to Robert, the final theory is perilously close to the *final solution* — by implication if not intent."

"And?"

"He dismissed my concern as unpleasant word-play and retreated into explications about molecular biology, something in which you seem exceptionally well-versed yourself."

"Well-versed in what I most fear! No, I'm at the doggerel level. I could spin out a couplet or two, but that's about it. I'm a bit of a sapient caterpillar, polyphiloprogenitive in my predilections, you might say. I creep slowly and devour small bytes as I go, but I am an omnivorous glutton. I might burst some day, I suppose, and become a butterfly."

Images of bursting made her uncomfortable. "In short," she said, "you know a lot but you've never studied."

"Not formally, no. I observe. Now, back to Occam. Your husband's death, it was almost certainly murder. The description of the facts you gave me before, especially in light of what you've told me today, leads to no other conclusion. The absence of a motive, the escape of the killer, they are unknowns in a separate equation. The event itself was clear. Someone ploughed a stolen car into yours from the side with sufficient velocity to assure lethal impact while allowing himself to escape unscathed and anonymous. Any explanation but first-degree murder introduces extraneous suppositions to account for his actions. His, yes, we'll suppose it was a male since there is nothing to indicate otherwise. The mystery and the event are separable. The crime is well documented. Motive remains unresolved. Motives in general are overrated in the resolution of murders."

"Sebastian." She leaned forward to see into his eyes and block out the soft beiges and browns that enveloped him in defiance of the winter outside. "Thank you," she said.

"Now let us strop the razor with another coffee." He made no move, so she got up and bought two more soy lattes and settled back opposite.

"Let us take as a given that your husband was murdered," he proceeded. "It is also a given that a woman roughly your age died in your presence by nefarious intent. Did you push her? It seems unlikely. You didn't know her and you are not, I presume, in the habit of pushing strangers under moving vehicles. Did you jostle her, did she jostle you? Let us assume it does not matter. An unknown activity caused the known to happen. No one has said that she tripped. Since perception distorts memory and memory distorts perception, it would strike me as reasonable to assume you were each jostled by a third party. She, to her death. You, off to the side. Certainly, you murdered no one, yourself. Now, what else is known? You dropped your handbag or it was wrenched from your grip and consequently she was identified as you? Did she look like you? Does it matter? It does. She literally looked more like you than you did! Your hair was dyed blonde. You were disguised. She was wearing a jacket similar to yours, walking your usual route. Now then, given your husband's murder as a precedent, it seems likely someone pushed her under the trolley, thinking it was you. And you contributed to the confusion, not only by leaching the natural colour from your hair but by leaving your bag and wallet behind. She was murdered and you were the intended victim. To think otherwise complicates the situation unreasonably."

Anna found his thinking perversely reassuring. His logical explanation of random chaotic events might have been little more than a coherent recapping, but his conclusions affirmed her intuitive grasp. What he said made sense of the inchoate particulars.

"Except…" she ventured.

"Yes, except that you did not own up to being alive when the police came to your door. That was a complication no one could have anticipated, although I'm sure your reasoning was sound."

"No, it wasn't. I was upset. My intellect, when I'm anxious, gives way to emotion. That was it, pure and simple — no, not so; anything but pure and not very simple. I was hiding from myself in a meaningless world."

"That sounds like a Sartrean manifesto, Annie. But the key question is, how are these incidents related? If we reject the possibility of coincidence, then you, Anna, are what connects them. Were you originally a target, along with Robert, and survived despite the loss of your baby? That must be terribly difficult to live with. I'm sorry, truly. Now, did you do something recently that invoked their wrath — let us call them *they* for the time being — did you arouse their need for vengeance? Perhaps for silence?"

"I thought we weren't interested in motive."

"Rationale, not motive. *How* would they justify killing you? We don't care *why* they felt it was necessary — only what they thought your death would accomplish."

"A subtle distinction. I'm not sure either a court or a corpse would find it convincing."

"A crucial distinction if we are to survive."

"*We*, Sebastian? You hardly know me."

"You dyed your hair for me. You thought I'd like it."

"Did I? Well, do you?"

"No, but it's a good thing you did. Vanity saved your life."

"I saw Peter Dearing give you the news of my death. You can't deny you were shocked."

"I can't. I don't as a rule have friends."

He confused her. He was ingenuous and soft-spoken, but he was also immodest and condescending; a self-conscious man who seemed not to care about the impression he made. She had not coloured her hair for him, but he had invoked in her a desire to engage once again with the world. She found him an emotionally complex stranger. Engaged, brilliant, naïve. In a time of desperate confusion, he seemed the only possible person to turn to.

"Sebastian, will you help me?" She tried not to sound plaintive.

He looked deeply into her eyes for a moment, then abruptly rose to his feet, pushing his chair back so forcefully it toppled with a clatter. "I have to go now," he said. "I need you to know I have never used the word 'polyphiloprogenitive' in a sentence before, I've never said it out loud to anyone." As if that were explanation enough for his departure, he walked away, wrapping his scarf securely around his neck as he moved out into the cold. When he disappeared from sight along Yorkville, Anna huddled into herself, baffled by his extraordinary behaviour.

She realized she didn't know him at all. Was he part of some conspiracy? Had she made him up? Was she herself an invention of her own mind like the feral protagonist in Abu-Bakr's ancient novel. Had events reduced her to the proverbial child on a desert island? She had a vast array of information at her disposal, but was it entirely separable from who she was? She felt bewildered and sickened and miserably alone, lost in a Kafkaesque world where even Kafka was missing.

For an instant she envied people who found their lives circumscribed by bits and bytes that had become the defining parameters of the human condition. She glanced around. Everyone in the café was online, some chatting and listening, some staring or preening, some typing with thumbs or forefingers, others picking out messages with their eyes on the monitor that their glasses projected in front of them, their eyebrows occasionally flexing, all of them filtering reality through texts and texting, tweets and ideograms, memes and quips and rejoinders, even the barista, who seemed to be falling in love through a site for lonely baristas.

Anna gazed into the dregs of her coffee. She felt alienated; from a different dimension. She looked around her again. Sebastian was standing in front of her. She realized she had been silently crying. She wiped away tears. She smiled wanly. He sat down opposite.

"I'm sorry," he said. "I seem to have lost myself for a minute."

"I know the feeling," she said. "Are you frightened? I don't blame you, you know."

"I'm back for the same reason I fled, because you asked me for help."

Wary of conflicted emotions, she said nothing.

"It would be hard to explain," he said in response to her silence.

Anna stared at her muddled friend. Sebastian was really quite beautiful. She uncrossed her legs, smoothed the material of her skirt over her thighs, and crossed them again. She took in a deep breath, held it, and let it ripple out slowly. Fear mixed with guilt, with a hint of desire; it was an odd combination.

"You will have to stay at my place," he announced. "They've probably figured by now that the dead woman isn't you. And *you* are. The confusion will lead them to assume depraved or felonious behaviour. The police will be, as they say, in hot pursuit. And they, the nefarious *they*, they will be close behind, if they are not already in the lead."

"You're scaring me, Sebastian."

"I intend to. For now, you need to consider *they* and the police are working together, even if the police don't know it. Since we have determined *they* were responsible for your botched assassination, I think we must consider we are now in the midst of an ongoing process to accomplish your death. You are in grave danger, and so am I."

She listened for ominous theme music to rise from the shadows. He talked like a Hitchcock protagonist in peril. In other circumstances she would have been amused. "They'll find out where you live," she said.

"They already know."

"Are you under surveillance?"

"Not to be paranoid, Annie" — he leaned forward and modulated his voice to a conspiratorial whisper — "but they know everything about us. It's all about information, the reduction of sovereign souls to statistics and quantifiable facts. We are amalgamations of data — as soon as the authorities learned to compare notes, to share files, to pool information, in nanoseconds we ceased being ourselves."

"The authorities?"

"The government, the universal corporate world."

"*Who* in the government, Sebastian?"

"Tax people, census takers, pollsters, statisticians, licensing agencies, healthcare agents, probably the police, although I've never been arrested — I'm assuming you haven't either — the transnational federal provincial municipal government people. And then, of course, the non-government agencies, ad agencies, retail agencies, banking agencies, insurance agencies. And social media. All of them. *They* are myriad beyond meaningful measure. They're linked electronically. Whoever controls the software owns us."

She shared his apprehension, although the proprieties of sanity in a vigilant world prevented her from articulating her anxiety in quite the same way.

"Sebastian, why are you here, really?"

"That's a big question. Locationally, motivationally, existentially?"

"Were you actually doing research on toads? I suppose if you were an authentic herpetologist, you wouldn't have needed my assistance. Is it simply a coincidence that my life has changed since we met or that we had coffee together two days before that woman died?"

"An *authentic* herpetologist, how glamorous. Well, toads were on my mind. I can't think why. Perhaps I was up the Amazon with Claude Lévis-Strauss. But no, I'm not enamoured of armpits. It's inexplicable, but not a coincidence. Events don't always follow causes in a logical sequence, but as Aristotle insisted, they nonetheless follow."

She wondered how many people in Toronto cited Aristotle so casually, or assumed their listeners would know what they meant. Or shared their fear and affection for a multisyllabic polymorphic word from a poem by T.S. Eliot: *polyphiloprogenitive.* She was flattered. And puzzled. Somehow, they had found each other, the last two people in the entire city, it seemed, who did not relate to the world by digital interface.

"*Real* coincidence," he said; he couldn't leave the topic unattended. "It is a dramatic device. The best movies and novels acknowledge coincidence for what it is. The best of the best, use its impossibility to develop notions of inexorable fate: 'Of all the gin joints, in all the towns, in all the world, she walks into mine.' Aristotle would have loved *Casablanca.*"

"Isn't fate by definition *inexorable?*"

"Retroactively, yes. Let's get out of here," he declared, rising again to his feet, this time flapping his arms in a gesture that indicated he wished her to join him. Despite being lean, he was awkward. He moved as if he were a temporary resident in his own body. "We'll go out the back way. Fortunately, a storm is blowing up. They'll never track us. There are too many prints. There's too much snow in the air."

She rose and followed, unsure whether he was valiant, a little demented, quite paranoid, or merely unusual. She was pretty sure Aristotle's actualistic ontology had been distorted, but she was no less charmed by the expediency of Sebastian's assertion that particular causes did not always precede discernable events. Good things sometimes happened for no apparent reason; *apparent*, of course, being the operative word.

They walked close, but not touching — there for each other if one of them happened to slip on the slush-hidden ice, but otherwise determinedly independent. By the time they arrived in front of a vast brick mansion with a mansard roof, manifold gables, and turrets adorning additions and wings, set back from Errington Lane in the heart of Rosedale, she was convinced there were people in what Sebastian had described as 'hot pursuit'. As if to confirm her fears, he suddenly took hold of her arm and pulled her away from the sidewalk into a narrow passage beside a tall cedar hedge leading along the side of the house. He guided her onto a side porch and into a vestibule. They climbed steep stairs that must have been for servants to pass unobtrusively in another era. It was like a secret route up to a hideaway where no one could possibly find them. When they reached the landing on the fourth floor, Sebastian huddled against the sloped ceiling, withdrew a key from his pocket, and let them into a small foyer, where they faced two steel-clad doors improbably secured by steel bars held in place with large padlocks. He extricated another key from his coat pocket and opened the door straight ahead, leaning the drop-bar against the wall. The door to the left would lead across the back of the house and remained secured. He reached into the darkness, and turned on lamps from a central switch, then guided her into attic rooms lined with shelves that were heavy with books, leather-bound and paperback mixed indiscriminately. More books were stacked on the pine plank floor, on the carpets, on tables and chairs. Anna felt simultaneously in alien territory and that she had come home, threatened and secure by the excessive security, reassured by the familiarity of books.

"Now, then," Sebastian said. "No one observed us come in. No one knows you're here." He seemed quite excited by the extremity of their solitude. "I call it The Cloisters."

"As in a cloistered monastery, or cloister, as in a walkway open on one side and closed on the other?"

"Cloisters, plural, many walkways within walls that conceal. This part was the living quarters for the emancipated Black servants two hundred years ago. They waited on the white servants and never appeared in the main parts of the house. As far as the family was concerned, they did not exist. Only the white servants were allowed to show themselves downstairs. The Negroes could not go outside except after dark, or on holidays when the family was in Muskoka. The outdoor help were always Italians or Dutchmen. Let me remove some of this clutter from the sofa, no, let me, I know exactly where everything is, I'm in the process of sorting. We don't want to disrupt my system. The drapes are closed, by the way, to keep out the light. You may peek through, of course, but don't leave them open. It's bad for my literary endeavours."

Anna gazed around her, trying to imagine the rooms without books. There were bars on the casements, massive locks on the outer door coming in off the landing, locks on most of the doors between rooms as well. Dust motes drifted in renegade shafts of light from the windows and all visible surfaces were coated in a fine layer, softening the edges of everything, making the entire place seem out of focus. Despite the dust, nothing was dirty. The whole bizarre labyrinthine set-up was chaotic but somehow exceptionally tidy. It was, on the whole, like being inside a bibliophile's brain, expanded to reveal its accumulated treasures and secrets.

"Have you been here a long time?" she asked.

"A couple of centuries."

My God, the undead. She sniggered to herself.

"My family," he clarified. "I'm neither Dorian Gray nor a vampire."

"Are you sure," she said.

"The house was built in stages as the Kroetsch family fortunes progressed. The first part was completed while George the Third reigned over us, and gable by gable, turret by turret, it accrued. Like Topsy, I suppose, it just grew and it grew. At the close of Victoria's *regni interminabilis* it looked like the hybrid monstrosity it appears to be now. Inside, of course, it has been quite modified, and this is my little aerie on top."

"And you own it? You're the last Kroetsch?"

"Apparently I am. Vampires and portraits don't perpetuate themselves. At least not in conventional ways. Now let's get you a coffee."

"We just had coffee."

"Then gin, will you have gin?"

She glanced at her watch: it had just turned noon.

"With a dash of vermouth, thank you."

When he came back through the creaking maze of passages that led to the kitchen, he had two martinis in hand. He gave Anna one and sat down beside her on the cleared sofa, which showed a network of depressions from books having been stacked on the grey velvet.

"Now then," he said. "You mustn't feel you're a prisoner, but I suggest you go nowhere for a few days. Actually, I insist. I will clear off my bed. I'll change the sheets if you'd like and I will sleep out here. I keep odd hours, but you may retire to your room whenever you wish. I will not be offended. You have in your bag a few clothes, I imagine. I will purchase whatever else you may need, just let me know. I will buy food. We'll cook. No ordering delivery; we are much too vulnerable. Do you have any sort of communication device? No. Good. Neither do I."

His restrictions made her feel uneasy and yet she was grateful.

"Who lived in these rooms before you?" she asked. It seemed unlikely that windows on the fourth floor would be barred for the containment of former slaves, however shabbily they may have been treated.

"Several generations of madmen," he answered without hesitation. "The last was Uncle Leicester. When he was no longer permitted to do extreme renovations or go out and hunt demons, he turned on himself. We locked him in here and kept him alive for a while, but it was hopeless. He died on this sofa, actually. Stabbed himself in the heart, dead before the knife stopped its forward thrust, I would imagine. A breadknife had found its way up from the kitchen. You wouldn't think a person could pierce his vitals with a serrated blade, but he did. We had it re-covered, of course. The sofa. It used to be pale green, chartreuse, in fact. I hardly remember him. We lived in the chambers below."

His casual chatter about self-slaughter made her queasy. She wanted to ask more about his family, about madness, about himself — facts to distract from the darkness hanging above her with piercing eyes and folded wings.

"You once told me you'd had a bout of near-madness, yourself. Enough that you were hospitalized," she said, nervous about violating propriety, anxious for clarification.

"Yes. No, I made that up to set you at ease."

"Really?"

"I assumed you'd be more comfortable thinking I was neurotic, even a little psychotic, than thinking this, as I am, is how I am."

"Ah, I am what I am. But you weren't." She paused for a moment to redirect the conversation. "Back in the coffee shop, you talked about Aristotle."

"I did."

"And about coincidence. 'There is no such thing,' you said. 'Everything happens for a reason.'"

"Two quite different propositions, coincidence and causality. The latter implies agency and intent. Coincidence, such as it is, is merely another name for correlations we don't understand."

"Like synchronicity."

"Ah yes, pseudo-physics and psycho-babble."

"But you do concede implausible phenomena sometimes concur."

"Oh, yes. But that doesn't mean there aren't *reasons* for their concurrence."

He spoke with authority, which she found both reassuring and condescending.

"Pascal's theory of probabilities," he continued. "It determines that a predictable outcome may come from analysis of random particulars."

"And?"

"Coincidence is in the mind of the person perceiving it. Did you know Pascal invented the mechanical calculator?"

"I thought the Chinese did."

"It was likely the Persians who came up with the abacus, if that's what you mean. Five-thousand-year-old tables were devised by the Mesopotamians, who used a sexagesimal system with a base of sixty, not decimal, like ours, based on the powers of ten. Please, don't let me ramble."

"You're rambling with relevance."

"All things are relevant, I suppose, but you really are gracious, Annie."

"I think," she said, "I think 'coincidence' is another word for metaphor. I believe in metaphors, Sebastian. I believe the genius of the mind is its ability to bridge the opposing sides of a trope, to make something new."

"You are back to Ezra Pound, dear soul. 'Make it new', Pound said. I am talking about 'coincidence' as *an unlikely spontaneous synchronic event where situations and conditions converge that have no obvious causal connection*. They can only be explained after the fact. That's what I'm talking about. You are talking *poetics*."

While his words were delivered in oral italics, with a playful irony that suggested self-deprecation, they were so deliberately chosen she felt them tighten like a noose, constricting her breath as she parsed their implications.

"I'm struggling to escape the consequence of conflicting causes," she responded. "Especially those *converging* on the singular effect of my own death."

"Which has not occurred!"

"Not yet."

"You want to identify connections that implicate you in two brutal murders but only so you can deny them. If you can't, you think you are doomed. But you're not." He paused, smiled.

"Explain for me, then, the coincidence that the woman who was murdered looked like me and that seems to be the reason she died."

"Anna, if you can explain a coincidence, it isn't one. So, back to Pascal's probabilities. From how you've described the woman, it is a statistical possibility that two such women would run into each other. Half of Toronto is female, you are both in the ethnic majority, your features fall within the accepted range of what might be called attractive, your ages are within the dominant range for adult pedestrians in downtown Toronto, you were both making your way through one of the city's busiest intersections, trudging through the snow like everyone else. It is a place where people of some, may I say, refinement, and people of little or none, intermingle. You, at least, if not your twin, were observing the world around you for efficient and safe transit. Neither of you was attending to an electronic device, not even e-glasses, it seems. This means you saw her clearly and noticed she looked like you. Quite likely she saw you as well, but might not have noticed your similarities — or maybe she did, maybe she saw you as a distortion of herself. In any case, if you consider the concurrence of sufficient variables, the possibility that you'd bump into each other becomes a statistical probability. I think it is more significant to consider your differences. How did you and the dead woman differ?"

*Only connect*, Anna thought, quoting *Howard's End* to herself. It is essential, it is impossible. I'm within seven removes of Kevin Bacon and a toad squashed along the Amazon stirs up a tsunami in Japan.

"Superficially," she said, "it was the colour of our hair."

"Exactly. The killer did not think to assess the quality of your jacket, your precise direction of travel, the finesse of your makeup and grooming. Given the context, your hair was a perfect disguise."

"But context is all. She's dead, I'm not, because our lives coincided at one particular point in time at one particular place."

"A place where you, Anna, were destined to die. Death attended your appointment in Samara, so to speak, but mistook you for a stranger."

"Death mistook the stranger for me."

"As you wish."

"Hardly!"

"As you wish."

He had a habit of repeating himself, which turned the most casual of comments into something decidedly sinister in their revised iteration. Her handsome ungainly brilliant conflicted errant knight made her feel both safe in his company and threatened — and paradoxically protective, as if at some point, she might have to rescue her rescuer, herself.

Distress unexpectedly registered in his eyes. Distress, curiosity, possibly annoyance. He spoke as if clarifying the answer to an unasked question, "When Robert Noyes died, I understand he was no longer involved in molecular biology. He was an academic administrator."

Once again, he was off on a tangent concerning her husband. Robert used his own name, of course. She used hers. Sometimes this created social awkwardnesses, but sometimes it seemed the only thing of which she could be certain, even back then.

"How do you know that?" she said.

"You must have told me. I'm not psychic, dear Annie. So why do you think he abandoned his research? He had a generous postdoctoral fellowship. He was on his way to scholarly stardom. Then suddenly he transformed into a bureaucrat. It seems an unlikely metamorphosis. There must be a story behind such a drastic change."

"Dramatic, not drastic. And no, there isn't. It wasn't that sudden."

"Perhaps it is a story you'd prefer not to share."

"Or one Robert preferred not to share. He stopped talking about his work a year or so before he gave it up. I didn't push. It was exceedingly complex."

"But you're very bright! Surely he didn't think you weren't capable of understanding."

"No, that's possibly what *I* thought. I realize in retrospect it wasn't the science, it was the psychology that daunted me. His emotional opacity enforced discretion. I've never forgiven myself for not delving deeper. But at the time it seemed I was respecting his privacy. Looking back, it seems I was exploiting it. Knowing nothing of what he was going through insulated me from his anger. When he was offered an administrative job, one that paid better than research, I encouraged him to take it."

"And to make up for your betrayal, you decided to have a baby and gave up on your academic career to work in the Public Library. Perhaps not in that order."

"I think we both imagined somehow, miraculously, we were going to become a regular family."

"You once mentioned he was involved in implants. Were they retinal implants?"

"They were, yes. Why on earth would you ask me that?"

"Bear with me." He held her in a piercing gaze like a predator lamenting the necessity of killing its prey. His intensity made her anxious; this confused her.

"He worked on the molecular level," stated Sebastian as if he were clarifying something for himself. Then he asked, "Nanobiotechnology or bio-nanotechnology?"

"Both. I'm surprised you know there's a difference."

"I looked it up. You told me he was trying to formulate a DNA computer of some sort."

"Specifically, to be injected into the human eye, a double-helix molecular device to transform light passing onto a defunct retina into electrical impulses that could be read by the brain. It was important work with astonishing implications, but he ran into snags."

"And suddenly he walked away from it all."

"Not suddenly, no. He withdrew into himself. It was agonizing to watch. And when he finally emerged—"

"From himself—"

"From a dark place in his mind where he had found refuge from God knows what, a place where I couldn't find him. When he emerged, he put his work behind him."

"Perhaps he backed away from it because he was more successful than he anticipated, not less. Perhaps that is what terrified him."

Terrified. It had never occurred to her. Perhaps Robert had been stricken with terror and she had given no comfort! She had read his behavior as anger not horror, as frustration not fear. Had one word, *terrified*, provided the key to unlock the barriers between them, even after his death?

While opening to this revelation, she simultaneously considered Sebastian's perverse suggestion that Robert's research had not been blocked by failure but by success. She had the uneasy feeling that Sebastian knew more about her situation than he had previously revealed. She proceeded warily. "How could exceeding his goals have had a negative impact?"

"Dr Frankenstein, dear Annie. Think about it. What if your husband had stumbled onto something as momentous as enlivening the dead? Mary Shelley's scientist recognized his *hubris* too late and his murderous monster ran wild. Perhaps your husband anticipated the impact of his discovery — would Gutenberg have proceeded with moveable type if he had known the Church would shrivel as a consequence and humanism would run bloody rampant? Would Victor Frankenstein have defiled death if he had known how deadly his invention would be? Would Einstein have proposed general relativity had he anticipated Hiroshima?"

"Robert was hardly working at the same magnitude."

"I'm sure Percy Bysshe Shelley thought much the same about his juvenescent wife's 'little' fiction, but it ended up capturing the changing world in ways his poetry never quite grasped. What if someone else anticipated the significance of Robert's work? Conceived of other applications? What if demands were placed on him that he could not live with?"

"You're suggesting the advances he made in his research were responsible for his violent death?"

"And for the attempt on your life, as well."

She said nothing. They were sitting close. He took out his reading glasses and gazed into her eyes.

"Ah," she said, quite abruptly, feeling liberated by a startling insight. "If we go back to Aristotle, the *premium movens*, the prime mover, is required by logic to be outside the primary action. You, Sebastian, are the most likely link in all this, the poet behind the metaphor."

For a moment he looked nonplussed. His dark eyes narrowed as he examined her abrupt declaration, as if it were an item on the table in front of them. He put away his glasses.

"You appeared in my life," she continued. "My life changed irrevocably. Suddenly I'm in danger, distressed, baffled."

"Whatever are you getting at, Anna?"

She had been so exhilarated at finding a person she connected with intellectually, who opened new vistas with his quirky esoteric undisciplined erudition, who challenged her to re-think all she had stuffed into her head over years of intense study, that she had seen him through a glass darkly, or, to adjust the metaphor, through rose-coloured glasses. She had let the thrill of cerebral intimacy obscure her judgement.

"You had a job to do," she said. "All this time in the library, you only pretended to read. You were observing me. You needed to know if I have special capabilities — computer access, perhaps, through a surgical implant. Am I my husband's experiment? After we talked, you decided my mind was not computerized. You reported to *them*, but *they* didn't take your word. It seemed prudent to eliminate me. Expedient. They chose to use a streetcar as their weapon. From your perspective, I resurrected in the library. How apt, when you think of it. Having betrayed me, now you wanted to help me. You felt responsible. But feeling responsible, you wanted to get away. You left unaccountably. You came back. We came here. Why? To save me? To betray me? Or because you couldn't resist being at the centre of whatever the hell is going on."

He sank back against the grey velvet, wrapped in menacing silence, and appeared to ruminate as if he were trying to think of a resolution to the dread that was closing around her. "No," he said, finally. "Me, at the centre? Not likely. You are the still point in this strangely turning world and I am a man of little importance."

She swallowed the rest of her martini and set the glass down on the coffee table. There was a slight rattling of glass on glass. Then she spoke: "Sebastian, have you brought me here to murder me?"

"How sordid, dear Anna, but no. Nothing so simple as that."

# Chapter Three
## Lost in the Funhouse

By the way she fitfully careened into consciousness, Anna knew she had been drugged. A discreet night-light cast shadows across the ceiling. She turned her head gingerly and spied her bag on a Queen Anne chair and her boots coupled neatly on the floor beside it. She was fully clothed; the same clothes. She rose unsteadily to her feet and walked into the living room. A pair of table-lamps glowed softly within parchment shades. She did not expect to find Sebastian and, indeed, he was nowhere in sight.

She carefully lowered herself onto the grey sofa, as if she might disturb some unknowable equilibrium in the universe if she moved incorrectly. After a few moments, she rose and went to the entry door. She knew it would be locked with an iron bar from outside. She explored the entire network of rooms and corridors. There were no other exits. For better or worse, she was secured inside a vault. Several times she called Sebastian's name, expecting no answer.

Her Georg Jensen watch was missing. It was an analogue piece, mounted on a broad silver band, a gift from Robert (she had asked for it instead of an engagement ring). She owned a smartphone, but it was at home. Her purse with her money and e-glasses was gone. Recent glasses came with audio components. Most people preferred to text in character clusters that defied conventional syntax and conveyed messages by short-hand suggestion, but it was possible to set them so that a voice whispered the time in your ear at prearranged intervals or in response to a glance at an image of a clock face.

It was dark outside. She had turned on overhead lights when she explored. She had no idea how long she'd been unconscious, but on looking through the drapes she surmised by the absence of illumination in neighbouring windows it must be in the long hours before dawn. She walked through the entire space once again, turning lights on and off as she went, failing to find anything to give her the time. There was no computer, television screen, telephone, radio, nothing electronic, not even a clock display on the stove. Nothing but books.

She went to the bathroom and the absence of urgency made her realize she had been unconscious for fewer than twenty-four hours. Time had resumed its flow. She winced at the word — time didn't *flow*. Pee flowed.

Seconds, minutes, hours, days, weeks, months, years, decades, centuries, millennia, were units of duration. Seasons, eras, eons, ages, were not so precise but still drew meaning from human experience and were in themselves only words. Time was perspective, time was perception.

Sipping coffee at the kitchen table, she thought about Immanuel Kant — not the man but his ideas, and not all of them, only ones pertinent to her situation. His scepticism concerning our ability to know the ultimate nature of reality seemed poignantly appropriate. Being locked in an elevated Victorian dungeon, absurdly she felt quite secure. She contemplated the various representations of time as *a priori* structures imposed by the mind. And then her distracted ruminations about time as a measure of consciousness broke down. An hour unobserved still passed in a sequence of instants and everything everywhere changed. Time was time, the word *was* the reality it signified.

She wondered if any word could mean something *perfectly*.

Philosophers, medieval and modern, she couldn't think who, some argued that words in ancient Greek quite literally embodied their meanings, and all Western languages since then constitute layers that must be decoded. She doubted Aeschylus or Euripides would have been so vain. She wondered if computer language was the terminal stage in linguistic derivatives — the ultimate removal of the word from the thing it signified, with no room for nuance, implication, or analogy. She wondered if words reduced to hieroglyphs by Optical Character Recognition had phonetic significance, or could they transcend, like Arabic numbers or Chinese logograms, to mean the same thing in different languages — 3 is three *est trois es tres ist drei yw tri*? She happened to know *yw* in Welsh meant 'is' and she guessed at *tri*, a curiously Latinate derivative, given the Romans occupied Wales in a perpetual state of seige.

In Greek, είναι τρεις. She saw graphic images of the words in her head but couldn't pronounce them. It's all Greek to me, she said to herself and smiled. *Graecum est; non legitur.* It is Greek; it cannot be read.

She sat with elbows on the kitchen table, thinking dialogically, as if she were engaged in conversation with another person.

"Quoting medieval scribes in Latin! This is all too esoteric for words," said the other person in her own voice. "You are a prisoner, for God's sake."

"It's the books."

"They're paper and ink; look around you, they're the walls of your prison."

"It's Sebastian. He encourages abstraction. He demands it."

"He's your jailer, Rapunzel. And you may not have noticed but he's aggressively absent."

"Aggressively?"

"You're locked in a tower."

"Isolation isn't necessarily bad."

"It is if you're buried alive."

"But not if you're dead."

"Which you're not."

"That's the point. He didn't kill me."

"Ergo, he's not your enemy? For a thinker, you're rather obtuse. Maybe it's time to panic."

"Why? He's narrowed my perimeters to comfortable proportions. With books! With an accumulation of knowledge like this I'd happily retreat from the world and grow my golden hair until it reaches the ground."

"It won't stay golden, Goldilocks. The roots are already beginning to show."

"Hardly, it's been less than two days. Fewer," she corrected herself.

"Barely one, but roots are relentless. The perimeters of your being at the moment are marked by an absence of clocks, doors with locks, and windows with bars."

"You realize it's difficult to tell us apart."

"Because we're bifurcations of the same personality."

"You can't think without feeling."

"You can't feel without thinking."

"Do we believe a word could mean something 'perfectly'?"

Her other self offered a Cheshire smile which drooped to a frown as she faded from view, out of mind.

"You're *perfect*," Robert would tease, insulting with a compliment, using a notion which as a humanist she found absurd. When he was working in microbiology, she argued that scientific progress, like all notions of progress, was predicated on fabulist daydreams of perfection. After he stopped, there seemed no point to the argument.

"You're a scientist," she would say. "You think out there somewhere is the ultimate answer. As with every religion, science insists there are brave new worlds awaiting us that will finally eventually retroactively give meaning to where and who we are right now."

"Do you really think science is a religion?" he would demand, as if the question was proof of its own absurdity.

"Science and the scientific method, the doctrines and dogmas of religion, they're myths designed to impose coherence on an inexhaustible world."

"You prefer meaninglessness?"

"Infinitely!" She rejoiced in her own irony, even though she was aware he had missed it.

Before he started working in the registrar's office, Robert began to lose whatever interest he had had in esoteric banter. For a few months he immersed himself in computer theory, so much so that their conversations shrivelled and died. Once away from the lab, he relaxed a little. He was no longer defensive about computer technology. It must have seemed pointless, like defending the invention of forks. Computers were perfect for what they did, indispensable for tracking student records, monitoring their profiles, balancing the ledger. She in turn stopped protesting her concern for their deleterious impact on cerebral function. Her fear was that the subliminal fusion of retinal and computer imaging would displace high-order consciousness, leaving the mind to operate on a primary level associated with animal awareness and the observation of spectator sports.

Gradually they stopped mediating their own versions of reality for the other's supposed benefit. For a brief period before the accident, they seemed content.

Occasionally, they read to each other and talked about art or listened to music. They favoured Beethoven and the Beatles, with a mutual abhorrence for opera and rap which, she convinced him, abused the intrinsic fluorescence of language. She argued an assault on the richness of words by reducing them to noise was a cultural aberration with sociological significance but little aesthetic value. He didn't argue. They agreed on the visual arts, but for different reasons. Both were enthralled by the hyper-realism of Alex Colville, Banksy, the Wyeths — he, because they conveyed a variant of the familiar world; she, because they eviscerated that world with surgical precision. Both inevitably loved Tom Thomson. She also admired the Québec abstractions of Paul-Émile Borduas and Jean-Paul Riopelle, while he thought them unsettling. She read Shakespeare to herself. Together they read mysteries out loud. He enjoyed the puzzles in Agatha Christie, the breezy bravado of Raymond Chandler. She was amused by Christie's excruciatingly bad prose and Chandler's louche and stylized wit.

As the diffusive effects of being drugged lifted with coffee, toast, the rhetoric of nostalgia, and time, Anna began to explore again, now looking specifically for a means of escape. Not that she wanted to escape. She had nowhere to go and Sebastian's behaviour, while unaccountably bizarre, was not overtly threatening. In fact, she wished he'd return — assuming he'd return alone, assuming he would not betray her again. If he had, in the first place.

The thought of betrayal took her back to the last thing she remembered before passing out, accusing Sebastian of complicity with her would-be assassins. Why the hell had he drugged her? She was annoyed that she had only now thought clearly enough to wonder. Did he have somewhere to go and didn't want her to worry? Was it misguided compassion, allowing her to get some rest? Was it to reinforce the walls of her prison? It apparently wasn't to violate her, not sexually, not yet, although she was wary enough of the world to take nothing for granted.

She wandered back to the bedroom and retrieved her patent leather boots, then she sat down on the grey sofa to slip them on, made herself comfortable, and contemplated the locked steel-clad door. Beyond it there were two others, three in all. One led down the steep stairs to the outside. The one on the left, now the right, she assumed it opened into a narrow passageway under the mansard roof between the exterior wall and the wall behind the bookshelves — she suspected that passage must cross the width of the house surreptitiously and open onto a parallel staircase for servants to access rooms on the far side. If egress was not also barred by a steel-clad padlocked door, those stairs would lead to another exit.

She got up and walked to the bookshelf on the right of the entry door. She moved over a few paces, until she was sure she had passed the point where the door outside was set perpendicular to the wall, then she squatted down and reached through, over volumes of matching leather-bound books with gilding along the edges of the pages like striated gold. She knocked sharply on the plaster wall. There were reassuring echoes, but she stopped suddenly, wondering if tenants downstairs, could hear the noise.

She had not considered that there might be other people in the building. The silence in Sebastian's loft was so absolute it could be heard as a whispering thickness, indistinguishable from the rush of blood, the soft murmur of breathing, the rustling of clothes emanating from the listener herself. If there were others downstairs, they might be ghosts. The entire space might be a voluminous crypt.

If she couldn't hear them, they couldn't hear her.

You have to believe in ghosts to make them real.

Carefully, so as not to do any damage, she lifted books a few at a time from the lower shelves and piled them on the floor. When she had cleared a full section, she wrenched the shelves free and stacked them off to the side. She walked through to the kitchen and found a bread-knife with a serrated blade and several garbage bags. Returning, she noticed through a crack in the curtains that dawn was beginning to invade the darkness outside.

Kneeling on a folded blanket, with sawing motions she etched into the ancient plaster the shape of a small doorway, then, pushing the knife until she forced an opening between strips of cedar lath, she plunged it through into the space between vertical studs of rough pine until the blunt end hit the lath and rough plaster on the far side of the emptiness. For the next hour she sawed and pried, pulled, broke and broke off, shards of tinder-dry cedar and chunks of plaster clinging with horsehair, until she could easily reach through to the inverse layers of cedar and dried oozing plaster. She restrung a floor lamp to cast light into the cavity and proceeded to cut her way through into the narrow attic corridor under the slope of the roof.

The more she worked the more anxious she became until by the time she crawled through into the darkness of the passageway she was frantic. She could see little to either side. She looked out at the warmth of Sebastian's apartment. The stacks of books glistened like pillars of gold, the worn Persian carpets absorbed in haphazard profusion the tangerine glow of the primordial pine plank flooring, the air itself seemed radiant with the beams of the risen sun playing through the narrow openings between the drapes against the thoughtful disorder of furniture and books. She wanted to turn back. She wanted to flee. She remained motionless.

An hour passed, or maybe ten minutes or half a day. She was chilled to the bone. The narrow space between the book-lined walls of Sebastian's aerie and the attic passageway had been insulated with dry shavings that were crushed down to clumps from the weight of gravity and time. A certain amount of heat leached through to where she sat huddled across from the hole but could not contend with the cold seeping in from outside. Finally, she crawled back into Sebastian's refuge and set about cleaning, sweeping, dusting, vacuuming, scrubbing, jamming dirt and detritus into the cavity between the walls, with some spilling into the corridor beyond, repositioning shelves, moving the lamp back to its place beside the sofa, until at last a person not looking specifically for a hole would never see it in the shadowy depths behind the rearranged volumes of leather-bound gold-enhanced books.

Surveying the scene, Anna realized that her project might be given away by good housekeeping. She decided the best course of action would be to vacuum and dust the entire apartment. If she were caught *in flagrante delicto*, as it amused her to describe what might seem an aberrant obsession, she would declare that she was simply bringing the place up to her own requirements for comfort.

She finished uninterrupted, put away the cleaning paraphernalia, and stood at the drawn drapes which she pulled back a little so she could peer outside. If she broke one of the small panes of glass — each was as old as the house with waves and swirling depressions and small bubbles embedded — and if she called out, she might be rescued. Or she might leave herself open to attack by whoever, whatever, was out there.

Although it was daylight, she thought of the ghost of Catherine Earnshaw, the icy hand grasping her own through the glass, and shuddered. She gazed at the uppermost branches of huge old maples which limned the sky with strands of darkness. Down on the snow-covered lawn, shadows were cast like striated pools from which the trees rose up in stark denuded majesty. The sun must be directly overhead; it was noon.

Anna picked out a book at random and sat down on the sofa to wait. Sooner or later, Sebastian would return. Despite having drugged her, he struck her as an honourable man. But why, then, the rising apprehension? Why had she created an escape route, why was she sprawled on the sofa with her winter boots on and her coat draped accessibly over the arm farthest from the door?

Her mind wandered and she followed — back to their discussion in The Coffee Café about glasses and roses. She was astonished at the scope of his knowledge, from semiotics to biotechnology. Autodidacts often delve so deeply into a subject they get lost in the quagmire or they peer down from the surface like an excited snorkeller but never don scuba gear to see what's actually there. He knew enough to be at neither extreme. He had a love of words that rivalled her own and no hesitation about playing among them. He was not a semiotician, but neither was she, not any more.

Her reverie shifted and she felt currents of warmth and loneliness and she smiled to herself.

Semiosis? One day not long after Robert had taken up his postdoctoral fellowship at the university, he had asked her to explain semiotics.

"I know what it means," he said. "I do but I don't."

"That's semiotics for you," she responded, then realizing his gravity, she shifted her tone. "It's the study of signs and how sign systems work. In a sense, its purview is everything everywhere and nothing at all." Her favourite writer at the time was Samuel Beckett.

"Like road signs?" he said. "Or symptoms of illness? Signatures? Military salutes? Signs of the Apocalypse?"

"And paintings and music and architectural styles, you name it. Natural signs, aesthetic signs, and signs by convention."

"Aren't they all by convention?"

"I suppose they are, in a sense."

"So, it comes down to language, doesn't it? Words and grammar, they're primary?" There was a tremor of suppressed desperation in his voice, as if the urgency was not merely to understand but to transform his understanding into factors in his own field inaccessible to Anna.

"To explore systems of signs you need language," she affirmed.

"Or whatever it is language does in the brain."

"What do you mean?"

"I don't know, I'm not sure."

"Robert," she cautioned. "Don't take me as an authority. I hardly know the difference between semiotics and semiology — one is European and derives from de Saussure's lectures at the University of Geneva, he never wrote them down, people transcribed them, and the other is based on the work of Charles Peirce at Harvard. Both deal with lexical signs, that's the important thing. My own specialty, poetics, is a sub-branch of an offshoot of semiosis, more or less, even though it came first. I mean poetics goes back to Aristotle, at least. You look really concerned? Is this something to do with your work?"

Sidestepping her question, he asked: "Semiosis is the study of signification, but what actually is a *sign*. Can a word, itself, be a sign?"

He was inviting her to lecture, to expatiate on her area of expertise, and she couldn't resist. She sometimes asked him to do the same, and until lately he rose to the occasion. These were their special moments of intimacy. Discourse didn't displace intercourse. It was more like mutual masturbation. Robert seemed generally satisfied with these encounters, while Anna's displaced desires were adequately suppressed.

"There's no such thing as a word *itself* — that's why yes, it's a sign. A word is a dyad, a two-sided code. The word 'rose' is a signifier — a specific sound combination in English — and what is signified by that signifier is a flower of a particular sort, perhaps one unique example or an entire genus, but it could also signify a flower in a text by Gertrude Stein, or a dead rose, a sea rose, a laughing rose, an evening primrose — those are titles of poems — or the word *rose* could signify the word, itself, as in the curiously meaningless title of Umberto Eco's exhaustive exploration of medieval theology, *The Name of the Rose*. It could signify Alice Munro's poignantly withering Rose, or Stein's friend, Rose. Or it could be a homograph, she rose at seven, or a homonym — 'lined up in rows' or 'he rows a boat' or succulent 'roes' on a platter, which itself could be either fish eggs or strips of Eurasian venison. I'm sorry, why is this suddenly so important? You look annoyed."

"Frustrated. Your obsessive precision is endearing," he said. "But a little discursive. I still don't quite grasp the mechanics."

"The mechanics?"

"Of the correlation between semiotics and thinking. Maybe I haven't sufficiently defined my confusion. I'm not sure I can. Does a sign *always* have two parts, is that how it works?"

Her remembering self recalled she had wondered about the word 'time', a singular instance in which — she had decided — signifier and signified merge. And perhaps they did merge in the entire ancient Greek language.

"Usually," she said.

"What," he went on, "what about, how would you deal with, 'Twas brillig, and the slithy toves / Did gyre and gimble in the wabe'?"

"'All mimsy were the borogroves'," she responded, delighted. "'And the mome raths outgrabe'."

"It's jabberwocky," he said. "It signifies nothing."

"Yet tomes have been written on Lewis Carroll's intent."

"You have signifiers but nothing signified. Surely those nonsensical words are incomplete signs. What do they do?"

"They don't *do* anything," she said. "That is the point. And yet they convey so much. You can nearly see the scene they describe."

"Nearly. What if I encounter a strange monolith in an utterly random context?"

"*2001: A Space Odyssey*!"

"Yes, yeah, and I don't know what this monolithic *thing* is. I have no name for it, no word to signify what I'm observing. *Something* is signified but there is no *signifier*. Again, it's an incomplete sign."

"Okay."

"Explain."

She remembered how curious he had been and what pleasure it gave her, even though he had seemed unaccountably solemn. Sometimes, conversation brought home how divergent their realities really were. They admired each other's minds for their capacity to think, more than for thoughts they conveyed. They had met in a bar at an academic congress where they had been attending separate sessions. She didn't remember falling in love, but it happened.

"In *Jabberwocky*," she said, "the nonsensical signifiers *are* the signified — as is often the case with poetry. The words don't project or anticipate meaning, they are themselves whatever was meant. Meaning comes to them. They don't invoke, they evoke. In Kubrick's film the monolith *is* the signifier. Whatever is signified is open to interpretation — think about poetry again, the monolith is an image that resists definition, an ambiguous premise in an aesthetic equation. Robert, you seem so serious."

"I am."

"Does this have to do with your research?"

"The completion of incomplete signs — yes, believe it or not, it does."

They never again talked about semiosis.

She walked to the window and looked through the bars. The dark rippled pools floating over the snow at the bases of the giant trees had slipped off to the right. Light cast through leafless branches made them seem turbulent. She knew the house must be facing south and it was mid-afternoon. She pushed Robert back into the dark place in her mind reserved for perished dreams, went to the kitchen and put together a lunch of poached eggs on toast. There were no fruits or vegetables in Sebastian's fridge. He either bought them fresh or didn't consume them at all.

After eating, she wandered into the living room and picked up a book Sebastian had been reading. A small piece of paper marked his place. He was not the sort to turn down the corner of a page or leave a leather-bound volume splayed open, yet he or someone had underlined a passage, albeit lightly in pencil. She glanced at the cover again. Montaigne. The sixteenth century French essayist. In English translation. The defaced segment was initialled in the margin with two letters. The first might have been an *L* for Leicester. Or an *S* for Sebastian. The second, in equally ornate script, was clearly a *K*. The passage read:

> Every sort of contradiction can be found in me. Timid, insolent; chaste, lecherous; talkative, taciturn; tough, sickly; clever, dull; brooding, affable; lying, truthful; learned, ignorant; generous, miserly and then prodigal. There is nothing I can say about myself as a whole.

At the bottom of the page, in the same florid script as the initials, the same pencil had inscribed: *Nothing that has not already been said.*

The graffitist sees himself mirrored in Montaigne's words, aggrandized and humbled at the same time. Unless he is being disparaging, which is doubtful. The essayist was sly, he defined himself between specific polarities as Everyman, certain he was more than the sum of his parts — as so he was, she thought, as so are we all, even Leicester the madman, even Sebastian, her sinister knight of the mournful countenance and impeccable diction.

She was restless; too distracted to read. She sat back on the sofa and wondered how Robert's work embedding double-helix molecules with the capacity to work as microcomputers could possibly relate to the process of signification in language. He had never explained, she had not asked the right questions. But he had more than a passing interest. He was intrigued, even challenged, and strangely edgy, as if either daunted by the seemingly nebulous concepts or frightened by their incomprehensible implications. Coming from the other extreme on the knowledge spectrum, her own interest was in signification as a poetic device, and this was secondary to her passion for literature as literature, philosophy as philosophy, and how they converged — not for the science of language or thought, but for the spaces and relationships between words, the links and correlations between propositions.

There was so much they hadn't talked about during Robert's crisis year. They only talked casually about his work in the registrar's office — there wasn't much to say — or about her work in the library — about which there was even less. During her pregnancy they talked about nothing else, preoccupied by the infinite particulars of gestation. And then came death and they never talked again.

The door shuddered and Sebastian entered with an armful of groceries. Brown paper bags; he was ecologically responsible. He greeted her with a spontaneous grin but couldn't hide deep lines of apprehension distending his face. He passed all three bags over to her while he secured the door on the inside with a single deadbolt. He took two of the bags and she followed him through to the kitchen with the third. It smelled of oranges and celery. After they set their bags down, he busied himself putting the groceries away, made a few comments about the freshness of the produce, and said he hoped she'd had a good sleep, had found something to eat, and having been surrounded by books he presumed she hadn't been bored. He offered a vague explanation for his absence. He had left very early that morning, he said, to run a few errands. Then he had had a doctor's appointment at Princess Margaret.

They both knew that was a cancer hospital. Undeclared social protocols determined queries about cancer invasive. No particular stigma attached to the disease itself, but the extent of an open discussion directly correlated to the level of intimacy between speakers.

"Hope everything was all right," she said.

"Thank you." He said nothing more. He had been gone most of the day.

They went back into the living room. He did not notice the entire apartment had been cleaned.

She sat on the grey sofa, he on a sturdy old wingback covered in matching grey velvet from which he cleared piles of books. He looked so worried, her first concern was to comfort him. She felt no urgency to receive explanations.

His features softened as he leaned back into the comforting embrace of the chair's wings, but he seemed distracted, attending to things known only to himself. She watched him with a mixture of affection and anger.

"Listen," he said, as if suddenly remembering she was there. "Listen." His face glowed in the indirect light streaming through a slit between the drapes. "You can hear the books talking to each to each."

She could hear nothing but the hush of the room.

"My books murmur among themselves, especially when I'm here on my own."

"Sorry to intrude," she said.

"You are cynical — don't ever be cynical or you will hear nothing."

"Agnostic," she said.

"Listen. They have discrete conversations, dear Annie, and despite the plenitude of words, it isn't cacophony. They seek out connections, they extol fonts and typography, they exchange phonemes and syllables, compare phrases and expressions, sentences, distinctive paragraphs, sometimes entire sympathetic passages, chapters, even volumes, whole volumes, can you imagine?"

Anna may have looked puzzled. She could hear nothing but she knew what he meant. Her puzzlement was more about him. How did this sweet, naïve, vulnerable man survive in a world where books had been reduced to artefacts and unfettered imagination was scorned?

His worried mask disappeared. She smiled encouragement.

"Sometimes this place is abuzz, swarming with words," he went on, rising to the implied invitation. "The voices of writers, living and dead, vying with the voices of characters from fiction, from history, biography, memoir, contemplative tracts, voices in rhetorical and expositional declamation, sometimes echoes of voices from previous readers, not voices cross-referencing or divulging intertextual locutions, the voices of the books themselves."

"It must get distracting, trying to sort them all out." Her voice hovered between gentle mockery and envy for his capacity to hear what she only imagined.

"But they thrive upon silence," he said.

"Now you're locked in a paradox."

"No, I defer to Yeats. Quiet the dog, he wrote, so Caesar can fix his mind upon silence and challenge the world."

"The dog?"

"The tumult of computers and pixilations and algorithms. The chatter of cybernatic pandemonium."

"Yeats couldn't have meant that, Sebastian. He died in 1939. And Caesar died before Jesus was born."

"He meant cerebral interference; words heard and not felt. Extraneous noise. Pity the person who thinks with his mind, he said. My voices I hear with my heart. They silence the dogs."

"It must be confusing," she said.

"Is that derision?"

"No, curiosity. I'm trying to understand."

"As Gide once opined, 'Please, dear Annie, do not understand me too quickly.' André, of course, did not write the words 'dear Annie'. They were only implied. And the rest was in French. *Ne me comprends pas trop vite*; something to that effect. Have you read *L'immoraliste*? Of course you have. In French? Of course. Or perhaps not. In any case, my voices are comforting. Like standing stripped to the soul before a choir of angels — you can hear every one with the whole of your being, all at the very same time. Think of a parabolic mirror and the sounds of writing as innumerable streams of light travelling parallel to the axis of symmetry, reflecting and converging on me at the curvature's focus. Think of God listening with helpless compassion to a million prayers simultaneously."

"A stripped soul, a trick mirror, and an impotent creator, they're playful analogies, Sebastian, but you're grandly avoiding my principal question. We really must get to it."

"It? Which is what?"

"Why the hell did you drug me?"

"Ah, that. I wasn't sure you would notice. You were exhausted. I can't imagine you slept very well the night before last."

"Why take my watch?"

"To give you back time." He retrieved the silver watch from his pocket and returned it to her. She set it on the table beside her, then changed her mind and slipped it back on her wrist.

"I thought you'd sleep better. Watches and clocks keep me awake."

"They're digital these days, Sebastian, they don't make a sound."

"It's not the noise. It's the anticipation. And yours isn't silent."

"It's a Georg Jensen."

"It's a mechanical analogue." He paused. "It was only a sedative."

"No, Sebastian, it was more than that."

"A strong sedative. I needed to be sure you wouldn't take off."

"You had already made that clear."

"I had no assurance you would listen to me, Anna. I wasn't sure I could dissuade you if you decided to go. I also took your purse."

"I noticed. With my money and my e-glasses."

"I didn't want you to leave."

She noticed he did not say he would return them.

"You locked the door. I couldn't have bloody-well left."

"No, sweet soul, you assumed I locked the door. In fact, I did not."

There was no way, now, to prove that was the case. "And why was it so important to have me stay?" she asked.

"So I can protect you."

"Really? From *them*? You're not my keeper, Sebastian."

"I'm your friend."

He looked so pitifully alone — a forlorn man at home among books but an outlier in the actual world. Brilliant, naïve, and dangerous, but not vicious or cunning. She rose to her feet and placed a comforting hand on his shoulder.

She stood facing the entry door.

"Sebastian, is there another way out or another way in?"

"There was no need."

'What about fire regulations?"

"That's considered a double exit. The second door leads through a servants' passageway, to stairs, descending to a garden on the far side. I keep it locked."

She gave his shoulder a reassuring squeeze and crossed to the entry door, which she opened after sliding the iron bar to the side. She stepped out into the vestibule.

Suddenly he was right behind her. "Don't!" he exclaimed. He placed a restraining hand on her arm.

"I wasn't going anywhere. Are you worried?"

Shaking off his loose grip, she pushed against the steel cladding on the outer door, then grasped the large iron knob and forged metal latch and tested. Everything seemed obdurately secure. The door that led to the passageway between the walls was fixed with a steel drop bar padlocked in place. The bar for the door into the apartment remained leaning against the wall.

They both stepped back inside. He slid the deadbolt across.

"They followed me," he said.

It took her a moment to realize what he was telling her. Then she began mumbling what sounded like an arcane mantra. "Ho-li-jee-zus." She repeated the phrase several times, articulating each syllable separately, draining the words of their meaning. She generally swore judiciously and if she were swearing now, she wasn't swearing at Sebastian. It was an existential statement, an awkward correlative to inarticulable emotion. "Do they have the keys for the outer door?" She banged softly on the steel surface of the inner one. "Where are your keys, Sebastian?"

He answered with hangdog defiance: "I gave them up, they have them. Three men sitting at the bottom of the stairs. They know you were here. I was carrying your handbag."

"Why didn't they come up with you?"

"It's a confusing place."

"They know that, do they?"

"I convinced them you'd left."

"Without my purse?"

"They've given me until nightfall to make sure you return."

"Or what?"

"Or they'll burn this place to the ground."

"But you've waited until now to tell me."

"There's a lot at stake."

She let the absurdity slide.

"They want me to come here?" she said. "Where I already am."

"Yes. Where they can reach you."

She glanced at her watch.

"We've got a few hours," she said.

"It gets dark early. It's winter."

She whistled with a deep intake of breath. "*They*, Sebastian, do you actually know who they are?"

"Not precisely."

He withdrew an antiquated plastic cellphone from his shirt pocket. "This is theirs. It's primitive but easy to monitor. They expect me to call you, to get you to come back. They assume we're more closely connected than I originally told them."

"Originally when? Before they tried to run me over with a streetcar?"

"Things have changed since then."

"Really?"

"They want you alive, now. They want to look inside your skull. It has to do with your husband's research. And then, after that, they may in fact want you dead."

She wheeled on him but he had already turned away. She followed him back to the grey sofa. The velvet looked drained of vitality in the muted afternoon light.

"What," she demanded, "what are they looking for? There's nothing special about my head, it's all pretty normal in there."

'That's what I told them. They wouldn't believe me."

"Normal," she repeated with a twinge of disappointment. "And now they *may* want me dead?"

He nodded. He was embarrassed, a strange reaction when fear or outrage or bewilderment might have seemed more appropriate.

Anna felt bleak. Could a person feel bleak? She was enveloped in *dread* — a word that ominously stood in for breath-constricting stomach-churning heart-palpitating mind-searing terror. Verbal profusion eased her soul — which she in no way conceded as a literal entity. She relaxed enough to consider the implications of Sebastian's terrifying confession and their possible options.

She looked at him sitting awkwardly beside her on the sofa. He seemed to have retreated into some obscure corner of his mind where he was safe. She smiled reassuringly and patted the back of his hand.

"Sebastian," she said. "They won't burn us out if they know I'm actually here, not unless they can auger the signs in my brain from grey-matter ashes. Sebastian?"

She could see in his eyes he was struggling to emerge from dark places in his head, from his refuge, his sanctuary.

"This building is worth more than our lives," he finally said.

"Not to me, it isn't."

"Nor to them. You are important, Annie. I don't want them probing your skull. I don't want to die myself, not prematurely. But we must save my library, we really must."

"You'd be willing to die for your house?"

"For what is in it, yes."

"Would you be willing to give me up, to turn me over to them, to save your books?"

"Possibly."

"Okay, I'm glad we've sorted that out. Now listen, Sebastian, the fact that you came in half an hour ago and have not made a single call — surely, they know I'm still here. They'll be coming any minute. We'd better leave."

"We can't."

Anna said nothing. She got up and put on her nubuck jacket. She stashed her travelling bag in a cupboard. She hadn't much confidence she'd be needing it. She led Sebastian by the hand over to the bookshelves against the north wall.

"We need to escape into a few good books," she said, smiling.

He smiled, confused by her smile.

She dropped to her knees and carefully removed leather-bound gold-embossed volumes from a shelf, a few at a time. She handed them to him. He glanced at the titles of each in turn before piling them neatly on the pine plank floor.

"Put them within reach," she said.

He didn't seem to know what she meant, but he tried to comply.

"Everything's very clean," he said.

"You noticed."

"I have a good cleaner. He comes for two days every two weeks. He's not due for a bit. Maybe I won't need him this month."

"Maybe not," said Anna. She imagined he had someone who was so new to the country, so unaware of cultural customs, that Sebastian's place would seem no stranger than any other wealthy eccentric's abode.

Anna removed the entire bottom row of books and then the next row and wiggled the empty shelf free. Sebastian was on his knees at this point and gasped in amazement. She urged him to crawl through the gap between shelves, to climb through the small doorway she had made between walls, and then she followed, tucking her skirt carefully around her to maintain decorum. Once through, she leaned back into the hole, slid the piles of books close, replaced the shelf and carefully reshelved the books with their spines facing out.

"There," she said, standing up in the dark space. "There," she repeated. The only other words that came to mind were the title of the first postmodern short story she had ever read, 'Lost in the Funhouse'. John

Barth's wondrously allusive title resonated with threatening ambiguity. She said nothing out loud.

Sebastian felt his way along the wall. Close to the back of the locked steel-clad door he found a rotary switch. He turned it and several bare-bulb lights in a series along the passage flared into glowering incandescence. He stared at Anna, gazing so deeply into her eyes she felt almost penetrated by his strange personality — not violated, but distinctly uncomfortable. He remained speechless.

Suddenly, the lights went out.

*They* had turned off the power.

She reached into the darkness and found his hand reaching out to find hers.

# Chapter Four
## Lost Horizons

In the instant between their hands touching and clasping, Anna envisioned herself there and not there, neither dead nor alive if no one could see her. She tried to concentrate. Time was out of joint. The past was more real than the present. She had visited Auschwitz once and felt herself virtually erased by the thronging of horrific events that had occurred before she was born. She had experienced comparable dissociation only one other time, when she had entered her grandmother's house by herself, after the old woman's funeral, and her Gran was there in the smells and the dust motes and the clamour of memories and Anna was herself, so it seemed, only spectral. And now, as she held Sebastian's hand and they stood facing each other in the afternoon gloom that crept past the books through the wall, as she gazed at his barely legible features and felt his breath on her cheeks, she and Sebastian seemed no more than ghosts in a place more real than themselves.

"What happened to the power?" she whispered into the darkness.

"The main breaker box is inside the door from the side verandah. That's where they're waiting. They figure, once night falls, they'll have the advantage with flashlights, even though I know the place and they don't."

"Will they?"

"Flashlights create the illusion you can see without being seen. I've seen a lot of mysteries — cops and detectives and women about to be murdered walk around in the dark, using flashlights to betray their location."

"But if they do that, we could fight back."

"There are three of them, Annie. They have guns. They have keys. Fight or flight — neither is an option."

"Foregone conclusions aren't fate," she said, her voice trailing off at the end.

Gradually, the light of the late afternoon ceased to penetrate the gaps in the curtains and creep past the books. The pale illumination in their attic redoubt faded to black. At first, they heard only a stirring, then voices excoriated the darkness from the landing on the other side of the steel-clad door. They froze, listening; suddenly an explosive crash ripped the air as their pursuers forced the deadbolt and shattered the doorframe into the apartment. The voices became louder, the three men conferred near the small hidden opening behind leather-bound gold-embossed books.

Anna and Sebastian released hands so they could shuffle in single file along the passageway. The roof was sloped too steeply for them to stay side by side. The floor creaked with low piercing moans. Each time they were startled, but even if they were heard the direction of the noise would dissipate through the walls and be impossible to trace. The building was structurally sound, the protests of old joists and planks were inevitable, almost reassuring, shrouding their location rather than giving it away.

After what seemed an interminable delay, they arrived at a landing that opened enough to accommodate two doors, both steel-clad and both, of course, locked. *Dead-end*, there was no other word more appropriate. There was nowhere to go, nowhere to hide. A single flashlight beam would reveal them completely.

But it would take the invaders a while to realize their prey had fled, to discover the opening behind the bookshelf, and to use Sebastian's keys to unlock the passage door. They settled down on the floor to wait.

"Sebastian?" she asked. It was time to settle final accounts. By confession, not combat. "Why did you betray me? What did you tell them?"

"They knew I was a book person. As I'm sure you'll agree, there aren't many left. They were dressed exceptionally well, they were cordial and reasonably articulate. They told me you were the enemy, that you worked in the Public Library to destroy people's interest in books."

"How in God's name would I have done that?"

"Haven't you heard? He's dead."

"How in heaven's — oh for God's sake, how did they ever convince you?"

"You don't use the library computers. You don't use universal Wi-Fi. You don't wear e-glasses or access the internet. You appear to depend on your mind."

"And?"

"They said your mind must be embedded with a microcomputer. They said you undermine books by making instant connections that no current computer could manage. Your mind is a preternatural organism, they said. It functions in defiance of logic and time — which, they insist, are inseparable. Logic. And time. They are both sequential."

"All this because I have implanted technology on strands of DNA in my skull?"

"Do you?"

"Don't be absurd, I was being rhetorical."

"I'm sorry," he said. For his question? For his betrayal?

She wasn't feeling up to pronouncing absolution. He hesitated. She nodded in the darkness for him to continue. After a minute or more, when they could only hear their own breathing, he did: "They explained that ultimately for such technology as yours to prevail, books have to be rendered obsolete. They told me they are out to save books. They call their project Fahrenheit 450."

"One degree below the ignition temperature of paper."

"Yes, in deference to Ray Bradbury's novel."

"And you told them I am a lexical cyborg."

"Not just restricted to language — not lexical but, well, I told them you appear to work in the spaces between words."

"That's called poetry, Sebastian."

"Not something they would know much about. I tried to explain there was something out of the ordinary about you. I may have used the word 'cyborg' in describing your capacity to make improbable connections. Then we went for coffee, you and I, we connected."

"And what you observed was me being human — an ordinary human mind functioning without electronic interference or augmentation."

"Yes, after our coffee together I told them that. Immediately, they tried to kill you. Apparently, I had confirmed exactly the opposite."

"So, you knew all along the streetcar incident was an attempt on my life. You weren't being the logical wizard I thought."

"The *logical wizard*. A paradoxical neologism. Quite clever."

"Did they see us the next day in The Coffee Café?"

"No, no, I didn't bolt because of them. I didn't come back because of them. This afternoon, though, they were here in the stairwell waiting for me."

"How did they know it wasn't me squashed under the streetcar? Especially since the police found my handbag and wallet?"

"Forensics, I suppose. Blood type, clothing, indicators of class, the fact that you turned up alive. They have access to police data."

"You do realize your Fahrenheit 450 buddies are out to destroy books, not save them. We're high enough above sea level in Toronto, 450 degrees would do it."

"Do what?"

"The incineration point drops, with a reduction in atmospheric pressure."

"I'm not much interested in common physics."

"What about the correlation between energy and matter in organic structures, like, say, the human body? They murdered my family, they tried to kill me. That's common physics."

"But they didn't succeed, did they?"

"Only partially."

"I'm glad."

"For which part?"

"You know what I mean, Annie."

"And now they've put me on hold until they can crack open my skull like a walnut. They're obviously offended by the unfettered brain, so after they let the air in and find nothing that doesn't belong, neither cybernetics nor soul, they'll bury me."

As if to make amends, Sebastian offered new information: "*They* are Vivuscorps, Annie."

"Who else!" It seemed too obvious. She glared as she considered the implications of his confession.

In synchronic accord, the lights came back on, pathetic low wattage spheres of incandescence spaced along the inner wall that made the passage vertiginous, like a vertical shaft with them perilously hovering near the top looking down.

Sebastian's face was directly under a bulb: he had been crying in the dark. She wanted to reach out and hold him, but that would have made his betrayal seem worse. She turned away discreetly. She reached down and brushed dust from her boots, stood up again and surveyed the setting. Beside Sebastian there was a small cupboard, waist high. Across from them was the locked door leading to a wing at the rear of the house. Barring their way forward was the locked door leading to a stairway running down to the garden.

"Where's that one go?" she asked, indicating the door to the side.

"Servants' quarters."

"The white servants?"

"Yes." He looked ashamed for the sins of his forbearers.

"And this?" she asked, pointing to the small cupboard.

"Laundry chute."

"Big enough for a person?"

"Good grief, not a chance."

"You're sure?"

"Absolutely."

She opened the outer door of the cupboard. There was another door at the back. She pulled it open and peered into a vertical shaft of yellowed boards that had been waxed and polished in the distant past. A length of frayed cotton rope dropped from one side of the chute.

"What's that for?" she asked, grasping the rope.

"There's a five-storey drop down to the laundry room in the cellar," he said. "Sometimes clothes would bunch up. Then the rope was flicked to set them free. When I was a kid, I lowered myself, floor by floor, all the way down. The other openings have been boarded up and built over. This one's for servants' laundry; nobody bothered to seal it. Their laundry was sent down in cotton bags so it wouldn't mix with family things."

Voices at the far end of the passageway struck them dumb. Someone shouted. Of course, with the lights back on, the little doorway she'd cut into the wall would have radiated light from behind the books into the apartment. There was a commotion at the far end, but no one risked coming through. Soon, keys rattled in the lock of the door from the landing.

"How old were you?" she whispered urgently.

"When I played in the chute? Ten, maybe eleven. Prepubescent. I got caught at the bottom and they locked me in my room for a week — a punishment I greatly enjoyed."

"We can make it," she said.

"Not me, not since, you know, coming of age. I couldn't even bend my old lanky body to get through the cupboard, never mind down the chute. Maybe you could, Annie. Let's give it a try. Let me help."

Before she could protest, he lifted her up from behind, tilting backwards so that her legs dangled into the shaft. She was not petite, but at 5'6" and 120 lbs she was slender — like most Canadians she used American measurements for personal data. She grasped the rope. Strands fell away in her hands. She twisted around to face the opening and reaching down she hiked her skirt up between her legs so it wouldn't rise on her hips, then she cocked her pelvis so she was awkwardly spread from one side of the chute to the other, her nubuck jacket providing an abrasive sufficient to stop her from slipping.

"Sebastian," she said. His face glowed in the light while hers was utterly in shadow.

"I'll be all right," he whispered.

He handed her the cellphone their would-be assailants had given him. She didn't want it. The police weren't an option. There was no one to call.

"Remember they'll be monitoring you," he said. When she tried to hand it back, he pushed her away. "Take it, just in case. When you get to the bottom, don't worry about the lights. No one can see into the house from outside. It's complicated down there, the exit route's impossible to explain. Just think like you're me. Gotta go, they mustn't see you're in there." He paused. "Anna, *amor est magis cognitivus quam cognito.* There's more we can learn through love than through knowledge. You've taught me a lot. Thank you."

He gently swung the inner door closed against the side of her face, then she heard the outer door snap into place, and then she heard voices. The voices grew louder. She heard thumps, shouting, muffled screams followed by ghastly involuntary groans. She couldn't bear the thought of what they were doing to him. She wanted out, to be with him; she pushed against the back of the door. He'd locked it from the other side. She pushed again, then shifted her weight to slip the cellphone into her coat pocket so she could get a better grip on the lip of wood extending from the cupboard bottom. The lapse in concentration made her slip. She scraped and bumped more than a body's length downwards before jamming against the polished wood to stop her descent. She grimaced, cringed in silence and listened, then finding the rope in the constricting darkness she held on and tried to relax. She took deep breaths. She could feel the warm air deflected back on her face. She was grateful she couldn't see the walls pressing in. She shifted, and with a sudden jolt the rope snapped. She began to slide, slowly at first. Suddenly the chute became wider and she plunged several feet, but with more room to manoeuvre she was able to spread forcefully against the walls and stop the fall. She had reached the third floor; the chute for the family's laundry was less constricted. She heard the cupboard door overhead rattle and she ducked her head under the ledge where the chute widened, just before a light beam flashed past her, waggled in the glowing darkness, and disappeared.

She lowered herself in painful increments until she was able to lodge a boot on a small protrusion where the chute had opened onto the second floor, gaining a few minutes' respite before edging down further. At the first floor, she felt for the ledge and relaxed her weight onto it, but it split off without a sound and she slid bumping and scraping against the polished sides of the chute until suddenly she plunged through an expanse of dark air like Alice and landed in a bin of wicker laundry baskets covered with frayed coils of rope, layers of disintegrating cotton bags, cobwebs, and dust. Lights flicked on and glimmered in dull profusion. She shuddered. She waited for the horror, the hysteria, to subside, then she slid awkwardly off the pile and lay prone on the ancient yellow linoleum floor.

Raising her head, she stared through the gloom. She spied a pair of old-fashioned cement tubs, several washboards hanging from the walls, various soaps and detergents in boxes that would have fetched money at an auction from collectors of domestic expendables. Exhausted, scraped and bruised, and frantic with pleasure at the relief from suppressed claustrophobia, she felt absurdly untouchably safe, surrounded by the cloying smells of ancient preserves, moulded potatoes, coal dust from ages past, and what might have been desiccated tea in the bottoms of ancient canisters left unaccountably open. No one could reach her, not even the Fahrenheit 450 thugs with impeccable manners, elocutionary finesse, and refined taste in clothing.

Sebastian! What happened to Sebastian? There would have been no point in executing him. There was no point in burning his house to the ground. It would just draw attention where it wasn't wanted. She hoped desperately he was alive.

She crawled across the cracked linoleum to a set of wooden stairs with the treads worn into shallow depressions and grasped the stair-rail to pull herself up to a standing position. She tried to brush off the dust and dirt from the chute, but ground it into her clothes. Pain was beginning to make itself felt, but there was nothing excruciating.

Images of Sebastian loomed in her mind. She needed to focus on herself. She was giddy and quivering as she ascended to a door that much to her relief pushed open quite easily. When she stepped out into the darkness the lights behind her went off and for a moment she was suspended in a strangely impalpable limbo, but when she took a further step forward the new room burst into light and she found herself in a runcible room with passages leading off through open doorways in eight different directions. Some of the doorways were very small, some large, some narrow, some broad. It was a high-ceilinged room. There were no windows. The walls were bare apart from ornate wall sconces, converted generations past from gas to electric.

She slumped to the floor, exhausted, disoriented, preternaturally still. She closed her eyes when the lights went out again. She rubbed her eyes with the backs of her hands. She saw herself on the yellow brick sidewalk in front of the house. The trees were voluminous with billowing leaves, the sky was brilliant blue, the turrets and towers surrounding the house, reaching up to the vast mansard roofline, shimmered in the summer sunlight. She was with Robert.

When she looked down, she was wearing winter clothes. They were dusty and torn. She was dressed unseasonably. Her boots were scuffed and far too expensive for a graduate student or sessional lecturer. She wore an excellent quality nubuck coat that was badly abraded on the arms. Robert was dressed for summer, like he always dressed before working in the registrar's office, in faded jeans and a T-shirt free of logos or messages and so clean she could smell the detergent. He did the laundry. She didn't argue. When she had lived with her grandmother, she usually did it. It was not a chore she especially missed. There was little nostalgia attached to the washing of bedding and clothes.

Robert was telling her about Sebastian Kroetsch, the man who had recently inherited the house and was doing strange secretive renovations inside. The Kroetsch family had given various grants to the university and underwritten part of Robert's thesis research on the progenerative capacity of DNA to replicate altered structural combinations. Robert had been there for a reception before the old couple died. Sebastian was home at the time, kind of skulking around the edge of the gathering, as Robert described him.

They had talked briefly and Sebastian had been surprisingly familiar with his work. Robert promised to send him some research data, which he did, but he never heard back. Then the parents had died in a boating accident near their cottage in Muskoka. Robert sent a note of condolence, written by Anna, but received no acknowledgement.

It seemed he didn't feel rebuffed or disparaged. He was apparently content, perhaps reassured, when people outside his discipline were daunted by what he did. He was an obsessive idealist, enthralled by his role as the catalyst in an alchemical process where, in the crucible of his laboratory, theory was transformed into things. Money or courtesy hardly concerned him, nor did benefactors interest him much. In those days, Anna believed, he was driven by an altruistic naïveté that a brave new world would come into being if he worked hard enough, sacrificed sufficiently, pursued his vision with relentless conviction, and let nothing dissuade him. Until, suddenly, he walked away from it all — as so often happens when dreamers wake up, when visionaries see around the edges of their visions, when reality becomes excessively real.

Robert smiled in the afternoon sun. Moisture glistened on his forehead. She smiled in return and told him about her grandmother's house in Waterloo County. It was not so pretentious as this one, but quite large and, from the outside, forbidding. Inside it was pleasing and comfortable and, she had laughed, on the whole quite a runcible home.

She blinked and moved closer to him. She could sense no dimension except time, but time was broken, swirling about in disjointed strands. The weather was balmy, but it was winter. The sun was radiant, but it was night. Robert held her hand, he listened to her chatter, but Robert was dead. He told her things, made connections that hardly registered, things without meaning until now.

Her perspective shifted. There was no light at all in the world. She felt herself plunge into the present.

Edward Lear's nonsensical 'runcible' crowded her mind, a word that refused to conform, and images swarmed through her head of Alice Liddell falling into Wonderland, of Ray Bradbury's Guy Montag grieving for Clarisse McClellan, and of Ambrose with Magda, lost in the funhouse among mirrors, surrounded by sleaze beneath the Ocean City boardwalk. For whom is the funhouse fun?

Anna sat with her back to the wall, trying very hard to resist thinking at all. Resistance was futile. Impressions of being trapped in a nightmare designed by Diogenes Teufelsdröckh filled her with dread and elation, displacing the other impossible things in her mind — he was Carlyle's philosopher-fool. Why him? She rose to her feet and the darkness shattered. Light dazzled. She heard voices drifting out through each of the doorways opening onto innumerable corridors, but it was only the hush of silence in an empty place. No, it was the voices of books conversing in whispers on myriad subjects, voices which rose in her head to an indecipherable din, so that she clapped her hands over her ears, but they continued to echo inside her mind.

She stood very still, continuing to listen, and after a short time the voices descended to a murmur and ceased. She clasped her hands and remained motionless until she was plunged into darkness again. It was comforting. She waved a hand in the air, the lights came back on. She surveyed this very strange chamber, and tried to decide whether it was magical, enchanted, and highly peculiar, or whether she wasn't herself or wasn't really there at all. The room lapsed into darkness again.

Movement from taking off her coat brought back the light. She folded her coat and placed it on the floor to mark where the cellar door blended into the wall so perfectly as to have virtually disappeared. None of the other doorways had actual doors. The air was surprisingly warm and very dry. She could smell books, she was surrounded by corridors of books even though none were in evidence. She recognized the elderly airs of old paper and parchment, the dull musty perfume of leather-bound tomes, the muted fragrance of factory-bound hardcovers with their prissy, clenched-knees aroma, the penetrating odour of paperbacks and their wanton cheap scent.

Gazing slowly around the hexagonal room, she selected a doorway at random. It was high and broad; dark, it was intimidating but, as she expected, on walking through a few overhead lights came on, congenially illuminating walls of books on either side. Behind her the room she had left turned black. As she progressed along the passageway, small rooms like votive chapels in a cathedral opened off to the sides, each filled with books. She stopped here and there to peruse, having forgotten entirely that there were pursuers in the building and she was their prey; having forgotten about Sebastian as the architect of this wondrous library or that he might be injured or dead. She pulled various books from their shelves and examined them. There seemed no coherent system to account for where they were placed. She tested to see whether the titles of adjacent volumes spoke to each other. *The Locked Door* beside *No Exit*, that sort of thing.

When she came to what seemed like the chancel, the floor was elevated and the ceiling dramatically descended so that she had to stoop through the door, one of three leading in a cruciform pattern away from the central nave. This corridor, also inevitably lined with books, led to another small room which had four doors, three besides the one she had entered. She walked through, and then through another, walking from room to passage to room, past chapels consecrated to unknown personages, up ramps and steps and down again, beneath low ceilings and towering ceilings (or high floors and low floors). Lights flashed on and off, marking her progress as she went. In each room, along each passage, in every alcove, beside each ramp and stairs, there were books in profusion, shelved in a neat but indiscernible fashion — much like Shakespeare and Company, the legendary Left Bank store in Paris, or the inimitable Scarthin Books in Cromford, Derbyshire, or the delightfully eccentric Highway Bookshop near Cobalt, Ontario. She had made modest pilgrimages to all three before she was married, and she'd once spent a week in Hay-on-Wye in Wales, discovering and rediscovering the joys of its myriad bookshops, afraid to miss a single one. She had wanted to take Robert there, but it never happened. As far as she knew, Hay-on-Wye had long since been turned into subsidized housing and the bookstores in Paris, Cromford, and Cobalt had collapsed under the weight of their wares.

Sebastian's explosive haphazard proliferation of books was an architectural representation of the undisciplined brain of a self-tutored polymath. The greatest university of all is a collection of books, proclaimed Thomas Carlyle, but he could never have anticipated anything so grand and arcane and wondrously inaccessible as Sebastian's Borgesian *bibliotheca cerebrum*.

She had been through innumerable rooms, large and small, with the occasional chair pushed up to a small table here and there; here and there a few large easy chairs covered in old leather had reading lamps poised at their sides. She may have doubled back on herself, but nothing was familiar. She had no sense of where the outer walls of the house were — never mind the exit — not even of whether or not she was in the main house or if Sebastian's labyrinth extended into the wings. She had no idea where the cellar door had got to, or the original octagonal room. She couldn't be sure which storey she was on. She had gone up and down so many steps, a few at a time or in multiples, and along so many passages sloping one way or another, she could not be sure she was anywhere at all. Surrounded by books, she was adrift in an Escher drawing, literally at sea among words. She tried to envision the house from outside, hoping she might better locate herself if she had a sense of the overall architecture. She was standing on the sidewalk, again, looking inwards. The house was vast, red brick, the brick was old, kiln-dried, more orange than pink or rosé. There were wings to either side of the main structure, which was flat on the top with gabled windows set into the slope of the mansard roof along the front. There were turrets and towers connected by several verandahs, making the main house itself seem in retreat.

She had to peer through dense foliage to see there were bars on the upper windows, though none on the others. The maples were in full leaf. It must be summer. She was with Robert. She remembered distinctly being with him before; she remembered the house, the sidewalk, their conversation when he had noted he'd attended a reception here, had gone in the front door, had met a strange young man his own age, one of the family. Sebastian Kroetsch. Although Sebastian had told her his name when they met, she had not made the connection.

She shook her head clear and moved with accelerating speed, frantically driven, passing among such an abundance of books she began to doubt if there was a reality beyond them. She came to a mirror at the end of a corridor. There was no other way to proceed. She pushed on the mirror; it was on a pressure-release catch and swung open towards her, it was backed by a short passage without lights that led to another mirror set at an angle. When she pushed that mirror, which appeared to be two-sided, it opened into a room filled with darkness. As soon as she stepped forward, however, lights flared. She was surrounded by a thronging crowd of shocked cowering people like herself. They were shrinking from strobes flashing in throbbing intensity from every direction. She had entered a dazzling room of mirrors angled every which way; she was surrounded by countless startled images of Anna Winston. Overhead, she was upside down, looking downwards. From below, her head leaned forward to peer up from below her skirt. But it was to the sides, every side, where she was most populous and, because the lights were flashing too quickly for the eye to fathom, she appeared in frighteningly incomplete fragments.

She was frantic, confused. Discombobulated. It was raucously disturbing to be in so many places at once, having so many facets, so many incomplete surrogate selves, like she wasn't in the world but the world existed as an extension of her.

If she sat down on her own image and sat still, she knew her multiple selves would disappear. She moved close to a mirrored wall. It was cold to the touch. She lowered herself onto the thick glass floor. It was cool as well. She waited, the lights went out. In the darkness, she was sure of nothing. Were her reflections still there, waiting to be animated?

Suddenly it hit her. His mirrored room was Sebastian's inversion of a priest's hole, a place where it was *impossible* to hide. Yet he would have designed a way out. It would be in the very place where signs were driven from the mind, where signifiers and signified were erased by the light, where the self was expunged.

She stood up and the strobe lights resumed in clamorous profusion. The mirror she had entered by had swung shut of its own accord. She forced herself to be analytic. She was surrounded by mirrors on a dozen different angles, ablaze to infinity. She squinted, she closed her eyes, her eyelids were pulsating screens, she opened her eyes, struggling to see through the glare. There were a dozen facets, twelve surfaces. Sebastian was wily. She edged forward through the vociferous chaos of light upon light, feeling her way towards the centre of the room. Suddenly the strobes stopped and the lighting became normal. She looked around. She was nowhere in sight, she had disappeared.

Sebastian was a wizard. His mind was magical. A*mor est magis cognitivus quam cognito*, she recalled his last words. She had much to learn from Sebastian.

The room was a six-sided star, the mirrors to either side of each apex, being necessarily set at less than ninety degrees to the other, reflected out into the open space of the room, but the reflections did not extend to the centre. There was a point where they only reflected each other reflecting. She had found her way into that limbo where nothing reflected back, the lights automatically stopped their insanity, and now, no longer there in the mirrors, she could relax, catch hold of herself, and think. Even below and overhead the glass was opaque. She was at an invisible place in a room where it was impossible to hide. It was the logical venue for finding an exit.

Anna turned slowly in rotation to survey each of the twelve facets of the star chamber in turn. She felt throbbing surges of relief, but with them came a renewed awareness that her life was in danger, that her perilous condition was not that she was lost among books but that she was being pursued for access to her brain — not her mind but, literally, her brain. She had to escape, she had to get out of Sebastian's Borgesian labyrinth, with all its doors and Möbius passageways and countless books strung out in paths that never converged. So long as she was inside the maze, she was trapped. That's how a maze works. The Minotaur comes in for the kill from outside.

All directions appeared the same. She anticipated hearing a voice.

"In a looking-glass world, you are somebody else."

The voice sounded distinctly her own.

"That is incredibly deep or lamentably shallow," said Anna, silently mouthing the words as she continued turning on an invisible axis, being careful not to step past the radius of invisibility.

"If you measure depth by ideas, I'm as shallow as paper. If you measure by feelings, I'm as deep as the words on a page. My feelings tell me you've tumbled down the rabbit-hole, dear Alice, stepped through the looking-glass, and you need to take Mr Dodgson more seriously. As Lewis Carroll, he is an amusing unsocialized and possibly degenerate fabulist, but as Charles Lutwidge Dodgson, he is a sensitive scholar in an insensible world, a logical positivist who is neither — not logical and not very positive. From the looks of this place, our Sebastian Kroetsch is a literal builder of dreams, a library of enduring dreams. You are the witness that makes them real."

"I hope he's alive."

"Dodgson expired at the close of the nineteenth century. He is dates on a gravestone in Surrey. Lewis Carroll is still with us, of course."

"No, I mean Sebastian," she said. "I'm really rather pressed for time at the moment. My life is in danger. Perhaps Mr Dodgson was murdered, but I am exceptionally lost — Sebastian, of course, when I say Dodgson, I mean Sebastian."

"Only when Tuesdays fall on Thursday afternoons, just before tea."

"Why are you here?"

"Because *you* are here, my dear Alice. We have wandered from one dream world into another and neither dream is our own. You are too logical, too positive, to notice, but Robert's dream has turned into a nightmare and Sebastian's into a metaphor."

"Standing for what?"

"For whatever is inside his head."

"I thought so," said Anna, not uttering a sound.

She stopped turning; she tried to envision how Sebastian might have imagined his mirrored room. To think like he might have thought. The door she had entered, the door to escape, would not be the same, yet they were identical mirrors in a chamber where nothing but mirrors was real. She walked deliberately away from the centre. The strobes flashed raucously. She suppressed the distraction and proceeded directly through multiple reflections to a single glass plane. She reached her hand out and pushed. Held shut by a pressure-release catch, when she touched the mirror surface it swung open and then with a counter-weight mechanism closed of its own accord. Each seemed to be the same, each opened into a different dark passage. She tested three in succession and the third opened into a corridor down which she caught a glimpse of the hexagonal room where she had found herself when she emerged from the cellar.

She proceeded to the room of doorways and found her nubuck coat lying where she had left it. She glanced at her watch. Sebastian had given it back to her. It was 11.20, just before midnight. She needed rest. She wasn't sure where she'd go when she escaped, but she'd need to recuperate lost energy, ease her sore muscles, and clear her head before getting there. She felt the urge to pee and with embarrassed repugnance descended into the cellar and urinated in the empty coal bin. She clambered back up the worn wooden stairs and settled on the floor, wrapping her skirt close around her thighs and lowering her head onto the folded jacket. Again, she thought of herself trapped in a nightmare conceived by Diogenes Teufelsdröckh, the tailor-philosopher in Carlyle's *Sartor Resartus*, whose logical nonsense and nonsensical logic called existence itself into question. She lay very still, the lights went out. She slept.

When she awakened, she waved an arm in the darkness and the lights flashed on. It was 3.30 in the morning. She rose gingerly to her feet and carrying her coat she made her way back to the mirror room. Bracing herself against the blinding menace of strobes flashing insistently in infinite regression, she shuffled across to the opposite side of the chamber. She figured the exit most likely lay farthest away from the hexagonal room behind her. She pushed a couple of dazzling reflective panels which opened into book-lined passages leading to other book-lined rooms. Through another she faced a shorter corridor blocked at the end by a door with a large framed mirror that distorted her image as she approached to make her seem unrecognizably larger, then small, larger and smaller, until she was expanded and reduced to an elongated broken blur. Anna had no doubt that was Sebastian's vision of himself in the outside world.

She feared the unusual mirrored door might be locked, but it swung open easily and she stepped into a conventional foyer. The door clicked shut behind her. By light from the street coming through the front door of the house she could see a small lamp on a *demi-lune* table. She felt for a switch but there wasn't one.

Intuitively, she clapped her hands. The light flashed on. She was surrounded by a vintage décor of mahogany, floral wallpaper, a pair of worn Persian rugs, and lace. The room was aggressively conventional. It would have been out of date from the day it was furnished. She turned to the door through which she had entered and was not surprised that it was locked. From the foyer, it looked like an ordinary ornate full-length mirror. Doors on either side of it were panelled: one, opening inward, appeared to access an empty closet, while the other, recessed and opening outward, apparently led into another part of the house. It was locked. In front of her was a heavy front door with lace curtains framing a small-paned window.

The room was decorated in whimsical detail with deference to Sebastian's own mythical mystical past among grown-ups who confused him. Stepping into it had been startling, like suddenly coming of age in a world transformed, when the world left behind seemed innocent in its exuberant complexity and very unreal. The anteroom's familiarity was curiously reassuring; its stolidity was curiously menacing.

She moved close to the front door and peered through the space between the curtains. This was a house from a time when there were porches. That was an image from a terrifying poem by Margaret Atwood. Maybe the poem said, 'verandahs', not porches; like saying carpets, not rugs. In the ambient light she could read a decal on the glass. She deciphered the reverse print and chortled to herself. It said: 'Property Surveillance by Sebastian Kroetsch and Associates'. He must have made it himself when he was very much younger. My God, she hoped he was alive. She wondered if he remembered meeting Robert. She couldn't imagine a world in which he was absent. Robert? Sebastian.

Footsteps on the verandah startled her. She pressed against the wall. She had left the lace curtains drawn back. She could hear talking but couldn't make out the words. After a brief conversation the voices receded. She moved forward and observed three men moving precariously down the icy rutted sidewalk. They got into a black Mercedes sedan but didn't drive off. Before she could think to avoid attracting attention, she clapped her hands to extinguish the lamp. She nervously peered out the window again at the black car under the streetlamp. Nothing moved. She settled on the floor in the foyer to outwait them.

Contemplating what she'd been through, she was fascinated by the revelations of Sebastian's character she'd encountered on her journey through his fantastical maze. Except in an institutional library, she had never seen such a vast collection of books, nor such an unusual space, anywhere. She struggled for a while, trying to grasp the nature of his cataloguing method. She was sure there was one, but it wasn't the Dewey Decimal System or any other she could imagine. She wondered what Robert would have made of this library. He would have been fascinated by the architectural peculiarities, by the challenges of having different builders work on different aspects, by the system of air vents and humidity controls necessary to preserve such a sprawling and vulnerable treasure.

She stopped herself. Robert was dead. God knows, he was brilliant, but his mind was hardly accessible even while he was alive. It was foolish now, false magic, to imagine she could think what he thought.

She had used the word 'magical' once in a forgotten context with Robert and he had demanded to know what she meant. This must have been near the end of his tenure with the postdoc, before walking away from science and technology — both were inimical to notions of 'magic'.

"Sometimes words signify in ways we don't mean," she had said. "Sometimes words are just words."

"And a good cigar is a smoke."

"Exactly. By saying 'magic' I meant *less* than the word intends, not *more*, and certainly not something paranormal, supernatural, mystical, fantastical, necromantic, occult, or enchanting."

"Much as you love to wallow in words," he had said, "you can't limit their meaning, can you! That's why I like mathematics."

She remembered being loquacious with Robert, but after his death she seldom strung words together except in her head or for library patrons on rare occasions. "I wouldn't want to limit them, Robert. But words in the right combination can be more precise than theorems and algorithms and hypothetical postulations. 'A rose is a rose.' How can you be more precise than that?"

"Since I have no idea what *that* means, I can't argue," he had said. She wasn't sure whether he was hurt or exasperated. "I can control numbers," he said. "You can't control language."

"That's what grammar is for, Robert. And figures of speech, parallel structures, juxtaposition, implication, tropes and symbols, similes, metaphors, metonyms, synecdoche, allegory, irony. But some words, of course, are James Deanish — rebels without causes or causes so deeply embedded they can't be discerned."

"For example?" he demanded. She was speaking in written English; no one used *discern* in a conversation, or *synecdoche*, or *necromantic*. Real people didn't speak that way.

"Names, proper names," she had explained, aware he was irritated. "Like James Dean, Robert. Like Beethoven. What does the word 'Beethoven' mean? A body of music, the life of a man? A few bars from The Fifth, an anecdote about deafness? Memories of a visit to his home in Bonn. A word-game: how many words can you spell from the letters in his name? If I use Beethoven in a sentence, my sentence necessarily puts limits on the possibilities of meaning. The word itself is limitless."

"What the hell does *that* mean — limitless?"

"If I say Borgesian, Kafkaesque, Orwellian, out of context, if you recognize the words, you know I'm referring to more than postmodern angst, psychotic dissociation, or authoritarian dystopian nightmare. If I say Lear and then the word *runcible*—"

"I think of runcible spoons." He laughed. "But I don't know anything more about spoons than I did."

"Neither did Lear."

"Edward?"

"King."

He looked puzzled. For a man who wanted to manipulate molecular structures, it seemed strange he found it so difficult to grasp innuendo, irony, or anything that said what it wasn't. She smiled to herself and felt tears burning her cheeks. Robert had wanted so desperately to understand the spaces between words which made language work. She wanted so desperately for things to be like they were. But time was broken. She wanted to fix it. She couldn't.

Footsteps crunched frozen snow on the steps. She crouched to the side of the door. She had hoped they had left. She heard shuffling on the verandah. It was only one man. She wished he would go. She felt secure behind the heavy oak door and angry at his persistence. He rapped tentatively. It surprised her there was no bell. Then he knocked sharply. She was startled. The light flashed on. She cringed in the mottled gloom. He knocked again, the light went off. He pressed his face to the window, with his hand shielding his eyes from the glare of the streetlamp behind him. She shrank back into the darkness, spectral in the cross-play of shadows. He pulled away a little so that the reflected light from the window illuminated his features. She could see him but he couldn't see her. There was no question about who it was on the other side of the door. It was her dead husband. It was Robert.

# Chapter Five
## Horizon Obscured

She rose unsteadily to her feet and watched in shock as Robert shuffled across icy debris on the verandah, shoes squeaking on the frozen snow as he descended the steps and walked into the pool of illumination under the streetlight. Her mouth hung slack, her eyes gaped wide, her breathing was forced and erratic. He turned when he reached the black car and surveyed the building's façade, then his gaze swung back to the main verandah and the front door behind which Anna stood trembling, hidden by reflections from the street. He opened the back door on the near side of the car. Smoke billowed into the cold night air and the glowing ember of a cigar flared briefly, filling the car with a fiery glow. Robert got in and pulled the door closed. Anna turned and stared into the gilt-framed mirror over the *demi-lune* table. She registered no familiarity with the shadowy agonized reflection staring back at her.

She moved against the opposite wall, reached into her pocket to retrieve the antiquated cellphone, and gazed at it for a while as if it were an alien thing. She turned it on. It cast a deathlike pallor over her agonized features. She pressed a button and in a barely audible voice she instructed the phone, saying "Help," and after a brief pause, "Police."

Following several abrasive buzzes, a genderless mechanical voice spoke into the darkness. "911, what is your emergency please?" Anna pressed the 'off' button and put the cellphone back in her coat pocket.

She did not think about what she had done. Her mind was empty, her skin icy cold, her breathing irregular, pulse racing, pupils dilated, eyes unblinking. Without any awareness of being aware, she was no longer herself.

She peered through the lace curtains. A police car with a flashing blue light rolled silently down the street. The dark sedan under the streetlamp spewed a cloud of moist exhaust as it started and sat idling. Another police car appeared from the opposite direction. Officers got out of each and approached the Mercedes. After a brief conclave on the driver's side, the dark sedan drove away. The police returned to their cars and left. It was the witching hour in the heart of the night. The street was aggressively empty, as if its denizens weren't sleeping but hiding indoors, waiting for the wagon to arrive, calling to bring out the dead.

The heavy door opened easily and locked behind her when Anna stepped onto the verandah. Despite the treacherous mantle of ice over the lawn, she walked quickly around to the smaller porch on the side. She entered the door leading up to Sebastian's apartment and was immediately surrounded by the stench of burnt cigars, expensive cologne, chewing gum, and male sweat. On the fourth-floor landing, the odour of scorched meat displaced the others.

She stepped into Sebastian's sanctuary and flipped on the switch for the lamps with the parchment shades. Sebastian was sprawled in the grey wingback chair. He was ghastly pale; his head lolled to the side. She pressed two fingers to the carotid artery on the distended right side of his neck and abruptly withdrew them, shocked to find him alive. She stepped back and stared. A vial of prescription sedatives about two-thirds full sat on the small coffee table beside him. His hands were draped over the arms of the chair. Clutched between what remained of the index and middle fingers on his right hand was the stub of a burnt cigar. Frayed shards of tobacco had melded with blackened flesh and charred bone. Beneath his hand was a soiled mass of crumpled documents, clearly intended to ignite a blaze when his fingers released their grip, but suppurating fluids had slowly extinguished combustion, leaving the cigar in his grasp.

She prodded the documents with her foot. They were pages, ancient, tinder dry, at the edges, remnants of the Montaigne essays in English translation. An empty Bénédictine bottle lay purposefully discarded on an incendiary strip of dry woven matting that had been dragged in from the kitchen. The bottle bore a blood-red simulated wax seal, and the label was boldly inscribed with the letters D O M, *Deo Optimo Maximo*, 'to God, most good, most great'. Had she not been in a state of shock, Anna might have tried to calculate how much Sebastian had consumed before passing out. She might have found the monastic slogan ironic.

She moved slowly to the window and pulled back the drapes. Her brain was functioning but her mind wasn't there. She felt nothing, thought nothing. There was no dialogue between her self and her soul, no judgement, no understanding.

Only the dead can be forgiven, said Yeats. Only the dead can be condemned. The words hovered meaninglessly before passing away.

She turned on the overhead light so the illumination could clearly be seen from the street, and picked up the sedatives, dropping them into her pocket. She pulled out the cellphone. When she linked to the police, this time instead of disconnecting, she set the live phone down on the table next to the unconscious Sebastian. Then she slipped out onto the landing, descended the stairs, and rushed to the sidewalk, where she turned west and then south, and walked briskly mindlessly into the night.

Clutching her collar close to her neck with alternating hands to stop them from freezing, she trudged down Yonge St., then over and down Church. On Church below Carlton, she stopped in front of an all-night café called The Greasy Spoon. She hesitated, then stepped into the vestibule inside the door. There were no customers, there was only a single figure near the back, leaning on the counter, reading a book. She hugged herself stealthily, shrinking into the shadows, but failed to avoid attracting attention.

"You come in," the man shouted. "You come back here, I'll give you hot coffee, no charge."

She shuffled, she said nothing as she edged past the counter stools to the rear booth facing the back wall. The man was wearing a soiled white apron. He had a close-cropped beard and a shock of jet-black hair. He brought her a cup of brackish coffee and a Danish pastry fresh the previous morning.

Anna put her hands around the heat of the cup and looked up, swinging her hair away from her face to see him. She nodded her appreciation.

He nodded back, leaned down, and looked at her closely, then spoke in a voice that registered confusion, amazement, concern.

"Dr Anna, it is me, this is Azziz, Azziz al Azzad. You do not look like yourself, my goodness, dear woman, you look terrible, your hair has turned blonde dirty white, you have been frightened very badly I think."

She stared into her coffee.

"Please," he said. "It is okay. You drink this. I will get you more, yes. What has happened, what happened?"

She took a few sips from the cup, then meticulously replaced it on the saucer as if it were ancient bone-china and might shatter. He sat down opposite. She bowed her head behind the curtain of blonde hair.

"Will you speak to me, Dr Anna? Please speak."

He looked beyond her to a girl who in an urban gesture of togetherness among strangers had slipped into the next booth although the others were empty.

"Here, you, please, girl, come, you must help."

"No thank you," said the young woman.

"Please, this is Dr Winston. Something is very, very, troubled."

The girl rose to her feet. She was no more than seventeen, possibly younger, with huge amber eyes and hair the colour of honey. The soft down on her cheeks accentuated the delicate contours of her features. Her coat was an oversized fake Army Surplus parka so big it threatened to swallow her in its folds. She started to leave, then turned back and, although Azziz al Azzad slid over to accommodate her, she slid in beside Anna, pushing her gently to the wall.

"She is dressed so poorly," said Azziz al Azzad.

"No worse than me," said the girl. "She's been through a lot, you can tell."

He looked at the girl sympathetically. Her coat was obviously not her own. Her sallow complexion needed a good scrubbing. She smiled radiantly at nothing. And in her eyes, he read untold suffering, as she might have in his, had she noticed.

"You are an angel," said Azziz.

"Let's push that hair back and see who's in there." She gasped. "Oh my God!"

"Your God?"

"There is no God."

"No God?"

"She has coloured her hair."

"I know. That is exactly what I said to myself."

"Agnes, it's me. Agnes, honey, it's me. Sweetheart, look into my eyes. You're seriously blonde. Sweet Agnes, where have you been?"

"She is not Agnes. She is a librarian. Her name is Anna Winston."

"I doubt that very much. But she is a good person and her name is Agnes. She calls herself Agnes Dei. We live at the Hostel for Ladies down along Front Street. Come on, honey, what have you done to your hair? Oh Agnes, you don't look like yourself. I've been frantic with worry. You just walked off and I didn't follow. Not past Yonge Street. People over there, they've got places to go. I heard a bunch of noise when I was walking away but I didn't turn around, then someone told me about that terrible accident with the streetcar and I was scared it was you, but then somebody said somebody at the hostel saw stuff on television and it was somebody else, some lady who owned her own house. So I felt a lot better. And now you're here. I've been worried, honey, I've been very very worried, I'm not exaggerating. Could I get a Coke, do you think? I just had a double-double up the street but it wasn't fulfilling. Real Coke, nothing nutritional. Not the Diet stuff. I need sugar."

Azziz brought her a Coke and a coffee for himself.

"How do you know her as Agnes?" he asked. "*Agnes Dei* means the Lamb of God. But she is Dr Winston and she is a secular person."

"Secular person?"

"She lives without God."

"Me too. And she's not a doctor, I don't think, for sure. I don't sleep with doctors."

"You are lovers?"

"Roommates. That hair don't fool me much. I know who she is. Do you like Shania Twain?"

"You do not wear e-glasses." He seemed to have suddenly noticed.

"No point," she said and smiled her brilliant meaningless smile. "Can't read or write. I'm severely dyslexic. Dyslectic, whichever. My brain didn't develop the right way and no one taught me. What about you?"

"Glasses, yes, sometimes," he said. "I don't wear them a lot."

"Agnes doesn't, anyway, either, because she's not all there in her mind, so nothing makes sense. She just kind of *is*, you know."

"She doesn't need them. She is a reference librarian."

"Not likely. Whatever that is, she isn't."

"It is someone who lives within books. For myself, at night when I work, I read many real books." He withdrew a pair of e-glasses from his breast pocket and flourished them for her to see, then put them away. "Dr Winston, she made me see that sometimes is important I rebuke the computers. It is a very great revelation. What do you think happened to her?"

"There are many explanations inside my head."

"Do you know the right one?"

"Yes, probably, I just don't know which one it is."

Coming up with no rejoinder, he said, "My name is Azziz al Azzad."

"They call me Rose Malone, so that is my name. I knew your name, already. I've been here before. You were wearing glasses, I remember. My God, she smells."

"It is a familiar aroma. Cigars, I think."

"Burnt meat. It's the same as we'd smell at the Vivuscorps Camp from burning garbage."

"You went to a camp?"

"Because I've got my dyslexia. They sent me there. It's a Vivuscorps charity. They looked after us pretty good. There were cabins. It wasn't just tents. We didn't have to read or write, there. They told us everything to do and as long as we did it, we were happy. I didn't like it," she said cheerfully. "That's where I met Agnes. She was a trustee, just following orders, and she didn't like it either. The stink was atrocious. We left, the two of us, just walked away in the night, right into the bush. It took us a month, giving our blood to mosquitoes and our flesh to the blackflies just to get the garbage smell out of our bodies and, after we smelt better, we walked out of the bush and the Sally Annes gave us clean clothes. And what about you, Azziz al Azzad?"

"It is a long story. I will tell you sometimes about me. What do we do with Dr Anna?"

"Agnes, Ms Agnes Dei. We colour her hair back to normal, that's first. You've got hair dye upstairs. We'll use that."

"How do you know I live upstairs?"

"Because you've got no coat. I can see into the kitchen, I can see empty pegs on the wall. No galoshes on the floor. I can see some stairs by the toilets going up. Or down, depending on which way you're travelling. And that hair colour of yours isn't real, that's for sure. You're grey at the roots and it's too black by half for your age."

'It is my own colour."

"Maybe a long time ago."

"Not so long, but okay we will take her upstairs."

Azziz moved awkwardly as he led them up to the door of his one-room apartment, then immediately hobbled back down to the café. Anna sat on the edge of the rickety cot. Rose discovered limited washroom facilities inside a closet; a cracked basin and cramped shower but no toilet. Azziz was expected to use the customer lavatories downstairs. She found black hair dye on a shelf and stripped Agnes to panties and bra. Her friend stared vacantly ahead, neither protesting nor helping. Rose rolled up her sleeves, unclipped a pink plastic cellphone from the waistband of her chinos and set it on the counter separating the kitchenette from the bed-sitting room, then moved her friend to the kitchen sink and proceeded to change her hair back to a crude semblance of the colour it had been. When she washed the dye out, it hadn't set. She did it over again, chattering like a trained stylist. This time she waited to rinse, and decided to use the shower rather than the kitchen sink. She reached into the stall and turned on the water, then guided Agnes under the flow, soaking herself in the process. Black spattered on the white enamel and sheeted down to the cracked cement pad on the floor, then swirled into the drain, reiterating the black and white images from a classic horror film Rose had never seen.

She tried to towel Agnes dry and dabbed at her own soaked chinos and sweat-shirt. She dropped the towels in a motley pile and led Agnes into the main room where she wrapped her in a grey blanket that had been folded neatly over the end of the cot. A tattoo of a miniature rose on a thorny stem showed through Agnes' opaque blue panties where the wet nylon knit was stretched virtually transparent over her left upper buttock. Rose touched the image with tentative fingers, then drew the blanket closed.

She found beard-trimming scissors, sat Agnes down on a chipped-paint ladderback chair and snipped gleefully at her hair, creating a hodgepodge of layered waves that made her look curiously gamine — like a brunette Janet Leigh in *Psycho*. By the time Rose was satisfied that Agnes looked like Agnes again, her body heat had dried her own clothes to a tolerable level of comfort. The room was a disaster, but instead of cleaning up she moved her friend over to the edge of the bed, swaddled her more securely in the grey blanket, and proceeded to wash out Agnes' skirt and blouse in the kitchenette sink. She strung a length of twine and draped the torn clothes over it to dry. She didn't try washing the sweater but shook it vigorously, rubbed a few darkened areas against themselves to spread out the smudges, and arranged it across the back of a plastic kitchen chair.

She walked to the bathroom and lifted the mirror from its nail over the sink and carried it back to the main room where she sat down purposefully beside Agnes who had been observing all the activities with expressionless eyes. Rose held up the mirror to her friend's face in front of her own, then dropped it away, then up to her face, and dropped it away, doing this again and again.

"Now you're here, now you're gone." She giggled. "Oops, you're there again, gone again, there." She did this, each time reappearing with a different facial expression, confusing identities.

Anna's eyes welled up with tears that streamed down her cheeks and into the corners of her mouth. Her first sensation of herself as a person since Robert's image had appeared in the window was the bittersweet taste of her own tears.

"My husband," she whispered. "Robert Noyes." She mumbled his name several times, as if the words were an invocation to summon his presence. "Noyes. No yes. No. Yes. Robert."

"Sweetheart, I don't think you got a husband, you've never been married, not even common-in-law." Rose stopped trying to provoke a response with the mirror. She spoke gently. She smiled, responding to the crestfallen look on Anna's face. Rose slid over and set the mirror down on the bed.

"My baby," Anna whispered, whimpered, as if the words weren't coming from her.

"No, honey."

"My baby?"

"Honey, you don't have a baby."

"She would have been," Anna paused, searching for the word: "viable."

"Honey, I don't know about viable, but there wasn't no baby."

After a prolonged silence, an inhuman sob rose from deep inside Anna and setting the mirror on her lap she moved closer to Rose and collapsed against her. Rose held her until she gradually stopped weeping. Anna wiped away the tears, blew her nose, and picked up the mirror. She grasped it with fierce determination, as if the image might slip away. She tried desperately to empathize with the woman she saw looking back at her through the glass. The object of her gaze was a stranger unconscious of the person who was conscious of her. Bewildered, she turned to Rose for affirmation that she was there, that she was real, a woman with a history to account for the horror she felt.

She set the mirror down on the end of the cot.

"My little girl," she said plaintively, but this time without crying.

"No, honey. They sterilized you when you were thirteen. Don't you know that, don't you remember? They told you it was a girl's right to have no babies. They called it a right of passage. That was before I got there. I hadn't been born. They reamed out your insides. You were a trustee when we met. You couldn't read, I don't think. You still can't read, or you don't, I never know which. You didn't have no baby except me. I was your little girl."

Rose wrapped Agnes in her arms and the woman embraced her and they rocked back and forth on the edge of the bed. "I was your girl, Aggie. Don't you remember?"

A shuffling outside the door presaged the arrival of Azziz with a tray. He seemed not to notice the black dyes smeared on his bedclothes or splashed on the walls of his diminutive bathroom or the ragged clothes hanging in his kitchen.

"I brought breakfast," he said. "My friend Farouk, he is my boss, he is here now. I am off my shift."

"We'd better leave," said Rose. "We don't want to be imposing."

"You stay," said Azziz. He couldn't take his eyes off Anna. "She looks very pretty. Perhaps you will cut my hair some time."

"Do you want to look pretty?"

"Oh, no, no, no," he protested.

The two women moved apart and he set the tray on the bed between them. He pulled up a scavenged antique ladderback for himself. They ate English muffins with pressed sausage, processed cheese slices, and slippery fried eggs. He had brought enough for all three. Anna sat rigidly upright, staring distractedly at the front window, seeming like she was trying to interpret a message in the accumulated grime on the panes.

"She is better?" he asked. "A little, perhaps?"

"She talked a few words. She made up like she had a baby but lost her."

"Oh, my goodness."

"She only has me."

"You are a grown-up."

"Am I?"

"Where are you from?" he asked.

"Wherever."

"Where were you born?"

"I wasn't. I just turned up."

"No momma, no daddy?"

"No." She smiled her huge vacuous smile. "Each time they'd see you get bigger they'd move you to another home. Finally, I ran away and lived rough on the streets, then I got as big as I'm going to get and I was sent to camp in Temagami. Then I came here."

"What is to live *rough*? I do not speak your vernacular."

"I don't speak vernacular, either. *Rough* is like living nowhere in particular, in the ravines, sofa surfing if you've got friends. You know, here and there, stayin' alive."

"Where is Temagami?"

"I don't know exactly, we never went into town except when we arrived and it was night." Her huge amber eyes fluttered with secrets. "So, are you, like, an Arab?"

"I am Persian."

"Where's that from?"

'From Iran."

"You told me you'd tell me your story. I love stories."

"Dr Anna, it is her story, too."

Anna squirmed on the bed and settled limply against the wall.

"She should sleep," said Azziz.

"Okay," said Rose. "Here are her pills. They were in her pocket."

"What pills, what do they do?"

"They're probably for pain or for sleep — pills always are. We'll give her a few and one way or another she'll get some rest."

Anna took three pills without protesting, seeming hardly to notice. When she settled back and closed her eyes, Azziz tucked a pillow under her head. Rose squeezed upright beside her. Azziz resumed his place on the chair.

"Now," said Rose. "You promised."

"Is there no more to yours?"

"I don't make a point of remembering my story. It's hard to have one if you can't be coherent."

"Coherent?"

"If there's no beginning or end and it doesn't make sense in the middle."

"Who told you your story is not coherent?"

"Agnes. Hers isn't either. That's why we're friends. I'm dialectical and she's not."

"I thought you were dyslectic."

"Dyslexic, that too."

"And if I tell you my story, will we still be friends?"

"Are we friends?"

"Of course. Our stories are not so different, I think. When Dr Anna saw me in the library, I also was a street person. Very dirty, confused, very angry. Living rough, as you say. I found shelter in the carrels and study rooms on Reference Floor Number Eight until someone complained because I talked out loud to myself in a foreign language. Canadians are very afraid of languages they don't understand."

"Did you?"

"Talk? Oh yes, I was lonely. Sometimes I wanted to hear a familiar voice."

"Did you understand what you were saying?"

"Oh yes, sometimes."

"That seems very reasonable. I often talk to myself. If I could read, I would read out loud so I could hear myself reading. Otherwise, I don't see the point."

"You are quite wise," he said.

"I don't know about that, but I can't imagine seeing words in my head and staying quiet. I'd want them outside where they can stand up for themselves."

"And so they would." Speaking about such things made him comfortable. "Silent reading is unnatural," he said. "Do you know in the Christian fourth century Saint Augustine observed Saint Ambrose scanning pages with his eyes without uttering a sound and he was astonished. It did not seem a reasonable thing to do. Yet Ambrose was absorbing the meaning. From that observation Augustine declared faith over reason was the only true way to find God. For the next thousand years Saint Augustine's piety sanctioned the hysteria of obsessive guilt and brutal redemption that outside the Moslem world is called The Dark Ages. In the west. The east is different."

"You speak beautifully, Azziz. I have no idea what you're saying but I believe you. Were you a preacher in Persia?"

"I don't think so, dear girl. Perhaps I was a student."

"I like how you talk. So what happened next in the library? How did you meet your friend, Anna?"

"Ah, well, a gentleman in uniform came to take me away. Dr Winston spoke to him and explained I was doing research, very eccentric, a visiting scholar. So then the commissionaire gentleman departed and I asked her some questions about who I was."

"Who *you* were? You asked *her*."

"Yes. She did not laugh or look afraid."

"Did everyone else?"

"Yes. I was a frightening man because I was frightened."

"And so?"

"She told me, 'I've heard you, you speak Farsi.' I did not know I spoke Farsi. 'Your satchel is a saddle-bag weaving from the Qashqai region of Iran. You speak Persian formally, yes, and Qashqai with your own people.'

I said I did not remember. 'The bag is very old. It is made with vegetal dyes. It is tribal, perhaps woven by your ancestral mother when she was a small girl — the weaving is loose in some places, it distorts the whimsical pattern. The abrash is random, the colour shifts are capricious. It is very valuable to you.' 'Yes,' I told her. 'Possibly you are right. I do not remember.' 'You walk awkwardly,' she said. 'You have bad testicles.' I was shocked. 'You have been tortured.' I did not remember. 'The service ribbon pinned with an American flag on your bag strap. It is white on black on garnet on beige,' she said. 'That is Canadian. The American flag is upside down. You do not like Americans. Perhaps you fear them,' she said. 'I do not remember,' I said. 'But you love Canada, you have a dozen maple leaves pinned on your Maple Leafs sweater and a single Star of David."

He stopped, lost in his memories, adrift among words.

"Is that the end of your story?" Rose appeared disappointed.

"She gave me one hundred dollars. She told me to get washed, to eat food, to throw my hockey sweater in the garbage and to buy from the Thrift Store some clothes suitable for a grown-up man." He looked past Rose at the sleeping woman. He got up and dug out another grey wool blanket from the bottom drawer of an old painted dresser that lacked three glass knobs, and spread it carefully over her.

"Didn't she worry you'd go out and get hammered?"

"Hammered? I do not drink alcohol. She would know that." He gazed at Rose, scrutinizing, assessing. "Here," he said, reaching over for a tea canister on the kitchenette counter. He withdrew some bills. "I want you to go and get clothes for yourself and your friend."

"That's two hundred."

"Inflation."

"But Agnes, I'm not leaving her."

"Agnes, Anna, whatever you wish."

"We don't need clothes." Rose smoothed out the bills and handed them back. "Thank you anyway. We'll get proper help when we go to the shelter. Now, please, could you finish your story?"

"Ah, is it not finished? No, I suppose it is not. Maybe when I die it will be finished, but for now it is, yes, incomplete. Then, so, now I will tell you more."

She grinned.

"You see," he said. "I went back to the library and she told me about my ancestors and everything in my life up to that very moment and she offered to help me find work. She had an acquaintance named Farouk who owned a restaurant. His son had been her student. He is now a lawyer in Calgary, Alberta. She brought me here, to Farouk, and here I am at The Greasy Spoon."

"Azziz al Azzad, please, please, pretty pretty please. Fill in the blanks."

"What? You want details. It is very private."

"I won't tell anybody."

"Ah, you are wonderful, Rose. Are you a virgin? I might want you to marry me."

"I don't want to be married, thank you."

"Well, Dr Anna told me my people were tribal nomads and the women wove beautiful carpets on portable looms. She told me I went to university in Baghdad, that is in Iraq, the next country over, and that is where I learned very good Farsi. Probably I studied psychology, perhaps philosophy, Jewish thinkers, although I am Muslim, and I studied English in Moscow. You can tell much by the structures imposed on the language you are speaking by the other languages you speak. She said I fled Iraq when the Americans attacked and worked as a translator, probably in Kabul, for the Canadian military."

"What does a translator do?"

"I would listen to a language being spoken and speak in another."

"And they paid you for doing that! I only understand about half what you say."

He laughed. "It is an imprecise art. Words in one language only imply words in another. They cannot carry their cultural and historical context with them. Idioms defy paraphrase, Rose."

"Like, explain. I've known a few idioms."

"I'm sure you have. Let's see? The expression 'Love nothing' could refer to triumph in tennis or the essence of Buddhism or a Franciscan motto or a nihilist rebuke. Do you see? As a French Jewish North African philosopher called Jacques Derrida once observed, '*il faut*' means 'it is necessary' while invoking '*une faute*' which means 'fault'. Sometimes words can mean opposite things. They are called contronyms — 'make fast' and 'go fast', or 'bolt the door' and 'bolt in flight', 'cleave to me', 'cleave from me', 'awful as awesome', 'awful as bad'. Translation is a precarious business."

"I have no idea what you just told me. I don't think you were very good at your job."

"Perhaps you are correct. I was arrested by American soldiers and through something called *extraordinary rendition* I was sent back to Iraq and tortured with water and electricity. That is their specialty — water to make you suffocate, electricity to make you choke on your tongue from pain to your testicles. A lot of leftover pain but no missing limbs. American special advisors, Colonel Steele and Colonel Hoffman, Dr Winston had read about them, perhaps it was them, they hurt me very much but I told them nothing. They threw me away. I wandered with nowhere to go. The women of Qashqai in Iran, my mother and sisters, had been murdered. I was a traitor for talking to the hated Americans. I ended up back in Afghanistan on the streets of Kabul. The Canadian authorities found me and bandaged my wounds and sent me to live in Toronto where I would be safe, but when I got here, I had PTSD and they released me from service with a little money, with no memories, and I was like dirt. And that is my story."

"Gosh," said Rose. "Did she tell you all that? Who told her?"

"I did. The way I clutched at my bag, it was something treasured from my grievously lost past. The structures of my languages told her much. The Jewish star on my bag — I admired maybe Freud, maybe Husserl, Arendt, Lévinas, Maimonides, Derrida, Kafka, who knows? As a Muslim, it was important to say. The Canadian service ribbon from Afghanistan, my contempt, my anger, for the American flag, ah, so much I had told her. My souvenir pins, one for each province and territory, there are thirteen, not twelve — they represented my struggle to reconstruct my shattered identity in relation to the alterity of Canada. Even the word, *alterity*, the fact that I knew such a word, it told her so much."

"It must be French."

"It is from Latin. It means otherness or other."

"Then why not say 'other'? Nobody says *otherness*, except maybe if they're drunk. And nobody says *alterity*, trust me, drunk or sober. So, where did you get all the pins? Was she right about your mum? Do you still have your balls? Are you secretly Jewish, are you cut short like they say? Why do they do that? Do you eat pork? Where is Persia? Really, I want to go there some day. Have you heard about Aladdin and his Arabian Knights, and the story of the sesame-seed cavern?"

"If it wasn't for her recognition of my otherness, the details of my alterity, I would not have the story of my life."

Rose gazed with baffled appreciation at this unusual man with his close-shorn beard, his ferocious shock of dyed black hair, and his generous smile.

"I'm glad you have discovered your story," she said. "I wish I had a *coherent* one to remember myself."

"You would be hard to forget."

"Excuse me?"

"Your story. Perhaps, some day it will come back." He rose heavily to his feet. "Why don't you rest now? I have places to go. You take some pills and sleep. I will be back in a few hours."

"Okay," Rose said. "Why not?" She pushed her hair back from her eyes. He picked up the prescription bottle and handed her a couple of pills. When he got up to get her a tumbler of water, he dropped the pill bottle into his pocket.

Rose crawled under the grey blankets and snuggled up close to her friend. She was asleep before Azziz had removed e-glasses from his breast pocket and methodically put them in place. He donned a warm duffel coat that had been hanging on a hook beside a second door in the back wall, this one leading into a dingy corridor with an exit at the far end. He picked up a set of keys from a cracked dish on the counter, lifted his Qashqai bag from another hook and slung the strap over his shoulder, then he pulled the door closed softly behind him and descended the stairs.

In the late afternoon, when the west side of Church St. was cast in deep shadow, Anna stirred, disentangled her fatigued limbs from the blankets and her friend's adolescent embrace, and eased herself onto her feet. She stood gazing at Rose's honey blonde hair, which was dishevelled and flecked with black. She reached down and touched the girl's soft cheek, shuddered from the weight of confusion, and turned away to retrieve her clothes and get dressed. She slipped on her boots without noticing the patent leather was abraded down to colourless dried animal skin in places along their outer edges. She had forgotten how they got that way in the laundry chute or perhaps their damaged condition was no longer of interest.

She walked to the door that opened directly onto the stairs, looked out cautiously and descended to the bathroom, where she carefully locked the door behind her. She used the toilet and performed perfunctory ablutions, pausing at one point to watch as the woman in the mirror ran fingers through her hair. Her movements were furtive yet she never broke eye contact with the woman observing her.

Back in the apartment, she locked both exit doors from the inside. It didn't occur to her that either could be opened from outside with a key. While she made a coffee she fiddled with Rose's pink cellphone on the counter, then lowered herself with studied deliberation into a stained overstuffed armchair as if she could not trust her muscles to perform without explicit direction. She looked around, taking in details, hoping that, by eliminating everything that was not herself, she could arrive at who she was.

After some time, while her companion, who was sprawled like a ragdoll on top of the blankets, stirred restlessly, a strangling dread began to close in as she realized that, perceiving everything that was *not* her, left only an absence.

She was afraid. She once had a husband who was dead, or she had a husband who was alive and wanted her dead, or his ghost was haunting her, taunting her, making her bitterly angry, miserably confused. She was a widow, or she had never been married. She had a friend named Sebastian who called her Anna, he might be dead. She had a friend named Rose who called her Agnes. Another friend who walked with a limp and called her 'doctor'. She had been tortured. He had been tortured. She was choking.

She couldn't swallow. Her breathing was constricted. She was choking on panic and horror and fear. She had lost her baby, her daughter was dead. Her friend Rose told her she had never been pregnant. She cupped her breasts in her hands, then let her hands fall to her lap. Had she never carried her baby inside her, had she never been married, was her husband dead?

If Robert were alive, if she had a baby, where was Robert when their baby died? That question grieved and enraged and baffled her.

"Honey, how're you doing?" A muffled voice spoke from the bed.

"I don't know who I am."

"Nobody does, sweetheart. That's why we have names."

"I feel like I'm coming out of a long long dream where I was somebody else."

"Maybe you're only dreaming you're awake."

"That doesn't help. If I don't know who I am, how do you?"

"What?"

"Know who I am."

"Honey, you've got a tat on your bum. It's a rose, named after me. That's how I know you're Agnes. You can't argue with facts."

A snowplough scraped and battered the pavement out on the street. Dishes rattled and cutlery clattered. Heavy footfalls on the stairs coming up from the washrooms and kitchen resounded like thunder.

Rose held up her hand. "Listen, Agnes!"

The footsteps stopped, the door handle rattled. Rose scrambled behind the armchair. She was shaking. Anna was shaking.

Suddenly Rose stood straight. She tousled her friend's shingled black hair. "What are we scared of, Aggie? If we're lucky, it will just be Azziz."

# Chapter Six
## Camera Obscura

From the perspective of whoever was at the top of the stairs, the two women were simultaneously inside the apartment and not there at all. The classic paradox of Schrödinger's cat held both possibilities were equally valid until otherwise proven. The wily Professor Schrödinger had meant to resolve a particular problem in particle physics but inadvertently accounted for how an unanswered phone delays death, not just the news of its happening. What is not known cannot determine what is.

Anna and Rose were equally perplexed by whatever approached. Anna sank deeper into the stained armchair. She didn't know if she was afraid. She was confused. She didn't know she'd been lost but she didn't know where she was. She didn't know who she was. She seemed familiar but her identity eluded her. The facts of her life were swarming like bees, grieving a queen before replacing her with another. She might have been Anna, she might have been Agnes, she might have been somebody else. She remembered Azziz al Azzad from a scrambled past; she didn't know they were in his flat. They were in peril, she and Rose. She knew her companion was Rose.

She might have tumbled into an alternate sector of the Jamesian multiverse where nothing existed that did not connect through experience. This would appear to include her. And yet, it now seemed more consistent with her present confusion that she was alive in two different worlds simultaneously, one superimposed on the other. There was the world where Anna carried wounds that drove her to the margins of madness; and the other, where someone called Agnes struggled to clarify herself in a miasma of fragmented conjecture. Except, Agnes was dead and Rose was her friend. Rose was Anna's friend, but friendship with Agnes and Anna seemed mutually exclusive.

Rose grasped Anna's shoulder and tightened her grip.

Another pair of winter boots fell heavily on the stairs outside. The door handle turned, a pick rasped in the lock, the door swung open, two men entered. Robert was not one of them.

The men were well dressed and nodded politely. Rose started to speak. One of them was wheezing. He had a burnt-out cigar in his hand. The man who wasn't struggling for breath put his finger to his lips. She continued for another half syllable. He put his finger to *her* lips and pressed gently, breaking the sounds she emitted into aspirant exhalation. She backed away and went silent. She knew how to survive in a hostile world.

"Anna?" said the wheezing cigar smoker. He lay a heavy hand on her shoulder, holding the crook of his free arm to his face to stifle a phlegmatic cough, then rearranged his e-glasses which he had knocked askew.

Anna said nothing. She had nothing to say. They took off their coats. They were waiting for someone, or for something to happen. A phone chimed. They were startled but apparently relieved.

"He says bring her there," said the man with the phone to his ear, while he looked down on the street. "Do what we want with the girl."

He snapped his phone shut.

"She needs me to help her," said Rose in a confident tone, implying there were unspecified female problems that might need her attention.

The men put their coats back on. They had not taken off their boots.

"Come on," said the non-smoker in a coaxing voice, looking out on the street again. "We'll go out the back way."

The men handed the women their coats. They had difficulty sorting out whose was the scuffed nubuck and whose was the parka. No one bothered to pick up Rose's pink cellphone from the kitchenette counter. The men bundled them down the back fire exit into an alley and around a corner to a delivery van blocking the lane. It had darkened windows and the engine was running. A small Vivuscorps logo on the driver's door sanctioned the obstruction and warned away thieves. The men helped the two women clamber up through the back doors into a sheet-metal box carpeted in a shag rug that was thick with the burnt-plastic stench of garbage and smoke. There was an ominous brutality in the men's purposeful silence. The van doors snapped locked from outside. The van lurched over frozen ruts onto Church St. and accelerated through salt-slush and sand-spray, heading north.

The window in the partition between the back and the cab was open enough for the odour of tobacco to creep through but not to admit voices.

The woman and the girl sat opposite each other. Rose stared hard at her friend. The van bumped over the pot-holed pavement. Rose glanced at the men in the front, then ducked her head and in a whisper asked: "Who are you?" She mouthed the words emphatically, perhaps fearing the wrong answer.

"You know who I am."

"You can't be Agnes and Anna, too. Not at the same time."

Anna thought for a bit, then answered solemnly, "I think I can. I'd rather be Agnes right now, but we're here because I'm Anna."

"Is it like living in parallel worlds?"

'Where did you ever hear about that?"

"*Star Trek*. Spock and Kirk turn sexy and mean in another reality, but that's only because they're not really themselves. They're in a mirror universe. They're only reflections."

"No, they're real."

"I thought it was all made up."

"Well, it is. But in their fictional reality the different worlds are equally real."

"Is that like it is for you? Are you fictional?"

"It feels like I am."

"Are you crying? Are you ascared of what these guys will do?"

"No, I'm not crying and yes I'm scared."

Rose skittered on her bottom over to Anna's side and sat very close.

"Tell me about parallel worlds. Does that mean you could be me? Could both of us be somebody else?"

Their bodies jounced against each other as they talked.

"It all starts with Aristotle and the *camera obscura*."

"Speak English, please. I'm not very good on the Greek."

"It's Latin."

"But Aristotle was Greek?"

"He was, yes. Anyway, the *camera obscura*. By passing beams of light through a tiny hole in a wall, the world appears upside down against a wall on the opposite side."

"Aristotle did that, did he? He proved there really is another world than ours."

"Not exactly."

"And you are in both, only different in each."

"I'd have to be; I couldn't be the same. You can't be what a man called Leibniz described as *indiscernable*, exactly alike, or you'd just be using different names for the same person."

"Was Leibniz with Kirk or Picard or Janeway?"

"He was hundreds of years earlier."

"Time warp! I watched a lot of reruns when I was young, you know, in foster homes and shelters and with street-friends who scored rooms."

"You're still young."

"No. Trust me, I'm not."

The van bounced violently and sent them sprawling.

"Was that an up bump or a down bump, pothole or tracks? Where do you think we are?"

"Right here," said Anna.

"How can you be sure?"

"Ask Descartes."

"I don't know him. Was he three hundred years ago, too?"

"Fifty years earlier."

"You certainly know a lot of old people."

"Yes, I do. Most of the people I know are dead."

"So, tell me, let's say you're Anna — and I think you are, you talk better than Agnes — and I'm with you right here, but what if you're also and at the same time Agnes in a mirror universe, and I'm with you there, then am I still me, or only my reflection?"

"Whoever you are, you're still you."

"But I'm upside down through the *camera obscura*, backwards in the mirror, and the same but different in a parallel world."

"And every instant that passes we change."

"You think so?"

"Identity is not a stable commodity."

"I don't think of myself as a *commodity*. I don't even know what that means. Do you have a tattoo?"

"Does Agnes have a tattoo?"

"I don't know whether she does any more."

"Rose?"

"Well, I saw it when I thought you were Agnes, so I figured she always had one. What about you?"

"Yes, I have my own."

"On your bum?"

"On my bum."

"Did you always have it?"

"I travelled when I was young."

"You're still young."

"When I was younger. I studied for a year in Rome and I fell in love with an Italian boy and at the end of the year we both got tattoos."

"In the same place?"

"Yes."

"Did your husband know?"

'It was before him. No, not the whole story."

"Do I know the whole story?"

"As much as I'm going to tell you."

"Listen!"

"What?"

"We're in the country. I can hear cows."

'No, you can't, Rose. You hear truck tyres on wet pavement."

"They're crying like cows going off to get slaughtered. Do they eat animals in the other world?"

"No," she said. "They're oil-free sugar-free salt-reduced vegans."

"Do you think we're going to the slaughterhouse?"

"I don't know where we're going. I'm not sure what's going to happen to us when we get there."

"Are you ascared?"

"You keep asking me that."

"Only twice. It makes me feel better if you are. And worse, too. Do you think they killed Mr Azziz al Azzad?"

"I hope not."

"Did they kill your husband?"

"I used to think so."

"What about your friend with the big house?"

"The big house?"

"The castle with the books."

"Sebastian. Did I tell you about him? I don't know. I hope he's okay."

"Do you think Agnes got squashed to death?"

"By the streetcar? Yes, I think Agnes died in my place."

"But not for your sins. Jesus did that. Except Agnes said we don't have any sins to speak of, so that was a waste — I mean, Jesus dying." When Anna didn't respond, Rose asked her, "Do you believe in Jesus and the Holy Ghost?" Anna looked into her eyes and smiled, then looked away. "No," Rose answered herself. "Neither did Agnes. Neither do I.'

Rose finally picked up on her friend's need for quietude. They sat close, each in her own way contemplative, trying desperately to be serene. Not a word passed between them for the next half hour, until the van glided along a newly ploughed country laneway and drew to a gentle stop.

They were hustled by their escorts with neither brutality nor solicitude past a gold-lettered sign declaring in antiquated cursive script that they were at a Vivuscorps Rest Centre. They entered a lobby painted clinical green and strode rapidly down a long antiseptic corridor past glass doors opening onto a random series of social gatherings, from middle-aged people playing bridge to grey-haired people, mostly women, doing yoga and Pilates, to lecture discussions including all ages, to school groups working on science projects, to nursery play-groups. Everyone was wearing red, the deep colour of venous blood, and everyone except some of the smaller children was wearing e-glasses, everyone including the staff.

When they passed through a large locked door, their escorts turned them over to two other unsmiling men who took away Anna's Georg Jensen watch and led them through another door, assigning them to a pair of dormitory-style bedrooms that opened onto a central area with tables and benches but no people or evidence that anyone had been there, except for rows of books shelved along the walls that from the wear on the spines looked to have been well-read by previous inmates.

"Where do you think we are?" said Rose after they were left on their own. She peered into a room that had a small label on the door. "It says 'Rose'. Do you think all that stuff is for me?" She pointed to the small piles on the bed consisting of towels, a toilet kit with a hairbrush, toothbrush, toothpaste, dental floss, tampons, tinted lip-balm, and deodorant, plus dresses that might have been Girl Guide outfits, except they were deep red, and cotton panties, bras, socks, and red plastic slippers.

Anna smiled wanly and nodded assent, knowing the same exact piles would be in her own private room next door.

"Do you think we should try to escape?" Rose asked.

"That's hard when we don't know where we'd be leaving from."

"Not that hard, not if we want to be anyplace else."

A voice with no discernable inflection to betray human origin spoke from the walls, directing them to wash up and put on the clean clothes. The robotic tenor of the message made it clear the instructions were mandatory. Using a communal washroom and the toiletries provided, they transformed into the curiously sexualized institutional uniforms.

They looked like the Belles of St. Trinian's. Anna wondered who would be Headmistress Millicent Fritton, given Alastair Sim was no longer available.

No sooner had they finished than two men appeared, the same two who had escorted them in, or two different men, it was difficult to tell. They led Rose towards a large door at the far end of the common room. Rose stared wildly back at Anna, her eyes flashing and her mouth agape, but she didn't scream. Anna followed. When the door closed in front of her, she turned and sat down.

The flung parts of her mind coalesced, the widening gyre of fear and confusion collapsed into clarity and she felt she could understand anything, everything. But when she turned her understanding into words, they became jumbled, sense skittered away, and she was left with a vacuum, as if she were at the centre of a visionary experience beyond comprehension, no less profound for its lack of coherence.

She gazed about, the room was empty. Rose's abduction had not surprised her. Nothing surprised her. She wondered where Robert was. Was he the new Headmistress Fritton? She knew he was close. She wondered what rough beast slouched in the shadows, its hour come round at last. Things fall apart. The centre cannot hold.

"The best lack all conviction, the worst are full of passionate intensity." The voice was Sebastian's. She had not seen him come in. She had not realized she had been mumbling aloud the words by Yeats. He continued,

> Mere anarchy is loosed upon the world

> The blood-dimmed tide is loosed and everywhere
> The ceremony of innocence is drowned.

She smiled wanly and paraphrased the closing lines, "And what darkness vexed to nightmare by a rocking cradle is dropped upon the world." He sat down opposite and reaching over placed a bandaged hand on her arm. She grimaced with empathy and touched the back of his other hand. "I'm glad you're all right," she said in a nearly inaudible voice. "I was worried about you. Does it hurt?"

He was wearing a red uniform, a masculinized version of the preppy ensemble prepared for the women.

"Annie," he said, as if reassuring himself it was really her.

"Did the police take you to the hospital?" she asked.

"The Vivuscorps people reached me before the police. They brought me here and finished their surgical repairs before I woke up." He wiggled his bound fingers like a child showing off a fresh cast. "My wounds have been anaesthetized, cauterized, sterilized, immobilized. There's pain but it doesn't seem real, like it's there but it's not really mine. The opposite of phantom-limb syndrome."

"That seems unlikely," she said. She glanced around at the books shelved along the walls.

"Everything here is unlikely," he said. "The Modern Library's *Hundred Great Books*, The World Library's *Hundred Best Books of All Time*, *The Guardian's Hundred Top Books of All Time*, various definitive compendia by Harold Bloom — you could read here to your heart's content and never really learn how to read. Not critically."

"Do you remember the actor, Alastair Sim?" she asked.

"He played Ebenezer Scrooge."

"And Millicent Fritton."

"Who?"

"The headmistress in *The Belles of St. Trinian's*," she responded.

"Why?"

"Because he could. Where in God's name are we?"

"We're at some sort of spa, a retreat for Vivuscorps people. One could assume we're being monitored."

"Right now?"

"Yes."

"Sebastian, do you have cancer?"

The abruptness of her question startled them both.

"Why?"

"You told me you'd been to Princess Margaret."

"There's nothing to talk about," he said.

"If you prefer."

"Life and death are mutually dependent." He paused as if wondering whether he'd said something profound. "It is only the transition from one to the other I dread, and even that, not overly."

"I'll take that as a 'no'. You don't have cancer. That's what I would prefer. Have you run into someone called Azziz al Azzad?"

"Azziz, yes, he came to my house. He tracked me through the label on my pills. They followed him back to where they found you at The Greasy Spoon or someplace called something like that."

"What about Rose?"

"I've never met anyone called Rose. How did you like my library? I was worried you might not like it."

Was he being cautious or wily? She couldn't be sure. "Rose is my friend. She's interested in parallel worlds. Since we just met, it seems a bit paradoxical, but I think she's known me for years."

"But Rose is a Rose is a Rose. Is she real?"

"Of course."

"You never know with a name," he said. "Spinoza argued that God is everything that is, but all that proves is that God is a word, a name, a signifier signified, so to speak."

"It's good to see you, Sebastian."

She meant that. His helter-skelter erudition brought her mind into focus.

"Your friend, is she *Star Trek* or Leibniz?"

"What? Oh, Captain Kirk's mirror universe, as opposed to infinite *compossible* worlds in the mind of God — both, actually. She seems interested in both. And in the multiverses of Arthur C. Clarke and William James, and Ray Bradbury's time paradoxes, which are really the antitheses of parallel realities."

"She must be a great reader."

"She doesn't read at all. She listens."

"Well, listen, yourself, and think about this. Since, according to Leibniz, God chose the *best* of all possible worlds to pursue his experiment with us, the infinite worlds can't possibly be parallel. It's all just a trick with words. Do you see what I mean? You said *a bit paradoxical*, a moment ago. You do know something cannot be a *bit* paradoxical, Anna. That's like being a little bit dead. Did you know Leibniz made computers possible by inventing calculus and binary arith-metics? What about Spinoza? Out of the pulver, the polished lens! He was ostracized as a heretic by the community of his fellow Jews in Amsterdam. He fared as a glass grinder and, like Wittgenstein four hundred years later, gave up his claims to a family fortune in order more freely to think and to write down his thoughts."

"Sebastian?"

He was telling her things! What, she could not determine. He was definitely speaking in code.

"Spinoza was a rationalist. He shaped Nietzsche's thinking on the 'will to power'," she offered, talking to apparent cross purposes. "He didn't believe in the immortality of human souls. He argued that God is an abstraction, fate is determined by necessity, and knowledge keeps our emotions constructively under control."

Sebastian nodded sagaciously, seeming relieved.

"Nietzsche noted how insane dancers must appear to those who can't hear the music," he resumed. He seemed to be offering encouragement, direction, obscured information. "Spinoza made microscopes and he made telescopes — to explore quantum mechanics and the infinite reaches of space. He sanctioned God as a concept which atheists could deride, if they wished, without condemning themselves to perdition or scorn. Long before he was appreciated, he died by the instruments of his own creation, from inhaling ground glass."

Sebastian was talking about making lenses to peer into micro-worlds, to gaze at the illimitable structures of the universe, to perceive God as a construct of human necessity and the soul as subversive. He was talking about Spinoza being a martyr to genius, sustained by his faith in the transcendence of the superior mind. He was talking about death. Sebastian was telling her about her husband, about fatal pride, *hamartia*, and about the strange and dangerous Vivuscorps world in which they were imprisoned. He was speaking in an extended and cryptic metaphor.

"I saw Robert," she said.

"I'm not surprised."

She gazed into the depths of his eyes but saw only darkness.

"I saw him at your place, Sebastian. He was one of the three men in the stairwell. You knew who he was; you'd met him before. Why didn't you tell me?"

"What?"

"That he was alive."

"I thought you'd be devastated. I was trying to affirm what you felt to be true."

"Why?"

"To protect you."

"From myself?"

"From the enemy within."

"Seriously, Sebastian. You could have told me."

"I'm sorry."

"And *Star Trek* doesn't apply."

"What?" He seemed puzzled.

"A faulty transporter divides Captain Kirk into good and evil selves who fight with each other — episode five, first season, it was called '*The Enemy Within*'. I don't have enemies. I have miscreants after me who want to hack my skull open, and would-be assassins waiting to dispose of the mess. *Enemy* presupposes adversarial systems at war. What I have are mindless opponents."

"Including Robert?"

"Especially Robert — he betrayed me utterly, hiding within death. And God knows why. God? Why?"

"You could talk to him if you want to. He's here."

"No!" She shuddered violently. "Not yet. I, I—"

She couldn't find adequate words, she couldn't place herself in an appropriate emotional context. The horrors associated with Robert's resurrection settled like the oppressive and indistinct layers of a nightmare slipping into the unconscious. It was good to be with Sebastian, even as prisoners together in a windowless room.

Awareness of their constricted surroundings brought images flooding back of Sebastian's marvellous phantasmagorical Cloisters, images she had largely suppressed through the trauma of the last few hours or days. Now, she felt curiously invasive as she asked him to explain such a place and at first, he baulked at her questions, then opened up but ultimately told her little.

"I have the resources," he said. "I give a great deal to charity. I live a solitary life. I am neither profligate nor dissolute. I spend a small portion of what I have on myself. It is an ongoing project."

At first, she thought he meant *he* was the ongoing project.

She preferred not to think of his vast edifice of books and mirrors and doors as a monumental indulgence. "A project — to become what? To do what?" she challenged. "It is a grand and complex illusion but what does it do?"

He seemed hurt, as if she had exposed a prosthetic limb that had been trying to hide from public view. Then he rallied: "If I disappoint you, dear Anna, you in turn disappoint me. You wouldn't wander about in the Sistine Chapel and demand what it does. It isn't about *does*; it is about *is*. It *is*. Forgive me for speaking in italics, but I do have a point to make that apparently you'd otherwise miss."

"The Sistine Chapel is a *public* building within the Apostolic Palace. It's where they hold the Conclave to elect a new pope. It has a function. I've been there. It's open to visitors."

"Actually, it was a ruin restored by Sixtus the Fourth for a select group called 'the Papal Chapel', and for them alone," he explained. "Yet frescoes by Botticelli, the miraculous ceiling by Michelangelo, his massive *Last Judgement* on the altar wall, other frescoes by Perugino and Ghirlandaio, the architecture itself, the furnishings, Raphael's tapestries — not the originals, they were stolen in the sixteenth century — all exist together as a singular work of such sublime genius, whether it is private or public doesn't matter. It is unique, splendid, itself, and the makers and the viewers and the users who use it will die, but it *is*, it exists. That's what's important, it exists."

"And we *know* it exists! But like the statue of Ozymandias, it will crumble in time."

"And the sun will expand into a giant red ball and collapse and by then all life will have perished from the face of the Earth. Meanwhile, important beyond consciousness, are the works we create because they transcend — what? Time. Yes, time. Having existed, they exist. Having been, they will be. Always. Their existence does not depend on perception."

"You sound like a mystic," she said.

"Most realists do. And you sound like a fatalist."

"Not at all," she responded. "Except in the broadest sense. I don't believe in fate, but in ends. Everything ends."

"Now you sound like a poet."

They talked for several more hours. Periodically he dropped a quotation into the conversation, usually a line or two of verse, mostly American, and as their conversation progressed from the poetic to poetics, he championed Archibald MacLeish's *Ars Poetica*, declaiming "A poem should not mean But be" as if he had invented the phrasing, although by his reverential tone he gave the poet full credit when he declared a great poem conveys silence — "Silent as the sleeve-worn stone/Of casement edges." Then he tumbled over his own argument as he turned to Wallace Stevens and argued that a poem is "the cry of its occasion — between is and was. And the theory/Of poetry is the theory of life/As it is, in the intricate evasions of as."

*The intricate evasions of as!* She marvelled at how Sebastian had used Stevens to echo her arguments for poetry on their first coffee-date, and how little he seemed aware of that fact. Neither of them tried to explain or interpret the lines they strung out between them. She was familiar with McLeish and Stevens but quoted sparingly so as not to impede the flow of their talk. When she did, she quoted McLeish, although she preferred Stevens: "a poem should be wordless/As a flight of birds… motionless in time/As the moon climbs." The image intentionally collapsed; her voice fell off. She tossed a line of Frost into the mix and receded. She listened. The art of the poet was to listen. With Sebastian, she thought of herself as a poet. It was lifeblood to hear the antinomies of poetry, that it was wordless and word-filled, clamorous and utterly still, and to share such contradictions with a metaphysical man unencumbered by arithmetic and science yet able to use both in his wondrous Ozymandian construction.

She was about to quote Emily Dickinson when the door through which Rose had been taken swung open, interrupting their charged conversation. Rose emerged, wavered, and collapsed onto the floor.

They raced to her. She was wet from the waist up. They helped her to a bench. Anna rushed into her room and returned with a pastel-blue blanket which Sebastian held while Anna stripped off the wet dress. Rose clasped her bra to her slight body as if it were a last vestige of modesty while they wrapped the blanket around her like swaddling clothes and draped part of it over her head.

"Rose, what happened, what did they do?"

"I'm out of breath, I can't breathe."

"You have the breath to say you're out of breath," Anna noted.

"To paraphrase the lovesick Juliet," Sebastian observed.

It had not occurred to Anna she had been using Shakespeare to create the necessary delay for Rose to catch her breath. Sometimes borrowed words simply appeared in her mind. They provided an immediate context while leading in directions that often surprised her.

"I didn't tell them anything, Aggie. I couldn't. I didn't know what they wanted." She coughed in spasms and continued. "They held my head under water. They poured water over a towel covering my face. I couldn't breathe. I still can't breathe, I think I'm going to die."

"You're not going to die."

'Maybe not yet. They kept asking about the police — what do I know about police? They think I'm a cop. I told them I can't read and write but they still thought I could be a cop. Who's this, is this the guy with the books?"

"I'm Sebastian," said Sebastian. "I am probably the man with the books. If you want, I'll teach you to read."

"Okay." She paused. "I'm severely dyslexic."

"I'm severely patient. We'll work on it. It'll take time."

"And words. It'll take words."

"Yes," he said. "A lot of words. I happen to have plenty available."

"Do you own them?"

"The words? No, they're on loan."

Rose looked down at his bandages and she asked sympathetically, "What happened to your hand? Did they hurt it?"

"I was apparently smoking."

"You shouldn't smoke. It's bad for you."

"It nearly killed me. What else did they want to know?"

"It was like a dog chasing its tale." She smiled at her curious ability to make a pun when she didn't know how to spell. "It was comical except I was drowning. They kept asking what I knew and I kept saying I didn't know because I didn't know what they wanted. Then they'd ask me again and I'd give the same answer. Over and over until I guess they got bored. I mean, if I started telling them everything, I know about everything, I'd still be talking and drowning, talking and drowning, until this very moment right now. Annie, you're deathly quiet."

"I'm thinking."

"Think out loud."

"Rose, Sebastian saw Robert. He's here."

"That's good, that's great. I was afraid you'd seen a ghost or a lookalike, looking like he used to look."

"Anna," said Rose, pausing discreetly for a moment before going on, "I'm glad he wasn't cremated."

"I signed the papers releasing his body, I'm sure of that. I was in a convalescent centre. They brought me the forms. For Robert and for my little girl."

"You weren't in a hospital?"

"No. it was a centre. I had to stay in bed for over a week."

"Did you see them dead?"

"They took my unborn child from me before I woke up and they put her in Robert's arms and they cremated them together. They told me that. I had a concussion, we got pretty banged up, and Robert smashed his face, so they kept me away."

"Was there a service?"

"No. He wouldn't have wanted it."

"Were you interviewed by the police?"

"I know people talked to me. They tried to reassure me, to make me feel better. It was beyond understanding, they said — as if ignorance were a consolation."

"Were you at the cremation?"

"No."

"Why not?" asked Rose. "I would have wanted to be there."

"I wasn't."

"Do you know how hot it's got to be to burn a dead body?"

"Rose!" Sebastian admonished.

"I don't want to know."

"Nine hundred degrees Celsius. We tried to burn a raccoon once, up at the camp. Somebody killed it. Nine hundred, that's what they told us."

"Rose," said Sebastian severely.

"It's okay," said Anna.

"Humans would be the same as raccoons," Rose affirmed. "Do you know, when they were trying to drown me, I just kept thinking about what we were talking about before and about how much I wanted to be in another world. Maybe one where there was fire instead of water and they burnt themselves trying to torture me with flames. Or else a world where there was nothing at all, so they weren't even there. But then neither was I, so if it's an empty world could you say it exists?"

"You were thinking this while you were being waterboarded?"

"Is that what they call it? I was thinking a lot of things, and would have said almost anything out loud, but I couldn't figure out what they wanted to hear."

Anna stared fondly at her young friend who had escaped into parallel worlds. A random thought drifted into Anna's mind, and as soon as she grasped it she remembered her talk with Sebastian about causality, when they had been in The Coffee Café. They had talked about Aristotle and he had insisted (both Aristotle and Sebastian insisted) that there was no such thing as coincidence and nothing was random, not ever.

"Rose."

"Yes?" Rose shrank slightly into herself.

"How did you know I was in The Greasy Spoon?"

"I didn't, it was a coincidence."

"I think you did. I think you came looking for me. How did you know Sebastian lives in a castle of books? I never told you. I was confused at Azziz's place but I could hear myself speak and I never said anything about where I'd been."

"I'm your friend, Anna. I was looking for Agnes. She died."

"Who sent you? Was it somebody from Vivuscorps?"

"No, Annie, I promise. I absolutely promise."

"Rose?"

"It was only the police and we lost them."

Sebastian had moved around to the far side of the table so it might have seemed they were closing in. Rose sat straight and defiant but with no indication of hostility.

"The police caught me. I was sitting in the shadows on the side porch." She looked up at Sebastian. "At your big mansion. I was waiting for my friend Agnes. I followed you there." She looked over at Anna. "I saw the two of you in the alley behind the coffee shop in Yorkville. I was looking for food in the bakery dumpster a couple doors down and when you came out, I couldn't be sure because your hair was different but, like, if there was one chance in a gazillion I'd found you, I wasn't going to lose you again. I followed and you were both walking really fast and the sidewalk was slippery as hell, and finally you went into the big house, so by then I thought it probably wasn't you after all because Agnes didn't know rich people with books, but I thought I'd wait around, just to be sure."

"How did you know about the books?"

"A couple of times you pulled the curtains back and I could look up from the street and see them stacked to the ceiling."

"I thought you were on the porch."

"I was, but I got hungry and cold, so I walked around a bit and I went for some doughnuts and coffee over on Yonge Street."

"Where did you get the money?"

"I had savings in my pockets."

"How did you know I hadn't left when you got back?"

"'Cause I kicked snow onto the walk by the house and I could see that only one person ever went out and it must have been a man 'cause the prints were large, so it must have been you, Sebastian — I can't call you mister since I don't know your last name — and so I waited. I wasn't going to take the chance I'd miss Agnes in case you were still her. Then those guys came in their black car and I hid behind the swinging sofa on the porch. They went inside the door to stay warm but I could hear them. Then you came back, Sebastian. Then they went out and in, a couple of times. Mostly they sat in their car. And I waited some more. I couldn't go anywhere without being seen and finally, long after dark, it was the middle of the night, and the cop cars came with their blue lights flashing and those other guys left. I decided it was about time to give up on Agnes and I walked down and along a bit and the cops picked me up for being where I shouldn't have been, dressed poor as I was, and so I explained what I was doing up there among the big houses, looking for Agnes. They told me they were looking for Anna. They showed me a picture of Agnes and said it was you, Annie, and they didn't think you were inside the house any more. They took me back to the house and told me to wait in case you returned, so I waited on the side porch some more and finally you came out the front door, but you went back in at the side, right past me, and then you came out pretty soon, and before the sirens and flashing lights came rushing up the street, we both got away and I followed you down to The Greasy Spoon."

She smiled sheepishly and, wide-eyed with apparent surprise, she articulated words that she had never before heard in her life: "*et sic finis fabulae*. And so my story ends."

Caught up in her recitation, neither Sebastian nor Anna noticed the Latin.

"You knew Azziz already," said Anna.

"I just knew his name. I'd been there before. He gave me some doughnuts, they were stale but he gave them for free, and donated a coffee to soften them up. When he asked me to help, that's when I got close and saw it was you. Well, it wasn't. I thought you were Agnes. And that's the whole story. Like I said, *that's the end.*"

"And the police, did they know where we'd got to?"

"They followed the phone they gave me. I'd never own a pink cellphone on purpose. And who would I call? And I'd never own a smartphone, like I'd throw it away, because how would I text — I wouldn't know what I'm saying? And yes, the police knew we were in there all day long. I think they were watching from the street to see where we'd go. But we went out the back way with the Vivuscorps guys. And I left my phone behind on the counter on purpose. I didn't want the police following us."

"It might have been good if they had. They'd know where we are."

"We're not lost, Annie. You're always in the last place you look for yourself. See, we're right here." Rose didn't know whether she was making a joke or not. "I live in a looking-glass world," she said. "That's what Agnes told me. And I'm never sure which side of the mirror I'm on. But I am what I am and it is what it is, I'm here and I hope I'm forgiven."

Anna thought of *the magical copula.* To counter her amusement, she looked at Rose sternly. "Tracking me for the police but not giving me up — that hardly qualifies for redemption."

"Oh, I've been redeemed a dozen times before breakfast. Sometimes it's a condition for getting a freebie. You don't have to believe, 'cause I don't, but you have to swallow your sins if you want the grub."

"Now that's Lewis Carrollish."

"I don't know about Carol, but I know the cops don't know for sure who you are. I was there with you all the way, you know, scared of whatever would happen. Ascared you wouldn't be Agnes, then scared you would be, and I would be somebody else and not me. A double agent, that's what they said, living in two worlds at the same time. I really was. I'm sorry, Annie, but at least I didn't tell them, when I was waterboarded, you know, that I was working for the cops."

"But you just did," said a voice speaking softly from inside the walls.

Rose and Anna and Sebastian instinctively cringed.

"By telling us nothing you told us a lot," said the voice. "Anna, it's me, I'm coming in now."

Rose and Sebastian stood up. The door at the back of the room swung open and Robert appeared. Anna glanced over her shoulder. He was smaller than she remembered. He looked sad. He walked towards the three of them. Rose backed off, perhaps sensing malevolence, and Sebastian, perhaps sensing power, stayed still. Anna remained seated, facing away from Robert. He moved around into her line of vision.

"You don't seem happy to see me," he said.

"I saw you through the door at Sebastian's."

"So I heard you say. I thought you'd be pleased."

"Shocked, distressed, appalled, not pleased. I was used to you being dead. I've known you as a dead man longer than alive."

She wanted to match the cruelty of his nonchalance with her own.

"It was for the best," he said.

"For the best! Four miserable years of sorrow didn't feel like the best."

"I was trying to protect you," he said.

"To cope with the death of our baby myself?" Her statement came out as a question.

"What if there was no baby?"

*We were waiting for her birth to give her a name, I never gave her a name.*

Anna swung around slowly on the bench and rose to her feet. She gazed into Robert's eyes almost indifferently. Then, in a split second, the bewilderment that had displaced sorrow turned to rage and she was at Robert's throat. Her thumbs pressed under his jaw into his oesophagus, pinning him breathless and gagging against the cement wall. Rose moved closer. Sebastian remained still. Robert turned blue. Anna released her grip and walked into her cell. Rose followed and pushed the door shut. Sebastian caught Robert before he collapsed and helped him to the exit, then he approached Anna's room and knocked gently before entering.

# Chapter Seven
## *Ego Sum Camera*

Anna and Rose sat on Anna's bed. Rose, wearing the pastel blanket wrapped around her shoulders and draped like a cowl over her head, looked like a pale gentile Madonna. Anna was stricken, yet stoic, like Socrates after the hemlock. Sebastian sat on a chair, facing them. He appeared thoughtful, not contemplative so much as confounded, both angered and mildly amused. They all leaned forward into each other's space, not touching but trying to connect.

"I thought I was going to eternity," said Rose.

"It's okay," said Anna. "You're okay, now."

"I know," said Rose. "Time would have disappeared."

"It didn't, you're here."

"I think I blacked out, but I always came back."

"That's good."

"I'm sorry, Annie, I didn't mean to betray you. I thought you were Agnes. I thought I was helping. I nearly croaked. Time nearly stopped. Then I would never have existed. Or would I? I don't believe in heaven very much, so after you're dead, if you're dead *forever*, then it would be impossible to have been here at all. I mean you can't measure *forever* from *now*. That doesn't make sense. So, if there's no beginning, then how could you tell where you'd been? And what about the big bang? I love that show — Sheldon's as smart as you and Sebastian."

"Eternity is by definition forever," said Sebastian, who had been distracted from his own haphazard meditations by her poignant metaphysics.

"It can't be," said Anna. Rose's words had captured her attention as well. "That would mean all time is eternally present."

"Eliot!" said Sebastian. *"Four Quartets."*

Before he could expostulate on T.S. Eliot's turn to faith or start quoting, Anna began to recite and he had enough respect for the words to attend them, despite their aesthetic austerity:

> Time present and time past
> Are both perhaps present in time future

"That's what I've been trying to say. Sort of," Rose interjected.

> And time future contained in time past…
> All time is eternally present.

"Yes, but," said Rose, "if all time exists at the same time, then it's just something we call wherever we are when we're there."

"Rose?"

"What? We can only ever experience things in the present, anyway," Rose continued. "The past is what we remember about an earlier present and the future is what we expect will happen when a new present arrives. So, there's only now. Like your friend Mr Eliot says, all time is eternally present."

"Although he might have meant exactly the opposite," Anna suggested.

"He might have been wrong," said Rose.

"Like a lot of religious converts, Eliot thought he was God," said Sebastian.

Anna couldn't tell whether his judgement was scorn or approbation. "He took God's point of view on the world," she said. "That's quite a different thing."

"God wouldn't mind," said Rose.

"What's your conception of God?" Sebastian addressed Rose. Again, Anna couldn't be sure whether his question expressed scorn or respect.

"I don't have conceptions," said Rose. "I don't think there's God anywhere." And then, making a leap inexplicable to anyone outside her own head, she asked Anna, "Do you think maybe your baby's not dead?"

Sebastian seemed to reel, but Anna remained merely discomfited. "I have accepted her death for four long years," she said.

"That was because you didn't know any better, but now?"

"Yes, I think perhaps she is alive."

"Don't you care?"

"Rose!" Sebastian moved forward towards her.

"It's all right, Sebastian. Yes, I care, Rose. If she was ripped from my body and raised by her father in secret, I can conceive of nothing more cruel. Of course I care. I am distraught and enraged. But, Rose, I am also more focussed than I have ever been in my life. If she is alive, then Robert and his allies should fear me."

Anna turned her head slowly and spoke to the walls.

"Fear me," she said, and repeated: "Fear. Me."

She was distressed by the histrionics of her own utterance, but drew strength from its unequivocal force.

"What do you think happens next?" said Sebastian, offering a distraction.

"I told you," said Rose, "I think we just die."

Discounting both Rose's dismissal of heaven and Sebastian's declaration of uncertainty, Anna said softly, "We wait."

If my baby was abducted from my womb and survived, Anna thought — but she couldn't go on, there was no end to her thought. Deep inside, her other self wept. Anna tasted her tears and shuddered.

For three days they waited in their windowless ward, measuring duration by the meals wheeled in to them and their need to clear their systems of waste. Snippets from Eliot threaded through Anna's mind the whole time, mostly from the early poems, whose dolorous lines excoriating modernity were more comforting than the platitudinous assurances of the later *Quartets*.

At dusk on the third day, when evening was spread out against the sky, two men came for her. She was strapped to a gurney. She caught sight of the fading light through a window as they wheeled her along corridors into another wing of the complex. Let us go then, you and me, before the taking of a toast and tea — she purposefully scrambled the words to avoid copyright infringement. Lying prone, unable to move, she came to rest in an operating theatre and people in surgical gowns fussed around her, then shifted her onto a table and left her on her own. Inside her head, a roiling mixture of Eliot blended with Lennon and McCartney. He who was dead is now living/We who were living are dead/What do you see when you turn off the light/I try not to sing out of key.

"Anna, Anna. Can you focus?" Robert hove into her line of vision, leaning over, peering into her eyes. "I need you to pay attention. Can you do that? You've had a light sedative. It'll make everything go easier."

"With a little help from my friends," she intoned. "Are you going to burrow into my skull? Poor Anna, alas, I knew her well, a woman of infinite jest."

"Anna, I need to talk."

"I will talk to you, Robert. I will kill you. You are already dead."

"There's no reason to hate me, Anna, I'm on your side."

"You took my baby away."

She tried to lift her head but it was constrained by skull clamps. Her entire body was immobilized. Her eyes flashed frantically, then the panic subsided and she stared deeply into his eyes, which were impossibly blue. Absurdly, he smiled, drawing the bruises under his jawline into the glare. He was dressed in pale green surgical scrubs.

"Anna, there was no baby. Don't you understand? That's something you invented. There never was a baby." He spoke softly. He placed the back of a hand against her forehead, then her cheek. He looked grief-stricken, like a man breaking apart from sympathy and pain. Or was it empathy and sorrow? Or something else?

"The accident?" she said. "I lost my little girl."

"There was no accident, Anna."

He whispered, with only the hush of the air in his throat forming sounds, to emphasize the urgency and truth of his utterance.

She was bewildered, disconsolate, strangled by heaven's held breath. She waited. Panic overrode the calming confusion from the drugs in her coffee at breakfast. He placed the soothing palm of his hand on her forehead, as if trying to quell the horror taking shape like a beast of the Apocalypse coming to life between them. She shuddered with spiralling despair in the widening gyre, she could hear her own wretchedness echoing as she plummeted into its depths. "This is how everything ends," she mumbled. "Not with a bang but a whisper."

"You're going to be okay. We're going to help you."

Help? His declaration hit like she'd been slammed against a wall, or dropped into the depths of an endless abyss. Poetry fled on the wings of fear. There was nothing more to lose.

"Anna. You need help. You walked into the side of a streetcar."

"Not me, it wasn't me."

"Yes."

His simple affirmative was devastating.

"Tell me my story," she whispered.

"You had a miscarriage. Can you remember? Four years ago. In your first trimester. It was traumatic, you couldn't get over the loss. Do you remember anything?"

"No." She was uneasy, anxious, oppressed by feelings unconnected with memories or thoughts.

"You couldn't go back to lecturing."

"I remember you quit your postdoc," she countered. Her need to participate in her unfolding story subverted the confusion and terror at hearing reality being reshaped with cavalier certainty. She was desperate for clarity.

"I shifted locations," he said.

"You moved to the registrar's office."

"I moved here."

"Not the registrar? You didn't work there?"

"No."

"You work for Vivuscorps?"

"They sponsored my research."

"I thought that was the Kroetsch Foundation."

"My postdoc was funded by Vivuscorps."

"Why did you keep it a secret?"

"I didn't know about them at first. Then it was like I went underground. I got wrapped up in my projects. You and I separated."

"We separated!"

"You kept the house. I moved up here."

"You disappeared!"

"I did, more or less. My work is extremely sensitive. It was a proprietorial move, nothing sinister. Just a matter of maintaining control."

"Control?"

"Keeping my work under wraps until it is proven effective."

"Effective?"

"Yes."

"Is it?"

"We'll see."

"Robert, you said 'up here'. Where are we?"

"In the country."

"I don't understand any of this? I don't know who I am any more. My friend Rose thinks I'm somebody else."

"And what do you think?"

"It's like I have all my memories, my history, my thoughts and my feelings, my own personality, but sometimes it seems like it's all a veneer overlaying someone else underneath." Possibly the sedative made her loquacious or perhaps it was the banal absurdity of lying exposed on a surgical table. "I grew up with my Granny in her brick house in Cambridge. Cambridge, Ontario. 231 Queen St., I remember it clearly. My parents died when I was very young. I went to school. I studied at the University of Toronto. I travelled and came back and studied some more and was married and we got pregnant. There was an accident, the car crash, and the confusion began. Ghostly spectres began swirling around in the depths of my mind, vague premonitions of the past. I know that's impossible but that's how it seems — presentiments of a future that occurred long ago. For a time, the spectres were no more substantial than dreams that disintegrate on awakening, but after the streetcar incident the shattered bits coalesced into elusive ephemeral memories of places, of people, of growing up somewhere else, visiting Niagara Falls, picking fruit in the summers, running away, being abused, badly abused, running, running away, again and again. Then somehow, I'm in the American south and then I'm in New England and sometimes I'm just floating. When I confront the spectres directly, they flee or dissolve into dust."

"Your imagination is getting the best of you."

"I'm not making up metaphors, Robert."

"Do you remember walking into the streetcar?"

"I remember a car accident, somebody hit us. They told me you were killed. I signed cremation papers for you and our baby."

"Tell me exactly what you think you remember about that."

"A person doesn't *think* she remembers. She does or she doesn't."

He shrugged internally — she could tell by his eyes.

"Our baby was crushed inside me, Robert. She died. They took her away, a baby girl. I was alone. You were gone. I worked in the library. I read my books. My memories are vivid, disjointed. Time was not linear, the past never is, but it wasn't linear in the present. Time was in fragments. I grieved and I grieved. I deconstructed. I could not reconcile the oppositions and differences defining my life but I somehow endured. I still had my independence of mind but I was incomplete."

"Anna?"

"You've told me I had an early miscarriage. How could I forget such a thing and remember the death of my baby who never existed? You say it was me who walked into the streetcar, but it wasn't me. I saw that woman. She was smashed on the pavement, she was somebody else, she was dead. I'm here. So why am I here? Why do you want to see inside my skull?"

Robert moved so close she could feel physical warmth seep through his clothes, penetrating the sheet that covered her immobilized body.

"To make you feel better," he said.

"I've seen *The Stepford Wives*!"

"Anna, what you remember as a car accident was a surgical procedure. We tried to help you. You were an emotional disaster. You wanted that baby so much, but it wasn't remotely viable, Anna. It was just tissues and blood."

She stared up at him aghast, incredulous, and for an instant she remembered the horror of her collapsed pregnancy and the harrowing malaise that had overwhelmed her, then she careened back into the present.

"Listen to me," he was saying. "You fell apart. You needed help. After we separated, I arranged to have you brought here. My work had progressed to the point I thought we could do something for you. Right here, in this room, we inserted a DNA microcomputer into your brain. It's okay, it's okay. It was programmed to suppress anxiety, to increase coherence, linearity — nothing too advanced or radical, nothing to alter your personality or delimit your mental functioning."

"It's inside me now!"

"Yes, it is. And it's helped you. We've been observing you, checking up on you from time to time. Your friend Azziz told us you were doing okay. Your friend Mr Kroetsch helped for a bit, then turned against us — he's very protective. They're both loyal friends, in their way."

"What about Rose?"

"Rose? We couldn't get through to her. I don't know that there would be much there, if we could."

"So you nearly drowned her?"

"We threw a bucket of water on her. The rest she made up."

"You asked her a lot of questions?"

"It was necessary."

"What about turning Sebastian into an incendiary device?"

"I've already taken a look at his hand. He won't lose the fingers, only the feeling in the tips."

"Robert, what is happening? Why have you got me here, why now?"

"You walked into the side of a moving streetcar, that's why. Then you tried to disappear. We need to know what's wrong. Why didn't you see where you were going? How could you have been so careless? Was it an intentional accident?"

"That's oxymoronic."

"What?"

"*Intentional accident*. And so what if I had an Anna Karenina episode? What's that to you? Ah, yes, of course. Your tiny computer was designed to prevent such acts of free will. You couldn't be sure if it was working at all. So you need to dig it out and take a good look in my head. Tell me, am I meant to survive?"

"I expect you will. It's a little trickier to remove than it was to insert, but I'm sure you'll pull through. We need to make observations. Don't think. Relax. Here comes the team."

"Don't you do the operation yourself?"

"Of course not, Anna. I'm a nanobiotechnician, not a surgeon. I direct, I observe. See you on the other side."

Robert stepped away and others closed in.

The last words in Anna's mind, beneath the anaesthetist's countdown, belonged to Rose, who had said as Anna was being wheeled away to the operating theatre, *if they try to drown you, remember, don't breathe.*

After an absence of time, she drifted into consciousness awkwardly. Her mind swarmed with words in a strange Hegelian dialectic, struggling against each other to be resolved as a whole greater than themselves, binary word-clusters — self and other, mind and matter, being and nothingness, meaning and meaninglessness, time and the silence of eternity. Hegel's own method of synthesis, where being and non-being were mutually dependent, or Derrida's deconstruction of *différance* in rejection of the violent hierarchy of contradictions, or Camus's arbitrary creation of meaning in light of the absurd, all seemed equally viable modes of conjecture to reach who she was. But when she almost recognized herself in the miasma of words, her mind darkened as if all thoughts were erased. She was not someone else, although her identity was indistinct. Her history and her memories were in conflict, yet both anticipated her present condition. Whatever in her mind had been subject to a machine was apparently no longer active, but she felt virtually the same.

She opened her eyes. She was in the intensive care unit where she had recovered after the car accident, the accident Robert told her had never happened. She was in the room where she had recuperated after the original implant procedure. She was in a generic facility with cream-coloured room-dividers sliding on metal tracks, clicking and whirling machines, and walls painted institutional beige.

Wherever she was, Robert was there.

"Anna," he said, letting the word of her name hook the air. "Anna?" he repeated, the rising vowel at the word's end turning it into a query.

"I'm here," she mumbled.

"It went well."

"That's good." She couldn't think of anything more to say. He needed reassurance, but she couldn't imagine why. After a while, she drifted off to sleep and when she woke up, she was alone in a convalescent room with a large window looking out on gardens and a field and a maple wood in the distance. From the looks of the uniform size of the trees and the absence of undergrowth she assumed it was a sugar bush.

As soon as she sat up, a nurse who must have been monitoring her came into the room. He brought her a light lunch on a tray, with a tulip glass on a thin stem and a carafe of light red wine, a Beaujolais Villages.

"I hope you slept well," he said as he adjusted her pillows. She might have been at a spa or entitled, rather than a captive patient convalescing after invasive surgery.

"Thank you," she said. "How long have I been here?"

"Since yesterday afternoon. I hope you slept well."

He said that already, she thought.

"Thank you," she repeated. "How long have I been here?"

"Since yesterday afternoon. I hope you slept well. I will leave you now so you can enjoy your repast in privacy."

Officiously programmed, she thought, but sufficiently self-determined to know when to leave. He reminded her not so much of a Stepford automaton as of a highly trained soldier, drilled until all personality was extinguished. She was thinking clearly. That surprised her. She had been thinking fitfully about Hegel and Derrida when she first re-entered consciousness. She had never been a Derrida *aficionado*, but his later inquiries into language and the experience of self intrigued her. And now, in a possible world where computers and consciousness merged through surgical intervention, he was perhaps more relevant than ever.

She touched the gauze wrapping around her head and felt gingerly for a wound, but the pain radiated from the pressure wherever she pressed. She ate her lunch: scrambled eggs, surprisingly firm, with asparagus spears perfectly undercooked, a Swedish coleslaw with just enough sweetness to offset the sour, and a Honey Crisp apple for dessert with a wedge of Ontario cheddar. She saved the wine until after she had finished eating, then rinsed with water, and savoured the fresh grapey flavours. It must have been *nouveau*, vinted the previous fall.

As soon as she was finished, the nurse came in and cleared her dishes. She was not only being monitored for sound, she was being watched.

She reclined comfortably against the pillows and committed herself to Jacques Derrida and an exploration of her autonomous self. The first word that came to mind was *aporia*, an irresolvable contradiction. Was she a primary example: a logical anomaly, simultaneously a spontaneous mind and the flesh-and-blood face of a mindless machine? The thought struck her as grotesquely amusing: all premises are false including his one.

She assumed Robert had removed the poorly functioning computer from her brain, but she was aware of the possibility he had replaced it with another that was clever enough to keep itself hidden. Was she the antithesis of Aristotle's thought thinking of itself, his syntactical representation of God? Was she a cyborg whose identity was irrelevant to its primary purpose? And why? To take over the world? To consume Vivuscorps products? To perpetuate the revisions they had made to the species?

During the next few weeks Anna paced within the confines of her room and occasionally stared out the window where she followed the progress of shadows as the sun moved across the sky each day, scorching the snow into porous white islets that dwindled and melted into blanched stretches of grass. Apart from diminutive movements in the sugar bush, which several times included a colourful line of small children with their guardians traipsing across the field in the direction of the boiling shack from the furthermost corner of the Vivuscorps complex, the only person she saw was her nurse, whose name was Kevin, and Kevin seemed always on call. She assumed he had a room next to hers where he conducted his own private affairs.

Then one day it was April.

Robert ushered in Rose and Sebastian to visit. He muttered a few cordialities and left the three of them on their own.

"So they didn't murder you," observed Rose with a grin. "I'm glad."

"Me too," said Anna. "Have you guys been here all this time?"

"We have," said Sebastian. "They're sending me home tomorrow. They've fixed up my fingers surprisingly well. Rose is staying."

"I'm going to look after you," said Rose.

"And when you're ready to leave, you're both coming to live with me at The Cloisters for a while," Sebastian explained. "I think it's best if we keep together."

"What do *they* think?" Anna asked, rolling her eyes.

"Robert told us it's okay."

"Did he." It was an observation, not a question. "Was it his idea?"

"No, it was mine," said Sebastian. "I think it was."

"Your hair's really short," said Rose. "I could trim it up a bit if *they* would lend me some scissors. They won't give us scissors over in our wing."

"Do they let you wander about or keep you in one area?"

"We can go anywhere we want," said Sebastian, then added, "if we want to."

"But we don't," said Rose. "We've got no way to get away from here and nowhere to go. Except for Sebastian's house, but that's far away somewhere else."

"How far?" Anna asked.

"Quite far," said Sebastian. "It's all quite disorienting, isn't it? Happy April Fool's Day, by the way — the festival of *Hilaria* according to the Romans and through a clerical error a day of merriment and foolery chronicled by Chaucer."

"In *The Nun's Priest's Tale*," Anna noted with comforting pedantry.

"Happy Easter," said Rose.

"The cruellest month," Anna observed.

"Breeding lilacs—" Sebastian chimed in.

"From the winter of our discontent," said Anna, keeping faith with her current fear of copyright violation by merging bits from *The Waste Land* and *Richard III*.

"But Shakespeare's trope celebrates the sun, while Eliot mopes about dull roots that winter kept warm," Sebastian offered.

"It's so good to see you," said Anna.

"You too, Annie, I missed you. I missed the chatter."

"I missed you too," exclaimed Rose. "More than words can say."

"Rose, Rose, Rose." Anna felt a transformative wave of affection that swept away all doubts about herself, her identity affirmed by the uncomplicated devotion of her friend. "Rose, are you all right?" she asked. "Did they hurt you?"

"That was a long time ago. They've been good to me since. Your husband apologized. He said it was all a mistake. He's a very sincere man."

"So was Cassius," said Sebastian. "Robert has that lean and hungry look. He thinks too much. Such men are dangerous."

"Idealists turn into zealots," said Anna. "Poor Robert, he didn't set out to be monstrous—" She stopped herself short and turned back to Rose. "What else did Robert tell you?"

"He told us about your baby. I'm sorry, Annie."

"Did he say I lost her?"

"He told us you were never completely pregnant."

"But I was. Maybe not then, but I was."

"Did you know Sebastian taught me to read?"

"He did! Just like that? So much for dyslexia."

"We just decided it didn't exist and it doesn't."

"Sebastian?"

"It seems her mind was geared up, fully wired, just waiting for someone to throw the switch. She's very good."

"I can read to myself, Anna, not only out loud. It's like there's a machine in my head."

"I've told her the machine is the writing itself, not the mind," said Sebastian. He moved around Anna's bed, with his back to the light streaming in from outside.

"That's what writing does," said Anna, responding warmly to the intellectual replenishment of Sebastian's company. "It takes mental events and makes them repeatable. It is a machine, of sorts."

"But words written down are alive. You said they talk to each other," said Rose, her confidence reinforced by a month of literacy.

Anna remembered Sebastian calling her attention to the conversational murmurings among the books in his attic refuge and how she had been overwhelmed by the rush of voices that coursed through the labyrinthine passageways of his library. Attending to the murmuration of books would quiet the dogs and free the mind so it could listen, really listen.

Sebastian's response to Rose's observation was simultaneously prolix and trenchant. "Print evokes numerous singularities of sensibility, each a spontaneous mental event. Words written down are signs standing in for the illimitable activities of the organic mind. Temporal constraints might impose limits to meaning in speech but there can be no end to the interpretation of texts, for each modifies every other beyond the limits of time. Print conveys the wonders of uncertainty."

"I don't know about that," said Rose, her ensuing quietude an indication she thought better than to offer an opinion.

Anna, however, invoked Rose as a pretext for responding to the terror she felt lurking beneath the abstruse erudition of Sebastian's rhetoric. He was afraid, and hiding behind words.

"Rose said that we only experience in the present," Anna said. "But every experience has a context and vocabulary, so in our consciousness of each experience are traces of past iterations and future projections, otherwise how would we know it was an experienced event?"

"I don't know about that, either," said Rose.

Anna leaned over to the edge of her bed and whispered secrets in Rose's ear, then she leaned the other way and whispered in Sebastian's. Secrets shared were a conspiracy, by definition. In the context of their hospice, among three such unlikely confederates, such gentle manoeuvres seemed empowering.

Anna sat back and explained her secret message in a conversational tone which ran counter to the sinister words, twisting their meaning.

"It would be an astonishing thing to merge the spontaneous singularity of the mind with a computer unrestricted by self-reflection." She paused, as if casually collecting her thoughts. "If the brain and the machine could merge in perfect harmony, without displacing or distorting each other, that would be truly *awesome*, as Edmund Burke might have described it." She paused to let the sinister gravity of her reference sink in, then added as an afterthought, "Especially if the mind in its own self-awareness were to display no awareness of the machine."

She touched her hand to the scar-lines on her skull, where the tiny wound beneath the hair was almost healed over.

"*Ego sum camera*," said Sebastian. "One might become no more than a lens."

"I don't know about that," said Rose. "But I'm glad my dyslexia's gone."

# Chapter Eight
## *Te Provoco Ego*

Left on her own that evening, Anna had trouble coming to terms with herself. Kevin had delivered her dinner and cleaned up. She had prepared for bed and pulled the curtains back sufficiently to peer at the stars. Now she was lying under a snug duvet, observing random points of light in the moonless sky, some from the beginnings of time, some from orbital satellites, and she contemplated *despair*. The word stuck in her mind. It threatened to define her. She tried to fathom what Søren Kierkegaard meant by the intransigent elusive despair that he called demonic, when the person despairing has an insufficient conception of herself. It seemed the conflicted Danish mystic found neither alienation from God nor from the world were so heavy to bear as the despair over awareness of all that is Other. Emmanuel Lévinas might have called it *alterity*. Kierkegaard described it as the poet's despair. He declared anxiety in essence a very good thing. Dread, *angst*, fear of death, might lead to self-knowledge and freedom. Heidegger intruded. Anna's thoughts leapt to the knowledge of personal death as a requisite for living an authentic life. Her mind circled like a dappled-dark-drawn falcon, espying fatal flaws in the conscious mind. These, as Leonard Cohen declared, were how the light gets in. She drifted off, humming Cohen's "true love leaves no traces", although she thought it an untenable sentiment, and the full day rounded into a sleep.

    Kevin must have come in during the night because in the morning her curtains were drawn closed and she did not awaken from the sun but only roused when he brought in her breakfast tray which, after briefly freshening up, she took at a table beside the window as he ushered Sebastian and Rose into the room. Rose perched on the edge of her bed. Sebastian pulled up a chair facing her. He looked tired, the lines on his handsome face had changed from expressive to structural, as if he had always been tired. Kevin brought two more cups and filled them with coffee for the visitors. It was all very genteel.

    "I'll be leaving soon," said Sebastian. "Robert has arranged for a car to drive me into the city. We're somewhere around Aurora or Stouffville, I imagine. He wants to observe you for a bit. He says you need to recover. You've had a prolonged episodic breakdown. Rose will keep you company and I'll see you both in a week or two."

"I've had a hole drilled in my head," Anna declared, bewildered by his perfunctory farewell. Did he not understand her allusion last night to the sinister ambivalence of Burke's sublime or to the pernicious impact of machines embedded inside a person's skull?

"Apparently to remove a cyst of some sort," he said.

She gazed into his eyes, searching for comprehension. Finding only uncertainty, she declared in a casual tone, intended to raise no concern in the listening walls but to make her situation unequivocally clear: "A foreign intrusion, Sebastian. A twist of DNA that wasn't performing its designated task up to snuff."

"Well, there's nothing there now, so get better, come home, we'll settle in, we'll have a fine time, a fine time together."

"You sound like a Hemingway character — 'we'll have a fine time' — I'm sure we will."

"Is it better if I say, *ego te provoco fortis in arduis fortis et liber*? That's my version of Hemingway's 'grace under pressure'."

"*I challenge you, be strong in adversity, be free*," said Rose while staring distractedly out the window at smoke curling through branches in the bush from the sugaring-off shack. "They must have been using propane, now they're burning wood for the flavour."

"Rose," Anna exclaimed, her alarm at her friend's sudden erudition overriding the need to process Sebastian's pedantry. "Rose," she repeated. "How did you do that?"

"Translate? I must have read it wherever Sebastian did. He's my teacher."

"Did you read it, Sebastian? It sounded like spontaneous Latin to me."

"That seems a contradiction in terms," said Sebastian. "We mostly use Latin because it's immutably dead. But yes, the coinage is mine, imperfect as it is. *Ego te provoco*."

"I guess I just translated myself, one word for another," said Rose, sensing she had aroused some inexplicable controversy.

"From Latin?"

"Translation is imprecise, you know. Words cannot carry their cultural and historical context from language to language. The undecidability of an idiom defies paraphrase. 'Love nothing' could refer to triumph in tennis or the essence of Buddhism or a Franciscan motto or a nihilist rebuke. Translation is a precarious business."

"Rose?"

"That's what Azziz told me. He worked as a translator."

"But those are his words, not yours," said Anna.

"I didn't steal them. I'm not even sure what they mean."

"You've remembered *verbatim* what he told you. You translate a language you don't even know. What's happened, Rose?"

"I learned to read, that's about it. I see words now, they're inside my head. Saint Augustine would approve. Don't be angry, Annie. I read stuff and hear stuff. I can remember perfectly but I don't always understand. My head fills up with signs and symbols and phonemes and tropes — I don't even know what I said just then. Can you help me? Sebastian is going. I'm crowded with thoughts but I need you to teach me to think."

"Azziz must have delivered his talk about translation before we got here."

"The past is all in the present — you know what I mean? It doesn't make sense, it's just there."

Rose inexplicably began to weep. Anna and Sebastian moved closer to her, each touching her as if she were some exquisitely breakable *objet d'art*.

"Dear Rose," said Sebastian. "You are like a deaf girl who can suddenly hear, and you're surrounded by Beethoven and Bach and the Beatles, all at the same time."

"And Mozart and door chimes," said Rose.

Anna and Sebastian looked from one to the other, knowing it was more than sudden exposure to the infinite stimuli of words, words hovering beyond temporality on the printed page, or words echoing from earlier conversations, that made Rose such a figure of pathos and envy. It was the perfectness of her memory that struck Anna as dangerously improbable, combined with the absence of a critical faculty to sort out the snarling circumlocutions, evasions, obscurities of undisciplined unfettered unlimited language. What frightened her was the certainty that this strange turn was Robert's doing. Rose was an experiment in progress.

Anna explained to herself as much as her friend: "Rose, reading print turns words into present-tense memories. What you read has already happened but it's happening now. It's literally *déjà vu*."

"So you're seeing something all over again for the very first time."

"Exactly."

"On a computer screen, in your glasses, the print comes and goes," said Rose. "In a book, on paper or papyrus, it stays, waiting to be read."

"Digital print has recoverability." Anna's mind tumbled ahead. "But it has no substance." She needed to clarify for herself what she half understood, but she doubted Rose could follow, for all her new-found capacity to download data and retrieve it unsorted at will. Anna continued, knowing it was foolish to place limits on Rose's intelligence, or limit herself to what Rose might comprehend. "Reading light waves directly is a different mental process than when you read inscriptions on paper, where time is suspended." She paused. "Configurations of hovering light are instantaneous moments in the perpetual present, Rose. Hard-copy print precedes reading and outlives it. I'm betting your experience with words on computers is ephemeral, fleeting, like hearing them whispered or whimpering."

"Very *ephemeral*," said Rose, toying with the word like a lozenge cradled against the roof of her mouth.

"You'll get the hang of it, Rose," said Sebastian. "The thing about words is that whether imprinted on a solid surface, displayed as a molecular arrangement of liquid crystals, or inscribed in the mind from sounds in one's ears, even the unruliest words are defined by their context."

"Derrida would say words circle around and define themselves," Anna proposed.

Sebastian ignored her and continued his colloquy.

"Rose, if I say a single word, *grave*, you don't know if I mean a hole in the ground or a serious situation, do you?"

"If there's a coffin in the hole, then it's serious."

"Ah, yes, well, if I say, *Henry's grave*, then you know I'm talking about death, right?"

"Not if Henry's being serious about something else."

"No, Rose, oh my," said Sebastian. "You're using the 's' on Henry to denote a verb, not the possessive."

"You didn't say which I was supposed to do."

"Well okay then, if I should say, *The grave of Henry is empty*—"

"Compared to the seriousness of Eleanor? Then he's faking graveness."

"Eleanor who?"

"Sebastian, you started this. Henry who? The one in the coffin pretending he's dead or the one pretending he's serious. You're very mixed up."

"And you, dear Rose, are impossible."

"Not as impossible as Henry and Eleanor."

Sebastian offered her a twitching smile that hovered between scornful affection for her simplicity and quizzical regard for her verbal refinement. He leaned over and kissed her on the top of her head in what he did not intend as a patronizing gesture. Then he kissed Anna on both cheeks, holding her head awkwardly between his hands, careful to avoid pressing the wound hidden beneath her shingled black hair that was growing out dark brown, a shade lighter and with subtleties the dye had obscured.

"I have to go now," he said. "I'll see you in a week or so."

"You take care," said Anna. "You look worn out."

"A few good nights in my own little aerie and I'll be fine. The constant surveillance wears me down — the walls watch everything here and inform us what they want us to do. It's hard to know whether we've become apparatchiks in a soviet organism, functionaries inside a created god's head, or strangers inside our own."

"Maybe it's all the same," said Anna and shuddered. The walls in her own cell listened, they observed, they measured and recorded every overt response, but they did not talk. Kevin responded but seldom spoke. He seemed to know so much about her, there seemed nothing to say. And yet he was not intuitive. He seemed robotic in his kindness.

"Sebastian, I will miss you so much," she said.

"Come see me soon, both of you."

He backed up as far as the door, then turned as Kevin, who must have been immediately outside, held it open, and he strode out into the hall.

"Bye, Sebastian," Rose called after him. "Thank you for teaching me."

Anna envisioned him already back in his marvellous home, wandering among endless corridors of books and mirrors and doors. His Sistine Chapel — a rich eccentric's fun-house, an inspired escape from reality. It seemed on reflection, when she was no longer caught up in its thrall, less visionary than an elaborate evasion. As lonely as she was, she coped by disappearing into intellectual peregrinations inside her own head. He turned his head inside out, projecting cerebral mysteries into tangible things. She imagined him prowling in his attic sanctuary, not quite furtive but not comfortable, either. She wanted to hold him, to comfort him, but listening to his footsteps fade, she knew she never would.

Anna picked out clothes from her dresser. Sebastian had been sporting preppy grey flannels with a red blazer that made him look curiously like a hand-tinted illustration by Tenniel for one of the *Alice* books. Rose was wearing the standard red tunic, designed to infantilize the wearer. Anna had a greater range to choose from but selected a red cotton dress in solidarity with Rose, although it was cut just above her knees and not to mid-thigh. Their own clothes had disappeared the first night they were there. The lack of coats or boots had been intended, no doubt, to indicate escape was not a reasonable option.

Anna moved into the bathroom to change. She had made the assumption that, in that room at least, she was granted the benefits of privacy — either because there was no hidden camera or because Kevin exercised discretion and chose not to watch.

"Let's walk," she said when she emerged in her red cotton dress.

They stepped into the corridor tentatively, but Kevin was nowhere in sight. Anna's excitement that her initial foray beyond the confines of her room would turn into a clandestine venture faded in his absence. She clutched Rose's arm, giddy with apprehension, as they made their way through a maze of corridors, walking briskly as if malevolent guardians might be in pursuit. They were thoroughly disoriented when they arrived at exterior French doors that opened onto a walled park where there were children at play, with a scattering of elderly people in wheelchairs arranged at unsociable intervals here and there amidst the shrubbery. The children, none older than four, perhaps five, were bundled against the spring chill and the old people were wrapped snuggly in tartan-fringed blankets. A number of caregivers in duffel coats moved casually among them, responding to the needs of the invalids but with a clear bias for attending the toddlers.

Anna and Rose watched through the glass, mesmerized by the mindless innocence of the young and the very old. Yeats' poem, 'Among School Children', came to mind as Anna observed — not measured lines or well-shaped images, nor as a sequence of revelation and epiphany, but in its entirety, the end and the beginning simultaneous in her mind. At sixty, Yeats had declared himself a paltry thing as he reflected on the inevitability of decrepitude, when even the best of ideas, are no match for death. The greatest passions cannot stand up against time. Platonic dichotomies, Aristotelian absolutes, Pythagorean ratios, his own stifled love, come to naught. But the poet's despair gives way to acceptance in the presence of school children who will one day know for themselves that all are parts of the whole — joy is inseparable from suffering, achievement from loss. Life and its termination are personal. Survival is in the dance itself, in what has been felt and done.

Anna gazed through an aura of death and of innocence, as if she were the object of the great poet's thoughts. She slowly realized she was watching something in particular, an anomaly in the randomness among the clusters of children. Although membership in the several play groups changed from time to time, one child in particular stood out. As she wandered, others would join her or fall away. She was the moving centre of continuously reformulating social structures, yet she seemed to be doing nothing special. It was a kind of enchantment that Anna might have expected to observe among swirling schools of fish or frantic birds in flight, but not among children, learning as they were to be neat in everything. Distorted lines of Yeats' poem settled briefly into her brain. What young mother would not look upon her child and see compensation for the pangs of birth or the uncertainty of setting forth.

> O body swayed to music, O brightening glance,
> How can we know the dancer from the dance?

"How old do you think that girl is?" she asked Rose. "The one without the glasses."

"The youngest ones aren't wearing them," said Rose. "I see who you mean. She's no more than four. What is it about her that makes her so different? She's dressed the same, she looks as pretty, she doesn't do anything special. Still, your eyes follow her, don't they? She moves like she knows exactly what she's doing and she's the only one who does."

"Do you know what I'm thinking, Rose?"

"Annie, she's not. Let's go." Rose tried to haul her friend away from the door. Anna resisted. She wanted to witness her past and future in the girl's face, to see a trace of Robert in how she moved. The girl glanced over a couple of times. Anna responded to her gaze by shrinking into herself. She felt icily calm and simultaneously on the verge of hysteria. There could not possibly be a connection. She had had a miscarriage. She did not have a child. This girl was a Vivuscorps ward. Anna felt waves of anger and bitterness surge through as she turned away and held tight to Rose's arm while they made their way down the corridor into a maze of other corridors and it seemed by random chance, they found their way back to Anna's room.

She stopped at the door and said to Rose, "I'm going to rest for a while. You'd better go and see if you can hustle up some lunch. Kevin will turn up as soon as you leave; he'll get something for me. She had beautiful dark hair like mine, Rose, and deep blue eyes like Robert."

"She didn't smile, Annie. I've never seen a kid that age who never smiles, not unless there's something terribly wrong."

Anna entered her room and drew the door closed gently behind her. She felt utterly bereft. The haunting loneliness she had endured from the absence of her child in the years and moments of her emptied life was intensified, not assuaged, by the prospect that the little girl was her daughter. But the possibility that she was not was unbearable. Anna cried and then she busied herself through the rest of the day, avoiding thoughts stirred by her troubled emotions. Late in the afternoon Rose came over for Scrabble. They didn't talk about their morning walk or about the child.

Rose wanted to discuss books, but Anna was unresponsive. Rose said she'd been reading Hemingway.

"He makes a few words mean a lot," she offered, trying to catch Anna's interest.

"Sometimes you can say more by saying less," said Anna and pointedly lapsed into silence.

Gradually, the meaninglessness of geometrically arranged words and letters reduced to numerical values drew them together. They tried to form sentences from the words on the Scrabble board which invariably, without articles and punctuation, sounded like inept translations from Russian.

Their foolishness made them laugh. They adjourned, had supper separately, and both went to bed early.

The next morning, Robert appeared after Kevin had cleared Anna's breakfast tray. He proceeded to admonish her for wandering about.

"We were just exploring. I need to get exercise."

"I'll see that Kevin takes you to the gym."

"I want Rose to go with me."

"I'll see that she's there. We would prefer she not come here any more."

Anna felt a familiar surge of panic.

"Robert, what did you do to her?" she asked. "She's reading now and remembering things. She speaks Latin, for God's sake."

"She thought she was being tortured. We let her think what she wanted."

"Did you!"

"We don't torture people, Anna. We asked her questions."

"Questions?"

"Somewhat vigorously, perhaps. After she blacked out, we inserted a molecular device to counter the dyslexic effect. It was a simple arthroscopic procedure, minimally invasive, but we felt it would be more effective if she didn't know what we'd done, so we could monitor her subjective responses objectively. I admit, bringing her back to consciousness with a bucket of water was crude. It was meant to distract her, to give her time until she got used to the changes in perception."

"And in processing. You boosted her access to memory."

"To enhance her mental capacity — not to make her think better. It took me a while to realize how bright she is. We added RAM so she can better recall and configure what she takes in."

"Or what is already in there."

"She's doing well. Don't worry about Rose."

"She's part of my recovery," said Anna. "I need her."

"Of course. She needs you, as well. You may meet at the gym. You can spend time in her dormitory if you'd like."

"I want her to come here."

"It would be better if she stays out of the medical wing."

"Why?"

Robert seemed nonplussed at being challenged so directly. She looked at this attractive young man sitting opposite her and realized how strange it was that she had reached a point where she had no residual feelings for him, not of bitterness for his ghoulish deception, not of hatred for how he had violated her, not of resentment for what he had taken away, and certainly not of affection. Kierkegaard's demonic despair that had caught hold in the roots of her soul had been transformed, since the discovery of the girl, into an elusive poetics of dread and renewal. She now had a focus and the will to endure.

Robert was no more than a lethal abstraction in the Vivuscorps monolith and a functionary of hardly more consequence than Kevin, although he was certainly more dangerous. She stared into his blue eyes. She saw herself in reflection. She was an object of interest. In one immutable instant, Anna's soul took flight — not as religious conversion or spiritual insight, but in the explosive discovery of seeing herself reduced to merely an object of interest in the eyes of a man who meant nothing to her at all.

In the room, nothing changed.

"Robert," she spoke after a long pause.

"Yes?"

"Have you ever read Søren Kierkegaard? You should."

"Probably not. I have no idea who he or she is. I don't know why I should care."

"Neither do I."

There was another long silence, which Robert eventually broke by wishing her a 'good morning' before he scuttled away. Those are pearls that were his eyes — and he, full fathom five, was lost in the depths of the sea and no magic could ever restore him. She knew that. As he disappeared, she ascended to the surface and breathed air, and began her long fight for the shore.

She had said nothing about the little girl. She thought the girl's eyes had flared brilliant blue in a display of acknowledgement when she looked in Anna's direction, but that could have been a trick of the sun. The girl might only have been seeing her own reflection in the glass, not looking through it. Anna would not have been able to bear giving Robert the power to declare their daughter existed while being able to prevent them from getting together. Nor could she cede him the power of pronouncing that her desperate intuitive speculation was wrong.

She felt unaccountably tired. Daylight streamed through the open curtains. Her overhead light banished all but the most intransigent shadows from the room. She dreamed she was enfolded in the arms of William Blake, whose visionary body became a muscular vegetative etching of Jacob wrestling with the angel of his mysterious and obdurate Lord — Jacob, whose name meant 'the believer who struggles with God'. She woke in a sweat, remembering only that Blake extolled levels of being, seven in all — he was not modest in his capacity to perceive — and he yearned for antinomies to be resolved, contraries to unite, opposites to reconcile, and harmony to rule over discord on each level in turn. She slept again and dreamed she and Blake, he of the beautiful bones and voluptuous body, were lovers, and he became Gabriel, who seduced her with the words of his ambitious and passionate Lord, and they had a child who had no physical presence but was a spectre of their desire, and when she woke up she felt a desperate longing, like an ache in her soul, except awake she did not believe in souls, nor visionary worlds, nor a God who would stubbornly resist unconditional love or selfishly turn it to his unaccountable advantage.

After lunch, Kevin took her to the gym. She felt very light-headed, almost faint, as if she had not awakened from her earlier dreams. On the way, she studiously observed the protocols and aesthetics that governed the entire Vivuscorps complex. She formulated a model in her mind that conformed to the laws of physics, trigonometry, and architecture, as she filled in spaces, adjusted for structural imperatives, and posited usage depending on form and location. They saw people along the way, mostly through glass doors, socializing, receiving instruction, consuming their day. Staff and guests alike were dressed in red, the colour of blood when it flows from veins and is reoxygenated in the open air with a hint of purple or blue before it dries muddy brown. By the time they arrived at the gym she had assembled a detailed mental impression of what she was up against. It was not Robert, nor Kevin and his cohort; it was not the building itself. It was the vast organism surrounding her that in so many ways was a world itself, a world in which the inhabitants functioned like cells in the bloodstream, nurturing other cells that kept them alive, oblivious to their place in the flow.

Rose was already there. They changed into red rompers with tiny skirts stitched at the waist to create the banal illusion of female frivolity.

Anna had been through a traumatic and exhausting morning. Her mind whirled with visionary precision, darting between the limits of transparency where everything was clear until it was not and the limits of opacity where nothing made sense. She was delirious and exhausted. She wanted urgently to tell Rose about loneliness, to explain how seeing the little girl had generated, from dread, illumination, and from fear, hope, and from despair, renewal. She grasped Rose's hands. She wanted to extol the brilliance of Blake, to have Rose understand. She wanted to discuss the obscurities of Jacques Derrida who scrambled through the gaps and fissures in her mind as he celebrated mad brilliant Blake as her mentor. Language flooded her brain. It was viscous, glowing, volcanic. As Nietzsche had argued, words no more than things can be certain until the molten rock hardens to stone.

In a phantasmagoria of fragmented logic and elliptical allusions, with Blake the madman and Derrida the trickster as guides, Anna slipped into senseless oblivion, collapsing in Rose's arms. Rose lowered her onto a gym mat. The walls must have observed what had happened but they were not interactive. No one came to their aid. Perhaps passing out was deemed inconsequential or was not unexpected.

After a while, Anna drifted back into consciousness but the visionary fervour had subsided. It was displaced by steely resolve and a solid grasp of necessity.

"Annie, you're crying," said Rose, who was cradling her friend across folded knees. "Honey, it's the strain, you've been through too much. Maybe you've got PMS. Maybe your mind's working too hard."

"Yes," Anna whispered. "I think so."

"We have to get you out of here, Annie. It's urgent." Rose mouthed the words inaudibly but Anna understood. "I'm coming, too," said Rose.

"Of course."

"I gotta keep an eye on you, Sweetheart."

"Thank you, Rose."

"If your mind's gonna fight with yourself, you need me as a referee."

Anna agreed without speaking. The more I find myself coming together and soaring among worlds that only Blake could have dreamt possible, the more I need Rose to keep me from flying apart. Visionary experience without a grounded perspective is fantasy. It's ineffable, impractical, unreal.

"Annie," said Rose, "can you get up? Maybe we should change. You don't need a workout, you need some rest. There are things I have to tell you about. They're important but we'll have to talk later. I'm not sure you'd understand right now. I'm not supposed to go back into the hospital wing but I'll help you get to your room."

"Give me a minute," said Anna. "What is it? Tell me."

"We'll talk later, when we can be private." The last part, she whispered. Then aloud she said, "I've been reading some more. It's not the same without Sebastian around."

"No, it isn't."

Preposterously, they lounged on the mat in their rompers and skirts and gossiped. They talked a little about Hemingway. Rose was intrigued that she liked what she'd read, despite her mistrust of the values expressed. Anna didn't say very much. The ambivalence of her own responses to Hemingway raised questions of moral and cultural relativism that she didn't have the energy to pursue. After a while, they went into the locker room to change, and when they walked back to the door leading out to the hallway Kevin was waiting. Without a word, he took Anna's arm and indicated by body language that Rose should go on her own to the dorm.

Later that night, while Anna was lying in bed, she ruminated over something that Rose had observed about her mind in a fight with itself, and about being so tired she couldn't think straight. This course of reflection made her increasingly agitated. Despite fainting, she had felt more certain of herself earlier in the day. In the darkness she perseverated uneasily about conversations with Robert. He had admitted to having inserted a molecular computer into her brain four years ago to suppress her depression, and had openly confessed that the surgical procedure to remove it was going to, and then had, occurred. Were her anxiety, her exhaustion, her random sense of dissociation, the manifestations of her violated brain in search of itself? Could Robert have placed another computer in her skull which was being taken as a pernicious intrusion by the host tissues? She felt pinned by unanswered questions like a bug to a board. Not quite. She feared she was fixed on the edge of a vortex and might never be drawn into the regenerative swirl.

"I'd say you don't seem yourself and neither do I."

It took a moment before Anna realized the voice was her own, familiar but speaking from a great distance away.

"I can no longer pretend to be in command," said the voice. "You were thrust into my sphere, cast adrift in a storm-battered sea, and I no longer wish to be the tiller, the compass, the wind, as we sail. I relinquish control."

"I don't think you ever had it."

"Well, I don't any more."

Anna struggled to sort through the metaphor.

"What about Robert?" said her other self, coming closer, whispering. "He seemed confused about the streetcar incident."

"He was trying to confuse me on purpose."

"You loved him passionately, unequivocally, when he was dead. Did you love him that much before he died — or does your hatred derive from losing the idealized ghost he'd become?"

"Don't be a bitch."

"Say what you will, I think you loved him best when he was gone. Now you have to seek surcease from sorrow… by insisting he is the embodiment of evil come to destroy us all."

"You're being redundant."

"To make the point."

"Our daughter, he took her away. He let me think she was dead, that she never existed, that she doesn't exist now."

"Maybe he rescued her from an emotionally screwed-up mother."

"Shut up. I mean it, shut up, shut up."

"Look, there was a time when you loved him for his commitment to his work.

"You said he was an idealist, wanting desperately to do good in the world."

"The tragedy is, he still thinks he's doing good, working for Vivuscorps to reroute evolution. Theorists record things, activists like Robert change things. But let's not kid ourselves. Robert is irredeemably wicked. He has gone over to the dark side with a vengeance. Sebastian once speculated, when I told him Robert had abandoned his project, perhaps he was too successful and the possible outcome was more than he could deal with. In fact, success drove him in the opposite direction, to commit everything to his cause, even his wife, even his child. From being Dr Frankenstein, he became Frankenstein's monster."

"He proposes to make humans more than we are and that's sure to be folly."

"He's guided by conviction, not conscience. It breaks my heart."

"He breaks your heart and yet you despise him."

"I fear him. It's gone past revulsion, the more I understand what he's trying to do."

"Explain."

"I wish I could but I can't. I don't have the words. Not yet. We'll see."

A commotion outside the door startled her. She rose, braced on her elbows, and listened intently. There was a scuffle and then scuttling sounds like small animals playing in the walls and then the door opened and Kevin stepped into the room. He was illuminated by the light from the hall that cast a long silhouette as Rose pushed him forward and stepped out from behind, with one hand urging the much larger man ahead while the other pressed an index finger to her lips, not calling for quiet but indicating control. Anna reached over and turned on the bedside lamp. Kevin stood impassively at the edge of its halo with his hands behind his back. A thin strand of white fibre passed around his neck and when he turned slightly Anna saw it was attached to loops of the same material bound tightly around his thumbs.

"Dental floss," Rose whispered. "It's amazing." She nudged a foot against the back of the big man's knees and he buckled in slow motion onto the floor. She clambered over and around him, securing his ankles, bending his legs, and bringing a strand of floss up to connect with the piece coming down from the back of his neck, meeting at his manacled thumbs.

"That should do it," she said. "Get dressed."

Anna was sitting upright on her bed with the covers clutched close. What she had witnessed seemed hardly credible, but Rose, while impetuous, wasn't reckless — she might undertake the improbable but not the impossible. The twinge of sympathy Anna felt for her guardian gave way to admiration for the measured violence of her friend's calm and methodical manoeuvres. By the time Anna had dressed and, in spite of Rose's half-hearted objections, applied a few dabs of eyeshadow, brushed on a modicum of blush, and added a flourish of lip gloss, all from the previously unopened makeup kit on her dresser, she was strangely equanimous, prepared now, looking her best, to reclaim her daughter or embrace the cruellest consequences for their rebellion, even her own death, whichever the case.

"Shouldn't we tape up his mouth?" Anna said as they approached the door into the hall.

"Don't worry," Rose assured her.

"I don't understand. How do you know what you're doing?" Anna spoke in a whisper, to which Rose quietly responded:

"I've spent my life in human warehouses, Annie, and on the streets, in hostels or camps. I know how to handle the big guys. Sebastian told me the staff here are conditioned to avoid violence and have no fear. They're easy to approach, especially in the dead of night, and there's only one for each section. I took them out one by one as I moved along."

"How, Rose? You're not trained."

"The Vulcan crunch. I learned it from Mr Spock. Thumbs at the base of the skull, sharp pressure inwards and up. They black out but just for a minute. That's all you need. We used to practice at camp. A girl died — you've got to be careful. And then the dental floss, do you know there are two hundred metres on each little roll and Vivuscorps buys only the best. It's strong enough for a single strand around the neck to keep the buggers as still as mice until morning. They'll get found alive, as long as they don't *garrote* themselves by trying to escape, but we'll be long gone, so let's go."

"How on Earth do you know about garrotting?" Anna whispered.

"In a dictionary, actually. You know, we don't have to be quiet. Voices in the dark aren't illegal, and anyway only Kevin can hear us. The walls have sensors but they're not alarms. They just let the caretakers in each section know what we're thinking if we're thinking out loud. I guess they record everything, but nobody will check before morning."

"I'd rather whisper."

"You're right. Whispering seems more appropriate for a clandestine op."

"Is that what this is? What's the wire for?" Anna touched a length of stainless steel coiled around Rose's left wrist. She was nervous in a context where dental floss had been turned into a lethal instrument. Rose fingered the coil before responding:

"Just something I picked up in the infirmary. It's suture wire for sewing up bodies."

Or strangling them, Anna observed to herself. She turned and followed Rose into the corridor which was harshly illuminated by overhead safety-lights.

"We don't want Kevin to know what we're up to," Anna said.

"Too late, Annie, he already does. Do you want me to kill him?"

"No!"

"It's okay, I wouldn't anyway. The only one we might want to murder is Robert. I'd let you do that."

"I'm very confused about Robert," said Anna.

"Well, he's planning on 'putting you down' in the morning," said Rose. "That's why it's better if we leave tonight. That's what I wanted to tell you."

"Rose?"

"I've been snooping. Sebastian called me his *indefatigable Torquemada*. I had to look that up; it means relentless. Tomás de Torquemada was the Grand Inquisitor of Spain, infinitely curious but fanatically cruel. I don't think Sebastian meant I was cruel, just exceptionally nosy. He's Torquemada, actually — we call other people names we fear most in ourselves. So, yesterday after breakfast I faked a godawful headache and then a blackout to see where they'd take me and it wasn't to the infirmary, it was to the hospital. They had me on an operating table, so I faked waking up. Robert wanted to poke about in my head. I told him it was a woman's problem, my blackout was menstrual, and men get confused by women talking about that kind of thing. His surgical assistant freaked out. Robert sent me back to the dorm. He and his people aren't interested in anything below the belt — no, below the shoulders. But, Annie, while I was on the table and they didn't know I could hear, he talked to a technician about you. This is what I wanted to tell you. He said *yours* hadn't worked. Yours? Too much damage had been done removing the old one. He said the *girl*, I guess that was me, was *dubious*, that was his word, and he said that you were *redundant*. Turns out your brain keeps overriding the device, instead of the device controlling your brain."

"Did he say *keeps* overriding or *kept*?"

"Kept, that's what he said. *Verbatim*. Like, it's all over. Of course, he could have *meant* 'keeps'. Whether he was using the subjunctive or indicative, I couldn't be sure. It's interesting how grammar is used to pinpoint our position in time, but it doesn't always work. So, anyway, they figure I may have been corrupted by reading, but then Robert said fixing my dyslexia was only a test. Their system works best when they start from infancy — because then the two systems are naturally integrated as the organic materials mature. I'm not sure what it all means, Annie, but I'm pretty certain he's going to eliminate you in the morning, and maybe me, too. So that's why I'm here. We're getting out. We're going to Toronto."

"We're going to get my daughter."

"Annie, you don't have a daughter. I mean, if you did, she's not yours. She wouldn't know you from Adam or Eve."

"Maybe not, but she might."

"We don't even know where she is."

"If you can deal with the guards, I'll lead the way," said Anna. "But no killing."

"Okay, they're just doing their jobs, so okay, one at a time as we go."

Anna had constructed an uncannily precise model of the entire institution in her head and by triangulating from where they had seen the children play within the confines of the walled-in garden, and from where they had observed the nursery when they had first arrived, and from the direction she had seen the kids traipse out to the sugar bush, she led Rose to a closed-off wing with cut-outs of a mythical bestiary taped to the door, mostly gryphons and unicorns, and a single giraffe with a knot in its neck. Rose had to render powerless only two guardians along the way.

"Annie, are you sure?" said Rose.

"I'm not leaving without my daughter."

Anna pulled the door open slowly and peered through. She took a step forward and then gasped. A very small girl was standing in the darkness to the side of the doorway, fully dressed with a coat clutched in her hands.

"I'm certainly happy you are here." The little girl spoke in a barely audible whisper. "I waited last night until breakfast and tonight until now."

Anna dropped to her knees and held the girl at arm's length, then drew her close against her breast and permitted herself a muted sob.

"I waited for a very long time," said the girl, as she pulled back just a little, struggling to breathe. "You're my mommy. I knew you would come as soon as you could."

Anna rose to her feet and scooped the girl into her arms. They scuttled along the corridor to an exit and stepped out into the cold night air. Anna and Rose didn't have coats. They were wearing standard-issue red plastic slippers. The girl was wearing red galoshes. She wriggled to be set down and she put on her coat, which she insisted on doing by herself. She insisted on removing her galoshes, revealing her own red slippers and thin white socks. She set the galoshes down on a bank of frozen snow and held her arms out to be picked up again. With her arms around Anna's neck, she squiggled closer and fell asleep before they reached the parking lot.

Rose tested several car doors and selected an opulent SUV which she easily opened with the uncoiled strand of wire from her wrist. "Rich people don't fix broken alarms. They pay for higher insurance," she whispered. "Here, let me hold her. I never learned how to drive."

Anna reluctantly let the girl go. She buckled Rose and the girl securely into place in the back seat. Then she settled into the driver's seat and stared at the dashboard.

Rose smiled, undid her safety belt and clambered into the front passenger seat. "You're not much of a thief," she murmured. She twisted down to reach under the dash. She swore a couple of times, and finally the car's engine turned over with a muscular purr and settled into a low rumbling idle. The owner paid extra for that; the engine was electric and silent. Rose returned to the back seat. Anna adjusted the wheel and the seat and mirrors and set the vehicle rolling quietly down the drive through massive wrought-iron gates that were always open and they drove away.

The little girl stirred. She looked up at Rose, then leaned forward to look at Anna. Her eyes in the reflected light from the dashboard panel were deep violet and her hair glistened black.

"What's your name," said Rose. "My name is Rose."

"Rose is a flower," said the girl. "My name is Anna."

Anna felt a tsunami of passion course through her body, her mind, the depths of her being. She found the girl in the rear-view mirror. "Me, too," she said. She reached back and took the girl's tiny hand in her own. The girl didn't smile. She looked disturbingly serious.

"I expected it would be," said the girl and, curling into Rose's embrace, she let go of Anna's hand and fell back into a deep sleep.

They parked the car near Union Station. It was early morning and the city was beginning to stir. With coins they found in the SUV's ashtray, they bought two fares on the subway up to the Rosedale stop. Anna carried her daughter as they made their way to Errington Lane where Sebastian's Cloisters rose out of the gloom into the breaking dawn like an enchanted leviathan ready to take on the world. With Sebastian so close and her child in her arms, Anna's entire body trembled from relief that was tempered by fear more profound than anything she had ever experienced.

She estimated it would take a while before the arrival of Robert, accompanied by his sinister companions and their murderous cigars. They wouldn't come to Sebastian's first. It was too obvious. The GPS locator in the stolen vehicle would lead them to the downtown core.

The door on the side porch was locked from inside. Rose sat on the swing sofa she had hidden behind so long ago when she was spying on Agnes. Clearly, the next move was not up to her. Anna held her daughter; she paced, wondering if they should knock, knowing that four flights up they would never be heard. There didn't appear to be a bell or buzzer. She led the way around to the verandah at the front and approached the huge door with its small panes of glass showing the lace curtains inside. It was growing light. She wanted to be out of sight, even if they had to camp in the foyer. She tried the door. She had a premonition it would be unlocked. It was unlocked. Had Sebastian been expecting them? Did he know they'd escaped? Setting her daughter down and taking her hand, Anna pushed through the open door and caught sight of the three of them, foundling spectres, in the gilt-framed mirror against the side wall. Instead of clapping for the overhead, she stepped forward and switched on a table lamp. Now, in the soft illumination, she and her companions seemed real.

She tested the mirrored door at the back. It was locked from the other side. If they broke through, they could hide in Sebastian's wondrous fantastical construction. She felt she could probably negotiate its mysteries but then, if she could, so could Robert and his associates, even if they had to smash it apart. She examined the antique doors on the east side of the foyer. She tried one. To her surprise, it opened easily. She scooped up her daughter and stepped into the darkness, feeling for a light switch with her free hand, supporting the girl's weight with the other.

She found an antique brass press-button switch. She pushed it on and the air flared into light. They were in an Edwardian room with older flourishes and a few mid-twentieth century concessions. Other rooms farther along and still dark could be seen in diminished perspective. Dust motes drifted in air currents, stirring faintly. There was no labyrinth. There were no books, no mirrored walls. The entire vast library maze had disappeared into the tremulous gloom of an old house redolent with the scent of powders and pipe tobacco, skin cells and lemon oil, the lingering remains of generations long dead.

# Chapter Nine
## Provoking the Devil

Anna turned out the lights. Enough early morning sunshine was penetrating through clefts in the curtains, they could see their surroundings. She sank into a plush armchair with her little girl curled on her lap and she smiled. She smiled because the girl was real. She smiled because Rose who had settled onto the carpet with her head resting on Anna's knee began dozing. She smiled because Sebastian had achieved the most astonishing simulacrum, a distortion of reality so real it bore no relation to any reality but its own. She did not doubt her memories of the library. She did not doubt it was real. But now it was gone. She grieved for the writers whose works were reduced to illusion. She rejoiced that their absence was a negligible cost for holding the small girl bearing her name cradled against her breast.

An unnerving thought crept through her mind that this also might be an illusion. The girl shifted her weight and Anna adjusted her arms to make her embrace more secure. The girl whispered a single word, "Mommy," not tentatively as an inquiry but as an assertion of fact.

"Yes?" said Anna, gazing down into her daughter's sleepy blue eyes. She pronounced the word, as in Maugham, the writer, not as in mum, to keep quiet. Were she English, she wouldn't have been caught dead pronouncing it that way. As a Canadian, she wouldn't be allowed otherwise.

"How did you know I was your little girl?"

Anna's eyes welled up with adoration — tempered by a fear that she intuitively recognized as the cost of parental affection, a fear multiplied by the imminence of real possible threats.

"I just knew," Anna said. "I looked at you and I knew."

"Thank you."

"How did you know I was your mommy, how did you know I was coming?"

"I calculated it had to be you."

"You calculated?"

Rose settled closer, shifting her weight against Anna's thigh. She was listening. The little girl spoke matter-of-factly.

"I know everyone has a mommy to become born, so I always knew someone was missing. There is a man who says he is my daddy, but I never believed him. His name is Robert. He never held me, not even when I was little. He would *interview* me. Every month he would come to ask me things and I just answered his questions. Sometimes he took me to places with bright lights to do scientific tests. I watched him when he watched the other children. He was interested in all of us about the same. I'm not anyone special. He doesn't really like children very much."

The little girl twisted around so she could see Anna's face in the pale light. Sure of her audience, she went on: "When I saw you looking through the door, your eyes kept searching and landing on me wherever I was, whenever I moved. I knew who you were *not*, since I know everyone at the Centre. You were observing but not like a scientist. You looked *conflicted*—" That was the first word the girl had uttered that struck Anna as eerily more than precocious, verging on sinister. "So," the girl continued, "I knew the connection between us was personal. You didn't come out to talk to me. You left, so I knew there was a fence between us. I have watched mommies with their children, and a few daddies, and I know they sometimes take their children away, so I calculated that you would come for me, but the fences at the Centre are mostly invisible, so I knew you would have to be invisible, too, so you would come during the night when everyone else is invisible, except the night-guardians — and me, because I stayed wide awake waiting."

The girl's capacity to articulate, to process her strangely analytic grasp of the world, frightened Anna. She wondered if all parents occasionally sense a distressing distance between themselves and their children, or was this only because she was thrust into an unnatural symbiosis, with someone she had presumed dead for the first four years of her life? The girl seemed exhausted from her exposition and with one tiny arm reaching around Anna's neck settled into a comfortable sleep. A stirring in the air and the subliminal whisper of slippers on the carpets caught Anna's attention. She glanced up with a confusing mixture of trepidation and relief.

A dark figure moved towards them, progressing out of the gloom that was heightened by the lambent luminescence through gaps in the drapes, the material itself being two-sided velvet and impermeable to light. By the casual gait and awkward comportment, she knew it must be Sebastian.

"I see you've brought a friend," he said, approaching the armchair and dropping a hand gently to caress the little girl's hair.

"Me," said the sleepy Rose without opening her eyes. "I'm her friend. This is her daughter."

"Ah, well then," said Sebastian.

"My name is Anna," said the girl, squirming onto her feet and holding her hand out to him. "I'm very pleased to meet you."

"And I'm pleased to meet you, Anna. Has that always been your name?"

"Not always. Only since I was born."

"Well, I think you are starting a new life," he said. "And that's a very grown-up name. Perhaps we should give you another."

"My preference would be Edward."

"I think maybe you should choose a girl's name."

"Well, Edward Bear belongs to a girl. Her name is Christopher Robin."

"I think Christopher Robin is a boy."

"How can you tell? I don't think you can. But if you prefer, I'd like to be Violet."

"Really. That's fine, a very good name. How old are you, Violet?"

"Four, last January the first."

"Were you born on New Year's Day?" He looked at Anna, who shrugged.

"No," said Violet. "February 7th. But now I've caught up and am four and a quarter. We are dated from the first of the year. That's how they do it with the kids with no parents."

"But you have parents."

"I do now but I didn't."

"What about your dad?" Rose asked.

"He wasn't a real dad. I have to pee. Rose, can you take me to the bathroom, please. Mommy needs to rest. She's quite a lot older than you and she drove the car all the way from the Centre."

Sebastian indicated with a nod of his head the direction where they would find the toilet, then settled down on a chair aslant to Anna.

"I didn't expect you," he said. "I was in my aerie upstairs. Given the time of your arrival, I gather you are on the lam, as they say, with a posse in hot pursuit."

"There's a warrant out for my execution, Sebastian. That's apparently what they do with failed experiments and redundant wives, of which I appear to be both. Can we stay here?"

"She doesn't smile, does she?"

"Will you provide us sanctuary?"

"Of course I will, if I can. I hadn't expected you to be fugitives."

"We have nowhere else to go."

"That is not very flattering."

"Sebastian," she said. "It never occurred to me to go anywhere else. Really. I don't know exactly who you are in my life but you're very important. You are my refuge. Thank you for being here."

"Well, as they say in *Exodus, ehyeh-asher-ehyeh.*"

"*I am that I am*," she responded. It was one of the few bits of Hebrew she knew. "Another manifestation of the magical copula," she said.

"And a revealing rhetorical flourish," said a voice deep within.

"Excellent," said Sebastian, pleased that she recognized Yahweh's response when Moses had questioned his holy friend's name and found he was God.

"Beware of men who quote scripture to position themselves," said the voice.

"God can be quite redundant," said Sebastian, as if he had heard the voice too and was seeking to offset an accusation of *hubris* with wit. "He can be obscurely precise. Or do I mean, precisely obscure?"

"More abstruse than obscure." She couldn't help but get caught up in his cerebral effusions. "I have trouble thinking of you in the role of Yahweh, Sebastian."

"At least you can be sure that *I am*, which is more than you can say about your erstwhile husband, who exists and ceases to exist as he pleases."

"Which is also like God." Her words whispered.

"Now, then," said Sebastian, who seemed anxious to shift the conversation back to human survival. "There is nowhere to hide in my labyrinth, nor up in my attic retreat, nor in this rambling concatenation of antique rooms. The Fahrenheit 450 crew will peer through the walls with sensors, then flush us out with fire, noxious fumes, or brute force. What you have seen of my home is only safe by convention. Walls collapse, glass shatters, locks break."

"What *haven't* we seen of your home?" She knew there had to be some aspect of his marvellous edifice she hadn't yet fathomed? "What haven't I seen?" she repeated.

"There are places no one can reach."

"Not even us?" she queried. "Then perhaps we should call the police. I'd rather deal with them than with Robert."

"They would be obliged to interrogate you in connection with the murder of Agnes Dei."

"I dropped my handbag, I dissembled about my identity, I don't wear e-glasses, and I went into hiding. That doesn't make me a killer."

"The problem with police, they are moral relativists. Once they've established your innocence, they will turn you over to Vivuscorps for summary execution. Police inevitably serve the dominant power."

"No one knows we're here. We have some time, Sebastian. We need to figure out what to do next."

"There is always time; time always is." He smiled as if a silly syntactical inversion could displace the gravity their situation required. When she didn't respond, he continued, "Perhaps we need to convince the police they don't want you. And to convince your husband and Vivuscorps that you are gone, inaccessible, possibly dead. Rose and I both betrayed you — that was a long time in the past but we might be able to play on that. If we turn our misdeeds to advantage, we can help you achieve, what should we call it, *perfect inconsequence*. You will signify nothing."

Was he reaching for Shakespeare, summoning *Macbeth* from the shelves in his mind?

"Can you make me invisible without making us disappear altogether?"

"Ah, you want Prospero?"

"What I want is for you to apply your wizardry."

"Such as it is."

"Such as it is, yes; to make us impossible to find."

"I will take that as a compliment to my architectural venture. My retreat is a perfect exemplar of *antinomy*, you know. I'm quite proud of it, really — reasonable propositions that are mutually exclusive existing side by side."

"I know what antinomy means. But do they exist side by side? Are they mutually exclusive? If there really are irreconcilable structures superimposed on each other — isn't your mansion a monument to the reconciliation of opposites?"

"Quite the opposite. Reconciliation would compromise the integrity of each. Think of the *Gospel of John*, dear Annie."

"I often do," she responded. She knew what was coming.

"Jesus says, 'In my house are many mansions.' That is a perfect analogue for my antinomous Cloisters — of course, in the up-dated variants of the King James Version, transliterators have reduced *mansions* to rooms. 'In my house are many *rooms*.' Missing the poetry, they miss the point."

"Jesus said, or is said to have said, in 'my *Father's* house'."

"The Nicene Creed pronounced hypostasis to be the nature of God; the learned conclave decreed that Jesus is his own Father and both are the Holy Ghost. So, my house and my Father's house are synonymous. Perhaps they had it wrong, of course, or perhaps John had it wrong; the Gospels don't always agree. In any case, my library is not going anywhere. A maze is a maze to amaze, you might say. My books are secure and my house has mansions within it."

She wondered if he knew that *mansion* in Jacobean usage, at the time of King James, could also mean 'a house divided'. Even today *mansion* is used by developers to describe luxury apartments in a subdivided home. The committee known as the Second Oxford Company which translated the sectarian Judaic scripture assigned to John was particularly given to elusory language (it also translated the *Book of Revelation*). Her mind teemed with possible counters to Sebastian's bookishness.

He paused, then lowered his voice as if he were about to share clandestine secrets. "The entire project is my personal statement about the gap between appearance and reality that has haunted philosophers since Aristotle, and which Vivuscorps has all but eliminated with their ubiquitous machines. If Robert's current DNA machinations are successful, the last phase will be complete — appearance *will become* reality and reality will be only as it appears, augmented in whatever way they choose. Time as a constant will collapse. Continuity will cease to matter. There will be no more objective existence outside our own skulls, nor imagination and mystery expanding our minds. Science will destroy critical inquiry. Art will wither and die. All our yesterdays will light the way to dusty death. Life will become no more than a tale told by an idiot, filled with sound and fury, and signify nothing. Until time, on our exit, resumes."

She heard *Macbeth* in his words and, moved as she was by his passionate eloquence, she did not pick up on the invitation to engage. "I've missed the obfuscation of your truly undisciplined mind, Sebastian." She paused before redirecting his thinking to more practical purposes. "We need a strategy."

"To do what?"

"To escape."

"There is no escape, Anna." Is this what the word-play and posturing were meant to conceal? He knew better than she what their situation was. Had he been trying to conceal inevitable catastrophe? Did he see himself as inviolable, a kindly distraction?

He glanced up at her and smiled as Rose and Violet returned hand in hand out of the gloom of the farther rooms. "Here we are," he said. Anna thought he spoke like an elderly uncle. He was at most in his mid-thirties, the same age as she and as Robert.

My God, she caught herself in mid-thought! How easily Robert had slid back into her mind, neither resurrected nor evil but simply as an integer with no meaning himself.

"Okay," Anna announced. "Okay," she repeated, rising out of her chair. "It's time we come up with a plan."

"Excellent," said Rose. "I like plans if they're good ones."

Violet released her grip on Rose's hand and shuffled closer to Anna, pressing against her thigh and reaching up and grasping the three longest fingers of Anna's right hand. Then she shifted her weight onto one leg, cocking the other at the knee, and waited expectantly for the adults to determine what would happen next.

"Here's one possibility," said Sebastian. "Since I do not drive, we call our friend Mr Azzad, we ask him to come and get you. He will take you to Pearson Airport or Union Station, anywhere so long as you are recorded buying tickets. Meanwhile I will inform Vivuscorps. No, Rose will call the police. They will track you. But Azziz will bring you back here. We need them to believe you've left, but I guarantee you'll have perfect sanctuary on your return."

"From the police, but what about Vivuscorps?" Anna asked. She was certain he had strategies he hadn't yet shared.

"Fahrenheit 450 will monitor the police, but after a suitable delay I will call them anyway to earn their conditional trust, and I'm sure your husband and the thugs he travels with — his *advisors,* is how he described them while bandaging my wounds — they will come here. I will be gracious. They will find no one but me. They will join in the pursuit and lament the police having lost you, especially when monitors will have recorded you purchasing tickets, and although there will be no evidence of you actually travelling, we'll contrive a sighting in Vancouver, perhaps, or Seattle, or London, maybe Shanghai. Vivuscorps is, after all, an international and virtually infinite conglomerate."

"You mentioned heat sensors. They'll know we're actually here."

"No, Annie, sensors will prove that you are *not* here. Trust me, experience and reality don't always converge. You can measure an absence by the emptiness left in its wake, but you can't know a presence if there is nothing perceived."

"Except," said Rose, "like it's a good plan, Sebastian, but we don't have a phone to call Azziz. Azziz doesn't have a car if we did. The police aren't all that easy to lose when they're after you."

She was saying the obvious, but the room with its Edwardian décor seemed drained of energy by her words. As they listened the emptiness resonated cruelly, like thunder during a drought.

"Where is my coat," Violet asked, her voice breaking the impasse.

"There," said Anna. "Here. Are you cold?" She squatted and picked up the coat from the carpet where it had slipped off the arm of the easy chair. "Let's get you warmed up."

"No," said Violet, "I'm warm enough, thank you." She reached out and took the coat from her mother. Turning the coat over in her hands, she unclipped a thick plastic buckle from the belt at the back that held two pleats in place.

"Here," she said, handing the buckle to Sebastian. "You may use this if you would like."

Anna intercepted and took the small rectangular blue plastic packet and turned it over in her hand.

"This is a tracking device," she said. "You knew that, didn't you?"

"It's so our friends always know where we are."

"Your friends?" asked Anna.

"Our guardians," her four-year-old daughter responded. "They are actually the people who friend us and care for our needs."

"Oh really," said Rose. "We used to call our guardians guards, and they were not particularly friendly."

"Our friends particularly were," said Violet. "But don't worry, Rose, alarms won't go off. Everything at Vivuscorps is done very quietly. They won't even notice until breakfast because we're all still asleep in our beds. I'm quite hungry, really. Do you have anything to eat, Sebastian?"

Anna grimaced at her daughter's *sangfroid*, and stared down at the plastic buckle-box. She pressed a corrugated section and the back flipped off.

"What have we here?" she asked.

"It's a phone in case we get lost," said Violet. "The ones older than me wear glasses and if they understand print they can text where they are, or they can just speak and their guardian hears them."

"There we go," exclaimed Rose. "Now all we need is a car. Do you have one of those up your sleeve?"

"No," said Violet, looking very serious. "There's only my arm in my sleeve. One on each side. Last night was the first time I have ever been inside a car."

"Violet," said her mother, "can you read?"

"Oh yes, very well, thank you."

"Did you have books at your home, at the Centre?"

"It wasn't my home. It is a very large institution. And no, I have never held a book in my actual hands. I saw them several times but we were not encouraged to pick them up."

"Then what do you read, Sweetie?"

"Just words, the words inside my head."

"Oh dear," said Sebastian.

"Do you mean they go inside your head when you read?" Anna asked.

"Like Saint Jerome?" said Violet as if he were someone she knew. "No, they're already there. I just read when I want to."

"Do *they* give you things to read?"

"No, I can bring different texts into my mind whenever I want. Mostly I like *Winnie the Pooh* the best. That was Edward Bear's real name. But I read grown-up books too, like *Alice in Wonderland*, which does not make a lot of sense if you are only four years old, and *Lord of the Flies*, which does make sense."

"You know what this means, Anna?" said Sebastian, his eyes wide with nervous excitement.

"Yes," said Anna. "We'll talk about it later."

"They can trace you."

"Through Violet? No, or we'd already be caught. If there's a DNA implant, I don't think it's a transmitter, not even a receiver. It's rammed full of information before it goes in."

"What about her GPS?"

"The buckle, it won't attract their attention until morning."

"I don't understand," said Rose. "What's going on?"

"Do you realize how smart this girl is?" said Sebastian, nodding towards Violet.

"Well," said Rose, "I don't think anyone knows something like that for sure. Whatever you see is what can be seen."

"As Wittgenstein explained," he said. "'The world is that which is the case.'"

"I don't know about him but it wouldn't surprise me if he's smarter than me. Violet too, but I'm more mature."

"You probably are," said Sebastian, leaning over and kissing her on top of the head.

Anna called Azziz al Azzad. After getting over his initial surprise at hearing from her, he allowed that it might be possible to borrow his employer Farouk's car. He asked if they had eaten and offered to bring some sandwiches of flat sausages and eggs in what passed for an English muffin.

"Thank you, my friend," said Anna. After they disconnected, she turned to Sebastian. "He says he'll bring breakfast."

"I'll get you a thermos of coffee. You'll need cash for tickets. I have some upstairs."

"Do you have an ATM?" Rose asked.

"An old-fashioned wallet. It will just take me a minute. The coffee is already brewing."

Anna involuntarily loosened her grip on Violet's hand.

"You go with Sebastian," said Violet, picking up on the sign. "You need to explore the secrets of his house."

Startled by the little girl's prescience, unsettled by her self-reliance, Anna was keen to explore Sebastian's *Wunderkamern*. She needed to understand. It was an extension of Sebastian's mind, crucial to their collective survival and perhaps to her sanity.

"You stay with Rose," she said reluctantly. Rose was toying with Violet's blue plastic buckle. "I'll be right back."

"Okay," said Violet. "I will tell Rose about Pooh and Eeyore and Christopher Robin. They're friends, you know, in a world where animals can talk like people. Children can hear them, but apparently grown-ups can't."

*Actually, apparently, conflicted, scientific, calculated* — it frightened Anna how comfortable Violet was with her unnaturally expansive vocabulary.

Anna fretted as she followed Sebastian through a series of rooms, each with a window on the right opening onto the lawn or the gardens although the drapes were drawn. Several rooms had corridors leading off to the left into shadowy intimations of other rooms, including a bathroom with the door open, showing a pale gleam of tiles and porcelain, copper and brass. They came to a mirrored door and stepped through into a tiny chamber lined with walnut panelling. Sebastian drew Anna close and pushed a small pressure-release panel which swung open to reveal a control console. Under his guidance, a door closed and the room went into gentle silent motion and after a short while came to an abrupt stop, opening onto the vestibule at the end of a familiar passageway beneath the sloping mansard roof on the fourth floor. A door on the other side of the elevator opened behind them onto a landing with a staircase descending between worn plaster walls. With both doors open, the elevator itself seemed merely an ornate passage leading to the stairs which presumably descended to a garden in a protected angle between wings of the house. Anna moved forward at Sebastian's urging, and after he turned the rotary switch on the wall to bring up the lights, she discovered herself standing beside the laundry chute cupboard through which she had escaped, leaving Sebastian behind, some six weeks before. She knew exactly where she was but could not comprehend where they had been, where they had left Rose and Violet, since she knew immediately below them was a labyrinth of books and mirrors and other illusions.

"Please, Sebastian. Explain."

"Have you ever been to the British Library in London?"

"Yes, of course. Not the new one on Euston Road, the old one that used to be housed in the British Museum."

"Well, you should visit the new one; it was built less than a century ago," he said. "That was my inspiration."

"The British Library? The books in their treasury or the building itself?"

"Come," he urged, somewhat brusquely. "We need to get a move on; Azziz will be here soon."

"We've got to talk about Violet."

"We will. But right now, we must keep moving."

She tried to distract herself by remembering her visit to the British Library as a graduate student and being handed an original book, etched and hand-tinted by William Blake himself, along with a pair of white cotton gloves and the polite admonition to read it with care. How do you read a manuscript with *care*, whether from the hand of a visionary seer or the mind of a spontaneous typist? How can you *not* read with care, whether the work opens infinite doors of perception like Blake's or shares revelations of the singular world of a profligate dreamer — Jack Kerouac had been working his way to the front of her mind. How could she conjoin in her distracted maunderings two such different creators, all the while getting coffee, which was superfluous to their plight, and cash, which was essential?

By the time they returned to the drawing room, having quaffed a quick coffee in his attic retreat and picked up some money, her eclectic cerebral detours had converged into a powerful feeling of affirmation that Sebastian's library was not an imaginary contrivance. Real books evoked a real edifice to house them. Just where the library had got to, however, remained a mystery.

As soon as they were together, Anna wanted to hold Violet in her arms and to pursue her inquiry into the efficacy of the infinitesimal computing machine synthesized on a strand of DNA that was apparently inside Violet's brain. But Sebastian maintained control, guiding them out the front door to wait for Azziz. They sat on a swing sofa and a couple of Muskoka chairs on the verandah.

"Violet has been telling me about Pooh bear," said Rose.

"He's not a bear, he's a boy," said Violet. "He just looks like a bear."

"I tried to tell her he's really a bear. His name is Edward Bear."

"But of course, he's not *really* a real bear," Anna interjected.

Rose looked perplexed. "He would be," she said.

"But he's not," said Anna. "He's fiction."

"But he's a real fictional bear," said Rose.

"He's Christopher Robin's imaginary friend," said Anna.

"He's a real imaginary bear," said Rose.

"He is not a bear," said Violet. "He is a boy of little brain who looks like a bear. And he likes honey. But his friend Christopher Robin is not very nice. He kills all his animal friends, if we concede he's a he. Winnie is dead in the beginning and they're all dead at the end."

"They're not dead, Violet, they're stuffed. They're toys," said Rose.

"You can't stuff someone unless he or she or it is dead. It's called taxidermiology."

"Do you have stuffed toys?" asked Anna.

"No," said Violet. "I've read about them but I've never seen one. It's hard to tell what they're like if you haven't seen one. At the end of the story, Christopher Robin carries his dead friend Pooh upside down by his foot as he goes upstairs. In the beginning, you can see he's already got another dead friend just exactly like him. He collects dead bears, but he plays with them while they're alive. It is a disturbing story. I'm not sure what I'm expected to learn from reading it."

"She is astute," said Sebastian. "And not, like Pooh, bothered by long and difficult words. But she is very literal-minded."

"Children are," said Anna.

Rose didn't seem at all sure.

"That is part of the process," said Sebastian.

"What process?" said Anna.

"The process of Robert's intention." He looked from Anna to Rose, then back to Anna. "Let me explain," he said. The absence of any objection he took as license to expose more about Robert than was suitable for Violet to hear, or possibly for Rose, or for Anna, perhaps. Or to admit to himself. No matter. He launched into a brief disquisition: "Whatever Vivuscorps may hope to achieve through Robert's zealotry, what he appears to be pursuing, himself, is *technological singularity*."

He paused. They waited, each in her own way.

"The term was coined by a Hungarian polymath of prodigious brain, John von Neumann, in the 1950s. It describes a point in our managed evolution when the human mind will be biologically and artificially advanced to a level of superintelligence beyond which there is nowhere to go, nothing to achieve, nothing more to understand. We, in effect, stop. Full-stop. Cyber-cerebral reality will be the apotheosis of the human mind — and its annihilation. Like Fukuyama's 'the end of history', it is the end because nothing further can be achieved. The problem is, if we reach stasis, we expire. Life without change or uncertainty cannot endure."

"Sharks have managed it. They haven't changed for millions of years," Rose offered.

"Exactly. The new us — we become self-perpetuating, cold-blooded machines."

"Why on Earth would Robert want that?" Anna demanded. She had always admired sharks as a species. It was a case of the protean copula, to be, once again: sharks were perfectly adapted *to be what they are*.

"I don't think he does," said Sebastian. "Robert is somewhat of a perverse visionary. He imagines a world where superintelligence, neither impeded nor enhanced by intuition, is the norm — even at the cost of our souls. He is too literal-minded to see such a loss as a probable consequence."

"Souls?" said Anna, startled by the religious turn to his talk.

"The awareness of ourselves that separates us from everything else, everything that isn't us. Nothing transcendent, nothing mystical."

She sighed and he continued, but his train of thought had been broken.

"Vivuscorps," he said, "Vivuscorps has given Robert the opportunity to make his vision reality."

"Why?" said Rose. "Why does he want it so much?"

"Because," said Violet, indicating she had been listening as well.

"Why?" Rose repeated.

"Because," Violet repeated. "It would be good to know everything."

"Not without understanding," said Rose.

Anna felt a chill run down her spine. Rose intuitively got it. Violet did not. Fullness of consciousness resided in the spaces between understanding, in the surprise connections that confounded intelligence, in the conflicting poetics of thought and emotion. It was in the fullness of consciousness that the genius of humanity lay, making humans a singular point in the cosmos where the cosmos was aware of itself.

"Neumann's 'technological singularity' means the end of humanity," said Anna. It seemed a simple straightforward equation.

"Or a new beginning," said Sebastian. "It's hard to say. I mean, Fukuyama wasn't right about history. History persists; it will never catch up with the present."

Their conversation lapsed into an uneasy silence. Eventually, Azziz pulled up out front. Anna motioned him to remain in the car. Rose called the police. It took several minutes to find someone concerned with the case, but then Rose was assured they definitely wanted Anna for questioning and she was asked if Anna had a little girl with her. The speaker had obviously been in contact with Vivuscorps, perhaps while keeping Rose on hold. Rose explained the three of them had escaped from the Vivuscorps Centre and that Vivuscorps was in pursuit. She told the police they were hiding at Sebastian's house and wanted police protection. Rose was adept at improvising when dealing with figures of authority. The police agreed to swing by later that morning. Their casual response suggested they were counting on Vivuscorps getting there first.

Azziz got out of Farouk's car, leaving it idling, and marched up the walk, to be met halfway by Rose. They talked with furtive urgency while Anna and the little girl were saying goodbye to Sebastian on the verandah. Azziz waved a solemn salutation and retraced his steps, clambering back into the car, while Rose declared that she would go with him on her own and, before Anna or Sebastian could protest, she had joined him and the car was moving down the street. Rose leaned out the rolled-down window and flashed Violet's plastic belt buckle, before settling back as the car disappeared into the shadows at the far end of Errington Lane.

"Oh, for God's sake," said Sebastian. "What is that foolish girl doing? She doesn't even have any money."

"*I don't know, I don't care, and it doesn't make any difference,*" said Anna in a deliberate voice to indicate she was quoting, then added for clarification, "Jack Kerouac — but my meaning is the opposite to his. It's an expression of hopefulness, not resignation. We're not beatniks, nobody has beaten us yet."

Sebastian looked at her as if she were demented, while Anna stared after the car. She drew Violet close against her leg. Lights in neighbouring windows suggested people were up and about. There were no other cars in evidence. Everyone in an area like this had private parking. It was a quiet residential street with broad lawns, towering trees in bud, moss greening at their ancient protruding roots, and the occasional crocus peering up from the darkness under the sod.

"Rose is resourceful," Anna said. "She took the GPS. Vivuscorps will be tracking her. I'm sure they'll head over to the bus depot and she'll slip the tracker between seats or give it to a lonely kid going home. If we're lucky, Robert's people will follow her trail to Sudbury or Sarnia before losing her completely."

"Did she tell you this?"

"No," said Anna. "I understand how she thinks."

"Even though Vivuscorps is inside her head."

"You don't think they'll know what she's up to, do you?" asked Anna, perplexed.

"I imagine their goal is not to monitor her world but to have her monitor theirs. The object is to control, to manipulate perceptions of reality, not to observe the observer observing."

"They'll have their hands full with Rose. She's learned survival strategies from birth —sometimes she'll obey the rules, sometimes break them, whatever is necessary. She's not a cyborg. Even computer enhanced, she is her very own person."

"Good. And Azziz will look after her."

"She will look after Azziz."

"Then let us slip inside. I think we have provoked the devil and in one of his guises he's sure to come calling very soon."

Once in the foyer, Sebastian opened the door between the mirrored panel leading to the star chamber and the door opening into the Edwardian parlour, revealing a closet hardly big enough for half a dozen fur coats squeezed together. Despite the odour of animal must, Jergens hand lotion, and lilac perfume, it was an empty space, panelled in walnut like the secret elevator at the far end of the concatenating sequence of antiquated rooms.

"Step in," said Sebastian.

Violet leaned up to be hoisted into Anna's arms and the three of them crowded into the closet. Sebastian closed the door, prompting a light to go on. He sprung a control panel open and pressed a button that sent their crypt into a gentle shudder. Anna could have sworn the walls moved as the three of them were thrust even closer. When the sensation of the elevator shrinking subsided, the tiny room dropped silently into the bowels of the earth. It stopped sharply, perhaps four storeys down.

"Now *this*," Sebastian said as the door opened, "this is my *sanctum sanctorum*. Welcome, Anna. Welcome Violet."

They stepped into an antechamber that was both subterranean and ethereal, filled with light and flowers, bounded by sheer walls of shining granite set obliquely against sedimentary walls of ridged limestone. The ceiling and floors were solid rock, carved smooth but not polished. The room was magical, enchanted and oppressive, wondrous and terrifying. Behind them, the elevator door had virtually disappeared into the wall. Off to the sides, similar rooms, equally surreal, were illuminated by indirect lighting, filled with lush vegetation, and circumscribed by stone. The light was pervasive. There were no shadows. A crystal-clear stream meandered beside the converging stone corridors and, despite the distance below the surface of the earth, the flowing water created a gentle zephyr that moved fresh air from room to room.

"Sebastian, is this another illusion?" Anna clutched Violet close to her breast as they moved slowly around the central chamber, peering into each of the luminous wings off to the sides.

"It is, but a very real one," he answered. "As I've explained before, just because something subverts the logic of perception, that doesn't make it fantastical but merely fantastic. My *sanctum sanctorum* is the materialization of a *trompe-l'oeil*. It is an authentic fake, a phenomenological trick, and very real."

"Are we actually underground?"

"We are safe, the flowers are genuine."

"No one can find us?"

"No one."

"Sebastian, are we prisoners? For all the wonder, this place strikes me as a panopticon with running water and relentlessly good air circulation."

"Bentham's *panopticon*! No, not at all. Despite his enlightened sensibility as a great reformer, Jeremy Bentham designed a diabolical prison, didn't he? Two centuries ago, the champion of individual rights over natural law — which he described as 'nonsense on stilts' — he imagined a building which in itself was an instrument of retribution, where no man, nor woman, nor little girl, was ever out of sight and never allowed to be merely himself, or herself. He deserved to have his corpse stuffed with straw and stashed under the stairs. As so it was, and still is, as far as I know."

Anna blanched, while Violet flushed with excitement.

"Is he really stuffed with straw?" Violet asked, her blues eyes ablaze.

"He's kept inside something they call the Auto-Icon at University College London. It's shiny dark wood and he's sitting up in a chair. They've had to replace his shrivelled skin with wax, but it's still his own hair, his own skull and skeleton, and he's wearing his original clothes."

"Sebastian, please!" Anna admonished.

"Ah, you would prefer we talk about the structure he designed for enlightened incarceration, not his feeble effort at desiccated immortality. Anna, I assure you, this is anything but a panopticon. Michel Foucault chose aptly in using Bentham's prison to describe our dehumanizing exposure to the tyrannies of information technology. But my *sanctum sanctorum* is exactly the opposite. This place is a self-sustaining environment. Water moving through the earth provides power and nourishment. The plants replenish the air. Simulated sunlight and a careful selection of crawling insects and worms reinvigorate the soil. There are no mosquitoes. Everything exists in a very fine balance, presumably until the sun cools and our planet rolls off its axis.

"I think the sun will explode," said Violet.

"Well, that is virtually forever, and until then, it is lovely that no human presence is necessary to keep it going. Unlike God, it does not need to be perceived or praised to endure."

The thought flashed through Anna's mind that he was dead wrong. This place was a Foucauldian contrivance. It was intended to simulate exposure to the disciplinary power of extreme visibility and to render the human and humane redundant. In their new hiding place, there was no place to hide.

"Sebastian," she repeated, "are we your prisoners?"

"As I suggested before, dear Annie, dear little Violet, it is not so simple as that."

# Chapter Ten
# The Devil in Detail

Anna had little doubt that Sebastian admired the notion of preternatural intellectual prowess, albeit without cybernetic enhancement. He was too much a man of books and the ideas their undisciplined indulgence encouraged to countenance computer interference in the freewheeling procedures of the human mind, but he was too much the entitled eccentric not to be fascinated by the possibilities of superintelligence. He was too much a realist to doubt his own genius, but he must have realized he was not a visionary driven to change the world for better or worse. He was a dreamer who dreamed of resisting its changes. His panopticon, she knew, was not built as a prison, no more than his star chamber was simply a clever construction with mirrors or his library a maze to house books. They were all monuments to the singularity of cerebral achievement that he hoped to attain by turning away from the brave new world of Vivuscorps, Fahrenheit 450, Robert Noyes, and nanobiotechnology.

Sebastian seemed studiously distant in the soft glare of his vast and pleasant cavern. Anna wondered if he feared his willingness to hide them might expose his project to the gaze of violated innocence and reduce it to an extravagant fantasy. She held Violet close, as if her daughter's warmth could compensate for her own rising fears. This place was itself a singularity of sorts — which she knew in mathematics as a factor, like infinity, beyond definition, and in fiction as a point of divergence where parallel worlds spin off on their own. It was peculiar how a word like 'singularity' could mean so differently.

Even though they stood with him at the centre of his panopticon, the watchtower, as it were, Anna had no doubt they were his prisoners. You can't be the observer unless you are also observed, if only by yourself observing. She wasn't sure Foucault allowed for egregious reciprocity in his metaphorical prison, nor Bentham before him, in his designs for a real one. The guards were subject to the dehumanizing protocols they imposed, the executioner to the horrors of death he inflicted. The biotechnologist was subject to the psychic dissociation he induced, the wealthy eccentric to the brutality of metaphors he constructed to make the world sweet.

"Sebastian," she said, "please, explain, be reasonable."

"Of course," he responded. He moved away from the sheer granite slab where the elevator door receding into the wall had left only a thin rectilinear cleft in the rock that outlined where the opening had been. "Ask me whatever you would like. I'm very proud of my modest hideaway. You're the first ever to see it since the last workman left."

"Wasn't he required to die on site like the architects of the pyramids?"

"This is not a crypt to commemorate death. Quite the opposite, it is my vision of transcendence."

"Transcending mortality?"

"Transcending humanity."

"Really?" She was curious.

"Do you know the lines from a somewhat obscure poem by Hopkins, Gerard Manley, the melancholic zealot? Possibly not.

> Thou has bound bones and veins in me, fastened me flesh,
> And after it almost unmade, what with dread—

"Flesh and dread. That is our human condition. We place it at the centre of everything. You might say this sepulchre is my way of transcending all that flesh is heir to."

"The poem is not so obscure, Sebastian, and it is about redeeming mortality, not its denial. It is a poem of affirmation. The next lines refute your complaint with the introduction of a God neither you nor I might acknowledge ourselves.

> Thy doing: and dost thou touch me afresh?
> Over again I feel thy finger and find thee."

"Please, feel free to walk about if you wish," said Sebastian with a sullen nonchalance that suggested he thought she had missed his point entirely. "Do you like all the flowers, Violet?"

"I do, I've always liked flowers."

"Sebastian," Anna asked yet again, urgency straining her voice. She wanted confirmation to make this place and their status real. "Are we prisoners here?"

"As opposed to where?" He paused momentarily to appreciate the existential depth of his own wit. "Prisoners? No, not in the conventional sense."

"Are we free to go?"

"I cannot allow you to leave. Your lives would be in grave danger."

"Then we *are* your prisoners," said Anna.

"We weren't free to leave the Centre," Violet observed. "Do you think we were prisoners, there?" She was addressing Anna. "We didn't have anywhere else to go."

"Thank you, sweet girl," said Sebastian. "That is precisely my point."

"Having no alternative is hardly the same as freedom," said Anna.

"Why don't we say you are my guests?"

"By coercion."

"By agreement."

"But if I do not agree?"

"I cannot allow you to die over a matter of semantics."

"Do you mean semiotics, perhaps? Your meaning is clear enough, but what it signifies is not." She reached down and took hold of Violet's hand, prepared to lead her into one of the gleaming otherworldly chambers off to the side. Then she paused. "Or do you mean hermeneutics, since we are obliged to interpret your meaning, given how you are using words to obscure your intent?"

"Stop thinking, Anna. Sometimes it is best not to think — why not simply live and, perhaps, enjoy? These chambers allow you to witness eternity. This is my dream of perfection — where it is not even necessary for the observer or the observed to exist. It is a perfect illusion of forever."

"Heaven as an oppressively ethereal detention facility!" she muttered caustically, mostly for her own benefit. "I find the notion of heaven oppressive, an insufferable negation of time and space, where we live, when alive."

Violet, who had been listening intently, intervened. "Sebastian, nothing can be *forever*. What happens when the lights burn out?"

"They're very long-lasting bulbs, Violet. They will outlast any of us."

"Even me?" she said and, shrugging dismissively, tugged on her mother's hand, trying to lead her away.

Sebastian shifted his attention back to Anna. He seemed to recognize her greater concern was not to avoid being captured by Vivuscorps thugs but to resolve dialectical differences. "Despite being a good distance underground, Annie, this is not the underworld. It is not Dante's Inferno, not Blake's Ulro. It is not Hell, nor is it Error."

"I don't know about Error but, as a recent Pope, much beloved by his minions, pontifically proclaimed, *Hell is merely the absence of Heaven*."

"Of God," Sebastian countered. "Hell is the absence of God."

"Does it matter? What's a heaven without God, or hell, for that matter?"

"It is terrifying, there might be no God," said Sebastian.

"More terrifying if there is!" said Anna.

"You might possibly be right."

Sincerity is the first casualty of theological disputation, she thought. After an ominous interval, she announced: "We're going for a walk."

Sebastian harrumphed. He shrugged.

Anna let herself be led by Violet from one bright airy grotto to another, each leading off from the central chamber and each disturbingly the same as the last, until, on one of their returns to the axis, they discovered Sebastian, who had been watching them, was no longer present. Anna immediately knew that he had risen back to the surface, that they were alone in this bright and sinister place.

With sudden anxiety at being abandoned, she grasped Violet in her arms and turned her shoulder against the granite panel concealing the elevator door, hoping it was on a pressure-release mechanism. As it pushed back with equal and opposite force, she realized, with the elevator having ascended, even if she got the door open it would only reveal the bottom of an empty shaft. Catching her breath and determined to reassure Violet, she set her daughter down and leading her by the hand proceeded on a more methodical exploration, hoping to find living quarters, bathroom facilities, a kitchen. If they existed, they were well hidden. There was nothing in evidence but flowers, diffused light, balmy airiness, a gentle rill of clear water, and rock that by design was an unsettling arrangement of crystalline glitter and the grey of primordial mud. So thoroughly had Sebastian expunged human particulars from his *sanctum sanctorum*, it transformed in her mind, as she knew he intended and to which she was in uneasy accord, into a rather grandiloquent argument against the entire humanist tradition. This place was not an elaborate display of manic depravity or secular grace, nor a metaphor of reality beyond time and a God freed of prayer. It was one person's monumentally indulgent attempt to declare humans redundant, to create a visionary world where the presence of the creator was absent and the centre was not Foucault's observing consciousness, or Bentham's, but the creation itself.

Anna found herself smiling. This was Sebastian's tribute to Heidegger, his challenge to Plato. She settled in the central chamber onto a rocky shelf that was softened by a luxuriant blanket of virescent green moss, and drew Violet onto her lap. Secure or secured, they were safe. The forces of evil, which to her mind were inseparable from Robert, his confederates, and the vicious Vivuscorps project, were temporarily restrained. Sebastian's eccentricity was holding them at bay. And the astounding vanity of his attempt to counter the entire Enlightenment without resorting to God on the one hand or science on the other, endeared him to her more than anger could suppress or revoke. He had not betrayed her. He had simply asserted authority as yet to be earned. He was socially awkward, inept. She hoped wherever he had gone, he was safe.

She looked down at her daughter against her breast and was startled to see Violet's deep blue eyes wide open, staring back. Anna was uncomfortable being fixed in another's disinterested gaze, even when the other was her own child. She peered along the wall hiding the elevator door to where water burbled softly against the rocks which arrested its flow, then looked back at Violet, who continued to stare as if some revelation were surely at hand. Anna needed to think. She turned Violet closer so the child couldn't see into her eyes.

Like a disappointed Christian, she grasped at a concept that she had found quite compelling but no longer believed. Not that she ever did. It wasn't a matter of weak faith but false logic. Since the accident, which may not have happened, she occasionally tried to resolve conflicted emotions by denying the breakdown of the bicameral mind. It was not so esoteric a strategy as it seemed. The preliterate brain as posited by a psychologist called Julian Jaynes separated mental activity from linguistic cognition. Anna tried, in effect, to transcend self-consciousness and directly experience her thoughts without the mediation of language. Fear, loathing, and confusion became more real than their causes. She could deal with emotional abstraction, the misapprehension that feelings were ideas without words — she could deal with ideas.

Unfortunately, Jaynes argued that bicameral absence of personal awareness preceded the innovation of writing, implying that all preliterate peoples were not yet fully evolved, and she found this contemptible. She wondered, could his hypothesis also explain Robert's demonic machinations for the achievement of superintelligence as the inevitable next phase in human evolution? Jaynes would never have known how repugnant people like Anna would find the reduction of the species to cyborg efficiency. But that was not Jaynes' concern. He was a psychologist, after all, and not much adept at ethics, aesthetics, poetics, or maths. For the moment, his theories of the divided mind gave her license to think without feeling, which she did, despite rocking her newly beloved daughter in her arms and basking in her child's warm breath as it rose to define the features of her own face.

Feeling Violet's warmth, the presence of the child who had grown in her womb, she wondered, with a brief burst of delight, could a single mind ever be truly bicameral except during gestation, when one mind grew within the boundaries of another? In a world teeming with binaries generated by our desire to impose order on chaos, the fusion of opposing sides of the mind in a singular function seemed inane. We live in a bilateral world. Binaries reduce the complexities of human experience to simplistic apprehensible equations. Dualisms of one sort or another allow philosophers to comprehend their own speculations, determine how artists receive their perceptions, how visionaries structure their dreams, sleepwalkers prove to themselves they are not asleep. Everything is whatever it is not, according to Saussure. Language as the agent of consciousness abhors singularity — it needs oppositions, dichotomies, contraries, contradictions, complementarities, antinomies, antitheses, inversions, to generate meaning.

And before language, there was no awareness of being aware. *Homo sapiens* lived in the perpetual present. There were no words to describe being alive. But long before writing, art was inscribed in the depths of caves beyond the reach of natural light and we discovered ourselves. Jaynes offered nothing more than a facile explication to account for the pleasures and terrors of interior silence. Anna hummed to herself, to her child. She rocked Violet in her arms until they were both on the verge of sleep.

Suddenly, what seemed like a deep exhalation of air behind them presaged the elevator door sliding forward before it swung open. From inside the cabinet, Rose gazed out with a wild unfocussed look in her eyes. She mouthed an indistinct expletive, like a shriek underwater. With her was Azziz, who leaned against her with one arm slung over her shoulder, his head lolling forward, saliva running from his mouth, blood spreading in a grotesque blossom from a black hole in the lower front of his shirt.

Anna rushed forward and helped ease their wounded friend out of the elevator and onto the moss-covered stone bench. Violet, without being asked, folded her coat into a pillow and slipped it under his head. Rose stood back while Anna peeled the soiled shirt away from Azziz's gut and felt around for a pressure point to staunch the surging blood. Rose collapsed in slow motion on the floor. Violet crouched down to cradle Rose's head against her knees while gently stroking her temple.

Without looking away from Azziz, Anna anxiously asked Rose how she was.

"I'm just scared," said Rose. Her voice trembled as she shifted into an upright posture on the stone floor beside Anna's legs, drawing Violet close to her. "I didn't get hit, the blood isn't mine."

"We've got to get Azziz to a hospital," said Anna. "He's bleeding heavily. I don't know how long we can hold it back."

"No one's going anywhere unless there's another way out," Rose said. "There's a madman up there with a gun."

"If we stay, Azziz will die."

"If we leave, we'll all die. He's a crazy man up there."

"Sebastian? Was it Sebastian? Maybe he didn't know it was you. He thinks he's protecting us."

"The shooter could see us better than we could see him. He was hiding in a room full of mirrors and lights."

"But you didn't actually get a good look at him?"

"Not really. He just shot. We don't use guns in this country, Annie. We weren't expecting a bullet. Is Azziz really dying?"

"It's okay," said Violet as she squirmed her small body around so she could look Rose in the eye. "This is a nice place. It's just like heaven, isn't it, Mommy?"

"I wouldn't say so exactly, Sweetheart."

"I would." Violet was being neither captious nor impertinent. She was stating a fact. "Almost, anyway. Sebastian thinks it can go on *forever*, but he doesn't know the light bulbs will eventually burn out. Did Sebastian hurt Mr Azziz?"

"Yes," said Rose. "I think it was him."

Anna motioned for Rose to slip into the position where she had been and pressed Rose's fingers close to the wound in Azziz's side. She tore a couple of long strips of cotton from the hem of her skirt and tied them together into a bandage. Squatting down by the moving water she peeled a mass of drenched sphagnum away from wet rocks and squeezed it nearly dry before wadding it into a clump which she pressed against Azziz and wrapped tightly to hold back the oozing blood.

"How do you know to do that?" Rose asked. "Wouldn't the cotton be cleaner?"

"Moss is absorbent and extremely acidic. It will staunch the flow and kill the bacteria. We can't do much about the internal bleeding except keep him quiet and very still."

Anna tried to scoop up handfuls of water from the rivulet in the floor but it sieved through her fingers. She leaned down on her knees and took in a big mouthful and held it until she could twist around and press her lips to Azziz's lips and then she released a slow trickle into his mouth. She did this several times and was surprised when he finally coughed and offered a strained indecipherable phrase in Qashqai or Farsi. Then in English he said quite distinctly: 'Thank you, Professor Winston. I will sleep now."

"We shouldn't have talked about how he was dying," said Rose. "I didn't know he could hear."

A faint smile drifted across the wounded man's face, a twitching of his close-cropped beard, and his features settled in a pained grimace as he lapsed into unconsciousness with his head nestled against Violet's folded coat.

"Let him be," said Anna. She was aware of the loaded copula.

She led Rose and the little girl into an adjoining chamber. They sat in a circle of three, Violet being determined to sit on her own, unencumbered by affection.

Anna addressed Rose in a whisper. "There's nothing we can do for Azziz but wait. What happened, Rose? I can't believe Sebastian could do this."

"Maybe if we told him Azziz needs help, maybe…" Rose let her voice trail off.

Turning to Sebastian seemed an unlikely course of action, especially if Sebastian was the shooter. In any case, there was no way of contacting him. This was a panopticon, not a sentient building like the Vivuscorps Centre where the walls watched, listened, and spoke. As far as Anna could tell, they were in complete and utter isolation. That was the point.

"What happened is, Azziz and I went away," Rose explained. "When we came back the cops were waiting like we expected."

"Did you go to the bus depot?"

"Union Station. I dropped the blue buckle into a kid's knapsack. I think he was boarding the Montreal train." Her voice became louder as she spoke. "We came back here and I told the cops — they were sitting in a car out front — I said you skipped out on me, you probably went to Montreal. So then they left. Oh, yeah, I also told them I was asked to house-sit for Sebastian. They were okay with that. You're a pretty low priority in their scheme of what's what — like maybe you switched identity with Agnes or maybe you pushed a derelict under a streetcar by mistake. They're not really sure why they're after you. Questioning is all. So, we knocked on a couple of doors but there was no Sebastian. The front door was unlocked and we wanted to hide in case the Vivuscorps heavies checked here on their way to the train terminal. You're a much higher priority in their scheme of what's what, you and Violet. They want to kill you, and me too. I don't think Violet, so much."

Rose took a few deep breaths. Anna wondered why Sebastian hadn't answered when Rose knocked. Why wasn't he watching behind locked doors? All explanations seemed equally sinister.

"I would like to know what happened next," said Violet, quite formally but in a voice tremulous with excitement. Anna walked quietly into the other room to see how Azziz was doing. He was still asleep. Rose seemed anxious to continue her story. As soon as Anna returned, Rose began talking again although, curiously, as if Violet were the primary audience.

"So, okay, Sweetheart, inside that foyer room — this part gets scary — the closet door was ajar, but so was the big mirror door with a crazy mirror on its backside, and since the closet seemed a dead end, we stepped through the mirror into a long corridor. It was very dark but blinding bright, like from strobe lights flashing at the far end."

"Which was it?" asked Violet. "Bright or dark? They're opposites."

"No, it was both, I remember."

"I thought you had a photographic memory."

"This was like watching a movie on fast-forward. You could make out the darkness and the light at the same time, faster than your eyes could adjust from one to the other. It's only your brain that tells you they're opposed to each other."

"Do you know you can see a lot more in the dark than the light?" said Violet. "I figured that out."

"Really?" said Rose.

"You can see the horizon by day but at night you can see hundreds of stars and they're billions of miles away."

"Billions of stars and galaxies and constellations," said Rose.

"Constellations aren't real," said Anna. She was relieved by the diversion — the more trivial, the better. "They're patterns superimposed on the universe by us, from our vantage on Earth."

"I'm not sure about that," said Violet.

"It's okay, Honey," said Rose. "Your Mum and I are worried about Mr Azzad. We're just making noise."

"What about girls and boys, are they opposites?"

"No," said Rose. "Look, if you see two ducks in a pond, you know they're ducks, not turnips."

"Or windmills," said Violet.

"Just because one is a boy duck and the other is a girl, they're still more like each other than anything else. See what I'm saying? It's the same thing with people."

"They supplement each other," Anna explained. "You can only tell for sure what is male by knowing what is not, and what is female by what is not."

"But there are no rules," Rose chimed in. "Sometimes men and women, males and females, overlap. They can't tell each other apart, so you can have a manly woman and a womanly man, but then you're just talking semantics."

"I'm four and a quarter years old," Violet interjected. "I have no idea what you are talking about."

Rose and Anna let their voices rise to a normal volume as they continued to talk about antinomies, anomalies, complementary and converse linguistic signs. They were painfully aware of Azziz's precarious condition — they were chattering to reassure him if he were awake, to comfort him with their sound if he were asleep, to defy or deny his suffering if he were in the throes of distressed semi-consciousness. They took it as a matter of course that Violet should participate in their discourse. Neither she nor Rose had had enough experience with children to recognize how preternaturally intelligent their diminutive colleague actually was. They talked not so much over Violet's head as through her, with Azziz always in the backs of their minds.

"Let's go back to your story, Rose," Violet prodded. "What happened next?"

"Well, it all got confusing. There's this room covered with mirrors going every which way, under your skirt and over your head and all around on crazy angles, and the mirrors were flashing like we'd been caught out in half a dozen thunderstorms happening at once. Except it was silent, like we were stone-cold deaf. And there was a man in the centre of the room who had no reflection, so I figured he was a vampire. I don't believe in vampires but I don't believe you can't have a reflection, either. Who knows what's real and what isn't? Azziz and I just walked towards him and he looked as dazzling as an archangel in a painting, but when we almost got to him and the lights were shining off him like crazy, suddenly he raises his hand towards us and there was a gun in it. He shot Azziz. He fired at me but he missed, so I tackled him low and twisted the gun from his hand and threw it away as hard as I could. It shattered a mirror into glittering splinters and he whirled around like someone possessed by the devil. I remember every detail about him, and yet I didn't see who he was. In all those flashing lights it looked like his face was on fire."

"It was a vampire devil," Violet explained.

"I'm pretty sure it was Sebastian."

"Why?" Anna asked.

"I don't know. I just knew it was him. Maybe because he was expecting us."

"Vampires know a lot of things," said Violet. "But I don't understand, why did he shoot you?"

"Exactly," said Rose. "Why? I was blinded by the light but he didn't bite, so maybe he wasn't a vampire, but who else could it be? Anyhow, I swung wildly and chopped him across his windpipe and he fell into the glare and while he was rolling around trying to breathe, I grabbed hold of Azziz, but he was lying like a corpse on the mirror floor, and I couldn't lift him, so I left him there and I raced down the light and dark corridor past the crazy mirror and out into the foyer, then through the door to the family part of the house. That's when I got really quiet and I listened and I heard shuffling, then the noises stopped and I waited and then I went out and there was Azziz, slumped over against the closet door. But."

"But what?" both Violet and her mother exclaimed.

"I looked out and saw someone coming up the walk to the front door, so I hauled Azziz into the closet. When I pulled the door shut a light went on and there was a panel on the inside wall that opened when I pushed it and inside there were buttons and switches, so I pushed a button and the light went out. I could hear voices in the foyer. After a bit, the voices faded. I felt in the dark for another button and then I heard a whirring sound, soft as can be. I found the light switch again and when I turned it back on, the closet had shrunk and it was still getting smaller."

Violet squealed. Anna drew a deep breath.

"I tried hard to brace myself against one of the moving walls and I propped Azziz against another, but he was slippery because he was covered in blood. The walls kept closing and closing until there was hardly enough room for us to stand facing each other, which we had to do because there was no room for him to collapse on the floor. Azziz whispered things in Arabian. I don't know if he was praying, but since there wasn't enough space to drop to my knees, and since I resent any God who would put us in this position if he also had the power to get us out, I sure as hell wasn't praying myself."

"I think God only exists if you believe in him," said Violet.

Anna's mind jumped to Saint Augustine, but immediately fell back. She was more interested in the story of survival than in arguments of a reformed libertine for faith over reason, with God above all.

"They made us sing about God and the little sparrows," said Violet. "It seemed to me if he saw them so clearly, he should have saved them from falling."

Memories of a childhood prayer flashed through Anna's mind. "If I should die before I wake, I pray the Lord my soul to take. Good God, good grief, what a horrendous burden to lay on a sleepy child.

"So, I twisted around to jam my hip into Azziz and stop him from sliding, and my hand landed on the control panel and I figured I should just press every button and hope for the best. We didn't know it was an elevator. We didn't know it was shrinking to just the right size to worm its way down a narrow shaft in the rock."

Anna felt perversely reassured to know the diminishing volume of the elevator cabinet had not been a trick of the mind. "How did you know it was rock?"

"Because we're here. Because it's the Earth with a capital E. We sure didn't know we'd find you guys, or running streams and underground sunshine. And here we are. Oh my God, I hope Azziz is okay."

"Where in heaven's name would Sebastian get a gun? It must be an heirloom. The Kroetsches were eccentric enough to own guns."

"Is it all like this? I mean, if he comes down to get us, it looks like we've got nowhere to hide," said Rose. "He could pick us off, one by one."

"If he wanted to do that, why didn't he do it already?" said Violet with unassailable logic.

"Well, he tried to kill me and he already did a good job on Azziz."

Perhaps hearing his own name, Azziz groaned from the next chamber. Anna rushed in to find him trying to sit up. Rose joined her and together they boosted him to a more comfortable position. He didn't look any better, although the blood had congealed and was crusting on his gut. Anna tore another couple of cotton strips from her skirt, which was getting unfashionably short, and they wrung out more sphagnum to replace the old, and re-bandaged his wound without trying to clean it.

Azziz mumbled his appreciation and then spoke in a voice that was surprisingly clear yet betrayed a great deal of pain. "What is the little girl doing?"

Anna looked around. Violet had carried a couple of rocks over to the granite slab set perpendicular to the wall in front of the elevator. She was arranging them in an attempt to make the elevator door impossible to close.

"That's so Sebastian won't be able to surprise us," Violet explained as she stepped inside the elevator. She picked up Azziz's Qashqai bag and tossed it towards them, then by adjusting the rocks to make them secure she disturbed the delicate equilibrium of the granite door. It began to swing closed under its own weight. She slid a rock forward to stop it, but the rock skittered aside and the little girl stared out from the interior as the door opening diminished and then disappeared.

Anna rushed forward. She shouted at the vanishing cavity. She called her daughter's names. Violet, then Anna. She screamed as the surfaces aligned and all that was left of the elevator was a line etched into the implacable stone. Horrified, she sank to the floor. Rose scrambled away from Azziz and grabbed Anna under the arms, dragging and sliding her back to the moss-covered ledge where Azziz had negotiated his pain-wracked body to make room.

Anna bent over on herself and huddled against the wounded man. Her deep sobs echoed from the surrounding chambers. Suddenly she lapsed into silence. Rose stroked her forehead with helpless caresses, then got up and began striding from dazzling white grotto to dazzling white grotto, each iridescent in the luminous wake of her movements. Frustrated and dejected, she settled back on the floor beside the limestone ledge. She drew Anna close and held her hand against her breast. Three outliers, a fugitive, a perpetual foundling, and a brutalized dying man. The little girl who might have completed their complement was grievously missing.

"Anna." Azziz spoke the word of her name like an omen. His rasping voice etched it into the air. "Anna? The little girl, she is your child?" His voice was harsh with pain. "She will be safe, that is my promise." The intonations of his English diction echoed the Farsi he had studied in Baghdad and translated in Kabul.

Extricating herself from Azziz's contorted embrace and Rose's steadfast grip, Anna struggled to her feet. Azziz convulsed as he shifted and settled back against Violet's folded coat. Rose moved up beside him and took hold of his hands.

"Anna," Azziz rasped. "I will die very soon. I must talk."

Anna stared wildly about, then bent closer.

"Sit here beside Rose, it is important."

"Azziz, I can't."

"I just need you to listen. Please, you must listen."

She struggled against hysteria with a clarity of thought that surprised her. Getting angry at Azziz for being mortally wounded was absurd. She knew her distress at what seemed like a request to hear his confessional was pathetically misdirected.

"Azziz, you must rest, you will be all right," she lied.

"I need to tell you, you were wrong about me. Please, I need your prayers."

"Azziz, we can talk later." Her voice was unsteady. She wanted to hear nothing to diminish her concern about Violet.

"Dr Winston, there is no *later*, not for me."

Rose began to weep.

"You must listen," said Azziz. "My heart will soon run out of blood. I need to tell you. I need to tell you the truth."

"It doesn't matter, Azziz." She was frightened by his insistence. She wanted to hear nothing of the truth, if it subverted or distorted the story they had created together that allowed him to suffer with dignity.

"Let him speak," said Rose through her tears. "It's not for us, it's for him."

Azziz went on, "The noise of the gun in the flashing darkness, perhaps being shot in my guts, I don't know — I remember terrible things. It is all more real than now. The American advisors, they took turns standing behind me, shooting their weapons close to my head. They shot past me, very close, they shot women and children. It is very real now."

"Azziz, you did not kill those people yourself," said Anna, trying to stifle horror without losing compassion.

"But I did, I did. After many practices, the Americans gave me a rifle and I shot women and children and old people and disbelievers and anyone they wanted to die."

"You were brainwashed."

"I was tortured by shock and by fear, yes. I was driven to depravity beyond the limits of shame. My Qashqai bag, I took from the corpse of an old woman I murdered. No matter how much I wanted to forget, the bag would connect me to those people I killed, like a scar from wounds I could not remember."

"Why didn't you shoot the Americans if you had a loaded gun," Rose demanded. She had stopped crying.

"I do not know."

"Were you afraid they'd shoot you first? Americans shoot people a lot."

"I know. It is part of their vision of perfection."

"They live in a perfectly dysfunctional fantasy," said Anna.

"Perfection is always dysfunctional," Azziz murmured. "They are constitutional fundamentalists. Visions should be written by poets, not politicians or priests."

"And interpreted by philosopher-kings," said Anna.

"But Plato—" He paused, searching for a word, or the strength to proceed. "Plato's Kallipolis is a totalitarian regime."

Anna drew up short. They were having a debate! In the face of death, the ultimate diversion. "Azziz, you must be quiet," she declared with vehement compassion. "Critiquing the American Constitution won't heal your wounds. And it's still the best instrument of its kind ever written."

"I told you, Professor, my wounds will not get better. Thanks to the ingenuity of special advisors in Iraq, I have had much experience in separating pain from cognition. There is nothing better I can do now than to die passionately, railing against the tyranny by zealots of secular texts."

"Azziz," Rose exclaimed, "you are not dead yet."

"Give me time, just a little, my Rose."

"Do you believe in prayer, do you believe in God?" Rose asked, as if impending death gave him a privileged perspective.

"God does not need me to believe in him."

Possibly mistaking his humility for equivocation, Rose turned on Anna. "Do you?" she demanded. She seemed to be accusing Anna of imposing her doubt as an impediment to Azziz's recovery. "You told me you don't."

"Pray if it helps."

"Perhaps we should."

"You go ahead, Rose."

"Can you believe in prayer but not God?"

"Desperation is not belief."

"I would like to believe, especially when things are bad." Rose spoke as if she were drawing strength from her capacity for doubt. "Thank God we live in times when you don't have to believe in the God you are thanking. I know they used to torture people who didn't — burning them alive until they were dead or promising eternal fire in hell forever." Her redundancy evoked terror and she added a declarative, "No!"

No, everlasting, thought Anna. Rose's last word hung in the air like a perverse iteration of Thomas Carlyle's everlasting negative. Anna realized Rose was diverting her despair for Azziz and her fears for Violet into angry grasping for a God who continued to elude her. Rose was not seizing Carlyle's *Everlasting No* so much as denying the *Everlasting Yea*. Anna reached out and touched the girl's hair which in the artificial light was the colour of sun-dappled honey. Rose gazed up at her with troubled deep amber eyes and Anna knew she was taking in more than she could process, feeling more than she could assimilate. Then Rose smiled her curious downcast smile. The soft down on her cheeks caught the glow in the air and made her complexion luminous. She looked almost demure, like a pre-Raphaelite Madonna.

"Rose." Anna's solicitude made the word sound enchanted.

"Anna," said Rose. Her soft voice made Anna's name seem like a prayer.

"Please," said Azziz, he spoke to Anna in a resolute tone. "Please, will you hear me?"

"I will listen, Azziz."

"After surviving rendition, you understand, they sent me back to Afghanistan to work again as a translator for the Canadian forces. I had opportunities to intercept messages — that is what a translator does, he massages messages, turns linguistic structures into parallel codes."

"Azziz, save your energy."

"For what, so I can live ten minutes longer? I translated incorrectly, I betrayed Canadians and their Afghan colleagues time and again. People died. I let them die. I sent them to be slaughtered."

"Azziz," said Rose. "How can you be such opposite things? You describe doing evil but I know you are good. I don't understand."

"Sweet Rose, they are not opposites. Evil is the work of the devil — he doesn't even have to exist."

"Well, he doesn't," she affirmed. "But good people do." She seemed to find their discussion a relief from fear and suffering and the moral distraction of prayer.

"No," said Azziz. "Good things exist, like charity, excellence, beauty, love, many good things but not good people, not many, a few."

Anna was in no mood for clichés, even from the mouth of a man desperate to be lucid as he edged towards nothingness. "Surely people have a choice to be good. Charity might be evil if it were done for the wrong reasons or achieved the wrong ends. Excellence is a judgement. Beauty is how something is perceived."

'And love?" he said.

"Love is nothing."

"Nothing!"

"Nothing in itself. Its meaning is always determined by context. That is true of all words, perhaps, but love is a singular name for infinite kinds of experience."

"Ah, Dr Anna, perhaps you are right. I am tired now. I must rest."

"Azziz, there is no proof that you murdered innocents. A gunshot in a mirrored funhouse evoked horror. The horror may have resolved into false memories."

"I also have no proof I did *not*." His voice was weakened and hoarse from talking. "But why would I dissemble? Forgive me, Anna, I have shamed you deeply."

"Azziz, leave it to your God to deal with what happened. Your captors cannot absolve you; your crimes are their own. Your victims cannot forgive you; the dead cannot forgive. We, here, cannot exonerate you; we can only accept who we know you to be."

His eyes were wide open. Glazed and unblinking.

He seemed to have expired while she spoke.

He had, she hoped, found final acceptance. In the absolute silence surrounding them, she could almost believe he had found peace.

With the two longest fingers of her left hand, she softly closed his eyes. She reached out for the Qashqai bag and, lifting his head, placed the bag over Violet's coat and gently settled his head onto the folds of its sweetly naïve ancestral design.

Rising, she turned away and leaned her forehead against the granite panel concealing the elevator, feeling the cool of the stone. Suddenly, the stone trembled. The silent motion of the elevator had set vibrations through the wall so slight they were barely perceptible. She stood back as the massive door slid forward from the polished wall and swung open on its unseen hinges. Azziz stirred. Violet stood in the centre of the elevator in a bright pool of light, wide-eyed with excitement. Anna snatched her daughter up into her arms. She held the girl passionately, fiercely, whispering snippets of affection and wonder.

"Mommy," Violet protested, "you're choking me."

"Where were you, oh my God, are you all right, are you all right?"

"It was unpleasant up there so I escaped. Is Mr Azziz still sick? He looks awful." The little girl struggled out of her mother's arms and by the purity and force of her tiny presence displaced the brutalized Azziz as the centre of their subterranean world.

"Anna!" the revivified Azziz called in a voice that had turned hoarse and was drained of all energy. "It is time."

Anna took a firm grasp of her daughter's hand and drew her close as she moved back to Azziz's side.

"See, Azziz, Violet is back."

"Close my eyes again. I cannot bear the light."

"They are, Azziz, they are closed."

"Is Mr Azzad going to die?" asked Violet.

"No," said Rose.

"Perhaps," said Anna.

"Yes," said Azziz. "But not alone."

"Rose, take Violet away," said Anna.

"It is all right, Mommy, I know what death looks like. I have seen it before." Violet gazed directly at her mother. For the first time since Anna saw her playing in the walled-in garden, the little girl smiled.

# Chapter Eleven
# Details of a Life

Violet, whose real name was Anna, gazed serenely at the face of the dead man. She seemed unperturbed by the stillness that transformed the lucent depths of living skin into a waxen mask. Perhaps at four years and a cluster of months she had no comprehension of death and found nothing wondrous about a man who was alive in one instant, filled with pain and opinion, becoming an empty cadaver the next. Or perhaps she had an innate sense in which death struck her simultaneously as banal and repulsive and so her reaction came across as indifference, such as a ewe might show for her stillborn lamb, a raptor for its quivering quarry, a gamester for an exploded cyber combatant. Or possibly, Violet knew more of death than her mother could imagine and felt even less than was conceivably possible.

Anna drew Violet closer on the stone ledge but Violet pushed away. In the natural hermeneutics of reading her child's face, Anna had focussed on the wrong story. She was distraught by the loss of her friend who survived a brutalized life only to die needlessly, but Violet's inscrutable gaze overwhelmed her with terror. Observing her daughter's pitiless stare, a chill passed through her that was deeper and colder than death.

"Anna," Rose interrupted. "We have to cover him up. We can't stay here no matter what."

"He's not going to hurt you, Rose. He's not here any more."

"I have a mind that says he's gone but my feelings say he's not. I don't believe in ghosts but I'm scared of them."

"Saint Augustine would have approved."

"I don't know about him, but if he's a saint and he believes in ghosts, I'm inclined to think we're right, he and I, and you're wrong for not believing."

"You're *inclined* to believe? Where did you pick that up?"

"That's the way Azziz used to talk." She nodded in the direction of the corpse without looking at it. "Didn't you ever notice?"

"I did, but from him it sounded—" She paused, then, determined to avoid condescension, she said in a kindly voice, "quite *different*."

Violet, who was standing close but ignoring their conversation, took hold of the corner of her coat that was folded under Azziz's head and slowly drew it towards her. Anna noticed the girl was careful not to touch the corpse. When the coat was almost free she gave it a little tug and Azziz's head bumped down onto the Qashqai bag and lolled to the side. It seemed like a gesture of indignation which Violet ignored. She shook the coat out and put it on and did up the buttons. Her action was all quite deliberate and little girlish — her ignoring the dead man, her playing dress-up with her own clothing, her facial expression of focussed determination.

"Why don't we at least go into another room?" said Rose. "We can think better, there."

They moved to a different chamber of the luminous catacombs and settled on a section of stone where the moss was most luxuriant.

"Violet, tell us what happened," said Anna in a soothing voice.

"The elevator went up," said Violet.

"And then what? You told me it was unpleasant up there. What did you see?"

"I saw Sebastian."

"You did!" said Anna.

"You didn't!" Rose exclaimed at the same time.

"He didn't have a gun," said Violet. "He was hiding. He made me hide too. Then he sent me back down here again."

"I thought you escaped?"

"Well, I did escape, but he didn't."

"Why not?" said Anna.

"Anna, we don't want him down here, not if he's going to shoot us," said Rose.

"What happened is," Violet continued, "the elevator went up to the closet. It stopped, the door opened and closed, and then it went up farther and the door opened again into a tiny dark room and Sebastian was there and he told me to be quiet because he had spy holes where he could look down into the foyer, and you had to be very quiet because the sounds could leak through."

"Well," said Rose, "if someone opens the closet door, they'd be able to see the elevator shaft and they'll probably know we're down here."

"No," Violet explained, speaking slowly and carefully so Rose and her mother could follow. "When there's no elevator, the doors are locked. And anyway, Sebastian explained to me, there are two elevator cabinets, one on top of the other. They are exactly the same, they both have moving walls — that's so they can squeeze smaller to fit down the hole. They can also squeeze your guts out if Sebastian wants that to happen. So, when one cabinet is up in the dark room where he's hiding, the other is open in the foyer, just below. It looks like an empty closet. When the upper one comes down here, the other is hidden in the elevator shaft in the rocks below us.

It's a magic trick, only it isn't really magic. Sebastian likes to make imaginary puzzles into real places and things."

"Did he tell you that?" Anna asked. She tried to envision a magician's box with two compartments that slid into place behind a single door so that a rabbit could be locked in one compartment, the box could be shifted, and the door would open on the empty compartment, the hidden rabbit being presumed to have disappeared — the basic mechanism behind a child's magic-shop toy and some of Houdini's greatest illusions.

"Yes, he did."

"Did he tell you what *foyer* means?" Rose asked. "It's French."

"*Je le connais.*"

"You speak French!" Anna exclaimed.

"*Oui,*" said Violet. "*Je parle français comme une Québécoise ou comme une Parisienne. Celui que vous préférez.*"

"Who taught you?"

"It's there in my head. I could speak a lot more if I needed to. It comes when I want."

Rose seemed amused. "Me too," she said. "At the Centre, I would read cereal boxes. I can quote them *verbatim*!"

"I don't read it *into* my head," said Violet scornfully. "It's just there when I want it. Some words are the same in both languages, like *foyer*, *rendezvous*, *weekend*, *différence*, except with *différence* there's an accent and you say it differently. Some people say *différance* with an *a*, but they mean something else."

"Derrida," Anna mumbled. She knew with utter conviction, now, that Robert had violated their daughter's brain at birth. She had been invaded with manipulated DNA to formulate a computer module in her head. Even if she were the most precocious of children, she could not possibly have known about Derrida's notion of *différance*. Knowledge so esoteric and abstract in a child was inconceivable. She realized with certainty that her child was a hybrid of sorts, a cyborg creation of cellular evolution and biotechnology.

Raw information had been downloaded into Violet's brain without giving her the benefit of context. The innate linguistic structures were there. She had acquired vast quantities of knowledge. But the capacity for analysis hadn't developed and most cultural structures were beyond her experience. She couldn't possibly assimilate all that they'd jammed into her, and yet there was no indication that she was being externally managed. Most of the facts that she would ever acquire were already in her head, waiting for circumstances to call them forward. The more exposed to the world she became the more inexorably her mind would slip into neural chaos. Literally, she would go mad from too much reality.

"Violet," Anna said, "do you know what *prestidigitation* means?"

"Yes."

"Do you know what *legerdemain* means?"

"They both mean magic, not the supernatural kind, like sorcery, but more like what Sebastian does by making his house into a puzzle."

"What do you think about *hermeneutics*?"

"In relation to Biblical studies or literature?"

"Just the idea of interpretation — how would you interpret Noah's flood? Or the gifts of the magi?"

"The end of a failed experiment, the beginning of another."

"Interesting."

"Yes, it is. Water drowns and cleanses. Gold, frankincense, and myrrh are symbols."

"Of what?"

"It's hard to say."

"What is a *symbol*?"

"A symbol is an uncomplicated sign, implied and inferred."

Anna trembled with fear, with affection. She drew her daughter close to her side and held her so firmly the little girl began to quake before pulling away.

Rose seemed aroused by Violet's squirming from a kind of distracted lethargy induced by the death of Azziz, by bewilderment at why they were where they were, and by perplexity over the little girl's intellectual gifts.

"Anna, we have to go now," said Rose, as if she had suddenly grasped some new aspect of the danger they were in.

"No," said Violet emphatically. "Sebastian says we must wait here."

"Tell me more about Sebastian," said Anna. "Why is he hiding?"

"Because he was shot."

"Oh my God, is he hurt badly?"

"I think so."

"How badly?"

"I think he was shot in the heart, but he says that is his least vulnerable part. He is covered in blood on his hands and all over his clothes, but he says he's not going to die. He says he is watching to see when my father leaves because then he will come and get us. That's why he couldn't escape when I did."

"Robert is up there?"

"My daddy has a gun. Sebastian says he shot Mr Azziz. Sebastian does not have a gun, so he is waiting for my father to go away and we're supposed to wait too."

"But if he's been shot, he might die," said Rose.

"Rose," said Anna. "We sit tight. He quoted Humphrey Bogart about his infrangible heart. He's telling us he's not dying. Meanwhile, the three of us need to avoid Robert no matter what. Robert wants to eliminate me as a failed experiment — scientists are pathologically fastidious housekeepers. They don't take used lab animals home as pets, they put them down. Robert needs to capture Violet. He wants to observe her, to see where he went wrong. She and I are experiments of the same vintage, but my brain was fully formed, hers was not — her brain might assimilate her modified molecules in ways mine couldn't. Her brain might explode for want of perspective. Mine didn't. We are both redundant but she is of interest. I am detritus. As for you, Rose, when they fixed your dyslexia and implanted your memory, I have no doubt they left openings for future access. They must have; it is inevitable they would. You are the product of more than four years of progress in their machinations. They want you most of all; they need to probe your head."

"Not bloody likely," said Rose. "They're not getting in there again, even if they stop me from reading and take my memory away. They're not getting any of us, nor Sebastian either, since he didn't kill Azziz."

"Here's what I need you to do, then, Rose. I need time to think. I need you to take Violet and curl up on the moss and sleep. If Robert has removed a micro-computer from my head because it couldn't compete with an unco-operative brain, or if he's put in an updated one like yours which my brain refuses to assimilate — no matter, I need what this place is supposed to provide, absolute solitude. Could you do that for me, could you sleep for a while?"

Without saying a word, Rose took Violet by the hand and led her into the next chamber, farther away from Azziz's corpse, and settled in for a purposeful nap.

Anna smiled like a benediction and began to think.

She thought about Sebastian.

Although their conversation seemed a long time ago, Anna recalled Sebastian telling her how the British Library in London had served as the model for his own fantastical library. He told her their new quarters on Euston Road was his inspiration. While she had never visited the place, she was familiar with its design. People had assured her no image could match the actual experience of a sheer-sided multi-storey glass building rising up inside the shell of another, quite different, building so that the stacks with their seemingly endless and ancient arrangements of books, a quarter of a billion in total, were contained within an envelope of emptiness that was enclosed by a functional contemporary superstructure, the whole being an optical paradox of space and solidity, age and modernity, scholarship and imagination.

The exterior of Sebastian's vast house was much as it had been when he inherited it, a red brick façade with porches and parapets and a mansard roof, but behind this was a single layer of rooms connected one to another with windows on one side and on the other the occasional small room to create the illusion of depth. Taken together, this antiquated layer provided concealment for the phantasmagoric library which was his free-standing version of the towering warren of books exposed behind glass in the British Library. The star-shaped room was ironic, a reflecting room in which he had no reflection. The room of different-sized doorways was also ironic, the openings had no doors and led into passages that ultimately came back to the same room — she suspected that room had an earlier history; perhaps it was designed by Sebastian's mad Uncle Leicester. The wall sconces were originally gas. Going a step further, she realized that this illuminated space deep in the earth was somehow an ironic complement to the sinister aspect of his mirrors and doors and labyrinthine passageways in the stacks that housed his books. He must have intended this subterranean refuge as his one true sanctuary, a place to read and think with complete invisibility. It was only a prison through the force of circumstance. It was only a crypt because their mutual friend had expired.

She had been thinking of Carlyle. Sebastian had mentioned the nineteenth century Scottish satirist in passing. This entire edifice was Sebastian's version of *Sartor Resartus*, Carlyle's extravagant metafiction, 'The Tailor Retailored', which illuminated the world of German clothier-philosopher, Diogenes Teufelsdröckh, as he collapsed and conflated all manner of genres and conflicting judgements into a wondrous existential absurdity that exposed the nature of truth by confounding the possibility that it existed. It was a lovely example of *poioumenon*, a term she savoured that described fiction concerned with its own creation.

In his own curious way, Sebastian had created a work like Carlyle's *Sartor Resartus*, that belonged in the company of Sterne's *Tristram Shandy*, Nabokov's *Pale Fire*, novels by Lessing, Fowles, Rushdie, Golding, and, most significantly, Samuel Beckett. Sebastian did not write, but he deployed books as a creative act, the object of which was to be only itself. She recalled her suggestion that it was his version of the Sistine Chapel. No, it was his novel, one never meant to be read, absurdist and wonderfully vain. But? Was he Teufelsdröckh, the brilliant fool, or Carlyle, his canny creator?

Having herself negotiated an esoteric and improbable inspiration for his project as well as its architectural mechanics, Anna pondered their present dilemma, hoping a resolution would spring to mind. As soon as she relaxed, it did.

Nearly a decade in the past, long before she met Robert, she had visited her Italian boyfriend's family home in Siena. His father had shown her an ancient corner cabinet and when he opened its doors she was astonished to look down a deep shaft and see in the glittering gloom at the bottom the surface of a stream. Carved into solid rock deep beneath the old city of Siena was a maze of channels that flowed from the tilted campo in the centre of town, forming an intricate cistern for the great houses to draw water.

Anna couldn't know that during the 1820s, before Carlyle began writing *Sartor Resartus*, the wealthy citizens of Rosedale near Balfour Ravine in the heart of Toronto had sponsored a project similar to Siena's. They privately commissioned a network of channels to be carved out by miners imported from Wales, to provide an abundance of deep spring water for houses on top of the Don Valley escarpment, where wells were prone to run dry. When water was eventually piped in from reservoirs, the water mines were abandoned and their shafts were sealed over, but in older homes like the Kroetsch's, access was still possible.

From the subterranean flumes of Siena and their historical legacy as a megalithic oddity, Anna's mind leapt to the clear taste of the water she had held in her mouth to salve the parched lips of Azziz. It had the crisp taste of purity. It was flowing gently towards the central chamber. She also recalled Violet's description of the elevator's magical construction. She got up carefully so as not to disturb Violet or Rose in the next chamber. She walked by the corpse of her friend, stopping to close his grotesquely gaping mouth as *rigor mortis* began to set in. Shuffling a little further, she leaned over and touched the limestone wall perpendicular to the elevator where the water disappeared at her feet into a small tumble of rocks. She could feel splashing so quiet through her fingertips that the surface gurgle erased the sounds. She turned and looked back into the illuminated chambers, recognizing in the textures of the rock that had been washed to an eerie softness the marks of stone-cutting adzes and chisels and, remembering Siena, she realized they were in a network of passages carved out long before Sebastian turned them into his *sanctum sanctorum*. These linked chambers channelled water. Sebastian's magical elevator had to shrink to accommodate the dimensions of a chute already in place, providing access to the tunnels below.

There had to be another way in, another way out.

She stepped into the open elevator cabinet and stamped on the floor. Despite being covered in squares of polished granite, it sounded hollow. Anna removed her belt and using the prong from the buckle she scraped at a seam between pieces of granite. The grout yielded reluctantly but soon she had an entire square which easily pried up so that she could see narrow metal joists and the inverse side of a ceiling below. She slid the square to one side and carefully pried a ceiling panel free and let it fall gently to the floor below. The motion triggered a sensor and the cabinet beneath her was instantly illuminated.

She went back out past the cadaver of Azziz and scooped Violet into her arms, rousing Rose with a prodding foot into the girl's ribs.

"Hey, what the hell, Agnes," said Rose, disoriented and annoyed by the disturbance.

"We're leaving," said Anna.

When they got to the hole in the elevator floor, Anna unceremoniously dropped down into the cabinet below, then reached up and received Violet into her arms. She braced her hands under Rose's feet and lowered her until Rose was able to slide the slab of granite flooring back into place. Unless someone knew what they were looking for, they would be unlikely to find their means of escape.

"Now what?" said Rose as she settled onto the granite floor.

"Is Mr Azziz still dead?" asked Violet.

"Yes, Honey, he is," said her mother.

Violet knew that death is *forever*. Forever was even more abstract than death. How could she relate such a fact to her own experience? Facts were just words, however indelibly imprinted, however intricately cross-referenced, until they became memories, until they became hues in the infinite spectrum of colours accessible through human perception. Anna realized when Violet said *she had seen death before*, she had been blasé because dying would have seemed to children so small an evocative episode, but nothing more than that, especially if quite a few died. Some children must have sickened and turned unnaturally still and been taken away. Others would have left the Centre in exuberant high spirits. Some children came back while others did not. In a world as limited as Violet's, how else could she interpret *forever* except as a period of arbitrary duration to be avoided if possible? Anna was chilled by the metaphysical simplicity that Violet could not possibly grasp — death was an irrevocable transition from something to nothing, being to non-being, time to eternity (which for Anna meant timelessness; for the religious and the childlike, it meant *forever from now*). Dying and not death were the ultimate singularity. Death had no meaning at all.

Anna opened the control panel and flipped several switches until the elevator door opened and they were confronted by a dark chamber with rough-hewn walls and water to one side streaming down a smooth angled surface which reflected an eerie light and illuminated in the down-stream direction the gaping entrance to a tunnel that disappeared into absolute darkness. This had to lead out. The water had to go somewhere. This tunnel had to have provided entry for stone workers and stone masons, miners and artisans.

Anna led the way with Violet in her arms and Rose followed a half pace behind, clinging to the sleeve of Anna's blouse. Soon the only illumination was the diminishing hole of light behind them, which cast the flowing runnel of water at their feet into a shimmering ribbon but projected nothing of the tunnel ahead except blackness. Anna shuffled, not daring to lift her feet from the packed debris beside the stream, as she followed the soft sounds of moving water. Periodically, by the altered echoing of their own noise she knew they were passing tributary tunnels and overhead shafts. Several times she lost her footing, but Rose caught hold of her and she didn't fall or relinquish her grip on Violet.

Even Violet said nothing. The hush of their breathing seemed a violation of something eerily sacrosanct about the otherwise absence of stimuli. They might have been floating through space or drifting on the surge of undersea currents, so little did their movements relate to their progress as they moved towards a gentle zephyr of fresh air.

Anna knew the tunnel must be heading east in the direction of a ravine off the Don Valley since water had to run downhill and there was nowhere else for it to go. Nearly imperceptible reverberations in the pitch blackness gradually coalesced into a staccato rush of distant traffic and she had a sufficiently jaundiced sense of Toronto to realize the implied speed and volume of vehicles meant it must be midday. Traffic was notoriously snarled for most waking hours and sparse only at night. She instinctively wanted to confirm her conjecture and raised her left wrist in the darkness, although she had not worn a watch for several months, since they took it away on her arrival at the Vivuscorps Centre. She could see movement. Trying not to disturb Violet who was still asleep, nestled against her shoulder, she waved her hand in front of her eyes to confirm the faintest presence of light.

"Rose, do you see it?" she whispered.

"What? No, yes, that must be daylight ahead. It's like a fine mist. My God, I thought we'd been swallowed up by the earth, eaten by monsters, drowned in the belly of the whale."

"You can't drown in a whale," said Violet who, awakened by their voices, wriggled against her mother's embrace, struggling to be released so she could walk on her own.

Within a few minutes they were at the side of an oval slit large enough for a person to squeeze through standing up, but to address it directly necessitated stepping into water sluicing past up to the knees, and it was blocked by horizontal iron bars embedded in the rock at six-inch intervals.

"Now what?" said Rose, her tone indicating confidence that Anna would resolve their dilemma. Then suddenly she exclaimed, "Look! Out there. I know where we are. Holy cow, we did it, Annie. All we've got to do is break through the bars and we're free."

"If we can't," said Violet, "we'll have to go back."

Rose ignored her pessimism. "We're in the woods of a ravine that opens down onto Bayview and the Parkway," she said. "I used to sleep out around here when the weather was warm enough, before they sent me to Temagami, before I met Agnes. There's a lot of rubble and stuff below, so the water just flows under it into the valley."

Anna was thinking. The rock debris blocking their exit wasn't naturally in place. It reduced what must have been the entry for whoever tunnelled through, the Welsh miners, the stone grinders, and tradesmen. The path through the darkness had been smooth and level, it could have accommodated small-wheeled vehicles for extraction of rock, the delivery of granite.

She knew nothing of the sedimentary upheaval of the Georgian Bay Formation half a billion years earlier that penetrated the Sunnybrook Drift in recent geological time, when humans were still becoming human, and provided a stable and relatively tractable medium for excavation and tunnelling. She knew nothing of the miners from Wales or the original purpose of the hidden passageways, but logic dictated that such a vast and intricate enterprise must have taken many workmen with donkeys or oxen — this was done long before machines were devised for such digging.

She stepped into the icy flow and peered out through the bars. The water slipping past her knees poured into crevasses in a slide of rubble piled on the outside, against the opening, overgrown with dense layers of mosses and lichen enriched from the waters below. At least two centuries past, the entryway had been blockaded, leaving the oval slot to prevent water from building up, and barred over to stop subterranean access by renegade adventurers to the finest private homes in the fledgling nation. Nothing had been disturbed in recent years. Sebastian's renovations, such as they were, must have been accomplished entirely by access from his house. Even the granite slabs had to have been lowered through the elevator shaft — all to create an inspired emptiness, like Claes Oldenburg's 'Placid Civic Monument' in Central Park, except Oldenburg had his hole filled in and smoothed over by gravediggers while Sebastian filled his with light.

Anna grasped one of the horizontal bars with both hands and focussed all her strength on trying to make it move but it was unyielding. With trembling hands, she released her grip and clambered out of the stream, stamping to release water from her red slippers.

"Are we still prisoners?" asked Violet.

"No, Sweetheart," said Rose. "Your mommy will look after us. Won't you, Annie?"

"Yes," Anna responded, then lapsed into petrified silence.

Time passed, no one spoke. Anna's mind seemed empty.

"I can get out," said Violet, interrupting the quietness. "I'm quite little, you know. I can squeeze through."

"And where would you go?" said Rose.

"Nowhere, I guess. But at least I'd be free."

"You can't go by yourself," said Anna, feeling absurdly confused by the choice of having her four-year-old daughter trapped inside the earth or free but alone in an urban wilderness.

"What month is it?" said Rose "Is it May?"

"Yes," said Anna, puzzled but not surprised by the *non sequitur*.

"Good," said Rose. "C'mon Violet, let's see if we can slip you out of here."

Before Anna could stop her, Rose had hoisted Violet in the air and stepping into the stream was holding her close to the bars.

"No," Anna screamed, but it was too late. Violet easily squiggled through and clambered onto the rocks on the other side. Sunshine gleamed on her dark brown hair and her blue eyes flared luminescent against her porcelain complexion. Anna's heart throbbed with affection and fear. She reached through the bars to grasp hold of her daughter's small hands.

"Stay there," she urged. "Don't move."

"Annie," said Rose. "My friend Solomon lives up the hill, just over a bit. He stays there most of the winter, under a tarp with snow piled up, but since he's got really old, they make him stay in a hostel, except now, if it's May, he'll be back there again. He can help. Violet's got to go and get him. You've got to let her go."

"Solomon who?" Anna demanded. This was the first she'd heard of him.

"He sometimes looked after me when I was little whenever he could. Usually, he's always alone except for his friends, Immanuel and Becket."

Disregarding the paradox, Anna realized there were no options. Reluctantly she released her daughter's hands.

"Violet," said Anna, "do you think you can do that? Can you go and get the man and bring him here?"

"I'm sure I can," Violet said.

"Okay," said Rose. "You see that path over there? You follow it up, not down, and you'll come to a camp with lots of bottles and cans and a blue tarp strung like a tent over some dead branches. Don't you go in. You just stand outside and call for Solomon. You tell him Rose needs him real bad, okay, and you bring him here."

"Okay," said Violet and without looking back she made her way across the tumultuous mound of moss-slick rocky debris to the path and vanished into the dense undergrowth.

An interminable ten minutes later, she reappeared, with a bearded derelict following her, a stooped figure hardly recognizable as human were it not for the fact he walked on two feet, which were wrapped in rags, and wore tattered filthy remnants of clothing. His face was weathered and deeply creased. He leaned on a cane or walking stick. As he moved across the boulders, he repeatedly poised it on the rough surfaces with a delicacy that suggested he was its accomplice, not dependent on it for aid.

When he reached the barred opening, he set the stick down and gently pushed the little girl to the side. "Immanuel," he said, addressing the head of a dog carved onto a burl at the top of the stick. "Stay. You stay. Now, Violet, you watch him for me 'cause he likes to wander."

Then he turned and peered thoughtfully into the dark cleft among the rocks. He grasped an iron bar to draw himself closer. Then he addressed the darkness.

"Good afternoon, ladies, I can't see you very well. Is one of you Rose? My little friend here says you need assistance and it would be my honour to oblige. Is it you, Rosie?"

"Solomon," said Rose in a confessional tone. "It's me, it is." She sounded curiously shy.

"Amazing."

"Can you help us?"

"Rosie, where have you been? And who is your colleague?"

"She's Anna, and we need to get out of here," said Rose.

"Well, then, let me consider," said Solomon. "So, now, let me see. The rocks had to be settled before the bars were inserted. That means they can be removed. There must be cement of some sort. Now, then, my grip is arthritic so here is my jackknife, his name is Thomas à Becket, that's with one T, not two, the martyr, not Mr Samuel Beckett, the Irishman, and if you break him, I expect you'll get me another, although we wouldn't share the same history, would we? What I think you should do is poke around at the end of this rod, the one in the middle, and find where the cement was put in. The cement will be coarse so it blends with the rock, but it will be old, so it will likely crumble with a bit of prodding. It would have been applied reaching in from the outside, and it will be in a groove shaped like an upside-down capital L to create a lock with the rock, and only on one side; on the other there will just be a hole. Find that L and dig away. Once you gouge out a few chunks of cement, then you can remove the rod by lifting it up and pulling it your way, simple as that, and then you may join young Violet and me and Immanuel out here in the sunshine."

Rose took the knife called Becket from the old man and without thinking stepped back and handed it to Anna, who followed Solomon's instructions and had an iron rod loose and removed in minutes. She helped Rose to squeeze through the gap and then clambered through herself. She scrambled straight over to Violet and gave her a huge hug, then turned to Solomon and hugged him so hard he wheezed with embarrassment.

"My, you do smell good," he said.

"I don't," Anna exclaimed.

"And you smell terrible, old man," said Rose.

"Cheeky little bitch. That's God's own perfume. Now the three of you, get on out of here. Don't tell anyone you saw me, and bless you for making my day very special."

Solomon took his treasured jackknife, folded its scratched blade, which had been honed to stiletto narrowness, into the worn wooden handle. He polished the wood against a trouser leg and when the other two were distracted, he handed it back to Anna.

"Slip this into the side pocket of that little skirt of yours," he said in a barely audible whisper. "Give it back when you can. You watch out for Rosie now, you hear. Watch out for Rosie. She's very special. None of us are who we seem."

She looked for an indication of his intent but the glint in his eye was impossible to decipher. He picked up his walking stick, addressing it as he adjusted the large walnut carving of a terrier's head, an Airedale, to the curve of his hand. "Come now, Immanuel, it is imperative, categorically, we take our constitutional, isn't it, old fellow?" Without further ceremony, he turned and hobbled across the rocks and moss to the path and disappeared out of sight.

"Thank you, Rose," said Anna. "I like your friend."

"Me too," said Violet. "But he talks to his cane, which is a bit unusual, isn't it?"

"It's his buddy," said Rose. "His confrère, his accomplice, and his confessor."

"It's not alive," said Violet definitively.

Anna was disturbed that Violet seemed unable to imagine Solomon's walking stick as a dog called Immanuel. Probably a terrier, probably an Airedale.

Rose said: "He looked after me when I was going through puberty. He was fierce and no one messed with either of us."

"Really?"

"Really."

"Didn't anyone worry about an old man with a girl?"

"Annie, we were so low-profile the agencies didn't notice us. We never seemed improper. That's what welfare doesn't like, *seeming* improper. And when we were in public we always kept moving. They don't like people like us being still for too long."

"But you eventually left him."

"He told me I got too grown up for us to be friends any more and then I got sent off to camp."

"Rose, Rose, go after him. Thank him, tell him how important he was in your life."

"He still is, Annie. He knows it and I know it. We don't have to say it. He sees that I'm doing well and I have you as a friend. He taught me a lot of things, you know what I mean? He would ramble on about the Categorical Imperative over and over and I thought he meant God, but I listened because I liked his voice and I didn't know what he was saying. Now, of course, I remember everything. It's all on file in my head like a bunch of old photographs, but it still doesn't mean very much. He'd often talk about Hair Doctor Kant and a Marshall called Mr McLuhan."

"How would he know about Kant?" Anna asked, not incredulous, given how well-spoken he was. "Was he a scholar?"

"I think he was a shoemaker. He worked in a little shop on Dundas St., but he sure knows a lot about books. He came over from the old country. Sometimes he said Poland, that was the country that made him; and sometimes he said Germany, that was the country that taught him; sometimes he said Israel, that was the country that saved him; and the United States, that was the country that nearly destroyed him, he said, by assimilation, he said. Canada was the country that left him alone. He had a family but he lost them and that's when he knew for sure nothing was real. Those are the important details of his life."

"He doesn't have an accent," Anna observed.

"When you have lived in so many languages, he used to say, they all sound the same in your head, so you have to live within each as if it were the only one you've ever known."

"What happened to his family?"

"I think they were lost in America."

"Did he ever say how?"

"No, he never did. She might have left him, they might have been killed in a fire, or maybe they just disappeared. Life is how you see it. He'd say that a lot. *Life is how you see it*, Rosie. 'Marshall McLuhan told me that,' he'd say. Then he'd argue with himself. 'No,' he'd say. 'It was Immanuel Kant. And Friedrich Nietzsche taught me to know when I was beaten and then Martin Heidegger told me not to accept it. And a North African Frenchman taught me to smile.' Sometimes he'd say the Frenchman's name was Albert Camus, who thought nothing had meaning but everything mattered, and sometimes he'd say it was that guy Derrida I've heard you talk about, who thought everything had meaning but nothing mattered. It didn't make sense at the time."

"Does it now?" asked Violet, ingenuously. "It doesn't to me." Violet seemed to have an uncanny grasp of their esoteric conversation, but confidence enough to admit limitations.

"No," Rose cheerfully confessed. "But I remember those names like they were kids in my school."

"Did you go to school, Rose?" The proposition seemed strange to Violet. Rose must have appeared wild and free.

"A little, here and there."

The three of them were sitting on the rock slide, with water rushing through the boulders and rubble beneath them. The sun shone fully on their faces, making them look curiously pristine and innocent. The occasional car passed through the ravine below, along Bayview. Far down in the Don River Valley a steady stream of traffic on the Parkway filled the air with the awkward swooping noises of automotive machinery in motion.

"Who is Immanuel Kant to you?" Rose asked. "He seems pretty important."

Anna sighed with relief to be at least for a moment on surer ground. "Well," she said, "there were thinkers called Empiricists who figured everything we know comes through our experience, and there were the Rationalists who thought that our reason shapes all that we know. Then along came Herr Doktor Professor Immanuel Kant two hundred years ago and he combined the two approaches by arguing that both sides were right, saying that we only know what we experience through categories of reason, simple as that, but at the same time he argued both sides were wrong since there is a categorical imperative that governs existence by moral laws beyond either reason *or* experience."

"Kant sounds like a guy who couldn't make up his own mind, so he made up everyone else's," said Rose. "No wonder Solomon talked about him so much. He made being human impossible to understand by explaining how simple it was to be human."

"Kant describes how we *interpret* reality through filters that impose structures on our experience." Anna wanted to go on, to describe the structural linguistics of Ferdinand de Saussure, the structural anthropology of Claude Lévi-Strauss, the cultural commentaries of Roland Barthes and Jacques Lacan. She restrained herself.

"So, like having a computer inside your head. Now we're getting somewhere," Rose exclaimed. The fact that Rose made the connection, offering an observation rather than asking a question, sent a chill through

Anna. "But if everything seems to be the way the computer says it is" — Rose seemed unintentionally to be critiquing the notion of categorical imperatives and positing the post-structural response — "and not the way it actually is," she continued, "the world isn't real."

"It is, but not the way we experience it."

"Annie, I don't want to live in an unreal world," Rose declared plaintively. "If I've got modified DNA in my head, it means what's happening isn't happening at all."

"We all experience augmented reality." Anna tried to be reassuring. "According to Kant, we're programmed by structures of consciousness — it's just that not all of us are controlled by algorithms and micro-machines."

"I don't like this at all. I don't understand."

"Listen, look, let's say every one of us experiences time and space as duration and dimension — time passes, geography contains us — but that's all in our minds. If we weren't conscious of time from some point within it, it wouldn't exist. If we aren't thinking about space, it contains only itself, so it doesn't exist either. Time and space are mental constructs. They're us, imposing our minds on the world. That's what we do, that's who we are."

"If we imagine that time is passing and space is a place, we make them exist. Neat, really neat. You and Violet and I make everything be what it is."

"We make it what we perceive it to be, which may not be what it is at all."

"But what if my computer brain filters out the good parts?"

"Or makes the bad parts better," said Violet, who had been listening intently, apparently trying to make sense of their fugitive dialectics.

"So long as no one can access your implant from outside," said Anna, "you're no different from anyone else, either of you, except you have remarkable photographic memories and an illimitable capacity for facts."

"What about you?" said Violet. "Do you have a mechanical brain?"

Anna shuddered. "If I do, it doesn't work very well."

"Because you can think?" Violet asked.

"Because she can think in poetry," said Rose.

"What does that mean?" Violet challenged her, peeved at apparently missing the point.

"My mind makes connections," said Anna. "Between armpits and toads."

"You're funny. So how come we don't wear e-glasses?" said Violet. "Everyone else does. Except Solomon, he didn't, and Sebastian, he doesn't. Is that why they're strange?"

"Azziz did, but not all the time," said Rose.

"Well, he doesn't need them now," said Violet. "He's dead."

Anna flinched, but Rose seemed not to notice.

"People get addicted to having micro-computers in front of their eyes," said Anna. "The next logical step is to put them inside everyone's head. That's Robert's dream."

"I don't understand," said Violet.

"Most people want to avoid their own minds," said Anna. Violet and Rose both looked puzzled. Anna realized, puzzlement had become the default disposition for Rose. For Violet, it was equanimity. "People want e-glasses to filter reality for them so they don't have to think. Kant can, but they can't. They just connect facts. If they can dispense with the glasses, so much the better."

"For who?" said Rose. "For whom?"

"I've never worn glasses," said Violet.

"You and I don't need them," said Rose. "We've got computers in our heads."

"No," said Violet in a small strident voice. "I think you are wrong. I am exactly like my Mummy — we just think very well."

"And I am like Solomon," said Rose. "I'm filled up with information but I can't sort it out and perhaps it will make me go crazy insane."

"Maybe you already are," said Violet, offering her rare and sinister smile.

None of them laughed. They sat very still, close to each other. They listened as the gentle wise ruined old man crashed through dense underbrush up the hill, moving away from them with Immanuel, going for his daily constitutional, scavenging for food, and then they listened to the sounds of interminable traffic swishing over pavement on the Parkway below.

## Chapter Twelve
## The Life of a Woman

Sunshine flared through the wind-blown trees rising from the edge of the ravine on the southwest, sending ripples of light across their faces. Rose and Violet seemed already to have forgotten being imprisoned in the catacombs behind them. Violet appeared more animated than usual, frolicking with the mindless delight of a bee among flowers, while Rose preened herself in the glow of the sun like a prize geranium. Anna's mood was not so harmonious. She was grievously aware of Azziz in his luminescent tomb, she was filled with concern for Sebastian, wounded and surrounded by mirrors and books, and she was breathless with trepidation as she considered Robert and his henchmen looming like raptors, waiting for them to appear in the open. Squinting at her charges with their sun-dappled faces and innocent airs, the gnawing fear that she'd lose them, the fear that they'd slip like a lost dream into the past they'd escaped from, filled her with dread. Her joy in their company deepened her distress.

 She could hear the city but she could not see it. Their seclusion in an urban ravine was illusory. They were exposed to the sky and it was only a matter of time before random surveillance would select them from the masses of data being processed to serve one civic function or another and their location would be picked up by Vivuscorps. She had never before paid much attention to invasions of privacy as drones and computers managed their collective behaviour, staggered traffic, directed emergency services, and generally kept watch for patterns of suspicious behaviour. For the most part, no one complained. Drones, so small they couldn't be perceived by the naked eye, were ubiquitous instruments of efficient civility, but their effectiveness was determined by available light. Larger drones, which generated their own illumination, could usually be seen and evaded. After nightfall, Anna and her little cohort would move anonymously out of the woods and through the streets, unfortunately with no safe destination in mind.

 Anna shrank from the sunlight that felt like it was searing her face. Edging away from Violet and Rose, she slipped into the deep shadows of an ancient renegade willow. Vivuscorps monitors would register nothing suspicious about the other two basking in the sun — sisters, perhaps, or a very young mother and her daughter (who didn't seem to notice that Anna was off to the side and obscured).

Anna settled back in the shade. She felt a chill from the earth running through her and she pressed her arms close to her sides, trying to contain her own warmth. As a coping strategy, she leapt in her mind to abstraction. She contemplated the geometrics of language and thought, then shook her head sharply and the words of her rumination scattered, but not before Einstein had displaced Euclid and she recognized time as the missing factor in explaining the dimensions of consciousness and understanding Robert's struggle to control it.

Of more immediate concern, she needed to understand what Robert had done to the minds of these girls. Both were prodigies, the older with too much experience in the world, the other with not enough. They were isolated in the present — Violet with insufficient memories to anticipate the future and Rose with a past that no longer coincided with the information crowding her mind, leaving her equally unable to anticipate what lay ahead. Anna would resume her place in time if they survived, while Rose and Violet would not. Her mind was sufficiently formulated before Robert's experiments began that she was the least malleable, the most expendable, and, she assumed, the greatest liability to his success. She would die first.

She retreated into metaphysics. She might not be Robert's peer in science and technology, but she knew aspects of the human mind that were apparently beyond his reach. He had been obsessively concerned with the relations between language and thinking. This seemed plausible for a researcher trying to quantify consciousness. He had been morbidly intrigued by the ways that words signalled differently in speech and in print. She realized this was to formulate equations between words and their function in order to build his diminutive molecular machines that would reduce cerebral activity to the wholly predictable.

She urgently wondered, was thought a phenomenon generated by language that formulated in the mind to be grammatically, rhetorically, poetically meaningful? Or did thinking stimulate consciousness in some sort of subliminal mystical sanctified machination of neurons that translated into linguistic coherence? Neuroscientists might argue that higher-order consciousness, which characterized *homo sapiens sapiens*, was inseparable from language acquisition. But did that mean language and thought appeared simultaneously? How did this ultimately bear on which took precedence, writing or speech? If thoughts don't exist in themselves, written down were they only as holy as the words of their origin?

Julian Jaynes argued there was no contest. It was writing that released us from the limitations of the bicameral mind before its two sides joined forces and gave birth to the branch of our species that *knows that it knows*, a characteristic perhaps unique in the universe. Jaynes at best offered a metaphor, no more authentic than the account of language acquisition in *Genesis*. Plato before him had not been so facile, although his *pharmakon* favoured speaking over writing, while Derrida, Jaynes's contemporary over two thousand years after Plato, by not buying into its premises rendered the argument about precedence pointless.

Grounded in philosophy and literature, Anna believed speech was for the most part a way of keeping lines open between communicants. But print was intrinsically more valuable because it transcended the presence of the writer or the reader to stand in potential on its own. Writing endured, set upon a golden bough to sing, while speech was fastened to a dying animal and died with every dying breath.

She was frantic with irony. The source of Robert's power was writing, it was words encrypted in a quantifiable mode that connected consciousness with the cerebral machinery of his DNA implants. Anna lived among words. Wittgenstein argued that we cannot step out of language, there is nowhere to go. Without words, Anna wondered, does the universe vanish? Does a dog *know* cats exist? She tried to think without words. The notion was meaningless. It took words to think about thinking. But thoughts reduced to algorithmic equations became things and were subject to external manipulation.

She seemed far away from the others. The more secure she was among speculative thoughts, the more haunting the despair they obscured. Yet there was time, there was time for indecisions, for a hundred visions and revisions, before the taking of a toast and tea. She was curiously aware that her mind was functioning on many levels simultaneously, co-opting Yeats, quoting Eliot, thinking linguistics, feeling joy and dread, doubting, doubting her own existence, defiant, angry, contemplative, anxious, vibrantly alive.

She leaned forward and looked through mottled shadows at Violet and Rose, both sitting with their faces raised to the diminishing sunlight. They were sweet and trusting and content, waiting for her to lead them down into the valley or up onto the plateau, wherever she chose. She would know the right thing to do next, the right thing to say. Speech was like touching and they wanted to be touched.

But Anna remained silent and listened. Although the Parkway was beyond their sightline, she could tell by the increasing volume of noise that the day was rounding out as workers headed home to the suburbs. Violet was becoming restless, although Rose seemed content to loll in the sun until crisp. Anna had been ruminative because that's how she survived, but also to avoid the inevitable decision about what to do next. If they did not move soon, the evening would close around them and they would be marooned in the darkness with only the lights in the distance and the sounds of the city to affirm their location in the night.

Her mind worked furiously, trying to comprehend the shifts in Robert's thinking that had made him turn monstrous, trying to recover directness in her own thinking that might help them survive. She seemed far away from the hillside and the more secure she was among words, the more haunting the despair they obscured. She realized that the connections in her mind which no instrument could possibly replicate was the result of *intuition*, that elusive capacity to bend time and break it, as described by phenomenologists from Husserl and Heidegger to Merleau-Ponty and Sartre.

She thought of the mind as Borgesian. It was filled with endless volumes in orderly rows, with words on neat lines and numbered pages, and those words waited patiently, ready to burst into a huge explosive cacophony of discontinuous meanings, allusions, implications, intimations, assumptions, facts, figures, theories, and nonsense. In the mind was the potential for wisdom and passion — in computers, no matter how integrated with cerebral tissue, like Violet's, or facile with implanted information and restored memories, there was no place for wisdom or inspiration. Computers imposed on the brain offered communication without community, self-immersion without self-sufficiency, howling of the dogs, a muted soul, and no spirit.

She shook her head vigorously, shocked at her capacity for evasion. The real world, pressed in. The fact that Rose and Violet seemed unconcerned weighed heavily. She wished Sebastian were with them. She wanted to share her thoughts, to speak them aloud.

"Do you think Solomon will bring us food?" she called out to Rose from the shadows, disturbing the girl's reverie.

Rose looked around, startled, trying to see where the voice had come from. "We didn't suggest it, did we?" Rose responded as if the truth were self-evident. "So no, probably he won't. You wouldn't like what he eats, anyway. It's mostly from dumpsters, fleshed out with roadkill roasted over an open fire."

"Did you ever eat squirrel?" Violet asked. "We had squirrels at the Centre. They came in over the wall in our garden. I saw a dead one once in the sugar bush. He was a baby, he'd fallen out of a nest. We weren't allowed to touch it."

"Sometimes, I couldn't always tell what we were eating."

"Let's go," said Anna. She started to get up. She was stiff from sitting so long. "We can't stay here." She would have preferred to go nowhere, but remaining under the washed-out shade of an ancient willow wasn't an option.

"Why not?" said Violet. "We have been, so far, and nobody noticed."

"Well, for one thing, we'll starve," said Rose. "And if Sebastian is in trouble, we need to help him. I mean, if he's not badly wounded, he'll bandage himself. But if it's bad, maybe he can't get to the hospital. He could be a prisoner and can't get away. He might not realize being wounded is serious and that he could die. I think he probably thinks he's immortal."

"Oh, I'm sure he's sure he's immortal," said Anna. "He just might not believe it's of any significance. We'll go back for him soon." She was on her feet, balancing awkwardly while circulation evened her blood.

"Do you really think Robert will give up when it gets dark?" said Rose. "You make it sound like street hockey."

"It is a game, Rose, of course it is. A very nasty game. There's a good chance they'll search through The Cloisters and find nothing at all; that's part of Sebastian's illusion. They'll find only what he wants them to find. But then they'll follow the natural cycle. When it gets dark, they'll get tired. They'll take a 'time out'."

'Did Sebastian *want* them to find me and Azziz?" Rose asked.

Anna wondered but let it slide. Their primary concern was to rescue Sebastian before he succumbed to his wounds or, even more likely, to his vanity. Despite the possibility that he had in his confusion betrayed them, she worried about him. Even though he had a propensity for imprisoning her, she felt responsible.

"We should go down to The Greasy Spoon until after it really gets dark," said Rose.

"Good idea," Anna agreed.

"Why are we going there?" said Violet. "You said that's where Mr Azziz worked before he was dead."

"Yes, Sweetheart, he did. I know the man who hired him when Mr Azzad was having a bad time in his life."

"Not so bad as now," said Violet.

"No. I got him a job with the owner whose son was a student of mine."

"Were you a teacher?"

"Yes, I was, before you were born."

Violet's curiosity was apparently appeased. She led the way across the boulder slide to the path, then waited for Anna to indicate which direction. They walked up through Solomon's camp, which was strewn with the decrepit waste of urban life, much as Anna had anticipated from Rose's description. They stopped by a small stream to wash, brush off their clothes, and finger-comb their hair. Anna and Rose removed their outer clothing and scrubbed vainly at blood smears which left dark unrecognizable stains. Violet appeared to have no blood on her dress and had discarded her coat along the way. They wrung their clothes and shook out what wrinkles they could, then donned them damp and clambered up over the edge of the ravine, cut through parkland, and made their way onto a street that led out of Rosedale. They crossed Bloor St. and almost immediately they entered a rundown neighbourhood where bedsprings, soiled mattresses, and derelict appliances displaced the manicured lawns, trimmed hedges, and topiary they'd left a few blocks north.

When they reached The Greasy Spoon on lower Church, Rose was elected to go in and see if the owner was around. Farouk was a content and generous Egyptian who had come to Canada at the time of the Suez crisis, the second or third one, and he had prospered, having put three sons and four daughters through university without a single anti-social incident among them. His wife, who was also from Cairo, was a dentist. She lived in Vancouver.

Farouk beamed hospitably as he rushed out to greet Anna and Violet. "Yes, of course, Professor Winston, you must come in. And the little girl, of course." He seemed not to notice that Anna's hair was in tangles, her blouse stained, and her skirt clumsily ripped across at mid-thigh, nor did he remark on the contrast with Violet, who appeared rumpled perhaps, but as if she had been prepared that way by professionals for a photo-shoot as a fashion accessory in *Vogue*.

Farouk led them to a booth near the back where Rose was already settled in. The few other customers paid them no attention.

"Rose tells me you are temporarily extremely without money," said Farouk. "You must have a good meal. I will make you my specialty hot hamburger sandwich with brown gravy and real mashed potatoes, and then we will talk."

After they ate, Anna explained as gently as possible that Azziz was dead. Farouk wept openly.

"He was such a very nice man," said Farouk. "He worked very hard. He was very quiet. He had a very difficult life."

"You were good to him, Farouk. He had nobody else."

"Yes, even my car, I loaned him my car. I don't trust my children to borrow my car. We will take care of the funeral as a business expense. Where is he now? Where is the car?"

"We will get your car back, Farouk. No harm has come to it. It is parked in Rosedale."

"Good, that is a very good neighbourhood."

"His body is underground." She had trouble explaining that Azziz had been shot, that his corpse was hidden in a subterranean cavern, and that there might be men with guns who would prevent its retrieval, all this in Canada, in Toronto, in Rosedale.

How he died seemed less important to Farouk than what happened to his corpse.

"He is buried underground, that is good. Were gentlemen there to wash his body? Did they do it an uneven number of times? Is he shrouded and lying on his right side? Has he been covered with earth? What other bodies are also buried in that place? Who owns the property, is the owner devout?"

The only thing to do was to lie; that is what his religion demanded.

"He is looked after, Farouk. We will go there when it's thoroughly dark just to be sure."

Anna was uncomfortable with overt displays of religious obeisance. She had little interest in funerals of any sort, agreeing with philosophers from Socrates to Sartre that once you are dead, that should be an end to it, the rest is just housekeeping. Allowing the illusion of acceptable practice made her uneasy. Leading Farouk to think the body had been honoured as Sharia demanded was a desecration of sorts. She did not enjoy religious charades.

"As you said," Anna noted, "he had a difficult life — although that makes it no less tragic that his death was so pointless."

"Pointless? Surely, he was not in disgrace? He was not shot by police?"

"No, but there was no honour. His death was capricious and arbitrary." She searched for a more appropriate word. "It was mundane."

"Life is mundane, professor. Death is sacred. Our final act on this earth is holy no matter what is the cause. Death is destiny. Bullets are an instrument of fate. I will try to contact his family and say he died well."

"They are already dead."

"Oh no, his cousins live in Scarborough, that is where he grew up."

"Scarborough?" Anna was incredulous.

"I know where that is," said Violet. "It's on the map in my head." She seemed mesmerized by the plasticity of truth and their oblique conversation about dying.

"It is a giant suburb of Toronto," Rose observed. She also was not interested in the obsessions of religious ritual. Dead, much as she abhorred it, meant dead, nothing more.

Anna struggled to understand. If Azziz was from Scarborough, then the man she knew, the man she invented, was the avatar of a tortured imagination, a fiendish and pitiable delusion.

"Yes, yes, Azziz was from a Greek family in Scarborough. His name was Jason Oniropolos. He had a bicycle accident as a boy. He was badly scarred. He attended McGill University. He studied Arab languages. His closest family died in a terrible fire. They were all burnt up except him. He was spared; he was on holidays from his studies to celebrate Greek Christmas with his family, but at the last minute he left to finish essays back at McGill. After the fire, he fell into pieces. An Imam in Montreal helped him. He converted to Allah, blessed be his name, but when he tried to visit the United States of America he was arrested at the border because he was a radical convert. American border agency and Canadian border agency were very cruel. They turned him back. He fell into pieces again. He came to Toronto and lived on the streets where you found him and sent him to me. That is the end to his story."

While Anna tried to assimilate the details of Farouk's account, Rose leaned closer to Violet and observed, "His family got burnt up." Then she quoted from lines in her mind, "The incendiary temperature for human remains is 900 degrees Celsius."

"I knew that already," said Violet. "But artificial joints and dental implants burn differently and bone doesn't burn, it turns directly to ash."

Rose addressed Anna, "You said he was from Iraq, Annie. Were you wrong?"

"He was from Iran. He worked as a military translator in Afghanistan. He was tortured in Iraq."

"No," said Farouk. "You and Azziz made up stories."

"He was Persian." Anna was bewildered and angry. "He was Qashqai. He spoke Farsi. He studied in Moscow and in Baghdad. He killed people. He murdered women and children."

"Oh no. I have proof. I know I am right," said Farouk. "Upstairs in his room, there is a book, it is written."

"What is written, what book?"

"It is writing in his own hand. He was telling his story. I encourage him to write down everything who he was. I will get the book, just a minute, you wait."

"We have nowhere to go," said Rose. "Could I have some apple pie, please?"

"Me too," said Violet. "With chocolate ice cream."

"Yes, yes," said Farouk. "You help yourself, look after little girl, I will be right back quickly." He disappeared through the door by the kitchen and ascended the stairs in front of the washrooms.

By the time Rose had served out generous portions of pie with ice cream — she insisted on vanilla for both, while Anna refused, being too agitated to consider eating anything more — Farouk returned with a large black binder that he opened on the table, pushing the dishes to one side.

Anna tentatively turned the pages. They were in English. She scanned the awkward handwriting, gleaning enough to confirm Farouk's story. There was no doubt, this was an authentic and painfully thoughtful account. She closed the binder and gazed all around her, finding everything had somehow become strange. She felt dissociated from Rose, from Farouk, and especially from Jason Oniropolos, the man she had known as Azziz al Azzad. Only Violet seemed real to her, familiar and strange because she was both.

"He shared his story with you," Anna said. "Yet on his deathbed he confessed to a vile rendition of what he had previously told me. I had already helped him invent an alternative reality, Farouk. Why would he revise it with a false confession? Why not tell me the truth? Do you know where his Qashqai bag came from? He seemed to treasure it. I thought it was the key to his identity. How could I get it so wrong? How could he mislead me so drastically? It seems evil. It is a betrayal. Why did he need to do that?"

"He told me nothing, himself," said Farouk. "I read this book in his writing. You know, he did not talk very much. One day, after you and Rose had been here, upstairs, and after those two men came, he gave me the book. He also gave me his bag which belonged to his mother. It was all he had left for her. It still smelled of burnings, so I put the bag away and his book, I read it, I thought that was okay, I am not to be guard for it unless I know what I am guarding. When you called and he borrowed my car, we both knew he would die very soon, so I gave him his bag, but the book I placed with his clothes and shoes for his family if he did not come back. I think you were very important to Azziz. I will get you other keys if you will bring my car back, please. Then you stay here. No one is using his room."

"No," said Anna with a vehemence that surprised her. "Our friend Sebastian needs us. I must connect with my friend. We will stay with him." She softened her voice. "Thank you," she said. "You have been very kind."

"They will know we are there," said Rose.

"Not if we can get inside without being seen. It is the best place to hide. There are infinite shadows."

"You can't hide in a shadow if it's your own," observed Violet without taking her eyes from Farouk, whose dark complexion and voluminous moustaches seemed to fascinate her. As an Egyptian, he must have appeared swathed in stories about pyramids and mummies and the wrath of God when the Red Sea closed over his people.

As Anna and Rose walked slowly up Church Street in the dimming light with Violet between them, holding their hands, Anna thought about Jason Oniropolos. His name struck her as curious. Glancing east as they crossed Bloor, she had an epiphany. On the other side of the viaduct, Bloor St. turned into The Danforth, Little Greece, with its plethora of restaurants featuring souvlaki, tzatziki, feta, and ouzo. While her Greek was meagre, she thought *Oniropolos* meant *dreamer*. Jason: gathering fleece. Of course, it was a pseudonym, a pen name. Why had she automatically accepted the authority of his text over the spoken words they had shared? Her perseverations on the matter, on the rock slide in the ravine, surged into consciousness. She was predisposed to accept writing as closer to truth. Speaking was ephemeral. Not surprisingly, she had accepted the written words of Jason Oniropolos over the spoken words of Azziz al Azzad!

She was shocked. The scope and diversity of the written word opened to interpretation in different cultural contexts. Sacred or secular writings, holy scriptures like the *Bible* or *Qur'an*, mystical political documents like the United States Constitution, frightened her when they were seen as closed and immutable, authorizing jihad atrocities, holy vendettas, the literal obscenities of the Second Amendment. She had accepted the black binder as a singular version of reality authorized by the death of its creator.

Clearly, it was a metaphor!

Azziz had sought to rewrite himself into fiction. Azziz was Azziz, his hand-written text was a *bildungsroman*. She realized it was not a portrait of the artist as a young man. Before Joyce named his alter ego Daedalus, after the dreamer who designed the treacheries of the original labyrinth, he was called Stephen Hero. The triumph, for Joyce was to establish his protagonist in the heroic role of artist. Azziz was in pursuit of something more poignant, a detailed account of his surrogate's emotional and spiritual education that he could grasp in ways his own sad life would forever elude. It was another way of coming to terms with himself.

She wondered whether he had indeed murdered children. She had no doubt that he was the victim of a monstrous and stupid war, that he bore the scars of torture, not a bicycle accident, that he was from Iran, not Scarborough, and had served in Afghanistan. Was it Americans who had hurt him so badly, or were they a trope for something more malevolent; perhaps his own people?

Leaving Bloor St. behind, they dipped into a short-cut along the edge of the Don Valley escarpment, keeping to the fringe between prosperous urbanity and Toronto's gesture towards wilderness. Anna shared her revelation with Rose. "That stuff about Azziz being from Toronto wasn't true, you know."

"I know," said Rose. "He was making it up."

"You knew that? How?"

"I just did. He wasn't Greek; I know lots of Greeks. That was just to give his character a more exotic complexion. He wasn't from here, not from Scarborough. I'd know if he was. It's just something you know if you've grown up on the streets."

"He was writing a novel. I think he pretty much finished it when he took us in. The story was a metaphor. He was trying to locate some of the horrors he had endured in a familiar Canadian context."

Violet stopped them on the spot. "That's quite complicated," she said. "You need to explain. Did he make up a fictional novel to get hold of the truth?"

"Yes," said Anna. "I think so, exactly."

"Well, that is a perplexity I will live with forever, until the day that I die."

"Which will be a long time coming, I hope," said Anna.

"Thank you," said her four-year-old daughter. "I appreciate your concern." She pursed her lips and popped them, emitting a non-verbal explosive expletive.

They resumed walking.

"Why?" Rose asked. "Why not write about what he knew?"

"This *was* what he knew. He was struggling to connect the terror of his memories with the reality of his present life, a kind of time travelling in reverse, to understand both worlds better. His invented self brought his two lives together."

"A person can be two people, Annie. Some people are. I knew he wasn't converted," said Rose.

"To Islam?"

"Yes, no, it's just what he was. Sometimes you could tell he had doubts, you could see the light shining through. A convert is inside a closed box, if you know what I mean. He's a guy who jumps in out of panic and pulls the lid down over his head to shut out the world. But Azziz was comfortable enough to have doubts."

"Can't women be converts?" asked Violet.

"Of course," said Rose very patiently. "When I use 'he', I'm submitting to grammatical convention."

"So there's no word for either/or, when it could be a she or a he?" said Violet, smiling ingenuously.

"Azziz told me English insists on our differences when it should reinforce how similar we are, and insists we are the same when we're different."

Anna listened to their curiously informed and abstract chatter as they turned up a brick-cobbled side street under the lush spring foliage of ancient maples. Her four-year-old daughter with the alarmingly expansive vocabulary and the foundling waif who hovered between untutored common sense and intellectual posturing, sometimes losing herself between them, and who had become her very good friend. They were Anna's world, making it more complete than it had ever been.

"So, are east and west opposites?" Violet was asking, then apparently could not resist adding clarification. "That's a trick question."

"North and south are opposites," said Rose. "But east and west aren't. No matter how far east you go, you never reach west. But if you go far enough north, you'll start going south."

"Why?" said Violet.

"You explain," said Rose, drawing Anna back into the conversational intimacy she was obviously enjoying (after a lifetime on the outside, looking in).

"It's all got to do with the rotation of the earth," said Anna, and proceeded to explain with extravagant hand gestures that got all three of them laughing, even Violet, who almost never laughed.

Suddenly, they were on Errington Lane in front of Sebastian's vast home, standing at the edge of a pool of light cast from a street-lamp. Anna grew very serious and drew them back into the shadows, opposite Farouk's car parked exactly where Azziz had left it. She toyed with the keys in her skirt pocket, which along with the old man's jackknife created a considerable bulge. She looked at the girls. She was tempted to pile them into the car and take off, but they wouldn't get far with the pair of twenties Farouk had slipped her, and she had no access to her bank accounts or credit cards without revealing herself to the *authorities* — a nebulous ominous term for the forces that threatened them.

"Why are we here?" said Violet, not embarrassed to ask such an obvious question.

"Well, Honey, we've got to help Sebastian," said Anna.

"And we should see that Azziz is buried correctly," said Rose.

"Okay," said Violet, satisfied.

But Anna wondered about the wisdom of returning to The Cloisters. Sebastian was safe in Schrödinger's box for the time being. She recognized that curiosity might be the key to their survival — they needed to know where Robert was and what he intended — but curiosity might also bring them down. She wanted to talk to her other self, the voice that spoke in her own words, the part of her that seemed to be leading them, following instinct, feeling premonitions, familiar with fear, embracing affection. This parallel Anna usually made her feel more alone, but here, now, they sailed close-hauled together as they rounded into the wind, even though in her mind 'thinking' Anna was still at the helm.

Anna felt the semblance of a cool breeze emanating from the house. The barred windows set into the mansard roof were pitch black. A subtle pattern of shadows on shadows against the walls and in the depths of the porches and porticos threatened with blackness. The curtained windows on the lower three floors glistened with reflected light but floated in a dark void. She resolved the mottled darkness into a coherent architectural form in her mind and proceeded to move closer, leaving Rose and Violet near the base of a giant maple as she moved up the walk to the front verandah. She felt their presence immediately behind her as she mounted the wooden steps. By the time she reached the door they were standing beside her, each grasping one of her hands.

She gave their fingers a reassuring squeeze, then released her grip and peered through the panes in the door. The light inside that penetrated from the street showed the foyer to be empty. She tried the handle. The door was unlocked and swung open when she pulled it. Most front doors in a cold climate swing inwards to accommodate a storm door, but the thick panelled oak on this one allowed a departure from the norm. They stepped into the foyer. She warned the others not to make noise that would set off the sound sensor and force illumination to expose them — to whom was uncertain since no one else appeared to be about.

The mirrored door ahead was open but the corridor and mirror room beyond were dark and forbidding. The door into the anachronistic parlour and adjoining chambers was closed, as was the closet door leading into the elevator cabinet. Both were locked. She glanced upwards, wondering if Sebastian was peering down at them through holes in the plaster scrolling on the ceiling. She gazed at the floor, envisioning the corpse of Azziz far below, stiffened grotesquely on his mossy bed, sealed in caverns measureless to man — Coleridge — did Sebastian aspire to the role of Kubla Khan? Was this his pleasure-dome, with walls and towers, a savage place where Kubla heard from far, ancestral voices prophesying war? Coleridge's words and images collapsed and rebooted into a poem of inspiration, treachery, and creative rage. The dome, the cave, the fountain of voices, Sebastian's infinite library, swirled into a vision of creative imagination rivalling Blake's. She was sure Sebastian did not see himself as the Mongol emperor but as Coleridge himself, the visionary poet and analytic critic. This house *was* his vision. It was his recognition of the garrulous gothic that pervaded contemporary diversions, from spectator sports to computer games to the mindless narcissism of social media, and it was his heroic effort to exploit these tropes of excess and turn them into a monument of suspended disbelief.

All this passed in an instant through her mind and suddenly she was startled, as were her frightened companions, by a brief shudder in the darkness and a flash of illumination as the door of the elevator cabinet swung open and a bloodied Sebastian, Anna's Coleridge, stepped into the foyer and clapped his hands to fill the room with blinding light.

"Anna, Rose, Violet," he enumerated their names. He was not carrying a weapon and despite the blood on his shirt and arms he appeared not to be wounded. Anna was fascinated that she had immediately judged their situation by contraries. He did *not* look menacing. He was *not* unhappy to see them. She smiled to herself and reached out to give him a (tentative) bear hug. Violet was already at his side. Rose hung back, a little more circumspect — understandable, given the violence she had been through and the surreal death of Azziz.

Extricating himself from the awkward embrace of Anna and her daughter, Sebastian turned to Rose directly. "I am sorry it has gone so badly for you, Rose. I have arranged for the proper burial of your friend. You are safe now. No one can harm you."

"Is that true?" Anna demanded, having recovered from the explosive relief at seeing Sebastian unarmed and uninjured, and needing assurance that The Cloisters would live up to its name.

"Of course," said Sebastian, taking one of her hands in both of his, bowing his head slightly and looking up like a supplicant, asking for neither mercy nor treasure but simple affection. "Trust me, Annie."

He withdrew a key from his pocket and, unlocking the door, led them almost ceremoniously into the drawing-room, then turned and extinguished the light in the foyer before closing the door behind them. He seemed rather obsessive but inconsistent in locking and unlocking doors. Or was that how he controlled the flow of traffic through his sprawling home? He adjusted the drapes to make them impermeable to the flow of light from outside, and impenetrable to the light flowing out when he turned on a couple of parchment-shaded table lamps.

"What happened, before, with Rose and Azziz?" she asked.

"In the mirror room, they were shot."

"Was it Robert?"

"He shot them, yes, with a gun — if I am redundant, excuse me. I am surprised a man such as Robert, with his scientific finesse, would use such a crude instrument — but he did. He knew he had wounded Azziz. He must have thought he had also hit Rose. He went searching for you, Annie, and for Violet and, of course, for me. If he found me, he would have had his map to the house. I am not a brave man under pressure. I would not be good at resisting torture if I knew the secrets to stop it. But he did not, of course, find me."

"What about the blood?"

"I hauled Azziz out to the foyer, then I saw company had arrived at the front of the house so I thought it discreet to hide. I went up. Rose took Azziz, she had been hiding, they went down. The blood is his, not mine. Then Violet came to see me, but I suppose you knew that. Of course you did. I sent her back. She would be safer with you. You were safe until I discovered you weren't."

"I could have been dead and you wouldn't have known it." Anna paused. "Schrödinger," she said, then muttered, she couldn't resist, "John Locke, David Hume, George Berkley. Consciousness defines reality."

"Empiricists," he responded, as if by labelling them he was putting them into historical perspective and somehow giving himself the last word.

"You were watching from above, I take it."

He shrugged in the affirmative.

Violet had been observing, listening intently to Sebastian but ignoring the words. Now, oblivious to his wielding of silence as a rhetorical device, she asked, "Do you have a mechanical brain? Or are you poetical like my mother?"

Sebastian laughed. "Oh, not at all like your mother. But I am equally enthralled with the capacity for language to reach beyond its own limitations, so that makes me what you might call poetical, in my own way, I suppose. And what about you?"

"I have a thinking mind."

"So, you make connections between words and the world. You make the signified signify. You make the dancer dance and cannot tell what she is from what she does. Is that what you do?"

"No, I just think. The words are there and I use them."

"But sometimes, what we mean is conveyed by what cannot be said, Violet. Then we force words together unnaturally, we make poetry by the explosions and silences when they collide."

"Despite Wittgenstein," said Anna.

"He denied his own silence in the end."

"Sebastian, abstraction is not always amusing."

"Look, listen," he said, picking up a worn book from the coffee table. He switched his attention entirely to Anna, leaving Violet comfortably ignored. "I was re-reading this. It is the most terrifying and honest novel about war ever written, *All Quiet on the Western Front*. When language falls apart, that's when it is most disturbing. Even in translation, the senseless horror comes through in this book when the sense breaks down, when the author leaves you with raw words, brutal connections, the inarticulable absence of meaning. "Listen." Sebastian picked up Remarque's novel and read several passages, purposefully allowing no emotion to shade his delivery. "Listen.

> Bombardment, barrage, curtain-fire, mines, gas, tanks, machine-guns, hand grenades — words, words, words, but they hold the horror of the world.

"There is nothing more to be added to the litany of mechanical obscenities. Near the end, he is even more succinct, making expansive equations stripped utterly bare:

> Shells, gas clouds, and flotillas of tanks — shattering, corroding, death.
> Dysentery, influenza, typhus — scalding, choking, death.
> Trenches, hospitals, the common grave — there are no other possibilities.

"Sometimes, what is said is inseparable from the saying. Here the speaker's consciousness has been so reduced by devastation, despair, death, fear, isolation, that grammar fails him, reason fails him, only words are enough, and the emptiness between them. Erich Maria Remarque is a very fine poet."

"Like Anna," said Rose.

"Possibly," said Sebastian. "Unlike Wittgenstein, who closed his *Tractatus* by noting, 'whereof one cannot speak, thereof one must remain silent'."

"What cannot be spoken cannot exist? I'm not sure about that," said Violet. "There must be something beyond poetry, even if it's nothing at all."

She's a four-year-old child, thought Anna. Going on five.

"I would agree," said Rose. "He is no poet, your Wittgenstein." She moved closer to Sebastian. "Anna told me about your magical library," she said. "That it's laid out like an Escher drawing—"

"How do you know about Escher?"

"Same way I know about Wittgenstein, I just do. M. C. Escher; stairs that go up and down at the same time, columns that rise and descend." She stopped herself. She may have realized her words didn't capture the artist's illusions. "Anna says your library is bigger than the house that contains it. I like that, but don't you ever get lost among all those books?" It was a practical question, the corollary of how could he find a single volume among so many?

"It is all one book, dear Rose. It is my *Divine Comedy*, my own dark woods, and I always know where I am, even if I don't know precisely where that is."

"That is very perplexing," said Violet. "A cryptic tautology."

"Indeed, and a play on the copula — that's a running joke I share with your mother. Your vocabulary access is coming along quite nicely, isn't it?"

"If I think it, it is there," said Violet, far more enigmatically than she could have intended as she turned Descartes on his ear.

"Now, that is begging the question," said Sebastian. "Solipsism in someone so small."

"Schrödinger," said Violet. "Size has nothing to do with it. How do you beg a question?"

"It is an expression. I don't expect you are fluent in figures of speech. They do not translate literally. They only have meaning by common acceptance."

"That's what all words do," said Rose. "People agree on what certain signs mean and we convey them by sounds or marks or signals. Am I right, with an r? Or do I write with a w, or is it a rite, with an i-t-e?"

"You are fun," said Violet, then returning to Sebastian, she asked, "How do you beg for questions?"

"Well," said Sebastian, "if I say, the *Bible* is true because God says it is true and we know God is right because the *Bible* tells us so, that is begging the question."

"And God exists because the *Bible* is the Word of God and the *Bible* exists," said Violet. "I bet you have the *Bible* somewhere here in your library." She, like Rose, took it on Anna's word that he had a fabulous library, since neither had actually seen it.

"I do, sweet Violet. I have several, including a *Gideon Bible* my mother stole from a hotel in New York when I was your age, and another by Mr Gutenberg, printed in 1454, and known as the B42 for the number of lines on the page. Mine is among the forty-nine still in existence."

"How do you find them? How do you find anything in there?" Anna interjected. She was astonished to know he owned a Gutenberg *Bible*, which suggested his financial resources were virtually limitless. She wanted to talk about it. Even more, she wanted to understand his system of retrieval. Without access, a library, no matter how stellar its collection, was nothing more than a repository of deteriorating paper.

"I have a system," said Sebastian. He spoke calmly, betraying no feelings of urgency. "There is always a system."

Rose, who was indifferent to their esoteric conversation about books, stood at the drapes and poked a finger between them so she could peer out. Suddenly, she exclaimed, "My God!" She stifled a scream. "Someone's coming."

There was a thunderous rapping against the outside door into the foyer which, although not locked, by the absurdity of convention formed a temporary barrier.

Sebastian scooped up Violet and, to Anna's astonishment, rushed out into the foyer. She pursued, with Rose close behind, and watched, bewildered, terrified, as he stepped into the elevator cabinet with Violet in his arms. He glanced back and their eyes connected and premonitions of horror passed between them. The elevator door closed as panes on the outer door smashed and a gloved hand reached through and unlocked it and the Fahrenheit 450 thugs strode into the foyer.

Without a word Robert walked to the closet door and to Anna's dismay pulled it open. The cabinet was empty. He reached inside and opened a panel. He knew what he was doing. He pressed a combination of buttons, dropped a coin on the floor, and closed the door. The cabinet Sebastian and Violet had escaped in had to be in the space above. If the elevator had descended into the catacombs, the outer cabinet door would not have released. Robert waited wordlessly; Anna, in terror. The door opened again, the coin had disappeared. The upper cabinet had descended but was also empty. Robert stepped in and closed the door. There was a gentle whirring, a break, and another whirring, and Robert reappeared.

"Take them through there," he said to his henchmen, indicating the dark corridor into the mirror room. "I'll find the girl."

He didn't himself acknowledge Anna or Rose. Rose glowered at him like an enraged animal peering through the bars of its cage. Anna couldn't recognize him. He was a malevolent stranger.

"No," Robert amended. "Get them out of here. We're done with them. Take them to the facilities at the Centre." He said the word *facilities* with sinister emphasis.

The two women were cuffed with their hands in front in plastic manacles. The smaller man who reeked of tobacco manhandled Rose out to the Vivuscorps van parked in the shadows. The other man took Anna by the elbow and guided her firmly but gently, although when the back door was open, both women were pushed roughly inside. The stench of burnt plastic and garbage enveloped them as they sprawled across the shag carpet floor. They both squirmed around until braced against the sheet-metal walls, facing each other.

There were no windows in the back part of the vehicle but windshield light came through from the cab and flashed on their faces as they passed streetlights and shop windows. Anna smiled sadly as she gazed at her friend whose honey-blonde hair fell in gossamer wisps across her face, offsetting dark amber eyes peering back with resigned forbearance. Never had Rose seemed so wistful and vulnerable, like a little girl caught dressing up in her wicked stepmother's clothes. The flaring illumination on her face brought out flashes of the most delicate complexion, the most poignant features, the most trusting and loving, long-suffering, and uncomplaining expression. It was a vision to break Anna's heart. She hardly gave a thought to her own fate. The abject terror she felt for Violet, for whatever lay ahead once Robert found her — Sebastian couldn't hide her forever, if that's what he was doing — was masked by her profound devotion in this moment to her young friend whose expedient value to Vivuscorps had obviously, like her own, come to an end.

The van pulled into a restaurant parking lot and rolled to a stop at the back, far from the other parked cars. Anna heard the two men argue briefly, then both got out. The odiferous one came around to the back, opened the door and peered in, poked viciously at both of them; to check, Anna thought, if they would instinctively raise their arms in self-defence, to see if they had somehow got free of their cuffs. Satisfied, he slammed the door and locked it from outside.

"What's next, Annie?" said Rose.

Anna squirmed until she was able to work Solomon's jackknife forward inside the depths of her skirt pocket, then she rolled back on her shoulders and it slid out onto the carpet.

"Becket! Where'd you get that," Rose exclaimed, thrilled, frightened by the implications.

"Solomon told me to watch out for you," Anna whispered. "I wasn't sure which way he meant it, watch over or beware? Maybe both. I love you, sweet Rose."

"Me too, Annie. You're the only one except Agnes. I never loved anyone else in the world except for you and Agnes and Solomon. And Violet, of course, and Sebastian in a way and maybe Azziz."

"We've got a bit of time to make plans," said Anna, uncomfortable even under devastating circumstances with too much emotion. "They've gone in for fried chicken, you can smell the grease in the air."

Anna swung around to pick up the knife between manacled hands. She opened the blade and it gleamed menacingly, reassuringly, an absurd lethal symbol of resistance. She grasped the handle and cut the plastic strap binding Rose's wrists, then Rose cut hers. They were still locked in. She took the knife from Rose and set it at the edge of the carpeting against the metal wall.

"Do you think you could squeeze through the window into the cab?" Anna asked. "It's a tight fit."

"I'm not leaving you."

"You could go for help."

"Maybe."

Rose managed to get her arms and shoulders through but could go no further.

"Damn, damn, damnit, Annie, pull me back. It hurts too much. I can't breathe."

"You can breathe enough to say you can't breathe."

"'How art thou out of breath.' That's what you're supposed to say. It's still from *Romeo and Juliet*. Oh Christ, I can see the smelly one coming. Pull, get me out of here, pull, pull."

Anna braced and pulled. She could hear clothing rip. Rose failed to stifle an agonized scream, as she fell free. When the back door opened, the two women were sprawled side by side in a tangle of clothing and limbs. The odiferous man jumped in. He pulled the door shut behind him. He dragged Anna to the side and as she tried to protest he struck her on the side of the head with an open hand, then punched her square in the face with a closed fist. He turned away, crouching under the low dome of the roof as he moved towards Rose.

"Now, let's see what we have here." He straddled Rose. She hammered at him with a fist made from clasped hands. He shifted his weight to pin her arms down, then he clubbed her head with his own fists, taking his cue from Rose to grasp them together and make a more devastating weapon. She did not cry out. A slight involuntary whimpering emerged from Anna as she struggled to remain conscious. The noises of Rose's pummelled face were not discernibly human as her flesh turned to pulp.

The man got off, removed his trousers, and knelt beside her. He ripped clumsily at her clothing. He tore off her blouse, her bra, he swore viciously. He punched and battered her torso until he was worn out. He slumped over, then he rallied and lifted her skirt and yanked off her panties, tearing them along the seams. He screamed. He rose to his feet, striking his head on the ceiling, and he began to kick Rose with mindless hysterical brutality, swearing, spitting out every word and phrase in the language that demeaned, deprecated, diminished women, until at last he collapsed exhausted and wept.

Anna shifted to peer through the cavernous gloom. What she saw was the grotesquely beaten naked body of her beloved Rose Malone, and between her legs, pulverized into a bloody mass, were the remnants of male genitalia. Her Rose was a boy. His ribs were smashed where breasts might have been, his face was not recognizably human, his dead eyes peered out from brutalized flesh, staring fixedly into the emptiness.

The man sobbed. Anna moved her hands stealthily across the shag rug until she found Solomon's Becket. The quivering man seemed not to notice her movement. He was slumped against the inside wall of the van. She got a firm grasp of the wooden knife handle in her left hand and rocked forward on her knees. She clutched his hair with her right hand. The man gazed up at her through the tears of his humiliation. In a single rapid motion, she slashed his throat from one side to the other, severing both jugular veins and opening his windpipe. As the back door of the van rattled open, Anna fell forward against Rose's violated body, showered in the spurting blood of their dying assailant, immersed in imagery of the dome, the cave, the fountain as darkness swept over her.

# Chapter Thirteen
## The Library of Enduring Dreams

Anna became aware of herself in the debris of her mind. Gazing out the barred windows at the dwindling night as dawn began erasing the stars, she tried to locate herself in the present. She wondered if she had first abandoned herself when she thought she had lost her child and husband four years ago. Had her life been so narrowed, as Robert insisted, that she had been mad before that? Was disconsolate sorrow for a miscarried child the basis of madness or was madness sanity in anguished disguise. Perhaps she had never been mad but rather bewildered because somewhere inside she knew nothing, not even death, was quite what it seemed. Perhaps sanity itself was a form of madness?

She knew she was at The Cloisters. She was in Sebastian's apartment. She tried to recall how she got there. She wondered where everyone was.

She remembered Robert was alive and she had a daughter called Anna. Sebastian was her friend. He was not her lover. She had another friend called Rose — it was a curious name for a boy. He was young, in his teens, he was dead. Her head throbbed. She scrambled away from the overwhelming imagery of death. How could Robert be alive? Her daughter's name was Violet. Rose was a girl. Computers were evil, neither mindful nor intuitive. They were not contemplative, meditative, ruminative, reflective, analytic, or aesthetic. A computer must be given a purpose. It could not search randomly on the twist of an instant for nothing. It could not contemplate nothing. It could not be programmed to replicate the human mind. The mind, however, could be programmed to accept the cognitive limitations of a machine. The mind could be reset to minimal function.

Why would Vivuscorps want to do that?

She discovered she was standing at the window. Through the new leaves, she saw Sebastian walking towards the house. Her head felt like broken glass. She was wearing a clean cotton man's shirt. By flexing slightly, she could tell she had on no underwear. She smelled of soap, someone had bathed her. She sat down on the bed and waited.

Before long, Sebastian appeared.

"I found an all-night store," he said, tossing a plastic bag onto the bed. In it were cotton panties in three different sizes, all light blue, and a hairbrush.

"Thank you," she said. "Why am I here?"

"Why are any of us here?" He seemed embarrassed by his own cliché. She looked at him strangely, as if he hadn't understood her question. "Sorry," he said. "Force of habit. When I'm with you, I turn existential."

"Aren't you, anyway, aren't we all?"

"Anna, I'm sorry about Rose."

"Is she really gone?"

"You were there. She was beaten to death."

Confirmation made her unutterably sad. She remembered everything. Not as revelation. It was just all there in her head. She knew she had killed a man. She remembered being drenched in his blood. She touched her clothing, looked down, relieved the blood was gone. She took the smallest pair of blue panties from the plastic bag and discretely slipped into them. She felt no remorse for having executed a murderer. She remembered the other man sliding her out of the van. He had wrapped her in a blanket he had retrieved from behind the seat in the cab. She remembered him dousing the van with gasoline from a red jerry can and setting the van alight. She knew the bodies of Rose and the odiferous man were inside the funeral pyre. She remembered a car being commandeered and the surviving Vivuscorps man bringing her to the side porch at Sebastian's. She remembered ascending the stairs, being carried, being washed, being put to bed.

Sebastian had not responded to her question. Why was she here? She had been taken away for disposal on Robert's orders. Why did the man bring her back to Sebastian? Was it proximity — this place was much closer than the facilities at Vivuscorps? Did Sebastian's home now offer sanctuary from Robert's authority? Was Sebastian a fantastical centre of order and reason in a sequence of events that had fallen askew? Was the Vivuscorps man horrified by his companion's grotesque violation of Rose? Or perhaps by his summary execution? Was he sympathetic or was he confused? Or indifferent?

"Rose was a boy," Anna said. "Isn't that odd?"

"Rose was a lovely person," said Sebastian. "I'm sorry she suffered. *Hora novissima, tempora pessima sunt.* These are the last, the worst of times. She has left us only her name. As Umberto Eco explained about calling his novel *The Name of the Rose*, departed things leave their names behind, perhaps nothing more. Rose is a lovely legacy. Rose is a Rose is a Rose. That is all we can expect."

"Rose was more than a word, Sebastian. I had not anticipated such pessimism, even from a nihilist like you. Quoting Dickens in Latin won't help."

"That wasn't Dickens. Those were the words of a medieval Benedictine monk, Bernard of Cluny. He said nothing about the best of times, only the worst. His tormented images of burning ice and freezing fire influenced Dante, they say. Of course, his treatise called *Contempt for the World* was satire. Not pessimism so much as merciless anger. I haven't yet given in to despair."

"What about Violet?" Anna asked, afraid of a rambling esoteric response, shocked yet not surprised when he confirmed her worst fears with a cryptic shrug.

"We will get her back," he said.

Yes, Anna thought. She felt sure that Violet was alive. The girl was too valuable as a scientific project to destroy. But if she were with Robert at Vivuscorps, what inhuman procedures might she be forced to endure? Or, even worse, as a neophyte shaped in his image, he might raise her to be like himself.

"Did Robert take her?" she demanded. He looked back at her with uncharacteristic intensity, as if he had made a major decision.

"Anna, we will get her back, I promise you."

"God, how can you promise? Vivuscorps owns half the world."

"I own Vivuscorps."

In that instant everything changed.

During the following moments, Anna tried to assimilate the devastating impact of Sebastian's announcement, while struggling to deny it. He gave her nothing to make himself easier to read. He had not offered a confession with passionate intensity or dissenting conviction to ease her fears, nothing to imply shame or contrition, and his declaration wasn't a boast. He simply seemed to have opened himself to a friend in a particular moment of need. Desperate to return to the reality where Vivuscorps was no more than a nightmare, where Violet was safe and Sebastian was indeed her friend, Anna reached for a contradiction that would bring his claim tumbling down — a crack that would let the light flood in.

"Why did they try to kill you, Sebastian? They beat you, didn't they?"

"I stumbled. I thrashed around a bit making noises to cover your clattering in the chute." He held up his burned hand so that the deep ridges of scar tissue gleamed like an ominous souvenir. "They left. I tried to take my life in an extravagant gesture that proved inadequate. My body juices seem to have bubbled and burst my seams and extinguished a fine Cuban cigar. It was supposed to drop and light Montaigne's essays on fire. I had a bottle of Bénédictine to give me courage."

"Why, for God's sake?"

"Because I needed it. Even when self-inflicted, death is an unpleasant experience. I'm sorry, dying. Death is nothing."

"And you were prepared to have all this consumed in flames?"

"An entire bottle of Bénédictine is not conducive to clarity of thought."

"But if you own Vivuscorps, why kill yourself, Sebastian?"

"Because I own Vivuscorps. It is not so simple as it might seem. Suicide seemed reasonable at the time. Cowardly, of course, but I tried to compensate by going out with panache."

"I'm glad you failed."

"Ah, you don't hate me."

"I didn't say that."

Whether villain or fool, she found him endearing. She was worried sick about Violet and devastated over the events in the van, but she knew Sebastian's status with Vivuscorps was the key to getting her daughter back. She indicated she was curious. She listened. Corporate high finance was not Anna's strength.

"Henry Ford built a car company. His offspring worked for the corporation and he was forever associated with the Model T. Timothy Eaton created an iconic store, but his stores ran the lives of his children. The first Kroetsches who came to this country were blacksmiths. By the second generation they forged farm machinery, by the fourth they were among the wealthiest families in Canada. The Kroetsch genius was to invest in technology, manufacturing, and eventually computers. By my father's generation, Kroetsch money was mostly in cybernetics or invested discretely offshore. Vivuscorps was my father's creation, but he was still a blacksmith forging on the smithy of his soul the uncreated consciousness of the human machine. That was his vision. I found it abhorrent. I was not groomed to succeed him. He died quite young in a tragic accident in Muskoka. As a child, I was diagnosed as autistic, which I was not, and bipolar, which I was not, and darkly eccentric, an aberration which I assiduously cultivated. They feared I might take after my doomed Uncle Leicester, he was actually my great uncle, but I didn't. My bibliomania was deemed sufficiently obsessive to keep me off the board of directors, and my profligate requests to fund my compulsive architectural projects were considered a small price to keep me quietly content until, through the shifting of corporate monies and managerial responsibilities, I found my life virtually controlled by Vivuscorps. And oddly enough, they see in me the potential to become the public face of the corporation. I am a Jay Gatsby of sorts, possessed by my possessions, but without his deplorably extravagant style or Hollywood looks. Neither tragic nor pathetic, not comic nor, indeed, ironic, I simply exist — or did so, until I met you!"

Was this meant to be a compliment? She could think of nothing more vacuous than to be cast as a Fitzgerald heroine, especially Daisy Buchanan, whom Anna considered irredeemably stupid and a low point in aspirational role models — or did he mean she redeemed him from the emptiness such a world implied?

"Did you know what Robert was doing?" she asked.

"With his original research on the synthesis of nucleic acid, yes. I initially found his work on infinitesimal computing machines interesting. But my fears grew as I followed his progress. He slowly changed from serving humanity to envisioning humanity in service to him, though he wouldn't have described it that way. At about the same time as Vivuscorps took over his project, I retreated from computers almost entirely. I could see where they were going with subliminal DNA modules linked to a central source. It sickened me, Anna. Ironically, when I was asked to monitor you at the library, another world opened for me, a rare world where poetry mattered."

"Why would you do what they told you?"

"It would have been difficult to refuse."

"You could have said, 'I would prefer not to.'"

"Ah yes, Melville. But Bartleby the scrivener died in The Tombs. I didn't know you then. I took the position that I would *prefer not to refuse*, given the consequences if I did."

"Which were?"

"I never found out."

"Did you know what Robert had done?"

"When? To you? Not when it happened, not when he took Violet, not when he turned you into his experiment. But when we all went out to the Vivuscorps Centre I caught up to speed."

"You knew where we were."

"So did you?"

"I mean the location? You'd been there before."

"So had you."

"To endure invasive procedures, not because I owned the place."

"One does not own in a corporate world so much as use and be used by it."

"You spied on us."

"At the Centre? No, emphatically not."

"Jesus," she said. She didn't know what to believe.

Was this what it was like just before death? You are left only with an infinite swarming of meaningless connections. There is nothing to think about, nothing to contemplate, nothing but notes with no music.

"How did your parents die?" she asked, throwing him off guard.

After a ruminative delay, he answered, "Their launch, it was called *The Corsair* after Barbary Pirates, whether as a twisted tribute to more than a million Europeans enslaved by North African marauders, or through ignorance, because they liked the sound of the name — their launch caught fire."

"Were you on board at the time?"

"I was. We were in the middle of Lake Rosseau. Muskoka. I was thrown clear by the explosion."

"Wearing a life jacket?"

"Yes." He offered a grimace of distaste she might have mistaken for a smile. "Why?"

"Just curious, Sebastian. Everything about you fills me with curiosity. And dread. Tell me about your cataloguing system."

"You seem to be wandering in all directions, poor Anna. I think you received a concussion. Jacob Hummel wanted to take you to the hospital but I thought you would be better off here."

"Jacob Hummel?"

"Jacob Hummel, the man who brought you back to me. The one you killed was Gabriel."

"But it was Robert who ordered *deletion*."

"Deletion? Delete Anna, delete Rose. I expect that was what he intended. Jacob Hummel saved your life."

"Gabriel and Jacob behaved like humans, it seems — the worst and the best of what humans can be. Robert seems outside the spectrum. He's psychopathic."

"Robert is a 'created' psychopath, extremely intelligent and narrowly focussed. He is a living machine, that's what *vivus corps* means, *the living dead*. Actually, he is ideally suited to their appalling designs. He frightens me far more than the automatons he is helping create. He is a man without conscience, capable of slow deliberation and flashes of insight — both qualities of mind that are already restrained by e-glasses and will be virtually destroyed by DNA implants, especially if they can be accessed by monitors outside the skull."

"You make him sound like one of us. The consciousness part, not the lack of conscience."

"Perhaps he once was."

"He doesn't have a cerebral computer himself, does he?"

"Far more monstrous than that. He was brainwashed. The methods go back to the Korean War, the Manchurian candidate grotesquely updated. He can think, but not so freely as he imagines, and it seems he cannot feel."

"How long ago…?" She couldn't finish her question.

"The process began before he met you, Anna, and continues to this day. Brainwashing is never finished. It is adapted and refined as circumstances require."

"Who does it? If you are not in control and Robert is not in control, who is?"

"*They*, Anna. *They*."

"For God's sake, Sebastian!"

"Anonymous corporate executives; men who control so much money, collectively much more than me, and have so much power, it terrifies."

"No women?"

"Curiously, none. Women seem less attracted to power for the sake of power and more for what it can do."

*He* is explaining this to *me*!" she thought

"That's why churches are run by men, often celibates, while women look after the poor. Perhaps at some level men who fear women simply lock them out. As you know, women are dangerous, the *Bible* tells us so. And the *Qur'an* and the *Book of Mormon*, as well."

He smiled a wistful sardonic smile, confusing her. Did he understand the irony? She wanted to hate him. She was being seduced by her own conflicting emotions. She wanted to trust him. The awkward affection that surged gently inside soothed her anxiety.

"You want me for your collection," she proclaimed. The words surprised her. She had been leaning in the opposite direction. "That's it, isn't it? You want to collect me."

"What on earth are you talking about?" Sebastian seemed genuinely confused.

"I'm a *reader*. You wanted an authentic book-sourcing book-reading accessible friend."

"Of course I did, I do. You make it sound like a capital offence?" He still seemed puzzled. "Who else can I talk to about Ludwig Wittgenstein?"

"Why would you want to?"

"Because you are a warm clever gracious inspiring conversationalist."

"I meant Wittgenstein. Why would you want to talk about Wittgenstein?"

"Why would you want to talk about Heidegger and Derrida and Sartre?"

"Who says I do?"

"Anna, you do. And Saul Bellow and Iris Murdoch. No, I don't want to collect you. I want to share my considerable library with you — and, such as it is, my mind. Is that so wicked? Your own mind darts around so fast, you need me as a baffle to slow your thoughts down so we can both enjoy them. Mine perseverates over whatever I've read and ties me in knots. I need you to cut it free. We are the last two such people in the world, Anna. We need each other."

"I imagine there are more, somewhere, just like us."

"Possibly. I suppose. If I perish, perhaps you will find them." He looked at her with the troubled eyes of a man who had already confronted his own death. She remembered his appointment at Princess Margaret. He smiled.

She had been sitting on the edge of the bed. She stood up and they walked into each other's arms and embraced. They did not kiss, but they pressed close, their radiant body heat creating an ineluctable fusion between them.

"I thought you wanted to be God," she whispered.

"Perhaps we all do. That's why we created him."

"No, we created him to fill the moral vacuum we imagined around us."

"If I were to be God, I'm afraid I would be like Milton's in *Paradise Lost*, unsympathetic, autocratic, and not nearly so persuasive or attractive as Satan."

"Robert is neither!" she said. This was not about Robert. This was about Robert.

"I wasn't thinking of Robert. We're not rivals, certainly not on a celestial plane. Robert is a figure of pathos. Myself, I'm more like Harpocrates, the Greek god of silence, a very obscure deity and a prototype, I'm sure, for the least engaging of the Marx brothers. Robert, if pressed, I believe he might see himself as a combination Adam and Eve, not a rebel angel but a primal human, a pioneer in, dare I say it, a brave new world."

"I'm more comfortable seeing him as Satan, Milton's Lucifer but without the charm. And you, you're a visionary of another sort, you're really the tyger, aren't you?"

"The tiger?"

"You *are* imagination, burning bright, and what dread hand dare seize that fire?" she said, then went on, oratorically,

What the anvil? What dread grasp
Dare its deadly terrors clasp?

You make me almost believe in a world beyond Vivuscorps' reach, a world of books where no one can touch us."

She wasn't sure whether she intended to mock or to laud, perhaps both. It pleased her to think of Sebastian as a *created* force, created by books and his capacity to absorb the words of their roaring; created by history and his determination to resist a distorted heritage; and most of all, his own creation, a man who stood proud in the world. Even his attempt at suicide was self-creation, not unlike the son of God who embraced his death because he could not die (or what kind of a god would he be if he did?). Sebastian turned his final act into a sybaritic melodrama as if he were sending up his own passing. He was the tyger burning bright in the forest of the night. It thrilled her to think so.

Once they pulled away from each other, she realized the intimate proximity had distorted her senses.

"How can you be so sure about Violet?" she asked. "Will Robert bring her here?"

"He will. He is coming soon."

"Here? With Violet?"

"I requested it. I sent Jacob Hummel to get him."

He had more power than she had imagined.

"There are things I think you should know," he said. "It would be better if Robert explained."

"That sounds ominous, Sebastian. Why did you let him take her?"

"I had no choice."

"Because she belongs to Vivuscorps or because Robert insisted?"

"Both."

He had less power than she had hoped.

She did not think Sebastian meant her harm. There had been opportunities for him to destroy her. But he was deeply involved in whatever was happening to her, to Violet, and what had happened to Rose, perhaps even Azziz. She was desperate to understand.

Sebastian knew more now and from the beginning than he had been willing or able to share. His knowledge empowered him but it also made him vulnerable. He opposed Vivuscorps and what he called their 'appalling designs', yet he wallowed in the wealth they afforded him to indulge in deconstructionist architecture, a vast library, and his own peculiar brand of social anarchy.

In spite of himself, Sebastian lived in what Heidegger defined as a technological *gestell*, not because technology prevailed over consciousness but because technology as an *attitude* made consciousness the measure of everything. By placing humanity at the centre of being, philosophers and poets and scientists ensured that humans remained on the margin of *Being*. Such teleology was what his *sanctum sanctorum* was intended to counter, expressing intrinsic finality beyond human perception, yet he was its victim. This was the same paradox that permitted Heidegger himself to ignore atrocities as an intellectual but participate in them as a dedicated Nazi.

Lines from *Casablanca* swept through her mind, 'If we stop breathing, we'll die. If we stop fighting our enemies, the world will die.' She looked at Sebastian. He was neither hero nor villain; he was Rick, watching Ilsa's plane disappear into the fog. 'Here's looking at you, kid.' Anna looked at him again, he looked inexorably sad.

Sebastian was clearly offended by the Vivuscorps drive to literalize technology, reducing sense and sensibility to receptive functions, thereby making the human machine predictable. Anna saw their success as the virtual end of everything, the end of aspiration and moral choice, the end of creativity and contemplation, the end of all that it meant to be human. Sebastian found their ambition offensive, yet the technology that would bring it about paradoxically allowed him, personally, to refuse subservience to the technological *gestell*. Technology enabled him to build his own fortress, his prison.

She looked at him and felt sorry for herself.

She moved past him and surveyed the living room and it came to her she had stashed her travelling bag in a cupboard, months earlier, before escaping down the laundry chute. She retrieved the bag and discarding the man's shirt with her back to Sebastian she put on a clean bra, a blouse and skirt, but she kept on the blue panties he had bought her even though they were cheap and had an uncomfortable cut.

They were sitting in the kitchen, eating breakfast when Jacob Hummel came in. He was followed by Robert with Violet, who was directed to stay in the living room where she perched on the sofa and picked up a copy of Dante's *Inferno* with fiendish engravings by Gustave Doré. When Anna made a move towards her, Jacob Hummel blocked her way. She tried to peer over his shoulder to make eye contact, but Violet was engrossed in her book.

"Sit down," said Robert.

Anna sat. There was no alternative. Standing would hardly constitute an insurrection. She waited.

"I have Violet with me," Robert said, as if she might not have otherwise noticed. "I regret what happened to Rose. It was not supposed to go that way."

"He tried to rape her!"

"He had not expected Rose to be as he was. Gabriel was humiliated. It is unfortunate."

"And what about me, what about Violet?"

"Violet has been successfully modified."

"Oh God!"

"I have upgraded her system. She was displaying counterproductive levels—" He hesitated, as if searching for words of evasion.

"Initiative? Free-will? Curiosity? Imagination."

"Yes, but we have that under control. It was quite straightforward. Your own surgery was a major cranial intrusion. What we observed enabled us to modify our procedures. Her operation was little more than an arthroscopic probe, minimally invasive. She was under anaesthetic for less than an hour. Her body had readily assimilated the synthesized molecule we inserted at birth but it had connective limitations. Her new analogue will override such deficits. More significantly, it will enable her cybernetic system to be accessed externally. Potentially. It is a real breakthrough. We are very pleased."

Anna wept.

She sat at the kitchen table and gazed through tear-filled eyes at this monstrous man who had been her husband, at Sebastian who smiled gently, at Jacob Hummel who registered nothing.

"May I see my daughter?" she asked, desperate not to break down completely.

"She is not your daughter," said Robert, then seemed to shift to a different subject: "You have been useful. Thank you for the last four years. You were the failure that proved we were on the wrong track. One cannot prove a theory correct in every instance, but a single failure can prove it wrong. Your brain matter refused to merge with alien material. You are the reason it was necessary to shift from synthesizing DNA to creating its analogue by using alternate proteins. DNA was displaced by what we call XNA."

She looked directly into his eyes, searching for her own reflection but, with the slant of the light, she was absent.

"It will be best for us all, at this point," he continued, "if you are *deleted*. Jacob Hummel will make the arrangements." He paused. "Jacob is better working without Gabriel. More efficient. He will be kind."

Recognition, at least, that he was talking to a human! Anna's world had diminished so tightly that she felt no panic, only incredible loneliness.

"Why not just set me free?" she asked. "Surely there are many who will never be enhanced because they're too stupid, too smart, too rebellious or reckless, too weak or too strong. Cast me outside the gates of privilege, beyond the periphery, let me and my daughter live with the rabble."

"Ah, but the 'rabble', they do not comprehend what they don't have. They will soon die off through inertia, their inability to engage."

"And you and your corporate executives — you don't participate yourselves, I assume."

"In order to guide we must stay apart. Think of us as the Vatican, the central authority of men who guide the affairs of both sexes through birth and vocation, procreation, familial relations, and death, not to mention eternity. Figuratively, at least, we are celibate. We avoid distractions. Meanwhile, the enhanced will dwell in sacred abbeys and rise beyond their own limitations. Your rabble will linger outside the monastery walls and eventually become carrion, and that will be that."

"Then let us join them there."

"No, I'm afraid it is impossible to let that happen. You are the worldly heretic, a threat to the chosen, a threat to the damned."

"Robert. You are speaking in metaphors, do you realize that? You see, you cannot kill poetry! Your vision will collapse because it literally cannot succeed. It is a medieval fantasy — symbols of the absolute do not translate into absolute ends."

"The metaphor is within your own mind, I'm afraid. What we are embarking upon is a very real transformation of the world and the place of our species within it."

"How grand! How pathetic!"

"I'm sorry you can't appreciate what we're doing."

"Please, let our daughter live."

"Of course. She must. But as I said, she is not *your* daughter."

Anger stirred deeply within, and intimations of dread.

"Robert, you can't deny a biological fact. Please, then, please, I need to say goodbye to her."

"It won't make much of an impact, I'm afraid. And, trust me, there is no such thing as a biological fact. There are only probabilities. You taught me that. You share DNA with Violet, my dear Agnes, but she is not your child."

Anna was slow to comprehend what he was saying. It was not a riddle. He was not clever enough. She glanced frantically at Sebastian. He seemed pained but not perplexed.

"Anna died," said Robert. "Anna was killed in a streetcar accident. You witnessed her death."

"I wasn't touched, the streetcar killed Agnes Dei, Rose's friend," she protested, with panic rising like bile and her breath tightening.

"Yes, she was Rose's friend. Rose was her minder."

"Her what!"

"Rose looked after Anna for us."

"Please, Robert, Sebastian, please, somebody." Images of Rose's battered body flashed through her mind, slush spurting blood, infinite mirrors echoing invisibility, caverns blindingly lit, images of Violet in the walled-in garden, fractured images filled her head with explosions of sound and fury. Yet there were no words. What we cannot speak, we pass over in silence — not because words fail us but because reality exceeds our grasp. At least Wittgenstein hadn't deserted her. Silence is as deep as Eternity, speech is as shallow as Time. Nor had Carlyle.

Robert, who could not have fathomed either philosopher's consent to the ineffable, said, "It will do you no harm to understand."

"But first you must understand, Robert." Sebastian, whose passivity had become increasingly threatening, spoke directly to her. "Bearing in mind what I told you before."

"What did you tell her?" Robert demanded, then sneered. "Your judgements don't interest me, Sebastian. You are an aberration. You were useful. Your family's money transformed us; especially Anna. Poor Anna. She could not keep up with the changes. She could not keep up. We were never in love but for a while we were convenient in each other's lives. She used to chatter on about Aristotle and Kant. I would talk to her about the infinite promises of microbiology and behavioural modification, about technological singularity and superintelligence."

"I remember," said Anna, trying not to sound plaintive when she added, "I do think we were in love, Robert."

"No, Agnes, you may think you remember but you don't. Let me tell you about Anna. Not you. Anna. Her life was a kind of lament. She always felt incomplete. She thought I might fill the gap, round out the story, and after she became pregnant, when the emptiness still didn't go away, I researched the genetic records and found you. It is a sad and simple story, a cliché, yes, but no less true for that. You and Anna were sisters, matched twins abandoned at birth by an adolescent mother. Anna was adopted by the woman she knew as her grandmother, who did not know you existed. Your birth mother married a good man and they retrieved you from the system. Remembering blood, memories of the womb, made you and your sister an absence in each other's life. Years later, your family died in a fire. You were studying at the time at Duke University in North Carolina. You were spared."

"I've heard that story before," said Anna, her mind grasping for coherence. "The part about the fire."

"You might have. I told it to your friend Mr Azzad."

"You knew Azziz?"

"Only in passing. I knew he had made contact with you at the library. I asked him to keep me informed if he saw changes in you. For your own good, I explained."

Nothing surprised her, not even the implied betrayal of her friends.

"And did he see changes?"

"No. He was an interesting man. He suffered with PTSD from experiences at the hands of interrogators in Iraq. But, please, Agnes, understand, even if Anna and I were once in love, that was not you. You had another life. You taught at Amherst College in Massachusetts. You never married. Your discipline was philosophy, but you published quite extensively in literary theory and cultural studies. It is not uncommon for siblings separated at birth to follow similar trajectories through life, despite widely divergent childhood experiences — especially identical twins. Anna and Agnes were natural clones, which from my perspective was ideal."

"And both had parents who died, everyone's parents died, Sebastian's parents died in a mysterious explosion, Rose had no parents, and Azziz, his parents died, too."

"Sometimes it is more convenient that way," he said.

"For whom?" The implications were horrendous. She shifted course, more comfortable with mystery than murder. "Was I abused as a child?"

"Who knows?"

"Violet is my daughter."

"Agnes, you are infertile. Rose thought you were sterilized but you just couldn't have babies."

"Violet is my daughter," she repeated.

"Genetically, yes."

"Please, Robert, if there is any truth in this, I need to understand."

"Ah yes, the need to understand, illusory notions of free will, the urge to make things *new* — isn't that what your poet argued. Mr Ezra Pound, he said about art, *make it new*. But nothing is new, Agnes, if no one perceives it. All such notions in time will seem quite barbaric, a passing phase. The world is changing, Agnes. We are not so important as we think we are. Your Plato put us at the centre, but we are no more than a flash of consciousness in the cosmos, we need guidance to control our primitive impulses if we are to endure."

"Agnes? Tell me about Agnes."

"Fortunately for us, Agnes, you went on sabbatical at the same time Anna was pregnant. Gabriel and Jacob Hummel abducted you, as it were. We resigned your position at Amherst on your behalf. You had apparently accepted a post as senior lecturer at Trinity College Cambridge — quite plausible, since that was the home of Bertrand Russell and Ludwig Wittgenstein, or at least of their dust, as they were dead before you were born. Like Anna, you were a loner. You had no relationships with the living that could not easily be severed.

"Anna's was quite a simple operation, as was your own. You were at the Centre for some time, both of you. We delivered Anna's baby and set a DNA microcomputer into her brain tissue and subsequently into yours. It was good to work with an infant but I wanted to try my procedures on related adults. It did not go so well with Anna. Cyber and cerebral realities collided. Her thinking lacked what one might call 'functional clarity'. So I made adjustments to yours through optogenetic modulation, laying in enough of her personal memories, while displacing your own, to make you seem authentic, at least to yourself. We left you with access to knowledge you had previously acquired. Poetry and such. If your personal memories sometimes seemed askew, your cultural memories restored equilibrium. It is not uncommon for people with strokes to experience a cerebral division, but it had never been done by surgical intervention. We were moderately successful with you, more than with Anna. We slipped you into her life, you might say. You did have trouble with self-awareness but your capacity for mental leaps was astounding. You were adept at extrapolation but you were not very good at logic, judgement, or critical analysis. No matter, we moved you out of the lecture halls to an appropriate post in the Public Library. You do not think so well as you think you do, but you managed to get by. You are disturbingly intuitive, although in matters of reasoning I would say you are error-prone. You told me once that elegance in thinking is always the best, but ironically you make things more complex than they need to be."

"And Anna?" She seemed to have made the shift in her mind, finding Anna a stranger although Agnes was someone she knew mostly through Rose.

"As I explained, she did not fare so well. I tinkered to suppress personal memories. We thought it better to turn her out. We are not unkind. We appointed Rose to keep an eye on her — I say appointed because we did not pay her. We arranged for them to be companions. Rose knew her as Agnes, since you had displaced her as Anna."

Agnes turned suddenly on Sebastian who was sitting at the kitchen table beside her. "Did you know about this?" she demanded.

He glanced down at the floor, then looked up into her eyes. He said nothing and looked away.

"Then why kill her?"

"There was nothing more to observe."

She felt a tighter breathing and zero at the bone.

"Why kill me?" she said.

"The same reason. Think of my work as surgical, Agnes, although I do not do the surgery myself. After cutting into flesh, it is necessary to clear away the moribund tissue and cauterize the wound."

"*Moribund* means dead. You murder the dead. That isn't efficient, it's redundant. She couldn't do you any harm. I can't either."

"Well, you see, Anna was becoming *aware*. Her natural intellect seemed to be suppressing the implant, much as yours had done from the beginning. Rose told us Anna saw you on College Street one day and recognized herself. The shock triggered something — we might call it *clarity*. A dangerous quality for an unstable mind. She went back the next day, hoping to see you again. Rose was told not to follow, but Jacob Hummel pursued her. I think she got confused. You had dyed your hair. Then, as you know, the streetcar incident occurred. I had hoped that would be an end to it, although you had been suppressing your implant more and more, but unfortunately you saw Anna before she expired. Seeing yourself mirrored in her similarly triggered a shock which, in your case, led to doubts about your own identity. These might easily, in turn, have led to exposing our project to public scrutiny. Sebastian had been observing you but we put Rose onto you as well. She believed she was working for the police, which she was, but of course they are working for us."

"Rose thought I was Anna. Agnes didn't have a tiny rose with a thorny stem tattooed on her buttocks. Or was that hers? Who had the Italian boyfriend?" She heard familiar sounds in her head, speaking in her own silent voice. 'It doesn't make any difference. Agnes or Anna, we're indivisible.'

"Yes, we are," she mumbled aloud.

"Pardon?" said Robert. "It is *your* tattoo, it was *your* Italian boyfriend."

"Anna or Agnes?"

"Yours. We made sure you both had a rose tattoo."

"And who had the boyfriend?"

'Does it matter? The point is, Rose could not tell Agnes and Anna apart."

"Did you know she was male?"

"Of course. Eventually. When I did the molecular implant to correct her dyslexia, it was hard to avoid noticing she had male DNA. As it turned out, the anomaly made her worthless as an experiment. It was one variable too many."

"So she too was disposable!"

"Gabriel murdered her brutally. We are not brutal. Gabriel deserved to die."

"No one deserves to die." She could feel her pulse surging. "Do you realize how mad your project is?"

"It is only madness if it fails. It won't fail. I have the power of Vivuscorps behind me."

"Don't you understand, Robert! Do you have any idea what you're doing? If the mind is fashioned by nanocomputers and social collusion to mimic machines, we lose our capacity to make poetry."

"Ah, poetry. You make something so trivial seem catastrophic. We don't all need to be poets, Anna. Agnes. Thank God for that."

"Thank God! Really?" She was arguing for her life. "You believe your work will return us to Eden, before moral choice defined who we were, before poetry was possible. Is that what you want?"

"I prefer Darwin to God," Robert exclaimed. "I believe in another transition like the one that made *homo sapiens sapiens* possible, fifty thousand years ago. We have been distracted for too long."

"Distracted! Is that what civilization has been, a distraction?"

"Yes."

"Oh my God! And Vivuscorps will save us from ourselves?"

"From wars and holocausts, depressions and dictators."

"From Sophocles? From Shakespeare? From Mozart? From Michelangelo, Bashō, Tagore, Picasso, Bergman, McCartney?"

"Yes, yes."

"For what, to be what?"

"Happy."

"Is there a word more bland than *happy*?" she demanded. "Is that what people want? 'O brave new world, That has such people in't.' Do you actually know what they're after?"

"Vivuscorps? Not poetry, for damned sure."

"Exactly, and without poetry we lose our capacity to be human." He seemed irritated but intrigued. She continued: "We live within language, Robert. Language is a system of symbols and signs we have to interpret, or the mind atrophies and our souls expire." Desperation pressed in. She had to make her argument more tangible. "The connection between the word 'rose' and an actual flower is utterly arbitrary; to grasp the meaning of 'rose' we have to be poets. Otherwise, words are just phonemes, mere sounds that signify nothing."

He stared at her with his head cocked like a terrier. For an instant, it was like old times, they were incomprehensible to each other and absurdly cerebral but vitally attentive. She felt a surge of affection. It immediately expired like a popped balloon. Memories of what it had been like between them were not even her own.

"Computers do not dispense with language," he said, the terrier, relentless. "They turn words into binomial equations, information packets that make probable connections. Connections, what more could you want?"

"*Improbable* connections! That's what I want. Poetry! Listen to me — neuroscientists like Gerald Edelman, archeologists like David Lewis-Williams, philosophers like Curtis White, so many others, they identify 'higher-order consciousness' as the function that marks us from all other animals, and *higher-order consciousness* depends on our capacity for symbolic memory. It is inseparable from language. Without language as a *living* thing, we would not be able to construct socially-based selves, we would have no identity, we would not be able to model the past and the future, we would live forever in the present, we would not even be conscious of being conscious. Like dogs by the hearth after the fire has died. Not even howling, just whimpering, then silent. You imagine you are expanding our minds with your cerebral machines, but you would be reducing us to brute awareness. You plan to manipulate neurotransmitters in the cerebral cortex but the spontaneous interaction among billions of neurons is the basis of poetry, Robert. Poetry makes *improbable* connections. Poetry *is* our genius. That is what makes us human. Your cyborg manipulations will reduce the mind to a brain, consciousness to awareness, metaphors to facts. We will become automatons."

"We will become content, when we have never before had the option."

"Content! Happy! Watching Saturday afternoon football *on weekdays*? Being one of Justin Bieber's one million intimate friends? Streaming facts *ad infinitum*, no matter how trivial? Thinking facts are thoughts? Numbed by too much reality, ceding control of our consciousness to others, our sensibilities atrophied, our minds infantilized, our curiosity murdered? Fifty thousand years ago, as you say, we stumbled into higher-order consciousness, developed language, made society, invented time, and emerged as the people we are — or, if you'd prefer, we left the Garden and set out into the endless precarious world east of Eden. In the next decade or so, you propose to seize control of all that we've become and bind it into binary modalities with algorithmic structures of encrypted DNA — you propose to banish us back to Eden, to change the nature of consciousness, to reduce our minds to their primordial function. Like dogs, we will be trainable. Mostly we will observe. And you see nothing wrong with this?"

"Change is inevitable."

"But not predetermined. We have agency in our own lives to resist. We have choice."

"And my choice is to work with Vivuscorps. Your own choices seem to have run out."

She looked desperately to Sebastian. Sebastian looked away. She looked at Jacob Hummel. He gazed through her like she didn't exist. She looked out at Violet who was absorbed in Dante's *Inferno*, her thoughts and responses undoubtedly shaped by what she saw in her head.

"We have spent enough time chattering, Agnes, or Anna, whichever you prefer. Jacob Hummel will take you to the Centre. We have excellent facilities there. We are very humane, whenever it is possible."

"May I speak to Violet on the way?"

"Yes, of course. Please don't upset her."

Sebastian stirred. It was as if, after taking refuge under a cloak of inconsequence through most of Robert's discourse, he had set it aside to become real again, a visceral presence.

"Jacob Hummel," Sebastian said in a very soft voice, "could you take care of Mr No-Yes."

Agnes watched as Jacob Hummel removed Solomon's jackknife from his jacket pocket. It had been cleaned off. Robert twisted in his chair to observe him as well. Only when Jacob Hummel unfolded the blade did Robert anticipate what was going to happen. He leapt to his feet, sending his chair clattering across the broad planks. Jacob Hummel stepped closer.

Robert lunged to one side. Jacob Hummel caught him on the fly, hoisting the blade into his gut so that Robert hovered momentarily before falling in a gasping heap to the floor, clutching his abdomen with blood sheeting between his fingers. His impossibly blue eyes found hers, perhaps searching for Anna. He moved his lips to say nothing. There was only a bubbling gasp and his eyes turned depthless.

Violet in the other room glanced up and peered through the open door but seemed unperturbed at the sight of her father lying dead in a shimmering pool of blood.

Jacob Hummel walked to the sink, rubbed at blood smeared on his sleeve and rinsed off the knife before folding the blade back into the stained wooden handle and handing it to Agnes who had risen to her feet and was moving towards the living room. He made no effort to stop her.

Sebastian stepped fastidiously around the corpse and wordlessly led Agnes to the sofa, where she crouched down in front of the little girl whose real name was Anna. Agnes closed the *Inferno* and set it to the side and drew the girl close. Only for a moment, then she stood up and faced Sebastian. He apparently had more power than she had thought possible. She wanted to speak, to exchange words, but she was so overwhelmed with raw emotion that she simply stared, forcing him to take a step back and look away.

She again felt locked in the perpetual present — time was passing but there was no past, there was no future, there was only the persistent everlasting now. She remembered both lives, Anna's and Agnes's, but neither was clear. She remembered her grandmother in Cambridge, Isabelle Klahr, and she remembered her parents in Welland, the always inseparable Homuths. She remembered studying with Chris Armitage at Duke and with Linda Hutcheon at the University of Toronto. She remembered teaching at Amherst and at UofT. She remembered meeting Rose with her honey-blonde hair and ingenuous smile at the camp in Temagami. She remembered Azziz. She remembered falling almost in love with Robert, almost in love with Sebastian.

Robert was a corpse. Sebastian was her captor. She had never visited Trinity College, although she knew it intimately through readings about Russell and his impossibly brilliant successor. She remembered meeting her daughter who named herself Violet, which was not the case.

Sebastian broke the silence.

"Come," he said in a kind voice. "We'll go down to the library."

Agnes took Violet's hand. Sebastian led the way out onto the landing. Jacob Hummel followed. Sebastian unlocked the door to the passageway between the slope of the mansard roof and the outer wall of his aerie. They all stepped into the constricted space. Sebastian turned the antique rotary switch and the lights came on and again he locked the door behind them before they progressed forward. Agnes could see that the hole she had carved behind the bookshelves had been repaired. They passed the laundry chute cupboard at the far end and Sebastian unlocked a steel-clad door to reveal the curiously ornate cabinet which on the far side opened onto a staircase descending between rough plaster walls. He indicated that Jacob Hummel should stand aside while he entered the narrow cabinet and pushed the pressure-release panel to reveal the elevator controls. He closed the door out to the outer steps, then beckoned for Agnes and Violet to enter beside him, with Jacob Hummel's looming presence assuring their compliance, before closing the interior door of the confined elevator cabinet, leaving Jacob Hummel on the landing. The little room quivered and descended in a silent gentle motion and came to an abrupt stop.

To Agnes's surprise the elevator door did not open into the antiquated mausoleum on the ground floor but into a transitional chamber on what she imagined was the floor above, leading to the byzantine stacks of Sebastian's library. He did not send the elevator back up for Jacob Hummel, who remained locked in the passageway above, where Agnes, or Anna, had escaped down the laundry chute. Jacob Hummel and Gabriel had taken Sebastian back to his apartment. Sebastian tried with a flourish to take his own life. When word filtered through to the Vivuscorps executives about what he had done, Jacob Hummel must have been instructed to preserve him from further harm, even from Robert. Especially from Robert.

Sebastian, whose name means *awesome* and *dreadful* and translates into Latin as Augustus, was an invaluable Vivuscorps asset, a powerless emperor who lived among books. The symbol of a world which they planned to obliterate, he was an Antichrist who would remain fixedly on earth as a generative referent, bearing witness to the ascension of resurrected souls whose lives had passed from their bodies through electronic portals into the mindless noosphere, into a new evolutionary phase of collective consciousness that would displace the wilful ignorance of religion and the hubris of scientific humanism — and for that Agnes was grateful — but would stifle awareness of being, or of Being, which was the one true ornament of the species. This, she abhorred.

Sebastian pushed them along: Agnes lost deeply in her thoughts, struggling valiantly to hold onto her sanity by mindfulness, however convoluted and painful, and Violet, sullen, seemingly oblivious to the dread filling the spaces around them as they progressed through passageways, corridors, and tunnels lined with volumes and volumes of books, all now as menacing as vipers, flashing venomous fangs as they passed.

The labyrinth *was* the minotaur. Books were the menace in a world where reality television displaced reality, sports broadcasting replaced activity, news programming packaged catastrophes and was, otherwise, fake, even when contrary to reason or experience, where social networks supplanted society, and one person could have a million intimate friends. Consciousness through literacy as the source of the soul was monstrously redundant. If Violet's was the first implanted cybernetic cellular system with the potential to be externally accessible, the next phase was already under way. The soul, even secular versions that would die with the death of their mentors, were archaic and would soon cease to exist.

With Sebastian in the lead, they finally arrived in a room of intimate proportions with three large easy chairs covered in worn leather and walls that were inevitably lined with books, these ones particularly ancient and venerable.

"Sit," he suggested.

Agnes tried to draw Violet close as she sank into a plush wrinkled chair, but Violet moved away and settled into the depths of a chair on her own.

"You want to know my system," he said in a challenging voice while he remained on his feet. "I think you will find it is pleasing in its simplicity and astonishing in its complexity." He paused, smiled, as if expecting Agnes to speak, but she said nothing. "Well, my inspiration is the rhizome. Do you know the *rhizome*? It is a polyphiloprogenative trope adapted by French philosophers Gilles Deleuze and Félix Guattari to signify a system where everything connects. It is a very Borgesian notion, the obverse of a maze which only offers the illusion of connection while actually preventing it."

Agnes was intrigued in spite of mounting dread.

"The system for access is very simple," Sebastian continued. "It is based on dates of acquisition. Books are filed in the order acquired. I have an exceptionally good memory concerning my investments. You might say, eidetic. If you name me the most obscure volume, I can instantly tell you the date when I bought it. Each date is a signal event in my life. And thence I know where to find it."

"But no one else can, Sebastian. The dates are special only to you. And if you expire, your library is virtually chaos."

"Yes, yes, it is all very vain, but then knowledge is, isn't it? A child starts with nothing in mind — Violet, of course, being the exception. A man or a woman, studies all his or her life to gather limitless facts and spin out skeins of infinite knowledge and then he or she dies. It is all gone. It is sad."

"And your pleasure-dome? Is it sad, as well?"

"It is a monument to the ways we have devised as a species to have endless conversations with the dead. It is how we may speak to the future. A library like this exists in the perpetual present."

"In commemoration of all we will lose under the aegis of Vivuscorps. A memorial to the end of civilization."

"Each age sees itself as the end. Perhaps we have finally achieved what our vanity anticipated all along." He drew himself forward in his chair and, stroking his chin in an unintentional parody of contemplation, he made an observation that seemed at first profoundly irrelevant. "My mad Uncle Leicester had the octagonal door-chamber built before he was locked away. It exists in the perpetual past. The doors in his little oeuvre led nowhere. I made them connect."

"*Only connect*."

"It is the heart of the entire organism."

"It is an empty chamber."

"Precisely."

How could precision be so obscure, she wondered?

"My mirrored star chamber is the future eternal. You are a multitude there in projection and not there at all."

Sebastian rose to his feet and drew an ancient text from the shelves. He took reading glasses out of his breast pocket and checked that he had the desired book, then returned the glasses to his pocket. He glanced down at his feet, rubbed his worn polished shoes one at a time against his trouser legs. Then, standing tall he flourished the book like a trophy and spoke. "*Felix culpa*, Agnes. If there is good in the world, it is because all things perish in the end. *Melius enim iudicavit de malis benefacere, quam mala nulla esse permittere.* Our curse is our blessing. Even a library has its own form of mortality. You see this. It is the 49th extant copy of Gutenberg's *Bible*. It is beyond value, yes. But, look, it is a physical thing. A thing, Agnes, nothing more." She watched, horrified, as he tore pages from the book, crumpled them, and tossed them in a pile on the floor. She tried to get up to stop him but he held a hand forward in a commanding gesture and she knew it was futile. She settled back as he continued adding to the pile, which glinted gold and vermillion from the hand-painted rubrics set against faded black type and yellowing paper.

"This building is my version of the *sublime*," he explained patiently, as if his words weren't touched with madness. "Not Edmund Burke's, who insisted the beautiful and sublime were antithetical — but you and I know enough to distrust binary oppositions. This is my humble reification of Immanuel Kant's sublime, where nobility, splendour, and terror may all be found as formless boundless qualities accessible to rational consciousness, if only we are willing to look. Look, Agnes!"

"But it's private, Sebastian. You have locked out the world."

He gazed at her dolefully. "Then I must revise the tale of the Fall. It is not a good world and never was," he said. "Consider the shattered visage of Ozymandias. Here on the borders of death, as Erich Maria Remarque describes our condition, nothing endures, not even pride. There was nowhere to fall *from* — if you travel east of Eden forever, encircling creation, you are still travelling east."

The manic thread of logic woven through the strange tapestry of incoherence he laid out before her was frightening. Somewhere in his mind, havoc made sense.

"Sebastian!" She was insistent. "Do you think we are beyond redemption? The world can be good. It is we who are not."

"Isn't it pretty to think so."

"No, it is grotesque."

"A Vivuscorps world is grotesque, dear Agnes. You, perhaps, are holy, in your way. As for me, my only course of action is despair."

He took a lighter from his pocket. She hoped he was going to light candles. She looked about. There were no candles.

"The apparition of these faces in a crowd," he said. "This place is filled with the faces of the dead — petals on a wet black bough."

He squatted beside the scattered galaxy of Gutenberg's *Bible* and set it aflame. Sparks flared like shooting stars. Violet stared, mesmerized. Agnes was aghast with horror: horror at the obliteration of the inestimably valuable *Bible*, at the impending holocaust that would consume thousands upon thousands of books, and at the inevitable, hideous, and arbitrary annihilation of their lives. Even Violet, did he mean to kill her as well? In a flashing moment of clarity, she wondered, is the point of such fiery destruction to eliminate Violet? Everything else, everyone else, is collateral damage.

Sebastian stepped back from the flames that flared and seared the ceiling and surged in waves across the carpets, lapping at the lower shelves with their tinder-dry burden. He reached out towards Violet. The little girl with the mechanical mind scrambled closer to hold his hand. He turned to Agnes and with a gesture commanded her to follow. The clouds of smoke and fiery heat drove them forward. At the elevator, Sebastian placed his hands on Agnes's shoulders and shouted a manic benediction over the enveloping din: "William Hazlitt declared poetry is all that is worth remembering." The heat was becoming unbearable. The roar of the conflagration shook the floor and made the walls tremble as row upon row of books burst into flames behind them. "Poetry is all."

"Stop," she screamed into his face. He held her immobilized. It was as if he were compelled to fill the fiery gap between them and eternity with words.

"Ignore Occam's razor," he shouted. "*Amor est magis cognitivus quam cognito.*" Then he added with unnerving composure, "*Lectio difficilior potior*. The most difficult reading is best."

With this final utterance, Sebastian pushed her into the elevator. When she desperately reached out for Violet, he pushed her again, violently, and she fell back and slumped against the far wall of the cabinet. Sebastian held Violet close as he leaned in to manipulate the control panel and stepped back with Violet beside him. The elevator door closed. Agnes's final glimpse of the little girl was smoke billowing around her and flames surging forward. The elevator quivered, slouched interminably downwards, and settled. The wall Agnes was leaning against slid open and she rolled back onto a wooden landing leading out to the garden on the east side of the house. As she rose to her feet, the door closed again, sealing her from the raging fire inside. When the heat pulsating through the elevator door became unbearable, she retreated in shock across the lawn with the house roaring behind her and merged with the gathering onlookers on the sidewalk along Errington Lane.

She stared into the inferno, numbed in holy terror. Such was the library of enduring dreams. It hardly registered when the emergency vehicles arrived. The fire brigade concentrated on preventing the fire from spreading. Time passed, the EMS people left. The mansard roof collapsed, the scorched upper leaves on the maples flickered and flared. She noticed the crowd had thinned. A few stragglers remained, some with their backs to the fire, focussed intensely on their e-glasses to help them process what they were witnessing. Off to one side, glazed with the light of the dying flames, a solitary man cast a long shadow that merged with the darkness behind him. It was Jacob Hummel. He must have escaped across the back passage, knocked through the repaired hole into Sebastian's apartment, and descended the stairs before they crumbled. He looked smoke-drenched, blood-smeared, otherwise unscathed. Despite her initial horror at seeing him, she felt a strange kinship. He too was a survivor. She felt for Solomon's jackknife in her pocket. It was good to touch something real. She turned her gaze to stare in the direction of the ravine where he lived.

The old man walked out of the distance towards her. He was accompanied by a little girl holding his hand. Agnes froze, struggling to believe. When they got close, the girl acknowledged Agnes but held back, indicating she wanted no fuss. Agnes wavered. "What happened?" she said, trying desperately to suppress all emotion that might distress Violet.

"My father and Sebastian and Jacob Hummel," Violet said. "It was 900 degrees Celsius. They burned up."

"But you didn't, Sweetheart."

"No," Violet agreed. "Neither did you."

And neither did Jacob Hummel, Agnes thought, but didn't draw Violet's attention to him standing between shadows and light at the edge of the scene. There was enough confusing information to process as it was.

Solomon, with a firm grasp on his walking stick, spoke directly to Agnes, calling her Anna. He explained how the girl had told him that she had squirmed away from Sebastian; or possibly he had pushed her away. She was so small she stayed under the smoke and she found the magical room where the upper elevator waited to carry her down to the catacombs. She had operated it before, she knew how, she had unusual presence of mind. Azziz still reclined on his mossy catafalque. A rime of mould made it seem like he had turned into stone. Even his neatly trimmed beard and dyed black hair seemed to have ossified. By reaching in, pressing buttons, then standing clear, she shuttled to the lower elevator, descended into the tunnel, and followed the water course out to the ravine. She walked up to Solomon's camp and told him what happened, exactly as he explained. Violet listened to her own words without interest and didn't seem inclined to elaborate.

Agnes handed Becket to the old man which he addressed with a few unintelligible words of affection before stuffing it into a pocket in the folds of his clothes.

"Thank you," he said. "I'm sorry about Rosie, he was a good lad."

"She was," said Agnes.

"Yes, she was. I loved her like she was my own."

Agnes gave his hand a squeeze. She turned and easing down onto her knees on the sidewalk she held the little girl at arm's length. Had Violet gone to the old man because he was there or because he was a vestige of the world being lost? Agnes wanted poetry, a symbolic gesture. She feared expediency. The fire gleamed in the girl's eyes. Agnes wanted to embrace her, to weep, to laugh.

The little girl offered a solemn impersonal smile. "The books are all gone," she said and twisted to watch the flames. Agnes shivered as Violet slouched forward and slipped through her hands. The Cloisters crumbled. The girl glanced back at her, sparks danced in her eyes. The girl resumed monitoring the fire. Agnes stared at the back of her head, the fine texture of her dark hair gleamed from the soaring flames and the lowering smoke-filled midday sky. Within the roar of the conflagration, she could hear the words, *mere anarchy is loosed upon the world*. She smiled; she chose to be Anna. She gazed around. Everyone was wearing glasses except Violet and herself, and Jacob Hummel who stood off to the side, and the kindly old man called Solomon. She felt a tighter breathing and zero at the bone.

# BOOK TWO: THE INVISIBLE LABYRINTH

# Chapter One
# In the Time of Borges

This is a time before everything means something else, when words are things and there is no difference in the mind between 'stone' and a stone. There are no tenses, no parts or figures of speech. Lies and metaphors are inconceivable. The graphic design on the wall of a cave is an auroch in flight. The rock breathes and snorts and clatters with hooves over rubble as the animal perpetually runs. Words and images struggle to break through the walls of time, carving cracks in the darkness. The human brain is preparing to explode with radiant and murderous light.

A woman stoops and enters her shelter. She remains bent over after her head clears the pole holding an auroch skin in place to keep out the cold. She has been gone several days; she is looking at something in the mottled darkness. Her eyes cannot focus and she rubs them with the backs of her hands. She kneels tentatively beside a rumple of shadows which is the body of a younger woman on a bed of sphagnum and she touches the cold lips with her fingers, then slips her hand under the covering and feels the hard chilled flesh. She stares for a moment at the dead face of her daughter revealed in strands of light that penetrate the sides of the shelter, animated by wind scattering sunlight through wavering spruce.

The woman rises to her feet and stands for a moment, then leaves and the door falls, closed, behind her. She stands full-throated in front of the shelter, letting the sunlight warm her breast. Her eyes are moist and her lips tremble until she closes her mouth and draws them tight over her teeth. When her eyes become dry, she turns and walks along a narrow path past several homes in dead-fall spaces among storm-battered spruce. When she arrives at a skin door that is larger than the others she stops and draws herself tall and then stoops and enters.

A man her own age, fully grown with good teeth, glances up. He continues to stroke the girl lying against his outstretched legs, soothing her, as if keeping her still. The girl is the same age as the woman's daughter. She looks frightened but the woman, showing her own fine teeth, touches her face and the girl shrinks submissively and lies quiet.

The woman utters a sound to the man that reveals a story they both understand although the details for each are different. The man shrugs. His lips form a snarl accentuated by his beard. The woman lowers herself, pushing the girl to the side across the sphagnum. The three of them touch skin to skin. There is no further movement until the man reaches out and stirs the small fire in the centre of the shelter. The man spits into the flames and wipes the drizzle from his beard.

The woman forces herself more firmly between him and the girl. As soon as the man's hand falls away from the girl, she gets up and quietly leaves. The man rises to his knees and positions himself over the woman and briefly invades her body, surges, and rolls away. He falls asleep. She leans forward and picks up a blackened boulder from the hearth, weighs it, and brings it down sharply, cracking open his skull. His eyes flare wide in the moment of his death.

She pulls a charred stick from the embers and holding it close to her mouth she blows it into flame and then reaching out she touches the flame to a brittle tendril of the uprooted spruce that forms the skeletal structure of the dwelling. She rises and walks into the dappled sunlight.

Behind her, the wood and dried mosses and desiccated skins blaze into an inferno that roars for some time and then collapses over the smouldering body. She picks up chunks of dried log that have been smashed into manageable pieces and throws them onto the fire. Bystanders move close and a few heave wood into the flames, until the charred remains in the collapsed shelter are no longer identifiable as a corpse, then they drift away. A few others hold chunks of meat skewered on green sticks over the embers and cook them to succulence.

The woman walks back to her own shelter, carrying a glowing coal on a small flat rock. She sets that shelter alight as well and sits close so the flames scorch her face and eventually, she gets up and stirs the embers until her daughter's body collapses into fiery pieces and mixes with burnt detritus and scarred clumps of earth.

It is evening when a man approaches and takes her roughly by the hand, forcing her to her feet. This woman whose daughter was murdered and this unlikely man who acceded to the leadership of their community are now a couple. Neither has a name. They have known each other since infancy.

The man she killed had been powerful and perhaps handsome. This man is more supple, well adapted to hunting for aurochs on the plains above their valley. He had once impaled a lunging sabre-toothed tiger on a thick length of dry spruce he had sharpened in a fire, offering his own body as bait. He wears the tiger's skin draped across his shoulders. She is slender as a reed, silent and quick, able to snare rabbits with her hands and to strip the skin from frog's legs with a single tearing motion as she breaks them away from their quivering bodies.

Inside his shelter, he touches her gently. She opens herself to him. Afterwards they sleep. Frozen rains begin to whirl outside in a high-pitched wail and their fire crackles in defiance beside them. Dusk turns to darkness. The flames of his fire shoot wavering bolts of light through chinks in his shelter out into the night. Towards dawn the air is thick with sound and they do not distinguish the earth breaking along the ravine's upper edge nor the groan of stiff clay slurry as it slides down the hillside like a rumbling wall and smashes into their shelter and buries them, clasped in each other's arms, and they disappear for fifty thousand years.

***

David thought, what is it like to be human? This was not a simple question. He was human, but how could he know what it was *like* to be a human being other than himself. He was fifteen. He was a cyborg, as were his friends. They had DNA microcomputers embedded in their brains at birth. The boys among them were sterilized if their genetic capacity to advance evolution were in the slightest doubt. He didn't know whether he had been sterilized or not. He assumed he had not, but it didn't seem very important. He was as human as any of his forebears since *homo sapiens sapiens* first emerged as self-conscious beings. A simple surgical procedure had given him advantages of cerebral enhancement that allowed him to access documented fragments of their primordial experiences, perceptions, and dreams. It also made the question of what it was like to be human an utterly isolating existential dilemma.

Contemporaries who were not enhanced were educated in parallel systems to perform the necessary services that kept the mechanism of society both fluid and stable, gathering garbage, driving transport, working as statisticians, working as lawyers, maintaining the necessary infrastructures. Their number was reinforced by shift workers coming through from the city.

For androids like himself, the world was bigger and more elegant, filled with dance and music and art, with words and language and literature, with thoughts and ideas and concepts, all of which made their lives astonishing, if somewhat predictable, because the experience of everyone happened in their minds in exactly the same way. They did not actually dance or make music. They listened and observed. They did not read books, they read *about* Shakespeare and Dickens and Yeats. They didn't study philosophy although they were sufficiently exposed to major schools of thought to recognize them when encountered. They could quote brief excerpts from Nietzsche and Derrida, from *Hamlet* or *Prufrock*, without knowing how inextricable were their words from the whole.

In fact, and David sensed this without knowing it: they were *too* schooled. They knew about everything as passive receptors but they thought almost nothing.

He contemplated his own place in the world from the perspective of being already dead, a condition not inimical to the teen sensibility. He envisioned his tombstone with a prolix epitaph in a bold but lower-case font.

**in life he suffered from a sense of unreality**
**dead**
**he is no longer the ghostly creature he was back then**

David knew he was cribbing from Herbert Ashe's obituary. The words were originally written by Jorge Luis Borges in his book, *Ficciones*. This was one of only two books David had access to that fell into the realm of 'literature' as defined by his mind-monitor lexicon. The other was *Wuthering Heights*. The impenetrable radiance of the first, the incomprehensible passions of the second, were treasures he shared with no one.

A third book in his possession was not literary. It was a tattered copy of *Tractatus Logico-Philosophicus*, a treatise on logic and philosophy, by someone called Ludwig Wittgenstein. The prose was so sparse, precise, and opaque, he did not pretend to understand, yet he immersed himself in it over and over, that somewhere in its depths he would discover an alternate reality he could believe in, since his own seemed illusory.

There were other books in the house, the secret cache in the attic from which he had extricated Borges, Brontë, and Wittgenstein. This was forbidden territory. The one time he had broken in, these were the first books he had grasped in the darkness before fleeing. He found it reassuring to know more were there if he needed them.

His entire world was Borgesian: nothing was what it seemed, nothing connected except by authorial decree, and everything implied something else. He presumed all literature was like that, beguilingly disorienting and cleverly arbitrary. He read Emily Brontë through a Borgesian lens which made her prose seem airily decadent. The same lens made Wittgenstein seem comical. The *Tractatus* intrigued him because it was both more expansive than so-called literature and more limiting.

He kept all three books stealthily, hidden under the mattress in the spare room he was told his father had used as a study.

His friend Lucas, sitting on the edge of David's bed, was staring into the middle distance. David knew by the intensity of his friend's rapid-eye movements, culminating in a self-satisfied grin that he had been watching a classic hockey game playing out in his mind. Paul Henderson scored the winning goal. Canada beat Russia. It was September 28, 1972. The ignominy of impending defeat was displaced in the final seconds by the euphoria of well-deserved victory.

"What're you watching?" David asked.

"Nothing. Just finished. What about you?"

"Nothing," said David. "I'm thinking."

"Does it hurt?"

"A lot," said David.

"It's not encouraged, you know."

"What is it *like* to be you, Luke?"

"What's it like to be *you*?"

"I don't know. I guess we never know what it's like to be ourselves. We're just what we are."

"I'm going home now," said Lucas and left.

David settled back in his chair. His mother had visitors. He didn't see who they were when he and Lucas came in. Their voices suggested an older man and a youth, perhaps a young woman. He couldn't remember the last time they had a visitor. Violet's behaviour had been strange the last six months.

His mind drifted from the world he knew to another and he contemplated the possibility of transparent tigers and towers of blood. Borges described these as indigenous features of an alternate world called Tlön, which was perhaps more real and possibly more reasonable than our own because it was put together not by a pathologically insecure God on a rigid schedule but by a committee of experts, a secret society of astronomers, mathematicians, biologists, metaphysicians, geometricians, and engineers, under the guidance of an organizational genius who then washed his hands, or hers, of the whole project and retired to an abstruse oasis in the middle-eastern sheikhdom of Uqbar, on the planet Earth.

He studied the poster on his wall featuring various icons of the greater and lesser religions. There were images of Jesus and Vishnu, gods incarnate in whom the finite and infinite merged, and of Buddha the teacher and Muhammad the prophet, but there were also sketches in smaller proportion showing regional and ethnic deities. MakiMaki and Ra **and** the Orenda and others. Across the top of the poster in florid letters were the words:

**GOD LISTENS**

and across the bottom in a more ominous script:

**you must have faith to believe**

He did believe, although he was uncertain in what. This was not the same as having faith, which had never seemed an option. Religion made him uneasy.

He did not understand. It was not expected. He leaned away from the poster to put it in a better perspective and sighed.

His friends had identical posters beside their identical desks in their identical rooms and all of them valued their posters as ornaments peculiar to themselves. Whatever its message meant to others, to each of them it was affirmation of their personal relationship with an indefinable God. Since their DNA implants did not allow for metaphor, for one thing to be *like* another, they necessarily believed conflicting religions were simultaneously true. The fact that the Christian Gospels differed and contradicted, subverted or refuted each other quite brutally, did not mean those who grew up in the Christian quadrant did not hold each to be sacrosanct. It had been that way for over two thousand years — nothing was about to prioritize the Gospels in order of verity. Paradox, the simultaneous holding of opposing beliefs, was fundamental to faith. Faith was fundamental to the acceptance of paradox.

Paradox was the meta-meme of the age, as 'efficiency' had been of his mother's and 'irony' of his grandmother Anna's. Everything before that was history. What fell outside the narrative scope of history never happened. David had recently discovered he could think about such things. History and text were coeval.

Unlike Irenio Funes who, as described by Borges after the young man's death, had been cursed with a memory so perfect that the details barraging his mind overwhelmed him, David could control the delivery of textual information through his DNA microcomputer, such that he was able to formulate the occasional platonic idea. Against the deluge, he could shore up his mind with abstraction.

Funes was so relentlessly receptive to incoming data that he could make out the infinitesimal progress of a human body ageing, of moisture evaporating, paint drying, oxidizing rust — and structured thought was impossible. David's experience of universal knowledge was more Proustian. From the scent of a sweet bun, a madeleine, he could summon a curiously ordered sequence of information and images that rounded to eventual completion. The process was diverting but of little consequence and occasionally left room to think. While he had read only one book by Jorge Luis Borges, another by Ludwig Wittgenstein, and another by Emily Brontë, the latter not yet to the end, he didn't know if others in his peer group had the same independence of mind. As far as he knew, he was alone.

He waited until his mother's guests had left, then walked downstairs and through to the kitchen. Violet was in the living room with its minimalist furniture and pale green walls, apparently talking to herself. He poured a glass of unsweetened oat milk and stood at the sink, looking out over Lake Ontario, wondering what lay on the other side. Road maps and topographical charts immediately came to mind, but he rejected them in favour of Ogle, which gave him access to the minutiae of people's lives, although in a disorienting blur, since he had no place in particular he wanted to see. In his mind, he scanned from Rochester to Niagara-on-the-Lake, where he plunged into a scene on Brock Street and narrowed his vision to follow a girl about his own age wearing a yellow sweater who walked with a flouncing gait. He dodged passersby to overtake her, hoping to see her up close. As he expected, each person he passed was disguised with a version of his own face, aged appropriately and modified for gender and ethnicity, but always an anonymous variant of himself. When he receded a little and shifted to the next block and closed in again, reversing his course to move straight towards the girl in the yellow sweater, he was excited to find her increasingly attractive, until he was close enough that Ogle blanked out her features and substituted his own and he was looking at a prettier version of himself.

He blinked and glanced down at a clay saucer in the sink. A pineapple sitting on it the previous day had generated fruit flies before being tossed into the compost. There was a new generation of flies swarming over the clay. He turned on the tap and a stream of water blasted the saucer and killed half a dozen of the insects instantaneously. A few others struggled in a thin pool of water on the bottom of the sink and then swirled to their deaths down the drain. Another dozen flitted in the air over the sink, waiting for a new place to settle, lay eggs, and expire. It struck David as an exceedingly morbid scenario but he couldn't turn away. He lunged with his hands and clapped, exterminating a few more, then he washed away their tiny remains and shook flecked fingers dry, sending bits through the air that spotted the window glass and distorted the clear vista of the Lake.

David wondered, what was it *like* to be a fruit fly? It really concerned him. He began to feel guilty for inflicting arbitrary death on creatures whose lives were of such brief duration, whose being was so tenuous, subject to extermination by mindless forces of water, of air, of drain systems, of clapped hands. But no, not *mindless* forces since he had initiated his own destructive action and he had a mind. Half a billion years of evolution — one swoop of a predator's hand. Oh God.

David watched the surviving fruit flies gather in a slowly condensing gyre of flittering dots and dashes. His hands tightened on the edge of the sink and he wept. He had often cried before, but weeping was different. It was something he did without witnessing himself doing it. He wept for what he had done to intrude on the natural procedures of evolution and not for the flies he had murdered, although that's what he believed he had done. He did not imagine them with tiny minds that anticipated tragedy or grieved or considered their mortal condition. He could not imagine being a fruit fly amounted to very much. He wept for disturbing the universe.

Then several tiny flies flew too close and he snorted so as not to breathe them in through his nostrils and he scooped his hands through the air, grinding his fingers to exterminate any that might have got entangled in the air currents between them. He gazed out the window and enjoyed the sun glimmering on the lake and forgot about weeping or the struggle to survive or about the girl in the yellow sweater in Niagara-on-the-Lake hidden behind the mask of his face.

In the living room, his mother was still talking to herself. When David rounded the corner from the dining area, he saw she was addressing her laptop. "Why are you using a screen?" he asked. "Can't you see it all in your head?"

She looked up at her strange and curious offspring. David was on the verge of outgrowing his childhood. He still looked like himself but she wasn't sure whether he was becoming passively handsome as his features settled into a permanently quizzical scowl, or was he deceptively serene like herself? He towered over her, still uncomfortable with his size. He was in that vulnerable indeterminate teen phase where he could become anyone, even a stranger. She patted the sofa seat beside her and he flopped down, legs outstretched, arms wrapped around himself, warning her that was as far as affection would go. Then he snuggled closer, but only for a moment, tilting his head to her shoulder before he abruptly sat upright.

"So, explain," he said. "Why the screen?"

"Simultaneity," said Violet. "Mind-monitors are Aristotelian, they provide information sequentially on command or through cause and effect. I need to break the chain. Sometimes it's good to think about things that don't follow from algorithms or simply don't make sense. Antinomies are a valuable research tool."

He automatically summoned a definition: *antinomy*, noun, a contradiction between two reasonable premises. Of course, a paradox.

"I thought science avoided contradictions."

"Science does. Scientists don't. We try to resolve contradictions."

"Doesn't that make you dangerous?"

"I suppose it does, but I'm a palaeoanthropologist. That's hardly threatening, just not very important."

"So, you're using the laptop to contemplate stored information in secret. You're trying to think without getting caught. That sounds like a clandestine op to me. Very important, highly covert, awesomely subversive."

"David, David. I'm trying to get beyond language to the beginning of time."

He drew in a deep breath. His mother had never appeared so vulnerable. He envisioned her statement in a variant font.

**I'm trying to get beyond language to the beginning of time.**

"Sounds like a tough one," he said. "If you wait, it will all become clear. You'll know what your stone-bones say because the option *not* to know is impossible."

"Perhaps you're right. I've finished my project. I was only on-screen for a bit of nostalgia. Soon, perhaps, we'll see how well I've succeeded."

"Soon, when?"

"As you've told me, yourself, time is relative, if you can believe it exists at all. What happened in the past, when language began, and what happened to me as a child are equally inaccessible. The future is far more opaque."

"*Impalpable* is what I called it."

"Of course. I'm the one calling it 'opaque'. And whenever it comes, I hope my work will be understood."

"By whom?"

"Everyone capable of understanding."

"Said she in her tautological way."

"Don't be pretentious, David. Use words appropriate to your age."

"Shoot, poop, damn. Is that better? Look, you're being solipsistic. Everyone you want to have read you, will eventually read you. 'Every man should be capable of all ideas.' You just have to be patient."

"By 'man' you mean women as well, I assume."

"Yes," he said, embarrassed.

"And you believe that, do you?"

"Pierre Menard, the most recent author of *Don Quixote*, an exact duplicate, word for word, line for line, of the novel written by Cervantes three hundred years earlier, wrote those words to his friend, Mister Borges, who recorded them in a book. What doesn't have the potential to be known will never be known. What will be known, cannot be avoided. Borges writes stuff like that."

"It's fiction, you realize."

"Think that if you will, Mother. I couldn't possibly say." He enjoyed being arch. It was out of character.

"I'm not belittling fiction," she said. "Stories can be more powerful than history, or anthropology, for that matter. They come closer to truth by fusing feelings with fact."

He gazed into her iridescent blue eyes and wondered what secrets lay behind them. His own eyes were brown to hazel, depending on the light.

"So you believe fiction could set the world right?" he asked.

"A novel is a world in itself. If we know what's wrong with one world, perhaps we can make it right in another."

"Have you been writing a novel?' he asked.

"You know it would be illegal and very dangerous. Why don't you go out and play?"

"I'm fifteen. Perhaps I shall go out and consort with friends, toke up, do molly, pour a few back, and have careless sex."

"How do you know about Borges? I'm sure they don't teach literary subversion in school."

"They don't teach literature, only *about* it. I read it upstairs."

"You're not supposed to read fiction."

"You're not supposed to own books."

"Nobody cares. Nobody has the patience to read any more. They were my mother's personal trove. They're locked away."

"Anna's books. I know where you keep them. I know the combination."

"You don't."

"Yeah, I do. So explain why didn't you just Ogle the site of your dig?"

"I'm looking at shots I downloaded last summer. Ogle shows you what's there in the present and I'm trying to see what was there, tens of thousands of years ago."

"By talking to a scanned image a few months old?"

"Exactly, smart-aleck. I'm in a dialogue with me."

"Who's winning?"

"It's a dialogue, not an argument. Between knowledge and experience, self and soul. Using imagination to plumb the depths of genetic memory."

"You're kidding."

"Possibly not."

"That sounds like fiction to me."

She leaned back and looked at him, looking for herself. He was a strange boy, attractive and extremely intelligent. He seemed out of place in an epoch of cerebral enhancement. He was uneasy with cybernetic interference, yet he had known no other way to be, so he was thoughtfully unhappy a lot of the time rather than a rebel or anarchist. It was difficult to explain to him that her work was highly unpopular in the circles of power that ran their lives. No one disagreed with the Darwinian origin of the human species, but many found contentious the idea that we made a sudden leap from protohuman to human through language acquisition. Such a sinister notion undermined the authority of the Company by suggesting that a mutation of such magnitude could have occurred without its intervention.

"How can you get beyond language to the beginning of time if it has no beginning?" he asked. "If there wasn't time, then nothing could exist."

"Or everything can altogether. Certain cosmologists argue the universe was once a singularity and the laws of physics didn't apply. Time could not exist back then. There was nowhere for it to happen. Then the Big Bang, as Stephen Hawking described it — the universe burst into motion, physics took hold, time began. Simple as that."

"Except as a scientist you're not talking about time on a cosmological scale. You're a palaeoanthropologist, you're talking about consciousness of time, a much more recent event."

"David! I think you've been paying attention for the last fifteen years! I'm talking about consciousness of time *and* about consciousness through language, which I absolutely believe are the same exact thing. Before there were words for time, it didn't exist as a linear dimension in our ancestral awareness. Everything was in the present, even the past."

He wasn't convinced. He wasn't sure if he disagreed with her line of reasoning or was simply resistant to his mother being an authority. He smiled with affectionate condescension. "And you argue our capacity to chatter came to us in a moment of illumination, all at once, like."

"Like, yes. It's not so radical as it seems. The human hand had the ability to grasp with its opposable thumb for eons before it shaped stone into weapons or tools. The capacity for phonemic diversity undoubtedly evolved long before language itself. Social developments did not originate in evolutionary process. They were the ingenious response of our species to spontaneous changes. We evolved because we are intelligent. We did not develop intelligence because we evolved."

"What about intelligence itself, though, where did that come from? Sounds like you're making an argument for divine intervention."

"God no, not at all, you know better than that. Intelligence came together as we acquired the means to survive. It was little more than a concomitant factor, like hairlessness and toe nails."

"And why does the Company think this is dangerous?"

"Who said it does?"

"You're talking to your reflection on a laptop and you've been doing it a lot. That seems covert to me."

"I'm afraid nothing in this world is disconnected, David."

"Who were your visitors?"

"Disconnected."

"Ha." He liked it when she was elliptical. She had been alternately buoyant during the last few months and quite depressed. She had been developing a secretive project. It was apparently a radical departure from her usual work. They never talked about it directly. He missed hanging out with her. She was regularly away on digs and over the last few months she had seemed in another world. He liked to think they occupied two sides of a complementary paradox. He hoped now that her project was finished; if it was, they would reconnect like they used to be, and she wouldn't retreat from Tlön to Uqbar, even if it were in Persia, perhaps, on his own planet Earth.

"You'd think this project of yours, this book, was actually going to change the world," he said.

"And you think only your precious Borges could write such a book as fantastical fiction. Words have impact, David. The chill of Orwell's phrase, 'Big Brother Is Watching You' is felt to the present day."

He shrugged and grinned. He had no idea what she was talking about as he walked back through to the kitchen. He thought she might call after him, to quote Borges herself, but he was already out the side door, thinking, *Time is forever dividing itself toward innumerable futures… sometimes the pathways of this labyrinth are bound to converge.* She wants to be there when futures converge, when all the narratives of history come together in a single idea. She wants that idea, the theory of everything, she wants it to be hers.

She stared at the primitive laptop in front of her. Only months before she had struggled to formulate narratives from the evidence displayed on her screen. Were fossilized remains of the two people she had unearthed the previous summer tumbled together when the ice-age retreated and run-off carried them from different eras down the slope to converge in the basin where she found them? Or did recent floodwaters expose them where they had originally been buried side by side? If the latter, had one died in order to lie with the other in death as a token of honour, devotion, or servitude? Or could they have been swallowed together by the earth in some misadventure of natural origins and been preserved in a posture of affection by the elements that killed them? A clutter of bones washed out of their graves had moved her to curiosity. To imagine the simultaneous deaths of embracing lovers sent a chill through her heart.

The screen showed the gridded layout of the dig from a perspective that foregrounded the intermingled sprawl of their bones. The evidence of soil around them indicated they were contemporaries. Relative differences in bone mass suggested a male and a female. Their story was open to imagination. Violet needed romance to stimulate empathy, to make their lives real. In violation of professional protocols, she needed to formulate answers, not perpetuate questions.

And so she had written how the past might possibly have been. Writing outside the proscriptions of cyber-reality was challenging. She lived in a time when words had again become things. Language displaced perception. What could not be named did not exist. Words signified words in exponential succession, images signified images. An auroch on a computer screen was a software composite that simulated a creature displaying all the facts known about aurochs, an exemplary auroch — or it was a beast clattering with hooves over rubble, reeking of blood-wet fur and snorting as it impaled the onlooker in a gesture of arrested violence and breathtaking beauty, with an uncanny absence of pain. The auroch was an information package or an illusionary stimulant, but not both. It seemed, the mind no longer existed where such fusion was possible.

From where she was sitting, she could see David and Lucas out front. By their postures, slightly turned away from one another, she knew they had merged their mind-monitors and were exploring factoids together or playing a game. She was relieved. She knew the Company was watching David. He was different. She did not want him to be *too* different, and Lucas was not.

As she knew very well, surveillance was the key to a functioning society. Ogle was everywhere, their cameras so tiny they were largely unseen. They monitored all forms of life on the planet, enabling necessary adjustments for the greater good — except in a few major cities, of course, each known by the same name, The City of the End of Things. These areas were isolated behind electronic walls and were being allowed to die off through natural attrition. They were largely ignored.

Some of the surveillance craft, drones named after male bees who hover to breed but do no other work beyond perpetuating the species with an occasional efflux of sperm, were said to be capable of tracking the genomic signatures of dangerous individuals and blasting them with a microscopic missile that left no more residue than spontaneous combustion might have done. This was so rare an occurrence that many thought it was an urban myth perpetuated as an incentive to keep civil peace. Others, however, found convincing proof in the inexplicable conflagrations that occasionally flared up where, they argued, unexpected materials had been caught in the line of fire and burst into flames.

Such was the case when Violet was exterminated shortly after David walked out to the street. She was in her living room with the pale green walls, perusing images of bone fragments, trying to perceive a particular pattern in their dispersal, and then she was a wisp of vapours and smoke. Not even her clothing was burnt. It simply collapsed, still warm from her body. She no longer existed.

In the attic, securely crated in a room with a combination lock on the door, her mother's books, Anna's books, exploded into a fireball and dropped through the attic floor, gathered force and plummeted into the living room as David came rushing in. He stopped short at the edge of the inferno, staring at the small pile of her clothes. Violet, he whispered plaintively. Mom, Violet. She could not wait for death. My God, he thought. Oh God. And in that instant he was struck by a collapsing joist that knocked him clear of the fire. Hot blood congealed around the wound in his head as he lay still as a fallen statue, and the fire raged like a funeral pyre, casting his body in dazzling light.

# Chapter Two
# The Labyrinth

He was lost inside a labyrinth consisting of a single invisible line that was endless, without direction or markers. He was contained in a deafening roar that might have been taken for silence. He smelled smoke, then the absence of smoke. Slowly his confusion resolved into an awareness of time, a sense of terror and elation, and the unbearable knowledge that his mother had been consumed in a fire. Relief at surviving collapsed. He opened his eyes and saw a woman who looked like his mother peering back, gazing at him with inscrutable sadness.

*This is a dream*, he thought, but he knew it wasn't a dream. He remembered a massive dull blow to his head in the instant his senses collapsed. He closed his eyes and the woman disappeared.

The antiseptic odours affirmed that he was in a hospital. He opened his eyes and the woman was gone. Perhaps he had been hallucinating, perhaps he was dead. Did heaven smell like a medicine cabinet? Had his mother come first to welcome him home? Was God too busy to greet him, trying to cope with an immediate knowledge of all that existed, exists, or would ever exist, hearing the prayers of every being ever gifted with language? Was the Lord distracted by excessive reality?

If there were no words, no prayers, no language to utter them, was God even possible? David's grief was unnervingly metaphysical.

He could not fully comprehend that his mother was dead. She defined him at fifteen almost as much as before he discovered his otherness when he was weaned. He was not ready to stand on his own. It was enough to make forays into the world at school and among acquaintances who experienced the same reality as he did. If he was different at all, it was because Violet was different and he could safely test his limits and potential against her. Without her, he was a gangly kid at a loss for whoever he was. He felt empty, aching from a mighty vacuum that sucked inside like a black hole threatening to swallow him.

He closed his eyes tightly, squinting to fight off tears. When he opened them again the woman was back in the room. She was a girl, half his mother's age. It was important to determine how old she was, to gauge what responses were appropriate. She had dark eyes, and his mother's were blue. His mother had been middle height, she was taller, leaner, more athletic.

Both were attractive but his mother tended towards prettiness, delicate despite her years on excavations in gruelling conditions. This woman holding his hand was unconditionally beautiful but not perfect, not flawed by perfection. Pale, with dark hair. Black-brown eyes. Her features were strongly defined, in exact proportion, cut with flowing precision, animated by an inner mobility that gave the unblemished surface demeanour a haunting vitality. And yet he could not read her expression. He could not read her eyes. He had no idea what she was thinking or feeling. She was intriguing, enchanting, enigmatic. She leaned forward and smiled. Was it a gesture of concern, an invitation to trust, or was it meant to conceal something inexplicably perverse or subversive?

He inhaled deeply to clear his head but the pain was unbearable. He could smell the woman's femininity — an intoxicating blend of pheromones and lavender so subtle and confusing he recognized it only as warmth, as intimacy, as nurturing, beguiling, seductive. His emotions were in raw disarray. He was appalled at his excitement in response to someone who reminded him of his mother, whose death he was grieving. Was sex usually this uncomfortable? Was this proof his mother wasn't actually dead? He had only seen a pile of her clothes swallowed up in flames. My God, he grasped at the possibility she could be alive. And no, he sank back into himself. He intuitively recognized the Company's signature work, even if he didn't understand its methods or reasons. He knew she was gone. Without explanation. Quickly and cleanly, were it not for the fire caused by his grandmother's hidden books. The Company answered to no one.

How could sex and death vie with each other inside him? Was this an affliction of puberty? He considered himself post-adolescent. He shaved quite often. His voice was deep enough his mother would imitate its broken rumble in fun. Was this maturity? He didn't think of himself as an adult. He was in transition. Was this what was expected in the grown-up world, that death and sex coexisted, not always, perhaps, but they could?

"My name is Grace," said the woman. "I am your caretaker." Did she mean guardian or guard? She paused, then added, "For the time being."

"Are you a nurse or a technician?" he asked.

"A little of both. Think of me as a surrogate."

"For what? My mother?"

"So you know, you remember."

He turned his head away. She was a representative of the Company. She was there to interrogate him.

"That's just as well," she said in response to his silence. "It will be easier to adjust."

His mind raced furiously but couldn't get traction. Adjust to what? The mystery of Violet's demise? His isolation in the world left empty by her absence? The searing pain in his head? Why did this woman remind him so much of her? Was she a surrogate parent? A surrogate for society, for the Company? Was she an avatar, the incarnation of a computer ideal or, as Hindus saw avatars, the incarnation of divinity itself? Was she an angel, a distraction? He had been taught to fear distractions, anything that would draw his interest away from mind-monitor primacy, anything that would stimulate imagination insight intuition speculative thought, anything that might disrupt his perceptions of things as they were intended to be. Was she a bridge to what had happened? With the solipsism of youth, he wondered, was it all *his* fault?

He looked at the young woman who called herself Grace. He imagined that wasn't her real name. She was too much an integral part of the hospital setting not to have given up personal identity. People working in healthcare, education, social services, the military, the sciences, engineering, generally worked behind professional pseudonyms. When they weren't at work, they could disengage, merge with the masses on line, in their heads, play war games, watch athletic tournaments, interact with serial dramas and comedies, all with comforting anonymity. Work meant detached engagement, leisure meant engaged detachment. Those not in the professions, from shopkeepers to trades people, bankers to clergy, were not called upon by their jobs to have personality or suppress it. They usually kept their own names.

"For you," the woman said. Had he asked? She wasn't as young as he thought.

"What?" he said.

"I'm a surrogate for you."

"I'm right here."

She smiled benignly. She was annoyingly attractive. Grief and pain did not mask the distraction. Behind her, the sun had fallen out of the sky. Evening was turning to night.

"You've had a nasty blow to your head. You need me to interpret."

"I speak English and French."

"You think you do. You don't necessarily know what you're saying." She seemed to be talking gibberish. "We need to know how badly you've been damaged. Do you know where the Orinoco is?"

"What?"

"The Orinoco."

"It's a river."

"Where?"

"Venezuela."

"It starts in Colombia. Can you tell me the capital of Yemen?"

"No."

"Think."
"Why?"
"This is a test."
"Of what?"
"Patience."
"Yours or mine?"
"Good answer."
"It's not an answer," he said. "It's a response. The capital is Sana'a."
"You had to check."
"No, I just knew," he said. "My lexicon doesn't seem to be functioning. Do you know where Faa'a is?"
"I'm asking the questions."
"So, you don't know."
"It's the airport in Tahiti," she said.
"*On*, not in. It's the Papeete airport *on* the island of Tahiti. Have you ever been there?"
"David."
"Yes?"
"Do you read books?"
"I have."
"Why?"
"Because they're there. That's what George Mallory said about climbing Mount Everest."
"Everest killed him," said Grace.
"It isn't part of his story."
"He died on the North-East Ridge in 1924."
"I remember now. They didn't find his well-preserved corpse until 1999."
"Are you reading that?"
"Right now? In my head? No."

She leaned over him. She smelled of lavender and almonds and warmth. He could see down her blouse as she tucked him in. He could see her breasts. He had never thought of his mother having breasts. He had never thought of breasts at all. Girls had boobs, his mother had clothing, shirts and sweaters, but he had never considered beyond the surface. Seeing this woman's breasts, he envisioned his mother naked. My God! Like a dog first seeing a human undress, it came as a shock that her outer layer was removable.

*That's a metaphor! Like a dog. Like: a simile, metaphoric. Words meaning something they don't.* He had puzzled over metaphors in Borges, in Brontë, trying to fathom how it was possible that language could be so precise. And here he had devised a metaphor himself.

She asked him more questions, walking around the room while she spoke, encouraging his eyes to follow her, sometimes approaching his bedside, sometimes stopping at the farthest wall to pose a riddle. The questions and riddles seemed random, they were always about facts. He answered as well as he could. He avoided metaphors. She came closer. He settled back comfortably. She massaged his temples, making his discomfort concomitant with pleasure, masking the horror, the rage, the loneliness.

He knew the walls were listening. He was used to being monitored. The only reality that mattered was this woman who seemed to be absorbing his pain, assuaging his misery. Displacing his memory.

Eventually she prepared to withdraw.

"Good night," he said. "Grace," he added. "I like your name."

"Thank you, it's real. I'll see you tomorrow. I'll leave the lights on. A nurse will be in shortly to give you something so you can sleep. G'night, David Winston, sleep tight."

The next morning when he woke, she was there. The intense pain in his head had disappeared and the dull spiralling ache had subsided to a kind of sonic interference that was annoying but not intolerable.

"You're doing much better," she said.

"Am I? Can you tell me what happened to my mom?"

"I was hoping you could tell me?"

He raised himself against the bank of pillows, reached over for a glass of water on the bedside table and took a long slow drink, never taking his eyes off Grace as she edged towards him, moving between him and the window so that her features were erased by the backlighting that transformed her into a dark silhouette. When she pressed closer, out of the glare, he realized the window was actually a simulacrum. It broadcast light patterns into his room that varied to simulate the shifting sun, the stars, the seasons, the weather. She was stunningly beautiful but she did not remind him of his mother at all. She seemed an embodiment of the generic feminine — a fantasy figure of no more substance than a website model or a porn-site mannequin, sensual and sexless.

"What happens to me now?" he asked.

"You'll probably be charged with murder and eliminated."

He gasped. She was serious. He couldn't imagine whom he had killed. The woman reached out and touched him on the arm, letting her fingers curl around his wrist before tightening her grip so hard that he winced. He looked to her eyes. What was she trying to convey? She said nothing. Her eyes were expressionless. She released her grip and dropped his arm onto the sheets.

"My mother?" he asked. "Do they think I murdered my mother?"

Grace remained silent. Her silence indicated that a case could be made.

"Eliminated?" he said. The timbre in his voice betrayed fear and confusion. "You think they'll execute me for a crime I didn't commit."

"Executions are barbaric, David. Erasure is humane. You will be put into an irremediable sleep — then, because you are legally beyond resuscitation, the laws of euthanasia will be duly applied. You are allowed to expire with the assistance of healthcare professionals. It is efficient and quite gentle."

"But I didn't kill my mother," he protested. "I'd give anything to have her back. I'd give my own life. I really would, Grace, you've got to believe me. This is crazy."

"That is a common response of killers, particularly in cases of incidental murder."

"Of course it was incidental. I didn't plan anything."

"Exactly, it was not premeditated. That makes it murder in the second degree."

"I'm a minor."

"That's not a defence. Since she was your mother, the laws protecting juvenile offenders don't apply. The law takes into consideration how dangerous it is these days to raise children. You are not the first cyberkid to break down. The perfectibility of consciousness is an imperfect process. Some people were simply not meant to evolve through enhancement. But enough about technicalities, David. I need details if I am to speak on your behalf, to plea for your life or offer a eulogy. I must know the truth."

*Time is endlessly dividing itself into innumerable futures. In at least one of them, she is my friend.*

"Did you determine my guilt from your questions last night?"

"We determined you cannot be redeemed or repaired."

She had been composing his eulogy, then.

A smile flickered across her face and disappeared. The mobility of her features froze into a mask. Of indifference, disdain? Of righteousness?

He motioned for her to come closer. She was already at the side of his bed so she leaned over. He knew the walls were listening. He tried to make it seem as if he were just trying to garner some human connection. He drew her down so that he could whisper in her ear, barely mouthing the words. A moment previously she had seemed robotic, but she smelled more alive than he thought could be possible. She exuded something unidentifiably mysterious, dangerous, empowering — a scent of oestrogen and almonds that made his head reel.

"Please help me." He breathed the words, hardly daring to make his plea audible, even to himself.

She stood upright, leaning away from him and glanced at the walls opposite before locking onto his bewildered gaze. "Yes," she said with a coolness that sent chills down his back. "Tell me about the victim."

"My mother? She was not a victim."

"She is dead. That would seem to make her a victim. She had you after she finished graduate school, I believe. Your father, do you know who he was?"

"A palaeoanthropologist."

"Like her, yes? He was her tutor," she said.

"Her advisor and then her colleague."

"He never lived with you?"

"I don't remember. He had his own study."

"But not his own bedroom."

"Of course not."

"You don't remember him well?"

"He left when I was two. I think he lives in France, now. In Marseilles."

"Did she have other male friends?"

"No. Except me. I was her friend."

"Were you?"

"Yes."

"Then why did you kill her?"

He was caught in an invisible labyrinth where all paths led to the same conclusion. If he couldn't see the walls, he would never find his way out. "How would I do that? Where is her body? Can you prove she's dead? Perhaps she just went back to the Perigord Noir in search of more bones. She's on a research sabbatical this year. Perhaps she just checked in to see how I was doing and now she's returned to her dig."

"Which is precisely where? The Perigord is a very big part of France."

"It's a secret."

"How convenient. But there are no secrets. And what's the attraction? What did she find?"

"Evidence of a romance, forty or fifty thousand years ago."

"Which? That's a ten-thousand-year difference."

"I'm not sure."

"Were you jealous?"

"Of what?"

"Of her work. She went off all summer to her excavations and left you behind."

"I was at camp in the Haliburton Highlands, learning native skills."

"Native?"

"First Nations, Indians. Anishinaabe. "

"Officially they no longer exist."

"We'd be told at camp that the sound of a beating heart is nature being conscious of itself. They'd say that's what it was to think like an *Indian*. I figure it was all just a chance to dress up in Tonto regalia and pretend we were savages like the people we'd driven to extinction. Dancing around fires with chicken feathers in our hair, wearing plastic buffalo-head masks that made us look like rabid cows — aurochs, my mother would call them — and wearing wampum belts we'd made from tropical seashells holding up terrycloth breechclouts smeared with shoe-polish blood."

"So you did resent her for sending you there?"

"She did what was expected of her. When I was younger, it was fun. Ordinary stuff took on an aura of mystery and excitement, like trees in a museum. Then it just became awkward. We thought we were emulating the native people, but we were trivializing them, reducing them to caricatures. My mother and I talked about this."

"Did she give you the vocabulary?"

"How do you mean?"

"Of dissent, the words to describe cultural crimes."

"Maybe. I always assumed the words came from inside my head. We talked about the difference between honouring and burlesquing the past, while in her own work she struggled to recreate inaccessible lives from two thousand generations ago. She promised she'd take me to her excavation site next year."

"You want to study anthropology?" Her voice echoed like she was mouthing the words, like the lip-sync was off, the way it sometimes is when there's a split-second electronic delay in an amplification system. As if there were a wrinkle in time. He shook his head vigorously and sent excruciating pain through his skull. He sat very still, the pain subsided, leaving a residual ache.

"Sorry," he said. "I got distracted. Forgot where I was and why you were here. So anyway, no, cultural and social anthropology don't interest me and there are so many Company restrictions on physical anthropology, there wouldn't be much point. Palaeoanthropology is no longer even taught at the universities. Violet thought it was a joke, that the study of extinct humans had become extinct."

"*Remember the future, forget the past,*" she observed.

"I know that's what they say. *Don't resist evolution. Natural selection is a choice. The ascent of man is in our control.*"

"Well?"

"I'm with Violet! I want to know *what* made us, *who* we come from, *why* we are. I mean, the past is equally distant from us, whether it's five minutes or fifty years ago or fifty thousand years. I want to go there." He recalled his last conversation with Violet — the past is irretrievable; no, it is inaccessible. There's a difference; and the future is impalpable, opaque, elusive. The future is inaccessible, as well."

"Confounding perspective is an effect of the mind." She smiled. "The past is obsolete."

"Aha!" David was excited. "Suppose the Earth was just dreamed up, like really recently, and we're part of the dream and we were instilled with memories of a personal and collective past that never happened. History books and libraries and genealogies are inventions. Perspective *is* the illusion."

"I've seen *The Matrix* or enough of it to get the idea."

"No, *The Matrix* stops time dead in its tracks. The encapsulated humans are stuck forever in 1999. They're locked in, but they're sufficiently real to generate power. Jorge Luis Borges credits Bertrand Russell with envisioning a world where humans are a fantasy and when the sleeper awakens and like Blake's Adam Caedmon we disappear, we are only particles in a dream. Perhaps the dreamer is God."

"Where did you ever get such things? Borges, Russell, William Blake? God? No wonder reading books is discouraged." She looked about, almost as if she were frightened, and made a display of scowling while simultaneously she offered a partial wink, encouraging him to continue.

"I've read bits and pieces, mostly quotations in random display. I haven't finished *Wuthering Heights*. And Wittgenstein's treatise, I've read the whole thing several times over but I'd say I'm just skimming the surface. 'Like a long-legged fly.'"

"'His mind moves upon silence.' Yeats, I believe. And you've read *Ficciones* in its entirety."

"Borges, yes. Did you know on Tlön their philosophers avoid truth in pursuit of amazement?" he said. "Tlön is a planet imagined into being by a committee of thinkers and dreamers, where truth is the biggest impediment to worldly fulfilment."

"Really."

"Yes. And linguists on Tlön insist that language is metaphorical. Words have no reality at all. Writers on Tlön were invented by critics. And things of substance efface themselves if no one perceives them — the ruins of an amphitheatre on Tlön have survived only because they were observed by a few birds and a horse."

"Why are you telling me these things?"

"Because I can."

"That's dangerous, David. Remember Mallory's North-East Ridge."

She clearly meant he was in danger, not that he was dangerous himself. She was still bent over as if shielding him from invisible forces.

"You are a strange boy," she said, standing upright.

"Thank you," he said. He had supposed as much. Although he had been brought up in New Town Number Eleven beyond the edge of Toronto, The City of the End of Things, he had visited there on several occasions and had seen people who lived in puzzling disarray. Their dwellings were a hodgepodge of architectural flourishes and failures, their clothing represented a miscellany of colourful and tasteless styles, their lives conformed to no discernible pattern. He suspected he was more like them than his Number Eleven cohort. This thrilled and dismayed him. He never talked about his strangeness, even to his mother. She tried to suppress her own strangeness and would have found it disheartening.

Grace moved around the room, seeming to be doing one thing while doing another, creating an aura of benign confusion. He watched her at first with curiosity and then apprehension. She was performing for the monitors. The walls of his room were an inversion of screens, embedded with innumerable microscopic lenses whose images resolved elsewhere into a precise replica of the scenes they were observing. They watched relentlessly and were watched in turn by analytic programs set to alert accredited personnel to deviance from a predetermined norm. He had heard the technology was being used in new New Town construction, since the need for privacy had been eliminated by DNA modifications which rendered privacy irrelevant. *If anything is secret, everything is secret; if nothing is sacred, everything is sacred.* That's what they said, and most people seemed to agree.

"What are you doing?" he asked.

"Nothing," she said. "Everything." Did her enigmatic response mean it was over, the assessment, the analysis, the judgement? "Here, put on your clothes," she said.

She threw him a plastic bag with a draw string and a label that had his name on it. Inside was a full complement of clothes that he had never seen before, all in his size. She seemed to turn away and ignore him so he slid out of bed and stripped off his hospital gown and got dressed. The watching walls were sufficiently amorphous he ignored them.

"Good," she said. "Are you ready?"

"For what? Do I get a last supper?" He realized he hadn't eaten since the previous day when he had lunch with his mother. He wasn't hungry.

"Come with me."

"Do I have a choice?"

"No, David, you do not have a choice."

He was tall and angular. She was also tall but lithe and light. It didn't occur to him to use violence in protest. Whatever she might have said to the contrary, she was a surrogate for the entire institution, for the Company itself. Resistance was futile.

"Is this it, then?" he said. He wasn't really afraid of death. Grace had assured him it wouldn't be painful. He had lived so little of life he hardly regretted its passing. Apart from killing a few bugs and endless rehearsals in computer games he shared with Lucas and their friends, his only experience with the terminal condition was in fiction. In the Borges stories, death tended to be dispassionate, violent, usually ironic, somehow surprising, and yet invariably fitting. In *Wuthering Heights*, as far as he'd read, Catherine Earnshaw was a beleaguered ghost and Heathcliff her tormented lover. Death was a romantic contrivance. He had not witnessed his mother's death. Only a commonplace wisp of vapour had marked her passing.

It was dying, not death, that appalled him. God knows, Borges's protagonists embraced the executioners' bullets, the assassin's blade, with equanimity and his mother had disappeared without so much as a scream. Heathcliff was miserable from the pain of someone's death other than his own. David did not identify with Heathcliff. He had never been in love and was not sure such a condition was possible.

He looked around the room. The walls were a pale institutional green. He hadn't noticed before — they were much like the living room walls at home, except these appeared slightly luminescent from the infinite number of complex molecule receptors embedded in the paint.

Grace took David gently but firmly by the arm and guided him to the door which slid open on silent bearings as they approached. They stepped into the corridor. The door closed behind them. All he knew of executions was from Borges. He expected an escort squad but there was no one in sight. Noise in one direction, where the walls gleamed and the light was antiseptically bright, indicated a sizeable gathering of people out of his sightline — probably guardians and healthcare workers, functionaries, administrators, actuaries.

Then he realized with horror, Grace was his escort. He wondered, was she also his executioner? A single person could administer the soporific injection. Were the others gathered as witnesses? The babel of convivial sounds suggested they were there to set him at ease. Their laughter became ominous. They were waiting around the corner to perform a humane civic function. The second part of the procedure, euthanasia, didn't need witnesses and was probably done privately as a prelude to cremation.

Grace threw him off balance by turning away from the chatter. She led quickly down a long corridor into silence and shadow. They took several turns. He lost his bearings. The walls were dull, the gloom became palpable until they entered a twilight zone with brighter illumination off in the distance. He started to speak. She struck out towards his face but stopped short of hitting him and placed a finger firmly to his lips, at the same time pressing into his arm and urging him forward. Her breast pushed against his flexed bicep, burning.

He flinched. She had looked like his mother, like a proto-female from before time began, like a pornstar, a virgin, an emissary from hell. She had come across as nurturing, haunting, sleazy, beatific, menacing. He relaxed into the pressure, where only the layers of their clothing separated their separate flesh. He was fleeing extermination and he was aroused.

At fifteen, it was the norm, he was constantly on the verge of arousal. He savoured words like *concupiscence, titillation, lascivious*. Social constraints or consanguinity — his mother was his only living relative, he had no siblings or cousins — kept rampant hormones in check. He cringed from contact with Grace, ashamed of his own twisted responses, but she drew him closer. He had to stop, to catch his breath. She released his arm and took his hand. He breathed again. They continued, moving towards the light.

There was a sudden cacophony of boots on tile behind them. A siren pierced the air. The halls burst into full illumination. Grace drew him into an alcove. He felt an impersonal almost anonymous sadness. What would Borges make of this situation? How would he rework it into a gnarled and elegant *ficcione*? A strange hybrid woman was leading him secretively from his place of extermination through Kafkaesque corridors of lightness and dark, and they had ducked into an alcove and were standing perfectly still, betrayed only by the synchronous beating of their hearts and the sprung rhythms of their respiration. Would Borges have them die in each other's arms like puppets in a poem by Yeats? Would he have the sleeper who had dreamed them awaken on a clear spring morning? How would he leave the reader wondering? Wondering what?

The clatter of boots faded, the posse had taken a wrong turn.

They waited.

Time passed.

*Perhaps the Company never existed, perhaps it never would.*

Where had such a notion come from? Possibly Grace was right. Perhaps he had read too much that didn't originate inside his head. Perhaps it was too much for the mind to bear, to read a writer who conceived an infinite library that would last forever — *illuminated, solitary, perfectly immovable, filled with precious volumes, useless, incorruptible, secret.*

Perhaps with divine modesty, as Borges described it, the Company eludes all publicity and its agents are secret, unknown even to themselves. In its silent functioning, comparable to God, it invites infinite conjecture as it orchestrates the cries of the wind, the shades of rust, the minnow's flash in the sun.

What on earth was he thinking? How did this make any sense in relation to death or survival? He was seized with cerebral sensations that demanded attention, more graphic in his mind than fear or sorrow or lust. But he did not know how to think, not in ways shaped by metaphors and imagination.

At last, Grace drew him close and coaxed his head down towards her lips, and all thoughts ceased. When she turned his head sideways, he was disappointed. She whispered into his ear.

"Soon," she murmured and withdrew, but not so far that he wasn't still aware of body warmth filling the air between them.

He peered into the middle distance of his mind, trying to read a blurry chronometer. He couldn't make out the figures. He wanted to count off time, even though he didn't know what they were waiting for. He was puzzled that she didn't synchronize their mind-monitors although they were close enough to enable the connection. Normally this function was reserved for family in close proximity, or intimate friends and lovers, but surely, she could override the protocols that kept outsiders from entering private headspace. If these didn't exist, interference would mount into the billions, but she was empowered by the Company, he assumed, and could easily have accessed his innermost world.

The more he tried to focus on time, the more obscure the numbers became. "Soon," she had said. That could mean anything or nothing at all, just a means of keeping him calm. Imminence is a condition of consciousness, he thought, whether in anticipation of death or apprehension over a moment's uncertainty. We are a species defined by what has not yet occurred, as much as by the sequence of moments that preceded our awareness of now. Then, now, soon. Through procedures of triangulation, refined to guide artillery fire in World War One by a British mathematician with the unlikely name of Jacques DeMarbois, we can usually locate ourselves on the axis of time. But Grace's use of the word 'soon' was obscured by context: *soon*, the execution, *soon*, the escape, or *soon*, the dreamer will awaken and all the atoms of the universe will collapse into a nugget of infinite density.

"Now," she whispered and pulled him after her out into the corridor towards the light. She turned to a door sitting so flush to the wall that it might have been easily missed. She opened it outwards with a double push that animated a pressure-lock mechanism, and closed it firmly once they were through and standing in total darkness. She flicked on an overhead light from a wall switch near the door. A flickering fluorescent tube mounted in a panel on the ceiling cast an appalling gloom that amplified their entangled shadows in every direction. The room was not much bigger than a closet, with a closed door on the side opposite where they came in.

It was wider than deep, more like a transitway, but with a residue of dust on the floor.

He tried the far door. It was locked. There was not even a keyhole. The door they had just come through had snapped shut, but in any case, they couldn't go back the way they had entered. All routes in any building eventually converge. The boot squad would catch them, for sure. She had led them into a dead end. That made no sense. She was trying to help him escape. Surely, she was. And yet she had expressed little sympathy over the death of his mother, detached sadness at his head trauma, and what retrospectively seemed no more than clinical warmth when he parried her questions. While she had not confessed to being a subversive, in helping him evade execution she was putting herself at grave risk. And for what? To save him? So he could be interrogated? Exterminated? He felt more vulnerable, not less, knowing they were evading the Company. They had moved from an orderly and predictable dispensation into the appalling uncertainty of decision and chance. The latter, he realized with horror, was exciting.

He looked to Grace. She seemed calm, in no hurry, under little duress. He looked around their small chamber. It was no bigger than a family crypt. The dust meant there was airflow. At floor level on either side was a register grill of some sort that must have conveyed heat or cold as the seasons demanded. This room served no present purpose, although it might have housed a circulation booster in the past. Even if the grills could be pried open, the openings were too small. She might make it through, but in this larger version of himself that he was hardly used to, he would never fit. He felt a sinking sensation deep inside.

"Can I speak?" he whispered.

"Of course," she responded in a normal voice. "The walls can't hear us or see us, here. We're in a connecting wing between two parts of the complex. It's scheduled for demolition next week."

"Where are you taking me? It doesn't look like we'll get very far."

"Oh, we will, David."

"Why? I don't understand."

"You had a nasty concussion. Your mind-monitor isn't working properly. It's not defunct, or they would have let you die, but it's definitely broken. They want to study you. There's more to be discovered from examining the wreckage of an apple smashed on the ground than from admiring fruit still on the tree."

"That's an analogy!"

"Yes David, good. You seem to recognize that language works laterally as well as in a linear sequence. You seem to have the capacity to think in ways that some might find dangerous."

"And you're leading me where, from Eden into the wilderness?"

"Something like that."

"How come *your* mind works outside the algorithmic paradigms? Did you get knocked on the head too?"

"Not exactly. We need to get you out of here." She reached overhead and grasped a cord hanging from the fluorescent light fixture. She had turned the light on with a switch when they came in. She tugged the cord and a panel on which the lighting was mounted swung down, revealing a ladder on the upper side and a cavity so dark it was absolute black.

"Why escape? So your side can pick at my brains?"

"My side? No, my *side* wants access to your mother's research."

He had not expected this. What had research on primeval artefacts to do with his injured cerebrum? "I don't know anything," he said. "She didn't talk about her work, especially since she came back last summer."

"We'll see." She climbed the ladder in front of him and he instinctively looked away as the flash of her legs was swallowed in shadows. Hesitantly, he followed until he was beside her. He groped for her hand, clasped it firmly, and followed as she stepped confidently into the darkness. They moved ahead for an interminable period, occasionally teetering on the edge of what seemed a metal catwalk. He couldn't tell if they were a few inches above the ceiling below or below the ceiling above, or hovering within an immeasurable abyss. The only sounds were the autonomic systems of their separate bodies and the abrasion of shoe soles on steel. When another sound intruded, they abruptly stopped.

He felt her body weight shift sideways and then heard a thud as her fist hit an invisible wall. She banged three times in rapid succession, then pushed David backwards into the darkness the way they had come. They waited.

Suddenly, daylight exploded around them. A great steel claw smashed through the wall. Before the dust cloud had settled, David clambered down through the rubble into an overgrown lane that had been used in the past for deliveries. He could hear Grace immediately behind him. An ancient Hummer with darkened windows was parked close to the construction machinery.

"Are they here for us?" he asked. She didn't answer. He looked over his shoulder, then wheeled completely around and gazed up through the swirl of dust into the cavity in the wall. She was nowhere in sight. He looked to the Hummer. She hadn't somehow slipped past him. She had vanished.

He approached a slender man in dark clothes who had climbed out of the wrecking machine.

"Where is she?" David demanded, his voice trembling.

"It's okay," said the man in a barely audible whisper. "Come with us."

David looked past him. In the distance was the figure of a woman. She was making her way towards the front of the building. He thought she turned and waved. It was surely his mother. He looked back towards the hole in the wall, then to the diminishing woman again. It was Grace. Perhaps. He couldn't tell by the clothes or the movement. She was in silhouette. Then the sun caught his eyes and she disappeared into the glare.

He heard a rush of words inside his head in Grace's voice or his mother's; they sounded the same. *There are no paths in the past that do not converge in the present. That is simply what happens, and of all possible paths in the present, at least a few will intersect in the future.* He watched where she had been, then turned away. We will meet again, I'll be older, and we will become lovers or friends.

The lean man in dark clothes held the Hummer's battered door open. David slipped into the dark interior; frightened, confused, and relieved to be free, if he was.

# Chapter Three
## The City of the End of Things

"In the seventeenth century, Bonaventura Cavalieri put forward the notion that solids are the superposition of infinite planes, thus anticipating three-dimensional printers. Since nothing two-dimensional can actually exist, Cavalieri's hypothesis necessarily called for the calculation of volumes of irregular spaces, without which architecture would never have progressed, as it did until the subversive doctrine of Letizia Alvarez de Toledo that *more is less* brought the building of buildings to a standstill." The old man sitting on a jump seat across from David paused to catch his breath, sort out the convolutions of grammar, and assure the esoteric breadth of his knowledge had maximum impact. "Only when pure mathematics displaced personality, did building resume without the destructive imposition of aesthetics, tradition, cultural context, or considerations of function. Form was determined by arithmetical principle, as it is to this day. And thus, we have this." He waved a palsied hand towards a dark-tinted window, indicating the passing scene outside or the whole of the world as he knew it. He was exceedingly ancient. Balanced at the edge of his seat, he was leaning on a beechwood walking stick topped with the carved walnut head of an Airedale terrier. "My name is Jacob Hummel," he said. "I'm pleased to meet you at last."

The man's mouth didn't move when he talked. At first David suspected telepathy, but then he realized the man's entire face was buried so deeply within a robust white beard that his lips were hidden in the hirsute foliage. His eyes danced with refracted light. They were as deep and dark as the sky on a starless night.

"Where are you taking me?" asked David, trying to connect with whoever was behind the mask of old age.

"Be more careful with words, David. We are *transporting* you into the city. We are not *taking* you anywhere. Would you like to get out? You may, of course."

David leaned forward and peered through a tinted side window. Now I see *through a glass darkly*, he thought. Out of habit he identified the phrase. *1 Corinthians, 13:12*. He wasn't at all sure what it meant, having always encountered it out of context, but the words seemed appropriate. And no, he did not want to get out. He sat back and the tinted landscape moved rapidly past on either side. Apart from a slight jouncing motion, the Hummer seemed stationary, a rectilinear bubble with torn upholstery and dented panels suspended over an invisible road.

It wasn't actually landscape he saw. It was a series of billboards showing pastoral scenes. Behind them, he caught glimpses of derelict structures built according to the architectural principle established by Letizia Alvarez de Toledo that *more is less*. Their functional circuitry was fully displayed in a maze of exposed wires and pipes and girders, all wrapped in tattered layers of transparent tarpaulins. Only mounds where foundations had not survived the loads placed upon them were left exposed.

"An illusory present, purposefully revealing decrepit remains of the past," the old man explained. "It's all to achieve what a free mind would call the Ozymandias effect. *What powerful but unrecorded race/Once dwelt in that annihilated place* — those lines are from a poem not as well-known as it will be."

"Shelley," David muttered — the open-ended statement of a questionable fact demanded closure.

"No," said Jacob Hummel. "His friend. They had a poetry contest. Shelley wrote about the folly of human vanity. Horace Smith prophetically described the future, when London would become a wilderness — all that remained at the end of things."

"It sounds like Shelley," said David, unwilling to concede but unable to dissent.

"The painted billboards are placed strategically, paradoxically to display the decrepit structures behind them and the ruins of monuments built by engineers who studied poetry instead of mathematics, designed by architects who studied art through the ages and knew nothing of physics."

"I've travelled this route before," said David.

"Then you realize that behind the billboards and the Ozymandian mementos and the Letizia Alvarez de Toledo ruins are catastrophically functional, geometric communities such as your own. You lived, I believe, in New Town Number Eleven."

"Wasn't that where you picked me up?"

"In the vicinity, yes. From the hospital one town over. I move about."

"How do you know me? I assume you do."

"If I didn't, you wouldn't be here."

David was trying to determine if the old man's response was flippant or profound when the Hummer baulked and swerved and came to an abrupt stop in the shade of an overpass.

"Jacob Hummel!" The driver exclaimed. "Quickly, now." His voice was pitched high with excitement.

The old man stepped down from the car and reached back, taking David's hand and guiding him onto the gravel shoulder. The three of them walked rapidly into the depths of the overpass shadows and stepped behind an abutment just as a thunderous explosion rocked the air. The earth shook, the clamour subsided, traffic resumed.

Where the Hummer had been, a few wisps of smoke and vapour swirled in the aftershock and drifted away.

"They're getting better," said Jacob Hummel, grasping his cane and raising the carved walnut terrier to eye level. He seemed to be addressing the dog. "But so are we, Immanuel, so are we."

David shrouded his confusion in silence. The ancient man beside him was quite stooped, with a tremor that suggested neurological disease and a grinding effect to his movement that indicated chronic pain. But his mind was engaged and his good humour, if inappropriate, was heartening.

"That was a drone. How did you know it was coming?" David asked. He realized his voice was shaking.

"It was as inevitable as death," said Jacob Hummel. "They monitored the Hummer, of course, but it is you they are after. From the time you came out of the hospital until the explosion was precisely fifteen minutes. That is the period they allow. They refer to it as the *fail-safe interim*. It lets them scan for all possible details and minimize collateral damage."

"Why didn't we stop under the overpass instead of before it?"

"The missiles can penetrate the molecular structure of a bridge — they pass right through almost anything in search of their target. There's no escaping them except deep underground."

"But we did."

"Because the little buggers are computer-driven. They're very stupid. Once they locate a genomic signature, they fix on its inanimate context, a house, a Hummer, whatever. There's a brief lapse after firing, before the missile strikes, when evasion is possible."

"So you live your life in quarter hour increments?"

"Only until we get home. The same electronic walls that prevent us from contaminating the Evolved New World isolate us from interference."

"So you're from the city?"

"Oh yes."

David caught a smile in the old man's eyes.

A battered Ford Fairlane pulled up. Two-tone, four-door sedan, white and robin's egg blue. David recognized it as a 1955 model.

The man who had driven the Hummer held a door open for them. The driver of the Fairlane remained behind the wheel.

"Get in," said Jacob Hummel.

"What about him?" David asked, as the man shut the door.

"Issy? Born with a defective genetic code. Brain wouldn't adapt to a cerebral implant, but exceptionally adaptive otherwise. They haven't caught on, so Issy blends in."

Issy slammed the door shut and stepped back as the Ford pulled away. David twisted to look out the back window. He watched in amazement as Issy removed his hat and shook out long flowing hair which flashed highlights of copper and gold as she turned and walked into the bright afternoon against oncoming traffic with an indisputably feminine gait. David had assumed she was male; now he saw her as indisputably female.

*Nothing is what it seems. The appearance of reality includes the distortions of its perception.* F.H. Bradley to T.S. Eliot to J.L. Borges. And thence to David Winston. *Was he shaping a Borgesian world after Borges had profoundly shaped him?* That was a question that threatened to haunt him for the rest of his life.

Simulated landscape flashed past the Fairlane, distorting perception of architectural travesties with meadows that featured synthetic sheep and streams shimmering with the promise of trout. The closer to Toronto, the more desperately bucolic the billboards became.

David had been on this highway before, on a school tour. It was an impersonal experience and largely assimilated. The point had been to show why designated metropolitan areas were deemed beyond saving and left to deteriorate in isolation. These areas were surrounded by electronic barriers and security scanners that weren't visible but he knew were impenetrable. Their bus passed through a portal in the barriers but did not enter the city itself. They skirted south and left by a transit portal closer to the lake where day workers filed through on foot. This was known as Checkpoint Charlie for reasons obscured by time and historical revision.

He stared out the window, aware the old man was staring at him. It seemed Jacob Hummel was poised uncomfortably in a jump seat expressly to hold David in his gaze. This made David uncomfortable. The old man showed no signs of being bothered himself by his ill-mannered behaviour. Jacob Hummel. The name was familiar, possibly from things his mother had said, perhaps referring to work or ancestral lore? She often talked in incomplete thoughts and memories. David had learned not to fluster her by asking what they meant. Queries would just make her lapse into uncomfortable silence.

"Why do they want to kill me?" he asked, turning from the dark glass to face the old man. He tried not to sound plaintive.

"Because you survived," said Jacob Hummel. "Your cerebral inheritance from your mother is unique. How you think and what you might know of her work on the origins of man come perilously close to challenging the Company's credibility — perhaps we will some day discuss this at length. They were not going to execute you at the hospital until after a thorough study of your brain in search of your mind. You would probably have died in the process. To them, you are already dead — a headpiece filled with straw and algorithms behaving as the wind behaves, quiet and meaningless, shape without form, shade without colour, between the idea and the reality, between desire and the spasm, on you falls the shadow, David. With us, there is life, with them, only death. There is nothing between."

The old man spoke the words as if they had been spoken before. This was the familiarity of poetic utterance his mother had told him about. He needed to recognize and accept the excitement of words transcending the limitations of language. He needed to listen.

Only when the old man responded did he realize he'd spoken out loud. "Listening is important," said the old man.

David said nothing. The old man continued. "Words become facts only in relation to other facts. A word only has possibilities of meaning until given a context."

"A good example is good," said David. "A good joke, a good skater, a good woman, good reason, good sense, good breeding, good will, feeling good, good looking, a good for nothing. Each good is unlike the others. Only in the void between them is their meaning refined."

"You've made a *good* point," said the old man.

"*Good* grief!" said David, smiling. "I took it from a *good* book—"

"*The* Good Book?"

"A book by Ludwig Wittgenstein. He was a philosopher a long time ago. I'm not sure if I've quoted him right or even if he wrote it or if it was an excerpt from something I read about him."

"I am familiar with his work," said the old man. "The words, they are your own."

In the ensuing silence, David tried to draw his thoughts into line. Jacob Hummel was from the city. They were going to the city. Was David being rescued? Would he be studied there as well? And then discarded? His mind wasn't working right. He felt no connection with the friends he was leaving behind, with his buddy Lucas, with school, with the home that no longer existed. He couldn't make out the numbers on his mental chronometer but he estimated they were approaching fifteen minutes since emerging from the underpass. As he squinted apprehensively, he became aware Jacob Hummel was still observing him.

"Fifteen minutes?" he queried.

"It's all right," said the old man. "They think we're dead. It will take them a while to pick up our signature again and by then we'll be out of their reach. We will be pursuing the primary categorical imperative which is to survive." He gave his cane a half-spin, turning the terrier head towards him. "Immanuel understands," he said.

"Immanuel?"

"Kant. Before he became a wooden Airedale with amber eyes, he was an eighteenth-century German philosopher who argued for the necessity of absolute moral laws."

"If he was German, why didn't he become a schnauzer," said David. "How'd you get the name Jacob Hummel?"

"I've always had it. And you, how did you get to be David?"

"It's what my mother called me. I could be someone else, I suppose, but Grace reassured me that's who I am."

"Grace?"

"At the hospital. She helped me escape. She brought me out."

"David, you came out by yourself. We knocked a hole in the wall and there you were. There was no one else, no one called Grace."

David felt a surge of panic. It subsided as he released himself from the past. He had to live in the moment if he were to survive. If Grace had existed, she no longer did.

His mind felt the way his heart did when he was exceptionally flustered. It skipped beats yet continued unabated to pulse blood through his veins. He wasn't aware of gaps in awareness or distortions in thought, yet there seemed to be inexplicable lapses and his head ached ruthlessly when he tried to focus.

He hardly noticed when they passed through a portal of armed guards. The roadside billboards disappeared, displaced by an actual landscape of refuse and rubble that gave way to modest buildings with small gardens scattered through the transitional area between the Evolved New World and what Jacob Hummel leaned forward to describe as The City of the End of Things.

"Our city could be heaven or hell, I suppose. It could be the place where natural selection came to a halt when Vivuscorps took control, or it could be the ultimate city beyond which there is nothing better. Or no place worse. The New Jerusalem or Armageddon. You will have to decide for yourself."

"Who is Vivuscorps?"

"That's what the Company used to be called. With divine modesty it has erased its own history, which leaves the possibility that like the air and the stars it always existed. The process is part of a larger movement to absolve us of history in general."

"We study history in school."

"Oh really? As a sequence of cause and effect?"

"No. Each event as a random occurrence. Nothing ever connects."

"So, cybernotes on a screen! The human story reduced to synopses, dispensing with the need for chronicles and memoirs, literature, the infinite narrative of our rise and undoing. How sad."

In that moment the old man seemed irretrievably ancient.

"How old are you, Jacob Hummel?"

"Ninety-six. Expecting to make one hundred and one."

"You must remember a lot."

"I've forgotten more. Some of it on purpose."

The throughway dwindled into a grid of residential streets lined with houses and rubble. Some of the houses were in immaculate repair, which made the derelicts and ruins among them seem like gestures of civil defiance. Eventually, the Fairlane rolled onto Dundas West, which was lined with commercial shops, half with their gutted interiors open to the street while the rest displayed outdated dry goods and mounds of plastic-wrapped fruits and vegetables behind glimmering glass. As they progressed towards the centre of the city, the number of pedestrians increased, dressed in every conceivable style, and traffic got heavier. None of the cars had been manufactured within the last fifty years. They were preternaturally gleaming. Most of the sheet-metal panels applied to cover rust damage were buffed and painted in clashing colours to create a harlequin effect. Pneumatic tyres had been replaced by discs of a solid synthetic, but otherwise the vehicles were mechanically authentic, not replicas, and, as Jacob Hummel explained, were known collectively as 'Havanas', after cars from the 1950s that crowded the byways of Cuba during an interminable trade embargo and continued to function well after the turn of the twenty-first century.

Leaning forward, David was astonished to observe in the distance a number of gargantuan humans striding across the cityscape. They were stark and yet languorous against a multi-coloured panoply of intense luminosity. He squinted in disbelief, then looked back at the old man whose impenetrable eyes and hidden features revealed forbearance or indifference, but not surprise. David turned again, half-expecting the giants to be gone, but instead they loomed closer in an orgy of writhing and preening. He knew about Jonathan Swift, he recalled brief passages from *Gulliver's Travels*, he couldn't remember whether from school or his own promiscuous reading. What he recognized as Brobdingnagian figures, ten storeys tall, soared up from the urban horizon on electronic billboards and in holographic projections, apparelled in shameless dishabille. They were as prurient and provocative as anything David had ever imagined, and on a scale beyond comprehension. He gazed in bewilderment at the garish display of vulgarity, dazzled by the overwhelming invasiveness of intimacy. It was like nothing he had experienced before. Sophisticated and gross, private and flagrantly public, exciting and demeaning.

Once in their midst, the car was surrounded by crazy-quilt patterns of light careening helter-skelter, like flames in a blast-furnace, transfiguring the pale illumination of the overhead sun. The Fairlane slowly progressed through a series of interconnected civic forums called Ford Place, nudging pedestrians of every possible complexion out of the way, people who spilled over from the sidewalks and seemed indifferent to traffic or to being shunted aside. The first segment of civic space was circular, with a spontaneous-performance amphitheatre embedded near the centre. This opened at the far side onto a large square populated with clusters of stylized cut-out sculptures of horses, double-sized and in varying thicknesses of stainless steel, explicitly echoing Bonaventura Cavalieri's declaration that a solid is the superposition of infinite planes. The groups of horses appeared to be gathered in earnest conversation, and large as they were, and as noble in appearance, they were reduced by the gross extravagance of their setting to relatively diminutive proportions while still making the carnivalesque humans milling about, who came up to the drape in their bellies, seem Lilliputian in stature and haphazard demeanour. The final space was an elongated triangle, where the two equal sides met at the farthest point before trailing off into random streets, and contained in their diminishing sector a sculpted family picnicking on a small grassy knoll, the figures in bronze, the grass of shredded aluminium.

The old man leaned with his chin on his hands which were folded in repose over the walnut head of his walking stick. He seemed amused by David's puzzlement at the slowly passing scene outside the car. This was not what David had expected from his earlier experience at the edge of the city or from his mother's descriptions of how life there was endured. He connected with the old man's eyes.

"You knew my mother, didn't you?"

"I knew your grandmother better. Anna Winston was the love of my life."

David turned away. He looked out again at the crowded pavement. He was relieved when the car eventually moved into a street on the farthest side of the isosceles triangle, passing the picnic scene on the way. As they moved beyond a large building, the light inside the Fairlane suddenly became muted. The garish, lewd, and exhilarating public space passed into memory, as if he had imagined the entire scene.

David was trying to come to terms with the old man's unexpected announcement. It seemed surreal that Jacob Hummel had loved, that he still harboured a profound memory of passion. David had never known anyone old and in that moment, it came to him that advanced age was not a separate condition. It didn't surprise him that the old man knew his grandmother, whose clandestine books they had kept locked in the attic. That would somehow account for the connection — David wasn't someone being rescued at random or being pointlessly abducted. The real shock was that the woman he had heard about as quintessentially cerebral had been the object of passion and possibly, in turn, had been passionate herself. What David could only describe as wonder echoed in Jacob Hummel's voice, resonant with the travails of a long life. Heathcliff and Catherine Earnshaw seemed horrifically magnificently real.

They crossed Church and then Jarvis, veered up a side street and pulled into a parking space in front of a modest Victorian townhouse attached to a row of similar houses fronted with uniformly ornate brickwork, each distinguished by the vivid colour on its large front door, each vying with its attached neighbours for a shade on the spectrum of visible light never before seen with such dazzling clarity. To further set them apart, each doorway featured side-windows and transoms of a different design, some with glass panes stained in complementary colours, some crystal clear, some darkly impenetrable — again, *First Corinthians* sprang to mind. As with the rest of the Bible, despite public admonitions to the contrary, no one cared if he knew or believed what it said.

As they got out of the Fairlane, David stared at the door of the house. This particular door was midnight blue. The sidelights and arc of the transom were so dark they appeared colourless. The car drove away.

Passing through the door and the foyer behind Jacob Hummel, who seemed to be supporting Immanuel rather than being supported, they had entered a vast and indefinite library consisting of innumerable pentagonal galleries, linked vertically as well as horizontally, as far as the eye could see. Interminable corridors and passageways, descending stairs and hovering stairwells, connected these chambers in an endless illuminated concatenation, each lined with books of every conceivable description. They had stepped into a Library of Babel, where books by their number and numinosity were more revered, it would seem, than reality itself.

Librarians bustled about, carrying bundles of books, pushing trolleys of books, passing volumes among themselves from gallery to gallery, from one story to another. David had seen enough of the world beyond the city limits to realize this was a recent construction erected behind the façade of houses facing the street. He did not know enough about urban culture or architectural tradition to recognize the houses had once been homes.

Standing against a railing beside Jacob Hummel, David gazed into the depths of the library, unable to see a structural end or bottom that signified limits. He assumed the collection was infinite, although he surmised that the number of different books to have ever existed was finite and therefore at some point in the library certain books existed in duplicate to serve the arcane needs of intentional redundancy, perhaps in case some single volume should be lost or stolen or irreparably defaced. And yet he knew that the library could not comprise all books, since some might yet be transcribed from memory and others retrieved from hidden grottoes like the Dead Sea Scrolls or from attics of readers the world had passed by.

"How do you know about the Dead Sea Scrolls?" Jacob Hummel asked.

Again, David had not realized he had been talking aloud — mumbling, perhaps, but with sufficient clarity the old man had deciphered his thoughts. His brain was not working properly. It was sputtering like a broken engine.

"My mother. When you know what to look for in your mind, it's usually there."

"Ah," said the old man. "Information is not there because you look for it; you look for it because you know it is there. I see."

"What is this place?" said David. "Why have you brought me here?"

"To escape death. You were about to endure vivisection and be exterminated. Where better to transcend annihilation than a library. This library, in particular. It is the universe, David, a simulacrum gathered into an inconceivable structure of words in every possible combination. Simply by being here, you are an essential element in the Cosmos. By *being*, as the philosopher said, you constitute *Being*. Among words, you can never die. Of course, some librarians think of the library as a cerebral facsimile and themselves as neural transmitters activated by synaptic lapses, and when all is as it should be, everything will cease to exist. Theirs is a form of existentialism now considered quaint. It is hard to know when the metaphor became real."

David scrutinized the galleries, looking for readers, and found not a single one in the interminable, perhaps infinite, maze.

"The library is concrete, then, but it is limitless. How can it be both?"

"What cannot be named does not exist," said the old man. "Since all possible words are gathered here in palpable form, there can be no existence beyond the library. The rest is illusion. That is what keeps us going."

"What if I want to read one of these books?"

"Of course, but you must find a duplicate copy. We cannot risk having even a single book out of order. Once inserted in its proper niche, it becomes structural. Removing it might bring the universe tumbling down. Reading is a dangerous pursuit, David."

"But surely there are lots of books you don't have. We had my grandmother's locked in the attic."

"Copies! A gift to your mother. Since the middle of the fifteenth century when Johannes Gutenberg conjured moveable type in his blacksmith shop, an alchemical process more yielding and munificent than turning base metals to gold, we have been inundated by copies and copies of copies *ad infinitum*. Most were destroyed, a few survive. Read one of those, by all means. It is not a crime here, in The City of the End of Things. But outside these walls, duplicate copies are rare, and out there in the Evolved New World they are considered subversive. Once a book is gone, it is gone. Anna's have now been destroyed. Who knows, perhaps that was their target and your mother was collateral damage. Like your mother, like Anna, those books will never come back. When people who remember them die, books and their readers might never have been. But here, in the library, the library remembers. It remembers everything ever recorded. You are a very curious young man, David. Proof, I believe, your cerebral machinery has been compromised. Your brain is defective. But never mind, yes, never mind."

David had met people with no idea of their own limitations. They couldn't conceive of someone, anyone, being smarter than themselves, or of ideas beyond their own comprehension. Gazing into the old man's deep-set eyes, he felt a renewed surge of panic. Was he, David, one of those? Was he truly damaged, defective, perhaps expendable?

"Come and sit down," said Jacob Hummel. "Immanuel is exhausted by our rescue mission, which seems to have been quite successful. We are in the library, alive, yes? What more could we ask for?" He led David to a small meditation room furnished with several comfortable chairs. Other such rooms, all of them pentagonal, were scattered throughout the library, along with rooms for the discrete elimination of bodily waste and eating booths to sustain the librarians during their Stygian labours.

"Tell me about my grandmother."

"Ah soon, yes soon, if I live that long. Did I tell you I would like to turn one hundred and one before I die?"

"A self-limiting ambition."

"Five more years. Five! You see, one hundred and one, one zero one, that is the binary notation for five. Five is the numerological sign for freedom in thought and action, for feminine energy and masculine strength. It is a prime number in both systems, binary and decimal, a nonsensical number and yet quite profound. Also, I don't want to die at one hundred. It would be anticlimactic. One hundred and one would be a triumph, for clearing a century, yes, and a tragedy, for expiring as my second century gets under way."

"What you're saying is you've chosen an arbitrary age to die. Soon, but not too soon."

"So you want to know about Anna?"

"My grandmother."

"I had hardly turned fifty when we met. She was in her thirties and very attractive. She was damaged, she had lost track of who she was. She had a friend called Sebastian Kroetsch; he had a lot of money, a great deal of money, and he lived in a magical house of mirrors and books until it burnt down, with him inside, the poor fellow. I was meant to perish as well, I believe. It was a matter of moral housekeeping, you might say. But I survived. Before Sebastian died, he helped Anna and her little girl escape from the flames. The girl, of course, was your mother, Violet. Violet had a primitive molecular computer implant. Her father surgically inserted it when she was born."

"My grandfather? He worked for the Company."

"Back in the days when it was Vivuscorps. Sebastian Kroetsch was a major shareholder but he didn't appreciate their intentions to sidestep the evolutionary process. Your grandfather was their primary agent of change."

"A revolutionary anarchist!" David found the words exciting, although he wasn't sure exactly what they meant. He had never given much thought to anarchy or revolution. They had seemed implausible concepts in the world he inhabited with his mother in New Town Number Eleven.

"Actually, he was a nanobiotechnologist."

"Really?"

"His name was Robert Noyes. He put molecular biology to the service of Vivuscorps before it became the Company, before the anonymous *they* who directed its corporate mission became a singular entity known by many as God."

"God!"

"For want of a better word, but let us not get distracted by trifles. Your grandfather laid the foundations for cyber-cerebral adjustments to newborns of your generation, David. Your grandmother was one of his first experiments and her greatest achievement was that she failed his expectations. Her brain eventually rejected outside interference, although she suffered in the process. Your mother, Violet, assimilated the cerebral intrusion but not without psychological consequences."

"But she recovered."

"Let us not get ahead of ourselves. She and Anna and I, yes, and an old man called Solomon who gave me this walking stick we both call Immanuel, we gathered in front of the fire, four of us, each in our own way bereft, and we watched as Sebastian's Cloisters burned to the ground. It was like we were the only survivors in a world hovering on the verge of extinction. Solomon was old and scruffy and damaged, an antisocial derelict who lived on the streets and in the ravines, and there was myself, a rogue I suppose, a bad man in need of moral guidance, which the old man provided for me so long as he lived. There was Anna, a beautiful, poetic, and sensitive woman who had lost track of her own identity, and, of course, there was Violet, a brilliant child with a malfunctioning brain. We moved into an apartment together, the four of us, funded by a munificent legacy Sebastian had arranged for Anna before his death. Sebastian had been in love with her. Before long, I was in love with her too. She had the mind of a philosopher, the soul of a poet, and a heart that was broken. How could a person not love her?"

"You looked after each other?"

"They welcomed me in from the margins and taught me to think, to love, to aspire. I learned to venerate books. I learned how to channel my passions. I learned restraint, coupled with ambition, I learned how to grow old with fierce resilience and here I am now!"

"But you fell in love?"

"Yes, and I loved Solomon as well, until he died, and Violet, I loved her."

"But Anna was your great passion."

"Of course, but the little girl was precious." His voice trailed off. He seemed lost in the past.

"Did she love you?"

"Your grandmother or Violet? No matter. Until Anna died and Violet disappeared, I was deeply loved. Those were good years when we worked on the library together."

"Disappeared?"

"The library seems empty without her, yet the work goes on as if it were always here, which it wasn't, of course, despite a number of librarians who believe to the contrary. Some are lost souls who wander from room to room in search of the very first book. They find its elusiveness proof there was no beginning. Fewer and fewer of them are able to read, you know. This means even if there was a first book, they wouldn't recognize it. So the myth has become a reality. The library existed forever."

David looked out at the endless interconnecting layers of corridors and galleries with their wraithlike keepers and searchers gliding through the light, hovering here and there in front of shelved books, or purposefully running gaunt fingers over the print on their spines. There were no fat librarians. Their physical lives, he surmised, were austere.

"As our work progressed," said Jacob Hummel, "a few of the labourers, a few stragglers off the street, a few scholars and teachers and poets, joined us. They were the first librarians. The Evolved New World took shape beyond urban limits and the Company declared literacy a social disease. People without enhanced brains were left to their own devices. Some fled to the city and took menial work, driving an outlaw urban economy based on animal appetites for hunger, shelter, and sex. It is a lewd and garish world, here, as you may have noticed. But in the library, all is quiet. We are in a state of repose."

"My mother grew up here, then? How is it we never came to visit?"

"Every family story is difficult, David. Those who deny it, their stories are often the worst. Solomon once had a wife and children. They died in a fire. He could not forget them so he did his best to forget himself. Even Rose — did your mother ever talk of her friend Rose? Rose was a foundling child Solomon permitted himself to love. When she became old enough to think for herself, he sent her away. Not until Anna came along did life seem a feasible proposition again. For Solomon. And then for me."

"You're living inside Solomon's story. What's yours?"

"Eventually, David. In due course. But the library, yes. Solomon, Anna, and I, we built the library with Sebastian's funds. We nurtured Violet."

"Nurtured?"

"We did our best to give her real experiences to balance the range and complexity downloaded into her mind at birth and updated when she was four — that was just before her nanomicrobiologist father perished. A rogue and saviour slashed his throat."

"Was it...?" David hesitated for a moment. "Was it you?"

"It doesn't matter."

"To him, it did."

"Only if there was irony. There was none."

"It was you, then. I'm not sure how I knew."

"Well, apparently you did. But, David, we are talking about your mother. Violet's childhood was *vexed*. A perfect word, 'vexed'. Your generation of cyber-cerebral kids hasn't had the same problems. The Company learned it was too much to expect the body to assimilate molecular machinery without cauterizing the receptor cells, dulling the interface between arbitrary input and actual experience, so implants were embedded in an altered more amenable environment."

"Which is another way of saying *more is less*. Increase receptivity by decreasing sensitivity."

"That would seem to be an example of *less is more*. Decrease resistance, increase information potential. You are a child of the Company, David — rationality is determined by reason. Such would seem to be a truism, but consider: the reasoning mind not open to intuition, imagination, insight, instinct, it is not open at all and quite irrational."

"That's a circular argument that proves only itself," said David. It did not occur to him at the moment to be polite. "You said my mother's story was vexed."

"Yes."

"Please tell me about her. Perhaps it will account for why I am *not* a child of the Company."

"But you are."

"No, and neither was she. We were outsiders, out there."

"And she was an outsider, in here, as well. Yes, well, until she was your age, everything was fine. Not ideal, but fine."

"What happened?"

"I cannot tell you if you think of her as your mother."

"What does that mean? Of course she was my mother."

"But you must think of her as a stranger, at least while I talk."

"Okay, please talk." He was anxious to hear of his origins, even if he had to deny them to do so.

"Anna."

"Anna?"

"Anna had two passions, her daughter and books."

"What about you?"

"Yes, I was here, and there was no conflict between us, but passion cannot endure a vacuum. We lived as man and wife. We were affectionate, devoted, but not passionate in our love. My first wife was a saint, she was good and simple and her death was a blasphemy. Did I tell you I had been married? Well, no matter. Anna occupied my life the way water fills a vessel. She was everything. And when Violet went missing after Solomon died, I felt Anna's magnified fearfulness and pain even more than my own. It never occurred to us Vivuscorps might have been tracking Violet's progress. We lived very low-profile lives, shaping Violet's knowledge at home to suit her experiences, occasionally travelling abroad as a family, spending Sebastian's vast resources discretely, tracing and acquiring and cataloguing books as the library expanded, until both the building and its contents exceeded the capacity of the most sophisticated systems to record them. When Violet disappeared, Anna wandered off into the depths of the library. Eventually there were rumours that her body had been discovered. It was desiccated or dismembered, depending on which version of the story was on offer, and expediently discarded. I never saw her again."

"Is this a true story?" David asked. He could not comprehend the extent of the library, so the fate of his grandmother seemed both plausible and absurd.

"Close enough," said the old man. "Close enough. Meanwhile, I searched the entire city for Violet, convinced if I found her Anna would return."

"Did you, did she?" He wasn't thinking of Violet as his mother — she was a girl lost in a bewildering City of the End of Things, unprepared for the evolving new world that had been tracking her life from beyond the city perimeters.

"Yes. One night I encountered her at Ford Place. Even then it was the heart of a wasteland, surrounded by electronic giants and video billboards. A flaming fire, terrible and bright, shook all the stalking shadows there, across the walls, across the floors, as from a thousand furnace doors, it filled the upper air. Poetry is the only way to describe the inferno where I found Violet. She was slumped at the feet of a towering sculpture of horses who were speaking among themselves. Collectively, they are known as Houyhnhnms, and Violet appeared intent on hearing them converse. She was mesmerized by the murmur arising from the people milling around her which she apparently took to be the sounds of equine discourse. I walked up to her. She nodded hello. She refused to come home. She seemed safe enough. There were shelters in the area. I had to resume my search in the library for Anna. The next day I went back. Violet was still there. For all I knew, she hadn't moved. The next day and the next she was there, listening. By then I was sure Anna was gone for good. I was determined to go back every day until Violet came home. But the next day she was gone. I paid several people I recognized as regulars to search for her. They walked off with the money. Then one day a one-eyed girl of about the same age as Violet took me to a squalid room on Yonge Street over a deserted store. What remained of Violet lay sprawled on a filthy mattress. She was too depleted to stand. Delirious, indifferent, she had been beaten and raped until even the most degenerate miscreants abandoned her. She reeked. She was wallowing in blood and vomit and semen and spittle and urine and faeces. I had never seen a human, living or dead, so degraded in all my life, not in the ghettos of Europe, the slums of Calcutta, the skid rows of America, nowhere. She had been reduced to garbage and left for the maggots and rats to devour. I sank to my knees beside her. I had begun to weep from the moment I realized it was her. My body shook with horror and rage and pity and when I took her in my arms, we both shuddered from the violence of my emotions and were soon equally covered in the excrement of the Yahoos who had ravaged her. I lamented with shrieking anguish to acknowledge myself one among the most pernicious race of odious vermin that nature ever suffered to crawl upon the surface of the Earth. I was a man in my sixties, but I carried her back to the library. We were a stinking mass and no one stood in our way nor came to our aid. I have small private quarters here, no one knows where they are except Anna and myself, and Anna was gone. I took Violet there and cleaned her and nursed her back to physical health, but her brutalized mind remained in the shadows of her unimaginable memories. A year later, she left. She simply walked out of the library and I was told she travelled to the Evolved New World to study. They had been expecting her. She left an infant behind.

David was stunned.

Jacob Hummel had cautioned him to resist making the connection between the girl in the story and his mother. David had been moved to pity and fear by the horrors the girl endured and yet he watched her tragedy unfold from the safety of the gods. Then suddenly, with the announcement of the infant, he was plunged onto the stage and the story was his own. He was stunned by the old man's revelation that any of innumerable anonymous fathers might have been responsible for Violet's pregnancy. He was rendered immobile, transfixed, to realize that the opposite of a virgin birth might account for his origin. He glanced furtively around the pentagonal chamber, desperately avoiding Jacob Hummel's unreadable gaze. In the theatre of his mind, everything had stopped, waiting on his response for the action to resume.

Finally, like holding live wires together to fizzle and pop as they fused, he forced the moment to its crisis. "Was it me?" he asked. "It was me," he asserted.

The Old Man stared into the inset amber of Immanuel's eyes. "No," he said quietly. "It was not you. The child was your sister, the girl you asked about, Grace."

"Grace!" David's mind reeled. "You said she doesn't exist." He wanted to lash out and strike the old man, to beat him down, to hurt him viciously, to be absolved through violence of his own twisted history. The old man remained poised on the interminable edge of silence, then responded.

"In the library," said Jacob Hummel, "there is nothing that does not exist."

David realized with horror that he was in the thrall of a mad man.

## Chapter Four
## The Cloisters

All stories are fiction, even the true ones. Language transforms actuality, distorts time, generates unforeseen meaning. An entire life may be captured in a phrase. An instant can be interminable. Stories occupy time and the rent can be taxing. Consider the Spaniard, Cervantes. He is rumoured to have collapsed in exhaustion midway through writing *Don Quixote*, thus accounting for the peculiar division between Parts One and Two of his opus. Many dramatists, including his English contemporary, Shakespeare, circumvented problems of fatigue by borrowing their stories from historical accounts. The high cost of narrative would seem to explain why David was saturated with fatigue and the old man seemed unusually wearied, even though it was still early evening.

David was distressed by the discrepancies in Jacob Hummel's story, particularly in regard to Grace, who may or may not be his sister, who may or may not have been sired by innumerable fathers. He was frightened by the correlation between the old man's declared passion for Anna and his concerned acceptance of her death as if she had been mislaid. He was numbed with uncertainty about why Jacob Hummel had rescued him from the Company, from the brutality of vivisection or the horrors of a tranquil execution. Dread instilled by the death of his mother all but drained him of the will to endure, leaving him in terror and ignorance, despite the soporific safety of the library and the enervating kindness of his host.

He was relieved when the old man stretched stiffened limbs and made his way to the door, clutching Immanuel firmly as if the philosopher were about to demur, the terrier to resist, or the stick to bend. David followed and the old man led him through innumerable corridors and galleries, up and down countless stairs, some with steel treads that clanked and some with thick oak treads that made the sort of muted noise which registers on the ear without a discernable source, and which the old man negotiated slowly and painfully without uttering a murmur of complaint. Each stairwell featured a painting or two, mostly by French impressionists, a few by Picasso, a Dalí, a Pollock, several Vermeers, and, of course, a number by Canadians: Tom Thomson, Lawren Harris, Jean-Paul Riopelle (apparently a favourite), Emily Carr, Cornelius Kreighoff, and Homer Watson. Along the way they walked past an incalculable number of books and past countless librarians who ignored them. Eventually, they came to a small private room no bigger than the meditation room they had been in, but furnished with a bed and a sink with running water and a writing desk with a straight back chair. Without a word Jacob Hummel indicated David should make himself comfortable, turned and left, shutting the door firmly behind him.

The room was bright, there were no light switches. The door had a handle, which David assumed would be useless. He was philosophical about his predicament — the deeper into the bowels of the library, the less real everything seemed. In any case, there was nowhere else in the present he would have preferred to be. Jacob Hummel had saved him from the Company, had guided him through the nightmarish distortions at the centre of the city and, bringing him to the library, had isolated him from everything familiar. It appeared that Jacob Hummel was in charge of his life.

Somewhere along the way he had taken the position that he liked the old man. That now seemed frivolous. Not that he despised him. He did not. You do not despise weather because it is inclement, or a table because it is hard when you stumble against a leg splayed at an unfortunate angle. He simply accepted, with a certain amount of discomfort, that Jacob Hummel had an agenda that included his own presence in the library but did not depend on his understanding why he was there.

Left on his own, David was no longer tired. The door opened unexpectedly and a trolley appeared with an appetizing supper, a towel damp at one end, and a full change of clothes. He took the time to wash up and get dressed before settling in to eat. When he finished, he rolled the trolley to the door. The door opened. The trolley disappeared.

He lounged against the headboard of his bed. He felt disconnected; curious, not anxious. He tried to summon a mental diversion, a game to play, classic hockey to watch, random bits of information to savour. Nothing came. His mind-monitor had broken down completely. It had always seemed integral to his functioning brain, yet without it, strangely, he felt enhanced rather than diminished. His mind raced to fill in the emptiness left by its absence. At present, Borges provided most of the material. Emily Brontë, whose sensibility struck him as slightly hysterical, contributed unfamiliar passions to complement the Argentinean's emotional austerity. Wittgenstein, without a text at hand, broke down into phrases so pellucid in the moment they meant nothing. His mother's stories of humans at the dawn of self-consciousness continued to excite his imagination, as they had from earliest childhood.

Isolation didn't bother him. The library was an intriguing relief from the parallel worlds that had occupied his mind since birth. He wasn't bored. Boredom was a concept he had never been able to grasp. He looked around.

A leather-bound volume with blank pages and a liquid-ink pen sat resolutely on the bedside table, inviting interaction. He took up the book and moved to the desk, sat down, and printed in awkward hand-script.

> If I am destined to remain in the library, then I must devise a plan for survival that will engage my mind, whatever is left of it, while allowing sufficient expenditure of effort to ensure my physical well-being, assuming I am to be fed properly and clothed adequately, and perhaps given the opportunity for socialization. I will write and possibly take up work as a librarian. Perhaps there will be relief for what I identify as sexual urges. I feel them quite profoundly now — much like a blind diver on a high board for the very first time: I am excited, scared, and full of anticipation. I don't even know for sure if there's water in the pool. I remind myself I am fifteen. There are things I do not know from experience and cannot understand from what I recall about sex education fed by my mind-monitor. I don't mean orgasm, of course. I've never connected that peculiar exhilaration with sex as a shared activity. It has always struck me as intensely private.
>
> If I must exist in undefined reality, then who better to model myself on than Pierre Menard, the author of *Don Quixote de la Mancha*. Violet and I discussed him in our last conversation. He was the most recent author of the novel in English that exactly mimics the work by Cervantes, word for word, line by line, as translated in 1612 by Thomas Shelton. It was Menard's major lifework, although he is equally revered for his brief invective against Paul Valéry's metric promiscuity (or was it David Valéry?), published in the *Journal for the Suppression of Reality*. (I recall such random data from mind-monitor browsing before falling asleep.) My favourite work by Menard, although never published, was a piece on verses that owed their effectiveness to punctuation and apparently caused quite a stir. (Perhaps my recollections are not so precise as I thought. The fact that this essay never saw daylight suggests, insists, it was available only through the mediation of Jorge Luis Borges.)
>
> To write *Don Quixote*, Menard informed himself of every aspect of Cervantes's life and times, his personality, his rivalries, his doubts and beliefs. Before undertaking his task of original replication, he had to learn ancient Greek and classical Latin and immerse himself in sixteenth century Spanish, both aristocratic and the common vernacular, as well as to acquire proficiency in the intervening languages of the chivalric tradition which he intended

to emulate and parody with breath-taking cruelty, good humour, and wisdom.

Upon reflection, to counter the pitfalls of parody I will avoid the Knight of the Mournful Countenance. Instead, I will take it upon myself to write the original *Hamlet*. To that end, I must expose myself to angst and indecision. To be an Englishman's Dane, I will not need to speak Danish. It will be enough to perfect my command of English through its growth, flourishment, and present decline. I must learn about Shakespeare's personality and times, his sources and resources. It will be a formidable task. Shakespeare had only to be Shakespeare, but I must inhabit his life without losing track of my own. It is a reckless and daunting challenge which I will take up with the utmost humility.

David set his pen down. He had never before held a pen in his hand. It was an archaic instrument but oddly satisfying as he manipulated its flow onto the page. He had never seen *Hamlet*. He had read only synopses. In his world, that was all that was available. Here, in the library, there was no doubt a copy of Shakespeare's version, the text against which he would necessarily hold his own for comparison, but as he understood the rules of the library, books were not to be removed from the shelves except by librarians. They were not to be read. If that were the case, then primary-source research seemed out of the question. Imagination must suffice, *The Tempest* or *Macbeth* might be more appropriate.

He discovered a small room off his own, little more than a closet, but it contained a toilet and shower. After performing his ablutions, he changed into striped cotton pyjamas stashed under the pillow and crawled into bed, feeling intolerably alone. He got up, walked over to the desk, sat down in the straight back chair, and opened the book he had been writing in. There was nothing. He stared at the empty pages, wondering where his words had gone.

"Why don't you get into your pyjamas," a familiar voice said.

"I am," he exclaimed, pivoting on his chair to see her. He hadn't heard her come in.

"No, David, you're not. If Jacob Hummel's disorienting procedures are this effective already, God help you."

She led him by the hand back to his bed. He sat down, she sat beside him, so close their clothing touched. He was wearing jeans and a blank T-shirt. She was wearing the same slim skirt and peasant blouse she had been wearing in the hospital.

"We need to get out of here, David."

"How did you get in?"

"The door isn't locked," she said.
"I thought it was."
"You believed it was."
"Tell me about Jacob Hummel?"
"He has plans for you."
"Grace?"
'Yes?"
"Are you really here?"
"Yes."
"Were you at the hospital?"
'Yes."
"Are you my sister?"
"No, not really."
"My friend?"
"David, we have to get you away from here."
"I'm okay, I'm comfortable. I've been remaking my world according to Borges. He's the only literary writer I've actually read. And a chunk of Brontë."
"Charlotte?"
"Emily."
"Try *Jane Eyre*."
"Can you read?"
"Of course. I've read Borges's *Ficciones* in the original Spanish."
"I believe it was not faithful to the translation."
She paused to appreciate the absurdity of his ironic inversion. "David, Jacob Hummel wants you to feel comfortable but he won't like you reading. He needs you to empty your soul and then you'll be his."
"I don't understand. He left me a pen and a notebook."
"So you could write, I should say, print, to distort and erase who you are."
"Why bother?"
"Brainwashing, David. He wants to create a vacuum inside your head. He wants to invade your mind with his own."
"It's already occupied."
Wit offered no comfort. He shifted so he could see into her eyes. He reached out and touched his fingers to her cheek, to her lips. His eyes welled up. He hoped desperately she was really there. He waited, hoping she would continue. She did.
"He is ninety-six, you are fifteen. When he dies you will have reached the universally recognized age of majority, assuming he lives as predicted to one hundred and one and assuming you survive."
"And then?"

"You are his designated successor. That's why he brought you here. The library will be yours. But only, of course, if you shape up as he wants so he can move in — quite literally, I'm afraid. He wants to occupy your brain and your life. He wants to be you. But you will no longer exist. He will be there in your place."

David was baffled. Did she mean he actually wanted to download mortality, to discard one body for another? Why would an old man with an infinite library at his disposal covet the life of a youth inexperienced in the world, someone with a damaged cerebral implant? How could one person control the accumulated knowledge of an entire species and want to become someone else? We are stewards, at best; even our own lives are on loan. How could he hope to exchange his for another? David thought he was going to cry. Unaccountably, he started to laugh.

"David!" Grace's alarm affirmed she was real, even more than the touch of her skin.

"It's okay," he said. He stopped laughing. His chest heaved and subsided. "It's okay, Grace."

"Did you notice the paintings in the stairwells?"

What an odd question, he thought, but he nodded assent.

"Did you notice anything peculiar about them?"

"They appeared to be excellent copies, all oils, all in similar gold frames."

"And the size?"

"Small, medium, large."

"One foot square, two feet by three feet, and two yards by three. No exceptions. And no, they are not copies. They were taken from the Art Gallery of Ontario and from private collections, 'rescued' before the Company directors commandeered them."

"Was that Jacob's idea?"

"Yes, after Anna disappeared. And it was his idea to cut them precisely to fit the frames."

"Cut them? Picasso, Vermeer? He cut them to size! Repudiating Anna's death by imposing his will on irreplaceable art!"

"As he intends to repudiate yours."

"My death?"

"Your life. By trimming the edges. He intends to shape you as an original replica of himself."

"Shades of Pierre Menard. My God, Grace." He stopped. He did not want to ask the question, he did not want to hear the answer. His query was oblique. "Jacob Hummel said Anna was swallowed up in the library, as if she had encountered the minotaur at the centre. It devoured her, didn't it?"

"The minotaur, yes. In the invisible labyrinth, the beast and its maker had become one. Jacob Hummel murdered the one person he loved more than life — more than *her* life, as it turned out, not his own — which, in his mind, had become inseparable from the library they were building together."

"How?"

"How did he kill her? It doesn't matter."

"Of course it matters," said David.

"They descended into the nethermost regions, where the rarest books are stored, books made of vellum and papyrus, texts impressed on clay panels, inscribed on bronze plates, books like the apocryphal *Gospel of Eve* suppressed by Epiphanius in the fourth century, and the *Archimedes Palimpsest*, a parchment codex from tenth century Byzantium, and, oh yes, of course, the golden tablets revealed in the nineteenth century to Joseph Smith, the original Mormon. It is an astonishing place, visited on the rarest of occasions to make a deposit. This time Jacob Hummel came back alone.

"Years later, he took me there, to a room lit only by candles. We paid homage to a desiccated corpse on a stone catafalque in the centre of the room. It was dressed in a flowing white gown turned grey in the folds, and with the remnants of a silk cord wrapped around its bony neck. He meant to remind me of my own mortality. Instead, my witness of Anna's remains inspired a profound loathing for him as my guide and a commitment to take on death as my enemy. And so I am here!"

"What a ghastly story. Is it true?"

"All except the parts I left out."

"Like what?"

"Like what? Well, there were stories that Anna wasn't herself."

"In the same way he proposes to displace me?"

"She sometimes called herself Agnes."

"So there was a confusion about names. Sometimes I call myself Henry."

"Do you really?"

"No, but if I did it wouldn't change who I am." David was determined to forge ahead. "Did he...?" He could hardly bring himself to put his fears into words. "Did Jacob Hummel also kill my mother?"

Grace reached out and touched his cheek, his lips, with the tips of her fingers. He shook her away.

"Grace, did Violet die—?" David stopped, collected himself, and continued, "Did she die so that Jacob Hummel could get to me? Was she collateral damage?"

"Possibly yes, possibly no."

"Which?"

"Possibly both."

"But then, oh God, then, you—"

"I know what you're thinking, David. And no. The escape from the hospital. I truly believed we were helping you. It took a while to realize his motives were invidious in the extreme."

"*Invidious.*" He knew what the word meant; its obscurity was evasive.

"Horrifically self-serving. I came here as soon as I could. It's more difficult than you think to travel between the Evolved New World and what is left of Toronto."

David didn't fully understand how Jacob Hummel intended to infiltrate his brain and inhabit his life, but he assumed the technology was not impossible. He knew it meant annihilation of the person he would eventually otherwise become. It meant death without dying. He could not bear that Violet had died for such a travesty.

But why would Jacob Hummel arrange to have the Hummer destroyed, risking his own life as well as David's? He framed his question on the basis of trust, not doubt, and Grace responded adequately by explaining the missile on the freeway was proof the old man's powers away from the library were limited. He could arrange to have a particular target obliterated, but he had no control over an autonomous system designed to destroy a renegade vehicle and its occupants. At best, he anticipated the indiscriminate cruelty of its design.

"Grace," David said, shifting directions. "What about the baby? Jacob Hummel told me that Violet's baby was you. Is that true?" The stories seemed to overlap like pieces in a jigsaw puzzle haphazardly shuffled together and he still couldn't make out the picture. She had denied being his sister, but there was a connection — he just didn't know what it was. She didn't answer and so, with the brutal naiveté of youth, he persisted, "Were you the offspring of my mother's rape?"

A look crossed her face that he couldn't interpret. There was pride and anger and shame. Not shame; resignation.

"Yes, I was," she said. "I did not have multiple fathers and no, I am not your sister. Leave it at that. Let's get a few hours' rest. We'll leave first thing in the morning."

"What time is it now?"

"Don't you have access to your chronometer? Don't worry, that's a good thing. Your damaged implant makes you unpredictable. Welcome to the human condition."

"What about you? Aren't you cerebral-cybernetic?"

"Yes and no. David, you can't take in too much, too soon. For now, let's say, perhaps I have learned to override my implant. You've taken a short-cut with a whack on the head."

"How can you possibly 'override' something that's merged with your biology at birth?"

"Well, in short, when the brain is injured — do you really want this, now?"

"Yes."

"Okay, listen. Star-shaped cells called 'astrocytes' apparently bridge gaps in brain function, allowing healthy parts to take over for defective bits. People literally with holes in their heads, through synaptic plasticity in the cerebral cortex, have spontaneously gained full mental and emotional capacity. By intense concentration, and using the mind-monitor to guide us, a few of us have been able to replicate the process and short-circuit molecular intrusion. The implant is still there, but disabled."

"You used it to disable itself. That's deeply ironic!"

"Deeply, yes."

"Now what?"

"Get into those pyjamas you thought you were wearing and sleep for a few hours, then we'll get out of here before anyone notices."

"I don't need sleep."

"But our route needs daylight."

David changed in his small bathroom and when he came out Grace was dozing on one side of the bed. He lay down beside her, pulled the duvet up and, basking in the shared warmth between them, fell into dreaming.

When he became aware of the light, he tentatively opened his eyes. She was sitting at the desk. He sprang unsteadily to his feet, struggled to establish equilibrium, to sort out where he was. She smiled and stood up as well, reached out and placed a hand on his shoulder.

"Before we go anywhere," she said, "I have come to realize as I watched you sleep, there is something you need to know. When Jacob Hummel talks about my many fathers, it's an obscene way of asserting what you might call my 'undifferentiated' status. I am, in his eyes, everyman. Or no-man. Perhaps I should say 'no-woman' and make the word 'woman' generic. According to him, it's much the same thing, being everyone and no one. But, David, the truth is, Jacob Hummel is my father."

David gasped, then exhaled and took in a slow deep breath. "I thought Violet was raped."

"She was."

"Oh my God." One question surged to the fore. "Did he kill Anna before or after?"

"It doesn't matter, it was all part of the same act."

"But it does matter. If Anna's murder came first, that would explain why Violet ran away. It would account for why she stationed herself under the giant horses — shocked to insensibility and immersed in decadence, as he said. She was trying to find some rationale for existence in the conversation of Houyhnhnms. But if the murder of Anna came after Violet's rape, it might explain why he killed her."

"David, we need to get out of here. I just wanted you to know, there is a bond between us. You have to trust me."

"Yes, but—"

"No but. Let's go." To make it clear she would brook no further delay, Grace opened the door and stepped out into the bright intricate network of passages, stairwells, and galleries. She turned and grasped his hand. "Trust me, David. I need to get you away from Jacob Hummel."

A few librarians walked by without noticing. David was surprised to see human activity so far into the depths of the library. He wondered how often librarians frequented the sepulchre where the mouldering remains of Anna Winston were at rest. Was there any place safe from their interminable ministrations?

"I know a safe haven," she said. "A sanctuary. It's not far but we'll have to walk."

He hesitated. "This place seems designed to confuse."

"I used to live here. I found you, didn't I? The librarians know where they are." She nodded towards a couple gliding by on their inscrutable mission. "Or they believe they do. When I was a girl, this was my playground. I know it like no one else, not even Jacob Hummel. He's old, he forgets where he's been, what he's built, why one gallery leads to another, but my mind was shaped by this place — it is ironic that a monument of words should be accessible through intuition, but I don't have to think my way out of here, I just know. Watch, we will come to an end."

They had been walking while she talked, climbing and descending stairs, crossing galleries lined with books from floor to ceiling, negotiating corridors, passages, intersections, and no sooner had she pronounced they would reach their goal than they found themselves standing before the back of a huge steel door undoubtedly borrowed from the vault of a major bank. Grace whirled a wheel, lifted a handle, shifted a lever, and the door swung open.

They stepped into a dank dark concrete tunnel penetrated sporadically by shafts of morning light cast down from grates high overhead. Without hesitation Grace turned right and they walked between rusted steel rails into a whorl of darkness that eventually opened onto platforms with the name CABBAGETOWN inlaid in grimy cracked tiles on the walls. They were at the first station east of Yonge on a subway spur line that had never been opened. A few safety lights led them up a disabled escalator to the main line and they lowered themselves onto the tracks and moved north, relieved when daylight again appeared from grates above. After walking for almost an hour, encountering a few fleeting shadows of derelicts and recluses who kept out of their way lest they be removed from the wet cement burrows they had chosen as home, after struggling through heaps of rubbish and piles of rat corpses, they at last reached the Bloor Street intersection. They descended, turned right, and progressed through the murky half-light of the east-west line where the tracks had been torn up and repurposed. Eventually, they stepped out into daylight, in a narrow ravine with steep embankments on either side. They walked on until the sky expanded down to eye level and the ground plummeted at their feet. Far below, the steel and cement wreckage of what had been known as the Bloor Street Viaduct leered obscenely.

"End of the line," said Grace.

They picked their way through a barbed-wire barrier and stood with the Don Valley spreading below them in an unlikely panorama of forest and fields, the woods dotted with tents and the spaces subdivided into a maze of small market gardens. Wisps of smoke curled up here and there through the trees and occasional gardeners worked on their plots in the open.

To one side of the precipice was a makeshift ladder attached precariously from the top so that it swung giddily under their weight as they descended. Then Grace led through underbrush and across derelict roadways northwards into what had been known as the Balfour Ravine. They scrambled up a steep incline of rubble, softened beneath layers of lichen and moss, until they reached a promontory, beside which, what appeared to have been a drainage conduit servicing the Rosedale mansions on the plateau above, loomed out of the shadows. Horizontal bars of rusted iron prohibited entry. What appeared to be a pool of water in the interior swirled out of the darkness with a quiet rush as it spread under the rocky slide beneath their feet.

"Your hideout leaves something to be desired," said David. "Apart from being inaccessible without a blowtorch, even if we could get in it looks like we'd drown. What's next?"

"I'm glad to see your spirit's back, although it makes you a trifle obnoxious. The water's only knee deep, it's enough to keep out rats and mice, and as for the rest, as one of our more strident prime ministers once said, if you want to know what's next, 'just watch me!'"

Grace squatted and took hold of an iron bar at eye level. She slid her hands along to one end and lifted it up through an inverted L-shaped fissure cut in the rock and pushed it away. She allowed one end of the bar to sink into the water and leaned the other against the rock at the side. She squirmed through the gap, head first, belly-side-up, grasping an upper bar from the inside and manoeuvring her shoulders, then her hips over the bottom bar, managing to keep her upper body dry when her legs and feet passed through, and dropped into the gently swirling water.

"Okay, sport, come on in, the water's fine." Her voice echoed, seeming to drift up from behind her shimmering silhouette as she stood in the jet-black pool. After he was through, she very carefully replaced the iron bar, locking it into its grooves.

She was turning their flight for survival into an escapade. He liked that. As they stepped up onto a shelf of rock and moved into gloom that turned to absolute darkness, guided only by liquid sounds of water flowing beside their shuffling feet, he tried to block everything from his mind except for excitement. He desperately wanted to immerse himself in the thrill of the moment. The barbaric death of his mother, the heinous account of the old man murdering Anna, his own imperilled condition, whether from Jacob Hummel's grotesque intention to take over his life or the Company's to dissect his brains, it all seemed remote in the pitch blackness of this dank rocky portal into the bowels of the earth. But the fear was there, trailing them through the convergence of a half-billion-years-old sedimentary upheaval that had been invaded by the Sunnybrook subglacial deposit fifty thousand years in the past, about the time when humans began to realize they were human, and where in the early eighteen hundreds miners brought in from Wales had carved through the rock, where forty-three years ago Violet had escaped from the inferno of a magical mansion which burned to the ground, destroying one of the great libraries of the world and consuming its owner, Sebastian Kroetsch, whose family had founded Vivuscorps. David wanted to escape into adventure but he was being pursued by primordial forces beyond his comprehension.

"I take it you've been here before," he whispered.

"Speak up, David, no one can hear us. There's a glimmer of light ahead. It isn't far now."

He squinted, then opened his eyes wide. He could see shapes looming in the shadows, a world of shades that gradually gave way to defined geological formations. These in turn transformed into geometric passageways as the light increased until they stood at the bottom of what seemed like a stone staircase down which water danced with awkward precision. To the right, there was a shaft lit from above. They stepped in and Grace preceded David up a ladder lashed to what must have been a track for an elevator and stepped out into a softly illuminated chamber with walls of polished stone and a floor thickly carpeted in vivid green sphagnum moss.

"The Cloisters," she said, helping David step out into the room. "You'll like it here."

Several people reading books were positioned on the moss but didn't take any notice of the new arrivals. Grace ignored them in turn.

David gazed awestruck at the illuminated space spreading out before them, deep under the surface of the earth. They were standing beside a gurgling pool of crystal-clear water that drained through smooth river rocks at the base of a wall, down the cascading stairway into the tunnel at the foot of the ladder. Most of the walls were gleaming panels of granite set into undulating layers of limestone. The ceiling of each chamber was inscribed with a rough patina of tool marks left by the Welsh miners who created a series of linked cisterns, and each chamber opened into another and another through brightly lit corridors leading off in several directions, until an illuminated haze made one indistinguishable from another. Each chamber displayed innumerable books stacked on tables in the centre and each was occupied by a few determined readers, eyes fixed on the pages of books grasped firmly in hand as if someone might wrench them away.

The readers, some of them quite elderly, were dressed in high school apparel from the mid-twentieth century, the men in cardigans and chinos, the women in pullovers and grey skirts. Most were reading on their feet, pacing in slow and deliberate circles. A few ventured into more anarchical courses, so engrossed in the texts that they occasionally blundered into walls. None seemed the worse for wear for straying from orbit and none acknowledged their error by looking up from the pages before them.

"Grace," David whispered. "What sort of a place is this?" He was astounded to witness such flagrant acts of reading. He had never imagined readers so obsessively and silently immersed in their books. He did not know unabashed literacy was possible. He watched in amazement as two readers entered the chamber and stepped around Grace and himself without looking up, before proceeding on a collision course that ended without incident because one of them sideswiped a granite wall and turned without taking her eyes from the page to retrace her steps while the other stopped short of the gurgling pool and lowered herself onto a mossy bench, all without noticing the interlopers.

"Can we speak?" David whispered.

"Of course. They won't notice," Grace responded.

"What is this place?" he repeated. "We're deep underground. It's daylight bright but there aren't any shadows. I'd say the humidity and temperature are perfect for, well, whatever it is that they do."

"They don't do anything, David. That's the point. They read. Mostly fiction. A few autobiographies, which are generally more contrived than most novels. Biographies and histories for their stories, I suppose. That's about it."

"And you figure we're safe here, hiding out in the open?"

"Like I told you, no one will notice. And we're not exactly in the open. Few people know this place exists and those out there who do know, don't care. Who, after all, would read narratives when they can read commentaries and summaries? If these people here are known at all, it would be as a lunatic fringe, one hundred and forty-four votaries whose real lives are lived out in the pages of books."

"Votaries?"

"Readers, zealots who have taken vows."

"Of abstinence?"

"Of submission, dedication, detachment. Theirs is a holy order. This sanctuary, their Cloisters, as they call it, is a secret creation — even Jacob Hummel doesn't know it exists."

David was incredulous. How could it be that Jacob Hummel didn't know everything?

"Originally," she responded to his quizzical gaze, "Jacob and Anna and Solomon set out to recreate the ancient Library of Alexandria, combined with Washington's Library of Congress and the venerable Bodleian in Oxford. Sebastian Kroetsch's house had burned to the ground, with him inside, surrounded by the ashes of innumerable books. His unfathomable wealth, to be used at Anna's discretion, funded their project. They were concerned, originally, with the gathering of every first edition extant in the world, not papyri or manuscripts or facsimile copies. As the Evolved New World metastasized, the library holdings grew to astronomical proportions which they concealed behind townhouse façades in old Cabbagetown. After Solomon died, Jacob Hummel became obsessed with its threatened destruction. He made it into a *musaeum*, as it had been in ancient Egypt, and decreed books to be inviolable artefacts, never to be opened and certainly not read.

"This horrified Anna so profoundly she conceived a parallel realm where reading was sacrosanct. The Cloisters was modified with Sebastian's funds from his *sanctum sanctorum*. Anna commandeered linked cisterns from adjoining estates to make his fantasy more vast than he could ever have imagined."

"And he, Sebastian, is he related to me, to us?"

"Not by blood. But his bounty — it was family wealth accrued through generations — with posthumous generosity enabled our progenitors to manifest diverging bibliomaniacal visions. This was Anna's separate project. The way it is now was her design. She even set up a fund to ensure the subterranean cataracts far below that provide the power, and the kitchens and facilities far above that provide food and linens for the votaries, will exist in perpetuity, so long as the number of Readers is restricted."

"To one hundred and forty-four."

"Precisely. A postulant applies for admission and becomes a novitiate who must read one thousand books before being accepted into the community of votaries — this gives us the magical number from the Book of Revelation sacred to literalist Christians and Muslims and Jehovah's Witnesses, as well as the endangered Raëlians and the burgeoning Church of the Literal Subgenius."

"So it's a cult?"

"Only from an outside perspective. Look around you and what you see is people who want nothing more than to be left alone."

"With their fiction, bumping into things. Even the darkest among them look pasty, and the palest, like walking cadavers."

"Wearing nostalgic sweaters," she noted. "I thought with your love of Borges you would relish living in a world like this."

"Strangely, I do, and that scares me."

"Well, settle in, you'll be here for a while. Enjoy yourself while you can. Try a novel and a glass of whiskey or two."

"I'm fifteen."

"Drink medicinally, David, not to get drunk — to dull the senses when they're a distraction, but only enough to get over being yourself, so you can get lost in a good book or two. Come along, we'll go to the refectory and then we'll find you a place to bunk down in the guest chambers."

"The what?" David heard '*gas* chambers'. He had studied the Holocaust as a cautionary tale, reduced to statistics and a few key phrases. From hardly more than a century in the past, words such as '*kristallnacht*', 'gas chambers', and 'final solution' conveyed how unmodified brains, left to their own devices, colluded in that most grotesque execution of unbridled Darwinian urgency. The past was inexcusable, the future unknowable. The present was unavoidable.

"*Guest* chambers, David. You see, people visit The Cloisters on occasion to contemplate lives in fiction. Most flee and quickly forget they've ever been here. A few stay on in service, working above or below, and only the very select have the opportunity to join when an opening becomes available."

The refectory was brightly illuminated, the food was ordinary, and the absence of voices was frightening. David squirmed, hearing the sounds of cutlery on plates, teeth grinding, moist mouths clacking, all magnified by the accompanying conversational vacuum. He was relieved to leave, and when Grace led him to a cell labelled 'Fforde's Eyrie', he was prepared to settle in for the night with whatever book the previous occupant had left on the bedside table.

But he didn't want Grace to go.

"Sit with me for a bit," he asked, trying to sound like an adult. "Tell me about Violet." Talking about his mother might help him relax, even lull him to sleep — or it might fill him with sorrow and dread and keep him awake. He wondered if the lights in the sleeping cells could be turned off. "Did she ever go back?" he asked, like a child requesting a bedtime story.

"To visit Jacob Hummel? No. To see me, only once. She had her own life in the ENW. After several years of remedial instruction, she studied at the university and lived in a dormitory. The DNA microcomputer in her brain was fully assimilated, but her mother's assiduous efforts to counteract cybernetic intrusions had left her anxious and restless. Nevertheless, she was able to function. She became, as you know, a palaeoanthropologist, immersed in the origin of words, when our earliest ancestors discovered their capacity for language."

"I know the story from there."

"Parts of it, perhaps."

"What I don't understand, why did she leave you behind?"

"Why not? I was Jacob Hummel's offspring."

"But hers as well. You said she visited you."

"It wasn't really a visit. She came back for my baby."

"*Your* baby?" He was incredulous. It had never occurred to him that this woman, hardly older than himself, it seemed, could have had a child.

Grace slid along the bed so she could turn to face him. "I was raped."

"My God, not by Jacob Hummel!"

"Just after I turned fifteen. Violet's age when he forced himself on her."

"But he was your father."

"Which makes me double damned, I imagine."

"Oh God, Grace, I'm sorry."

"Don't be. Perhaps it turned out for the best."

"How could it?" His mind stumbled. He could hear dazzling colours, see unaccountable music. "No! My God, Grace. Oh my God! Violet came back to get *me*?"

"Yes."

"You are my mother."

"I am."

"And my sister."

"Yes."

"And Jacob Hummel?"

"Your father."

"My God, oh my God."

"No," she said. "Not God."

# Chapter Five
# We are the Dead

Imagine the primeval woman who suffocated under the unstable earth. She is creating words with her infant daughter. It is fifteen years before they die. They amuse each other, tossing sounds in the air. It is a game with no rules. As the girl gets older, the two of them sit in the sunlight or in front of the fire and click consonants, ululate, hiss sibilants, resonate vowels, and whistle, delighting in distinctive patterns. Sometimes the patterns are strung together. The woman and her child play with sound-clusters until sonorous shapes slip into memory where they are invoked at will. Music comes before words. Words come before meaning. The permutations seem endless. Sometimes the sounds attach to objects through imitative affinities, aural evocation, emotive stimulants.

After a few years the woman and her daughter share a vocabulary that allows preternatural communication between them. They live at the edge of their commune but others are enthralled, overhearing their music and words. Being gifted with curiosity and imagination they imitate the sounds in the privacy of their auroch-skin homes, sometimes roaring with laughter or screaming in fear at the unintended capacity of their efforts to invoke things even when the things are not there.

Soon words become the currency of play among the children and creep into the primal activities of adults as they hunt and gather and struggle against inclement weather. Within a few years, their group has achieved a consensus on sound equivalents for many of the items around them and that changes forever their relationship to the world. The girl and her mother, meanwhile, formulate verbs that enable divisions of time, as well as procedures of logic and abstraction. This changes their relationship to themselves.

By the time the girl is half her mother's age and her closest friend, they have taught, by example and imitation, their entire settlement to communicate in ways that neighbouring groups of humans find useful to emulate and the new tool of language spreads exponentially, eventually to the farthest reaches of the world, although at least one robust branch of their kin with sloping foreheads and recessive chins cannot comprehend the new phenomenon that enables the weaker more cautious *homo sapiens sapiens* to prevail at hunting large and ferocious animals whose fat stores are essential for survival as ice encloses the world.

The younger woman becomes anxious by the ways their words give them command over their world but separates them from it, as well. She ceases talking except when no one but her mother can hear. It is too intimate and estranging an experience to share. On a particular day, she disappears. Predators in the woods surrounding the valley are rare. Most have been driven to extinction or wariness by the wiry interlopers who chatter with furtive urgency, then fall into menacing silence, only to leap from the shadows, screaming and flailing with weapons that extend their strength and their reach. Always, the humans are outsiders. Their talk and their tools make them perennial invaders.

It is not exceptional for humans to vanish, although few venture far from the cluster of homes on their own. Humans hunt or gather fruits of the earth, in the company of others. Occasionally a couple will run off to live by themselves or to join a gathering of humans more amenable to their own peculiarities. When one person disappears, it is often because the lone hunter, the solitary gatherer, has been assaulted by his or her own kind and left to die.

Her mother searches for two days and on the third discovers a crack in the earth where odours of burning pitch drift upwards into the open air. She walks to the edge of the nearby ravine and descends, clutching exposed roots for support, and settles by a cleft in the rock face. After a period of consideration, she ventures into the mottled gloom. She had lived in this chamber herself after her own mother died. It is here that her daughter had been conceived and was born. Once they left, she had never returned.

She moves back from the main chamber and darkness closes around her, pressing from every direction. A crevasse near her feet echoes from pebbles she kicks as she shuffles across accumulated guano, scat, rushes, and brittle dried hides. She stops and calls, and receiving no answer returns to the harsh sunlight outside. She grasps a gnarled branch with a knot on the end where it had broken away from a struggling pine. It is caked in dried resin. She removes a small case made of perforated shells that is hanging around her neck and blows across the tinder inside until it bursts into fire which she touches to the resin, transferring the flame before smudging the living coal and retying the pendant, restoring it to its place as an ornament.

Passing through the initial chamber with her torch flaring wildly, carefully avoiding the gaping crevasse, she proceeds into the darkness and discovers amidst the leaping shadows an unfamiliar corridor that leads deeper and deeper away from the entry. There are layers of loose dirt under foot and evidence of bears who had dragged killed prey into the earth. Her torch casts erratic shadows over a patina of pawprints and bones and dried faeces as she edges forward. She is surprised that animals would eliminate waste where they eat. She detects the occasional fresh human footprint superimposed over the detritus. They are leading in only one direction, deeper into the bowels of the earth.

The woman scans for flakes of ash on the cavern floor. If her daughter has a torch, she will be safe from bears. The woman is relieved to find ash. There is only one set of prints. She shuffles on, gazing in wonder at the rock formations. She creeps through low passageways and sidles along narrow openings, always keeping the footprints in sight, until she hears a soft wordless song emerge from the flickering darkness. Thrusting her torch ahead of her, she crawls under a low-slung boulder wedged between two sheer walls and comes out in a chamber with flaring light limning the body of the girl who is facing the wall, singing softly and shuffling in a slow and erotic dance.

When the lights of their torches merge, the girl turns. She acknowledges her mother with a shy smile, then steps to the side and gestures to an auroch racing on the stone, with her palm curiously held in the direction of the wall as if she were making a gesture for the animal to stop. The auroch is a living thing, caught in mid-stride with its massive head flung back against an outer flank in wild exuberance as the slender forelegs paw the air and its hind legs kick out at the emptiness in pursuit. The woman gasps to see a sentient creature transformed from rock into flesh. Her daughter reaches and touches the auroch and the woman shudders as their torchlight sets the stone trembling. The girl caresses the animal's shoulder with stained fingers, reaches down between her own legs and scrapes congealing blood from her inner thighs, mixes it in the palm of her other hand with spit and charcoal from a burnt-out torch, and dabs the mixture onto the flesh of the beast, making it flex and ripple with movement.

This is the girl's first blood. This is the word made flesh. The woman's daughter has given birth to something authentic that stands for something else, and the woman suddenly understands how the sounds they have filled with meaning since her daughter's infancy have given them power. She understands how language works, how symbols are as real as their referents. Stone painted with blood and ash is still stone, but the auroch exists. In her mind, it is a living beast caught in a moment of time. She understands that she is a human aware of herself in the world, and with this new power, *homo sapiens sapiens* is forever estranged, even from herself.

\*\*\*

Organic materials scraped from the cave painting in the Perigord Valley with meticulous care, the way flecks of colour might be lifted from a

Renaissance masterpiece to authenticate its origins, were sent for analysis by the palaeoanthropologist who found it and were determined to have originated between 45,000 and 50,000 BCE. The scientist who made the extraordinary discovery was Violet Winston from New Town Number Eleven near Toronto in the Eastern Canadian Sector of the Evolved New World.

Until Grace's words ripped the air, she was thought to have been David Winston's mother.

The past and the future sheared away from each other, leaving David suspended between. He gasped for breath. Without thinking about it, he knew that sometimes human lives contained lines of division, where everything preceding a revelation was prelude and everything after was postscript, a supplement. The shock of losing his mother was suddenly more harrowing for being not only in response to death but to deceit. The world around him was unrecognizable. If his personal history were fiction and the alternative to what lay ahead as a damaged cyborg were to be occupied by the mind of a madman, the child as father to the man, then this was one of those moments when everything would change, change utterly. He shook in terror and awe, fear and excitement.

In this moment, he thought, *a terrible beauty is born.* Yet like a shadow of cloud on a stream, his life resumed. He gazed at his reflection in the woman's eyes, fixed and shimmering. The person before him was not his mother's replacement. She was a genetic source, young and beautiful, a woman who appeared to be his friend and he felt loathing mixed with affection. She could not fill the vacuum left by Violet's death — her revelation made his emptiness more painful. Far from rising to their connection, he felt isolated, beyond the reach and shuffle of time, standing on the edge of the universe looking in.

"David?" she said. "Did you hear me?"

He lost the image of himself in her eyes.

"David, there is no point in being angry with me," she said. "You have the same genes as you thought, they're just in different proportions. Please understand, I was a child myself when I had you. I had never been outside the library on my own. Violet and Jacob Hummel talked when she came for you, but I wasn't included. I didn't know she was my mother. I didn't fully understand he had raped me. They decided it was best for you to leave. She took you away and it broke my heart. I had played and prowled like a feral animal in a wilderness of books. All my life. I couldn't read. I didn't know what to do, if anything. If anything."

She had his attention but strangely not his compassion. His stomach churned. He recalled there was a time in prehistory when thoughts and feelings were believed to originate in the gut. Violet had told him that. It seemed plausible.

"After you were gone," Grace continued, "I was bereft. I searched for you, David. I slipped out again and again. Toronto was more grotesque than rumour and guesswork had led me to expect. For the first time in my life, I met different people — not librarians but scholars and derelicts, addicts and craftsmen, toilers and wastrels. It seemed inevitable when I eventually found a renegade teacher: I asked him to teach me to read — in exchange for purloined books."

"You stole from the library?" David was disturbed to think she would violate the sanctity of Jacob Hummel's fortress, but he was also aware that Jacob Hummel had violated her profoundly, in a way he could hardly imagine. 'Rape' was a literary term and a criminal offence. It had no personal meaning for him, drawn from actual experience.

"I only took second editions. My teacher was a reject from this place, from The Cloisters. He didn't care what the books were about so long as there were words on the pages. He didn't direct me to read critically, only to read everything, to devour print. The more I read the farther afield I ventured outside. I explored the most sordid and edifying reaches of the city, discovering the hidden glories, the luminous bright spots, finally coming to The Cloisters, myself. The reasons for my teacher's exile and for my own eventual flight amounted to much the same thing. He wanted freedom to dream among words. I wanted to experience a world where books were neither prescribed nor proscripted but always available. Do you see what I mean?"

"This must have seemed like paradise. They read here, they read anything they want."

"But they must."

"Or what?"

"They wither and die."

What the hell did she mean? She smiled a familiar inscrutable smile. It reminded him of Violet. He shifted on the edge of the cot and looked around, assessing his cell. It was austere, not to the point of sensory deprivation but there was nothing to distract the solitary mind from reading. He glanced down at the book on the bedside table. *Gulliver's Travels*. He would read it after she left, but he did not want her to leave.

His initial fury at her revelation faded. He knew she could never replace Violet, nor did she seem to be interested in doing so. While there was no maternal connection, this cloistered cavern she had brought him to was like an illuminated womb. He felt on the verge of being reborn. Neither human nor cyborg hybrid, he did not belong in the nightmare world of the city, nor in a world ruled by the algorithmic constraints of the Company.

He would be something else. Seized by the moment, he would seize it in turn. To do what? To read, to think, to spend his days in contemplation. He could imagine nothing more exciting. *Aye* — the words came to him from a précis of *Hamlet* — *Aye there's the rub*. He could not imagine anything that had not been imagined. When he once checked the word 'rub' on his mind-monitor, he had discovered it described an imperfection on a lawn-bowling green. That satisfied him at the time although he subsequently wondered what lawn-bowling was and why on a green. He had no idea *rub* could be an impediment to suicide, as Hamlet declared it. Dictionaries were of necessity literal, especially cerebrally implanted ones that sacrificed hermeneutics for efficiency.

"Perhaps we should both get some sleep," said Grace. "We'll talk in the morning."

"About what? I like it here."

"We'll talk about that. Sleep well, David."

She stepped out into the brightly lit corridor. He felt an inexplicable surge of panic. Why was his cell called 'Fforde's Eyrie'? Jasper Fforde was one of the great writers of the last century, obsessed with *Jane Eyre* — an eyrie or aerie was a raptor's nest, inaccessible and dangerous or safe, depending. Maybe the point was, there was no point. David busied himself preparing for bed, using the small private bathroom and donning the cotton pyjamas he found in a dresser against one of the polished granite walls. They were folded beside a high school cardigan with a large letter 'A' over the heart — at this point, an intended incentive. The uniform of votaries he assumed was forbidden to visitors, novitiates, postulants, or service staff. He settled in to read and had finished book one of *Gulliver* before the lights flickered and, after a delay of five minutes, were extinguished. At first, he was blinded by the darkness, but the illumination from the hall outside cast an eerie pall through the open doorway and he drifted into sleep, fearing how small-minded he must seem, preferring fictional Lilliputians to the silent company of others in The Cloisters.

For the next few days, he talked to no one. Grace did not reappear. He ate in the refectory, sitting with a handful of other dedicated visitors and postulants at a table beside novitiates who were not engaged in serving the votaries or postulants and guests. No one spoke or acknowledged his presence. Otherwise, he remained in his cell and read Jonathan Swift.

The second day, the first full day without Grace, he fretted and found little comfort in Book Two of *Gulliver*, feeling diminished by the monumental project absorbing the people around him. He wondered if the extreme isolation, surrounded by others in similar circumstances, was anything like the sensation of death shared in a natural catastrophe. The third day, his attention shifted from himself and he worried about Grace.

He wondered if she really were his mother or if that, too, was a lie. On the fourth day of her absence, his stress was mollified when he came to realize how rational the behaviour of everyone in The Cloisters seemed, in contrast to what he had seen of the meaningless worlds overhead.

On the morning of the next day, he awakened with Swift's fabulist fiction clutched in his hands and realized he had fallen asleep while reading before the lights went out. He finished the last few pages before getting up. When he returned from breakfast, *Gulliver's Travels* was gone and another book had appeared in its place, the infamous murder mystery, *We Are the Dead*, by the Canadian writer, Margaret McRae. He began to read and soon forgot entirely about Grace's sinister disappearance or his own situation, estranged from the world, and instead of anxiety about either he felt nothing at all and was relatively content.

He finished McRae's novel before noticing the blurb on the back cover explaining that between submission of her manuscript and its publication the author had been strangled by her lover, thinly disguised in the closing pages of her novel and exposed as the killer, subsequently arrested both in fiction and fact for his crimes. The interpenetrating narratives reminded David of a Borges *ficcione*, but he did not pursue the connection. Instead, he moved on to other novels that were lying about on various tables and took to reading while strolling beside the rivulet from one ethereal illuminated subterranean chamber to another, or while comfortably ensconced on a moss-covered ledge in a shadowless alcove. Time disappeared and the only urgency he felt was to join the conclave of readers as a true votary and forswear forever the reality of existence beyond words.

One day in the refectory he approached a severe grey-haired woman dressed in a particularly shabby cardigan who was eating with a book propped on a stand in front of her. He stood by her side but she took no notice, so he coughed and then he tapped on her shoulder. Since she still did not seem aware of his presence, he spoke in a loud whisper, "I think you are in charge," he said. "I would like to become a novitiate."

"You already are. Read nine hundred and fifty-three more books. You have only read forty-seven."

"Forty-eight. I read Jorge Luis Borges before I arrived."

"Have you finished *Wuthering Heights*? I don't think we need concern ourselves about the Wittgenstein treatise. There's not enough narrative depth to bother with: but Brontë you must finish. Ah yes, all of the Brontës."

She knew his reading history. She must have been aware of his presence all along.

"Emily first. I will if I can find it."

"Good. And when you have reached one thousand, we will proceed." She returned to her book. He realized he had been dismissed.

That evening he wondered what the woman had meant by *proceed*. He wondered where Grace had got to. He wondered what all the people in the world were doing who didn't read books. Once in bed, he drew the covers up close but a frightening chill ran through him and he started to shiver. He wasn't able to read with his arms restricted by blankets, so, instead, he thought about reading. He realized his mind was engaged while he read, and his emotions were stimulated, but they were not his own thoughts or emotions. He hadn't really been thinking and feeling on his own since he arrived at The Cloisters. He had been bearing witness to the thoughts and feelings of others, formulated in words on the page. Recognizing his doubt for what it was, he quickly dismissed it. Like the stages of grief, there must be stages in cutting oneself off from the world — contemplation, commitment, isolation, regret, anger, submission, acceptance. Doubt or regret could be taken as perverse affirmation of what he was doing. God damn it, he thought. Let us *proceed!*

The next morning at breakfast the postulant or novitiate beside him mumbled his name into her porridge. Instinctively, he avoided looking in her direction but cleared his throat, indicating he had heard her and acknowledging it was dangerous for them to be observed in conversation.

"Don't you recognize me?" she murmured.

The other novitiates focussed intently on the books propped in front of them, determined not to notice her talking. David gazed around the room. It was only the votary Readers who were a threat and they seemed habitually indifferent to distractions. He leaned forward and turned his head sideways, trying to bring her face into focus. Her hair was close cropped but it was discernibly copper and gold against her scalp. Her eyes were a piercing green. She was his age, perhaps a year or two older, and despite having originally taken her for a man he found her exceptionally pretty. He couldn't recall her name.

"You drove the Hummer," he whispered. "What are you doing here?"

"Rescuing you. Again."

"Once was enough," he responded. Three novitiates across the table looked up from their reading and glared. David glowered back at them and their eyes dropped to their books. "I like it here. I don't need rescuing."

"We'll talk later."

He glanced up and saw they were being monitored by the steely gaze of the authoritative Reader he had approached at dinner the previous night.

"I'll come to your room," the young woman mumbled through clenched lips. "Tonight."

The middle novitiate opposite looked up again. She had a stark featureless face. She expressed fleeting scorn before dismissing them with a flick of the eye and went back to her reading.

Abruptly a very stout middle-aged woman across the refectory rose to her feet, clattering the dishes in front of her as she hoisted her bulk against the table. The room fell deathly silent as everyone stopped eating or turning pages and stared. The woman's cardigan was ill-fitting. Despite her size it was too large and awkwardly draped from her shoulders. She cleared her throat, inhaled phlegmatically, coughed to avoid choking, and announced, "My name was Charlotte and I have finished one thousand books from beginning to end." She paused for the impact to resonate through the room. "I am wearing a cardigan tonight and ask to be nameless henceforth and to claim my right to be moved to a Readers' table." She sat down and after looking quickly around, resumed reading.

"That was simple," David whispered. "But no name? Don't any of them have names?"

"Look over there," said the girl with the copper-gold hair. She nodded in the direction of a lean woman in an exceptionally shabby sweater-jacket. She coughed and rolled her eyes. David realized she was indicating the man two places to the lean woman's right; an older man, obviously a former athlete but now sallow and gaunt. The man closed the book in front of him and for a moment stared into the empty middle distance. Then he stood up and, leaving his book on the table beside his partially consumed bowl of porridge, he walked through between the tables and out of the refectory.

"Where's he going?" David asked.

She seemed to take courage in the subdued din that the old man's precipitous departure had generated and spoke in a normal voice, only slightly muffled by her hands cupped in front of her mouth like a school-kid.

"Oblivion," she said. "He's being *displaced*. We won't be seeing him again. I'll tell you about it tonight. It's not complicated, but it's hard to explain."

"Who is he?"

"Nameless, of course. I think they called him 'Tiger' up there, on Earth, or maybe it was *The* Tiger." David realized with a shock that he had forgotten they were buried deep underground. "I think he was popular in high school and he never got over it. Kind of a burnt-out case. He retreated into books and spent most of his life in The Cloisters. Took him a long time to reach a thousand because he used to read Faulkner over and over. He made the mistake of confusing reading with thinking. With living. I imagine he's ready to go."

"What do you mean 'go'? You said he's being 'displaced'."

She stifled her response. Silence occupied the room. Their conversation had come to an end.

That evening, David was too restless to continue *The Red and the Black*. Stendhal couldn't compete with Issy — he finally remembered the girl's name. He tried *Huckleberry Finn* for a while, then switched to familiar territory, perusing the pages of a pristine copy of *Ficciones*, reading Borges's paragraphs at random, just enough to evoke their entire context which he knew almost by heart — like a child unable to read who turns the pages while reciting the text from memory.

As 'lights out' approached and she still hadn't appeared he began to worry. Had their tablemate with the featureless face reported them? To whom? Had Issy forgotten, or decided better of coming? Was she safe? If an elderly man could be *displaced*, couldn't a young woman be dispensed with as easily? Was she really here to help him? Was she an emissary from Grace? Was Grace alive? Were mothers expendable? He had forgotten entirely that he wanted to spend his life underground among stories. He felt panic as it rose to despair. A chill took hold and to shake it off he decided to retire under warm blankets piled high for the night.

After brushing his teeth and washing, before David got into his pyjamas, a slight rapping on the door frame presaged the girl called Issy, who stepped quickly into his room. He realized he was no longer chilled.

"Hi," she grinned. "Do you want to have sex?"

David gasped and held his breath and forced himself to exhale and breathe through his mouth. He was afraid his nose would make whistling noises. He didn't know what to say. She couldn't be serious. She was barely old enough to drive. Did she know how to do it? Had she done it a lot? Oh God, he felt extremely fifteen.

"It's okay, David, it was just a suggestion."

He didn't know enough about these matters to be inhibited by lack of experience. He was merely confused. Sex as an actual event in the Evolved New World was medicalized or animalistic, something accomplished in clinical conditions determined by laws of reproductive necessity, or furtively, which usually preceded a slide into decadence that ended with exile to the city. To recognize sexual urges was natural, to submit to them with a partner was savage. Shame and secrecy were displaced during puberty by incessant information. Masturbation bore no relation to sex. Gaming algorithms had been devised to quell and dissipate unruly passions. Most of his peers remained sufficiently distracted until their early twenties, when they were encouraged to visit hygienic Company-controlled bisexual brothels where they learned orgasmic control.

"I'm Isabelle," she said as if revealing a secret.

So Issy meant Isabelle. There seemed no relationship between the words. Issy was sibilant, crisp, like the voice of a snake. Isabelle was soft, like the echo of far-away chimes.

Issy, or Isabelle, took off her pullover and settled on the end of his cot. She folded the sweater over drawn-up knees in a move that was modest and flirtatious at the same time, concealing her legs while accentuating their lean muscularity as she smoothed the material over her thighs.

"Don't mind me," she said. "It's the influence of being outside. Too much Toronto. The City of the End of Things, it's a sexual wasteland; semen flows in the gutters, discharge stains the pavement. It's really quite sordid unless you like that sort of thing."

"Do you?" he asked, fearing she would say yes; fearing she would say no.

She shrugged.

"David," she said. "I'm a bit of a chameleon, I blend in wherever I go. Right now, I'm a novitiate who has been watching you for a couple of weeks. You didn't notice me. No one notices anything here except the Reader Superior, the woman you walked up to at dinner last night. The one with the permanent scowl. You need rescuing."

"That's sad," he said.

"You don't want to leave?"

"No, the chameleon thing. If you blend in so easily, you're nothing on your own."

She reached out and touched his hand. Her moist eyes were the colour of emeralds. Her lips were full, intimating petulance, but firm, promising strength. The sheen of her coppery hair glistened in a halo of light. With her legs curled under, she sat upright, leaning casually against the granite wall. A plethora of line-drawings and clinical explanations of coital conjugation shimmered in David's mind like a windswept sand-castle crumbling under its own weight. He desperately wanted her, without knowing quite what he wanted, but the promise of orgasmic ecstasy shared with this woman, this girl, threatened to overwhelm him. He jumped to his feet and strode the few paces across to the far side of the room.

"Tell me," he demanded, as if she might refuse to respond if he wasn't aggressive, "what are you doing here?"

"What are *you* doing here?" She shifted the emphasis with a sweet and menacing smile.

He was angry at her for arousing urges that disrupted the contemplative life he was prepared to embrace, and annoyed for her intrusion with questions that forced him to think. The lights blinked. He expected she would go. She needed to get back to her cell. She made no move to leave. Instead, she reached behind her neck and unclasped a silver necklace with a single pendant and laid it on the bedside table, then she patted the bed and drew herself tighter as if to offer him space beside her.

He picked up the pendant and placed it in his palm to examine it more closely. It was a pebble of some sort with a feline in flames etched into its surface, or perhaps a bit of the stone had worn away in an interesting pattern by the passage of time. He handed it back to her.

"You'd better go," he said.

"We haven't talked," she said. "It's important. I've got things to tell you."

"Such as?"

"Well, for starters, why we need to get you out of here. Grace sent me to get you."

"It was Grace who brought me here."

"She didn't expect you'd settle in so well."

"I like it. If it's a matter of choosing real life or fiction, I choose this."

"Do you know what will happen to that sallow man?" she said.

"The one being *displaced*?"

"Do you know what that means?"

"Retired. He's old."

"Not as old as you'd think. He will be eliminated." She paused for dramatic effect. "Put down."

"Put down! Euthanized?"

"Executed by the woman who has replaced him."

"Seriously?" She was no longer smiling. "Is it because there can only be one hundred and forty-four in the sacred order?"

"It is an unholy order, David. He will be exterminated by whatever means he and his replacement agree upon. Usually, it's by poison. Hemlock is a classic. Or by suffocation. Occasionally, when the redundant Reader resists, it is done with an old-fashioned straight razor kept stropped for the purpose. An elderly woman once insisted on being crushed under books and every one of her colleagues participated by bringing the weightiest hardcover volumes they could find and giving them to the novitiate to pile on her emaciated body until the old woman expired. They removed the books posthumously very quickly, of course, so as not to contaminate them with putrefaction. Another man leapt from a stack of Jane Austen novels in various editions, with a noose around his neck. He dangled and strangled like an emancipated marionette. He apparently diapered himself first and no copies were damaged."

She seemed to enjoy the grotesquery. The stories made him sick.

"What happens if the old man refuses to co-operate?" he asked. "The usurper looked very unhealthy." He meant flaccid. "The man looked resilient."

"When you are at the top of the list and your time is over, which is determined by seniority, by length of stay not age, you die. You do not fight back. How can you? You have no moral resources of your own. You are nameless, a cipher, you are nothing but memories of all the conflicting things you have read."

David sat down on the cot, turned so he could look into her eyes, to see if there was any chance she was making this up, wondering what purpose she could possibly have. The lights went off. Instinctively, they reached out to each other and entwined their fingers in a gesture of mutual support.

"Where's Grace now?" he whispered.

"Speak up. Just because it's dark doesn't mean the walls can hear any better. We're surrounded by solid earth. Limestone, actually, with baubles of granite."

"She's my mother, you know?"

"So I heard."

"Is she all right?"

"All right? That's hard to say. She defied the power of Jacob Hummel, then she violated the laws of The Cloisters."

"By bringing me here? She told me this was a sanctuary. A haven in the heart of the earth."

"It is, but if you decide to leave, it turns into a dungeon."

"The guy who taught Grace to read, he left."

"He was a novitiate. He failed out."

"Did Grace leave on her own? Originally, I mean."

"She came back for your sake."

"Was she a votary?"

"On the verge. But she refused to kill the girl she was meant to replace. Instead, she helped her escape."

"Really?" The selflessness did not seem characteristic.

"Really. If the gathering realized who she was when she brought you here, she'd be dead. The brutality in a story-book world is absolute. Once she knew you were safe, she had to get away. She asked me to come in and keep an eye on you; if necessary, to intervene. And here we are. You're prepared to erase yourself and I'm, of course, subject to extermination if they catch up with me."

"But you're a chameleon, right? And I'm indelible."

"As you wish."

"You said Grace displaced a *girl*?"

"A girl who was born here in The Cloisters, whose parents were executed because they were lovers — her father, on discovery, her mother, after giving birth. The girl grew up among books. She was a Reader, of course, entitled to wear the sweater. She was sixteen when she was displaced."

"There must have been others with more seniority."

"But they had not read as much. She was the only child in here and she had reached childhood's end."

"That wasn't fair."

"You are very sweet, David. But what is fair had nothing to do with it."

They edged closer to each other in the semi-darkness. He could feel her warm breath on his cheeks. She smelled of sunlight on lavender fields, she smelled of mist.

"The girl," he said, his voice shaking. "Was it you?"

Her silence was a resounding horrific assent. She set the pendant and necklace on the table. He could feel her heart quicken as the muted light softened the walls of his cell. The bright rectangle of illumination shining at the door seemed like a blockade, ensuring their privacy. They edged closer.

She disentangled their entwined fingers and taking his hand she slipped it inside her blouse and pressed his palm to her breast. The flesh felt soft and firm, warm, cool, and contoured. In the curve of his grasp her nipple nuzzled into his skin. He pulsed his hand nervously as she pushed against him. They tried to undress each other. Their clothes seemed evasive and alien. Her bra in particular confounded him and she had to take over. Once they were free of clothes in the darkness, she calmed him gently and with excruciatingly slow movements she kept him on the edge until she was ready, then released them both into astonishment, before slowly bringing him back and drawing them together through the same ecstatic procedures again, and then again, before both fell asleep.

Morning came when the room suddenly filled with artificial light. David rose first and looked down at Isabelle sprawled across the ravaged bed, a pilgrim soul in repose. He had never seen a naked woman — except diagrammatically, abstracted, piecemeal and labelled, or in reproductions of paintings where suggestive bodily parts were redacted — never whole, as a human, bemused, vivacious, and wanton. She rose languorously, stood beside him for a moment, stretched, laughed at his gaping expression, and disappeared into the bathroom.

# Chapter Six
## Plato's Brother

"I cannot remember a time before reading," she said. "When I first became aware of the world, it was through words on the page. Written language was the source of remembered experience. I grew up believing the world was a phantasmagoria of characters and situations originating in print. The subterranean experience down here was an illusion, representative of a rumoured but inaccessible existence in another dimension I knew only from the resounding footfall of passersby overhead who didn't realize I existed."

"You could hear people up there?"

"I was speaking figuratively. Do you know Plato's Parable of the Cave? No, of course, your access monitor is down and you never bothered to check out classical philosophers when it was working."

"Wittgenstein, 1889-1951. A contemporary and classmate of Adolf Hitler. Nietzsche, 1844-1900. An inspiration for Hitler. Kant, 1724-1804. Rationalism, empiricism; he laid the way for Hitler — and for those who defeated him. Those three, and name recognition of a few others. I was not attracted to earlier philosophers soaked in religion or doubtful of being. I skimmed the classics but not much more. Tell me about Plato."

"He liked to tell stories. The Parable of the Cave was one of the best."

"As a story or as philosophy?"

"Both. Imagine living your whole life a captive underground, chained facing away from a fire, and all you know is garnered from shadows cast on the wall of cut-outs manipulated by puppeteers who are hidden behind your back, between you and the flames. Behind the puppeteers is a crevasse providing access to the world outside. Now suppose you break free. You turn and crawl towards the light. You are blinded by the fire, then dazzled by the sun. What you see out there is a spectrum of colours beyond your imagining. You creep back into the cave because that is your home, but you see the shadow world differently now as silhouettes cast from books, images only made real by the mind."

"Your horse seems to have changed riders in midstream. Shadows have become words, the puppeteers have become writers."

"My story and Glaucon's reflect on each other," she said.

"Glaucon?"

"Plato's brother, the interlocutor whose earnest ignorance inspired the parable. According to Plato's *Republic*, Socrates told the story of the cave to Glaucon."

"Then why is it called Plato's Cave? Why not give credit to Socrates or to Glaucon?"

"Because Plato wrote it down. He could call it whatever he wanted."

"Out there in the actual world, the writer is philosopher-king. And you say this was your story as well."

"Living in The Cloisters, I didn't know there was anything else. It was not until Grace arrived that I realized there was light beyond writing, a light upon which the votaries had wilfully turned their backs. She made me see writers as puppeteers standing in front of a flame, in front of the sun at our backs. This was exciting. Grace and I shared books. We talked. We made critical judgements about writing that soars, and writing that plods. It was all very subversive. She explained that books were echoes of a world outside, which the votaries chose to leave. Grace was here as a seeker, not to escape. She was born and raised in the library, where no one reads, so The Cloisters was a place to discover herself. There was much at stake. She was a careful reader — she was dismayed by indiscriminate reading. She taught me the difference between losing myself in books and finding myself. She showed me how to read with a *critical mind*, which in The Cloisters was heresy punishable by awareness of mortality and death."

"Not only did she refuse to erase you, she taught you to separate yourself from the text." He wanted to reassure her that he followed her discourse.

"I owe her a lot, David. By the time we ascended into the open, I felt I had already been there. Yet nothing prepares you for the dazzle of the sun when you have been surrounded by shadows. Afraid and in awe, you promise yourself you will never go back."

"But you did," he said. "You came back for me."

"That is the trouble with parables. Sometimes they collapse in the face of necessity. The point was not in the details, David — I was trying to say too much too briefly."

"About yourself?"

"About readers who are moulded by the medium at the expense of the message — about writing, unable to dance, that merely delivers."

"About reading without becoming an attribute of the book being read," he said. "Okay, you sure as hell broke free. I mean, that was you, right, you were driving the Hummer. The old man told me you could move around out there because your brain refused to adapt to its implant."

"I never had an implant. I was born here, remember."

"Why did we leave you on the side of the road?"

"You were being extracted by taking my place. Your malfunctioning implant would have read on the scanners the same as my natural brain. I was expendable, you weren't."

"In whose bloody judgement?"

"Jacob's, of course. I made my own way back as you can see. Crawling face down in the mud."

"Really."

"No. I went out through Checkpoint Charlie down by the lake. Most transients don't have implants. They go over by day to the Evolved New World, for dangerous or tedious work. They're checked randomly."

"They could've checked you."

"But they didn't."

At this point, they were talking in her cell rather than his, but the rooms were the same, down to the tiniest detail. Despite the provocative exchange of glances when they had risen that morning, neither had mentioned the previous night. Their love-making, however, cast a shimmering light over every moment for David and he found himself smiling foolishly, even when she was in the most serious and convoluted explication of Plato's theory of forms. In contrast, she seemed to have entirely forgotten their tryst and treated him like a long-standing friend in need of enlightenment.

They had already been to breakfast, sitting side by side like strangers. The refectory was oppressive. The quiet clatter of dishes and mouthing of porridge, the dry turning of pages and occasional throat clearing, accentuated the gloom. David noticed the stout woman who had proclaimed herself a votary the previous night was now seated at the same table as the Reader Superior, forcing the others to make room. What struck him as more sinister, the gaunt man with a nickname that echoed from his previous life had not returned. The Readers on his bench had expanded their personal space to close up the gap left by his absence. Even more disturbing was how easily Isabelle submerged herself into the collective, with the terrifying conviction that the Readers were too absorbed in their own proclivities to recognize her as an outsider who had once been their youngest Fellow.

Grace had sent her to save him from himself, afraid he would allow his personality to be erased like the Tiger's had been, like the others who followed the Order's commitment to submission, dedication, detachment, the annihilation of self. Seduced by books, he had nearly succumbed. Seduced by Isabelle, he was prepared to resist.

Isabelle had glowered at the novitiate with the featureless face who was seated directly across the table, making a display of ignoring them.

"What are you thinking, you utter twat?" Isabelle had declared, then turning to David, she mumbled, "A fine Shakespearean insult. It makes people uncomfortable. Not you, you twit. Her."

"Oh." He had heard neither 'twit' nor 'twat' spoken aloud before this.

Once they were back in her cell, just the two of them together, he relaxed a little. That's when she launched into her Glaucon analogy and in a fog of erotic distraction he forgot about danger until there was a sudden rap on the door frame, there being no actual door.

David's impulse was to ignore the intrusion, but Isabelle walked straight to the opening and, as she did, it filled with the drab sinister presence of the Reader Superior.

"Isabelle," said the woman. Her utterance of the name had an unexpected impact on David's rescuer-lover. Isabelle's shoulders sank, her head tilted, she seemed instantly submissive. "Did you think I wouldn't recognize you?" said the woman. "You are a foolish girl, Isabelle, a silly child. I knew you would return. Whatever incentive was promised by that vile woman who took you away, I knew you would come back."

David was bewildered when Isabelle sank deeper into herself like a contrite child. Where the hell was the young woman who taunted the smug novitiate across the breakfast table, the girl who made love to a virgin boy like she was salving a wounded soul, the young woman who risked returning to the cave through shadows and flames to take him back to the light? He was losing her, he felt terror mounting inside.

The Reader Superior turned and walked out into the brightly illuminated corridor. Isabelle and David followed in her wake. David doubled back and retrieved the pendant and necklace from the bedside table. He caught up and placed it around Isabelle's neck. They moved through a series of chambers linked like a panopticon to give the impression, despite being far beneath the surface of the Earth and surrounded by rock, that from any vantage an observer could see in all directions without limit, as the soft dazzling light swallowed details and created a receding encompassing haze. Everywhere, they passed Readers reading and books piled on tables waiting to be read. David channelled his fear into fascination for their immediate acquiescence to the unspoken will of the woman who glided ahead of them, betraying her advanced age with a slight hobble in her gait, a slight stoop to her shoulders, a woman no one seemed to notice as they passed, yet to whom all deferred by moving slightly to the side as if they might be a little in her way.

When they stopped in front of a massive door, David realized with shock that this was the first closed door he had seen since entering The Cloisters. The sight of it seemed a personal affront. The absence of doors to the cells had left him oppressed, not as an assault on privacy but for the assumption that no one's life in this nether world was of sufficient interest to merit surveillance. But this door was an insult, especially since it appeared to be locked. It was a declaration that he was not a free agent, here of his own volition and able to go wherever he wanted. He watched the woman with mounting resentment as she withdrew a key from her cardigan pocket and unlocked the door. It did not occur to him as an option to resist when she ushered them through and closed the door behind them.

They had abruptly entered a different reality. Gone was the eerie luminescence of The Cloisters, with its sheer granite walls reflecting the absence of shadows and its moss-carpeted floors and burbling stream and niches and alcoves for undisturbed reading. They were in the chill embrace of a tunnel cut through natural formations of rock, illuminated by a few incandescent bulbs strung on an overhead wire. The walls glistened with moisture and echoed the slightest sound, even their breathing, the thumping of their hearts, the shuffle of their feet over finely crushed grit as they moved through the gloom towards a crude stairway carved into the stone at the farthest extreme of their narrowed dark vision, steps rising upward into a flickering light which, as they approached, revealed itself to be flames lapping against the stone walls.

When they reached the top of the stairs, they found themselves inside an inferno illuminated by three huge wrought-iron braziers that throbbed with fiery cinders topped by dancing flames that emitted a low-pitched crackling roar. A single attendant with a dead cigarette hanging from his lips stoked the fires, heaping coal on the flaming braziers from a bin hacked into the rock on one side of the chamber. On the other side was a single door made of heavy oak planks reinforced by strips of iron studded with hand-forged bolts. At the far end was another door, presumably leading to the world above. Even hell must have an exit, if only so its minion could step out for a smoke.

"Welcome to Hades," said the old woman in the worn cardigan. She had to shout over the roar of the braziers. "Call me Lucy."

"I thought you were nameless, the Reader Superior," David responded, mouthing his words so she could see them in the enveloping din.

"Down there," she nodded behind her. "Here, I am Lucifer." She drew them closer. "It is a pseudonym, of course, in keeping with the literary pretensions of maintaining hell on Earth to punish the wicked before they can escape into death. What do you think, Isabelle? Is it not a marvellous creation?"

"It's amazing what bad taste and money can do," said Isabelle, speaking normally yet clearly audible despite the noise. "I never imagined there could be such a place. It's right out of a novel."

Lucy seemed pleased. "It's taken from contemporary horror fiction or from classical mythology or from the religious sensibility of pre-Renaissance Italy. It could be an invention of Dante and the Popes he despised or the despicable daydreams of Donald J. Trump."

David was puzzled. Isabelle seemed to be restored to her earlier assertiveness, the Reader Superior was proving to be a pedant, and this place called hell was a nightmarish vision either conjured by the devil or possibly to summon his presence. David had no reason to think the devil existed, nor that he didn't. Belief in the ineffable was not to be confused with faith. **GOD LISTENS** was an admonition to encourage acceptance, not superstition. Religious instruction was not meant to inspire or redeem but to foster submission. For that, Jesus was useful in the Canadian sector of the Evolved New World, historically more convenient than Vishnu or Muhammad, Odin, the Orenda, or Ra. No better, no worse, but useful.

David's thoughts on the rhetorical function of religion in the world of his childhood's end occurred in an instant. He needed to focus on the present. He gazed through the burning light. It seemed like the air was on fire. His eyes caught Isabelle's. For a moment they connected, one damned soul with another, then her gaze shifted and he lost her. He looked to Lucy. She seemed on fire herself. She had cast off her cardigan and loosened her blouse and her flesh flared crimson and yellow and blue, the same as the stone walls throbbing around them. The man charging the braziers ignored them. He glistened with sweat, busy with his Mephistophelian labours.

"Isabelle, David," shouted the woman on fire, who seemed so much more alive as Lucifer than she had among Readers as their nameless Superior. "If you would step in here. Both of you. Isabelle, my dear, the inner room is for you." They moved through the open, oak doorway, the door swung shut heavily behind them. Immediately, the roar of the burning air vanished. They were surrounded by the muted light of a single bulb dangling from a wire, a myriad of shadows which leapt in unison as they moved, and by an oppressive stench. David's eyes took a moment to adjust to the gloom. He was sickened by what he saw: death's twilight kingdom — a littering of human corpses in varying stages of decomposition. Some were draped from shackles set into the stone walls, some sprawled limpidly across the crushed cinder floor. Most were nearly naked, a few were overdressed in rags they had stolen from the dead, and most were virtually sexless, ambiguous in their degraded condition.

"Isabelle?" he whispered, afraid to speak out loud, as if that would make the horrors more real. "Isabelle?" he repeated softly.

Isabelle said nothing but moved ahead into a brightly lit grotto filled with stacks of mouldering books, a narrow cot with a filthy grey blanket, and a cracked porcelain sink beneath a rusted tap. There was a chipped chamber pot on the floor and a reading light attached to the stone above the head of the bed. Lucy, as the Reader Superior called herself, closed the thick glass door which was a mirror on the inside but transparent from outside. There appeared to be no handle. Isabelle looked back but would be able to see only herself, while David and Lucy observed her in illuminated detail, every pore and skin crease exposed to the glare. Even her golden hair seemed scant and unpleasant in the ravaging light.

"Isabelle," he whispered to her image through the glass, but she was in a silent world of her own and could not possibly hear.

"She will become nameless, dear David. She will read and read and read and lose herself reading. As for you, you will observe. That is your fate, to watch your friend disappear, to become nothing yourself. The Duc de La Rochefoucauld once said, *Le soleil ni la mort ne se peuvent regarder fixement*, 'neither the sun nor death can be looked at steadily'. There is such a thing as too much reality, David; more than the mind or the soul or the eyes can endure. You will become nothing yourself. I'm sure you know the story of Glaucon. When challenged by Socrates to return to the cave, he realized reality in the world of the sun was ephemeral, that authentic experience was evoked by the shades in the world of language and words. You will both be in the shade. You will both expire content."

David was sure, from Isabelle's recent explication, that Lucy had the parable wrong. She likely misunderstood La Rochefoucauld as well. But David had no doubt her predicted outcome for Isabelle was a distinct possibility. Isabelle had been formed by fiction from birth. She might easily revert to fiction if reality failed to intervene. She would literally become what she read.

"Why am I being punished?" David asked. He couldn't help Isabelle if he didn't understand what was in store for himself. He gestured to the dead bodies scattered into the farthest shadows. "Were *they* being punished?"

"Of course not," Lucy declared. "They were merely indecisive."

He could see she was not about to explain. "Will I be released?"

"That is up to you. You will be fed and if you choose to keep your friend alive, you will share your food with her. Since there will only be enough for one person to survive, how long either of you lasts will be up to you, David. You will watch her read, but you cannot read yourself. There are no books in the antechamber to hell."

He felt frantic, panicked by confusion. "I don't understand."

"This is what will happen. You will eventually die or go mad or you will return to The Cloisters with your personality erased, having poured out your soul to Isabelle, who will not even know you are here, or you will be returned to Jacob Hummel, who will displace your mind with his own. He will empty your brain and insert himself. Those are your options."

"You know about Jacob?"

"More than he knows about me."

"What about if I just say I'm sorry?"

"A quip in the face of catastrophe! Always revealing. Isabelle has had a dangerous influence already. But you have nowhere to go, David. Your mother is dead. You are a pebble cast on a pool. You have sunk to the bottom and the ripples grow smaller and smaller and soon they will smooth over completely. You have heard the mermaids singing, each to each, they will not sing to you."

"*But those are pearls that were his eyes.*"

"Yes? And?"

He was bound up inside. "I don't know," he mumbled. "I don't know. Shakespeare's Ariel, Eliot's Prufrock? Is it all the same?" His voice trailed off. References without meaning, great writing reduced to quotations shorn of their context, this was the legacy of his education under the Company's aegis.

"You have nothing to remember if you don't have the words. And no future if you have nothing to read. Watch Isabelle, perhaps you will see a few passages over her shoulder and through the glass darkly. They will give you comfort and time, or perhaps not."

Much as he abhorred this woman, he preferred her odour of brimstone and roses to the malingering stench of death when she slipped past him and out the huge oak door. "Don't leave," he called, too late. There was a flash of flames as fire washed over her and suddenly, he was alone, surrounded by bodies in all stages of decomposition reaching out from the shadows towards him. He turned to the illuminated glass fronting Isabelle's cell. He could see her already buried in a mildewed copy of a narrative by Thomas Carlyle. He banged on the glass with his fists, then with his open palms. There was no response. He sank to the floor and wept.

The tears were self-pity and quickly dried on his face. He was angry at himself for submitting to emotion. His mother had taught him that exaggerated feelings could be indulgent distractions from dealing with whatever their causes. His mother, Violet! The Reader Superior had said his mother was dead — she didn't know that Grace was his actual mother. She knew Jacob Hummel well enough to be aware of his demonic design to implant his mind. Apparently, she did not know the relationship between Jacob Hummel and Violet, Jacob Hummel and Grace, Jacob Hummel and himself. She was dangerous because she knew too much but, paradoxically, she was dangerous because she knew so little.

Convoluted thinking, combined with his horror and fear, exhausted him. He walked about, shuffling carefully amidst the decomposing human detritus. He would have to clear a space to stretch out for sleeping. This burial chamber, charnel house, cavern, crypt, mausoleum was warm enough from the fires outside the oak door, but he would have to 'borrow' some clothes from the least putrid bodies for bedding. He sucked in his gut and began sliding corpses around. Some fell apart as he pushed from his knees with closed fists. Exposed skin and sinew and protruding bones were uniformly covered in a green haze of mould. The bodies with the thickest layers smelled least but were more likely to disintegrate under pressure.

He stripped clothing from several of them. He was careful to pick less soiled materials while avoiding what appeared the most recent, which brought death too close to endure, or the oldest, which had absorbed death into their fibres. When he accumulated a sufficient pile, he walked over to the one-way mirror and was startled to see Isabelle had retreated to her cot, Carlyle still absorbing her attention. When she was leaning against the glass door, he had been able to peer over her shoulder and read with unnerving clarity. Now he could only see letters dancing in reflection as her eyes flickered across the pages.

A rattling noise alerted him to the arrival of dinner. A slot opened at the base of the oak door and a tray, briefly glistening from the inferno, turned instantly drab as it slid into the chamber — which suddenly, for acknowledging its living inhabitant, had transformed from a charnel house into a dungeon. David sniffed at the food. It was a generic stew and smelled surprisingly good. He ate less than half, then knocked on the glass door into Isabelle's grotto. She couldn't hear him. He found a drawer at the foot of the door which opened on one side by sealing at the other like an air-lock, so things could be passed through but sound could not penetrate. With the handle end of the spoon, he scrawled the letters of his name on the tray and slid it through. She read his message, stood up, and smiled sweetly at her image in the mirror. He moved into her direct line of vision and smiled in return, feeling wretched, knowing that she couldn't see him. But at least she knew he was there. She returned to her cot and read Thomas Carlyle while she ate.

When she returned the tray, she had scrawled the words 'hi there' in the residual food with her finger. He didn't know what more he had expected.

She rolled her grey blanket into a bolster, turned out her lights from a switch by the bed and instantly disappeared. He turned away from his sudden reflection in the glass and settled onto his foul-smelling bed of rags, then got up and walked to the far side of the chamber where he relieved himself against the wall and returned to his bed. He decided to leave the dull light turned on, lest in the dark, he mistook himself for a corpse.

Lying on his side, he immediately closed his eyes to avoid looking at the cadaver stretched out facing him an arm's length away. Its flesh was not yet corrupted. Its clothing was worn but relatively clean. David opened his eyes again and peered through the gloom at his companion. Taut features highlighted the sharp creases of skin drawn tight over the front of the old man's skull. His hair was wispy with a slight curl. The cartilage of his aquiline nose pressed against its leathery sheath. His lips were narrow, moist from the humidity, with teeth pressing them open in a sustained half-smile. His eyes were sealed beneath folds of skin, his lashes pale. He had one arm at his side, the other draped over his own body, meeting at clasped gnarled hands, once-athletic fingers curled into each other like tendrils of aged vegetation.

So emphatic were the features of death, David had not recognized until this moment that this was the gaunt sallow man reputed to have been called The Tiger, formidable in his youth and universally admired for his quick and caustic wit before succumbing to books. He had been displaced. Isabelle had said he would be eliminated by agreement with his successor. Lucifer had said most of the occupants of the charnel house were victims of their own indecision. David wondered, did this mean the old man didn't accept death, that he had to be cosseted inside a crypt until he expired, or was it simply that he couldn't make up his mind how he wanted to die? How could he be dead so soon? He had been expelled only the previous evening.

The Tiger burped.

David flinched. He understood that gastric and intestinal gases could animate a corpse in an illusory gesture of restored mortality. It was only this and nothing more. What a ghastly trick — and feeling forlorn he muttered: "May we both rest in peace, my friend."

He reached out and touched the letter A sewn to the man's cardigan, trying to establish a perverse rapport. He pushed on the sweater to see if he could evoke another burp.

"If you do that again," said the corpse, "I shall be very pissed off."

David scrambled up on his haunches and raised his hands towards the corpse as if preparing to ward off a blow. The old man's eyes opened, one at a time.

"I'm not going to bloody well get up to greet you," said the man, his dry mouth making the words crackle. "The honour is yours. Now leave me alone. I'd like to pass on, uninterrupted."

"I can't leave," said David. "There's nowhere to go." He was terrified. What if the other cadavers were about to awaken? He forced his gaze away from The Tiger and surveyed the room, imagining that skeletons could walk, that entrails would slither back into the gaping holes in decomposed corpses, that putrefied sinews could bind, mouldering flesh could quiver, wizened eyes could penetrate the gloom, that they would all rise together and seek him out beside the former high school star lying prostrate beside him, anticipating his own imminent death.

"Why aren't you dead?" David said. He had just been wondering why the man wasn't alive.

"I've been asking myself the same question," the man chortled. His eyes were an impenetrable slate blue. "It's certainly not for want of wanting. I think it will just take time. Your friend in the grotto, what is she reading?"

"How did you know she's a she?"

"By the sounds when you came in. I recognized her by the sounds of her breathing, her movements, her particular projection of silence. We once shared the same table in the refectory. We shared certain books. What is she reading in there?"

"Thomas Carlyle. The headers on the pages say *Sartor Resartus*."

"The ponderous nonsense of Diogenes Teufelsdröckh, yes, good. As I remember, she's read it before. It is delightful, yes, very postmodern."

"Postmodern?"

"Post. Modern. A fusion of genres, a clash of attitudes, a discourse on its own making."

"But he died before there was such a thing."

"Possibly he did. But only before it was named. Did you know he was much concerned about great men and how they made history? No women, as I recall. But I would argue, and I'm not a great man, that history was made by writers and the stories they tell. History is not memory but text. In any case, the man was a terror."

"You say that with a hint of admiration."

"He wrote *against* the abolition of slavery, he wrote *against* democracy, he wrote *against* God."

"And you admire him?"

"I admire the force of his mind, not the ideas they produced. And he was a man after my own heart, or I after his, because he believed in the written word — despite giving primacy to heroes over books. They are the soul of mankind, all that remains when 'material substance has altogether vanished'. Everything we are, he said, is in the pages of books. For such thoughts, I forgive him his fascism."

"Like Hitler?" David couldn't recall very much about fascism, itself.

"Carlyle died in the 1880s, the same decade Hitler was born. A coincidence of numbers, nothing more."

"You seem talkative for a man who is about to die for a number."

"Huh? Ah, the one hundred and forty-fifth Reader. Yes, do you know, over a hundred years ago, in Herr Hitler's reign, there was a terrible place called Auschwitz where a million people were exterminated, a million, but one hundred and forty-four successfully escaped. A hundred and forty-four. That is significant."

"You identify with the ones who didn't survive?"

"No, nor with the rarity of those who did. I am the one too many. Singular. I am one, the essential component of all numbers."

"Until the next *one*, then you will be one hundred and forty-six and anonymous."

"Which as a Reader like me is tremendously appealing."

"You're surprisingly talkative."

"I can be — if not, giving up talking would have been a small sacrifice. I once liked to talk. Trust me, I was charming if the need came up. Now why don't we agree, I am a sensitive man and it's time to leave me alone?"

"Do you want some food? There's still a little left on my plate."

"I want nothing. I need nothing. I desire nothing. Nothing, nothing, nothing. So, please do not intrude any further."

"Your replacement didn't kill you?"

"We agreed I would die passively."

"By refusing to live?"

"With no food, no water, no whiskey, and nothing to read, it will only be a matter of hours. I was well on my way before you people came in."

"Why here, like this?"

"I knew such a place existed, there were rumours."

"Do Readers gossip?"

"Of course. Behind closed doors."

"But there are no doors in The Cloisters."

"There are if you know where to look. There are places where some of the votaries exchange critical chatter about books. I chose never to indulge. The last thing I wanted was to share my responses with people who considered themselves my peers. But I listened, and purporting to talk about Dante, they would describe the furnace beyond the oak door. It is fed from the coal bins of wealthy estates two hundred years old. Some claimed to have had glimpses into this corpse-littered crypt, meant to strike them with terror — or longing. Yes, longing, I suppose. Look around. Each set of decaying remains is one of my fellow Readers, a grisly familiar, each an exemplar of death's empty promise. Where better to die than in a cemetery, surrounded by corpses of redundant people I never bothered to know?"

"You are a sad old man."

"Pathetic, but not sad. I have done with reading now. I wish only to join their insignificant company."

"They're only shades of the living," said David, feeling quite smug. "Shadows cast on the wall of our cave, animated by our own minds. Do you know about Plato's brother?"

The old man bared his teeth and smiled. It seemed a gesture directed at himself more than David. "Glaucon, yes. He never fully understood what

Socrates told him. Plato was showing how empty is the world of experience. Our lives are populated with shadows of corpses."

"No," David declared with confidence reinforced by his limited experience and knowledge. "Surely Plato was challenging us to turn around and look into the light."

"Read more, young man. There is no light. There are only flames burning cold at our backs."

The Tiger seemed prepared to lapse into silence, but David was not quite ready to let the man go. "If there is no escape from this place, how could you trust rumour, how could you be sure it existed?"

"Because it must. If it can be conceived, it exists. The cavern out there is a transit on the way to the surface. The executive branch lives in a fine mansion when they are not re-reading ancient fictions in The Cloisters below — or so I've been told. They are a very secretive group, known only to themselves — a literal Conclave, otherwise known as The Book Club. The Reader Superior is, you might say, their bishop. Together they have constructed hell — the inferno provides power, and it is a symbolic reminder of the world we've all given up beyond books, and this crypt is a symbolic reminder of the world after death. The Conclave have to pass through, pass by, each time they emerge from The Cloisters, each time they return to its comfort. But enough, now, you have exhausted me. Let me be, I would like to die."

"Do they turn out the lights?"

"Not completely. You die in the darkness you have made for yourself. Come in. I will show you something different from your shadow at morning striding behind you or your shadow at evening rising to meet you. I will show you your life in a handful of dust."

With that, the gaunt sallow man who had been a popular athlete in his youth closed his eyes and assumed the demeanour of a corpse. He had not displaced thinking with reading as Isabelle supposed. Words inscribed on a page had clearly transformed into a fury of sounds in his mind. But now, all he wanted was silence.

David settled back onto his filthy bedding and faced the glimmering rectangle on the far side of the chamber. He got up and returned his tray to the slot at the base of the oak door. It was almost immediately pulled out into the fiery glare. He returned to his bedding but, before shutting his eyes, he surveyed death's other kingdom. He felt hollow inside, his soul shrivelled.

Before David fell asleep, The Tiger, having exhausted himself in conversation, expired.

# Chapter Seven
## Odysseus Ever Returning

The girl who creates aurochs avoids people. She refines compounds made with animal fat, blood, clay, ochre, and charcoal. Her mother brings visitors into the depths of the cave to witness her creations, but only when the girl isn't there. This desire to work undisturbed translates into magic. The girl is thought to make flesh from her dreams. She is believed to conjure an auroch from nothing, grazing, in flight, at bay. The paint flows with finesse from the tips of her fingers as she turns it to flesh and sinew and bone. To the girl, it is the auroch itself that is magic.

The more people who arrive from distant communes to witness her work, the more desperate she is to retreat. For months and then years she hides deep in the cave where sunlight can't touch her and her skin turns the colour of ivory with a luminescent sheen from the smoke of the fires her mother keeps stoked for warmth while she contemplates aurochs. Periodically, she ventures to a place near the cavern entrance where a sliver of sun penetrates through a narrow crevasse and watches as it slowly sweeps across her legs and torso.

Sometimes she sits on the fur mats on the floor of her cave and arranges pebbles in the dust in rigid designs, sometimes she rocks herself asleep and awake and asleep until she collapses onto her side and her mother covers her naked body with an auroch robe. Sometimes she eats the berries and meat that her mother provides and she gazes into the middle-distance teeming with aurochs. Sometimes she and her mother chatter while they eat together, trying out phonemes, contriving modifiers, verb tenses, metaphors.

One day in an indeterminate season, with no warning, the mother brings three young men into the heart of the cave while the girl, now a young woman, is dreaming of aurochs. When she sees them approach, she turns her back and addresses the stone, searching for creases in the rock face that promise the curve of a twisted neck, the surge of a shoulder or haunch, any part of an auroch waiting to be freed. She mixes pigments and begins to paint, and the arm muscles of one of the three young men twitches in unison with her movements and he looks past her nakedness to the metamorphosis of rock into paint into pulsating flesh as she manipulates the shadows and spectrum of light, and he cannot separate what she makes from who she is as she works in the firelight. The other two watch her pale body flicker and they shrink in annoyance and fear and contempt.

The woman who brought them into the cave pushes the boy most stricken with repugnance towards the pale apparition. The girl drops and he moves forward and takes her with little more than a clumsy thrust, rises, and stands apart in the shadows. The next shrinking boy is pushed forward and falls on the girl while she is still down on the fur mat, resigned to the breeding ritual orchestrated by her mother. He takes her in an instant and rises triumphantly, then recedes into the shadows to join his compatriot. The third young man, without urging, steps forward and first touches his fingers to feel the auroch alive on the wall, then bends to the young woman and gently touches her skin until she moans softly against his shoulder and spreads to invite him into her, where he lingers and then comes with a quiet surge. He rises and joins the others. The girl's mother leads them away through the tunnelled convolutions of rock, out past the big crevasse where the bodies of two of the girl's fathers had been cast into bottomless darkness only moments after conception. The third, the woman had allowed to survive. These three she now discharges with a perfunctory shrug and prepares dinner for her daughter and herself of tubers cooked inside a roasting goose and succulent slabs from its breast.

The girl rises and goes back to the auroch and fashions a calf stumbling in its tumultuous wake. In another season, in the chamber near the opening outward, her newborn shivers, gasps, howls in a single cry, and dies. Her own mother takes her dead infant from her arms and wraps the small body in a lamb's skin and sets it away from the fire. The girl rises and walks with her mother to the opening of the cave and is blinded by the sun. As her eyes adjust, she sees colours she has long forgotten and shapes that move with the breeze. Her pale skin quivers in the open air. She picks wildflowers in bloom from close to the entrance. The two women turn back into the cave. The girl picks up her baby cocooned in its wool and cradles her burden against the flowers pressed to her naked breast and walks alone deeper into the earth, carrying a small torch in her free hand. When she finds a secret grotto, she crawls through and sets her bundle down, wipes away tears from her cheeks, and unwraps the shroud. She plucks petals from the flowers and spreads them in delicate patterns over her baby, gently wraps her again, and places rocks around her to protect her from the idea of predators, then walks out into the firelight where her mother wraps her in an auroch hide and together they make their way up to the sunlight.

\*\*\*

*History is a nightmare from which I am trying to awake.* Everything everywhere led to this moment. David was thinking about energy and matter back to the beginning of time. Everything had to align as it did, without an erg or an atom out of place, for him to be here in the anteroom of Hades, where he calculated he had been for a week. Two meals a day, by content determined to be breakfast or dinner, porridge or stew, with a squat pitcher of water. He kept the water for himself, since Isabelle was drinking from the tap in her cell. Everything else he shared.

At first, he had gagged at the surrounding stench of disintegrating flesh, especially from The Tiger, whom he had hauled to the farthest corner of the chamber. He found it difficult to hold down his food but, like anything, he got used to the miasma and in the last couple of days, drained and discouraged, he had taken his full portion before giving Isabelle hers. She was dependent on him for food. She had no way of knowing it came from him. He was dependent on his unseen jailers. Each of them, he and Isabelle, had been thrust on the forefront of a different history into this convergence of autonomy and reliance. Their keepers were equally minions of chance and change that led them to, now.

He walked into the radiance of the glass rectangle on a path he had cleared through the charnel waste and touched his fingers to the cool surface. Isabelle was sitting on the grey blanket folded on the stone floor with her back to the mirror so he could read over her shoulder.

David tried to concentrate on the present.

The past is a singularity, it cannot be changed. The future plays out with infinite connections that only converge when time catches up. A blue-green butterfly swoops in the tundra twilight, and David is aware of the coolness of glass. Both moments happen, come together in his mind, and pass as they must. Self-consciousness, the blessing and curse of his species, has led him to a modest epiphany about being in time.

Isabelle was reading *Ulysses*; not a Latinate translation of Homer's *Odyssey* but Joyce's modernist vanity fair set within and all about Dublin during the progress of June 16th. He had read along with her for a couple of hours the previous day, but after their shared dinner he was relieved when she closed the book on the words of Stephen Daedalus that had resonated in his head through the night: "History is a nightmare from which I am trying to awake."

At the end of two weeks, he was a changed young man. He no longer thought about history and how it conspired to make him a prisoner at the edge of Hades. He no longer worried about stuffing his excrement down a drain hole in the floor and washing it away with cupped hands brimming with water from a small putrid pool in the back corner of the cave. He just did what he did and took little notice when Isabelle excreted into her chamber pot and then washed her waste down the cracked porcelain sink in her cell. He no longer imagined what future lay waiting in texts yet to be written about this pathetic semblance of life: eating, eliminating, reading over a starving young woman's shoulder, sharing his food and drink. When she stripped and washed herself with bunched-up clothes at her sink and spread the clothes over a rickety chair to dry and lay back on her bed, naked, and touched her body with her finger-tips as she read, he felt what her fingers felt and he was frustrated when she fell asleep, but it didn't occur to him to finish on his own.

By the end of three months, he believed she was him, they were the same person. When he watched through the glass, he thought he was observing his own reflection. He had no history. He had awakened from the nightmare of history. He no longer existed.

Together they sometimes read two or three books in a day. New ones appeared in her cell, in exchange for those already read, when they both were asleep. Gradually, they approached death by starvation, lack of sunlight, mental fatigue, but neither thought much of their compromised state, being so thoroughly immersed in fiction that their bodies seemed of trivial consequence. In emulation of her fastidious habits, he had started to keep himself cleaner, washing in the foul pool and sponging off with his T-shirt that he dampened with a few precious splashes from his meagre ration of drinking water. She had not acknowledged his separate existence after the first day when she had scrawled an offhand greeting on their tray. She seemed content to waste into nothing. He was vaguely perturbed by the prospect.

Isabelle had seen no one but her own reflection in the mirror. David had seen no one since Tiger had died except Isabelle, whom he mistook for himself. On this particular day in mid-June, they were reading a book by Jorge Luis Borges. She had haphazardly selected *Ficciones* from the top of a pile, but before they finished, she took to her bed, from where she continued to read for two and a half more days. Her progress through the pages was excruciatingly slow. He knew the stories line by line and could follow along, taking his cue from the way her eyes marked the paragraph proportions.

When the book fell forward across her breast, spread-eagled against a splayed spine, and her eyes remained open, gazing fixedly at the empty mirror, his knees buckled beneath him and he sank into the bedding he had some weeks ago moved to the base of her door so he could be nearby while they slept. He figured she had just finished "The Sect of the Phoenix", lingering over the part close to the end that describes God being as *delightful as cork*. The secret of the sect, which Borges leaves hidden, remains wholly elusive. It is beyond description, yet all words refer to it.

What does that even mean? He had been following the text inside his head, but he was muddled when she stopped reading.

In search of something substantial, he turned back a couple of stories in his mind to a certain image: *upon a courtyard flagstone a bee cast a stationary shadow*. Yes, he remembered — while Jaromir Hladík thought — I'm in hell, I'm dead, I've gone mad, time has come to a halt. And in a sense Hladík was right: God had stopped time for a year between the snap of firing squad rifles and the course of their bullets so that Hladík could finish composing his *Vindication of Eternity*. In that protracted instant, he mastered each new hexameter, honed fresh symbols, perfected divine references, and as he condensed, amplified, omitted, incorporated primitive earlier versions, he grew to love that courtyard and those soldiers, and when he finished his work a drop of rainwater continued its journey down his cheek, the bee moved, and Jaromir Hladík completed a terminal shriek and the world died.

David shifted uneasily on his bedding. The light from Isabelle's cell projected a rectangular glow across the oak door opposite. He remembered every detail of the Borges story. Each was part of his own history. He felt a revelation creep through his viscera and up into his head. He, himself, *he* had a history! He had a past signalled by words — not only the words of Borges but the words of the entire universe as it converged in his consciousness. Weakened and miserable, he knew who he was. Like disappearing ink reappearing in the heat of a flame, he was visible again.

A fiery shimmer rattled at the base of the oak door. The dinner tray slid through. David hobbled over to get it, then suddenly stopped, returned to his bedding, and slouched back determinedly, intent on falling asleep. He woke when his breakfast delivery clattered against the untouched dinner tray. Isabelle's light was still on. He peered into her cell. She was standing at the mirror, smoothing her hair which had now grown into an oddly becoming golden nimbus. She had washed and smoothed her tattered clothes. Her face was pale and drawn but her eyes gleamed. She seemed to be searching in the mirror for David's eyes. Then she moved back to her bed and lay down on her back with her hands folded across her breast. She was imitating a corpse.

He settled back, slumped awkwardly against the glass door. Eventually the red glare beneath the oak door accompanied by rattling indicated the breakfast tray was being removed. A hand glistering with fire, with a copper bracelet tight on the wrist, poked through. The hand extended, groped, took hold of the dinner tray and removed it as well. Time passed until finally the heavy oak door swung open on its massive hinges. David's charnel house flooded with fiery light. He shut his eyes, waiting. A foot kicked him sharply, catching him in the solar plexus. He emitted an involuntary groan, rolled a little, played dead. The last few months were a rehearsal for that. Through nearly sealed eyes he watched as Lucy, the Reader Superior, bent over and grasped his ankles. She hauled him away from the glass-mirror door which she then opened by some mysterious mechanism and moved into Isabelle's brightly illuminated cell, where she leaned on the closest pile of mouldy books to catch her breath. She had removed her sweater and her skin glistened from the heat like the crackling on a pork roast.

David rose up behind her, stepped quietly forward, and clubbed her with clasped fists across the side of the head. She crumpled without a sound. He rushed to Isabelle's bedside. She was still, beatific, absent. He leaned down and kissed her forehead. He was afraid to kiss her lips; they appeared like a wound. She stirred. He stood upright. She smiled and opened one eye in a sustained wink, then the other. She seemed to have no idea who he was, if he wasn't herself.

After binding Lucy to a disjointed corpse that was held together by disintegrating synthetic fibres and putrescent ligaments, David took a secure grip around Isabelle's waist and together they shuffled towards the roaring inferno beyond the open oak door, leaving Lucifer moaning behind them. The grim idiot there, stoking the braziers, offered a fleeting grin and nodded in the direction of the door at the end of the chamber. It wasn't locked and as soon as it closed behind them, a gentle surge of air seemed to draw them forward through a concatenation of stone passageways, all well lit, smelling musty like an ancient root cellar, and up a series of stairs until they passed into a room made of brick with windows along the upper edge of one wall. They were in the basement of a very large house. Through the glass they could see blue sky and the sunlit branches of maple trees wavering shades of verdant green. For a moment David was blinded by the natural light, but the sensation quickly passed as they climbed more steps to a door that opened into a rotunda with a huge staircase and doors and halls leading in every direction. They were in the central foyer of a Victorian architectural monstrosity.

"What money and bad taste can buy," Isabelle exclaimed.

A woman dressed in servile livery tried to step around them, bound for the door through which they had exited. She was wearing a thick bracelet of hammered copper. It didn't seem to strike her as unusual that two such derelicts, dressed in grave clothes and covered in grime, were standing awkwardly in the middle of a grand mansion. She was carrying a tray with a bowl of stew, a squat pitcher of water, and a half-bottle of red wine lying on its side, a cabernet sauvignon blend from France. David scowled. The tray was obviously meant for him, but wine had never made it into the mausoleum. He wondered if she usually shared it with the man stoking the fires. And cheese, there was a small slab of cheese. David liked cheese more than wine, but cheese had never found its way to the crypt, either. The woman didn't recognize them. She had fed them but never seen who they were. She had reported them no longer eating, probably dead. Still, she was bringing more food. Apparently, no one had told her not to.

Isabelle clung to David's arm and gazed into the cupola high overhead, apparently looking for the sun.

"Are you all right?" David asked.

"It's all so unreal," she said. "How well do I know you?"

"Better than you think. I'm not sure where we are but we need to get out of here." He looked at an over-sized seated bronze statue in a niche by the north wall, done after the manner of Michelangelo's Moses but dressed in a bronze Edwardian business suit, looking solemn but less pontifical than Moses and without the ambiguous horns protruding from the top of his skull. The imperious set of the head indicated the homage by the artist was intentional. The bronze knees gleamed from years of being rubbed by patrons of the mogul's retail empire, before the statue had been removed from the lobby of his flagship store by descendants and found its way into this private home, now the retreat of the Conclave, this covert executive sector of votaries who called themselves The Book Club.

Across from the bronze figure an open doorway, with the inevitable bust of Pallas Athena poised on the lintel, led into what was evidently a sprawling library. As they prepared to move by, David glanced in, paused, and entered. No one was at the reading tables or perusing the shelves of books, but four middle-aged bridge players were seated at a square table near a window overlooking the garden. None of them seemed to be enjoying the game. They looked up at the shamelessly dishevelled young couple. David noticed on a side table a Spode platter of egg-salad sandwiches, white bread, the crusts removed, accompanied by Waterford pitchers of juice, one excessively orange and the other obscenely purple. He nodded towards the table. The bridge players shrugged, more or less in unison, and went on with their game. David and Isabelle ate their fill and choked back draughts of the saccharine liquids before leaving. The imaginations of the resident executives had apparently been saturated by obsessional reading to the point that their unsavoury visitors seemed merely a ripple of fiction. They apparently didn't know or care that Lucifer, their Reader Superior, was missing, or that her captives in hell had escaped.

David and Isabelle stepped outside onto the sweeping wrap-around verandah and took in the luxuriant scene — carved shrubs, dramatically poised boulders, pollarded linden trees, vivid splashes of colour orchestrated into a visual symphony of floral design, verdant manicured lawns rolling down to a boxwood hedge at the edge of the sidewalk. Nature enhanced; reduced to an expression of human vanities.

"David, this is the world, isn't it?" She seemed to have adjusted quickly to becoming the principal inhabitant of her own mind. "You read about places like this," she said.

Was she being whimsical? "Now how do we find Grace?" he said.

"She's safe," said Isabelle. "But we're not, since we neglected to kill Lucifer. We didn't lock the big oak door into the crypt, did we?"

"It might have self-locked, but the woman with the copper bracelet will have found her by now." He looked at her curiously, wondering if she would actually have accepted Lucy's death so casually. "You seem to be doing a lot better," he said.

"Egg-salad sandwiches, white bread, no crusts, lots of mayonnaise, and vile sugar water. Junk food putting on airs, but junk food, for sure."

"For a girl at death's door, you're surprisingly fit."

"I worked out in the dark — I didn't want you to see me wasting calories when you were so generous with food, I figured you must be sharing. Between sensory deprivation and the richness of the words I was reading, there was no room for *me* — physical exercise allowed me to believe I was there. At least when I began to lose my mind, I knew who I was losing."

"You knew you were eating from my rations of food?"

"Of course. Everything on the plates was divided so neatly. Half carrots, half gruel, half portions of everything except water. You knew I had water. It was diabolically consistent with everything I had read about Hades. Too much compassion would kill you first and then the food would stop coming and I would die of starvation. Generosity would kill us simultaneously, more or less. Hoarding for yourself to survive, sacrificing me, well that would never have occurred to you. I doubt if you even countenanced the hope that I'd die first, relieving you of responsibility."

"It never crossed my mind."

"Of course it didn't. Our lives were interdependent so it seemed reasonable our deaths would be contiguous as well — all of which makes me think we'd better get the hell out of here while we can."

There was a commotion behind them. Looking back through the screen door they could see a crowd of minions and executive Readers, swarming like frantic bees having misplaced their wounded Queen.

Isabelle took hold of David's hand and they slipped along the verandah, down a set of side steps, and eased across an emerald croquet pitch into a cedar maze where, as evening settled around them, they were overcome by the strange sensation of knowing exactly where they were and being lost at the same time. David dropped to his knees and peered between the rows of thick cedar trunks. He found a place where they could worm their way through to the next open walkway and then to the next and the next until they arrived at a wooden bench at the centre. This struck him as either the most obvious place to hide or, like being inside a Trojan horse in full view of the enemy, the most deviously obscure.

The sunlight continued to fade and David realized the open air was beginning to penetrate sensibilities dulled by the foul vapours of their captivity. Isabelle had been fastidious in her illuminated cell, but without soap or a change of clothes her protocols for cleanliness had gradually diminished until in the end her skin was embedded with grime and her clothes were threadbare and stained. David, quartered amidst rot and dreck, with putrid water and no mirror, was considerably worse.

"Come on," he said. "The noise out there has died down. They've stopped searching. They assume we're gone."

"The chase has only begun, David. She'll let Jacob Hummel know we're on the loose. I doubt he was even aware we were broiling in Hades. I don't think he knows The Cloisters exists, never mind hell. I'm sure he was content to have you settle in like the Cheshire Cat with a few good books, to ripen like an ageing cheese until you were ready to be consumed."

"Mix metaphors much?"

"What about cellared wine? Do you see yourself as a sun-drenched sweet sauternes or a fulsome old-vintage Bordeaux?"

"What in God's name are you talking about?"

"I'm on fast forward and rapid reverse at the same time. Give me a few minutes."

He gazed up at a pale disc of the moon contending with the twilight to make itself visible. He drew in a deep breath and marvelled at how reassuring he found their intermingled odours to be, like a shared cocoon of familiar and intimate smells, his own virulent from living with putrefaction, hers with more personal strains intimating incipient death. He drew her close. He thought about how a passage from Borges had invoked his personal history and brought him abruptly back from the edge of insanity and he marvelled that Isabelle, with very little history of her own that had not been gleaned from novels, was coming back, perhaps in jagged little steps but moving to the clear. In a mind so shaped by borrowed narratives, how would she know who she was when she got there?

"Come on," he repeated. He led her by the hand and keeping the moon as a fixed reference, since it moved imperceptibly through the sky on its own weird trajectory, he edged into the dark cedar shadows of the labyrinth and recorded in his mind every twist and turn so that he could build from where he had been a map that by a process of elimination eventually led to the outside. There was no one about. Night had already sunk into the thick rich grass and it glistened like ebony beneath their bare feet as they dashed across an open swathe to a gate in a high brick wall and slipped through, finding themselves in another titan's garden, this one even grander but now fallen to ruin.

"There once were giants," he whispered.

"What?"

"They lived on these overwrought estates."

"Brobdingnagian," she said.

"Yes, they are, they were."

"Swift, *Gulliver*. Laestrygonian—" she said.

"Homer. *The Odyssey*," he responded.

"Cannibals," she said. "Gargantua, his son, Pantagruel."

"Rabelais," he muttered.

She looked puzzled.

"I was reading over your shoulder."

"Ah," she giggled.

"People like the guy who owned this place weren't satire or myth." He talked as they progressed over the weed-choked lawn. "They were behemoths who commandeered natural resources, leviathans of manufacturing and merchandising, titans of commerce and technology, hedge-fund hustlers and information tycoons. We studied them in school. They eventually lost everything, most of them, but before they did, they lived in ghettoes of wealth and privilege in neighbourhoods like this."

They were at the mansion's front door, their clothing gnarled with burrs. David pushed. The door gave way. They stepped inside and moved towards a glimmer of flame at the end of a long central corridor. As they got closer, it became apparent the light was a candle on the centre of a large mahogany table. Two shrivelled old people sat, one at either end, their huge flickering silhouettes cast on the walls behind them. They were ancient and each was intent on dawdling over food at the centre of Royal Crown Derby chargers. There were several larger plates of a similar design, set formally, as if waiting for guests. Each had a dollop of food, each covered with a fine layer of mould. Whoever they were expecting, if anyone, it seemed unlikely these two would be allies of The Cloisters conclave.

David and Isabelle stopped in the doorway. Their feet were still bare and the floor was littered with shattered bone china and splinters of crystal.

"Excuse me," said David.

The wizened old man threw his plate, which arced unsteadily and settled in a clatter of shards immediately in front of David, its contents sliding away and continuing on course to splatter across his feet. The pungent odour of cat food rose and caught in his nostrils like barbs of Velcro.

"Is this your house?" David asked.

"It might be. What do you want? We don't have any," said the old man.

"Are you friends with the people next door?" It seemed prudent to ask.

"Which side?"

"Either."

"Doesn't matter. Despise them all. Lawnmowers and snow-blowers, everyone has 'em, they disgust me. Nature never meant us to take charge with machines. Would you like some wine?" He held his hand out in a beckoning gesture and indicated an open high-shouldered bottle, a crystal decanter with a silver stopper, and two tulip-shaped crystal glasses on a silver tray. "The last of our claret from a very fine cellar. It may taste a trifle of tannin after more than a hundred years, but it is still one of the greats. Help yourselves." He paused. "It's a once in a lifetime opportunity." He smiled enigmatically, ominously, as he turned to his ancient dinner companion. "You don't suppose they are dangerous, do you?"

"No," she answered. "Not yet. He's just a boy; she's a girl." She held up her hand in a commanding gesture, directing the old man to rescind his offer of wine, indicating the young couple should resist. David carefully shuffled through the debris on the floor so he could read the water-stained label on the empty bottle, which had clearly been partially-consumed in a previous sitting, since the decanter was only half full.

**Château Mouton Rothschild,** *1945, Année de Victoire*

Victory for whom, David wondered? He knew very little about fine wine; he knew very little about a war that ended well over a century ago.

"Would you like to clean yourselves up?" asked the old woman. The shadow behind her loomed larger as she drew herself upright, setting her platter of cat food aside and rising unsteadily, then thinking better of it and settling back on her chair. "Just go up those stairs. Take this candle. We only use it for atmosphere. We know our way in the dark." She pointed to a monstrous staircase behind them. "Go sharp right and down the long hall, through the big door, and then turn left. You'll have privacy there, as much as you need. The first room is the bathroom. The dressing room is attached. Extra candles are on the vanity along with a box of matches. You're fugitives, I take it. Don't worry, you're quite safe here. No one visits." She smiled with perfect implanted teeth and her eyes sparkled in the wavering light of the single candle. "Off you go. You both smell very unpleasant, not natural odours at all."

"That's death and the fires of hell," said Isabelle.

"Yes, dear, whatever the case, now go and wash up."

The old man called after them, "You'd like it, you know. 1945 was a very fine year. For Mouton, probably the best."

"Later," said David over his shoulder. Although not a drinker, he was intrigued. He had heard certain fine wines can outlast the lives of their owners, improving towards perfection all the while.

When they passed through the massive door in the upstairs hall, it was like stepping into Miss Havisham's private quarters. Time stopped. Motes stirred up by their movement swirled gently in the candlelight. Generations of spider webs across every corner caught the light softly. The details surrounding them seemed curiously indistinct, as if they had stepped into an alien reality that strangely resisted perception. They moved into the bathroom together. The fixtures were porcelain, a century old, and cleaned to gleam an unnatural pale green. There was no electricity, but the water drained down from a solar unit and was tolerably warm. David showered. Isabelle lolled in a tub brimming with suds. They were open with each other's nakedness but a little shy, like strangers in a public bathhouse or lovers from the distant past briefly rekindling an affair. Dressing was an adventure. The clothes in the walk-in cedar closet were relatively dust-free but hopelessly out of date, at least fifty years old. They were in surprisingly good repair. Despite their own emaciated condition, David and Isabelle both found the fit was adequate. By the time they were fully dressed, wearing fine leather shoes, and had finished grooming, they looked as well turned out as a young couple in a dated fashion magazine, photographed by Steichen or Karsh or Annie Leibovitz or Avery Snell — each of the greats, time-specific but unnervingly vital.

When they blew out the other candles, time resumed flowing and they moved like spectres from another era back out through the large door into the hall at the top of the stairs. Standing close to a massive baluster, with the candle on its silver holder balanced on top of the rail, they turned to admire each other and be admired. A gust of fresh air surged over them. The candle flared and went out, leaving only a glowing strand of wick and then total darkness. Their hands grasped and drew them together into an awkward embrace. The building seemed to have disappeared. They remained poised, very still, in a vast dark chamber of silence. He could feel her heart thumping. She smelled of flowers and sunshine.

"The front door is open," she whispered. "Someone else has come in." She pressed so firmly against him he had to twist and brace against the balustrade railing.

"It's okay." He drew out the vowels, trying to be soothing.

"I'm not afraid," she hissed. "I'm angry. Our gothic hosts told us no one visits."

"We should be afraid," he whispered. "Whoever it is, is coming for us."

"For you. I don't think they care whether I'm alive or dead."

"That must be lonely."

"You care," she said, kissing the side of his neck.

He wondered if what he was feeling was the beginnings of love.

"We'd better get out of here. It's too quiet," she said.

They descended the giant staircase one step at a time. David clutched the candlestick in one hand and kept the other on Isabelle's shoulder as she moved a step below him. The place echoed with an ominous hush, except for the distant sounds of the city through the open front door. There was no sign of intruders.

The dining room was empty. The tray with the fine claret had disappeared. The dusty Royal Crown Derby chargers seemed likely to have joined their predecessors on the floor — the noise of their smashing would have been muffled upstairs. The old couple were gone. There was an eerie stillness, but the flickering light of a candle showed through from the kitchen on the far side of the dining room. With Isabelle in the lead, they shuffled across the Heriz carpet glittering with broken china and crystal, past the mahogany table towards the light. At the kitchen door they were brought up short. The candle on a sideboard cast huge shadows of the old man and old woman across the far wall. Beside a laminated maple utility island in the centre of the room, their bloodied corpses dangled from nooses looped over a suspended bar, from which various tarnished copper pots also swayed in the muted light. With their feet just inches above the floor, they had been strangled from the force of their own weight by a double garrote that was embedded so deeply into their flesh their throats appeared to have been slashed. Blood glistened black and orange on their bodies in the wavering candlelight. Flashes of brilliant red crept across the floor beneath them.

David touched his extinguished candle to theirs, doubling the ambient light. Isabelle reached forward and touched each of their hosts on the cheek with the backs of her fingers in a gesture of wordless grief. David saw them as figures in a grotesque scene arranged by a necromancer — a habit of disengagement he had developed living for so long with death as his sole companion in the bowels of hell. Recognizing her gesture, he felt guilty for using imagination as a shield. He tried to see beyond the banality of horror. He wondered if the clothing he and Isabelle were wearing had once been worn by the shrivelled old couple in their prime, if this had been their ancestral home, if they had a history, if they ever had children? He wondered if they were too impoverished to buy food from the market gardeners in the valley, or did they prefer the convenience of canned cat food with their fine vintage wines?

Isabelle was staring at their faces. Their features were distended by pain and asphyxiation but curiously they did not look unhappy. Their deeply crenellated lips were pulled in a final gasp for breath but their eyes were strangely fixed in a serene gaze in each other's direction.

David moved around to the other side of the kitchen and his knees bumped into a human arm. The fingers of a hand clutched the air. He gasped and swerved back to retrieve one of the candles and returned for a better look. Sprawled in the shadows across the benches of a built-in breakfast nook were the bodies of two men, each as if grasping for air. On the table between them were the silver tray and the empty crystal decanter. A tulip glass lay on its side in front of each man; they were broken but the pieces not scattered, as if they had simply been released and allowed to tip over.

Attracted by his focussed attention, Isabelle tore herself away from the suspended corpses and carried the candle from the sideboard to examine the new set of bodies.

"They've poisoned themselves," he said. "Toasting the death of the old folks."

"Killing time, waiting for us. To kill us."

"You figure?"

"They strung the old people up together, but they killed the old man first. He wouldn't tell them anything. And then, for her, why talk? She had no reason to keep on living. She told them nothing. And she liked us, remember — she wouldn't let us drink the wine."

"From the looks of it, they died at the same time — but I like your story," he said. "It's very romantic."

"It's always better to die in a good story," she said. "At least they had a chance to enjoy their prized wine before they added the poison. The irony is, they were about to commit suicide when we wandered in. Their choice was to die. It is only the means that was altered. When these guys figured we were here — maybe they heard water running, this house was built before indoor plumbing, the pipes were retrofitted, probably noisy — they killed them both. After all, it was us they were after."

"Jesus," he hissed, drawing the word out like an evangelical expletive. "There are very bad people in the world."

"And a few very good ones." She leaned down and prodded the body closest to her, pushing at a bag attached to its wrist, then straightened abruptly. "David, he's carrying explosives! They were having a last drink, toasting the corpses as proof of their zealotry before abducting us and destroying the evidence." She squatted to examine the contents of the bag more closely and stood up abruptly again. "There's a timer. It's set to go off. Now!" She grabbed David's hand. "Come on. This way. No, this, it's closer."

They plunged into the gloom towards the back screen door and without trying the latch smashed through with a force that sent them both sprawling across the porch as the building behind them exploded and fiery debris raged all around. The sound of a thousand thunderbolts shook them like dry leaves as they skittered and tumbled from the force of the blast down the collapsing back steps into the overgrown garden.

# Chapter Eight
## June 17th

Isabelle cradled David's head on her lap, rocking to the rhythm of their synchronized heartbeat. A slate shingle had caught him across the side of the head and knocked him unconscious without breaking the skin. Despite her long ordeal with sensory deprivation and a barbaric diet, her nocturnal regimen had kept her relatively fit and she had been able to drag David away as flames twisted into the shattered night-sky. She hauled him over smouldering grass past shimmering bushes and into the mottled shadows of a ravine. Struggling to keep her grip on him as they skidded down the embankment, they came to rest against a stump at the edge of a stand of spruce. She had twisted around to hold him against her and now she looked into his eyes for coherence.

David stirred to the wail of sirens as they converged in front of the house. He was mesmerized and vacant, sprawled against Isabelle as if the world had moved on without him. His eyes flickered while he struggled to inhabit his mind. His lips moved. He spoke slowly, from far away, like whispering down a long tunnel. "Do you hear sirens?" he asked. "Stop up your ears with beeswax. Quick now, be perfectly still."

"David, it's okay, David. We're hidden. No one can see us. We'll wait until the fuss dies down."

"I always liked the sound of bees." He started making a high-pitched whining noise. She put her hand lightly over his mouth but laughed, certain they couldn't be heard. "You've had a bump on the head."

A pall of anguish swept over his face. "Did anyone die?"

"They were dead before the explosion."

"What about Violet?"

"That was a lifetime ago."

"Not so long."

"Why don't you sleep?" she said.

"Not if I've had a concussion."

"I don't think you have. Get some rest."

"The sky is on fire."

"Let's both sleep."

She shuffled him over onto his side and spooned against him. The breeze picked up; the clouds of spark-laden smoke swirled through the spruce. She could see in the far distance below, between the tree trunks, a line of late-night traffic snaking along the remains of the Don Valley Parkway. The sirens became louder until the sounds were impenetrable. It was no longer possible to think. The orange glow overhead gradually changed to black and eventually gave way to starlight, although the sirens continued to tear at the night. She dozed and when suddenly the sirens fell silent, she awakened and immediately realized that David was gone. She scrambled up the embankment and gazing across the seared lawns and scorched shrubs, past the glowing ruins, she saw him standing on the sidewalk beside a small van.

There was no one else there. In recent years, catastrophes away from the centres of population failed to attract attention. Before the Company abandoned the Cities, any gathering that distracted people from their individual computer-enhanced responses was considered a prelude to insurrection and strongly discouraged. It was prudent to avoid gawking at a burning mansion. No one gathered at fires or road accidents any more.

"There's nothing here," he said when she approached. "No fire engines, no people, only this guy playing the sirens on loudspeakers. I think he's leaving now."

She was unaccountably livid. She banged on the door of the van. A window rolled part way down.

"Where are the trucks?"

"This is it, ma'am. No one's burned up, the fire didn't spread, a bit of grass flared in the wind but it burnt itself out."

"There are four bodies in there! What in God's name have we come to?"

"Your friend said they were dead before I arrived. Ashes to ashes. There won't be much left of them now. It's all over. Gotta go." He started the van and set the vehicle to roll gently out from under her grasp. She let her hands drop, one from the edge of the roof and the other from the top of the window glass.

As the van moved along the street past The Cloisters executive mansion, the sirens gave a final whoop-whoop in salutation. Isabelle looked back to see that David had wandered off and was approaching the smoking remains which had once housed giants. She ran after him and hauled him away. They moved north; he did not resist.

Circling around, they came out on Yonge St. and turned south. Dawn was breaking in the east and as the light increased, they picked up their pace, alternately walking and running, to get as far away as they could from The Cloisters, the library, and Jacob Hummel's malevolent reach. A few old cars cruised between potholes, but pedestrians were rare. It was still too early. When they got to the financial district, the dismal anomaly of opulent architecture in extreme disrepair spoke of the great upheaval that now seemed all but forgotten — a revolt over monstrous bonuses bankers and brokers paid to themselves for shifting monies in cyberspace, a revolt that brought the financiers to ruin, and left no one the better.

The grand entryways of banks, once more formidable than cathedrals, were now inhabited by derelicts wrapped against the cool of a mid-June morning, before the sun had warmed the day, when they could walk about nearly naked and forage for food in small shops, makeshift dumps, and momentarily unguarded market gardens, of which there were an astonishing number, mostly hidden from public view.

Off Bay below King, they veered up a broad flight of granite steps and into an open courtyard surrounded by abandoned office towers, more exposed to surveillance now that the city was fully awake. They pressed forward and mingled with the haphazard swarm of squatters among tents and tarpaulins laid out as a garrison encampment, with neat garbage-free lanes, small tents to the fore and larger communal tents towards the edges. A fountain rose at the centre from which passersby drank clear water scooped in their hands, creating innumerable whirlpools with enough collective force to scuttle the paper boats of children playing like gods from the edge.

Seated on the parapet surrounding the fountain with its tumbled planes of natural stone thrust belligerently into the air and bleeding water in crystalline sheets, David was amazed by the sensation that he was in another world entirely, one neither formulated by the Company nor composed of whatever it abandoned. He gazed over the heads of the people of the encampment, busy at their morning rituals of eating, chatting, and doing their ablutions. The points of reference, the office towers and sky, were all part of the same region and told him nothing about the significance of where they were. He had glimpsed open water when they walked down Yonge St. and imagined a lake at the bottom of parallel streets, probably a continuation of the same Lake Ontario that formed the southern boundary of New Town Number Eleven. He was disconcerted to find himself oriented less by his senses than by residual knowledge.

"Isabelle," he said. "What now?"

"We wait."

"And?"

"We're safe here."

"What are we waiting for?"

She ignored his question, seeming intent on observing the crowd and leaving David adrift among his own thoughts.

What if the world we take to be real is an invention no more than a few moments old, inhabited by newly created people who have had memories instilled in their minds and anticipate the future based on a past that never existed? (This was Bertrand Russell's hypothesis, according to Borges.) David shifted to think about parallel realities. He especially focussed on Tlön. He would be a scientist, there, moved by amazement rather than theories and facts. What if Tlön is reality and Earth is a fiction? What if the library is endless and everything else is confabulation, being read into being by a Reader we choose to call God because we have no other word for a consciousness able to conceive our existence? Do the people in this garrison know they exist? Do secondary characters in a dream know they aren't real? He panicked. What if he was in the dream of somebody else? He remembered as a child, when he pretended to be dead, such absolute power amazed him. By thinking it so, he could make the world disappear. In those moments, he remembered wondering if he were God.

A woman appeared in the crowd, pale with black-brown hair. She was moving towards them. Others stepped aside to allow her to walk unimpeded. She was wearing a cowl. David looked around and realized some of the denizens of this concrete encampment were wearing hoodies or cowls. Not all and not only women, not enough for the coverings to constitute a uniform or article of religious observance, but enough to suggest sensibilities in common.

The woman stopped directly in front of them, pulled her head covering back just a bit, and smiled. It was Grace.

David leapt to his feet to embrace her, but she turned away brusquely. Violet would have given him a huge hug. Grace was not Violet. David was confused by the impersonal response but reassured by her clear sense of purpose as she walked away, indicating they should follow. Near a sheer granite wall inscribed with graffiti they descended an immobilized escalator into a barren subterranean courtyard as big as the one they had left. Grace strode across the cavernous open space and led them through a broad doorway into what must have once been a commercial bank, down another flight of stairs, along a brief corridor, and through an opening into a huge vault with the massive door missing.

"It's like the door we escaped through in the depths of the library," David mumbled.

"It is, it was," said Grace, who overheard him talking to himself.

He couldn't imagine how they had moved it but, since it had been installed in the first place, they must have been able to break it down to its constituent parts. They? Jacob Hummel and his cohort. Book people, librarians.

In the outer chamber of the voluminous vault and off to one side was a cluster of people crowded around a large table, conferring with clandestine urgency. They acknowledged Grace with silent deference. If the encampment above was a garrison, this was HQ and evidently, she occupied a command position.

"Okay," Grace said, turning towards Isabelle and David and lowering her cowl again. "We can talk now."

"Were we being watched out there?" David inquired. He knew, of course, that they were. He was looking for reassurance.

Her response was ominously lyrical. "The Ogle cameras are everywhere, even in the city — sometimes you'll see them catch edges of sunlight, like random snowflakes as harbingers of an incoming storm." Then in response to his perceived apprehension she added: "As you know, they look but don't see — not unless you're in a particular subset that has attracted attention, and even then, the surveillance is periodic. Monitoring every cerebral-cyborg out in the Evolved New World, their resources are too stretched to bother with anachronisms in here. You're one of us, now, and we're of limited interest. We prefer to keep it that way."

Listening to her, he found it unsettling that this was his biological mother, distressing that they had the same father. His life-mother, Violet, had told him a French palaeoanthropologist by the name of Rejean Dupuis had been his father, but since M. Dupuis disappeared when David was small, their relationship never struck him as significant. Not having a real father, he didn't know that he needed one. And now, having discovered that a vicious old man was both his grandfather and his father through incomprehensible acts of violence made him angry but generated no feelings of kinship with the woman who was his half-sister and mother by virtue of rape, an act he could not comprehend. My God, he shook his head, how sordid, how absolutely irredeemably sordid. He was angry with himself for having been born.

He felt like a fool for the thought.

He felt like a fool for the facts.

Three women, bound to each other through the vicious predations of a single tyrant like they were sisters, and he, the soul of pathos, he was the boy set by fate to redeem, witness, adorn their shattered lives. To deny his birth — Shakespeare's Lear could not wound his Fool more than this.

"David, did you hear me?" Grace shook his arm. Startled, he looked not at her but at Isabelle. Grace had been talking and Isabelle was holding his hand, squeezing his fingers until they hurt.

"David," said Isabelle. "Listen, she wants to know if you've been hurt."

He turned and addressed Grace quite formally. "My life-story was nearly erased by fiction."

"I sent Isabelle to retrieve you."

"And we ended up in Purgatory."

"In Limbo, David."

"With fiery furnaces and rotting corpses. It was hell."

"But you were cleansed by the fires, unharmed by the dead. It was a cautionary reminder of our inevitable end. *Hominem te esse memento! Memento mori!*"

David immediately translated. "*Remember that you are human*! My mother used to tell me that. It was her way of countering religious cant. *Remember that you will die*. That was her way of denying the power of computers."

"Religion is something the Company encourages, of course. You have a fine memory, David, considering your own computer is defective — perhaps we're more akin than you think. The woman you called your mother wanted to subvert your cyber-cerebral implant by forcing you to think like a human and not a machine, much as her own mother Anna had before her. And, as for me, I override my implant as an act of will. It's still there, I have access, if need be, but I'm in control. That's what Violet wanted for you."

The three of them were standing awkwardly in the middle of the vault. Isabelle listened but did not participate in the curiously impersonal conversation. Suddenly, Grace addressed her directly. "You have done very well, Isabelle. You've brought him to me more or less in one piece." She paused it seemed for effect. "Now, go away."

"What? Who?" Isabelle appeared baffled.

"No," David protested.

"The past is over, girl. From this point on, we begin again, David and I."

"You don't understand," said David. "Belle stays, we're a team."

"No," Grace declared, her voice like steel.

"It's all right," said Isabelle. She looked deeply into David's eyes but whether to deliver a message or register futility he could not determine. "See you, David." She wheeled away and strode out the massive door before David could stop her.

Grace had her hand on his arm. He felt powerless, enervated from prolonged captivity in the charnel house with inadequate food, no sunlight, and a mind enfeebled by fiction. Despite having been insulated by a mirror from the rampant death he had endured, Isabelle could have fared little better. He pulled sharply away and was surprised when he couldn't break Grace's grip.

He would find her. He knew he would find her. Meanwhile, he had to sort out his situation with his biological mother, this woman who had been so kind to him and was now so unaccountably severe.

"Do you know the expression, 'Blood is thicker than water'?" she asked.

"I do. What about 'love is stronger than death'?"

"Don't be silly. If you love the girl, that's fine, it will pass. It always does. Meanwhile, let me show you around. It's important you understand what we're doing."

He recognized he wasn't much good to Isabelle until he recovered his strength. Isabelle knew the city, she would be fine. She'd need to recuperate, too.

Grace edged him towards the conference table and the conspirators turned their attention from their secrets and rose to their feet. With a gesture of one hand, Grace indicated they should sit down again. With a slight nod of her head, she made it clear they should not yet resume their colloquy.

Without saying a word, Grace established herself in David's mind as the organizational genius in charge of a secret society, here gathered, of engineers and astronomers, metaphysicians, mathematicians, and, perhaps, ethicists, who were designing the new planet of Tlön. If they were following the format established by Borges, there would not be a medical or a military person among them, no politicians and no lawyers. Furthermore, Grace would ultimately remove herself from their machinations and retire to an obscure oasis in the middle-eastern sheikhdom of Uqbar on planet Earth, where she would pursue other dreams, but only after this project was complete.

David's fantastical overlay of fiction passed through his mind in an instant as Grace cleared her throat. It was a futile grasp at coherence in a situation where nothing made sense. Zero plus zero is zero, *ad infinitum.*

"This is my son," Grace announced. Strangely, she glanced upwards, as if looking through the ceiling of the vault into another world entirely. Then she lowered her gaze and smiled and nodded. "And these," she said, with an inclusive sweep of her arm, "these are my *colleagues.*" She put the word in oral italics, implying a seditious cohort.

"Colleagues in what?" asked David, turning to address her privately.

"In the struggle."

"I've seen no evidence of armaments."

"Nor should you. The barbarians at the gates of the city are us. We're on the inside looking out. So long as we remain in a state of apparent confusion the Company is indifferent to us except as a source of cheap labour. They're merely a force to contend with, like gravity; too amorphous to ignore, too powerful to subdue. No, my colleagues and I are the Committee for Public Safety, we have organized a form of passive resistance."

"Resistance to anarchy or to indifference?"

"We are dangerous and highly subversive, but not at all violent, David. We are historians." A mumbling rumble from the executive table indicated displeasure at Grace's disclosure. She guided David to the far side of the vault and continued. "I mean that literally. Our job here is to make the present inevitable. The Historian, with a capital H, is arbiter between the infinite complexity of the past and the singularity of an unresolved future. To control what happens we must control what happened."

Underlying her conviction was a ferocity that puzzled him.

"Come with me," she said. "I'll show you."

"Why?"

His question clearly surprised her.

"Because our work is important."

"But why me? I'm not important."

"Ah, but you are."

No further explanation appeared to be forthcoming. He was unsettled by her answer, it struck him as sinister.

He followed her through a door at the back of the vault shaped like a giant unblinking eye and up a flight of stairs between cyclopean walls of dry-set stone into a broad corridor with a warren of cells opening off either side, each with a scrivener, wearing a monocular lens, poised over a light-table at work with scissors and wax adhesive on various texts.

"What're they doing, besides messing around? Your troops in the courtyard are subtly menacing, but these guys look about as dangerous as dandruff."

"Those people you call the troops are citizens in search of order. They're waiting."

"Waiting?"

"For the work down here to be done."

She led him into one of the open-ended cells. The man at the table sat back and gazed at them through rheumy eyes. His face bore the creases of age and extreme concentration. He put a hand to his beard and stroked it pensively but remained silent.

"Explain, your project, Thirty-One. Our young colleague needs to understand just how dangerous we are."

The old man cleared his throat, as if he hadn't spoken for days. "Spies penetrate enemy lines, code-breakers break down enemy codes, intelligence-gatherers monitor the enemy's mind. We penetrate, break down, monitor, and then we transform. Enemies become allies.

"And who is the enemy?" said David, intrigued by how the clarity of the man's answer could be so opaque.

"Why, us, of course."

"Then who is in danger?"

"Us. It is not complicated."

The old man turned back to his work, apparently oblivious to David looking over his shoulder. He had an open copy of Brunel's comprehensive *Chronicles of the Great War* in front of him which had been published to commemorate the end of hostilities almost two centuries ago and was taken as the definitive history of a definitive world event. The volume was open to 'The Battle of Verdun', with its account of how Erich von Falkenhayn, working on the direct advice of the Kaiser, had attempted in the winter of 1916 literally to bleed the French into submission — at a cost of 400,000 dead on either side. Such 'tactical attrition', largely forgotten except by French sentimentalists, was being manipulated. David leaned closer, permission implicitly granted by the presence of Grace at his side.

Narrow strips of printed paper had been cut from an identical companion volume and were being arranged on the light-table, then set aside or invisibly waxed over original text to alter the meaning. As David watched, 800,000 dead were reduced to 'regrettable setbacks' and the barbaric implications of 'tactical attrition' became the more tolerable but equally obscure 'strategic difficulties'. General von Falkenhayn came across as efficient and humane, the Kaiser as shrewd. The French were dauntless. Verdun was an unavoidable conflict in which the antagonists benefitted equally and nimbly endured — all but the 800,000, whose bodies were ground into dirt, thought David.

David had never heard of Verdun.

"Thirty-One is our First World War specialist," said Grace, just loud enough to be audible. Braced by her words, the old man's posture straightened and he briefly paused to survey his achievement.

"War cannot be avoided," he explained, without turning.

"So we make it palatable," Grace said. "A struggle between heroes with anonymous casualties. No winners, no losers. When Thirty-One finishes, The Great War will seem almost benign. Just ripples on the surface of history."

"Benign?" David was incredulous. He had been taught from earliest childhood that war was inexplicably complex, inexcusably horrific, irredeemably demeaning, a grotesquely unconscionable holdover from our most primitive and savage condition and the shame of our species — until cybernetic enhancement transformed us.

"It's a matter of perspective," Grace said, leading him out into the broad corridor. He realized each cell occupied by a revisionist scrivener had been a retail outlet in a subterranean shopping mall. Some still showed remnants of their former function, fragments of signs signifying Coach handbags, M.A.C. cosmetics, Cole Haan shoes, a variety of specialty food stores. No book or magazine shops. Reading hard-copy had gone out of vogue long before the collapse of the cities (some suspected the two were related).

"You told me in the hospital, you wanted access to Violet's palaeoanthropology research. Is this why? So you could rewrite the distant as well as the historical past?"

"I understand she made prehistory accessible by writing fiction, so yes, I'm interested. But how do we reconstruct something that never happened?"

"Her version is probably closer to truth than history." The thought pleased him. "But she's gone, it's gone, so that's the end of it."

"Nothing that begins ever ends, David."

He wondered at the ominous implications of what she stated as a simple fact while they ambled past numbered cells with occupants working on texts dealing with a variety of subjects. Next to the Verdun project was a much younger man cheerfully rewriting a history of the Great Depression and in the cell next to him two women worked with feverish concentration to humanize the Holocaust. Across from them a scrivener was amending Caesar's *Commentarii de Bello Gallico* to expunge all references to the slaughter of a million Gauls, and further along a portly old man in cell Forty-Two seemed to be working simultaneously on *The Outline of History* by H.G. Wells and all four volumes of Winston Churchill's *A History of the English-Speaking Peoples*. Sitting on a side table were copies of Clarendon's, Gibbon's, and Macaulay's histories, as well as Darwin's *The Descent of Man*, along with six volumes each of Churchill's *The World Crisis* and *The Second World War*. Forty-Two seemed to be the only scrivener at work on multiple books. David was intrigued and drew Grace into the man's cluttered cell so he could question him.

"This is a lot for one person to handle," David observed.

"He has already finished with Mr Wells but needs him for reference. Churchill is formidable. Not since the Venerable Bede has a single author captured the whole of history from an English perspective. Wells tried and failed but Churchill, by his own admission, succeeded."

"What about other perspectives?" David asked, more amused than confused. "The world wasn't actually an English invention."

"Nor was it Winston Churchill's," Grace conceded. "But we have to deal with history as written, not things as they actually were. Someone once noted that Churchill wrote brilliant autobiography — disguised as a history of the universe."

"That would be Prime Minister the Earl of Balfour who said that," muttered the portly man at the light-table without looking up. "Better known for his astute observation that 'nothing matters very much and few things matter at all'. Possibly a more profound statement than Churchill's millions of words put together. Makes one think of Jack Kerouac, actually. 'Nothing makes any difference.'"

"Ignore him," said Grace, as they moved along. "His work has affected his mind. We'll probably have to replace him."

When they came to an intersection, with mall corridors leading in different directions, David urged Grace to sit with him on a small bench and asked her to explain further what the history project was all about. "You can't really change the past," he said.

"Of course you can. We revise history continuously, with each passing moment. Here, we're merely pursuing a particular agenda rather than letting infinite revisions accrue at random."

"So, how do you handle Mr Churchill?"

"How does one handle Winston? We make him humble, of course. The Second World War becomes a game of conflicting ideals. We amend or erase statistics. Fifty-five million civilian casualties are expunged from the records. The fire-bombing of Dresden is conceived as a project to eradicate poverty, the Allied refusal to bomb Auschwitz is described as a move to protect the camp's transient residents, the arch-enemy Hitler is re-inscribed as a misguided man of the people in opposition to Churchill, the articulate aristocrat."

"Even I know you can't sanitize Hitler."

"We can juggle his attributes, displace the less savoury with the heroic, accentuate his visionary acumen and political zeal, his love for Eva Braun, his thwarted talent as an artist, his affection for dogs. If we can turn slavery into a peripheral aberration and genocide into an ill-conceived civic project, do you really think we can't reduce Hitler to a video-game avatar and fascism to a totalitarian ripple? And, of course, the Pacific Theatre becomes a sequence of tropical war games sandwiched between territorial misunderstandings over Pearl Harbor and a Japanese cultural transition accelerated by Hiroshima. And then there's Viet Nam. And all the wars since. We have much to do."

It struck David as a massive undertaking, but he could not grasp whom it endangered, although thirty-one proclaimed it a dangerous pursuit and Grace indicated it was of strategic importance.

"Okay, explain. You haven't brought me here just to be your witness. So, what's happening?"

"Bear in mind, there are sections in the mall devoted to religion and science, and to sports, of course. This isn't just about making war seem tedious and evil banal. Science is reshaped into a welter of fortuitous accidents instead of an inevitable structure of progressive discoveries — do you see, science moves away from coherence? Religion, by contrast, is bad in itself. From its earliest manifestations in the caves of our forbearers, veneration of the ineffable as an expression of collective hysteria has wrought evil on humanity. We invented the word *soul* to signify the mysteries of the preconscious/postconscious mind, the word *God* as a consolation for death, and *faith* to counter intellectual curiosity, our innate desire to know. We turned religion into the scourge of mortality. Here, we make it merely a bore."

"And what about sports?"

"The ultimate diversion. Mostly we juggle scores and minimize achievements."

"So you are rewriting history to make it benign, science to reduce its coherence, sports to eliminate the excitement, and religion to reveal its absurdity. Why? Who cares?"

"The so-called Evolved New World."

"The Company? How can changing a few books effect anything?"

"A single emended copy of each book we alter will be returned to the library—"

"Jacob Hummel knows you have them!"

"He does." She paused. "He does. Before we return them, we make digital copies of our own. These are insinuated into the Company's servers through a virus that eliminates competing data." She paused again to ensure he grasped what she was saying. "Imperceptibly, we change the past that is available to the cerebral computers of the entire population out there. We call it the Goebbels Initiative. By controlling information, we control their world."

"But if your copies of record in the library are also altered—"

"In the future, people will see where we've changed history, but it will be a version of history that allows them to exist. They will be grateful."

"Is there a polite way for me to ask, why bother?"

"Ultimately, we will be in charge of our own world and their world will collapse. Our weapons are word-byte revisions meant to undermine their reasons for existing. The Company's power is based on the conviction that humanity is hopelessly gullible and vicious — a radical change in evolution was imperative. But we show that mankind was gentle, science chaotic, sports and religion distractions."

"So the Company folds and the Collective takes over, with your power based on an alternate past."

She smiled.

"But the world will be no better off," he continued. "We simply exchange one totalitarian state for another, equally dependent on cyber-cerebral manipulation."

She steered him around to retrace their steps. When they reached the giant eye at the back of the vault, she stopped.

"This is a lot to take in, David. In a few years it will all become clear."

He was bewildered. He wanted no part of either world. The Company and the Committee for Public Safety seemed equally oppressive."

"Come along," she said, propelling him forward. "There's someone to see you inside." They stepped out of the shadows and around a steel partition into the main vault chamber. There, in the centre, waiting, was Jacob Hummel.

"Welcome, boy. I'm here to take you home," said Jacob Hummel with a hand outstretched towards them, his beard twitching with pleasure, while with his other hand he held Immanuel Kant up to eye level, as if to share his pleasure at the reunion.

David looked around. Grace had disappeared. There were only themselves.

# Chapter Nine
# The Ghost Sonata

Before the woman who was buried under the earth-slide reaches puberty, long before her own daughter is born, the home she shares with her mother turns into a funeral pyre. She has been foraging for berries left to dry on the vine by migrating birds and when she returns, their lean-to hovel has buckled. Tendrils of flame flick along protruding lengths of shattered poles, smoke seeps from beneath auroch hides that gather the body of her mother under their acrid folds. The simmering haunch of a giant elk lies heavily on top. The girl gazes at the smouldering ruin, enthralled by the carnage, confused.

She knows the infirm or inept receive a share of the communal bounty before hunters are replenished or their own families fed. Her mother, deemed eccentric, perhaps even mad, has received a generous portion of the most recent kill, but the weight of a gift tossed carelessly, the force of snow, the weakness of rotting supports, have collapsed their shelter. Glowing embers on the hearth have turned their home into a seething furnace.

The girl pulls hides from the wreckage, keeps the least damaged and throws the remainder aside. When she reaches her mother's remains, seared and roasted like the slaughtered elk, the corpse smells succulent. The girl touches her fingers to her mother's seared breast and to her own mouth, but instead of salivating she gags. She wraps two skins around the crumbling body as winding sheets and ties them securely. Then she hauls the grisly bundle along the base of the cliff to a narrow opening in the rock and manoeuvres it into a cavern littered with layers of dried animal scat. In the gloomy depths of the cave, she peels the shroud back and looks at what's left of her mother's face, before rolling the wrapped body into what seems a bottomless crevasse.

She returns to the site of their devastated home and tears chunks of flesh from the roasting elk and eats without satisfaction until she is satiated. Only then does she realize how cold she is, despite warmth rising from the ruins. Her grease-covered fingers are frost-bitten to the bone. She pulls a smoking remnant of auroch hide from the wreckage and wraps it around her hands. The pain as her fingers thaw makes her scream, but no one can hear. Their home is away from the deepest part of the valley where others live and no one has noticed that her mother has died, swathed in billows of smoke and the aroma of cooking meat.

The girl moves into the outer chamber of the mortuary cave. She does not venture deeper into its recesses until years later, when she is searching for her own lost daughter. No one she knows lives inside the earth, recognizing that caves are the homes of bears and cave lions and ghosts of the dead. She lays out salvaged skins over the scat on the floor. They are late-winter auroch hides, filled with holes from warble flies that have gnawed through the animals' flesh from the inside to drop and pupate in the warming spring earth. The hides have been cast off by the families of hunters as worthless, although arranged in layers they serve adequately as shelter and robes for mendicants who cannot supply their own. The leathers and furs of smaller animals which the girl has captured as long as she can remember do not cover sufficiently to be useful, except for the swaddling of infants, but they are soft to lie upon, stretched over sphagnum moss.

The girl forages for food close to her cave, setting sinew snares for rabbits and wrapping their skins around her feet. She binds several auroch hides that are scarred by smoke and perforated with holes around her thin body and begins to follow the hunters at a distance and watches them work together to make their kills and flense the skins from the carcasses and strip the flesh from the bones. Sometimes when she approaches close enough, they throw scraps of meat her way, and she devours small uncooked bits but saves larger pieces to take back to her cave and roast on a stick, and the savoury smoke finds its way through fissures in the rock overhead and eventually out to the open, flavouring the crisp winter air.

Winter rounds into spring, spring warms into summer, summer dwindles as autumn descends. With urgency brought on by the shortened days and the growing chill, she gathers discarded skins of wild sheep, bringing them back to her cave from the hunting fields. Their hair is still dark but beginning to thicken and the warble flies remain subcutaneous. The skins become supple by scraping away residual flesh with the sharp edge of a cracked human shin bone retrieved from a stranger's cadaver. She places them on top of the smaller hides to make luxuriant bedding. She would not be allowed to carry off the auroch skins or elk at this time of year, nor the rare woolly mammoth skin, which the hunters use to clothe their own families so they can survive the leering cold wrapped in bulky folds that are loosely bound with sinew made from shredding the dried membrane stripped from their kills.

When the girl walks through the village in the depths of the valley, many cringe in their hovels until she passes. She cannot know how they fear her courage; she lives in a cave like a beast. She cannot understand how oppressive they had found her mother's behaviour, dwelling at the edge of the community like a half-domesticated grey wolf with her cub. She cannot know how threatened they were by her mother's disappearance or unsettled by her own unnatural capacity to live by herself.

In a world where imitative behaviour generally offers the best assurance of survival for all living things, the most minor infraction could easily mean death. Yet the girl resists conformity. Being raised by a mad woman, she has never learned the essential behaviours that allow her species to thrive. Driven by the same appetites as the others but free from absolute constraints to conform, she is eccentric, defiant, resilient, liberated through ignorance, empowered by curiosity, innovative, aware of herself, fearless, and she endures.

For the most part, the girl keeps to herself. Sometimes she imitates the world around her. She stands in the wind on clifftops, swaying like a tree; she emulates deer prancing and rabbits leaping; she gurgles and giggles like spring run-off coursing down the cliff-face to enter the stream in the valley below. Sometimes she follows a trail of leafcutter ants carrying bits of foliage under dense thickets she has to claw her way through. She watches spiders for hours and days as they create their webs, twitching with fascination as they bond one strand to another. Sometimes she observes female spiders devour their mates during or after copulation. She knows which is which because she understands the females deposit eggs, the males die. She monitors her own menstruation. She feels awkward at first but empowered. She identifies with the female spider; she knows her blood will make children. Perhaps from observing her mother, perhaps it's just something she knows. Her mother was still bleeding with the cycles of the moon when she died. Menopause is an incidental factor of age in her species and seldom achieved.

The girl is intuitive, observant, inordinately free to think as she wants. Although she and her mother wore cast-offs, she has observed women in their village scrape and dampen and knead the auroch skins over and over, each time letting them dry in the sun before working them further, until they are supple enough to drape over human bodies, the first layer with the hair turned in and the second overlapping with the hair turned out. It is as if their own bulky flesh has grown fur, providing they move carefully so the coverings don't slide free from their sinew bindings. She knows how to make robes, but as she sprawls between bringing in loads of dried wood, she rests on fly-riddled auroch skins and gazes at the holes made when flies dropped to the earth. She examines their patchwork of moulting fur and despairs of a winter confined close to her cave for want of adequate clothing.

She picks up a length of sinew that has dried crisp from being left too close to her fire and pokes it through holes near the edges of two dilapidated skins and draws it forward until a kink in its lower end catches and the skins come together by magic and undulate as she tugs on the thread. She plays with sinews, using more supple strands, and binds pieces of hide together until they seem like the skin of a single large animal, which she draws over herself as if hiding and marvels at the sight of firelight shining through perforations like stars among low scudding brown clouds on a moonless night.

The next morning, she selects quality skins of smaller animals from her bedding and sets about forcing holes along their outer edges with a stone-sharpened shard of elk antler. Then she retrieves sheets of dried backstrap membrane she has scraped from chunks of retrieved meat and shreds them into sinews which she works with animal fat until they are pliable. Finally, she threads softened sinew through the holes to make smaller skins bigger and roughly in the shape of two humans, as if they have been skinned from the corpses of hirsute giants with their hands and feet and heads cut off, and she begins to sew these together, leaving openings in the envelope of leather for arms and legs to slip through from the inside, and a slit wide enough at the bottom to admit a person's entry.

Her fingers are nimble and her broken nails are thick and sharp and no one has shown her that what she is doing, following intuition, is aberrant behaviour. Living the meanest of lives gives the girl time to create. Living alone gives her freedom. By dusk of the third day, she has added tubes of hide for arms and contrived a warm coat that extends from her neck to her feet. With a bandana of fur tied over her ears and rabbit hides bound around her feet, she ventures out into the chill autumn air and breathes in the cold, and excited by her own body warmth she strides down the narrow path into the village.

Seeing an unfamiliar beast approach with movements that belie its gigantic size, most villagers flee to their shelters, although the braver among them take up sharpened poles and burning brands and stand their ground. They are not a timid species. They do what is necessary for survival, hiding or fighting as their nature demands.

A boy throws his spear while the monster is still out of range. The spear clatters on the frozen ground at its feet. The great beast laughs and they are amazed when they realize who is inside the strange animal. And frightened. But curious. They approach cautiously. A few tug at her coat. She smiles. She has never smiled before in public. She is invited into the best hunter's house. She has never before been in anyone's home but her own. She sheds her coat like a moth slipping out of its chrysalis and stands naked in the firelight, as the villagers crowd into the dwelling to gasp and grunt their amazement at the transformation. The men feed her choice morsels of meat softened in the flames; the women anoint her newly formed woman's body with grease from a bowl made of a mastodon skull with the holes stopped up by wads of grass and clay. They wait politely until their ministrations are complete, then all examine her coat. Some press the edges of their own robes together, but when they release the pieces fall open again, leaving gaps exposed as expected. They laugh and slip out into the cold autumn air. There is much to consider.

Before the winter solstice, the girl has shown the village how to sew. She still lives alone in her cave, but now she receives choice pieces of meat and the most succulent tubers in appreciation and is growing round and plump. She is sad her mother is no longer alive except in her dreams to share her contentment and revel in her absence of fear.

One spring evening as she sits by her fire, binding two small prongs of elk antler to short lengths of sinew before slipping each prong through a hole on different sides of a robe to make a fastener, she hears a commotion near the cave entrance. The sounds are strange but familiar.

She thinks of the female spiders she has watched.

She waits and a man enters. He is the first person to venture into her cave since she made it her home. He is very young, her own age. He is nervous. He lies down beside her. She helps him, takes him in. It is over quickly, after a surge of discomfort neither had expected. He rolls away. She reaches closer to the fire and wraps her hand around a shaft of sharpened antler and brings it forward and plunges it through the side of his neck. There are noises still gurgling from his mouth and his wound when she drops him into the crevasse at the back of her cave. She returns to her bedding. There will be two more. It is believed that three are necessary. The second enters. He is twice her age. He takes so long he begins to weep. She plunges the antler into his gut as he lolls to the side. She disposes of him in the same fashion as the first, waiting by the crevasse this time until his body smashes into the bones and debris at the bottom.

She calls softly and the third man enters. Firelight shimmers off the walls of her cave, making the stone seem fluid, luminescent. He looks around for his predecessors, peers into the shadows, then shrugs and proceeds, kneeling by the girl and stroking her hair away from her forehead. He bares his teeth. It is an ambiguous gesture. Although he is older than her and a powerful hunter, he is wary. She smiles. He strokes her breasts experimentally, squeezing them gently to test their consistency. He touches her between the legs, he touches himself, both gently. He lies down beside her and invites her onto him. She draws him inside and he stays utterly still until, moving slowly, she explodes in unexpected elation. Then he grinds under her weight until they both come together. He grasps her wrists and spreads his arms, holding her pinioned from below. When their heartbeats fall into synchrony, he shifts her to the side and rises. He stands looking down. She is not a woman to live with, but she will be the mother of a child he knows must be his. She and her infant daughter will move out of the cave, into an auroch-clad shelter that she builds for herself on the spot where she and her own mother had lived. The man will never lie with her again. It is too dangerous and he already has a woman in the village, but he will hunt for her and keep others from intruding on her solitude. He will accept that his two missing friends have disappeared. He has begun to forget them already.

After he leaves, she squats close to the fire. Tears roll down her cheeks. She does not understand grief. She misses her mother. She slides the small prongs of antler from the skins they are holding together. Their bindings of sinew slip off and they fall to her mat. She picks one up and with a sharp edge of obsidian carves a groove around its tiny circumference. She does the same with the other, then binds them again with fresh sinew. She inserts each toggle through holes in two separate skins. Satisfied with her work; confused. She begins to doze off, then awakens abruptly and detaches her new contrivance and tosses it across the chamber, where it slides over the edge of the narrow abyss into the gravesite below, and a woman called Violet, digging through the detritus of time, will find fossilized antler pieces scored around their circumference, the sinew long gone, buried under bones turned to stone and thick layers of rubble and dust, forty-five thousand years closer to the end of the world.

\*\*\*

David walked beside the old man rather than behind him. He yearned to go back to New Town Number Eleven, to live under the Company's dispensation, to walk through the front door of his home by the lake and find Violet waiting, pretending she wasn't, smiling in spite of herself at his return. He yearned to be with Isabelle in their anonymous cell, naked in one another's arms. He wondered which path he had taken had led to this present. Was he here as a matter of choice? His own? Grace's? Isabelle's? Jacob Hummel's? Was he here as a narrative or thematic necessity through the contrivance of an inconceivable author, an elderly prodigy poised on the edge of his universe, peering through rents in the fabric of time?

Jacob Hummel said not a word beyond his initial salutation until they passed through the townhouse door, painted midnight blue with dark sidelights and a hairline crack in the transom. Once in the small foyer that opened onto the vast and possibly infinite library, Jacob Hummel addressed him. "I have followed your adventures in wonderland, David. I admire your curiosity and fortitude. I might have done much the same at your age, had I had your opportunities. So, now, then, we must come to some sort of agreement. We have the future of *homo sapiens sapiens* in our hands. We have the recorded past at our disposal — and what is the future but fulfilment of all that preceded? We must work together, be of one accord, merge our fates with the fate of the world."

"You don't really believe all that?"

"Which part? About the importance of the library? Of course I do. About our merged destinies as humanity's best hope for survival? Yes, I do. I think that is something worth believing in, better than God. Oh yes, for sure, better than God. But we must work together. The father, the son, we must become one."

"Isn't there a missing third?"

"The Holy Ghost, the eternal feminine, what do you suggest?"

"I think you are a dangerous and degenerate old man."

"Ah, the rape myth. I should have known."

"You deny it?"

"There is nothing to deny. If something did not occur, to proclaim one's innocence has no more validity than to acknowledge one's guilt."

"I would have thought I am the living proof."

"Ah, the will of the father, incarnate. Good, good, but come, I want to show you something."

"You have no power over me. I refuse to be your prisoner."

"Of course. You may walk away whenever you like. But first, there is something I need you to see." All the while they talked, the old man had been leading David down interminable flights of stairs, along endless corridors and through innumerable open galleries. David could conceive no alternative but to follow. At last, they passed through a room lined with exceedingly ancient texts and came to a chamber lit with flickering candles. An ornate catafalque of sculpted stone rose from the paved floor at the centre of the room. On top of it a glass reliquary contained a desiccated corpse, a grotesque *memento mori* in grisly repose on faded velvet cushions of indeterminate colour, clothed in the remnants of a mottled grey gown, with a silk cord embedded in the parched skin of its bony neck.

David stifled a retching sensation as he gazed on the remains of Anna, his grandmother, in a state of suspended putrefaction. Since the time when Grace had seen the old woman's body, it had been laid out formally and surrounded with glass set in mullions of carved oak. This was all that was left of the woman Violet had venerated yet fled in a cloud of mystery. David wondered, if the rape stories were not true, why would Violet, the woman he knew as his mother, why would she have abandoned her own mother and designed a life for herself in the ENW as a palaeoanthropologist? He gazed at the horrific face, searching for a hint of the person who had once animated its dried sunken features. Finding beneath the ghastly mask only death, nothing more, he shuddered and turned away. As he did so, the candlelight caught an edge of personality in the crease by her emptied eyes.

So, he reasoned, the old man must come every day to replace the burnt-out candles, to protect Anna from disappearing into the darkness.

Jacob's eyes were glazed, perhaps just with the rheumy moisture of age. After a long shuffling silence, the old man backed away, merging with the shadows, then turned and led David into a gloomy antechamber lined with ancient texts.

"Did you think visiting this mausoleum would induce me to stay?" David asked, not at all sure what the old man's intentions had been in bringing him into the very heart of the library, which was as overwhelmingly moribund as an infinite collection of books not meant to be read.

Jacob Hummel indicated they should sit, drawing two ladderback chairs from the shadows at the edge of the room and setting them face to face. Once seated — the old man with awkward dignity, the youth at the edge of his seat — the old man proceeded. "I live too much with the dead, David. My mind itself is a ghost — it haunts my beloved Anna and won't let her go. It haunts my books, peering in here and there as I pass a familiar volume, trying to reconstruct the world as it was or should have been. Now, this is my case: I cannot be a ghost among words of the dead for much longer. My body is wearing down with despicable acceleration, although I have every reason to believe my mind is intact. I need you desperately, my son, to take up my work, accumulating the memories of our species, our multivariate histories and infinite fictions."

David was startled. The old man's declaration seemed almost reasonable. "But surely," he said, "you don't want me to displace you. You mean it the other way around — you want to take my place yourself."

"How very abstract. Have you not ever felt you were born for an epic life? That is what I'm offering you, something very concrete to fulfil your ambition to do some special thing. You will be who you are but no longer alone. If my implantation is successful, I will join you. You will have access to my knowledge but can block me out if you wish. I, in turn, will have access to your potential. In the past, very rarely, twins were allowed to be born who were conjoined at the head. Do you know, they would think independently, they were individuals in their own right, yet when one would eat, the other could taste the food, when one would dream the waking one remembered the dreams?"

"And what if one were to like music and the other was tone deaf? Would one soar to a Beethoven sonata while the other heard unpleasant sounds? Would they not both hear cacophony? Beethoven plus noise is just noise. Our minds cannot be coached into merging."

"You have much to learn," said the old man. "We will learn together."

"To think like you?"

"Is that so frightening?"

Suddenly David blurted words he had never before said aloud: "*The Ghost Sonata!*" With satisfaction born of a mild revelation, he continued: "That's why it's all so familiar. Jacob Hummel. You've taken your name from the mysterious stranger in Strindberg's play—"

"You have seen this play?" The old man seemed incredulous. A boy from beyond the city could not possibly have had such an exotic experience.

"Yes. No. A critic's description. In point form. But enough to recognize that the world you offer me access to is a nightmare of stifled souls."

"No, the play is about metamorphosis."

"From beauty to bondage, to mummification, misery, silence, suffering, death."

"You remember as you wish."

"That was my point, Jacob Hummel. You would give me knowledge unearned, just information no better than computers supply. And you would feed on me as a parasite, a source of cellular rejuvenation. In turn I would lose all sense of my self."

"*Self?* Do you mean *soul? Personality? Essential being? Life-force, spirit, transcendent identity?* Soul is an illusion, dear boy. Self is an illusion, a grotesque indulgence. A sham, a romantic contrivance, wish-fulfilment in a word that is freighted with obscurity. If I were to have dementia, if you were to have a concussive blow to the head, selves and soul would disappear like dry leaves in a hurricane."

David was restless. He had no wish to debate psyche or soul in some Faustian arrangement with a mad Mephistopheles. He wanted desperately to get away from the library and search for Isabelle whom he feared he might never find in this chaotic City of the End of Things. He rose to his feet. The old man had told him he was free to leave. But he was unable to resist engaging in some sort of dialogue. Although repulsed, he found the old man's thoughts irresistible for the thrill of rhetorical engagement that he had not experienced since conversations with Violet, where ideas were often abstruse and yet alarmingly personal.

"If I understand the story of Dr Frankenstein," said David, "his creature became a monster because he was a composite of cadavers with no soul of his own. I'm leaving," he declared.

Before he could turn away, the old man responded. "Perhaps we should look at one more thing. You might call it an incentive to rethink your situation." The old man drew an electronic device from his jacket pocket and flashed a screen towards David, who took the device in his hands and gazed at the image. Only a slight flutter of light across her features made him realize it wasn't a still shot. A person in a coma is somehow less animate than a person asleep, as if the cellular structures beneath the skin are already progressing towards death. Isabelle lying in state looked almost serene, almost dead.

"What in God's name have you done?" he gasped.

"She is in suspension, David. She might easily expire or she might not. A long life awaits her or eternal sleep. It is up to you."

Isabelle lay on a bier of velvet cushions inside a glass box similar to the casket containing Anna's desiccated corpse. Her arms were drawn over her breast with her hands folded in the awkward pose favoured by morticians. Her face bore a waxy pallor, with a slight smile imposed on fixed lips and no sign of emotion about the eyes. Her face looked sculpted, like ice with warm sunlight casting a sheen over the surface.

"The casket is humidity and temperature controlled. She can stay like that for a very long time, so long as she is not disturbed — and so long as you do as I wish. She will be very well cared for. Eventually, you and I will merge and together we will decide whether and when she should recover her life. In the meantime, she will endure."

David was stunned, like a fly swatted in mid-air, mindlessly reeling as the collision of terrible forces sends it ricocheting in haphazard distress. The image of Isabelle was grotesquely disturbing, but it was the old man's measured explanation that shattered his equilibrium.

"Where is she?" he demanded.

"Out of harm's way," the old man responded as if Isabelle were a floral arrangement. He added almost as an afterthought, "It is better you do not find her. The instrumentation is carefully calibrated to keep her in suspension, but if it should be disturbed, I'm afraid she will perish. It would be your fault entirely, of course."

David sank back on his chair in exhaustion. If he had ever learned, growing up, to act upon his feelings instead of suppressing them, he would have murdered the old man, throttled him without a shred of remorse, but instead his feelings spiralled inwards like an imploding galaxy.

"Anything," he mumbled. "What do you want?"

"Your time. Literally."

His words hung in the air like a Calder sculpture, massive and weightless, turning and turning in a delicate balance from conflicting forces drawn in by their motion to reveal realigning facets of possibility. All of them lethal, depleting, horrific.

Questions of time and timing swarmed through David's mind. How long did Isabelle have before the cellular breakdown and controlled regeneration necessary for her survival in a dormant state would turn to necrosis and metabolic collapse would become irreversible? Death would set in, it was indeed a matter of time. How long did he have before invasive surgical procedures would commence in preparation for his function as the cerebral host to an offensive alien presence? Would it be by increments, by attrition or radical conquest? Short of abandoning Isabelle outright, he could see no alternative to co-operating, as time unravelled towards some inevitable end.

"Where?" he repeated, his voice trembling. "Is she here?" He gestured with an outstretched arm that could have been indicating an adjoining room or the entire library complex or the city itself, or, indeed, the entire world as affirmation of her continuing existence.

"All in good time, David. You are a fledgling, rushing in a fury of feathers with no understanding of gravity and no destination in mind. If you fly, the sun will burn your wings, my boy, but you have nowhere to land." He paused, seeming pleased with his distorted classical allusion. "I simply want to spend time with you. You are my future as well as my past. We will get to know each other. Is that so evil? I do regret having to employ your friend's survival as an incentive, but that is only until you feel the wind under your wimpling wings and learn to soar at a level that will not melt the wax holding your feathers in place, nor compel you to crash. I simply want to spend time with you. We will walk and we'll talk and we'll get to know each other, as we should. There is nothing sinister about that."

"Apart from extortion based on my girlfriend's life!" He had decided he was in love. "This is a very unpleasant plot, old man."

"Life is a plot, David — but you and I shall no longer be *in medias res*, you in the opening scenes and me in act five. Together we will step off the stage and assume the role of dramaturge."

"I meant plot as a conspiracy."

"All plots are conspiracies, David. All conspiracies are plots. You have read enough novels to know that."

"From the author's perspective, perhaps. But we're not on an equal footing here. I'm the hapless protagonist; you're writing the last chapter yourself."

"The penultimate chapter. The finale is yet to come. In the end is my beginning — quite literally, one hopes."

"Only when you plunge into the fiction, yourself. In such a beginning is our mutual end."

"Grace told me you might be difficult."

"Grace doesn't know me at all."

"You dropped from her loins. I think she knows you more intimately than anyone alive."

"That's not saying much, since you killed my real mother."

"Violet was a surrogate. And I did not kill her. The Company did."

That is what Grace had said. David protested, "It was at your behest."

"What a quaint word, 'behest'. You sometimes speak in an oddly archaic English, David."

"As did Violet, my mother. We lived in a world of our own."

"I understand you did well in school, you had friends, a friend called Lucas, you were a model cyber-cerebral child."

David was horrified at the old man's informed presumption. "You do not know me at all."

"Nor do you, David. You do not know yourself very well. That is what we must try to remedy, one way or another. Grace warned me."

Grace, mercurial — saviour, benefactor, captor, betrayer, yet always the same. She could never have been his mother, and it was inconceivable to think this despicable desperate Mephistopheles could be his father. He was bewildered by the mythology of his origins. There seemed only one way to resolve the mysteries of the Gordian knot.

David rose to his feet, shuffled awkwardly; he was still hurting from captivity among the cadavers. He moved to Jacob Hummel's side. With quivering fingers, he clutched the old man's ancient grizzled neck and slowly relentlessly squeezed until his own shaking stopped and the old man's glistening eyes glazed grey before, with a final shudder, he collapsed into himself, suddenly diminutive, hardly more imposing than a discarded piece of garden statuary exposed to the elements through inclement seasons. Only saliva seeping along the creases at the corners of his mouth betrayed that he had only moments before been human.

# Chapter Ten
# MOAB

Jacob Hummel was dead. There was nothing to suggest he had ever been other than dead. Being reduced to a corpse was the consequence of a life voraciously and brutally consumed, and so opportunely did death become him, it seemed a natural condition. David loosened his grip and the old man slid off the chair which fell sideways and clattered as he slumped to the floor. David looked around; everything seemed unfamiliar. He had become a footnote in someone's posthumous autobiography, someone he didn't know.

He turned away slowly, walked back into the crypt, and stood close to the glass reliquary, placing one hand on top to shield Anna's squeezed features from the flickering glare of the candles. This was his own flesh and blood, diminished to dry membrane stretched over bone. For the first time in his life beyond childish speculation, he realized what it was to be mortal, destined to ignominy and decay. Yet he couldn't quite grasp his deadly inheritance. The future was capricious. The accumulated deaths of ten thousand forbears were no guarantee that his was inevitable. Consciousness could not fathom its own absence.

Gazing at the remnants of hair shrouding Anna's skull, at her yellowed nails as creased as antique ivory, he thought about the bones his mother Violet had dug up in the Perigord Noir, fragments of a woman's cranium, phalangeal-joints of her fingers turned into nubbles of stone, and he wondered if that ancient woman was also his mother? How did Isabelle fit into the sequence of mothers and death? She was not quite a woman if age were the criterion, nor a mother — unless all women are mothers by virtue of a doubled twenty-third chromosome. Assuming their coupling had not led to conception, and if Jacob Hummel could be believed, she was not quite dead.

He shuddered, aroused from morose contemplation by the image of Isabelle suspended as it were over death. Numbness at his core was displaced by fear, not remorse, as he struggled to quell rising panic. Surely, she was close at hand. Whatever power and influence Jacob Hummel might have had out there in The City of the End of Things, or even in the Company's world, he had been most in control right here where he ruled like a papal oligarch. Where better to keep Isabelle in bondage? Clearly the old man would want his evil machinations to pass unnoticed. His venerable status, reinforced by the canonized remains of Anna, his co-founding partner, would collapse if the extent of his malevolence were revealed. Yet as far as David could tell, swarms of anonymous Librarians had access to the most obscure corners and crannies of this immense edifice. Where, then, was a redoubt so sacrosanct that no one would think to intrude?

David surveyed the crypt. There were two doorways, the one they had entered and the other leading into the antechamber where Jacob Hummel's corpse lay sprawled on the stone floor. David left the candlelit glare of his vigil post beside Anna's crystal casket and walked the perimeter of the room, sliding his hands along the walls to catch any hidden seams that might reveal a secret door. Finding nothing, he returned to the centre of light and glanced down at his expensive borrowed shoes, noting how they scuffed against the base of the stone catafalque without revealing a mark on the leather. He leaned down and touched the stone, tapped on it; it was genuine but showed a resilience that suggested an absence of mass.

He pushed at the slab with his foot. It moved slightly yet it refused to move further. David had played enough video games with Lucas to know there had to be a secret release mechanism. He ran his fingers along the oak mullions and found a piece at the base of the casket that felt less solid than the others. He tugged at the wood strip and it levered open. The entire catafalque shuddered when he put his weight to it and rolled silently to the side, revealing a gaping grave underneath.

Removing a candle from a wall sconce, he descended a narrow stairway into the darkness, his heart thumping in apprehension. He peered past the glare of the candle at another casket and approached cautiously. The crystal mirrored the flame and his wavering reflection. The casket was empty. Hope and dread gave way to horror. The image he'd been shown had lied — time out of context continued — she was already dead. Her body had been discarded. Arresting the progress of death was a cruel illusion.

He crumpled across her vacant coffin and sobbed in grief and frustration. The candle dropped to the floor, light all but extinguished from the narrow room except for the grave-shaped shaft through which he had descended, and a meagre slot of incandescence down a narrow passageway off to one side. He hurried up the steps, retrieved another candle, and descended again, this time walking directly past the empty glass casket which caught the candlelight prismatically as he passed, and proceeded down the illuminated slot to what turned out to be a steel door.

The door was locked from the outside with a simple latch. He slipped the latch to the side and pulled the door open. And there sat Isabelle, slouched comfortably in an oversized easy chair with a book in her hands. She looked up and spoke in gentle admonishment.

"Where have you been, David? I've been waiting. With George Eliot for company. She's really quite amazing, very witty, very sardonic, an astonishing vocabulary, but a little prolix by current standards."

He fell to his knees in front of her chair and embraced her awkwardly with his face buried in her lap. He cried into the folds of her skirt. Then he stopped, wiped away his tears, stood up, drew her to her feet, embraced her as a man embraces a woman, driving all contraries from mind.

While Isabelle cleaned herself up in the bathroom of her subterranean apartment, secret tomb, abysmal dungeon, David moved out through the darkness and climbed the grave-opening into the crypt to retrieve Jacob Hummel's body from the antechamber. The old man's remains were pathetically light. David carried him down and met Isabelle beside her own empty casket. Together, they lifted the glass cover and arranged Jacob Hummel on the bier of purple cushions, then replaced the glass. David picked up the walking stick with the Airedale head and amber eyes. Immanuel Kant. Experience determines all we can know, he thought. Space and time are the only reality. Where had those notions come from? He had only read excerpts of Kant. He would have to read more. He looked at Isabelle. She took Immanuel from him and set the stick down. Without saying a word, they turned away and ascended through twists and turns to street level, where they exited the library's Georgian front door.

They had only a few hours, perhaps a few minutes, until Jacob Hummel was found missing. They walked rapidly along the street out of Cabbagetown, but began to run as fear took over, until they spied a nameless theatre marquee south of Ford Place displaying the words,

NOW PLAYING

Exchanging glances, they ducked past the closed ticket booth and made their way through a small crowd in the lobby. The house lights flickered as they progressed down the left aisle. The theatre fell into darkness and a murmur rose from the crowd. They tried vainly to slip past a throng of latecomers but were pushed into empty seats in row L. Their space in the aisle immediately filled with moving bodies jostling for a better vantage.

A collective gasp through the darkened theatre accompanied a tracking strobe as it picked out a costumed character striding across to the front of the stage. He moved in staccato flashes that made him seem like a celluloid figure in an ancient movie. At centre stage he stopped. The curtain went up behind him and revealed a well-lit cast of characters wearing costumes from various theatrical periods of the western world including ancient Greek, late

Roman, medieval, Elizabethan, Restoration, Victorian, several distinct eras of the twentieth century, and contemporary.

The rakish dandy at centre stage raised both arms in a petitioning gesture. "Friends, Romans, countrymen," he declaimed. "I come to bury—"

"Falstaff," someone shouted from the audience. "Sanguine coward, bed-presser, horseback-breaker, hill of flesh."

A woman stepped forward from stage left dressed in a toga with purple edging and whispered loudly, "How now, sweet creature of bombast! How long is't since thou saw'st thine own knee?"

A rumbling of pleasure from among the cast rolled out over the audience. A lean middle-aged man rose from the dress circle and before the roving spotlight could reach him, he cast words towards the stage: "They are as sick that surfeit with too much as they are that starve with nothing." When the light flashed over him, he took a modest bow and sat down.

A boy dressed in bell-bottoms minced neatly to centre stage and shouted in a jagged falsetto: "In the room the women come and go, Talking to Michelangelo." He nodded his head in the direction of the dress circle. "Full fathom five thy father lies; Those are pearls that were his eyes," he concluded before retiring to stage right.

A voice rang out from the gods: "He is superfluously tall. *Middlemarch*. George Eliot."

"That's a rarity," Isabelle whispered. "Giving credit. He's showing a tactless lack of confidence."

The entire company meanwhile surged to the centre, closing ranks, and declaimed as a chorus, "Tyger, Tyger burning bright, In the fortress of the night."

A woman in row B leaped to her feet. All stopped, silence rippled, until the spotlight found her. Then she turned slowly, dramatically, to face the audience and spoke in a perfect Burnsian dialect: "Wee, sleekit, cow'rin, tim'rous beastie, O, what a panic's in thy breastie! I wad be laith to rin an' chase thee, Wi' murdering pattle."

"I think it's going to turn Tragic," Isabelle observed, *sotto voce*.

As if in response, the chorus declaimed: "Does the whale worship at thy footsteps as the hungry dog; Or does he scent the mountain prey because his nostrils wide Draw in the ocean?"

"How now, brown cow!" These deep-pitched words came wafting down from the gallery.

"No. More likely it will turn Comic," Isabelle whispered.

"The Daughters of Albion hear your woes, and echo back their sighs," declared the chorus, unable to hear her.

A slight woman two seats along row L from Isabelle rose to her feet. The light caught her immediately. "Alas poor Yorick, I knew him, I really did."

"There's the question, that's it," someone shouted out of the darkness.

The principal actor, dressed in dark pantaloons and a white blouse, stepped out of the cluster at centre stage and seized the moment: "The way a crow shook down on me. The snow of dust from a hemlock tree."

"First we take Manhattan, then we take Berlin." This, from an ingénue with clown make-up. "I thank you for the monkey and the plywood violin."

"Irony, perhaps," said Isabelle. "They never intentionally do Romance."

"Out, damned spot! Out, I say—" rang out from the dress circle. A murmur of approval subsided by the time the light successfully found the small man with the huge voice who intoned as an aside before dropping back into his seat, "Hell is murky!"

His lover beside him rose to the light and bellowed: "Who would have thought the old man to have so much blood in him?" He paused. "Not I, *Pas Moi*," he declared as the light moved on, leaving only his mouth visible in the darkness.

David leaned close to Isabelle and whispered, "Beckett," then felt immediate embarrassment, not sure whether he was showing off or lacking confidence.

A Regency dandy near centre stage began to enunciate: "I caught this morning morning's minion, daylight's dauphin, dapple-dawn-drawn Falcon, in his riding of the rolling…"

"He left some words out," David whispered.

"It's all from memory. They do their best."

An elderly actress wearing little make-up walked slowly to stage right, capturing everyone's attention, then whirling around she called out, "Someone must have slandered Joseph K." She paused, then sternly continued: "I wish my father or my mother had minded what they were about when they begot me." She slumped to the stage in apparent exhaustion and finally breathed out as barely a whisper: "Many years later, as he faced the firing squad, Gabriel Garcia Márquez was to remember that distant afternoon when his father took him to meet the Emperor of Ice Cream, while cheek by juke the jitter chatter fell." At this point she feigned death. Two stagehands, or perhaps coroner's assistants, hauled her away.

A man and woman in scarlet loincloths strolled to the front of the stage. He declaimed, "Oedipus, Wordsworth, Ezra Pound, they're all mother-lovers, life's only a sound," and she, responding, said: "How can we know the dancer from the dance, without a little seltzer down his pants?"

"They're ad libbing," David whispered.

"But no one's caught them. Isn't that super."

"I guess it is," said David, bewildered. It was one thing to leave out words and phrases; it was apparently another to add them. "I don't really see the point."

"There is no point, that's the point. They come together to share what remnants of literature they can recall. There doesn't have to be a point, David. Art *is*. That's the point. *Art is*."

"How can we know the players from the play without a program?" he paraphrased Yeats.

"Easily," she whispered. "If they come in costume, they must be actors, they go on stage. If they're not dressed up, they must be the audience, and they self-select their seating alphabetically, A's to the front, M's to the galleries, Z's in the gods."

"We're in L."

"Why not?" she said with a grin. "You can rename yourself as often as you wish."

A wail from stage left walloped the air. "Yellow mother custard, semolina pilchard, elementary penguin."

From the right came the response: "I've never seen a diamond in the flesh."

And from the left: "Boy, you been a naughty girl you let your knickers down."

Together: "Sitting on a cornflake, see how they snide."

In the orchestra, a resonant contralto and soaring soprano merged: "The slithy toves, all mimsy were, my beamish frumious bandersnatch, oh borogoves, oh borogoves."

"They rehearsed that," said David. "They got the words wrong in unison."

"They're trying to tell their own story in art," Isabelle said defensively.

"All art is autobiography," he declared. "We do what we can. The rest is madness."

"Are you quoting someone?"

"Several, no one, perhaps."

They simultaneously looked along row L to see movement in the far aisle. Two men were moving erratically, occasionally picked out of the darkness by the roving house spotlight splashing past them. They were searching.

"Time to go," said Isabelle. "Keep low."

Crouching, they struggled down the crowded aisle, past stage right, and out through an exit with the EXIT light burned out. The final words they heard, before emerging into the glare of daylight in an alley glistening with garbage, echoed after them: "Of shoes and ships and sealing wax, quoth

Ubu Mere, and never ever more." They immediately began to run. Isabelle took the lead. David had no sense of where they were going. Once on the street, she led full speed down several blocks towards a corner building with a huge sign composed of what seemed like innumerable bulbs, many of them burned out so that the sign was hardly legible. The bulbs turned out to be damaged metallic discs awkwardly reflecting the sun to declare,

### Charing Cross Covert Book Emporium

Entering the Emporium was like slipping into the memory-bank of someone who used to haunt shops crammed with books of every description stacked in baffling profusion, shops that reeked of dust and dried paper and the odours of book-lovers' bodies, shops ill-lit but with soft chairs here and there under low-wattage lamps, peopled with clusters of strangers conferring about what they had read, were reading, and what to avoid because of tedium, pretentiousness, indelicate or awkward prose. Such shops no longer existed in the Evolved New World and David was certain were rare in Toronto and would be subject to sanctions if ever revealed. What better way to hide than in plain sight? No one would dream a storefront emblazoned with the sign of its nefarious contents would actually hold, within it, nefarious content.

They squeezed past what David had taken to be strangers conferring but turned out to be readers gathered around clerks who expounded on what they themselves had read. It seemed these clerks were not employees but unpaid interns whose lives were given over to books. A few readers responded by offering preferences and judgements and suggestions of their own, but for the most part anyone with much to say wore a label indicating their elevated status.

David and Isabelle worked their way through the helter-skelter stacks and conversants, taking in snippets of prattle as they progressed. David decided this was the most splendid place he had ever been and forgot they were fleeing for their lives.

In a gloomy section devoted to hard-cover books, mostly leather-bound, some subtly emblazoned with smeared streaks of dust, smatterings of successive bilingual exchanges hung in the air.

"*Bitte* chocolate," someone said, suppressing a laugh.

"*Ensuite* bonbons."

"*Dies* dies." The first word was pronounced *dee-ez*. David remembered reading that Archbishops dream in Latin.

"*Gestalt* and pepper," said the voice they had first heard, toying with German. After a contemplative pause, she continued: "Rise and *schön*."

"*Combat de* whores." There was a collective giggle as David and Isabelle moved out of range. They progressed along a series of narrow passages until finding themselves at an impasse, blocked by a small group in the earnest exchange of phrases that taken out of context seemed to mean nothing.

"Unequivocal past participles."

"Pluperfect preferred."

"Liking gerunds."

"Syntactical function determines determiners."

"Adverbially deranged."

"Subjected nouns, objecting correlatives."

"Trope, cantor, gallop."

And so on. David leaned over, and whispered to Isabelle, his voice tremulous with wonder. "Semiotic syntactical semantics?"

She smiled up at him and politely pushed through the knot of grammarians, with David following close behind.

"They once read a lot, some still do, they want to talk about books. Those people back at the theatre don't know this place exists. This particular group gravitates together because they can't get beyond units of construction. You'll find other groups talking font sizes and paper weights or sentence lengths and diphthongs. What they all love is the cut and thrust of literate discourse."

"They're not making sense."

"They gather among books and connect. Doesn't that make sense?"

Seeing further clarity was unlikely, he shifted direction. "Where are we?" he asked.

"Exactly where we should be," she said. She drew him behind her through a casual ensemble whose sallow complexions suggested they hadn't seen sunlight or soap on a regular basis for a long while. "Government intelligence," one of them said, letting the oxymoron dangle in the air while its meaning caught up.

"Political science, creation science, science fiction," someone else said.

"Bart-hes Bar*th*," said a girl on crutches as they squeezed past. "*Re*fuse ref-use. Patients patience."

"In*val*id inval*id*," was the response, followed by awkward clarification: "Adjective/noun."

"Quite unique."

"Fuck! Fucking fucker's fucking fucked." Pause. "Expletive, adjective, noun, adverb, verb."

"I hope you're not referring to me," said the girl with crutches as an aside.

"Timorous temerity! Ambiguous homonym."

"I'll sanction that."

"Fast, break-fast, make fast," said yet another, his voice coming through horizontal stacks of miscellaneous volumes from the next aisle over.

"If you have to explain, it doesn't count," Isabelle mumbled as they disappeared into a deep alcove jammed so precariously with books it seemed impenetrable, yet she pushed through, squeezing and twisting, until they emerged at the other end into a room that looked for all the world like the private study of a particularly fastidious scholar in one corner of a small bachelor flat.

"Here we are," she said. "We're safe here. Although I do have a place of my own, this is where I sometimes stay — except when I'm off rescuing you, of course."

He ignored the affectionate dig. "Does Grace know you're here?" he asked, a little alarmed despite the sense of security exuded from books throughout the shop being exchanged and discussed and critically assessed by minds free of cant and computer mechanics — books alive and being *lived* in ways he could hardly have imagined except through ancestral memory.

"Of course she knows. That doesn't mean she has access. You can't walk in off the street. You can't browse to purchase, not for the last generation or more. Admission is by invitation, invitation is by reputation, reputation is conferred by tests administered so secretively no one knows when they are being tested. Most are turned away as insufficiently literate. If they insist on coming in, they disappear among the aisles of books and are never heard from again. Even if librarian thugs knew where we are they wouldn't dare enter. Everyone here is a critical reader. This is the locus for the reading elite, those alive in the world who truly love books for the words they contain. Quite unlike The Cloisters, which is for readers in the shadow world who lose themselves among narrative diversions from reality. Here the books complement life like a redundant thesaurus; they don't displace it. Here it is the words themselves that define experience. This is fundamentally different than places for obsessives concerned with rare books and readable books and books currently under revision. It is a very special place, David. In some ways, this vast little shop is the power centre of our vast little world and so exclusive it is inviolable. Welcome to my safe-house."

He tried to parse her explanation, uncertain about the pointillist discussion of semantics and semiology he had heard passing through as the basis of exclusivity or the source of power. "So you live here?" he asked.

"Sometimes."

"Did Jacob Hummel know you were here?"

"He did. As you know, he's dead."

"I'm sorry." He paused. Guilt had not set in, although he felt uneasy in anticipation, and badly that she seemed vaguely bereaved. "I had no choice."

"It doesn't matter."

"Of course it matters."

"He had hoped to get to know you, David, but being a prudent man he had made provisions for an untimely demise. Quite wise, given his age and the possibility he couldn't get through to you in time."

David was disconcerted. "How well did you know him?"

"It doesn't matter. It's all in the past."

"Nothing ever is," he declared.

She smiled and urged him to join her on the small sofa.

He remained standing. "I didn't realize you and the old man were close. That changes everything."

"Well, I was. And nothing has changed. See, look around you, look in my eyes. Nothing has changed except your perception."

He gazed into the depths of her piercing green eyes. He was searching for himself but in the distorted reflection he saw only a stranger. He had never before had to deal with the disorienting afflictions of romantic engagement.

"David, please sit down. Let me explain. You know my story. You believe you know Grace's story and Violet's but you don't, and you don't know your own, and you don't know the old man's, which is yours more than you think."

"Jacob Hummel was a fascist lunatic and I'm the bastard of a bastard; the sum of rape, squared."

"If that were true, I'd have more pity for the mothers than their child."

"I wasn't asking for pity."

"Asking and hoping are two different things."

Even while struggling to comprehend wilful defilement as a sexual act and the possible source of conception, he had never doubted that the man he had murdered was a rapist and therefore unconscionably bad. By contrast, there was no one he trusted more than Isabelle and she was casting doubt on the vile account of his origins. Could her truth mean the justification for his crime lay solely in the old man's Faustian designs on his *soul* (a term of convenience for his nebulous *self*)?

"David, exactly what did Jacob Hummel tell you about Violet and Grace?"

By this time, he was seated on the sofa beside her. He looked around as she had suggested and wondered whether there were other apartments like this, tucked away in the bowels of the Charing Cross Covert Book Emporium. Then he began to talk, at first hesitating among the words, as if uncertain as to where they would lead, but eventually in a flowing narrative that replicated, even embellished, the grotesque details of Jacob's story about Violet's sordid rape by multiple assailants and her recovery from unimaginable squalor, her subsequent giving birth to Grace and her transcendent flight into the Evolved New World, where she channelled her brutally damaged psyche into the study of ancient human remains and raising the child of her child inevitably to be, like herself, uneasy with cerebral cybernetic hybridity.

"The part about Grace growing up in the library is true." As Isabelle spoke, she held both David's hands in her own. He stared at their entwined fingers. She tilted her head to try and see up into his eyes but he shifted his gaze. "And Grace is your mother, that part is true. And Jacob Hummel was your biological father."

His eyes flickered, caught her glance, and gazed expectantly.

"When Grace was fifteen, a couple of emissaries came from the Company. They wanted to negotiate a settlement with Anna and Jacob. The Company wished the library to be closed down. They considered it a threat to the survival of the Evolved New World. Here was a repository of books that might not be subject to the reductive power of algorithms, books that might one day provide the foundation for a revolution against cyber-reality that might drag cyber-enhanced humanity back into the abyss of natural selection. The Company's *angels*, as they called themselves, or *demons*, as the Librarians described them, acknowledging that their powers were limited within The City of the End of Things, allowed that the library might remain open providing no one actually read the books, conceding that books might be of unforeseen value as artefacts in the distant future.

"Anna, having kept silent to this point, protested. She was executed with a single blow. Jacob, shocked beyond grief, immediately acquiesced to the Company's demands, trying to protect their library as best he could. For surety, he offered them Grace, to take to their world as a hostage. Grace, who had been observing the exchange, was aghast. She accused him of whoring her out. She believed he had traded Anna's life for the library and was offering her up as well."

"Sounds like it," said David.

"Or he was honouring Anna under desperate circumstances by preserving their library and he was trying to save Grace by sending her off to a safer world. It depends on your perspective, David. Anyway, the two messengers stayed the night. They dined with Jacob Hummel and Grace, who insisted on serving them the best wine from the cellar in the depths of the library, the chamber that eventually became Anna's crypt."

"And your own."

"Jacob had no intention of killing me," said Isabelle.

"How do you know all this?"

"About the past? I just do."

"I mean, seriously. It's life and death knowledge from before you were born."

"David, you don't want to know. Not right now."

'I do!"

Following a frightening moment of hesitation, she continued. "Eventually, Grace set me free; she introduced me to the world beyond the confines of books at The Cloisters. That's when Jacob sought me out. He was fascinated by the notion of a reader unspoiled by actual experience, a mind and a memory shaped solely by books. He became my mentor. He used to come here, to this place, in disguise. We drank countless coffees, and he'd tell me how to apply life to reading and reading to life. We became good friends."

"Oh my God. You must hate me."

"For killing him? No, he forced you to do what you thought best at the time. He should have known better than to come between lovers. I grieve his passing, of course."

"I'm sorry, Isabelle."

"Let me get back to the dinner. It was a charade, everyone pretending Anna was not lying dead in the adjoining room while her killers and her husband and grand-daughter dined in style. At one point Jacob slipped out of the room and bound a silk cord around Anna's neck."

"A bit macabre."

"It was. He was affirming something — that Anna's death was his fault, that she would not have died were it not for him. He tied it so tight, there was no mistaking his intent. When he went back, Grace was decanting the wines herself. She made sure they drank a great deal. She couldn't read the labels but she knew their images. I believe they consumed bottles of Ch. Mouton, 1945, and Ch. Petrus, 1961, neither of them actually Médoc *Premier Grand Crus* but the best Bordeaux had to offer, and they feasted on food commandeered from veggie grow-ops in the valley. They finished with a '67 Ch. d'Yquem sauternes. In the morning, the angel-demons, saturated and disoriented, left without Grace. And while this was going on, Grace conceived the idea of you, David."

"What on earth?"

"You. She had loved Anna. She loved Jacob Hummel. She was a foundling herself, her mother having apparently abandoned her by the blue front door as an infant. The library was Grace's world and her home and she saw it was in grave danger. She desperately wanted continuity.

Confused and determined, she plied the old man with more drink and eventually took him to bed and, as they say in the Bible, she lay with him. He wasn't aware of what he had done or when she arose, but she conceived that night."

David gasped.

As Jacob Hummel's son, he was begotten by deceit and conceived in the womb of a girl deranged by distress. His birth was Borgesian in its mythic complexity. The old man's death was the stuff of classical tragedy.

# Chapter Eleven
# The Secret Chapel

The stone comes alive as cave lions overtake one another in endless succession around the cavern circumference while the girl paints frantically in the concealed chamber where she has laid her baby to rest. The stripes on their fur are visible in rippling shadows. Their massive size is shown by un-devoured carcasses of aurochs and elk beneath their leaping contours. Their speed and agility are caught in a whirl of torchlight swaying in the darkness while the grieving young woman exorcises their furious beauty into colour and movement that sets the stone trembling. Her mother tends to her with supplies of ochre and charcoal and blood mixed with animal fat, or with food and water to be shared amidst the feline threnody for the dead infant child.

One day, and she cannot know when since days inside the cave are indivisible, her mother arrives pushing her torch and a bundle of food ahead through the narrow crawl-space into the chamber and finds the
girl seated in the dwindling glow of her fire which she has not stoked or replenished. Their eyes flicker as the girl soundlessly directs her mother to survey the completed chapel, like Michelangelo's in Rome two thousand generations later, a distillation of genius so vast and intimate the viewer becomes pure consciousness, transcendent and inseparable from the power of the vision conveyed. What will eventually be called the aesthetic annihilation of personality, Calvary's turbulence, the uncontrollable mystery of creation, is in that chamber an expression of grief and renewal unlike anything the earth has seen. Mother and daughter, filled with fear and awe from the lions around them, turning and turning in a widening gyre, stop when the girl breaks away and leads to the exit. She urges her mother to go ahead through the narrow passage; her mother complies with trepidation, fearing the girl will block the way between them and perish surrounded by her whirling memorial, but the girl follows and together they close off the chapel with boulders and gravel and wads of clay worked into mud with drinking water carried in a bee hive sealed by layers of its own wax. Even to them it seems the chamber might never have existed.

They clamber over rockfalls and through hollows and fissures into the cavity that was the girl's first studio and then further towards the surface of the earth to the chamber that had been her mother's refuge after her own mother died in a fire before the girl was born. The girl has crafted a few aurochs here, to engage with her mother and be shown to visitors who don't warrant a deeper tour into the depths of creation. The older woman has spent a lot of time here making clothing from hides while the girl has been working on her lion project which they both recognize is an attempt to displace the loss of her baby, not the infant herself but the harrowing gap left by her absence; not to honour cave lions which are the humans' chief predator but to honour death, which is more powerful than lions or love. The girl does not pause by the glowing coals of the hearth but continues to the gap in the rock that opens onto a vista of the valley below. She kicks a piece of woolly mammoth ivory off to the side as she goes. Her mother picks up her sewing implements, an awl made of elk antler and a scraper of cracked human bone, a few pieces of ivory along with a rolled bundle of membrane to make sinews, and together they venture into the sunlight and traipse down and over the worn forest path by the side of the river until at the edge of the commune they come to their ageing shelter of auroch skins draped across logs propped against a cliff, built on top of the charred remains of the funeral pyre of the woman's own mother, who herself was feared and thought mad because her mind was estranged from reality around her.

For the next few months until winter falls upon them, the girl joins her mother in sewing clothes for the hunters whose partners are better disposed to gathering autumn berries and to drying fish, flesh, and skinned fowl in the wind and the sun. With the first snow, the girl takes three lovers and conceives. In the seasons that follow, mother and daughter share companionable chatter, creating word patterns that signify parallels to details of their lives. Occasionally their sounds conjure the carousel of lions still whirling in perpetual darkness, their eyes gleaming, their silent roar deafening. They sing by the fire and chew hides into leather, and their song keeps the circle from ceasing to turn.

Late the following summer, the girl gives birth to two boys and a girl. One of the boys is stillborn. The families of the fathers attend the birth and the girl falls into abject sorrow as two of the families each take an infant to suckle with aunts because the girl is depleted and does not immediately lactate and the lives of the babies are precarious. The girl does not recover and is distracted by visions of lions as they swirl through the depths of the earth which she never again enters or smears with contours of charcoal and blood. Her mother who had killed two of her own lovers discourages her from further progenerative encounters.

She is surprised when several years later a man comes in while her mother is absent. He reveals his intent in the streaks of light that penetrate the sides of the shelter, animated by the wind scattering sun through a stand of wavering spruce between her home and the river. Sex and death seem much the same and she is murdered for her apparent indifference. When her mother finds her body, she goes to the man's home and lies with him and kills him. By the next morning she too is dead, smothered by the restless earth in another man's arms.

Twenty thousand years later, after glaciation reaches a maximum and begins its rapid retreat, melt-water run-off floods the valley and scours the landscape of soil and vegetation. Another twenty thousand years sees the waters dwindle as the ice recedes northwards and the river flows much as it had eons before. Lichens and algae, mosses and grasses, bird droppings and natural detritus build up the soil until trees take root; first alders and trembling aspens, then towering conifers, and finally beech, maples, and great oaks in abundant forests. *Homo sapiens sapiens* had fled the cold while the hardier Neanderthals stayed and adapted until it was too late — they did not have the skills or technology to hunt the diminishing fauna and they perished. When the proto-humans return, carrying remnant Neanderthal genes within them, they flourish, occasionally discovering echoes of their distant heritage. No one finds the cave where the woman had made clothes from animal skins while her daughter made art until palaeoanthropologists from New Town Number Eleven in the Evolved New World dislodge a few boulders, causing a small landslide, and discover the entry revealed by the adjusted surface of the planet.

\*\*\*

Through a narrow subterranean fissure, deep in a nondescript passage, Violet pulls away rocks to clear an opening. Prying with her spade, she hits an oddly displaced chunk of river clay and feels a momentary breeze on the back of her neck as it crumbles. As she clears a space large enough to squeeze through, the smell of charred wood and oestrogen emerges from the darkness ahead. Her colleagues and assistants have retreated for lunch near the river. Violet skips eating, herself, relishing the time on her own in the bowels of the earth, when every discovery is mysterious and generates wondrous emotional stirrings. The discoveries of colleagues are facts to be catalogued, deciphered, and stuffed into boxes for future withdrawal in support of a theory. Her own are episodes in the continuity of human experience. By herself, she is a dabbling dreamer, Democritus perhaps, while among others she is a studious polymath like Aristotle, Leibnitz, Einstein, Sagan, or Schreiber. As a scientist, she knows the odours that waft out of the narrow passage are distorted perception. As a sentient being in continuous conflict with her cybernetic implant, she knows she will find ashes ahead and walls, scanned by her flashlight beam, will reveal heartrending flourishes of movement and colour. This is not something she wants to share. She knows she is being subversive.

Anticipating the desired impact, she crawls forward, hesitates as she enters a small chamber, and moves carefully, illuminating her way step by step on the fine-powdered floor until she reaches the centre, then stands tall and shines her flashlight beam on the wall and turns slowly, turning and turning in the direction of the animals' movement, until she is dizzy and switches off her light. In the palpable darkness she can hear the rush of the lions, fur whirring in the breeze, the hush of their breath throbbing in rhythm with her beating heart. She has never felt more human.

She switches on her flashlight again and slowly circumnavigates the room, mesmerized, examining each lion in turn, pausing to identify the carcasses of elk and aurochs that they leap over in a steeplechase with no beginning or end. There are so many lions, some superimposed over others, that they seem like innumerable facets of one large whirling animate creature, with her, perceiving, surrounded by rock and energy inseparable from their terrible beauty.

Her feet strike an object and she flashes her light down to see boulders in a tight circle and knows this must have been the hearth where the artist warmed pigments and drew light. The dusty clay is discoloured with streaks of carbon near the rocks but lies undisturbed as it has been for tens of thousands of years. Nothing, no person or animal or elemental disturbance has penetrated this chamber since the girl conjured a whirl of lions to fill the void that engulfed her.

On the far side of the fire's dark residue, Violet's light catches a strange configuration in the dirt. When she moves closer, she recognizes the hint of a human footprint. Giddy with excitement, appalled at her unprofessional carelessness, she sweeps her light across the entire floor and recognizes her own bootmarks standing out from dwindled contours that turn out to be a chaos of footprints indicating two people, from their size likely women, with the smaller ones fully arched suggesting youth. In the shadows away from the hearth another mound of rocks reveals by its shape the grave of an infant. Violet starts towards it and then stops. The sound of her own weeping fills the chamber and stirs the lions to leap faster and higher until they seem to overwhelm her and she sinks to the floor, fists clutching at clay as it sifts through her fingers.

A voice calls through the rock. Suddenly she is at the opening of the passage she came through, stepping carefully not to crush footprints, and crawls the long passage to the entrance of the tunnel and gazes out, shining her light into the eyes of her colleagues. "Nothing," she declares. "Dead end." She urges them to return to the principal dig, deep in the crevasse by the side of the main cavern where they have found human fossils and curious bits of antler with rings etched into their sides.

Once she is alone, Violet piles rocks across the narrow low entry and pushes dirt and sand and a paste made from clay dust mixed with cold coffee from her thermos, supplemented by urine, into the remaining fissures until a seal has been made that will resist even the seepage of air. Then she walks away as if the cave of swirling lions never existed except as a trick of perception.

Back in the outer cavern, with the voices of a work party wafting up through the crevasse dulled to meaningless phonemes by the churning sounds of a propane generator, Violet sinks onto the soft floor of sand, guano, and vegetative detritus. She gazes at aurochs that leap on the walls as if in rehearsal for the riotous profusion in the secret chamber she has already discovered, created by the same artisan who brought the brute power of lions to life with such feverish intensity — she knows this, in the same way she would have recognized a recovered painting by Michelangelo, from the ways flesh pulsed beneath painted skin. The artisan was an artist long before art migrated into an end in itself, and the artist was a woman. She knows this by the way the smaller footprints covered the floor from every perspective with deliberate randomness (the larger prints, a mature woman, more flat-footed, possibly a caregiver). She knows the artist was a woman by the subversion of anatomy to motion in her art, form to pure function, that speaks of a visceral truth she is convinced few men could grasp, however moved they might be by the facts.

Swarming in concentric circles, like the scratchings on a reflective surface that arrange themselves neatly behind a candle in patterns owing more to perception than the source of the light, what she had seen in the funerary chamber merged with the maelstrom she had endured long ago, sprawled on a filthy mattress, consumed by lovers, rapists, dischargers of bodily fluids, all before Jacob Hummel lifted her out of the filth. It is a memory so appalling she had refused it admission to consciousness in the interim, and yet fused with the riot of lions it came forward as an ordeal she no longer had to endure.

Feeling secretive and free, she struggles to suppress her explosive heartbeat, to subdue her turbulent breathing. She envisions the young woman as a visceral memory, ecstatic in the throes of creation, a young woman at the base of an opening gyre that includes all the women who lived in the period between them, a young woman who was perhaps among the first humans to be aware that she was aware — and Violet fears she herself could be among the last. She walks out into the broad valley and along the well-trodden path by the river, determined to shield her progenitor's soul from the implacable light of science in the brave new world that promises an end to their species.

*\*\*\**

David scanned the small apartment, looking for signifiers of personality, anything to indicate this was more than a transient residence. Even in New Town Number Eleven he had a few keepsakes scattered about in his room, along with the ritual poster of exhortation, **YOU MUST HAVE FAITH TO BELIEVE**. Theirs had been the only house he knew to display *objets d'art trouvés*, which is what Violet called them, artefacts brought back from her various expeditions, stalking prehistory. On the mantel of their simulated fireplace had been a small case in which she displayed her most recent acquisition, a small fossilized antler prong circumscribed with a shallow circle. The anthropology department at the university had dismissed it as a meaningless trinket since it fitted no established criteria. It would have been destroyed, he assumed, in the fire that consumed her scattered remains.

He gazed around Isabelle's rooms, looking for something to connect with; he was unnerved by the anonymity of the décor, much like the hotel rooms he had stayed in on the few trips he had taken with his mother.

Although he acceded to the strange notion that Grace was the woman who bore him, he still thought of Violet as his mother. While he searched for indicators that would mark this apartment as personal territory, he wondered about his father, the man he had righteously murdered. If Jacob Hummel was not the depraved rapist he had been led to believe, David realized the unspeakable crime of patricide placed him beyond redemption. By violating natural law at its most elemental, by defiling social law and desecrating the most fundamental laws of religion, he had offended humanity itself. The monumental horror of what he had done began to emerge from the shroud of shock. With no words spoken, Isabelle responded by stepping back, disengaging, becoming an apparition, both strange and familiar.

"Isabelle," he said plaintively.

"David. I'm here."

She approached closer. She was now wearing knee-length socks rolled at the top. They were wool and impossibly green. She wore a strange flared skirt, also green, and a scoop-necked peasant blouse. He didn't speculate on her underwear. She looked like an exotic insect; her clothes hung loosely from her recent weight-loss in hell like an amorphous exoskeleton, but out on the street she would blend in. He liked insects.

"What do you know about Jacob Hummel's intentions?" He struggled to make his voice firm.

"In relation to what?"

"To me! He planned to erase me."

"No, not exactly. He had a dream that would benefit you both."

"You sound like you believe it."

"With the help of scientists who work for the Company he wanted to share your mind. He had no intention of wiping it clean. He wanted to exploit your peculiar capacity to live within words like a poet and think like a sentient machine. He wanted to share in the legacy that he and Anna passed on to you through Violet."

"You're saying, *share*. That sounds worse than I imagined, having someone else in my head while I'm still around."

"David, the process has already begun. Once he knew you were safe in The Cloisters—"

"You told me he didn't know about The Cloisters."

"He knew we were there."

"And he thought we were *safe*? Being confined in a dungeon with human cadavers, sharing my food to keep us alive?"

"He thought a session surrounded by the offal of death would make you more flexible, especially if I were reading myself into oblivion close by. When he was informed you weren't breaking, he became worried that his own mind was slipping. He arranged with his people to download his cerebral activity, latent or actual, everything he took as the limits of consciousness that could possibly be formulated into cybernetic equivalents. It was all entered into a specially prepared cloud accessible only by computers under his management."

"But we've seen him since then."

"Of course we have. As I said, he simply began the transition. He was counting on death, when it came, to be of no consequence. And it doesn't need to be, if you come around — as I imagine you will, since you have already made the huge commitment of killing him. How could you resist? You would defeat death together. Think what he offers you, David: wealth beyond measure from Anna's mentor, Sebastian Kroetsch; wisdom from infinite reading; inexhaustible memories; the benefits of vast experience."

"And in return, he gets from me, what?"

"Youth, vitality, innocence, the benefits of so much potential."

Her attitude confused him. This was the girl he loved, yet she seemed to accept the invasion of his mind by an occupying force, however benevolent, as a reasonable thing. Even more perplexing, she accepted that he had murdered the old man as relatively inconsequential.

"Did he know I would kill him?" David asked, afraid of the answer.

"He knew, one way or another, he would push you over the edge. He was confident your affection for me would lead you to capitulate or to retaliate. If you gave in, we could have all worked together. Since you didn't, you have a responsibility to bring him back. I cannot imagine life without Jacob Hummel."

"You sound eerily like you were in love with him — he was old enough to be your grandfather."

"Great-grandfather. Ancestral father. And yes, you might say we were in love. I was a creature created by books and he was a man devoted to books, a man who saw in their pages a world born of the human mind more ordered and authentic than the randomness of temporal reality. He read me back to myself. Do you understand that? Of course I was in love with him. When he shared his dream of controlled reincarnation, I saw our future *writ large* — Plato used that expression to describe the nation-state as a composite entity, but for me 'writ large' holds the utterly romantic notion of unified being — Jacob, you, me, merging as one."

"An unholy trinity."

"I would not call it unholy."

"What you and I had, it meant nothing?" He was crushed.

"On the contrary, it was everything. I discovered you were the perfect host for Jacob, as he had anticipated. To have you as my lover and Jacob sharing the bond between us, I could not have wanted for anything more."

"I seem to have been reduced to a medium of exchange."

"No, no. You're of vital importance. Let me tell you about a vision by the poet William Blake of creative perfection. Blake described three lovers. There was the poet in time and space, that's you. There was his twin, whom he loved; she was his inspiration. And there was the spirit of whom they were composite parts, he was the principle of creation, the rage to make something new. The union of all three was necessary for the poet to forge a work of art that could redeem the world."

"His version of the Holy Trinity," said David. He knew Blake. He had read the poem *Jerusalem* over Isabelle's shoulder in the antechamber to hell. While the poem baffled him, he had been caught up in its mystic complexity and awed by the hand-tinted drawings that seemed reckless in their resistance to the conventions of art. Perhaps he had understood more than he knew, for he responded with disconcerting coherence. "Each of the three in Blake's vision is as much constrained as attracted — inspiration is the poet's twin, incest stands between them; the spectre has no physical body, his attraction to either cannot be consummated. The two males, in any case, violate social decorum. A variation of Sartre's *No Exit*. The failed revolutionary, the infanticidal nymphomaniac, the predatory lesbian — no satisfaction, no escape."

"*Infanticidal nymphomaniac*! How very erudite."

"Existential," said David, hoping that would block the necessity for clarification, yet in spite of himself he added, "Blake and Sartre, they both describe the impossibility of perfection and the desirability of its achievement."

"But we don't need perfection, David. Don't you see? We just need to *try* for perfection."

He looked at her with a mixture of affection and anger. Did she really think he would submit to sharing his mind with another, especially an old man utterly set in his ways? He could not imagine how they might coexist. Would they be in the forefront of consciousness at the same time or take turns? Would they argue? Would youth become a slave to old age? Or age to youth? Would he be a stand-in for inconceivable lovers, would she come to love him with the passion she felt for the old man? Would Jacob be absorbed into the younger man's being? Or would David Winston be absorbed into his?

She was so eager to make this happen, and his residual affection for her was so strong, he felt guilty for his pedantic hesitation to participate in the resurrection of Jacob Hummel.

A small revelation intruded.

He had observed that nothing in Isabelle's apartment offered a point of connection. It was like a corporate room in a dream. When he woke up, he'd be gone. Nothing was real. She was an illusion, an avatar of his father's desire. She was a projection of the old man's gruesome ambition, meant to seduce David into acquiescence. He had fallen in love with his own father, with himself.

She was doing strange things to his mind. He had to get away, to grow up and take possession of whoever he was.

"I'm going," he said.

At some point in their conversation, he had walked across the room. He turned to the door off the kitchenette and pushed it open, stepping out into a gloomy maze of passages arranged helter-skelter with elite readers here and there, gathered under stolid pools of illumination, talking earnestly about matters of syntax and semantics.

She called after him, "David, wait!" But he kept going until, pushing through a door at the end of a book-stuffed alcove, he suddenly found himself standing in full sunlight on a deserted side street. The tinkling of myriad metallic discs on the overhead sign sounded from around the corner. He moved under them, out into the flow of pedestrian traffic. A few elderly cars, Havanas, mostly of Japanese and German origin, urged their way along Bloor St. towards the centre of The City of the End of Things.

He trudged along in the same direction, hoping Isabelle would catch up with him, fearing Isabelle would catch up with him. He cut down to Dundas without thinking about where he was going, and when he approached Ford Place two men closed in on him from either side. They were large enough, the three of them formed a formidable phalanx and people stepped to the side to let them pass.

"The proceedings have begun," he said to himself. His curiosity about whether they were going to the library or some other facility was satisfied after they entered the Cabbagetown, when they rounded a corner and he recognized the endless row of Victorian townhouses with ornate brickwork and brilliantly painted front doors. They stopped in front of the midnight blue door with sidelights and a transom so dark the glass appeared colourless. He felt almost like he had come home. The men stopped at the base of the steps.

"Go ahead," said the shorter one. "We don't generally go in there. Too many books." His explanation seemed reasonable; he gave a slight push and released his grip on David's arm, propelling him up the first step. David stopped, then shrugged and continued. The door opened before he pressed the latch. He entered the foyer and was confronted by Grace who stood in front of the vast and indefinite perhaps infinite library with its innumerable pentagonal galleries.

"You don't seem surprised to see me," said Grace.

"Nothing surprises me any more, *mother*." He mouthed the word 'mother' like he was unsure of the meaning.

"Good!"

She led him through labyrinthine shadows to a part of the library he had never seen. It was high, not low; an aerie, not a crypt. They passed through a door she unlocked into a large and modestly appointed apartment with interior walls reduced to bare brick and old wooden beams, with ductwork and conduits showing — a very dated, mid-twentieth-century modernist exposure of structural form surrounded by geometric modules of open space. Somehow serene and uncomfortable at the same time.

"Here we are," she said. "This is where I grew up."

He looked around, realizing as she spoke that much like Isabelle's small flat in the Emporium there was little evidence of a resident's personality. No keepsakes, artefacts, *objets d'art*, no whims or passions in evidence; an intellectual triumph, architecturally superb, and emotionally bleak and austere.

"No books," he observed. "Strange, for a library."

"After Anna's death, Jacob didn't read very much. Even before that, this place was a refuge *from* books. I was allowed to wander the library at will but never permitted to read. Being kept in the dark was a symbolic act — everything in Anna's life became symbolic as she aged."

"You remember her well?"

"Oh yes, I was fifteen when she died."

'And when I was conceived.'

"Yes, that too. Fifteen."

"That's what I am now."

"I know. You don't think I'd forget, do you?"

"My birthday? You haven't remembered one yet."

"Just because you didn't know I existed doesn't mean I forgot giving birth. It's not something that slips the mind."

"But apparently my conception was a casual event."

He was prepared to be admonished for insolence but not for the sadness that swept over her face before it resolved into a mask of forbearance. "No," she said. "It was very deliberate. I had never been with a man and have never been with one since. Do not be confused. It was not incest. He was my father in name only. He meant to displace the countless fathers who might have been mine from a welter of anonymous semen. When the angels of the Company murdered Anna, I could not bear that he might die as well, then or ever. I determined that I would provide him with provisional immortality. Hence, you. And his agreement to the absolute proscription of books in order to protect their continued existence, that drove me to reading — something until then that had seemed redundant, close as I was to readers like Anna and Jacob who shared the benefits of books with limitless generosity."

"Did you also conceive his project to rejuvenate himself at my expense?"

"That's something fathers do. Him, perhaps a little more literally than most."

"By moving in."

"It would eventually have been a blessing for both of you."

"Somehow I doubt it."

"You're very strange, David. You must learn to adapt. When I returned to the fold, fully literate, Jacob was not enraged, he was proud. He adapted. He assigned me to supervise the revision of history, and in turn I initiated the procedures that led to his present transition, which awaits completion, of course, through you." She uttered the last word with sepulchral resonance that chilled David to the bone.

"You said Anna wanted to keep you from reading as a symbolic act," he said. "How can illiteracy be symbolic of anything except ignorance?"

"It was a personal symbol, signifying horrific events in her own life."

'It was selfish to impose it on you."

"No. Perhaps. I was happy, I liked being surrounded by books."

"Even if you couldn't read them?"

"The world was real just like it was. I didn't need to turn it into a text. It wasn't until after Anna's death that everything changed."

"You made yourself pregnant with Jacob's child and you became obsessed with reading. You seized reality and then you tried to evade it. By reading, by running away."

"Yes, both. But I only ran away and learned to read after he insisted we give you up to Violet."

"That was pretty despicable — for you, if not for me."

"Necessarily callous, perhaps, but committed. It was the opposite to what had been done when Violet first left and took me, her infant, with her. Jacob brought me back, but not before I had been implanted with a DNA microcomputer."

"Which you claim to override by sheer force of will."

"I had the advantage of illiteracy. That's why Anna kept me from reading. It reduced cybernetic intrusion."

"Rather paradoxical, given that Anna resisted external control by her own voluminous reading."

"She wanted to protect me from the book-borne demons that haunted her. And you, dear boy, were the third way. When the ENW took you in, you were altered to give you full access to your enhanced resources. You had no incentive to transcend your mechanized brain."

"Which it seems has now been damaged beyond repair. But my situation was apparently more subtle than yours, *dear* mother. Violet taught me to turn my cybernetics to better uses than they were intended. With her as my model, I was learning how *not* to abandon my species."

"How grand that sounds."

"But true enough that she died for it."

"Did she? Well, perhaps she did. You loved her, didn't you? And she loved you. She gave you a childhood that I could never have given, nor Jacob Hummel for that matter. Believe me, growing up in The City of the End of Things, childhood is difficult. In the library, impossible."

"*Born with nothing, she gave me everything.*"

"You are paraphrasing the apostle, Paul. Jacob wanted to name you after that strangely dispassionate zealot. He hoped you'd grow into the name. Instead, you became a poet in potential and possibly a philosopher king."

"Ambitions to which I would never aspire."

"Well, forget the Bible, forget Aristotle. Neither are very important. You'll stay here for a while. It's comfortable, with all the amenities, and there will always be a book on hand, but only one book at a time. The best way to get a reader to read a particular book, make that the only book available. I think we'll start you on Saint Paul — the entire compendium."

"The King James Version, please."

"By all means."

"How long will I have it?"

"As long as it takes."

To do what, he wondered, but he only smiled.

"You're amused by this?"

"Not at all. I'm terrified."

"You have strange ways of showing it."

"I'm a kid. An hour ago, I thought I was in love. Turns out I'm a surrogate."

"For Isabelle?"

"For Jacob Hummel. In Isabelle's affections."

"I'd be careful of her."

"I'm sure she'd say the same about you. So now that Jacob's dead, which one of you controls the mind he's put on deposit?"

"Again, you seem oddly amused."

David looked at her through narrowed eyes. "We've created a Greek tragedy, despite the Hebrew zealotry implicit in its structure. And Jacob Hummel's tragic flaw appears to be that he's dead. Or is it God who has died? As for me, no Hamlet, I, but only an attendant Fool."

"You're talking nonsense."

"Because sense makes none."

"You're being absurd."

"Then leave me with my Bible and I'll make myself at home."

Apparently deciding it was not worth her effort, trying to decipher his attitude, Grace rose to her feet, prepared to leave. "You are a strange boy," she said.

"And as a man, in short, I am afraid."

"Of what?"

"Of everything, of course."

A knock on the large wooden door preceded its opening and Isabelle stepped into the room.

"You have been listening," Grace observed, apparently not surprised.

"Jacob needs him to be fully functioning," she said.

""I'm sure you do as well," said Grace, with a smile.

Isabelle turned to David and addressed him, *sotto voce*: "Are you all right?"

"All right all right all right," he whispered in a confidential response. "Those are pearls that were his eyes."

"Who, David? Do you mean Jacob Hummel?"

"Jacob is dead."

"No, he's here."

"That's very mystical. He must be a wizard."

"He is, David. Listen!" At this point they were talking at a conversational volume. "Listen," she repeated and turned to Grace. Grace turned to a mirror and nodded assent at her own reflection.

Someone behind the mirror switched a switch and a voice recognizably Jacob Hummel's but betraying its simulated origins spoke into the room.

"David," the voice said, "it is good to know you are with us."

"You're dead."

"Literally, yes, I suppose I am. But I'm also alive within cyberspace, quite aware of my present condition. Self-consciousness, David, knowing that I know. That presumably means I'm still *homo sapiens sapiens*, just a little light on the *homus*."

"*Homus* means 'shun'. I'd say you're heavy on *humanis mortali*." David was surprised at the pedantry the old man evoked. "You know," he said. "The whole death and mortality thing."

"Without you, David, I am a cybernetic equation. With you, within you, I can become a cellular organism once again."

David felt rebuked for his insolence and said nothing.

"You must co-operate," Jacob continued. "Otherwise, you will be guilty of murder."

"A threat and a plea rolled into one," David observed.

"As your father lives within you, so you shall live within him," was the cryptic response.

David stared intently at the mirror but could see nothing beyond his own reflection. He was getting used to moral obfuscation arising from tenuous premises. He yearned for the maturity, the depth of experience, to cut through to the essential truths necessary to sort out which way to turn. But he yearned to be a child again, to step away from responsibility and leave the decisions to others. Most of all, he yearned to be himself as he was in that moment. He did not want to be someone else.

"I killed you once," he said to Jacob, still staring at his own image in the mirror. "I can do it again."

"You killed me? I don't know what you mean. Who killed me?" The simulated voice betrayed human dismay.

David looked to Isabelle and Grace. Grace shook her head as if he had committed a social blunder. Isabelle coloured deeply and turned her back to the mirror.

"Don't you know how you died?" David asked.

"It doesn't matter," said the old man.

"That is very magnanimous," said David. "Do you think I could see you?" he asked. He was curious to know what a man would become when he was no longer a man.

"You've seen computers before. I'm just a voice in a box."

"From Kansas, I imagine."

"No, no, David. Dorothy was from Kansas. The wizard was from Nebraska. Don't you remember? Toto tipped over the screen." The voice gave a mechanical chuckle that sounded like an equipment malfunction.

David gazed deep into his own eyes, trying to imagine someone looking back who wasn't himself. "In the meantime, what am I supposed to do until you give up," he said?

"We'll talk about books."

"Why not." This made as much sense as anything else.

"We need to get to know each other, David. It would not do for me to share a mind not amenable to my own, nor you to yours."

"You want to soften me up," David observed. Despite having been abducted, he had trouble taking the voice purporting to be Jacob Hummel as a valid threat.

"Or to toughen you up. It's much the same thing." The voice was disquietingly conciliatory.

"Either may take a good deal of time," David observed.

"Time is the one thing I have in abundance," said the voice. "In cyber-reality, there is sequencing but no such thing as duration. One instant follows another, but their length, whether a millisecond or eons, does not matter at all."

"It sounds a lot like death."

"And you've been assigned to read 'The Book of the Dead'."

"The Bible?"

"It is called that, yes."

"I'm not afraid of death."

"Nor of the Good Book?"

"I only know it in excerpts. I'm looking forward to reading the original," said David.

"The King James version is poetic but hardly the original. Death or the Bible, you know little of either."

"I know that death, the last enemy, is a feeble adversary. You had me locked up with death, old man. I have looked death in the face — in juvenescence a tiger, then toothless, decrepit, and finally putrescent."

"All the more reason for me to return. I miss being human, David. I miss being alive, which is something only you with our common genes can give me."

"Perhaps you should skip a generation or two and inflict yourself on our descendants."

"Which you intend to sire with my beloved Isabelle?" His assumption made David blush with anger. The old man continued. "No, David, I may have all the time in the world, but Isabelle does not. She grows old as we speak."

"So do I," said David, looking at Isabelle, disappointed to find no response. He could fall in love all over again. He didn't think it would be difficult. Clearly, however, Isabelle would need time to adjust. Meanwhile, Jacob Hummel could serve as a bond between them, not a barrier.

"That's enough for now," said the disembodied voice and immediately was swallowed up in its own small echo.

The apartment door swung open, the two women stepped out into the brightly illuminated corridor. The door closed with an abrupt smack and the metallic sound of locks sliding securely into place echoed softly through the room.

"Belle," he whispered in her wake. He did not know how to be in love. It was difficult and confusing.

David looked down on the coffee table. A single book, the King James Bible in a black zippered cover rested on the polished mahogany surface. Unsure whether to formulate a joke or a prayer, he decided to settle for silence. But his mind kept whirling until the maelstrom of his emotions merged with an image that Violet had secretly shared after her last expedition, a vision of the chaos and comfort of lions.

He was soothed by the brute beauty of the image and opened the venerated book at page one, determined to read until anarchy descended on his inexhaustible world.

## Chapter Twelve
## The Sleeping Room

Over the next few days, David read the King James Bible when he wasn't soaring above alien shores in search of a parallel world, looking for Tlön with its transparent lions and towers of blood, or looking for some other world that Borges had never imagined, or perhaps had imagined but kept to himself, a world where David was David Winston but different entirely, safe from the predations of an agèd invader, a young woman desperate to make him the proxy lover for an old man who was dead, or a mother who seemed to hate him as much as she loved him. At times in his mind, he hovered like a kestrel scanning for minnows or mice and sometimes he tumbled into the wind, but then he returned, again and again, to the five-hundred-year-old version of a much older text and was enthralled by the lift of the sacral language when it swept over his wings, baffled by how it could keep him aloft. Beauty not veracity was the key to its value. Believe all or not at all; the windhover soaring on wimpling wing would rise through the firmament or plummet to earth. There is no in-between.

When Jacob Hummel next appeared as a voice in the mirror, coughing softly as a prelude to speaking, David moved close to the glass and engaged the eyes of his reflection. After acknowledging a cordial greeting, he asked for an explanation as to why he should bother to read when his mind was overfilled as it was.

"But you did, didn't you? You read. You did not have to. Can you imagine a reader not reading if there is time to consume and something to catch the attention?" His voice sounded disengaged, as if he were thinking one word at a time. "A cereal box, a tattooed slogan on shrivelled skin, a ketchup-stained label. It is unnatural for a reader not to read. So tell me, how did you like your book? I gather you've finished it."

"It ends with a curse. I had never realized how deeply disturbing it is."

"The Book of Revelation? It is uncompromising drivel, of course, 'the ravings of a maniac', as Thomas Jefferson described it; paralogisms not worth the time to consider. No, I mean the entire book or, to be more precise, the book of books, since it consists of many."

"I was enthralled with the poetry but shocked by its meaning," said David.

"You presume to know what it means? That is interesting. What disturbed you the most?"

"I think the discovery that God is unlikeable."

"Most gods are, they don't need to be liked."

"But there is no room in his scriptural story for an alternative. There is no ambiguity. If he's to be taken literally, as clearly intended, he's a fiendish incompetent megalomaniac. How can a holy book endorse incest and slaughter, infanticide, fratricide, genocide, dragons and giants, the last days, end times, original sin, a God who exterminates all living things, save a few inexplicable favourites, a vicious chauvinist, hateful, spiteful, and jealous God! There is nothing to redeem him."

"Apart from the death of his son?"

"Which was meant to atone for his failed creation in a barbaric exchange."

"Perhaps it was to atone for Him. You are angry, David. At yourself, perhaps?"

"Possibly."

"For having accepted as sacred mere words?"

"For having skimmed the highlights that sustain doctrine and dogma without giving their context a critical thought, for having assumed value and virtue amidst vapid platitudes and trite parables, for accepting belief as the basis of truth. I find the Bible odious in almost every respect, and myself for even momentarily accepting its worth."

"Did you?"

"No, actually not. But I might have."

"Perhaps you should fault the world that venerates words emptied of meaning through myth and poetics. The Evolved New World exploits minds dulled by religious cant to deliver their own brand of thoughtless devotion, but from earliest Romans to American Republicans, the precedents are numberless. Religion is toxic, a moral soporific in small doses, lethal in large. No, my dear David, it is not up to you to feel guilty for the set of the human mind. Your Biblical namesake, you know, was a tyrant, a poet, a king. I doubt you will ever qualify as a tyrant, but you share with poets and kings the weight of the world on your shoulders."

"I hoped I was named after a poor boy who made good in a novel by Dickens."

"Biblical origins are not so mundane," said the old man.

"More poetic."

"Exactly."

"And yet," said David.

"Yet, what?"

"You fault the Bible for myth and poetics."

"'Consistency is the hobgoblin of small minds.'"

"Your memory is not perfect! Emerson said 'a *foolish* consistency'."

"Words are meant to be managed. And your capacity to follow a line of reasoning, I might say, is not perfect either."

"Back to the Bible, then. Poetry and myth are the source of its power. It is written, presented, *as if* it were true. It is not offered as a grand metaphor; it is what it is."

"Ah yes, and 'I am that I am'," said the old man's voice with sepulchral certainty.

"That's how God identifies himself to Moses, I know, but he also conceals himself in a burning bush. And each of those presentations is given as a literal fact. The enigmatic words and the flamboyant trope, they are equally God."

"What are you saying, David?"

"Only that scriptures must be read literally, to have any meaning at all. If in the beginning was the word, as John in his Gospel proclaimed, and the word was God, then the words must be true. It could not be otherwise. But if a single word is false, it has to be fiction."

"And if it is fiction?" demanded Jacob's voice.

"Then an entire religion is an abyss into which hundreds of millions have cast their lives in blind hope for redemption from the guilt of self-consciousness and the sure knowledge of death."

"You exhaust me, David. You are quoting a source I don't recognize."

"Maybe. I don't know."

"I'll leave you for a while. We'll talk again soon. You have another book, I believe."

"*Through the Looking Glass.*"

"Good, good. And its prequel, both in one volume. Be wary of subliminal messages."

David thought he detected laughter in the depths of the mirror, but his eyes still glistened from his anger over a miscreant God, the power of words, and an insatiably credulous species. His mouth remained set in defiance as he edged away, stricken with the realization that to all intents and purposes he had been talking to himself.

Then he glanced at the cover illustration of Alice and was captivated by Tenniel's drawing. He already knew Alice from his time in hell. He had followed her adventures over Isabelle's shoulder. If anything could lift him from the darkness of scripture it was the innocence of unrestrained wit. But he hesitated before picking up the book. There was much to consider.

What had Jacob Hummel accomplished in their previous conversation? It seemed absurd to think the old man simply wanted him to be a better reader. Was it an opportunity to merge minds, however briefly, in a discussion of texts? Did he really hate the Bible? Did he really hold God in contempt as a whirling beast born out of the darkest recesses in the human mind?

He shook his head, scattering his thoughts, and reached for the curious volume by the Oxford don who called himself Lewis Carroll, for want of a better disguise, and he began to read. Quickly, he lost himself in the sensical nonsense of a wonderland world contrived as deviously as Tlön or Laputa, Oz or Eden. By the time he had progressed half-way through the second book he wished someone would show up for him to discuss what he was reading. He would have preferred Charles Lutwidge Dodgson, as Lewis Carroll was known in life, but Jacob Hummel would suffice. He was bewildered by the volatility of words and wished desperately to share his uncertainty. He would have preferred Gertrude Stein or Wittgenstein, both of whom understood that a word is a word, or Shakespeare, or any of a number of poets from Donne to Dickinson who refused to believe that that was the case.

And just as he was beginning to think he would never again have a real conversation, this as punishment for keeping his mind to himself and not opening it to an intruder, a voice proclaimed its presence from the mirror.

"Have you finished with Alice?" Jacob asked, kindly.

"No," said David. "I don't see how anyone could finish with Alice."

"You may be right or, possibly, wrong."

"Inside my head she seems infinite. Yet the pictures and words make her very particular."

"Oh, she is most particular. And frumptious when sloeful, I think you'd agree?"

"That's quite Tweedledum to say so," said David, pleased with himself.

"Which seldom I do! When I use a word, it means whatever I choose it to mean, neither more nor less." The voice in the mirror paused. "Words do have a temper, though, some of them do, particularly verbs."

"Adjectives are more amenable," said David. He couldn't remember the exact quotation, although he could picture a number of adjectives on a number of pages.

"David, you have been on your own too long."

"I have been with Alice."

"Which is much the same thing."

"Have you ever noticed how sexy she is?" said David. "Not the words but the drawings."

"Oh, I don't think so."

"Look again."

"Well, we know Dodgson was judged rather harshly for his inordinate attachment to Alice Liddell, mostly by latent paedophiles, I imagine, and there are incriminating readings of the books, themselves, written by prurient scholars who have turned Freud into a bludgeon of sorts. But really, Sir John Tenniel's illustrations project an innocence that would seem to absolve the author and his works of the most abhorrent suspicions. It is universally acknowledged, they are endearing."

For once, David felt his youth gave him an advantaged perspective. "Have you ever seen those heart-warming Victorian paintings of naked children warming themselves by the fire or cavorting like nymphs in fields of flowers?"

"Have you?" said the old man in surprise. "Covert prurience, nothing more."

"Look closely at Alice," said David. "The little-girl body in her frilly dress has the worldly face of a jaded adolescent. Innocence and experience in a singular package, just look. You read the words in light of the images and see the images in light of the words. The little virgin sprawled ingenuously about the pages, the worldly young woman gazing out through a mask of constraint — a perfect correlative for wordplay that refuses to mean as it could in the mind of a girl who means far more than she should."

They didn't talk much more. The old man seemed tired. His voice was strained around the edges sufficiently to remind David of his advanced age. After Jacob switched off, David continued to stare at his own reflection in the mirror. He was intrigued by how Jacob Hummel's voice rose out of his own image as if the words originated inside his head. He would gladly have continued their conversation.

That evening he finished *Through the Looking Glass*. There was no one around to discuss it with. He was lonely. He missed Jacob's company. He slept fitfully. In the morning there was a new book on his bedside table, a play by Shakespeare. He knew the bard's entire canon but had not actually read a full play or seen a performance. In the Evolved New World, Shakespeare, like the Bible, was a source of historical facts. Only the uneducated would not know about them, only subversives would actually read them. David was quite able to quote both out of context, where their words could effectively be used to mean just what he wanted, no more and no less.

He worked his way through *Titus Andronicus*, which he knew was a minor play. He often took breaks to wonder when Jacob Hummel would arrive or where Grace and Isabelle, going their separate ways, had got to. After an excellent dinner, when the silent waiter had taken away his dishes, he framed himself in the mirror and almost immediately Jacob began to talk.

"It's good to see you, David." Jacob's voice still sounded tired.

"And you too," said David.

"But of course, neither of us can, not actually."

"Can't you see me?" David asked, addressing his reflection with surprise.

"I have the transient capacity to process sensory stimuli into coherent recognizable patterns. I am not sentient at the present moment. I cannot seem to make new memories — although my recollection from before I was downloaded is quite impeccable."

"But you hear me now!"

"It is a cybernetic illusion, I assure you. What have you been reading? Shakespeare, I believe. What did you think of him?"

"Him? He's great. *Titus Andronicus*? A fraud. It's presented as one of his earliest plays but I doubt if he ever sat through a single performance, unless in derision or drunk. He may have acted in it; he didn't write it."

"My, David, that is a strong critical opinion."

"The play is an extravaganza of blood and gore. It has no depth; it's a jumble of words, neither a farcical tragedy nor a tragical farce; it is bombastic, splenetic, and cruel; dubiously amusing, abysmally empty. There is no poetry, no Shakespeare in it at all."

"Good, good," said the old man. "We must talk more about books."

"That seems to be the basis of our relationship. That's what we do."

"Yes, we must."

David was concerned. There seemed to be a slight syntactical disconnect between them. "Do you remember talking about Alice?" he asked.

"In Wonderland? I'd like to. I'm very fond of Alice."

"What about God and the Bible."

"I know something about both. You must read the Pentateuch, the first two of the five, for certain, and the 'Gospel of John'. The rest is superfluous. The Book of Revelation is bilious junk."

"Jacob, when was the last time we talked?"

"I don't remember, exactly. It was in the library, I believe."

"We're in the library now."

"Are we? Ah, well, it is impossible to tell, isn't it?"

"No, not really."

"I gather I've been in this room for some time," said Jacob.

"I can't see what room you're in," David responded.

"Well, no, neither can I. I remember coming into a chamber filled with computer paraphernalia. I seem to have misplaced Immanuel somewhere. You were not on the other side of the mirror, then. Now you are, so time has passed."

"You're in a computer?"

"Well, yes and no. I'm in a box, a cage, a cloud, you might say. I'm in cyberspace. I can summon myself into being at will."

"To inhabit the disembodied consciousness of Jacob Hummel as he was before he died."

"When he was downloaded, yes. And no, I do not inhabit his mind. I *am* his mind, I am myself. I am what I am."

"We've been through this before. You are who you were. But that's all you are, who you *were*."

"You make it sound rather dreary and sordid. You are quite the necromancer, chatting even though you think I am dead."

"That doesn't make you alive, just interactive. Don't you remember dying?"

"Not actually."

"Do you remember who killed you?"

"Of course not. After death you remember nothing."

"You told me that, wherever you are, there isn't duration."

"Time in my world has no dimension at all. The present is a transient, theoretic; an arbitrary point on an endless line."

"But there is a line. The order in which things occur, that's vitally important."

"Did I tell you that?"

"You did."

"Believing in something is what makes it true. That is the basis of religion, you know."

"Something a few days ago you held in contempt," said David.

"Did I? Well, I'm sure religion will get on, whether I am a believer or not."

"Let me try to explain what's happening to you, Jacob. It is a matter of sequencing. You are presently locked in a box to which, by genetic accident and clever design, I have the keys. And you will never be older than you were when you downloaded your mind."

"I didn't erase, I duplicated."

"But the original is gone. The past is ephemeral if there is no present to give it perspective."

"David, as Descartes declared, *cogito ergo sum*. I think, therefore I am."

"A brain in a jar, in a box, in the ether; dissociated from reality since the day it was set on the shelf."

"Then you see how important you are!"

"Unless I escape again."

"Did you ever try to escape?"

"From the hospital."

"I helped you, didn't I?"

"I also escaped from this place to The Cloisters. Grace helped me."

"You liked it there too much. I sent the girl after you and you ended up in a chamber of hell."

"The girl. Her name is Isabelle. Yes, you sent her and we escaped from there, too."

"I was very fond of her. Where is she now?"

"I thought you would know."

"I haven't encountered her in quite some time."

"Nor Grace?"

"No, not Grace either. Would you have them drop by?"

"That's up to you, Jacob, not me. You saw them a few days ago."

"No, you are mistaken."

"And in the following days we talked about God, we talked about Lewis Carroll. I showed you the pictures of Alice, I held them up to the mirror."

"I think I will retire now. Don't go away. I'm sure I'll be back."

David grimaced at himself in the mirror. The fiercely controlling old man had turned into a haunted ghost. Aristotle's *hubris* and *hamartia*, blinding pride and a fatal flaw, these were the primary attributes of Jacob Hummel and his project for conditional immortality. Yet David found nothing tragic about him. Locked into the receding past as he was, Jacob had become a figure of pathos. David even allowed to himself that he had grown fond of his diminished abductor, a response Aristotle would have scorned.

The next morning, in a particularly desultory manner, David followed his routine of washing, dressing, eating, and settling in with the latest book left for him while he slept. Given his thinking of the previous night about classical tragedy, he was unnerved to find himself fingering a copy of Aristotle's *Poetics*. Did the old man know his mind so well? Had the invasion already begun? He recognized the Stockholm syndrome was taking effect as if in a stranger. It wasn't sympathy for his captor so much as complacency with his condition that seemed to be taking over. David had no desire to fight the disembodied voice of an image in the mirror. He began to formulate points in a conversation, preparing for their next encounter.

\*\*\*

After the girl is murdered and her avenging mother suffocates with her new lover beneath the shifting earth, her infant children, a boy and a girl, are carried away by their adoptive families in a great trek across warmer plains that stretch to a vast river flowing between the rising and setting sun. As the seasons progress, their party migrates to a great saline sea where they settle on the estuary. By the end of their arduous journey, the children are approaching maturity. The boy has learned to be an excellent hunter and is welcome company in any shelter; but the girl, while strong and exceptionally capable, is not at all social. She keeps to herself as much as possible, sharing in food, shelter, and work, but spending a lot of time on her own, on solitary expeditions, foraging for sustenance and sleeping under the stars or in shallow caves carved by the elements into the soft stone of the area.

On a midsummer day when she is far from home, exploring the steep hills sloping away from the sea, she sights a cave lion slinking through the underbrush. At first, she thinks it is a furtive shadow, but when she sees an eye flashing through the leaves her fears are confirmed. The lion is tracking her on a parallel course, unfamiliar with the scent and behaviour of this strange nimble animal with flapping skin. Even with its massive size and jaws that can seize a deer in mid-leap and break its neck on the run, the lion is wary, by instinct anticipating the unexpected. In the interval provided by this defensive anomaly the girl has time to think, which is the primary defence of her species.

She can't see the ruff around his neck but she knows he's a male. Female lions pursue their quarry in groups, usually in the open, while males are solitary hunters and use the layout of natural terrain to their advantage. She turns his strategy against him by clambering higher up the slope into tangled scrub, forcing him to drop back and follow the course she sets for them both. When she is confronted by a sheer bluff, she searches out a small plateau at its base between two large outcroppings of rock. The lion can only approach from one direction and at the same elevation.

She moves with deliberate composure and gathers an armful of twigs and sticks. When she reaches the back of her plateau, she removes a case made of perforated clam shells that is hanging from her neck and blows across the tinder inside until it bursts into fire. She touches the flame to a cluster of dry twigs and smudges the living coal inside the shells before restoring her ancestral pendant to its place as an ornament.

Once her fire is blazing, she takes advantage of the temporary respite from danger to haul a pole from the edge of her safe zone back to the fire. The pole is dead pine, the wood is dry but firm, most of the branches are broken away. It is large enough she can only lift one end but light enough she can wield it quite easily when the lower end is braced against the earth. She repeatedly sears the tip, burning and scraping until she smooths the charred wood to a point.

She roasts and devours the hind quarters of a rabbit she had snared the previous day and carried in a sling over her shoulder. She has no water. She needs to force the issue with her predator before thirst makes her foolish. She extinguishes the protective fire and drags the pole forward in front of the smouldering coals, planting the blunt end with a few roots still showing against a boulder, piling stones to secure it in place. She pivots the charred end upwards and slides herself under it until the point is poised well above shoulder height. She temporarily fixes the pole in place with a brace of sticks lashed with sinew. The landscape will force the lion to attack within a projected wedge of open terrain, but when it happens, she will have to bear the weight of the pole in order to aim the point with lethal precision.

The surface of her fire grows cold, the vermillion embers crumble, gall themselves black. There is not even a wisp of smoke to indicate where the few remaining coals cling to their warmth. She waits through sunset. The dark of a moonless night closes around her, then opens to a skyful of stars. She listens. She can hear the air breathing, or is it her own breath or the restless breathing of the lion? She can hear his heartbeat, it seems to be inside her chest. She is desperately thirsty, she wants to sleep. She can hear the lion sleeping, its rough breath purring in dream. She smiles. There is a bond between them. She dozes, sitting upright. She awakens abruptly, she senses movement. The stars are washed out of the sky by the first hint of dawn. She moves under the pole next to the brace.

When he comes, he comes swiftly. The only sound is the muffled thud of the brace falling away as she raises the weight of the pole on her shoulder. She peers into the blur of darkness as the lion leaps high through pale air at the furious centre of a blood-curdling roar. She shifts her weapon as the arc of his flight expands, his massive form turns to a whirl of dark destructive energy. She lurches back and a few degrees to the side. There is a piercing scream — the lion, the girl; agony, terror. The lion, caught in mid-air, impaled through the gut, hovers above her, in a maelstrom of rage and despair, and then lion and pole, both irreversibly broken, crash down, pinning the girl under a mound of throbbing flesh, whimpering, blood, charred wood.

He twitches and shudders in violent death throes. The girl cannot tell where the heaving carcass ends and her own body begins. She is drenched with warm blood. The lion's head is twisted, his face is close to hers, she can see herself in his eyes, she can feel his hot ragged breath. She pushes to free herself, the lion cries out. She lies still and waits. His breath washes over her. He moans, she weeps. His breath smooths out. Then he is dead. She flexes and fidgets and worms her way from under his body. She drinks blood from his wound, lifting it to her trembling mouth in cupped hands.

She lights another fire. It is not necessary, the sun has risen, but it gives her comfort. Other mammalian carnivores, with the exception of the unscrupulous wolverine, will recognize the feline scent of the mighty leviathan and scatter, perhaps catching a scent of death as they turn away. But wolverines are opportunistic and tend to binge, storing fats to cope with inevitable privation. They are scavengers and the smell of the lion's spilled guts will attract, although the scent of the lion itself may keep them wary, especially when reinforced by the smell of his human companion who reeks of death.

The girl sleeps on the open ground but is awakened by the screeching of carrion birds and the buzzing of flies. She stands and gazes at the animal she has killed. Even sprawled on the ground, he rises half way up the height of her body. She takes an obsidian blade from her sling-bag and after the difficult initial cut, she flenses the lion with meticulous flourishes, slicing deftly under the skin and peeling it back, proceeding solemnly, showing deference to the great beast even in death. She cuts carefully around the head and pulls the skin back, removing residual flesh with a scraper made from a cracked human tibia.

No one in her community has killed a cave lion before, although a decade ago a woman had been carried off and devoured in front of her adopted daughter. The incident was never acknowledged. That was the best way to honour such passing. The wilderness consumed as an expression of power, allowing a form of transcendence.

Her daughter was nearly five at the time, nearly old enough to fend for herself. The entire community watched out for her, making sure she did not starve and had sufficient clothes to survive the bitter cold that descends further upon them each winter, but no one knew how to salve her wounded psyche, assuage her bitterest fears. The lion became the girl's secret talisman for the incomprehensible fury with which it merged with her foster mother.

When she was ten, she carved the crude shape of a lion from stone, small enough to nestle in the palm of her hand. The carving showed the fearful lineaments of a voracious animal while the edges were softened by what seemed like a flurry of flames, transformed in the girl's memory from the screams and blood spewing out of her mother's body. She worked a hole through the stone and wore it as an amulet. Abandoned by the woman she knew as her mother, she walked alone under the grace of the lion.

When the girl who is now fifteen and has killed the beast awakens in late afternoon, she chases away the carrion birds and rolls the skinned carcass into a depression in the earth. She digs a loose canine tooth from the skull, surmising the lion must have been quite old, perhaps losing a little of the cunning that might have given it the advantage. She looks to its claws that are fully extended in death. Lions walk on all sixteen toes. With no concept of numbers, she recognizes symmetry and admires his feet, even with the fur stripped back to the pasterns. He must have been magnificent in his prime. His claws are smoothly curved and razor sharp, but his toes are calloused and worn. She decides there is more honour to her prey if she leaves his claws than to take one. She rolls a sheet of congealing blood onto a smooth piece of stone, before piling rocks on his remains in a huge mound.

She sits by her fire and pokes a hole through the root of the canine tooth and taking a cord of leather from around her neck she adds the tooth to her clam shell casing and the pendant that could be a lion amid flames that she had fashioned from stone when she was ten years old.

She picks up the shaggy head which she has removed from the skull. It has been baking in the sun but it reeks when she holds it high in the air. A zephyr sweeps in from the distant sea and displaces the smell with memories of the lion's warm breath washing over her while he died. She smiles. The skin of a lion contains its invisible essence and she is determined to keep it to make robes, and to keep the skin of his head to stuff with dry grasses.

She spends the night close to the fire working on the skin, singeing the remaining tendrils of flesh and scraping its inner side smooth and pliable. When the sun appears, she bundles her skins and moves away from the direction of its rising. She walks for days, chewing the lion's congealed blood, drinking water from puddles and rivulets. She knows there is a lone wolverine following her, desperate to attack, but a wolverine is the most cunning of animals and will keep its distance until certain of its own safety. It will follow her until she shows a moment of weakness and then it will strike. She wears the lion skin over her shoulders; it drags on the ground behind her. The head-fur is rolled up and strapped with her sling to her side. She is confident the wolverine will not attack so long as she keeps moving. It has been a good summer, meat has been plentiful, he will not be desperate. When she finally approaches the river, she knows he has slunk away to find a quarry not protected by the scent of a lion.

Swarms of flies have been attracted by the animal skin that has not been fully worked into soft leather and by her own sweat-streaked skin beneath it. After she fords a branch of the river onto the estuary, the flies become worse. She stops by a slough to smear mud on her body, but still the insects attack, so she drapes the skin over her shoulders again and draws the lion head over her own, with twigs inserted sideways to give it shape and allow her to breathe. She continues walking, exhausted, like a beast slouching towards home, hardly able to see through the eyes of the lion, guided by the feel of landscape passing beneath her feet more familiar the closer she gets to the end of her journey.

A cry rings out that a lion approaches. She is too depleted to wriggle out from under the skins. A band of boys and young hunters who have been grooming themselves in the shade recognize that the lion is strangely injured and offers no threat. They rush at her with spears poised, but she seems so feeble they leap over her and on top of her, working themselves into a frenzy, and they kick at her with bared feet and they scream with excitement when she groans, which confirms the beast is alive, giving proof of their courage.

The entire community is watching, uncertain what the death of this strange slouching creature will mean. After a powerful blow from one of the boys, a hand emerges from under the lion and flails at the air, followed by a mud- and blood-soaked human head with blazing eyes. There is a collective gasp. The lion has swallowed a human whole and is releasing her. The oldest man and woman rush to the girl and draw her free and she is born again into the world. A young man her same age comes forward and lifts her in his arms and carries her to a shelter he shares with his adoptive parents.

No one seems to recognize the girl. It is as if she has been transformed, born into adult being from the womb of a male lion. The girl she had been seems forgotten. The young man cleans her and cares for her and after a few days he carries her to a new shelter he has built from driftwood and auroch hides and lays her on a bed made of the lion fur which he has worked to chamois softness. After a few more days she awakens, fresh and powerful, and gazes at the lion's head which he has filled with grasses and shaped like a living lion, except for the gaping eyes, and hung on a supporting pole. She reaches for the necklace and grasps the small case of perforated clam shells. It is cold. The tiny fire inside has burned through the tinder. She touches the canine tooth of the lion, then holds the flaming lion amulet in her palm and squeezes, feeling its power, and with her other hand she takes the young man's hand and squeezes. She smiles. There is a bond between them.

# Chapter Thirteen
## Notes in Time

Violet held a flute carved from woolly mammoth ivory across the palm of her hand, wondering how music had shaped human minds. In the distant past, where she was most at home, patterns of sound were transient. Long after they were formed into words, the patterns were eventually encoded in print; literature and history were born. Patterns of rhythm and echoing harmonies, however, remained locked in the moments of their performance. Song died on the lips of the singer, notes faded as they drifted from shaken strings towards stillness. The body did not create the dance, it became the dance that music created and stopped when the music ceased. Music was cerebral because it existed only in human response to its genius. Unlike language encoded in libraries or images embedded in paint or in stone, music lasted only in memory or in mathematical abstraction on a chart or a score for others to follow. But then came sound recordings and in a transformation as radical as Gutenberg's press, almost every moment of human consciousness was now accompanied by music. Violet stopped thinking. Her fingers curled around the ancient flute carving; the ivory was still warm.

\*\*\*

The young man and his lion-bride pack up their skins and tools after their first child is born and turn away from the primal community where they are feared and revered and walk to the left of the rising sun until they have climbed rolling hills, past where the lion is buried, to a height where on a clear day the horizon shimmers from the distant sea. They settle into a shallow cave with a cleft near the back that draws smoke up through the rocks overhead and with a small stream tumbling through the rocks close by. Together, they pile boulders into a wall across most of the front and drop auroch skins from the upper edge, making a nearly impenetrable barrier against inclement weather but allowing the balmy zephyrs sweeping in from the far-off sea to embrace them when the weather is good. They have seen a few humans on their journey, a single Neanderthal hunter, and a great deal of game, as well as gardens of berries and grains, fruits and nuts, all within easy reach.

In the evenings they sit by their fire inside the cave or outside in midsummer and share sounds with their baby, their child, their children. She uses words but he is awkward with language so he makes music, sometimes from his mouth, sometimes with sticks and bones, and then with fledgling flutes.

Imagine this primordial family in front of their home, resting on skins, the older children having dragged the cave lion's head out from its niche, playing ferocious giggling games. The woman is sewing hides into warm clothes in anticipation of winter which is still a long way off. The man has had a good hunt, bringing back the haunch of a deer — he left the rest for wolverines or the humans who he knew watched from the shadows. He sits partially in the smoke to ward off insects. He takes up a splinter of ivory the length of a child's forearm and begins working it with a shard of obsidian. The ivory is from a wounded woolly mammoth his birthmother and her mother had put out of its misery. He does not know this, only that it has been the one possession that he has always had. The lion-woman carries in her folded sling a small piece of ivory from the same tusk as her own ancestral inheritance. On a shelf in the rock near at hand are earlier versions of the man's work, a polished tube he had carved from the femur of a young cave bear and a length of bone from a mute swan wing, both with holes along one side.

After he has finished hollowing and polishing the ivory, he takes up the other tubes, one at a time, and plays them as flutes, testing the sounds made when he moves his fingers over and away from the holes. Then he grinds two punctures into the ivory and tests the sound. He takes up the other flutes again and plays. He is searching for a true correlation of the distance between holes and the quality of sound. He grinds out a third hole, then a fourth and a fifth, all within finger reach but at variant spaces from each other. Working on into the night, with only the fire tended by the woman to fend off the darkness, he achieves a diatonic scale with the eighth hole. As dawn obscures the night sky with first light, with the children asleep and the lion-woman at his side, he polishes the ivory, reaming out the detritus inside and smoothing the holes. Then he puts the flute to his lips and plays.

His music sweeps down through the valley. Their children rise from their sleep and fall silently into place at his side. The older ones hum. The woman smiles and smiles. Other humans far away, even the lone Neanderthal hunter, who will never see his own family again, are caught up in the music's unearthly embrace. And east of Eden they have made a new world and settled for two thousand generations to come.

***

After several days dipping into an anthology of quotations, David was disconcerted to find he enjoyed perusing discontinuous word clusters swarming with indeterminate meaning. Taken out of context, with only the names of their authors to identify them, they seemed curiously reduced to amusing baubles. He took pleasure in their allusive emptiness.

In his next conversation with Jacob, the old man recognized every quotation David offered, yet he could not expound or expand on its origin. It seemed he had a selectively eidetic memory, recalling the most obscure things in the most precise way. The library in its infinite complexity was the architectural equivalent of his apparently limitless brain, and like a library with books that no one is permitted to read, his mind had become a prison of sorts. Far from holding infinite worlds on offer, it has locked them away.

"I enjoy talking about quotations," Jacob said.

"It's like watching tropical fish in an aquarium," said David. "There's something tragic in watching how beautifully they move in their confined little world."

"Have you ever seen an aquarium, David?"

"I can imagine the sadness."

"But words in quotations, they're inside you as you read them. They're not something you see from outside."

"Possibly," said David. "Perhaps it's the opposite. We're inside the words and they threaten to drown us."

"Well argued, young man, although our aquarium metaphor has collapsed. We live inside borrowed words. Quotations and aphorisms and slogans, yes. But all words are borrowed. We don't make them up unless we're creating sheer nonsense like Edward Lear and his runcible spoons or Lewis Carroll with his jabberwockery snarks. Look, what we're really talking about, the subtext of our conversation, is the dissociated sensibility. That's what T.S. Eliot called the bifurcation of thought and feeling, that's what happens with words."

"Sometimes, Jacob, you make me realize how much I miss being fifteen."

"Ah, but you are."

"Not with you surging inside my head. Let's start with 'sensibility'. I figure that 'bifurcation' means a division or split, although I don't know why you don't just say that."

"Dividing, splitting, bifurcating, each has an edge of its own, like knives in a drawer. As for sensibility, it is a faculty unique to our species, or was. It's been with us since the dawn of time — the dawn of human self-consciousness, to be more precise. It is our capacity to experience complex aesthetic stimuli emotionally and intellectually at the same time. Consider music. You do not *think* your way through Brahms or the Beatles, not without destroying their works. Nor do you merely *feel* them like a reed in the wind. Sensibility describes your capacity to *experience* their music, and of course sensibility can be refined through critical learning and further experience. But you're making me sound like a pedant. That's not something anyone wants to become."

"Not surgically, at least."

"Then I shall cease to lecture."

"No, I'd like to hear more. When does Eliot say thought and feeling became separated?"

"Never. It is our ability to respond to them and to express them at the same time that we've lost. He suggests the loss began quite abruptly when the metaphysical poets were in vogue. In the time of Shakespeare, poets like John Donne, especially John Donne, wrote thoughts as experience. When he said in a sermon, 'The bell tolls for thee', his congregation did not have to think, now what does that mean? It simply meant what it said. When Macbeth declares, 'Out, out, brief candle! Life's but a walking shadow', the death of his wife and the wretchedness of our mortal condition merge. Not even the groundlings at the Globe could avoid feeling this thought. They were not brighter than the average university sophomore of today. However, for them the words simply meant what they said, they did not have to be analyzed, their impact came from within."

"And then it all changed? The printing press, universal literacy, words ceased to be things."

There was a long silence. David knew he was on the right track, quite excited but a little confused. This had started with his query about feeling like he was living inside other people's words. He wasn't sure he followed the sequencing of their conversation but he was thrilled to engage Jacob Hummel as if he were a living presence in the room. Finally, the old man drew himself out of his reverie and continued.

"There was a sea change, yes. By the eighteenth century everyone in the British middle class read books. (We're talking about the English language so we'll focus on Britain.) The abstraction of language was epidemic. Consider Pope, consider Swift; brilliant thoughts, dazzling words, but little to feel beyond amusement or outrage. The reader thinks about feelings, about Arabella's wrath, about Gulliver's confusion, but does not feel what they think. Even in Swift's infamous 'A Modest Proposal', the eating of babies arouses revulsion, but the idea meant to be grasped has less to do with cannibalism than social policies and political conventions. You might say the ideas expressed are supra-textual. They come about through self-conscious reader response. Critical analysis, you might say."

His voice seemed to dwindle, then he went on. "In retaliation, romantics like Wordsworth and Keats, men of great sensibility and limited thought, gave primacy to passion, and, and," he lapsed into silence.

"Sometimes we just read," said David. He found himself smiling at the pleasure he took in their esoteric conversation. He wondered if the old man in the mirror noticed his smile.

"And it becomes harder and harder to distinguish the good from the bad," said Jacob. "Readers in The Cloisters don't even try. In some ways, genre writing is closer to the metaphysicals than most literary writing. A good mystery or spy thriller, a good bit of verse like 'The Cremation of Sam McGee' or 'The Highwayman' or most of Longfellow, a lot of Tennyson or Kipling, of course, simply are what they are. You *experience* them. There is something primal about Agatha Christie's yarns, although her prose is terrible. Poe's 'The Raven', Joni Mitchell's lyrics, different as they are, are exhilarating, but both show contrived feelings and sketchy intelligence, at best."

"So, like Marshall McLuhan said, print changed everything."

"The mechanical press — but the impact of printing began long before Gutenberg. Reading, after all, began thousands of years ago. Literacy changed our minds incrementally. The bifurcation of sensibility began with language itself. Reading exacerbated the division. There once was a time when words were things. They meant what they said. I understand certain aboriginal communities into the present era cannot lie, their languages will not permit it. That doesn't mean the people are inherently honest, any more than the rest of us. It doesn't mean they avoid symbols and metaphors. It means the word, the symbol, the metaphor, they're literally truth. They are facts, and that is all that is the case, as Ludwig Wittgenstein said."

"Meaning what?" said David. "Have you actually read Wittgenstein?"

"Have you?"

"In snippets," said David.

"Quotations. Fish in the aquarium."

"I understand him a little."

"One cannot understand Wittgenstein a little. I'm not sure one can understand Wittgenstein at all. But let us consider, a word has no meaning itself, it has only the potential for meaning. It becomes fact at the intersection of grammatical deployment and semiotic invocation (think of these as horizontal and vertical axes, at whose intersection the word is impaled, still squirming). As Samuel Beckett might have said, to speak of nothing is something. What cannot be put into words cannot exist."

"Cannot or does not?"

"A good question, David. The dissociation of sensibility began with the first words ever exchanged. A drawing on a cave invoked the feelings of being in an animal's presence. Let's say there is an auroch like the ones your mother discovered in France. Viewers look at the beast on the wall and share an experience, even if there are thousands of years between them. But a word, the word 'auroch', that's different. *Auroch* names a primeval bovine of one sort or another and the word may be passed from person to person. They do not originate the word. They *borrow* it. It evokes an actual beast only through learning, through context. The word is no longer the thing. Do you want me to continue? You don't find this tedious?"

"Some of the best stuff is."

"How very wise you, sometimes, can be, David. Well, it took eons for the drift of feeling away from thought, with words and images hovering between. Think of the multitude of human-hand silhouettes bursting from the stone walls of caves in Argentina's *Cueva de las Manos*. They are perhaps ten thousand years old. Have you seen them?"

"In pictures?"

"In pictures, of course. And do you remember how much emotion they express, although the thoughts that inform them remain irretrievably obscure?"

"I saw all those hands, some laid over each other, as a celebration of human self-consciousness. There is a joy in their tumultuous multiplicity that sets the stone trembling."

"Or perhaps it trembles in terror as souls of the damned, imprisoned inside the stone, clamour to break out. They are damned by their emerging self-awareness, they struggle with language, and against it, to gain dominion over the earth that engulfs them. They are reaching for the light, to stand over the stone, the earth, and compel it to yield."

David said nothing. Both extremes seemed equally plausible but both could not possibly be true. Jubilation and desperation. Perhaps that is the human condition, he thought, to know both, simultaneously.

The old man had moved on, allowing insights to gather in erratic progression. "You see, David, language, at first, was a tool for survival," he said. "With the leisure provided by agriculture and technology, feelings and thoughts gradually became two separate functions of what Julian Jaynes misleadingly calls 'the bicameral mind'. With writing, introduced in Mesopotamia, the split was complete. Incidentally, the Mesopotamians wrote down the story of a great flood a thousand years before Noah. *Gilgamesh* preceded the *Torah*. And here we are, now. With bifurcated sensibilities."

"But the metaphysical poets, they resisted?"

"A few always have, before them and since. Consider Lucretius. Consider Dante, particularly the *Inferno*. There have been a number of gifted metaphysicians since Donne and Marvell, including Hazlitt, the essayist, Emily Dickinson, Eliot himself, and the man he called *il miglior factor*, the superior maker, Mr Ezra Pound. These are people who struggled to merge thought with feeling in their words and conceits. Winston Churchill was another; a passionate intellectual if there ever was one. Such writers are rare, of course. Unless you and I can be the exception, they are all in the past."

"As of when?" David asked.

"What took the printing press five hundred years to accomplish has taken only decades in the age of computers. We have become comfortable living inside other people's words, so much so that the environment has become us! However, it is no longer stone."

"The computer environment?"

"We no longer find ourselves within a few good books, as we did in a lifetime of reading. We feel with our hearts and think with our brains, forgetting they're both metaphors for the *mind*. We live in cyberspace among the electronic detritus of civilizations that preceded us. *We neither think nor feel, we perceive.* In a frightening way, we have come full circle from the age of the cave artists. But there are gods now who control the world of our transformation. The Company, the Company, ah yes, yes, the Company."

"Are you all right, Jacob?"

"No. Never. Never, never, never, never. Perhaps I'm worn out. It is exhausting to be here when I'm not."

A slight change of the pressure in the room marked his departure.

David settled in for the night. He thought about music and drifted towards sleep amidst the strains of John Lennon's posthumous 'Imagine'. The last thing in his mind were the musician's own words, *God is how we measure our pain.* Or did those words shape the world his mind was in?

The next evening when the old man appeared David made a request.

"I'd like to read books of my own choice. Do you think that would be possible?"

"If we can agree on what your choice would be."

"Then it wouldn't be my choice but ours."

"Which might be for the best."

Jacob had the knack of making David feel comfortable as the solitary occupant of the room. He also had the knack of slipping words like a noose around sentences and pulling them in unexpected directions.

"Jacob, yesterday you mentioned Ezra Pound."

"Did I? He was a genius in his youth but deeply troubled when he got older. A fascist and a lunatic. The poem in English that most closely approaches perfection is his two-liner, three if you count the title which, of course, you must. Listen. In a Station of the Metro:

> The apparition of these faces in the crowd;
> Petals on a wet black bough.

"Utterly simple, but so complex it wraps Dante's *Divine Comedy* in its strands; utterly primal, a triumph of despair. Thoughts and feelings are inseparable, the words are what they describe. Journey into the underworld, stations of the cross, the constancy of change, ghosts, ephemerality — you can parse it and analyze it, but in the end, the poem stands utterly on its own, an authentic aesthetic experience."

"So why don't you describe it as perfect instead of *approaching* perfection?"

"Zeno's paradox. You may approach perfection but you can never reach it."

"Zeno's paradox?"

"There are actually a number of them. Nine, to be precise. The most profound and fundamental concerns Achilles in a race with a tortoise."

"Why Achilles?"

"Indeed. Why a tortoise? Never mind, Achilles gives the tortoise a head start. Each time Achilles reaches where the tortoise started, the tortoise has moved on. Ergo, he can never be caught."

"Achilles can simply step over him."

"Her. The tortoise is female. And no, logically Achilles cannot do that. In every phase of the race he must first reach where the tortoise was — but each of those times the tortoise, of course, has moved on."

"You are describing the limitations of mathematics and logic in an irrational world," said David. "Consider Pound's poem and the notion of perfection in reverse. The poem is perfect; you may now define perfection based on the poem."

"That is an analogy, not a definition. Listen, David, another of Zeno's paradoxes describes Homer having to walk the length of the garden in half increments. He walks half way, then half of the remaining distance, then half of that and half of that, *ad infinitum*. He will never reach the far side. That's known as the *dichotomy paradox*."

"Why not the Homeric paradox? Or an Achilles variant? Or Zeno's other paradox?"

"Why not Plato's or Aristotle's? They both played with Zeno's propositions. Do you know, Zeno also proved motion is an impossible illusion? An arrow in flight in any instant of time is motionless. If it is motionless in every instant and time is a sequence of instants, the arrow cannot be said to move. Think of watching an old-fashioned film being run through a projector: each image is static, yet rolled before the lens in a stuttering sequence the eye puts them together and the image appears to move."

"The film moves through the projector," said David.

"But each image is static. Pixels display movement in much the same way, through static arrangements in a sequence so rapid perception displaces reality."

"A paradox Zeno might have anticipated?"

"Paradox confounds reason. And the senses. It does both."

David smiled. He imagined the man he had murdered. He could not connect him with this wondrous venerable dissociated mind adrift in cyberspace, locked inside a mirror, slowly receding.

"I understand Pound's best poems were written while he was imprisoned in a cage," David said.

"*The Pisan Cantos*, yes, they were created in a cage that was exposed to the elements, where he was treated like a rabid dog. He completed them in the asylum where he was sent to avoid execution."

"After broadcasting vicious propaganda for the enemy through the war. I'd say he got preferential treatment."

"Well, he was a good poet, just not a good man. And he got too old too soon," said Jacob.

"Is there any other way?"

"No, no, quite right. It is always too soon to get old."

"One could avoid it by dying young, I suppose."

"Or you can fight it. We'll do this together. It will be a grand gesture. We can defeat death. We can unify the mind."

"By surgery?"

"By merging my experience, your potential. Don't think of it as dying but as a procedure necessary for our shared resurrection."

"I'm not afraid of death, Jacob."

"You're fifteen."

"I've seen old people who are happy."

"Ah, what fools those mortals be! An agéd man is but a paltry thing, a hank of hair, a piece of bone, the remnants of a dry season fluttering on a broken stick. David, my dear Saint David, you cannot imagine. One day you notice a bit of crêpiness on the surface of the skin. It disappears almost immediately, but you saw it. Years go by, the crêpe has spread over your arms and legs, even to your face, it doesn't go away. More years pass, your neck becomes ropey, your hair grows thin, your eyes water mercilessly or get dry as dust, sex and sexuality are a bittersweet mockery, you become conscious of breathing, you hear your heart beating, your strength diminishes and your recovery from exertion takes longer and longer, your joints become stiff, your muscles grow sore, your memories are vivid but often elusive, and your mind is full to capacity with combinations of numbers and words, but most remain meaningless because the processor has slowed and functions erratically. You finally reach Shakespeare's seventh stage of life. *Sans* what? *Sans everything*."

"But look back at what you've achieved, Jacob. Surely there's comfort in that?"

"My achievements? When Yeats gazed at the image of a Muse on his Nobel Prize, he declared he had been young once and beautiful, as I might say of myself, but now I am old and rheumatic, he said, and nothing to look at. My Muse moves perpetually towards the dayspring of her youth, perpetually receding. No, David, at best old age is a test of character. How well does one measure up, enduring what cannot be borne?"

Again, they fell into silence. There was an indecipherable murmur which David had learned was the signal of Jacob's departure. Then David heard what he thought was a sob.

"Jacob! Are you still there?" he called. He shouted again. No answer. Silence. He realized the sob had risen from his own throat, escaped through his own lips.

He continued to cry. He wanted to be with Jacob, to merge with him now, to give the man presence, to give himself access to his beautiful mind. He called out again. With no response, he became frantic. He banged on the mirror with his fists. He wheeled around, looking for something to break into Jacob's retreat. There was a floor lamp with a heavy base beside the chair he most often sat in to read. He picked up the lamp and swung the base against his own image in the mirror. The glass shattered. David stared into the gloom of an empty room. There was nothing on the other side of the mirror at all.

Emptiness can be more oppressive than profusion or presence. Never does such a vacuum overwhelm as in the home of a deceased beloved, never so desolate is a missing child's room than after the body is recovered. Like a stone rolled away from the tomb of a stranger, the shattering glass meant nothing yet the gap it revealed tipped the world off its axis. Before the clatter of shards splayed through the darkness had settled, David realized the world had changed.

The old man was an electronic wraith. David had formed a relationship with an equation of algorithms and residual data accessible in the shape of an old man's life. This was the future, a dead man with more presence than the living. Could the dead who were contained in all the books in the library be released on the world? He shuddered.

He was ecstatic and alarmed in equal measure. He didn't quite understand the revelation at hand. He envisioned an army of the dead rising from their graves and swarming the streets of New Jerusalem, and yet he thrilled to the thought that Violet's vision of a brave new world might be fulfilled, where the best of human consciousness from the past would be restored and the species might yet be renewed. Slowly a feeling of horror spread over him. He recognized how grandiose his response might have seemed to a mirror that proved to be empty when it was shattered. What, after all, had he expected?

He knew the old man was dead since he had killed him. He knew the old man had downloaded his entire cerebral existence, turned himself into a database, a cybernetic clone of himself. He knew that this *thing* the old man had become was locked in the receding past, not embedded in molecules of glass in a mirror. He knew the old man could only be resuscitated by entering the mind of a living person, apparently one carrying his own particular combination of genes.

David rocked back on his heels. He peered through the glittering remnants that framed the dark emptiness of the adjoining room. It seemed like visiting the scene of an infamous catastrophe, where the past was more real than the present, more palpably real than he was himself. The ghost was more real than the person. The mirror had used molecular transmitters to draw the old man's presence from a source located somewhere else. The question was, where? And who was in charge? Who was the dramaturge directing the exchanges between them? And to what purpose?

As if in response to his questions, a light flicked on in the empty room and Grace walked into the glare. Until that moment it had not occurred to David that he could have escaped through the shattered mirror. Grace looked at him, retreated, and reappeared through his unlocked door and closed it behind her. She held out both hands to him, taking his in a solicitous gesture that unnerved him. Was she offering condolences for the latest passing of Jacob Hummel, his father? Approbation for his breaking free of an evil genetic obligation? Pleasure at seeing her son?

"Well, now, David," she said cheerfully, then waited for a response. He said nothing. "You seem to have destroyed Jacob's window on the world. He is gone from us — for the time being at least. It's a shame. I'm not sure what happens when continuity is broken."

"I hope you figure it out. Meanwhile, you don't need me. May I leave?"

"Yes, of course, but where will you go?"

"To find Isabelle. Maybe home."

"Your home was destroyed. Isabelle has moved on. I'm sure she no longer has an interest in you, David. Especially now that you have destroyed her beloved Jacob."

"I broke a bloody mirror!"

"You killed him again. The best we can hope is to slow his fading as time closes around him. The longer he is locked in the past, the more difficult it will be to retrieve him. We do not want Jacob to remain in storage like an autobiography gathering dust. You will be necessary of course if we are to bring him back. This time, the implant will not require the acquiescence of the host, I'm afraid, especially if the mind of the host is displaced."

"Let me understand this. Next time around, once you put the pieces of the mirror together—"

"Not literally."

"Whatever! You intend to find a way to invade my mind, to occupy it, displace it, erase it. He in effect will live; I in effect will die."

"You grasp these things very quickly."

"Thanks, Mom."

"So, I think you should settle in. I'll get you a good book. What about poetry? Perhaps *Paradise Lost*? Or some rousing good prose? Dickens? *David Copperfield*?"

"'If Barkis is willin''.'"

"What on earth is a Barkis?"

Jacob Hummel would have picked up his allusion to a kindly miser's awkward proposal of marriage in Dickens. Isabella would have smiled. This woman, Grace, was not a reader, not in the same way. She lived in a singular world and it wasn't the one commonly occupied. She was obsessive and delusional. David felt better with the diagnosis. At least he could name the monstrosity he was up against.

"You can appreciate our problems, David. Jacob has been dead for some time."

"I was there for the event," said David.

"Oh," she laughed. "No, David. You killed a corpse. Jacob Hummel died several years ago."

David staggered slightly and lowered himself into the depths of a leather sofa. He looked at her pleadingly. She sat beside him, on the edge, knees cocked and body turned so that she faced him from a higher elevation.

"Does that really surprise you so much?"

"Surprise is hardly the word. Do you mean dead, as in stone cold deceased? If he's been dead since I've known him, then who have I been, what have I...? My God, it seems my mother is a succubus and my father was a zombie. It's comical, if it weren't so pathetic."

"First of all," she snapped, taking the labels literally, "I am not a demon of any form, succubus or otherwise. Your conception was a brief psychotic act, not seduction. And Jacob never became a zombie. Quite the opposite — he was a mind whose body had deserted him. He died of natural causes long before you appeared on the scene, this scene. You were a schoolboy."

"Until a few months ago."

"Well, this was several years in the past. His body died."

"Does Isabelle know this?"

"There was no need to tell her. She is not important."

"What a cruel thing to say. Of course she's important."

"Not in the way we had hoped."

"Really! But you let her develop her crush on a corpse. You're sick."

"He was old, his mind functioned well. It's not like she wanted to have his babies."

"You used her!"

"I don't see how. She kept him content, engaged with ideas of the most extravagant and subtle sort — she has an interesting mind. I'd say she used *us*."

"You kept him going by artificial means and she didn't notice?"

"Neither did you, David."

"He just seemed old. I had nothing to compare."

"And neither did she."

"How could you do it? That's not a moral question. How could you sustain the illusion?"

"It's complicated."

"I imagine it would have been."

"You're part of this now, so let me try to explain. We have the technology with cellular implants providing the necessary stimuli to keep a dead body in motion. We were doing that with the organs of lab rats in the late twentieth century. We are able to do it with humans, but unfortunately, we cannot stop the ageing process, itself. As a separate procedure, we have been learning how to keep the mind functioning after its host is dead. There are problems, of course. A deteriorating body without a mind is an abomination. A mind stored on a shelf, however, is a comparable horror. Our dear Jacob Hummel was the first instance where we managed to prolong both, at the same time. With his blessings of course. But his body was ageing too fast, it was a terrible distraction, he was too old when we started. You did not kill him, David. You hardly touched him. Feeling your anger and fear, it was more than he could bear, his system simply shut down."

"He died, or died again, because of *his* emotions?"

"Jacob was a man of great intellect and a man of great passion. Anna brought these together in the life she devised for them here in the library. After Anna's murder, after he was compelled to enforce the edict against reading, his capacity for thought and for feeling bifurcated — do you know that word? Ah yes, I see that you do. You might say he eventually died of a dissociated sensibility. I realize, of course, your recent conversation together was about such things — the dissociated sensibility, the bifurcated mind, yes. He wanted you to understand."

She had been monitoring their sessions.

"He loved you, David. He knew our work had not reached the phase where merging was a practical possibility, but he saw you as his genuine heir."

"Genetically, I suppose I am."

"And you disappointed him."

Her remark felt like a slap.

"How?" he murmured. Then he flared in anger: "I think he murdered my mother, my *real* mother. I know he took me prisoner. He tried to brainwash me. How in god's name can you say *I* disappointed *him*?"

"By not growing up to *be* him. It's a common complaint among fathers about their sons."

"I never even met the man until a few months ago."

"He followed your progress. Violet kept him informed."

"Parenting at arm's length; very Victorian. I was an experimental project to him. Fortunately, Violet was totally hands-on. She was my mentor and friend. And you know what, I'm happy the way it turned out."

"With her being dead?"

"That's not what I meant."

"If she was actually your mother, that would make you an orphan."

"But never a foundling. I know who I am. I got that from her. I don't much like the planet we live on, but I'm happy enough with myself."

"Do you realize how radical that notion is, the notion of contentment? Here, in the city, happiness is not an accessible aptitude — it's more like a skin condition that appears arbitrarily and clears on a whim, leaving acne scars in its wake. No one aspires to happiness in The City of the End of Things."

"What do they want, then?"

"Nothing. Nothing. Out there, in here, no one wants anything at all. That is the tragedy of our times. People simply endure."

David was about to offer a rejoinder in defence of *simply enduring* when the door opened from the corridor. Isabelle strode across the room as Grace rose to her feet, clearly about to speak.

With a closed fist, Isabelle hammered a blow that rendered the other woman unconscious. As Grace slumped to the floor, Isabelle grabbed David's hands and hauled him to his feet.

"Happy Birthday," she said. "You're sixteen today."

"What the hell are you doing?"

"Getting you out of here."

She turned and strode to the door with David in tow. There seemed no doubt in her mind that she was an unstoppable force. She was small, lithe to his lanky, sleek and quick, and confident in her movement. He followed her into the passageway. Grace had said she wasn't important.

She was.

## Chapter Fourteen
## The Primrose Garden

Flying out of Marseille, Violet shaped much of her new book in her mind before touching down in Toronto. She had been ruminating all summer about violating the protocols of palaeoanthropology research by entering the hidden cave on her own, without following proper procedures to avoid contamination, without documenting everything, including the impact of her own presence, and then sealing its wondrous kaleidoscope of whirling lions from her colleagues and the world. Keeping its secret a secret. Everything she had learned from Anna, and from Jacob through the trauma of her late teens, and from the university and established criteria of scholarship, came back to haunt her with the immensity of her indulgence. Yet instinct told her she was right. She had honoured the girl who had made such magnificent art long before the concept of art was conceived. She had allowed her to be human again.

Violet knew she would have to share her discovery eventually. If natural conditions after forty or fifty millennia should damage or destroy such a creation, she would consign herself to the nethermost regions of hell. Even more important was the notion of sharing. As a scientist and a humanist desperate to maintain the strength of her species in the face of restrictive revisions imposed by the Company, she believed it would be the work of the devil to keep such a treasure to herself. The only way to redeem the woman who made the whirling lions from oblivion or careless erasure was to write her story, to give her a knowable personality in an authentic context. Violet felt a connection between them. Imagination would fuse them as one. Rather than becoming a cluster of details filed in a document folder or universally accessible in cyberspace, the girl and her kin would exist again, but this time in a world of words.

Violet thought of Blake's paradigm. She would be the poet in time and space, bringing learning and experience to the project. The girl was the muse, inspiration, the vision embodied. Her leaping lions would provide the rage, the energy, to drive their creation to closure. Violet was a scientist. She would write a novel and use fiction to capture the truth.

Just before leaving Marseille, her old friend at the *Institut d'études humaines préhistoriques*, situated on a lane running parallel to rue

Baudelaire, had asked her opinion on three artefacts that were recently discovered in a small cave near Grasse, otherwise known for its lavender perfumes. While at the same depth in the accumulated dirt and debris as a few fragments of human bone that he had already dated as among the earliest of *homo sapiens sapiens*, he was not at all sure they were connected. One was the fossilized tooth of a cave lion that seemed to have a hole bored through to make it a pendant of some sort. Another was apparently the remnant of a flute, perhaps the earliest musical instrument ever discovered. It was carved from a fragment of woolly mammoth ivory and showed three holes and parts of two others, suggesting the possibility of even more, spaced to indicate they were likely not caused by the bite of a predator.

The third piece he found more puzzling. It was a pebble about the size of a walnut, a little smaller, and seemed to have been shaped into an animal form. There were markings incised that might have occurred from natural wear but could also be indications of a feline in motion. The possibility of it being a carving was enhanced and confused by edges that seemed deliberately rippled, as if stony flames enveloped the tiny beast. Gentle scraping revealed a cleft that could have been made for a necklace thong, yet Violet's colleague was more interested in microscopic fragments of mother of pearl embedded in the stone. They appeared to be charred and were exceptionally fragile, almost transparent, worn through with fly-speck holes from ageing. Although unaccountably far from the Mediterranean shore, they were from seashells not freshwater clams. He was fascinated by the implications; she was captivated by the art, although not at all confident that it wasn't her mind creating the feline image.

When her colleague saw her off at the airport, he gave the piece to her as a parting gift. His name was Rejean Dupuis. She had loved him since they were graduate students together. They were much the same age and much alike. He too sometimes violated protocol, usually on a very small scale, simply to prove to himself the Company was not in absolute control. She had not learned to be an intellectual maverick from him, but he had quietly fostered her subversive quirks. The gift was not necessarily confirmation that he thought the pebble meant nothing.

She sometimes thought they would have been ideal partners, had their personal histories been different, but he had returned home to Marseille, had married an ordinary woman, and had several children. She, in turn, had remained in New Town Number Eleven, suppressed her past, and raised David as her own. Occasionally, over the years, they connected, which gave them great joy and made them both sad.

When she got home, she had the cleft in the pebble filled with a loop of silver through which she strung a silver necklace with a rectangular clasp.

This was to become her prized possession and only ornament, not a talisman but a marker, a reminder of her place in the sequence of passing generations.

The tooth from a cave lion seemed strong evidence of hunting prowess, but it was the flute that had most intrigued her colleague. It was significant for its apparent age. Tests were being run to see if it could possibly coincide in age with fragments of human bone. What seemed most astonishing was the material from which it was made. Given that it must have been carved with flint or obsidian, it would have had to be worked from a relatively fresh piece of ivory, but there were no woolly mammoths in the region of Grasse at the estimated time it was made. They were cold weather animals and avoided excessive warmth, close to the inland sea. Another small piece of ivory nearby seemed to be from the same tusk. It had been smooth, possibly from handling, but not shaped or incised. They had to have been transported from far away, a journey of weeks if not months or years.

Her colleague was writing a paper on the flute, hoping others in the field would add to its provenance. She had stood in his office, staring out the window. Across an expanse of water that shimmered like shook lace, she caught sight of the storeyed Château d'If, set stolidly on its austere and sun-dappled islet. From this perspective the medieval fortress seemed carved out of solid stone, with no windows or doors in evidence to belie the illusion. Even the massive curved planes of its towers suggested that it had arisen from bedrock when it came into existence at the behest of one François I in the middle of the sixteenth century. She smiled to herself at her esoteric fantasy and realized something that changed her life.

The Château d'If was as familiar to her as anything in her childhood. It was redolent with history and fiction. This was where Alexandre Dumas had imprisoned Edmond Dantès for fourteen years in solitary confinement, the last eight under the secret tutelage of old Abbé Faria, whose corpse Dantès displaces to make his escape before finding the treasure of Monte Cristo which allows him to dedicate his life to goodness and vengeance.

The Château d'If was real to her long before she knew it existed. That was the power of story. And while François I was an obscure king born in 1515 and long since dead, Edmond Dantès, in his misery, and the Count of Monte Cristo, in his brooding and benevolent glory, merged as living characters in the present tense of her imagination. Figures in history, or prehistory, she realized while still holding the ivory flute, were dead, were dust. Figures in the imagination were ongoing and real.

On the plane, Violet fingered a small artefact, a fragment of fossilized antler marked around its circumference with a narrow incision. She had found it among a stash of human bones, deep in a pit off the main cave in the Perigord region of France, where they had discovered magnificent drawings of aurochs and other animals several years ago, the site where they had returned to explore, near where she had discovered the hidden cave with the maelstrom of lions. Why she carried the antler piece with her, she wasn't sure. Subversion of some sort. There had been another just like it; she had given it to Rejean Dupuis.

She listened to the drone of the engines and the soft rush of air through the plane. Relaxing deeply, she thought she heard the flowing reverberations of a single flute. She could feel its notes in her blood. Music flowed through her body and curled through her mind. It was like voices in a dream that turn into nonsense on awakening. She could not make out the tune. She smiled, she knew what she had to do. Listen to the music until it made sense and the sense would be swallowed up in the sounds.

Violet became restless; she wanted to take all that she knew and wrap it around the artefacts until the story of people at the dawn of civilization was accessible to readers at the dusk. The girl in the lion-cave deep in the earth, the antler buttons — she realized that's what they must have been, some sort of toggle or fastener — and the findings in the cave near Grasse, a thousand kilometres away, they were part of the same story; the human bones, the ivory flute, the pebble that looked like a lion in flames. The bones they had found under the mudslide and the bits of bone she had seen in Marseille, she was certain that mitochondrial DNA would prove them closely connected. A sequence of women, the beginnings of language, of music, of buttons and clothing, of art, it all came together. Four generations of women. She was the fifth.

\*\*\*

Isabelle led them along the same route Grace had taken when they escaped to The Cloisters, through the bank vault door set into bedrock and onto the abandoned subway line. Neither spoke a word. Isabelle never showed hesitation. David never doubted she knew what she was doing. By the time they surfaced at the Bloor and Yonge St. exchange, he was quite sure he was in love again. In the open air, he held her by the shoulders at arm's length.

"I don't feel sixteen," he said, admiring the sunlight tangled in her hair.

"How old do you feel?" She smiled as if they were on a first date.

He looked around for dangers that could destroy his mood, then back into her piercing green eyes. "Seventeen, I'd say. Seventeen sounds good."

"Well, you're in your seventeenth year, same as me. Congratulations, c'mon."

He released her shoulders and followed, feeling neither mature nor a child. She led him west through the milling people until they came to a side street and turned down a lane named after bpNichol, a twentieth century poet. She stopped at a rambling garage of some sort, converted to a studio. A faded hand-painted blue sign on the red-brick front read: Carriage House: Books. Above was a discretely chalked wooden sign that had been lacquered against the weather:

### Gallery of Egregious Semantical Errors

They turned through a Dutch door and found themselves inside a spacious room criss-crossed with a maze of small wooden desks. At each sat a person of indeterminate age, each in the ill-fitting ethnic dress of a Torontonian; sweaters over T-shirts, blue denims, open-toed sandals with socks. Each was bent over printed documents. Some were perusing books, others newspapers, magazines, old letters, advertising flyers. Each had a notepad poised on the desk and made occasional entries.

A curiously ordinary anomaly struck him as oddly significant — despite Toronto, the city of the End of Things, being the most diverse melting pot in the world, these people were apparently of a single pale ethnicity, representing the long-since merged genetic diversity of the British Isles. They were, he realized, the self-defined 'norm'. By definition, what they were doing was subversive, even seditious.

"Where have you brought me?" he asked, for the first time dubious about her intent.

"We're not staying, not right here," she said. "Don't worry."

'I'm not. But what are they doing?"

"Finding mistakes."

"Oh," he said. There was no point in asking *why*?

She answered anyway. "They have a mission to root out bad English."

This time the question seemed appropriate. "Why?" he said.

"Like Everest, because the errors are there. These people are zealots and purists. The English language is gloriously dead, they say. Like Latin. And they want to weed out necrotic aberrations."

"For whose benefit? Does anyone care?"

"Yes and no. Jacob and Anna in their prime celebrated *living* English. They abhorred 'language by law', as in France and Québec. Legislation is a sure way to kill words. But they could not abide careless usage. They mourned the passing of *whom* and the death of *who* made them weep in despair — even the erudite use *that* for *who* nowadays and no one uses *whom* any more. It's as dated as *thee*."

She turned to the desk closest at hand. "See what she's doing? She's compiling a list. In this case, they're spoken elisions and phonetic distortions.

artic, anartic
infastructure
strenth
vunerable
Febuary
libery
chimley
punkin
indict
syncophant
elphanunt

At the next desk a man was pondering a complementary list of words with superfluous intrusive phonemes:

filum
triathalon
elum trees
inflammable
irregardless
ironical

"'Ironical' and 'inflammable' are variant forms," David observed, speaking to no one in particular. 'Filum' and 'elum' are regional dialect and no one is obtuse enough to say 'triath*a*lon' or 'artic'." He didn't know what to do with 'indict'.

"So what?" said Isabelle, nodding towards the woman sitting at the next desk over. She had two words featured, underlined, and contained within horizontal columns of exclamation marks:

!!!!!!!!!!!!!!!!!!!!!!!!!!!!!!
!!!!!!!!!!!!**ec-setera**
**nuculer**!!!!!!!!!!!!!!!!
!!!!!!!!!!!!!!!!!!!!!!!!!!!!!!!

Following, was the single notation, **penultimate**, then a blank line, then:

alot (thanks)?
most everything (regional)?

At the bottom of the page, she had added as an interrogatory postscript the word **bigly?** and then, by appending her signature, seemed to take personal responsibility for the errors she'd noted. She was sitting hunched into herself, staring at the page, quietly weeping.

A cluster of desks near the far wall were devoted to missing apostrophes and redundant commas. David knew this because they were huddled together under a sign that declared:

**Apostrophe's, and Commas**

Piled all around were stacks of local newspapers, small-town weeklies, advertising leaflets, and various commercial brochures. David wondered what they did about the Oxford comma, an aberrant intrusion he preferred that came before the final item in a sequence of three or more, conjoined by a conjunction, usually 'and'. Oranges, cars, and porcupines. The final comma was essential for clarity, to avoid an undue bond between the latter two items at the expense of the first. That's what Violet taught him, although teachers used to mark him down for using it. But he persisted.

As the two of them made their way through the orderly tangle of desks, he noticed other lists. Several ran for pages and were drawn from novels concerning vampires and dragons. One was a list of semantic and syntactical errors in Shakespeare's plays and another tallied up Shakespeare's misuses of words and abuses of grammar in his poetry, especially the sonnets. They overlapped, David suspected. The last list that he saw before they went out through a back door brought a smile to his face. It was long and some of the selections were words that he found confusing himself. He had been required in school to memorize their differences:

| | |
|---|---|
| crocodile alligator | mammoth mastodon |
| fusion fission | imminent immanent |
| biannual biennial | incredible incredulous |
| fewer less | famous infamous |
| principle principal | compliment complement |
| obligated obliged | extent extant |
| discrete discreet | calvary cavalry |
| practise practice | ravel unravel |

And listed, to the side of the page:

| | |
|---|---|
| suede swayed | execute (a person) execute (a manoeuvre) |
| staid stayed | your you're yore |
| maid made | cleave to / from (contronym) |

there their they're    odd awed
its it's               enjoin to / from
precede proceed        mould in a dish / mould a dish

While across the bottom were the words:

stand watch, wrist watch, black watch, watch over, watch out, watchword

What on earth would they do with these lists? That begs the question, he thought (demands or evades?). To wit, to a wit, not a whit.

He had caught a glimpse of paraphernalia from an antiquated book bindery in an adjoining room. From the stacks of books with uncut pages, he assumed it was operational. I suppose, he surmised, they deposit their lists in bound copies in the library and then start over and do them again?

These people were a strange lot, but at least they were pursuing a passion and fulfilling an ideal, however weirdly conceived. Given the condition of the world around them, it didn't much matter if their feelings and ideals were incompatible, at odds, out of sync. What they were doing was a significant diversion from reality. He envied them their commitment.

He looked at Isabelle. They seemed to have fetched up in a leafy brick-walled courtyard edged by gardens with profusions of flowers (plural intended), and a crushed gravel floor that crunched as they moved ('fetched up' was the antiquated term that came to David as he looked around for an exit). The air was eerily quiet, as if they had moved into another country, another world (the gateway to the planet Tlön?).

"Maybe we should talk," he said.

"About what?"

"Well, you punched my mother, you knocked her senseless."

"It'll give her a nice break from over-thinking so much."

"Did you know I'd sent the old man plummeting into the past?"

"It doesn't surprise me. When I arrived this morning, you had already broken the looking glass. I often visited, you know. I'd watch you through the mirror while you talked to Jacob. It gradually sank in, Jacob Hummel was a wondrous illusion. He was important to me, he had filled a gap, but I realized I was there to see you, David. You were the real thing. You *are* the real thing. This morning, I stayed in the shadows. I listened to your conversation with Grace. She was candid, I'll say that for her. She said I was dispensable. Well, to hell with her. She said they had upped the stakes — you weren't being groomed as a host, you were going to be sacrificed. I figured it was time to get you out of there. And here we are."

He looked around. They were surrounded by carpets of yellow primroses, highlighted with clusters of violets. Spring flowers. He wondered if it were spring. He had lost all track of time. Or was the courtyard a controlled micro-climate? He glanced up; there was a transparent canopy overhead. The garden wasn't a metaphor. He was getting used to metaphors. In this small corner of the world, the seasons were subject to human design. The courtyard was much bigger inside than would have seemed possible before walking through the gallery to reach it. On a stone table near the centre was a plate loaded with tiny madeleines and a large pitcher of lemonade, with two glasses. The cakes might have been for the lexographic minions to nibble during their breaks, but the glasses, there being only two, seemed meant for David and Isabelle.

It could be any time of the year except winter. No snow. His birthday, he'd just turned sixteen. Then it must be October.

Isabelle poured him a drink, they ate numerous madeleines and gazed at the primroses and violets growing amidst mounds of brooding moss. He noticed a small door through the brick wall at the far side of the garden with letters carved on the stone lintel: v.a.l.

"What does that stand for?" he asked.

"*Verum Ad Libris*."

"What a shame."

"Really?" she said. "It means 'truth through reading'."

"Roughly speaking. It comes closer to: 'books against truth', or maybe 'truth against books'."

He looked around again at the primroses and violets, embarrassed by his pedantry, but also by his imperfect command of Latin.

"I have several pressing questions," he said.

"Shoot."

"Did you order the lemonade? There are only two glasses."

"That's the policy of the Gallery. It's to encourage intimacy in sharing insights, one-to-one encounters during the breaks, and to avoid the conspiracies invariably generated by group discussions."

"About semantics?"

"You'd be surprised how rules of language melt through consensus."

"I would be. So, another question — surely the joy of language is that it's alive and as a living thing it's bound to be imprecise and ambiguous. I mean, Chaucer used '*ain't*', Shakespeare brilliantly broke rules, the King James Bible pulsates with pleasing and powerful redundancies. So, what's the point?"

"For years, dictionary publishers scrambled to issue updated editions. When the ENW took control, the language was considered closed. Only as a finished thing could English be rendered into digital paradigms, otherwise the mathematics would collapse and we'd end up with nothing but meaningless numerical equations. English, the dominant language in our sector of the world, was frozen."

"So, these people in the 'Gallery of Egregious Grammatical Errors' are working for the Company."

"Oh no, you mustn't think that. They're trying to preserve what's best by identifying what's bad. There's a difference between cleansing the wounds and washing the corpse, so to speak."

"So to speak." The analogy seemed obtuse. "Here's another question for you. Grace kept talking about 'they', about 'we' and 'they'. Who is she working with? It's confusing. You and I left abruptly and she was unconscious, so I didn't have time to ask her."

"If I knew the answer, I'd tell you. I just know she's dangerous — at this point, lethal for both of us. Next question?"

"Who killed Jacob Hummel?"

"The first time? No one. He simply died. People do. I was with him."

"I thought Grace said that was before your time."

"I don't know why she'd want you to think that."

"To make you seem as stupid as me."

"For not seeing through the mask?"

"Death's mask? I didn't either."

"I knew him well. As he died, he made me promise to find you. He had been monitoring you all your life."

"He said it like that? *'Find David Winston'*."

"I believe his words were: 'Dear girl, look after my son.'"

"His death spiel was a rounded thought in perfect grammar?"

"David, don't doubt the power of syntax to finish a sentence in a dead man's mouth. That's what he said, then he died."

"Okay, a final question: who are you?"

"I am who I told you I was. No secrets. Well, secrets, but no lies. You are my lover, I am your friend."

He had never thought of himself as a *lover* nor heard himself described that way. He blushed. They finished the lemonade and she led him to the small aperture in the far wall, leaving a hush of flowers in their wake.

Crouching to get through the door, they came out into a comfortable ground-floor studio with brick and beams showing, festooned with tribal carpets, mostly from the Caucasus and Persia. Rugs were overlaid, one across another, covering broad planks of ancient pine. They were hanging from the walls, revealing narrow slashes of brick between them, and draped over railings and tables like multiple takes of a painting by Vermeer. They exuded a warm smell of wools, slightly acrid and unnervingly intimate. David had never experienced anything to compare with the swarming of colours, madder and ochre, indigo and pistachio, and the overwhelmingly embracing cacophony of lines, curves, spandrels, medallions, figures; symbolic, abstract, and familiar; peacocks, splayed dragons, people, bodehs, camels, chickens, triangles, goats, and discs; with fields sliding off under borders and boundaries poised around teeming oases.

He was breath-taken. He grasped her hand.

"Is this where you actually live?" he asked, tremulous with excitement.

"Yes," she said. "The flat in the book emporium wasn't mine. You like this? No one wants these rugs — they're all too old."

"Too old for what? They're beautiful beyond anything I've ever seen. You live in a great library of carpets. It's amazing."

"They are nice, aren't they? Nineteenth century and earlier. Tribal. You can see the work of individual women in the weave, in the strength of the warp and the weft, and especially in their subversive whimsy. They don't reveal their stories so easily as books, but if you open yourself to read them as sensual experiences, their stories are infinite."

"Magic carpets," he said. "Can we stay here a while?"

"Thank you," she said. "Yes."

They settled in on a plush leather sofa. He turned sideways to face her. Sunlight streaming in through one of the small windows high overhead, caught in her copper-gold hair. The corners of her eyes crinkled softly, framing depths of green that refused to yield his reflection.

"I think it's time we take a few steps backwards and descend Jacob's ladder," she said. "Think about this, David." She paused, framing her ideas carefully. "You need to know where he began. His pillow was bedrock."

"I don't understand."

"There was a time when people saw visions, David. Jacob wanted us to get there again. When language was literal and words were not labels but things, when images weren't projections of human perception but objects of experience, themselves, then dreams and visions were parallel versions of whatever was real. People still see visions, of course, and I don't mean the jackass evidence that God is a dunce, where Jesus and Mary turn up on pieces of burnt toast. I don't mean the hustlers like Swedenborg or Joseph Smith or L. Ron Hubbard who created religions from inspired fantasies. Just the opposite. I'm talking about people who overrule their visions with reason.

"People dream, but we *know* dreams have no substance. People see things that aren't there, but we *know* they are optical illusions, tricks of the sun or the psyche. We dismiss magic because we *know* it's absurd. We overrule imagination from childhood onwards with intellect. If I see a burning bush, I don't think it's God, just light-waves refracted with a particular flare. Or perhaps shrubbery someone's set aflame."

"I thought you were going to tell me about Jacob Hummel."

"Which was a name he borrowed from a Strindberg play."

"The stranger in *The Ghost Sonata*."

"Well, as I'm trying to explain, Jacob saw visions. Not revelations, which are intellectual epiphanies and their meanings are instantly clear. No, he saw visions. A vision eludes rational explanation."

"A moving staircase, Jacob's ladder connecting earth and high heaven, with God caught forever in transit."

"Nothing so banal, David. He told me he had three visions in all. The first, when he was still a student, commuting to university from the east end of the city. He was married — did you know he was married before? — and they had a small boy. One day they were swimming in Lake Ontario, out near the Eastern Gap. His wife was reading, he was reading, the boy was playing in the shallows. He looked and saw the boy, then an edge of the lowering sun caught the horizon and an explosive glare turned the horizon to flame. Blinded, he glanced down at his book, the letters danced on the page in a meaningless jumble, he looked up again. The boy was gone. Just like that, it was over."

"Blinded by the light. My God."

"He dropped out of his graduate programme. Philology held no more interest for him. His wife grieved through the winter and in April, the cruellest month, she took her own life. Lilacs didn't bloom by the dooryard that year. He turned to the Company for existential coherence. In their employ, he suspended moral awareness. What began in a vision of sunset flames ended with him settling into the mindless role of a corporate thug."

"What was the boy's name?"

"I don't know. Why?"

"I suspect it was 'David'."

"That is so sad," she said.

"What was his second vision?" Deep down David never believed the old man had murdered his mother. Somehow, hearing of his family's horrific demise reinforced his confidence in his own intuition. Jacob Hummel, whoever he was, had a history.

"This one is harder to fathom. It is a vision of blood. He and an accomplice were transporting two women in the back of a van. It was a job they were doing for the Company. One of the women was a teenager named Rose. When Jacob wasn't present, his accomplice tried to rape Rose and when he ripped off her underwear, he discovered she was a boy. The man was humiliated; he beat Rose to death. The other woman couldn't stop him, but when the beating was over, she took out a knife she had hidden away and she slit the rapist's throat. While blood was still sheeting from his wound, as he writhed in his death throes, Jacob reappeared. He took in the scene at a tortured glance, picked up the blood-covered woman and placed her in shadows before setting the van with two corpses on fire. Later, he stood close to the woman and watched as The Cloisters burnt to the ground. He stood with her and her small daughter and their friend Solomon, their lives fused like molten metal forever."

"The woman was Anna, wasn't she? The little girl was Violet. The flames were the conflagration that demolished Sebastian Kroetsch's mansion."

"Yes, and Anna's name might have been Agnes, and Solomon was the owner of a walking stick called Immanuel which eventually went to Jacob."

"Where is it now?"

"Here!" She reached across a table covered by an exquisite Caucasian rug rippled with abstract designs and pulled Immanuel from the shadows. "He would have wanted you to have this," she said.

David took the cane tentatively, like shaking an invalid's hand, and held it up so the amber eyes connected with his own.

"Thank you," he said.

"Transfigured by his vision of blood washed away by the flames, Jacob turned to a truer calling: he dedicated himself to Anna, or Agnes if that's who she was, and he took up her dedication to books as the panacea for humanity's future. Yes, and he took up her commitment to revise Violet — after the macabre machinations of her father, Anna's first husband, who had embedded Violet with an experimental DNA microcomputer long before the kinks had been worked out."

"Hers was defective."

"Not like yours. It worked. But Anna and Jacob were able to countermand its influence."

"A bit like Grace with the next generation of implants."

"Grace was never implanted."

"What, what? Why would she insist she was?"

"The appearance of power."

"But she passes through the scanners at the boundary."

"Because the Company has given her special dispensation."

"And the third vision?" He had heard Grace's version of what it must be — when the Company angels killed Anna. "Is my origin at the centre of it?"

"Your conception story? I believe your father was in no state to notice. As for your nativity, it was only a signal event in retrospect, and, when it was, you were shipped off to live with Violet."

"But Grace gave birth in the library, right? I was born there?"

"No, Colonel Mustard in the kitchen."

"What? Pardon?"

"Nothing. A parlour game, something we played in the evenings."

"Who's *we*? People here, in the subversive collective?"

"This is my home."

"Why are they all WASPs?"

"To create a diversion. To keep the spies guessing."

"What? What's diverting about a bunch of neo-British pedants?"

"Well, if that were true, it would be amusing, don't you think? But take another look out there in the bindery. You were so distracted by the lists of Egregious Errors, you didn't notice how many of the people making those lists were in white-face and wearing borrowed clothes. There are Pakistanis and Indians, Indonesians and Filipinos, Kenyans, Nigerians, Egyptians, and Turks. They're all disguised as Brits. It's a post-colonial joke."

"Not all of those were in the Empire."

"Maybe not the British empire. That isn't the point. It is part of our effort to create confusion for the Company monitors."

"Because you plan to overthrow the governing powers of the Evolved New World with better grammar, correct diction, and subversive racial stereotypes?"

"No. With our refusal to submit!"

Her fierce inflection made him realize how serious she was. He wanted to steer them back to Jacob Hummel's third vision. He stood up, by gesture inviting her to join him, and leaning on Immanuel he led them back into the courtyard. They sat on two stone chairs and he poured more lemonade.

Isabelle seemed hardly to notice they had moved. "Your mother, David — when you were taken away, she buried her grief in books."

"I thought she was forbidden to read. She didn't know how."

"Until a renegade reader got her started. Then, reading spread through her like a rampant contagion, but she had developed a formidable immune system. It did not displace her life as it did for those in The Cloisters."

"Where she rescued you from extermination."

"Exactly. She was able to resist the power of books to subsume personality. She took time off from her work with the Committee for Public Safety."

"And saved you out of the goodness of her heart?"

"Is that so unlikely? Before long, she went back to the Revisionist History Project. That's where I connected the two of you — well, she knew you already but I didn't know that. I'm told her work in the Project is important. It seems perfect for her. Think of the implications. If the past is a contrivance, the present must be absurd, moral values are relative to the moment, goodness and evil no longer exist. What's left? A woman whispering to herself, her voice like the wind in dry grass, rats' feet over broken glass—"

437

"—who crossed into death's other Kingdom! I think her soul died years ago, perhaps in the battered womb of her mother. She didn't *rescue* you from The Cloisters," David said. "I think she was sent to retrieve you for a particular purpose."

"For what?" Isabelle seemed startled by his radical conjecture.

Resounding in the hollows of his mind were Grace's own words, *she is not important in the ways we had hoped.* He hesitated, he did not want to hurt her, but she needed to understand.

"I think you were part of a plan," he said. "They had heard about you, the girl in The Cloisters. They thought you would make an ideal host for the rebirth of the old man's mind. You would *become* him, Grace would be your regent — not consort, I don't think her interest in you was sexual, but who knows. And it wasn't about books, it was about power. She freed you, she groomed you. She thought she could control you. You and Jacob connected. He obviously liked you as a *destination.* You wouldn't have had to know what was happening. You would have been a perfect pairing. Except for one thing. You weren't a proper genetic match. Your chromosomes would have rebelled at the intrusion and shut you both down."

Isabelle was obviously caught up in his revisionist conjecture. He waited for a few moments, then continued: "The host brain had to embrace the invading mind on a cellular level. Yours wouldn't work. Neither would hers, of course. Much as she wanted to claim Jacob as her father, he wasn't. There was no link between them, in spite of the fantasy that he was her father. But as her child with him, I was a match."

"Providing there was no interference to the transfer on a psycho-social level," Isabelle said.

"Exactly. They needed my co-operation for the continuity no one else could provide. Perhaps the old man knew all along, perhaps that's why he turned me over to Violet, so she could raise me the way he wanted himself to become."

"This doesn't seem real," she whispered, unable to catch her breath. "It's too complicated, too cryptic."

"Would you have agreed to take my place if it could have been done?"

"To give him a home, to share my mind, possibly yes. My sense of myself was mostly from books. I don't know. Oh my God, I really don't know."

A pallor settled over her face as he talked. She seemed stricken with horror, as if being told a death sentence had been commuted to unending torture in the deepest most soul-searing regions of hell. Doré's etchings of Dante's *Inferno* could not be as devastating as the images that must have swept through her mind. There was nothing to redeem her corrupted memories of the old man's affection.

"How do you know this, David?" she asked, her pale lips trembling, eyes flickering like spent embers.

"Think with your gut," he said. "Don't sort out your emotions from facts. Let them build on each other; review what you've been through with your feelings."

She reached out to him across the small table. Warmth spread from their clasped hands and colour flowed back into her face.

"David, your account makes total sense, but your proof is absurd. Feel, think; think, feel. Guts don't form theories, brains do."

"In a strange way, you were meant to be me," he said.

"And you were my stand-in."

"Will the old man ever return?" David asked.

"No, there's an unbreachable barrier of dead time now. He's gone."

"But we could bring him back," David announced. "We could draw on his mental archive and write him down as a book."

"Genius! Yes. We will, oh God, oh lovely, he will exist, a being in Being, he will *be* again, he will continue forever among words. That's what he always wanted. We will do that together."

"His third vision! We'll bring closure," he said.

"No, his third vision was the life flickering and fading from his beloved's eyes. His first vision was of water turned into fire, his second was of blood turned into flames, his third was death as he saw it in Anna's eyes. He envisioned their library a raging inferno. What he saw was worse than her dying, it was the death of the human soul. Left to pursue their goal on his own he had to take responsibility. He strangled her corpse with a silk cord."

"I'm not sure I follow the logic."

"Guilt works in mysterious ways. It leads some to deny responsibility entirely; some to assume it obsessively. Logic and reason don't always coincide. After Grace slept with him and drew his seed, he saw her as the Devil Incarnate, he saw you as Gabriel, the rescuing angel, who would seize back the power to make the library viable again, a vast living organism, as a library should be. He was willing to die so that you could succeed him. That's where his vision became visionary. If we can write his story, capture his life in words, we will make the future inevitable."

David felt humbled, he felt exalted and confused and outraged. He had never wanted to be more than he was. He sank against the stone chair. Waves of violets and primroses cascaded gently towards him, riffled by a breeze so imperceptible it could not be felt on his cheek. He wondered what Jacob's real name had been. Perhaps it, too, was David, a long time ago.

## Chapter Fifteen
## Tlön Revisited

It was a time before people had names. There was no concept of numbers or size. A hunter knew the precise heft of a spear, the exact speed of an auroch in flight. She knew to the last drop of blood the maximum weight of a venison haunch she could carry. She knew the colour and scent of a gangrenous wound. Such knowing was invariably felt more than understood but change was afoot, a remarkable mutation at hand. The capacity to formulate words had existed for hundreds of thousands of years, yet the arrival of grammar was sudden. When syntactical structures occurred in the brains of a few in the Perigord Valley, it might have seemed madness. Words grew like apples from blossoms on branches that determined their use and they propagated with unearthly profusion. The human larynx created the sound but a new chromosomal twist created the noun, the verb, their derivative forms. And as words became things, spoken and remembered, our species discovered the intersecting notions of time and consciousness. We discovered we existed. Forever a part of the world, forever apart.

*** 

Violet stared at her keyboard. David was upstairs in his room. She scrolled through what she had written and resisted pressing 'delete'. She had decided the best way to make her story inevitable, based on the facts she had put together from research, was to organize it chronologically as a sequence of events happening in the lives of characters who were already as alive in her mind as family or friends, the couple who raised her, the man who saved her, the colleagues she worked with, or even her son. She knew her characters as if they were blood, so it seemed unnatural to leave them nameless. Astronomers named galaxies, microbiologists named microbes. She decided to call the woman who avenged her daughter, 'Anna'. The daughter who created a whirl of lions to rival the Sistine Chapel, she named Rose after a childhood friend who was murdered. Rose's daughter would be Violet, after herself. David would be Violet's twin brother, her partner and the father of her children. The convolutions of incest, real or implied, reflected the bonds among them and, not in her mind, their sexual relations.

She would not use the names in her text but they would help her keep track of their lives.

She could hear David and his friend Lucas upstairs. She encouraged them to spend time together. Lucas was an ordinary kid in every respect and she hoped David would recognize, in comparison, his own idiosyncrasies. She did not want to teach him to be different — she was not sure if such a thing were possible. She hoped he would come to realize his DNA implant did not function like those of his peers. He was, in effect, a cyber-genetic mutation. Far from being dulled, his feelings were refined to an uncomfortably high degree. His capacity for thought extended well beyond the limits imposed by cybernetic protocols. He didn't know about, and the Company monitors apparently had not picked up on, his radical capacity to be what once might have been considered high-functioning 'normal'.

She let her mind drift into the other world, where David and Violet, as she thought of them, were sitting at the front of their shallow cave, basking in the glow of a summer sunset while their children romped on the grassy slopes. David played his flute softly and the notes drifted down the long valley, picking up resonance as they curled like smoke through the trees and the underbrush. Animals stopped in their tracks and listened, a few humans gathered close to their fires and smiled. The lone Neanderthal listened and moved closer, stalking the sounds to their source. When he breached a cleft in the forest, he saw children playing in the grass. He stooped low into the shadows and waited.

The woman stood up languorously in the diminishing sunlight. She caressed her man's shoulders while he played his trilling mellifluous tune, then she went into the cave to retrieve a robe for each of them. The children followed her without being summoned and climbed into their bedding of auroch hides and a lion skin that was getting old but exuded an odour of primal warmth. She sat with the children for a while, humming along with the strange ethereal music of the ivory flute. When it went silent, she thought nothing of it. She caressed the baby's forehead, hoping she wasn't coming down with a fever.

The woman with robes in her arms pushed the skin door back and went out. There was still enough light to see the Neanderthal hunter stooped over her man, passing the flute back and forth from hand to hand, apparently trying to determine where the music had come from. David lay sprawled with his head smashed open in a dark stain that glistened in the sunset like a pool of flames. Violet roared with incomprehensible pain, she staggered backwards into the cave and gathered her children behind her. She and her oldest girl and boy each grabbed a stone-tipped hunting shaft and held them poised with lethal unwavering intent at the door.

The Neanderthal didn't try to come in. The woman moved slowly to a slit in the door, shivering with rage. The killer had pushed David's body to the side and taken his place on the stone bench. He still held the ivory flute in his fingers. He turned when the woman came out, she moved slowly towards him. A large club lay across his knees. It was made from a branch that had been sheared from a tree with the knot still attached which had been shaped into a murderous protrusion by repeatedly burning the surface and rubbing the charred wood against rock. The bulbous end glistened with the viscera and blood of its victim sprawled at his feet.

He beckoned her to come to his side. He seemed oblivious to the hunting spear in her hand. He ran his own hand across his throat in a gesture of vulnerability. He held out the flute in her direction and rattled it, as if trying to shake the music free. She moved backwards into the cave, drawing her children with her. She had never encountered a Neanderthal at close quarters before. She knew he was the lone hunter who lived in the valley below. She and her man had sometimes left a cache of meat for him, although he seemed to fare well enough on his own. They had shared the knowledge of him with other humans, imitating his slow powerful gait, and no one seemed to hold him in fear. Nothing in his behaviour indicated aggression. Perhaps he had been driven to murder by loneliness and the haunting strains of the flute. During the night he remained on the bench, gazing out over the valley.

At dawn, Violet and the older children walked out, ignoring the interloper, and gathered David's body, which they dragged off to the grass sward on the closest slope and buried with a mound of rocks piled over to keep him safe from scavengers. When they returned to the cave the Neanderthal was gone. He shortly returned, lumbering up the hill with a broken branch laden with ripe figs which he set down on the stone bench and offered with an open-hand gesture. Warily, the woman ate and her children followed suit.

After a few days, when their stores of dried meat were diminished, the Neanderthal left and returned with the haunch on an auroch, freshly killed and crudely slaughtered, and they roasted the entire piece on the fire and feasted, tearing chunks free and smearing grease that oozed from the meat across their faces and rubbing their hands through their hair.

That night the Neanderthal and Violet slept under the same robes at the back of the cave. Near dawn she slid out from under the skins and walked to the front of the cave where she took up the lion's head and quietly removed the branches and grass stuffing and drew it over her head. She picked out a spear, felt the sharp stone tip with her fingers, and slipped stealthily through the flickering darkness back to her lover. He rolled over, looked up, offered a fleeting grin, then shrank back into the lion-skin covering as she drove the spear through his chest, deep into his heart.

Violet learned to play the flute. She had watched David by the hour and before long his notes were filling the valley again and their family endured for two thousand generations, born from a mad woman and her daughter who created sewing, invented buttons, and avenged her own daughter, who made lions and aurochs from paint and stone, from shadows and light, and whose surviving children merged with a lion, struck out on their own, and made haunting music from an ivory flute.

This had been worked into the final section of Violet's story, which began with the woman who thought herself mad because clusters of sounds and contours of light played out as patterns in her head and she didn't know what to do with them, and who died under the weight of her commune's generosity. She described the secret cave, which made it no longer a secret. As a visionary place within fiction, she made it accessible through words. She concluded with music reverberating endlessly, ever and ever fainter but still to be heard, like radio waves sent into space on an infinite journey. She had seen the painted lions, they swirled inside her mind, and she had heard the music, she could hear it still.

She thought she would throw David a party, just kids from the neighbourhood, including Lucas, of course. Her lovely son's forbearance over the last few months had been remarkable. He coped with her clandestine behaviour, knowing she was breaking the rules, and cheerfully put up with her obsessive work habits. Since she last came back from the Perigord, she had been distracted, caught up in the throes of creation. She realized how outrageous that would have seemed, had she spoken the words out loud. She was a scientist. It was not her imperative to create, nor to lose herself, find herself, in the throes of creation.

She believed she had written a novel. She wondered if anyone anywhere wrote novels any more? Had she been working in a vacuum, drawing from data and documents, driven by inspiration and desire, guided by imagination, memory, and dream, as she fused feelings with sense in ways long forgotten, except on occasion by a poet or two?

***

The warm acrid smell of innumerable rugs filled the air, giving their lovemaking an aura of earthiness and mystery unlike anything he could have imagined. If he should live to a hundred and have countless lovers, something he could not envision, making love would forever evoke the embracing odour of antique tribal carpets stacked in profusion in the heart of the city. For days he was content, confident that Grace and her sinister cohort would have no idea where to find them.

Sometimes they took their meals out in the courtyard where a lovely couple seemed to have been diverted from their work on egregious linguistic and lexical errors to cater for their every need. Vincent and Amy spoke softly, and never about anything grammatical, yet they conveyed such dignified assurance in their bearings that David felt sure they were in service to some larger purpose. In fact, the more comfortably he settled in, the more likely it seemed that those working in the old bindery were all serving a cause he couldn't quite grasp.

"What's going on?" he asked Isabelle, horrified that he might be breaking the mood. "They're doing something more than it seems."

"Everyone is," she said.

"They treat you like a leader but you don't lead."

"Being led is the last thing they need. You'll notice no one is deferential; they are courteous, considerate, gracious, and very committed. They have given me a home and I give them a focal centre for their emotions."

"Why?"

"Because I need a place to live. Oh, well, because their work is so distractingly tedious, I remind them of their need to be human."

"Grace taught you this?"

"Grace taught me how to be human. Books taught me how to be humane."

"But you despise her."

"And love her, yes, both. Perhaps we'll invite her for biscuits and tea."

"Surely she doesn't know where we live. Shouldn't we lay low for a while?"

"We have been, but she knows. Now it's time we move on."

"How?"

"How does she know? Did you really think when you came into the city you were beyond the reach of the Company? We are contained inside an electronic shroud, David. We can't get out, without special dispensation such as Violet had to do research, such as Jacob Hummel had in order to confer with the Company executives, but they can see in. Universal ogle devices are no longer just miniature drones whose information can be summoned into individual consciousness. That still exists, of course, but there are molecular refinements which move through the air like an invisible fog. We are constantly monitored. Our information is collated. By computers, of course. No mind made of tissue and fat could process the quadrazillion facts generated every hour of every day."

"And you're telling me Grace has access to the analyzed data."

"We have the advantage of knowing she knows we're here."

"Advantage to do what? To escape and escape and escape. Is there nowhere she can't reach?"

"First of all, we are so deeply observed, there is so much detail at such close quarters, they can't actually see what we're doing. Computers are stupid, David. The babel of noises created by the Gallery for Egregious Semantical Errors creates such a hubbub of interference, all words spoken or written in the immediate vicinity go unresolved. They read out as visual and audible static. In fact, I can say *subversion, rebellion, books, anarchy, dissent* and no alarms will be raised. Such words without context are meaningless to the monitors. The absence of syntax renders them mute. Day after day, the people here repeat their lists and discuss them, but each day each one makes a different list. It generates chaos and chaos is a very good thing."

"This place is a safe house," he observed. "The Emporium and the Theatre were distractions for residents of the city. This place, it's an oasis."

"It is."

"And that's why you collect tribal carpets from Persia. To create a hubbub of images."

"No, I collect them because I like them."

They were nibbling madeleines in the courtyard. He could smell the richness of multi-hued natural materials through the small open door leading into her home.

"Isn't this cultural appropriation, turning artisanal works into artefacts?"

"They were being discarded. I saved them."

"That's what the British Museum used to say about the Elgin Marbles."

"And when they were returned, they went into storage. They were blown up by terrorists. Photos suggest they were beautiful." She sounded angry. "My rugs still exist. By preserving them, I increase the chance they'll be shared and endure." She sounded hurt.

He felt badly.

"David," she said. "Books don't always have pages. Each rug tells volumes — stories, information, passions, symphonies of aesthetic complexity — each draws from tribal tradition and the weaver's skill, her whimsy and discipline always just a little at odds. If this were the end of the world and I were the last woman on earth, you wouldn't object to me retrieving Michelangelo fragments from the rubble of galleries and museums."

"Even though you're not Italian! No, okay. It's your woolly library and it's teeming with interest. I love your collection." He paused. "Isabelle, I love you."

She gazed into the depths of his eyes and echoed his words. "I love you, David." She paused. They let the silence wash over them. Then she continued: "Together we will kill your mother, David. We have to kill Grace."

How had they moved so precipitously from a discussion of tribal carpets, through a flash of affection, to matricide? Incredibly, Isabelle smiled.

He turned and walked slowly into her carpet-filled ground floor studio and dropped onto the leather sofa. She sat down opposite.

"Why?" he asked. "Doesn't that seem extreme?"

"My genes rejected efforts to implant Jacob's mind and she inevitably found her own cells no more amenable. She believes only you, David Winston, can provide literal access to his mind while I can provide access to his affections."

"But that's absurd at this point — right? I've already killed my father."

"But you didn't."

"I tried."

"No, you didn't, David. You didn't. Listen to me! We are in a position, you and I, to kick-start history into action again. Not by dwelling on Jacob's death, he is irretrievably gone, but by countering the end of history, the death of books. We can do this, but Grace stands in our way."

"That sounds rather grand," he suggested, torn between affection and disbelief.

"Look, listen, let me explain. Since our species first settled east of Eden, we have been guilty of original sin. Social evolution displaced natural selection; we became our own creation. Forgive the Biblical allusions, but blasphemy is sometimes the best metaphor — God lost his grasp on things; humanity lost its grasp on things; the Company has seized control."

"Do you really think the Evolved New World is all that radical? It just seems a lot more organized than the city and without the obsession for books."

"Most of the city doesn't know books even exist, or ever did. You happen to have fallen among the few who do."

"Fallen? Been pushed."

"In any case, words in print can change the world!"

"Oh, come on," he said.

"Ah, but they can. Think of *Uncle Tom's Cabin*, *Magna Carta*, the *Q'uran*, the American Constitution, Aristotle's *Poetics*, Shakespeare's tragedies, Augustine's *City of God*, *Gilgamesh*, the *Bible*, *Harry Potter*, the list goes on with diminishing returns until all the words ever recorded are covered. Jacob Hummel believed that, even after he died. Anna believed it. Their dream was to counter the Company. I believe Grace subverted the dream. Perhaps it's too late and we have already lost our humanity. Her revision of the species is almost complete."

"Unless we kill her."

"Yes, David, listen. She will always conceive herself as Jacob's offspring, not as a child of multiple assaults by anonymous cretins. She won't give up. She will kill you to inhabit your life."

"Herself?"

"She's desperate. She'll try, you'll die."

"Did she murder Violet?"

"She was responsible for Violet's death! Violet had faith in you — she believed you'd grow up to resist Armageddon, the end of our evolutionary span. I only met her once but she told me that. I was with Jacob. She made me promise to look out for you. I fell in love on my own. She believed in you, David."

"Grace killed Violet."

"Yes."

"Okay," he said.

"Okay what?"

"Let's go, let's kill Grace. It's the least I can do."

While it was still early, the next morning, they cut across side streets to Yonge and approached Ford Place from the north. David had Immanuel firmly in his grasp, as neither for physical nor moral support, but simply because he would have felt incomplete without him. The Houyhnhnm sculptures had their regular gatherings of misfits and miscreants hanging about in their shadows. The Brobdingnagian figures striding provocatively on electronic billboards struck David as bland in the white morning sunshine. When people got too close, he flourished Immanuel, but they moved aside because he appeared disabled, not because he was menacing. A few people they passed seemed to recognize Isabelle, who was wearing a bright orange micro-mini with a striped sailor T-shirt, three-quarter-sleeved as a concession to the October chill. She smiled that sort of ferocious half-smile that warned them to keep their distance.

David looked around as they passed from the square to the circle. This was the very centre of decadence yet it seemed no more vulgar or dirty or sinister than most parts of the city. A few couples were fornicating in the shadows of the sculptures, one guy was exposing himself on the speaker's podium, dancing to inner music, and several girls they passed were clearly soliciting, with another consummating her sale in the lee of the old subway stop. For the most part, people were doing nothing. That in itself was an aggressive act, he thought, to clearly do nothing at all.

When they came to the midnight blue Georgian door in Cabbagetown with its dark side windows and transom, he thought again of *First*

*Corinthians*. Sometimes it was necessary to see through a glass darkly, if only to cut the glare from the other side.

They entered and stood in the vestibule. He paused to consider the Escheresque galleries feeding off like so many arteries through the body of Jacob's vast mausoleum. They seemed to represent David's wildly conflicting emotions. He thought how effectively all those other Georgian doors in the neighbourhood successfully faked the impression of access to individual homes. The books were as real as he was, yet the library itself was a giant illusion.

There was no one in sight to greet them. Isabelle led the way as they descended through pentagonal galleries into the crypt. They found Grace standing in the flickering candlelight between Anna, decrepit in her crystal coffin, and Jacob, whose ancient remains had been moved and settled in suitable repose inside a similar reliquary. Grace remained still, with her head bowed, one hand on each casket.

"Grace?" said Isabelle, as if she were in doubt.

Grace looked up.

"It's David and Isabelle."

"I've been expecting you." Grace edged forward, sliding her hands along the caskets until each was over a decrepit face, shielding the grisly features from the flickering light. Multiple shadows cast by the candles slithered along the walls as she moved. "I see you've brought Immanuel."

"It's time," said David.

"Yes, perhaps it is."

"You killed my mother."

"Violet was *my* mother, David. I killed my own mother."

"You are an evil woman."

"No more than most. We all have the capacity for evil. It is the books, isn't it? That is why you want me dead. Books that might have saved us from a soulless future, I have turned books into weapons, haven't I? I regret that. I miss the old man. I regret his passing. I had hoped to have you in his place. I regret that I won't. They tell me he has deteriorated, he has slipped too far. The Company no longer has use for his mind. If you had opened yourself to give him a home, he might have been with us still. But you didn't, he isn't. I regret that. He's gone, the books are useless."

"They're not," David protested. "They can still be read. There's a revolution coming, it needs your support, they need these books."

"David!" Isabelle exclaimed. "David," she warned.

"Don't be naïve, Isabelle," said Grace. "If you expect a new world order to grow out of your primrose garden, forget it. We cannot monitor what you've been planning but with a certainty we know any place that blocked our monitors was subversive. Shortly after you two left the Gallery for Egregious Semantical Errors it became a hole in the ground. It is gone."

"No!" Isabelle protested. "You didn't, you can't."

"We can and we did. The historical revisionist project has likewise been blasted from the face of the Earth. No more Committee for Public Safety. The Cloisters has been obliterated, all but the deepest tunnels, which have been sealed with strategic explosions. The Book Emporium wasn't worth the trouble, it will collapse under the weight of its own pretensions. The theatre, 'Now Playing', as I called it, will also be allowed to dwindle as memories fade. They are merely diversions, no more significant than a football match or a public execution. Bread and circuses. Sorry about your carpets."

"You bitch," David snarled, shaking with rage.

"I will kill you with my bare hands," said Isabelle.

"Since you brought no weapons with you, I assumed that was your plan all along, dear girl. Now let me explain something. Our beloved Library is about to explode. It is too much a fortress even for Company drones to demolish, so it has been packed with explosives and wired. It is a bomb stuffed with innumerable books, some of which are not what they seem. Many have pages between their covers but some contain powerful incendiary devices. And you and you and I, we will go with it. Did you notice there are no librarians around? I sent them away, but *we* cannot escape. When I remove my hands from the crystal caskets, the release in pressure will detonate a bomb which will set off the others. If I do not release the pressure, the bombs will go off anyway, ten minutes from the moment you entered this room. We have three and a half minutes to go. Say your farewells, hold each other if you wish, the young in one another's arms, yes, a delightful way to die. As for me, my service to the Company is complete, my time is done. No regrets. Ta ta."

"Isabelle?" David said her name as a query: can all this be real?

"If we run, we can't make it, David. There's not enough time. If we make a move, she triggers the bomb, there's no time at all."

"It seems you have a dilemma," said Grace. Her voice was mechanical, her words rehearsed.

"You're my mother," he said, moving close to her.

"You're my son," she acknowledged.

Isabelle slipped close behind him until she was between the caskets, then thrust her hands down on the crystal surfaces.

"Okay," she whispered.

David grasped his mother by the neck, shook and throttled and twisted. Her eyes rolled back, her lips grimaced, she gagged and gurgled, and then she was dead. No bombs. Isabelle had displaced the pressure.

"Now get out of here, David," she said.

"No time."

He stripped off his shoes, shirt, and trousers and placed them on the glass above Jacob's body. He pulled at Grace's clothes but her corpse refused to give them up. "Your boots," he yelled. "Belle, give me your boots." She nudged them off without releasing her pressure on the crystal. He leaned down and grabbed them and placed them above Anna's wizened face. He laid Immanuel across the crystal, then tore her striped T-shirt along a seam and stripped off her micro-mini, adding them to the pile.

"Not much material there," he muttered, nodding towards the bright orange skirt. "Do you think that'll do it?" he said.

"Let's see." She took her hands away from the caskets.

No explosion. She lifted Immanuel. No explosion. She handed him to David.

"It was one of my favourite skirts," she said. "Okay, I'd say we have a minute or so, c'mon."

"Where?"

"Follow me."

They scrambled through the rare books room and along passageways lit by emergency lights and reached the vault door in forty seconds. Once out on the tracks, they ran madly towards the abandoned Cabbagetown station. Before they got there the earth trembled, then rumbled, then shook violently like they were at the centre of some terrible holocaust, and copies of all the books in the world turned into an inferno of flames and whirling debris.

Standing on the subway platform, lit only by a safety light, wearing nothing but panties and briefs, they started to laugh. They held each other so closely, the flames sweeping down the subway tube illuminated no space between their nakedness and dissipated before reaching them, leaving them roiling in sweat. They couldn't stop laughing in spite of the deaths of all those books and the words within them. They shook and shuddered as laughter turned to tears and they wept against each other and collapsed to the cracked tile floor and slumped against the cracked tile wall and stared straight ahead into the gloom. They held hands with a desperate joy that confused them.

At last, he said, "I'm sorry about your carpets."

She snuggled into him. "I'm sorry about the deaths of Amy and Vincent and all those others, and the primrose garden. I'm sorry about the books. At least she spared the librarians. I'm sorry about the historians."

"Me too. I, I, we, you…" His words dwindled into silence.

They reached the surface naked, filthy, scratched, and bruised. The sun swirled crimson through a huge black cloud mushrooming over

Cabbagetown. Behind them, another cloud darkened the sky above Rosedale where The Cloisters had been. They walked down Yonge St. hand in hand, oblivious to the October cold or to their primal immodesty. When they came to the Square at Ford Place, under the huge horses surrounded by looming neon giants, they felt oddly comforted. Young people came forward with clothes and wet towels and washed them clean and dressed them warmly and gave them food to eat and beverages to drink and left them alone. David took the lead as they walked on towards the smoking column rising out of the ground in the financial district.

"Is it the Evolved New World you want to get us to?" asked Isabelle when they took a break by slowing their pace.

"Yeah," said David. "If we're going to change things, we do it out there. The city of the End of Things reminds me too much of Jacob Hummel's last days, sinking into the past with no grasp on the present."

"David, you have to realize, before they turned him into an animated corpse, he never let go of the future. He was a sad man burdened by an excess of living. But you know, we connected, he and I, we trusted each other. He told me about his plans for you to inherit his wisdom — it was not immortality he wanted, it was continuity." She paused, then hummed, "*I am he as you are he as you are me and we are all together.*"

"*Boy, you been a naughty girl you let your knickers down,*" David tunelessly intoned. "I am the walrus — I'm surprised you know the words."

"I don't know what walrus you're talking about. Nobody wears knickers, or admits to it. *You and we are all together* is something the old man used to hum. *Sitting on a cornflake, waiting for the van to come.*"

"I like *Hey Jude* better."

"The readers I knew didn't listen to vocal arrangements. A distraction from pure music, they'd say, although they didn't listen to instrumental music either because there were no words. The lyrics of most songs are doggerel pretending to be poetry, they'd say. Leonard Cohen was the exception. His lyrics were poetry pretending to be doggerel. *Divine affection,* Jacob used to say."

David knew only the Beatles.

"Tell me more about Jacob's plans," he said, realizing they were evading the dangers awaiting as they approached the boundary between the city and the ENW.

"He had no doubt that Grace worked in the Company's interests."

"Yet he loved her?"

"Sometimes. He knew you were destined, he hoped you were driven, to kill her, to murder your mother and continue his dream. Yes, but he could not have foreseen the destruction of his library, the obliteration of his beloved books."

They had come to a chute between two walls that funnelled through barriers, familiarly known as Checkpoint Charlie. On the other side was The Evolved New World. There were unbreachable turnstiles for pedestrians to pass through, people from the city who worked at dangerous or trivial jobs on the other side. To the south was Lake Ontario. To the north the wall was topped by electronic sensors and weapons, patrolled by squadrons of lethal drones. The highway he had first come through with Jacob — my God, that had been Isabelle at the wheel; it all seemed so long ago, events in another life — the highway was for vehicles cleared in advance. People like Jacob had permission to transit if they were known to work in the Company's interests. Unless, of course, they were carrying illicit cargo; a renegade boy, a survivor. Then they were obliterated at fifteen-minute intervals.

Did Jacob arrange for the Hummer to be blown up to emphasize the division between worlds, his capacity to transcend them, and David's dependence on him when they travelled from one to the other? Was it a concession to Grace's ambition? Was it to establish a memorable connection with Isabelle? Or was it simply an expression of the Company's power?

Evening was closing in. Most of the turnstiles built with giant cogs of rotating teeth were closed until dawn. There was a line-up of night-workers shuffling through the gloom and David and Isabelle took their place among them.

"The dream?" he asked.

"It's your dream now," she said. "Continuity, books, the integrated sensibility. Oh God, David, he could not endure the death of the natural mind. His dream was for minds to be free of computers, cybernetics, and cerebral controls."

The line was snaking forward. She seemed increasingly nervous. "What is it?" he asked.

"I can't go through, David. No credentials. You can, you must. Their scanners will read your implant. You'll be okay."

"You're coming," he insisted.

"David, no, listen, I've got something for you."

The line shuffled forward, nearly out of the shadows.

"You're coming," he insisted.

"David, you don't understand. They will kill me. That bunker there, they'll take me in and erase me. Please, no."

She reached behind her neck and released the clasp of her silver necklace, then drew a pendant up from between her breasts and dropped pendant and necklace into his palm. He had seen the pendant before. It was an unusually shaped pebble, unusually inscribed. A feline in flames, or perhaps a bit of stone worn away in an interesting pattern by the passage of time.

"My mother," he whispered. They were close to the floodlights which countered the fading daylight. "Isabelle, Violet gave you this." It was not a question.

"Jacob Hummel took me to see her. You were upstairs with your friend. She entrusted me with its care. David, it was more than a gift. She had finished her book. She contacted Jacob for help." As they entered the sphere of light, Isabelle twisted the clasp on the necklace, revealing a thin memory chip inside. "This is her novel, David. She called it *À la recherche extrême du temps perdu*. That wasn't a title, just a name she borrowed from Proust. It doesn't have a title, not yet. That's up to you. She believed if the story of the past were known, there could still be a future. It's important you believe it too. This is the real reason the Company killed Violet. They thought her death meant her book was permanently erased. They don't know this copy exists."

She resealed the clasp, reached up and placed the necklace around his neck, draping the pendant onto his chest.

"I love you, David. Show this to the world. Share Violet's ancestral memories. Recreate Jacob in our own voices. Everything will change."

She slipped back among the shadows.

He grabbed at her, he grasped her arm, he hauled her into the light. She struggled, he unfastened the necklace, heaved her over his shoulder and, clutching the pendant in his fist, he tucked the walking stick with the walnut head of a terrier under his arm. She kicked and squirmed but he held her firmly as he pushed through the brightly illuminated night-workers and strode into the security maze inside Checkpoint Charlie. He was counting on their equipment being unable to recognize his implant was defunct. He nodded towards the scanner and addressed the guards. "Bitch tried to make off with my mother's jewellery." He waved the necklace and pendant. She squirmed, he whacked her across the buttocks. "She's a bloody thief, get out of the God-damned way. She's going for demolition."

The guards stood back as he pushed through the stolid mass of workers on the other side and out into the evening sun which glared in his eyes. Beginning to flag under the weight of his burden, he trudged forward until they rounded a corner. He moved off to the left onto rocks piled in the distant past as a breakwater. She had stopped wriggling. He set her on her feet. She slapped him across the face, gently but with enough force to be felt.

"We both might have died," she scolded. Her copper-gold hair glinted in the falling sun. Her piercing green eyes were moist with emotion.

"Yes," he said. He returned the necklace to Isabelle's neck and put his arm around her. "'To set the stone trembling,'" he said. "There's our title, and that's what we'll do." Daylight was slipping into the water offshore. When they kissed, the passion of their embrace pushed the pendant between them. The necklace and the words of its roaring crept through their flesh like a promise. They slipped into the pages of a novel as tiny waves lapped against stone by their feet, echoing the notes of an ivory flute, and the tumbling sun left a spiral of lions shaking the evening horizon.

# Author's Note

*To Set the Stone Trembling* is in some respects a summation of my life. The following provisional obit is another.

John Errington Moss arrived on Feb. 7, 1940; departure, to be determined. He will leave in his wake a life thoroughly, often fretfully, enjoyed. He grieves at the thought of separating from his beloved wife, Beverley Haun, but is grateful for the wondrous decades they shared. He vowed at eight to live a life of adventure and did his best to do so. Honoured with a BA, MA, MPhil, MSDT, PhD, and Fellowship in the Royal Society of Canada, he retired as *professor emeritus* to write eleven modestly-acclaimed mystery novels, after publishing twenty-some books on Canadian culture, arctic exploration, and experimental literature. He lectured from Rome to Tokyo, Tasmania to Greenland, the Canaries to Polynesia, throughout Canada, the U.K., and much of Europe, and held guest professorships in Berlin, Leeds, Mysore, Dublin, and Vienna. At various times he reared horses, raised dogs, kept swans, bees, chickens, and a few cats; redesigned, carpentered, plumbed, wired, and restored old houses; replicated colonial furniture. He was a scuba instructor (PADI and SDI), a fervid oenophile, an inveterate traveller, and a determined endurance athlete. He swam across the Hellespont in 1962; Boston Marathon, eleven times; competed in: the original Kona Ironman, 1987; Canadian Ski Marathon, touring gold and Coureur des Bois gold bar; numerous treks in the Arctic, including twenty-eight days alone on the Barrens; many long-distance loppets closer to home; long walks with his redoubtable Beverley, including coast-to-coast crossings of England and Scotland—Hadrian's Wall in 2013, the Wainwright Trail in 2017, Scotland in 2022. In his youth he worked as a canoe tripper in Temagami, at the Aldwych Theatre in London, and as a stand-in for the principal character in *Lawrence of Arabia*. In latter years, he renewed his passion for bees with Trembling Stone Apiary, and loved nothing more than to work on his '54 SeaBird, a gift from Bev named Corsair after the identical launch of his childhood summers with his beloved Aunt Beth in Muskoka. He grieves at having to leave his beautiful daughters, Julia and Laura, after sharing with them the infinite joys and complexities of their childhood, enduring the terrible loneliness as they grew up and away, salving his sadness with pride in their achievements as they attained doctorates, professional stature, and had fine children of their own (Julia's Clare, Maddie, and Olivia, with George Zarb; Laura's Simon, Owen, and Charlie, with Fred Cutler). He has no regrets at sharing thirty tumultuous and enriching years with their mother, Virginia Lavin, honours her achievement as a clinical psychologist, and revels at Bev's PhD in cultural theory and publication of a definitive book on Easter Island. He shares Bev's grief for the loss of their infant son, Jack Austin, and is saddened to leave her daughter, Beatrice, and son, Joel, Bea's husband, Pedro de Silva, and son, Diego. Proud of his Moss, Clare, Pattinson, Cameron, Errington, and Erb heritage, he has always thought of himself as lucky to have had such interesting parents as George Moss and Mary Clare, and such diverse siblings as Richard, Steve, Liz, and Erry, all of whom shaped his early life, mostly for the better. He grew up in Blair, Ontario, fifty feet from his chosen burial site and fifty feet from the grave of his ancestor, Christan Erb, the founding father of Waterloo County, whose Pennsylvania family purchased their land from the Mohawk Nation. His life has been touched by many; he anticipates the inevitable end with forbearance.

CPSIA information can be obtained
at www.ICGtesting.com
Printed in the USA
BVHW031536010422
632794BV00005B/14